CANARY ISLANDS MYSTERIES

BOOKS 1-3

ISOBEL BLACKTHORN

A MATTER OF LATITUDE

CANARY ISLANDS MYSTERIES BOOK 1

For Vivienne Fisher, in loving memory
As citizens, we all have an obligation to intervene and become involved—it's the citizen who changes things. - Jose Saramago

1

CELESTINO

THE OCEAN HEAVES TO ITS OWN PULSE, ANGRY AND INSISTENT, FORCING its bulk against the rock; my wet and salty companion, silent, even as it roars. The tide runs high, the wind cyclonic, waves spill their spray into the fisherman's hut through the window cavity. The boom as each wave hits sends a lesser boom through me.

I'm using a wooden table with a missing leg as a barricade. Also occupying the fisherman's hut are two backless chairs and three wooden crates, their slats rotting and brittle. In a cracked plastic bucket are short lengths of frayed rope, discarded as useless by their owner, along with scraps of fishing net, tangled and no good to anyone.

I huddle in the back corner of this cold cell of a room with all the detritus, for all the good it's doing me. I can hear the canine, sniffing and whimpering outside: my stalker. The cavity should have been boarded up against the wind and the spray that coats everything in salt. My only comfort, it's too high for the dog.

The cavity must be too high for the dog or it would have leaped in for the kill by now. Unless it's building up the courage or figuring out its approach. I don't care to think about it. The barricade would be useless against that snarling beast, but I'm not crouched down here on the cold stone floor hiding from a four-legged enemy.

I reassess the condition of my body. I'm not in good shape. The dog bite on my left calf is bleeding through my jeans. I can feel the blood, sticky and warm. My left arm is a mess. Broken at the shoulder, it hangs, limp and unusable, the pain throbbing in time with my heartbeat. If I move, even a fraction, daggers of agony radiate through the whole of me, eclipsing the searing pain of the burns I received exiting the car, burns on my face and my hands.

I managed to get far enough away before the whole crumpled metal carcass went up in a ball of flame, despite the rain that had started teeming down. The wind that came with the rain sent the flames my way, scalding patches of exposed skin, singeing my hair.

The dog can smell my blood, my weeping flesh. Hungry, feral, it shouldn't be out here where there is no other food but me.

I'm as hungry as you are, buddy.

The accident is stuck in my head on replay. It was a miracle I got out. How the hell I managed to grab my rucksack is anyone's guess, but I was motivated by its contents, or one particular item among the rest, my daughter's birthday present. What happened? The storm happened. I knew it was coming, it was the talk of the island, but I thought leaving at midday would give me ample time to drop off a painting to a regular customer, a Swedish doctor with a smart villa in the little village of Mancha Blanca, and make it back up the mountain to my wife's parents before the birthday party. Erik was insistent he wanted the work this weekend. And I needed the cash, not least to recoup the cost of what was inside that pretty wrapping paper. I was on my way to the party when the impact occurred.

That stretch of road is narrow and flanked by dry stone walls. Drivers shouldn't put their foot down, but enjoying the lack of hairpin bends, they do. I didn't see the vehicle that ran me off the road at the intersection and slammed my car into a wall. No, I definitely didn't see it coming. It was a large vehicle, that is all I recall, much larger than my own little car that flipped over and spun and came to rest upside down.

The driver sped away and I was alone in the wind and the rain. I got out as fast as I was able, a sixth sense telling me that was no accident and the driver would come back to make sure of his success.

Paranoid thoughts maybe, but then again, maybe not. I wasn't taking any chances.

Besides, the stink of petrol was strong and the hiss and sizzle under the bonnet augured only one thing. My car was going to explode.

Nursing my bad arm, I walked, heading off up the road and into the rain and the wind, following a natural sense of direction away from the village and down a lonely track that led as far from other people as it's possible to get on the island. I trudged along, determined, not thinking straight, my instincts telling me to head in a direction no one in their right mind would head in a tropical storm. The dog joined me as the farmland gave way to lava scree on both sides of the road, or at least, that was when I became aware of a scrawny, bedraggled-looking mongrel trailing behind.

I ignored the dog and kept walking, arriving at the coast and a fork in the road about half an hour later. My mistake was to pause to get my bearings. I was assessing the best way down to the cluster of fishing huts when the dog seized the moment and attacked me from behind, sinking its jaws into my calf. I hurled the rucksack at the dog's head, it was the only weapon I had, and it was sufficient to startle the dog. It released its grip, giving me enough time to reach down and fumble around in the grey light for a rock hoping there'd be one. My hand curled around hard stone and I hurled it at the beast's flank. I detected a thud and a yelp. Taking no chances, I found another rock and then another. The dog scuttled off. Heaving the rucksack on my right shoulder, I limped down the track to the east and pushed on doors until I found one open.

I knew once I'd settled into my damp corner of the hut that I was trapped. That the moment I headed back up the track I would be exposed, visible, vulnerable to a second dog attack. I also knew that whoever had run me off the road would want to make sure I was dead.

Or maybe they thought I *was* dead.

I soon would be.

The dog, my companion, had made me a prisoner. It can't get in and I can't get out. How long can I ride this out?

I have water, at least I have fresh water, a whole two-litre bottle, unopened. It added extra weight to the rucksack. It was the primary reason that first blow hurt the dog. I have snacks I carry with me on the road: chocolate, protein bars, nuts, treats for Gloria, a picnic of sweet delights now my rations.

I have two options. I can walk back, or I can stay here, eating and drinking what I have, and wait until some holidaymaker or fisherman comes by, and hope they do before whoever ran me off the road arrives to finish me off.

What am I thinking? No one comes here in winter. Not in weather that brought the ocean right up to the fishing huts. No one would think to come here. Only me. I wish I could turn back the clock and tell my feet to walk in another direction, towards the village, towards safety and civilisation. But I had my reasons and those reasons still hold true.

I am cold, my clothes are drying on my body. I huddle, trying to trap my own heat. The only parts of me that are generating warmth are my burns, my shoulder and my calf.

The calf wound bothers me. I need to bandage it to stop the bleeding. What else is in the rucksack? I reach in and pull out a little scarf. I hesitate. Part of me doesn't want to tie my leg with Gloria's dress ups. But it's silk and will tie tightly so I use it.

Satisfied I've done all I can, I sit on the cold concrete, bring my knees to my chest and lean against the wall. I shiver. My teeth rattle. Every movement sends red hot pain through my shoulder.

Delirium takes hold. Sleep comes in snatches. When it does, I dream. I dream the dog has my leg in its jaws and chews at my living flesh as though I am already dead meat. Part of me watches on in terror as the demon dog salivates and moans and growls and licks at the gash in my leg, savouring the taste.

With dawn comes fresh fear. The rain has gone. The dog has not. It guards my hut like a beacon to anyone passing.

2

PAULA

I REPRESS A MOMENT OF IRRITATION, WISHING I HADN'T AGREED TO HAVE Gloria's party at my parents' house. It was so much larger, they said, and tidier—something else I can't dispute. Yet it's the last house on the northern edge of Máguez and although scarcely two kilometres from Haría, no one will want to risk the drive. A tropical storm, a rare event on Lanzarote, has chosen this very afternoon to lambast the island.

All I can do is wait and hope. I've no mobile reception and I never thought to give the guests my parents' number.

There were numerous warnings. The weather bureau saw it coming for about a week. The little supermarkets at each end of Haría's plaza were both busy when I drove past earlier, locals stocking up on essentials before the storm struck. By then it was already raining. The media advised people to stay at home once the storm intensifies, avoid the roads, and if the road to Yé is any indication, so they have.

Perhaps we should have cancelled, or postponed. I considered it, but Celestino questioned the veracity of the warnings, and my parents said they would never cancel a birthday party over a bit of inclement weather.

The guests were due at two and it's gone half past. I stand at the guest-bedroom window, peering into the grey for cars emerging from down the road. The thickness of the wall, about a yard of basalt, affords some comfort. I lean against it, the stone cold against my skin. An irascible wind funnels through the gaps in the casements. The shutters, open and fastened to the façade, judder and clap. I'm reluctant to venture out to close them. It would be too much like sealing myself in.

Gloria is in the kitchen, oblivious to my concerns. Her ebullient little voice bounces around the farmhouse walls, off the concrete ceilings twelve feet high, fragmenting into a confusion of numerous little voices, her simple bold talk obfuscated by its own echo.

Angela and Bill are keeping her entertained.

I should join them and make the best of things, but I can't help holding fast to my post at the window in the absence of Celestino.

He usually keeps good time, although when I went to the studio I understood he wanted to complete the island landscape on his easel, a commission for a Swedish doctor who owns a villa in Mancha Blanca. Finding him crouched over the work, I arranged my face into something I hoped appeared accommodating, but he didn't look up. It's a complex piece, a dance of earthy tones in the style of Matisse's fauvist period, Celestino yet again shunning as a source of inspiration the Picasso-inspired works of Lanzarote's beloved César Manrique in favour of Picasso's rival. Even then, behind his back I observed the work with grudging admiration. When he said, 'Quiero terminar esta esquina,' and pointed at the bottom left corner, adding a polite but firm, '¿Vale?' I knew it would have to be okay, the Swede is keen to take possession and we need the cash, even though I also knew he'd be late for his only daughter's birthday party. Leaving the studio, I struggled to hold back my displeasure.

The storm intensifies as I watch. The soft branches of the shrubs in the front garden, normally sheltered from the prevailing wind by arcs of stone wall, are receiving a lashing. In the field across the road some newly planted maize is already flattened. It's a harsh irony that a storm, with its deluge of rain, damages the island more than the long dry spells. All that rainwater lost to the sea. Taking in the thick cloud hanging low, the volcanoes shrouded in grey, it's a scene anathema to the bright blocks of sunny colour found in those depictions of the island in paint and photograph alike, depictions coveted by the tourists. I fold my arms across my chest, shove my hands up the sleeves of my dress and pinch my flesh. Cheap and cheerful, isn't that what the world wants? A cheeriness reflected in Manrique's abstract artworks. But not in Celestino's. Instead there's a brutal truth in his paintings; he refuses to sweeten the pill. Celestino, where the hell are you? I stare into the grey harbouring a vain wish that the sun will shine for my little girl's birthday.

Gloria comes bounding into the room in the pretty dress Angela insisted on buying, holding up her drawing gripped in two hands. 'Look, Mummy! Look!' I make my lips stretch wide. 'How gorgeous! Aren't you clever.' I ruffle her hair. She's a bright and animated child. She has her father's thick dark hair and proud face atop the fine-bone frame she inherited from me. Her eyes are large and inquisitive, yet she's as content in her own company and in that of her family, as she is playing with the other toddlers in the neighbourhood.

Gloria gives me the painting then takes my hand and tugs. I allow myself to be led away. Satisfied her mother is following, Gloria lets go and runs back to join her grandparents.

'I don't suppose ...' Angela says upon my entry into the kitchen.

'Nobody is going to drive up here in this, Mum.' I gesture past my father and the windowed doors, to the patio where the rainwater pools, repressing my annoyance that my earlier misgivings over the wisdom of holding a party in a tropical storm were overridden.

'But Celestino should be here. It isn't like him to be late.'

'He's finishing the commission,' I say flatly. 'I imagine it's taking longer than he thought.'

Angela smooths her hands down her apron and turns away to the sink. She's a petite woman, a little stooped, her short grey hair thinning around the crown. Beyond her, the depths of the kitchen look gloomy. An unusually long room lined with flat pack shelving units and makeshift benches, the challenges of installing a modern fitted kitchen too much for the previous owner. Maybe it's her way of proving to the world she's assimilating to local ways by choosing not to renovate. The only change she's made is the acquisition of a large dresser with cupboards top and bottom, positioned at the table end of the room. The landline is perched at the end beside a silver-plated letter holder.

Angela follows my gaze. 'Have you tried his mobile?'

'Last time I tried it went straight to message bank.'

I survey the table, strewn with paper and crayons. Bill has drawn up his chair close to Gloria's, her chair's height raised by a plump cushion. Gloria leans forward and reaches across for the bowl of potato crisps. I push the bowl closer and watch the grabbing hand, the mouth opening wide, turning away at the crunch and chomp.

Angela goes to the fridge. 'What should we do?' she says, more to the contents than to me.

'Wait, I guess.'

Out on the patio, the rain sloshes down; the drain in the far corner failing to cope, the water around that end already ankle deep.

'You did tell them all two o'clock?' Bill says.

'They're not coming.' Exasperation rises. 'I know I wouldn't be. Not in a deluge like this.'

I picture Kathy and Pedro and their three daughters battling it up the hill from Tabayesco. Pilar and Miguel and their two boys have even further to come. They won't make it out of Los Valles, the rain surely falling most heavily on the mountain.

Gloria reaches for more crisps. I catch the anticipation in her eyes. I'll have to explain somehow. Promise we'll do something special on a different day. Tell my parents they might as well make the most of the afternoon and start on all that food. There are the presents to open, the cake to cut. And Celestino is bound to turn up eventually.

'Shall we...?'

'Shouldn't we wait a bit longer?' Angela says. 'For Celestino?'

Her gaze slides away from my face and settles on the phone. As though summoned, I go to the dresser and press the receiver to my ear. Silence. I put a finger in my other ear to make sure.

'The line's dead.'

The word catches in my throat. I glance at my watch. Bill does the same. It's three.

'Put the radio on, Angela,' he says. 'We'll catch the news.'

'What for? It's in Spanish.'

'Paula will understand.'

The broadcaster speaks rapidly. I snatch at words. I wait until the report comes to an end then gesture to my mother to turn it off.

'It isn't good. Haría is the worst hit. The barrancos are raging torrents. Roads have become rivers, many impassable. There are reports of rock falls and landslides. A few cars swept away.'

'My word,' Bill says beneath his breath.

'Thankfully, no injuries reported, so far. And all flights since midday have been diverted to Fuerteventura.'

'It's sure to pass over,' Angela says.

'Until it does, Celestino will be stuck where he is.' Wherever that might be.

We fall into silence, gazes settling on Gloria's painstaking attempt to solve a jigsaw puzzle.

Bill leaves his seat and stands by the patio doors. 'I thought when we moved here we'd gotten away from all the flooding.'

'It's rare and it never lasts long. Things will soon dry out.' My hopes of forestalling a tirade are dashed at the full stop.

'Not like those poor buggers back home,' he says, turning back to the room. 'Can't imagine how they'll get those houses dry. Sodden they are. Think of the mould. We got out just in time, Angela.'

'Oh, Dad.'

Since his retirement, he's become prone to grumbling over 'the dismal state of the world' as he calls it. The recent floods that inundated villages and towns in England alarmed him more than almost anyone we know. I share with my mother a wish that he would switch off sometimes and relax. So much negative passion can't be good for his blood pressure.

I hoped my parents' move to Máguez would bring them both peace of mind; that the warm sunny climate and the invigorating ocean breeze would enliven their spirits.

In the months after Brexit, Bill and Angela sold their Suffolk home and bought the old farmhouse, moving in time for Gloria's second birthday, my persuasive efforts of the previous two years at last paying off. It was the mild climate that swayed them. Plenty of opportunity to be outdoors. They were holidaying on the island one time and they had taken a walk around the village. A retired high school teacher, Bill began to see in Lanzarote the tranquil lifestyle he craved. Although I suspect the climate was just the catalyst, the deeper reason his attachment to his only granddaughter.

I thought the new climate would help Angela move out from beneath the shadow of her depression that took hold when she was retrenched from her job as school secretary in her early sixties. The move has certainly lifted her spirits, but not in the way I anticipated. It is a fascination for gardening in a dry and windy climate that absorbs Angela. She marvels over the ease with which dracaenas and succulents grow and she's developed an avid affection for cacti.

Much to my dismay, although not to my surprise, she hasn't developed a similar adoration of Gloria. For Angela is as indifferent as she was with me when I was young, consumed by guilt that she should be doing more, yet steadfastly not acting on that guilt.

It is Bill who has taken to Gloria, and Gloria to Bill. Watching him help his granddaughter insert the last puzzle piece, watching him take her hand and lead her to the main room, I can't help feeling warm inside. The way he bends down and points at the long table filled with fare, the way Gloria responds with a look of awe, the lifting of her face to his as if for approval. The way his face lights up at her smile. Gloria has taken years off him. He is a large man, with a tendency to carry too much weight, his serious nature showing on his face in downward curving lines and in the furrows on his brow. Around Gloria, there's a bounce in his step and an enthusiasm for life's small adventures, for sharing with Gloria every single detail of the day, myriad little observances. Gloria mellows his heart. Although he will always rail against the injustices of the world. In that, he shares with his son-in-law, Celestino, something meaningful and important.

Celestino.

Who should be here.

Even if he were, there is no denying Bill offers Gloria something Celestino can't: his complete attention. Not that Celestino doesn't care. Although I can't count the times I've told myself in the face of mounting dissatisfaction, that he has to work hard to produce and sell his art, especially since there are the three of us. Alone he may have survived adequately if frugally, but with a wife and a child the burden is great. That commission for the Swedish doctor; we'll have to live off those Euros for a month.

In an effort to push away my cares, I grab a handful of toasted maize kernels and take in the room, recalling the relief I felt when my mother relinquished all notion of shipping to the island the vintage furniture, replete with a tatty Chesterfield lounge that never fitted in any room it was put. Between us, Bill and I managed to persuade Angela to part with all her old pieces, selling some and arranging homes for the rest. Here in Máguez, they have resorted to furnishing their home via Ikea, the effect—modern, clean lines, plain colours— in keeping with the roughly rendered walls of brilliant white, the polished timber floors, the overall simplicity of design.

Hanging on the longest wall is one of Celestino's larger pieces, a sketchy rendition of the island's northern landscape, which they tried to buy but Celestino insisted they have. Along with the sight of it hanging there like a chimeric representation of the artist himself, annoyance at his absence gives way to concern. Perhaps the road out of Haría is truly impassable. Or the commission is taking far longer than he anticipated. My self-reassurances can't replace a nagging thought that something dreadful, even catastrophic has happened to my husband.

I put on a brave face and suggest we play a game to keep Gloria amused.

'What shall we play?' Angela says, directing her question to no one in particular.

'Laloply!' Gloria cries.

'Laloply?'

'She means our Monopoly.'

'Good plan,' Bill says and goes to fetch it.

It is a game far too old for Gloria, but she loves it. I make space on the kitchen table. Angela brings in some party fare and pours everyone a soft drink.

'Lemonade?' Bill says, entering the kitchen and eyeing his glass.

'There's rather a lot of it.'

He doesn't respond to the subtext as he lays out the board, making two piles of cards in its centre and lining up the players on 'Go'.

There is no Old Kent Road or Mayfair to be seen. Instead, arranged in a logical sequence of rising wealth, are the various locations on the island, everywhere from budget holiday complexes to the luxury locales of Costa Teguise, Playa Blanca and Puerto Calero. Stations are replaced by tourist sites, all of them created by Manrique and up for sale like the rest of the board. Celestino has painted a little scene in each square. The result is a visual feast of marinas, beaches, palm trees and volcanoes, and many and varied streetscapes. Houses become holiday lets, and the hotels resorts. The players Celestino carved out of clay, little figurines of islanders in native dress, a dog, a pirate ship and a high-domed wide-brimmed hat. He customised the Chance cards to suit, with the exception of 'free parking', the 'go to jail' card and 'income tax'. In keeping with his own worldview, bank errors in the player's favour have become sweeteners and kickbacks.

He created the game after he found the original Monopoly in my parents' sideboard when searching for placemats for a family dinner, and insisted on playing afterwards. Bill and Angela were just settling into their new home at the time. What began as a tentative introduction to the game became, thanks to a bottle of single malt whisky, rowdy and intense. Towards the end, when Angela was bankrupt and I struggled with half a dozen mortgaged properties, Celestino lost Mayfair and Park Lane to Bill and won a new friend, the two men forming a bond where previously existed common civility. That was the night Celestino introduced Bill to the story of the island's corruption. I recall the many hours Celestino spent in the following weeks designing the new board, with Gloria leaning over him engaged in every step; the day he brought it over to Máguez for a trial run, and everyone agreed it was much better than the original.

Gloria climbs onto Bill's lap and chooses the ship. Angela takes the hat and I pick up the dog. The game is helped along by Bill's enthusiasm but it's strange to be playing it without Celestino. By the time we've all bought up the various streets, promenades and boulevards, Gloria's attention wanes.

Outside, the wind and the rain are unrelenting. The afternoon rapidly gives way to dark. Conceding an early defeat after having to mortgage Famara Beach, Angela goes about putting the lights on.

'Those shutters need closing,' she says to herself, emerging from the guest bedroom and heading to the front door.

'I'll do it.'

Angela promptly turns back.

An angry wind roars up the valley, flinging the rain at everything in its path, slamming the unlatched shutters closed, narrowly missing pinching my fingers. There's nothing to see beyond the stretch of small, cultivated fields that fan down the hill to the village centre. Low cloud obscures the mountains. Run off from the roof gushes from a drainage outlet, eroding the soil beneath, creating several muddy rivulets which carve their way down towards the garden wall.

I duck back inside, determined to steer my attention towards my daughter, although I soon find I have no need. Gloria has decided to entertain herself by running around the house in search of her grandparents' cat, Tibbles. Bill's doing.

'Is he under your bed?' he says as she runs towards him.

She about turns and runs off to the guest bedroom.

'No, he's not there, Granddad,' comes a little voice.

Then she reappears, breathless and beaming.

'What about under Nanny's bed. Have you tried there?'

And off she goes.

After several more attempts she says, 'Granddad, where is he?'

'I'm not telling.'

'Please.'

'You have to find him. He has to be somewhere.'

Another unsuccessful attempt and Gloria drags Bill off to help the search. After a short while, as Gloria tires of the game, Bill leads her to kitchen, to the cupboard under the bench. Before long I hear, 'There he is!' and Gloria reappears with Bill cradling Tibbles in his arms.

3

REMINISCING

WE WAIT ANOTHER HOUR BEFORE HELPING GLORIA OPEN HER PRESENTS.

'Let's start with the smallest,' Bill says, lifting his granddaughter onto his lap.

Angela passes the gaily-wrapped packages one by one. I stand back and watch. Amid squeals of delight and lots of frantic ripping, out pops the rag doll I bought at the local arts and crafts market, the play dough I found in a shop in Arrecife, replete with a small wooden rolling pin and some pastry cutters, and a selection of picture books that were on special in the supermarket. As the gift size increases so does the value, my parents indulging Gloria with an arts and crafts kit in its own special carry case, a memory game, a toy toolset with workbench, and finally, leaning against the wall beside the table, a heavy duty, plastic cubby house.

'Thank you,' I breathe, moved by their generosity, if at once diminished by it. In such moments, when my nose is pressed up hard against my pecuniary circumstances, I face afresh the knowledge that if I returned to England, endured the travails of single parenthood in an existence without Celestino, I would be sure to provide my daughter with something more than a hand-to-mouth lifestyle. Not that material circumstances could outweigh having a father in day-to-day life. Besides, my parents are here. I smile and make all the right noises thinking Celestino should be here too, to watch his little girl delight in the unboxing, his mother-in-law gather up all the wrapping paper, his father-in-law set up the toy workbench.

As the evening wears on and the storm shows no sign of abating, the waiting becomes intolerable, unease vying with irritation inside. Several times I catch my parents exchanging worried looks. Looks that suggest all manner of suspicions and speculations.

Together, the three of us keep Gloria busy until her bedtime. The moment Gloria's eyes close and her breathing steadies, I hurry to the telephone. The line is still dead. My home-phone answerphone normally kicks in on seven rings. I picture it there on the kitchen bench making a shrill noise that no one can hear. In a wild moment, I think of dashing out to the call box in the village. Angela hovers. Taking in that strained face, I put down the handset and say in as convincing a voice as I can muster that he must be stuck in Haría. 'The storm will have worn itself out by morning,' Bill says by way of offering comfort. It isn't long before they retire to bed.

LATER, when the others are sleeping soundly, I open the front door and fix my gaze on the driveway barely visible in the rain. Lightning illumes the night in sharp bursts of grey, thunder roiling in the wake. The cool wet air chills me and too soon I'm forced to close the door, well aware that through the thick wall of all that dark grey Celestino won't appear.

It's childish to blame, I know that, but standing in the dark of my parents' living room it feels as though Celestino's absence on Gloria's birthday is symbolic of all that frustrates me, precipitating a release of the pent-up emotion I've been feeling for years.

It isn't Gloria's fault. How can it be? I have no desire to wish away my own child, but there's no escaping Gloria, more than Celestino, has trapped me on the island. Moving overseas to be with the man of your dreams is one thing, falling pregnant to him another.

My thoughts take me down familiar tracks. If only I hadn't booked those two weeks on Lanzarote; if only I hadn't taken the coach trip north to Haría; if only I hadn't been lured by the novelty of an art exhibition held in a former underground water tank; if only I hadn't been enchanted by the artist himself; if I hadn't accepted his offer of dinner and then, finding myself with no way of getting back to my hotel, stayed the night. If I'd done none of those things I would never have fallen for Celestino.

It's no use. Gloria is a fixture in my life and takes up all the space in it.

I spy in the dim a toy cat on the floor beside the sofa and pick it up for a cuddle. Gloria consumes me in a way I couldn't have anticipated. I'm still a little stunned. The best that can be said is that she's the product of a brief period in my life when I rent myself open and let in a wild wand of change.

No one would ever call me reckless, which made the move all the more unusual. Although, despite my specialism in tourism, back in Ipswich I was little more than a glorified receptionist and I'd begun to find my work uninspiring, the eager visitors pushing through the information centre doors even more so. I booked another holiday to Lanzarote to spend more time with my new love. When Celestino expressed a wish for me to be by his side, I resigned from my job and moved to Lanzarote, with hesitation, yes, but also with resolve.

Then, just as I'm trying to adjust to things, I fall pregnant.

I head through to the kitchen, recalling with anguish and a measure of embarrassment the desperate solitude I endured in the aftermath of the birth, absolute whenever Celestino was at work in his studio, which was more often than not. Those early months were dreadful. There were days I wondered what I was doing on the island. In my depressed state, I was slow to make friends. Kathy and Pilar, both close to Celestino and young mothers themselves, offered support, but it took me a great deal of courage to accept it. Looking back, I feel vindicated with Pilar in the light of the language barrier. She spoke little English and my Spanish was rudimentary. With Kathy, it was the opposite. I didn't want to mix with other expats. Besides, Kathy and Pilar were both still in their twenties, with all the attitudes and interests typical of that age, and motherhood came to them with astonishing ease. In my mid-thirties at the time, I couldn't help feeling an outsider in their company.

The rain pelts down, the storm determined to unleash its tyranny. Untroubled, Tibbles rubs himself against my bare calf. I draw up a chair at the kitchen table, setting the toy cat on a place mat to stroke the real one on the floor. Finding him in an affectionate mood, I pick him up and nuzzle his fur.

I mustn't judge myself too harshly. I made a valiant effort to learn Spanish. With language acquisition my confidence grew and it was very early on in Gloria's second year when I felt compelled to earn some kind of living. That was when I realised my job prospects on the island were little short of laughable. There was no chance of me resuming a career in tourist information. My language skills were far from adequate.

They still are.

Besides, to work in the tourism industry is to work for the enemy as far as Celestino is concerned, and that will be grounds for divorce. It's a hypocritical view since he sells his artworks to the very tourists he doesn't want on his island. Not that I ever broach the topic. I wouldn't threaten my marriage in that way, and I don't dispute Celestino's point of view; I share it. If I didn't, I wouldn't have married him, would I? But the sacrifices I find I have to make are enormous.

I'll never forget the day I managed to gain work as a shop assistant for an Englishwoman trading in tourist bric-a-brac in Costa Teguise. Celestino's mouth fell open when I told him, then it clamped shut when he discovered to his annoyance that I wouldn't be dissuaded. Not long after, the woman fell ill and retired. I had a short spell filling in as hotel receptionist at a resort in the same town, a job I secured by chance when I went to collect my last pay. I can't believe the trouble I had convincing Celestino he had no right to tell me where I could and couldn't work. He was much happier when I took the job of cleaner of a holiday let in Punta Mujeres. The job was closer to home but not at all to my liking. He doesn't seem to mind my current position either, waitressing at a restaurant in Haría on Friday nights. It's a job from which I take little satisfaction. The clientele, mostly Northern Europeans, are gauche, and I struggle to smile at their banter.

Last night was especially bad; a drunken Frenchman's audacious pinch of my arm caused me to drop the plate of grilled fish I was carrying, the fish landing in the Frenchman's wife's lap. Unluckily for me, the proprietor of the restaurant, Eileen, whose warm heart usually calms her fiery temper, hadn't witnessed the scene, and berated me in the office out the back. It was as much as I could do not to walk out.

The rain eases. I lift Tibbles off my lap and go to the fridge, hoping a glass of milk might make me sleepy. The lit interior is a little emporium of leftovers and small treats. I can't help comparing it to my own, a stark representation of the lifestyle of the wife of an artist.

It occurs to me as I reach for a glass that I didn't know much about Celestino when I made the decision to be with him. I thought the mainstay of his creative life was the little paintings he sold at the local markets and the occasional exhibition. I found out much later that he was having a dry spell after losing his studio space to a property developer from Alicante, who bought the semi-derelict building to convert into holiday lets and turfed Celestino out. About that time, the local mayor offered up an artist-in-residence position for an indigenous painter. Celestino accepted: with qualms, with reticence, yet also with relief.

Gloria was toddling by the time Celestino found another studio. A British civil servant went broke when barely into the renovations of a former gofio mill and was finding the building impossible to sell. Celestino got wind of the place, and after some negotiations, the estate agent persuaded the owner to let one of the downstairs rooms. At the time, it seemed a heaven-sent gift.

My single example of the togetherness we've shared in the last two years, is one I contrived. The mill is a short walk from our home in Calle César Manrique. At lunchtimes, with Gloria in one hand and a basket of bread, cheese and fruit in the other, I amble down past the little covered market and town hall, and then take a detour through the plaza for the shade. At the end of the plaza I stop and wait for traffic to pass before making a dash to the mill on the next corner. Calle San Juan is one of the main routes through the village and never that pleasant to navigate by foot due to its narrowness and near total absence of pavements. There I stand, an English woman in her late-thirties with a small child, known to the village as Celestino's wife, neither a stranger nor accepted as one of the island's own, occupying a curious in-between place in the social fabric of the north, with my sandy hair, lightened by the sun and pinned back, limbs tanned, a large portion of my face obscured by my sunglasses.

I never go anywhere without my sunglasses. In the sunshine at any time of year I find the whitewash that coats just about every building on the island far too glary. I've become oversensitive. I never used to find the ubiquitous white so dazzling. Bearing a child seems to have changed me in unexpected ways.

I knock and push open the old mill house door—never locked when he is at work—and battle my way inside with our child and our lunch, always to find my husband absorbed before his easel, paintbrush poised, the accoutrements of his craft scattered all around him on benches and chairs. And when he sees me he stops, swings round and kisses first me, then Gloria. '¿Qué tal?' he asks, and I describe the little events of the past few hours: the laughter, the tears, the tantrums.

This morning, I drove to the studio instead and, leaving Gloria in the car, I dashed inside to make sure Celestino remembered when the party was due to start. He reassured me he wouldn't be late. His utterance seems far away from me, a lifetime ago, but I can still hear the hint of reproach in the tone. I picture him at the studio behind his easel, but it makes no sense that he'd still be there. More likely he's at home in bed, sound asleep after a good day's painting, not all turbulent inside like me. It's ungracious of me to think it, yet I can't understand why he didn't move heaven and earth to get to Máguez.

I take a long slow draught of my milk, feel the cool creaminess coat my mouth. Setting down my empty glass on the draining board, instead of somnolence it's annoyance I feel, almost exasperation over the way Celestino insists on living his life. I see in his passion a sort of wilful recalcitrance typical of the teenage boy, while berating myself for holding that view. After all, I chose him. I knew, even back in Ipswich as I prepared to leave my job and sell my house, what sort of life I faced in a village like Haría with an artist like Celestino.

On Lanzarote, the lot of the artist is made all the harder by a tourist market oriented to the light, the novel, the bargain, the memento of a short stay. Celestino's art is heavy, primal, and often confronting. He produces works to please himself, to honour his ancestors, not to cater to the tastes of holidaymakers. Fine art; I can accommodate that, or so I once thought. Besides, wasn't it my passion for the island, for the complete transformation of a life, and my yearning for something different that propelled me forwards, saw me relocating to make a go of things? Yet I knew nothing about Lanzarote beyond its tourist enclaves and its numerous museums and its stunning landscapes. I could have had no idea the impact Celestino's vehemently upheld indigenous identity and his resultant attitude to the status quo would have on our lives.

I rinse the glass and return to my seat. Listening to the relentless howl of the wind, I stare into the dark of the patio. Celestino's absence makes those early memories more present to me, one in particular, the first time I encountered in him not just the qualities of the politically motivated outsider, but the dark passion that comes with it.

It was a Saturday in February and we were at the Haría markets in the plaza. He'd scored a good pitch at the church end, in the dappled shade of one of the laurel trees. Me, an ungainly eight months pregnant with a baby neither of us was prepared for, was seated in a fold up chair, a loose cardigan wrapped around my belly, my face hidden behind newly acquired sunglasses. The plaza was filled with tourists ferried up by coach from the island's southern resorts. The trips were popular, the itinerary including a tour of César Manrique's last residence. The morning was sunny and warm, and most were out in their shirtsleeves. A musical duo were entertaining traders and browsers alike. Celestino's artworks were selling well. He'd knocked out a series of framed landscapes, for once broadly appealing and the price suited the average budget. His finer works, those larger paintings he created with enormous love and care, served more as stall decoration, a lure. Celestino was in a buoyant mood, engaging in pleasant banter in English and Spanish as he unzipped his belt pouch to add the euros. I sat back and smiled, fielding inquiries from the women who noticed my belly. Celestino joked I was good for trade.

By lunchtime, long queues had formed at the food stalls. The front of Celestino's stall was crowded as a result. He'd just begun to pull two of his paintings from the front edge of his display, when a boisterous teenager rammed into an old woman clutching a large bag. The woman toppled sideways and almost collided with a small child. In an effort to regain her balance, she reached out for Celestino's table. A watercolour landscape, one of Celestino's prized creations, toppled and crashed to the ground, the glass in the frame shattering, a shard tearing the paper.

There were the apologies and the woman offered to pay for the damage, but of course it was an accident and Celestino refused to accept recompense. These things happen, he said. But after that he was on guard and his mood darkened. A short while later, before he had a chance to recover from the loss, an enthusiastic couple came over and marvelled at his works, handling first one painting, then another. They quizzed Celestino on his methods, his background, his entire creative life story, then without making a purchase the woman handed Celestino a leaflet advertising an art exhibition, telling him he should get himself down to Arrecife to check it out.

The moment they were gone, Celestino crunched the leaflet in his hand and tossed it on the ground behind him. I was curious but it was too far for me to reach. Seeing my outstretched arm, he said, 'Leave it.' I was stunned. My distress must have shown on my face behind my sunglasses. Celestino qualified his remark, but not with the comforting platitude I'd anticipated. Instead he said, 'Bah! My work is as good as his.'

'Whose?'

'Diego Abarca. He isn't even a native.'

'Does it matter?'

'Of course, it matters. It matters a lot. Especially when he's made himself one of the DRAT brotherhood.'

'The DRAT brotherhood?' He made it sound like a conspiracy.

'El Departamento de Recreación, Arte y Tourismo. The Cabildo's champion,' he said with a dismissive flick of his hand. The Cabildo is

Lanzarote's island government. 'DRAT was established to promote the island's culture. So how come Diego Abarco gets the funding? He's from Andalucia!'

He went on to explain from his acerbic perspective that DRAT had transmogrified over the decades into an arm of the power elite, concerned more with pomp and ceremony than supporting hard-working artists, especially those of the alternative scene in the island's north.

'Does Diego live in the south?' I asked.

'He lives in the pockets of the rich, Paula.'

I was left none the wiser. All I knew was, much to Celestino's transparent vexation and my private displeasure, the privileges, the patronage and the funding were largely denied him and he was left to labour on unsupported.

Although as the weeks slipped by, there were times I couldn't help suspecting the situation had more to do with his own bellicose attitude. Times when my evening would be taken up listening to him vent. 'The politicos have no interest in the arts. But they do like to decorate their jobs. You see, Paula, the international arts scene provides much better opportunities for them than anything local and grass roots.' I did see. I'd heard him say it many times before. His eyes would narrow, his lips curl around his words. Manrique had been a people's man too, champion of the island's unsung artists and architects. He would have been as incensed as Celestino to see how far from his own ideals some had taken things. I often have to remind myself of that.

I knew from the moment I moved into his house that he had an interest in fighting corruption, but in those early months while I was pregnant he devoted a great deal of his time to me and my needs. We were, after all, in love, but the birth of Gloria seemed to flick a switch in him and he reverted back to his old habits. Perhaps until then he hadn't quite trusted me. Maybe he felt excluded from my affections once I had a baby in arms. Whatever the reason, Celestino began to spend hours of every evening on his computer. And when he readied for bed, I was treated to a diatribe on the latest scandal in what I was quick to realise was a corruption culture second to none.

What's the point of perpetual indignation? I don't like to see him chewed up by it. Not when he has a wife and a daughter by his side. I wonder sometimes what matters to him most. If the sacrifice he's making, all three of us are making, is worth it. But he sees hope on the horizon, through the younger generations, those who, unlike their parents and grandparents, have travelled overseas and gained a university education. Their forebears might be submissive and averse to change, he would say, but the young are not. They even have their own political party: Somos. It is for the young that, when he isn't in his studio creating art, Celestino campaigns to expose the island's corruption. Name and shame is his motto. 'Corruption always makes the poor poorer and enriches the rich.' Seated there in my mother's kitchen, I can almost hear him say it.

The rain stops. I go and open the patio door. Out in the cool night air, raising my face to the wind, observing through a break in the cloud the stars in the night sky muted by the streetlights of the village, my frustrations give way to a sweeter memory, one long forgotten.

I was about seven months pregnant, all flushed and contented and filled with anticipation. It was a time when Celestino had delighted in my presence. At night, while we lay together in bed, he would stroke my hair and in a voice smooth and soft he'd tell me of the places he wanted to show me, special places hidden away. Most of all he spoke of a string of beaches on the coast of the island's south, the beaches of the ancient mountains of Los Ajaches, accessed via the little village of La Quemada. He would describe the first beach, how it lay at the foot of a secret valley carved out of the mountainside by an ancient barranco. An unspoilt and inaccessible place, part of one of the island's most protected areas. He said the beach was among the last remaining on the island where the waters were calm enough and safe for swimming. Where the tourism juggernaut had yet to reach. Lying beside him, feeling the soothing touch of his hand, his breath warm against my cheek, the little beach sounded like paradise. Once I even drifted to sleep and dreamed I was there.

He promised to show me, but I was too heavily pregnant to make my way along the steep and rocky path, and then the baby came and we never went.

Suddenly chilled, I close the door, vowing to myself we'll visit the little beach at the first opportunity, the moment Celestino comes back.

4

TENESAR

Hunger gnaws at my guts. I take a sip of water and eat half a protein bar from my meagre rations. It makes little difference. My shoulder vies with the throbbing in my calf, a competition of pain. The impact of the collision and the terror in the aftermath are stuck on replay in my head. It's a jolt, a wake-up call. I've got too close and they don't like it. Another part of me smiles in grim satisfaction. It'll all be worth it if I can get out of here alive.

At least the burns on my face and hands have eased, and the dog has gone. About mid-morning, I watched the scruffy, brown-haired beast head off up the track and disappear. Although he could be still out there, but he won't smell me on the wind; there's a light north-easterly blowing off the land.

I need to head outside, not least to relieve my bladder. First, I need some sort of weapon. Risking the noise, I hurl one of the crates at the wall. The impact loosens the nails' grip. Feeling the joints wobble, I put my good leg inside to hold the crate still and yank at a plank with my good arm, wrenching it free, leaving two rusty nails protruding from one end. Weapon in hand I ease open the door and step outside.

The ocean is still heavy after the storm, the tide high, waves crashing on the basalt reef, sending up fountains of spume. To the west, where the rock pools at the bottom of the cliff make for enter-taining scrambling at low tide, the ocean thrashes. To the east the coastline arcs around a cliff. Facing the cliff and sheltered somewhat by the reef is a small beach of black sand.

Coursing up an incline to a low cliff, the village comprises about fifty small houses and huts arranged higgledy-piggledy around an arterial T intersection, one almost atop another. There's another house, nestled at the cliff base further west, and a few more sitting proud on rocky outcrops close to the waterline. At high tide, an occu-pant of one of those houses could cast a fishing rod out a sea-facing window.

Many of the buildings in the village are abandoned, others run down, the salty air eating into the whitewash, revealing the render in patches of speckled grey. It's the most inhospitable looking place, situated on the edge of a lava plain beside a barren volcano, but on a hot summer's day, when the island bakes, here is cool and secluded and families from nearby Tinajo come for weekend breaks and for the fishing.

In early spring, in a storm, no one is here but me.

I walk cautiously up a flight of stone steps and enter a small street. I try a few doors. None open. I take care where I place my feet, leaving no footprints. Maybe it's paranoia, maybe no one is watching, but as I reach the top of the street, I lean against a wall, peering round.

The main street is empty. I cross over and make a hasty dash for the next side street, and again try a few doors on the left. I wander back, trying the doors on the other side. Confidence grows as I reach the intersection and I'm planning to head down the main street when I detect the steady thrum of a car engine on the wind.

It has to be heading this way. I wait. The noise fades, then gets louder. Damn! I hobble back to my bolthole, careful of footprints, avoiding puddles and soft earth. With the door shut behind me, I re-arrange my barricade which is looking too much like a hidey hole, pulling away a couple of chairs and a crate. Satisfied, I crouch behind the table and wait.

The sound of the engine gets louder and louder until the vehicle is right outside the hut. Then the engine dies and a car door slams. There's no second slam. Safe to assume one person, then.

A shadow passes by the window. The guy has some height. I keep my breathing shallow. Soon I hear a voice, as though he's phoning someone, followed closely by a bark. That was definitely a bark. There's a scuffle, a shout, the car door slams again and the engine roars to life.

I exhale, relieved, but not for long. That mongrel dog has saved me, but whoever came here will assume that animal has an owner. They'll be back.

I try to calm down, conserve my strength, but my earlier suspicions are confirmed. That was no car accident and now, whoever tried to kill me is making sure I'm dead.

It doesn't take long for my thoughts to settle, first on Pedro, and then Paula with the sickening realisation they're both in mortal danger.

The bastard! If this is who I think it is, then I know what he's after. He wants to retrieve documents he believes are rightfully his, but in truth, those documents belong in a court of law. The problem for Pedro and Paula is this guy will stop at nothing to find them.

Pedro, I can rationalise. He knows the dangers, he's been in on this anti-corruption campaign since the beginning. But not Paula, my dear sweet Paula. She's as innocent as they come. What have I done to her? Will she realise soon enough? Will she join the dots? Or will she believe I died in a car accident and go on with daily life grieving and oblivious. What will she think? How will she act?

For the first time in my life I feel like praying. Guilt consumes me. I've neglected my wife and child, and for what? I automatically reach for the stone Paula gifted me at the end of her holiday when we first met. To remember her by, she said. Polished obsidian and I had it mounted on a pendant and I've worn it ever since as a necklace. But my hand reaches around my neck and it's bare.

Horror has me in its grip. I've lost her necklace; am I going to lose her as well?

The day wears on. My thoughts return to survival. How long do I stay here? As long as possible; I'm being stalked by twin hunters. Will

help arrive? I figure it'll take a while, days even, for the car to be identified, if at all. After yesterday's storm the authorities will be stretched.
In the meantime, what will Paula do? In the end, she's all I can think
about.

Oh, Paula!

5

HARÍA

THE ROOM IS DARK, THE WEAK LIGHT OF DAWN BARELY SQUEEZING through the chinks in the shutters. Beside me, lying on her side and breathing steadily, Gloria sleeps. Under her arm is the toy rabbit Celestino's favourite uncle gifted when she was born; once plump, furry and white, with ears all straight and true, now much-loved, one-eyed and grey, the ears droopy, fur thin from the wear of a tight hand.

My eyes feel puffy and I remember crying as I lay beside Gloria, small tears of frustration over her disappointing birthday party, which transmuted into a gush of anguish over the vicissitudes of my married life.

The wind has dropped and I can't hear any rain. Still dressed in yesterday's clothes, I slip out of bed and go to the kitchen. Angela, an early riser, is making coffee.

'Sleep well?' she says without turning around.

'Sort of.'

I take up the chair at the table's end. Hoping to hide the puffiness around my eyes, I direct my gaze at the window. Thin mats of cloud drift across the sky.

'I need to nip back to Haría. Check on the studio, and the house.'

'At least eat something first.'

Angela comes over and hands me a cup brimming with milky coffee. I feel her eyes on my face as I take it.

'Mum, can I leave Gloria with you?'

'It will be our pleasure,' Bill says, entering the room in his brown check dressing gown.

I wrap my fingers around my cup, feeling the warmth penetrate my skin.

He hovers. 'Try not to worry. There's bound to be a reasonable explanation. Something to do with the storm.'

I can find little reassurance in his words and when Angela sets down cereal and toast I can't muster the will to eat.

THE ROAD GLISTENS, puddles yet to evaporate on the stretches still in shadow. The narrow streets of Máguez are empty save for the odd car parked up hard against a whitewashed wall, but that is not strange. The village with its ancient, cuboid farmhouses, their shutters and doors the same shade of green, maintains quietude when the rest of the island swarms with activity the whole year round. Like Yé and Guinate, two tiny villages a few kilometres further north, here the tourists are few and they pass straight through.

I head south. Before long, the village gives way to open fields edged with low stone walls. Despite my eagerness to discover what has happened, I drive carefully up the steep rise that separates Máguez from Haría, avoiding the silt smears on the road. At the crest, the village of Haría begins, and I wend my way down more narrow streets, built for feet and the occasional cart, streets scarcely wide enough for two cars to pass.

Down in the village centre, I park outside the front yard gates of the old mill house, mounting the right wheels on the pavement. I have to wait for a slow stream of oncoming cars to go by before opening the driver's side door.

Celestino's old blue car is nowhere in sight.

Mine is a Renault, a white ex-rental hatch and I dislike driving it. When I moved to the island I hadn't wanted a car. Right through my pregnancy I was determined to rely on Celestino and buses. Even now, I spend as little time as I can behind the wheel, having regretted buying the vehicle the very day I drove it home from Arrecife. I took the scenic route via Teguise and up over the mountain, Peñas del Chache, to find the vehicle losing power down the switchbacks to Haría. I had to freewheel much of the journey. The alternator had died.

I push the mill-house door half-expecting it to open, but it's locked. I push again to make sure, thinking the rain might have caused the wood to swell, but it doesn't budge.

The windows facing the street are shuttered, and the only access around the back is through the front yard gates, which are always padlocked. I knock and wait. Knock again. I can hear a faint echo inside. I press my ear to the door but hear nothing more.

'Celestino.' I call as loudly as I dare, taking a quick glance up and down the street.

I knock and call again. No response. I do my best to quell the tension tightening my chest, reasoning away an image of him prostrate on his studio floor. People don't get murdered in Haría. They just don't. And he's in good health. People don't drop down dead in their late-thirties. It's unheard of.

I return to the car and drive on a short way to the tiny church of San Juan, set in a swathe of tarmac at the convergence of several streets, making it easy to turn around and head back the way I came. The village looks as it does on any other day, aside from the moisture on the parts of the road still in shade. Closed in by dwellings and high, whitewashed walls, it's impossible to assess the storm damage. It's only when I pull up outside our home that I see that the barranco opposite, usually a dry stream bed, is wet and littered with debris, and part of the wall on its far side has collapsed. Storm water must have risen to the height of the road; silt fans out, drying as the day warms.

The street is still. No sign of Celestino's car, but he usually parks in the garage round the back. Anticipation stirs in my belly. I'm across the street and out the front of our little old house in a second. I push my key in the lock and take a breath as I open the door.

The hallway is dark. I remove my sunglasses as I step inside. My eyes are slow to adjust to the dim. I almost trip over one of Gloria's toys. I curse and shove whatever it is to one side, realising as I do that Celestino is almost certainly not here; the door to the patio is as I left it, closed.

I pull open the door and nudge a wedge of wood under its base.

The wind rustles the leaves of the tree in the patio centre. Rainwater brims in Celestino's chunky pot plant saucers. On the far side of the patio, a canvas chair left out is half dry.

Foliage sparkles in a sudden burst of sunshine, shards of white brilliance. I wince and turn and squint, the morning sun too bright on the kitchen wall. I go in to find the room as I left it; uncommonly clean and tidy, with the dishes washed and left to drain, the pans put away, the bench tops clear of condiments; and the shelves above, cluttered with jars of this and that, arranged in some sort of order. On the small table set to one side of the room are three green placemats, Gloria's plastic cup drained of its contents, and a few coloured pencils that belong in the tin on top of the small bookcase nearby. There is no indication that Celestino has been in the room since I left for Máguez yesterday. When I open the fridge, the level of milk and juice look about the same and there is no food to be taken, just a near empty jar of artichoke hearts, another of pimientos in oil, and a half-used bottle of passata.

I deposit my bag, sunglasses and keys on the table and check the bathroom, accessed via a short passage off the kitchen. Finding the room undisturbed—toilet seat down, shower curtain drawn back, lid on the toothpaste—I go and unlock the back door which opens into the garage. The absence of his car comes as no surprise—he drove to the studio and has clearly not returned home—but disappointment prickles anyway. The atmosphere of this new reality I find myself in feels surreal, as though I've entered a life belonging to someone else.

I lock the door and make my way through the kitchen and the patio to the main hallway. Gloria's bedroom is on the right. It's in its usual disarray, her toys strewn across the floor, bed covers crumpled in a heap in the middle of the mattress.

The door directly opposite leads to the two tower rooms: a small square living room, with main bedroom above. The wooden staircase set against the near wall renders the living room even smaller. There's nothing noticeably different, no empty coffee cup, no open book lying face down, or any other evidence of Celestino's recent presence. What did I expect?

I climb the stairs cautiously, a tread at a time, taking in the sharp creaks as each tread yields to my weight. This is the last room in the house, the only place Celestino could be if he's here at all. I stop halfway and brace myself, forcing myself on, wanting to find him, craving the relief I would feel at the sight of him, and not wanting him here all at once, for if he is here, in what state will he be? Unconscious? Dead? Ridiculous thoughts, I tell myself, as I reach the last tread.

I don't know how to feel when I see that our bedroom, like the rest of the house, is exactly as I left it. The bed made in a haphazard fashion, clothes dotted about on chairs, on the floor. It is impossible to tell if any of his are missing. The books on each of the bedside tables appear unchanged. I check the wardrobe and his chest of drawers. All look normal. I go to the window overlooking the patio at the rear of the property. No sign of Celestino's car in the laneway.

Finally, I turn to his home office crammed into the far corner of his side of the room. The old wooden desk he borrowed from his studio in the mill house seems no different. The drawers are locked as anticipated. Glancing at a small pile of manila folders on the floor underneath I hesitate. Knowing how annoyed he'll be if he discovers I've riffled through his papers, I leave them undisturbed. Besides, I doubt he would leave anything that private lying around. The desk top is empty save for his computer and, open atop his keyboard, the letter acknowledging receipt of his application to secure a commission of indigenous artworks for La Mareta, a stately home soon to be opened to the public.

With the letter in my hand, I sit down on the bed, my search of the house complete. I take in the DRAT letterhead, feel the weight of the paper. The letter is a harbinger of hope, our future salvation locked into its print. The winner will be announced in eight days. I can't help feeling Celestino's absence as a betrayal. As though he's run away to escape the responsibilities that might lie ahead of him if he won. It's a ridiculous thought but even as I dismiss it, my mind traipses back to the worst days of our marriage, to a time when my frustration over our hand-to-mouth existence peaked.

IT WAS A FEW MONTHS AGO, and the local newspapers were filled with coverage of La Mareta, the first articles detailing how generous King Felipe VI was in gifting the former royal residence to the island, journalists singing the praises of all the dignitaries concerned. I was reading one such article in the local paper when Celestino walked into the kitchen and dumped his satchel on the table.

'La Mareta, another example of Manrique's genius,' he read aloud over my shoulder.

'It'll attract tourists in their thousands.'

'Bah!'

I looked at him strangely. Surely even he could see how the island benefited from using Manrique as its emblem. Yet he wasn't alone in his attitude. An editorial in the same edition went on to cite a growing sense of injustice in the hearts of activists and community groups in the island's north. Yet again, the ordinary people were shut out.

The media now had another angle to cover and the following day the La Mareta coverage was front-page news. For weeks after, the complaining and campaigning and protesting went on. Celestino ignored it all. Whenever I broached the topic, he waved it away with one of his dismissive scoffs.

Yet the campaigning proved a success. An opportunity arose, one shrouded in controversy and debate, for another artist to display their work in one small section of the residence. When I read the news, I could scarcely contain my excitement. I hurried Gloria into her shoes and walked briskly to the studio to tell him.

'What's up?' he said after I pushed open the studio door and stood panting. I'd carried Gloria for half the trip.

I proffered the newspaper folded open at the article and explained in hurried sentences. The criteria were strict. The artist must be native to the island and all artwork must be identifiably of authentic indigenous merit.

'It's made for you, Celestino.'

'It is?'

'You must apply. Surely you can see that.'

He wore his intransigent face. Even as he turned back to the work on his easel, I urged and cajoled, pointing out that the commission would sustain us for months if not years, and it would establish Celestino's reputation and give him the prestige he so needed.

'Paula! Stop it!'

I froze. I'd never heard him yell like that before. Defiance rose up in me and I folded my arms and tilted my head to the side and told him that once La Mareta opened, in all likelihood coachloads of tourists would stop coming every Saturday to marvel at the Manrique residence in Haría. Privately I knew they wouldn't but Celestino hesitated and I knew I'd got through to him.

As much as he couldn't help but admire the late César Manrique, he despised the way one solitary man claimed all the attention, albeit posthumously, leaving little room for any living artist to make their mark. He especially despised the way this harsh reality was ground into his soul on a daily basis by the trickle of tourists passing by our house on a post-Manrique ramble about the village. Even then, I spent several tense weeks wondering if he'd go through with a submission.

I PLACE the letter back on his keyboard. One quick glance around and I head downstairs without a clue what to do next.

The coffee I drank for breakfast on an otherwise empty stomach has left a cloying taste in my mouth. I go and brush my teeth. Moments later, I'm hungry. Without a second thought I down the last of the orange juice in the fridge, straight from the carton. After the toothpaste, it tastes bitter. I throw the dregs down the sink, leave the carton on the bench, and fetch a glass from the highest shelf, far from Gloria's reach. The flagon of water we store on the floor under the sink. It's almost empty. I fill my glass and put the flagon on the bench beside the juice carton. As I swill my mouth I collect my thoughts. It's possible, not likely but possible, that Celestino is still at the studio. I have a vague recollection of a spare key. But I'm standing right by the phone: the logical next step. I don't want to alarm our friends or appear to be overreacting but given the situation, there seems no choice. Pedro is Celestino's closest friend. I dial his number first.

Three rings and his wife picks up.

'¿Hola?'

'It's Paula.'

'Espera un momento,' she says in carefully enunciated Spanish. There's a long pause. I hear scuffles in the background and Kathy's muffled admonishments. Three daughters, six and under—must be a handful by anybody's measure.

'I'm sorry,' she says, at last coming back to the phone, 'but we couldn't make it yesterday. The storm was crazy.'

'That's okay.'

'How did it go?'

'No one made it.'

'That's no good. Poor Gloria.'

'She's fine. She didn't seem to mind. My father kept her entertained.'

'¡Ay, los abuelos!'

Did she really need to show off her Spanish like that?

'I have a present for Gloria. I'll call in with it next time I'm up your way.'

'No rush. Look, this might sound like an odd question but have you seen Celestino?'

'Celestino? Why?'

'He didn't make it either.'

'That is strange for him to miss such a special party.'

'I know. I haven't seen or heard from him since yesterday morning. He was finishing a painting and said he'd come later. But he never showed up. I'm worried, Kathy. I'm thinking of calling the police.'

'The police? Calm down, Paula. Have you checked his studio?'

'I went there. It's locked. I knocked but no one answered.'

'Maybe try again. He might have gone up the street for some fresh air. You know what he's like when he's working on something.'

'But...'

'He'd never put his art before his daughter,' Kathy says as though finishing my sentence for me.

I can't help wishing he would feel the same way about his wife.

'Don't worry Paula. He'll turn up.' There is a brief moment of silence. Then, 'I have to go. Pedro's at the market and I said I'd join him with the girls. Aye ...' her voice trails off as she attends to a commotion in the background. Then she comes back to the phone with, 'We're just heading out the door. Hasta luego.'

'Bye, Kathy.'

'Hey, maybe Celestino's there too. I'll have a look around.'

'Would you? Thanks. Please call me if you find him.'

'Of course.' And she hangs up.

I have an almost identical phone conversation with Pilar.

'Something urgent must have come up,' Pilar says in that reassuring tone people put on at times like this, a tone I'm already finding tedious.

'Then why hasn't he phoned?'

'He probably ran out of battery.'

I spy his phone charger plugged into the wall over by the kettle.

'I expect you're right,' I mutter.

'I better go. Miguel's outside clearing up. We lost a section of wall.'

'Is the house okay?'

'Sure. Thank goodness. And yours?'

'All good.'

'Don't worry, Paula.'

'I'll try not to.'

Fernando hasn't seen him either. He curates for a museum in Teguise, and is busy cleaning a new acquisition when I make the call. 'He'll turn up,' he says, and abruptly rings off. The flippant tone of his voice seems dismissive. Yet perhaps he's right. Perhaps they are all right, and I'm worrying about nothing.

I can't think who else to call. Kathy and Pedro, Pilar and Miguel, and Fernando—they are Celestino's only friends. Celestino, I discovered once I started living with him, is an intensely private man, maintaining his reserve with few exceptions. He interacts with his fellow villagers in a cordial manner, as though they are acquaintances; scarcely evident he's known them all his life.

Standing alone in the kitchen of a house two hundred years old, situated in an ancient village on a narrow tongue of land barely three miles wide, I feel excluded; not only from aspects of Celestino's life, but from the island I now call home. My reaction is strong, surprisingly strong, and I struggle to contain it. He appears to me now an absent presence. I sit down at the table, giving my mind the latitude it seems to want, as though through my recollections I'll have much more success in manifesting the real man.

It was impossible to grasp when I first arrived how guarded the Lanzaroteños were when it comes to outsiders, especially in the relatively isolated villages of the north. The old ways are almost a distant memory, the island having long given itself up to tourism. Is a deep-seated resentment alive in the hearts of not just Celestino but many a local, especially the artists? Why shouldn't it exist, fed by a knowledge of the perpetual injustices meted out against the people and their land? But it does nothing to alleviate how I feel, sitting in the kitchen with the phone in my hand. If I belonged, if I could enter the closed world of the locals, then I'd have a far better idea of what to do next. He might be inside the home of any resident of Haría, doing heaven knows what.

Then again, if I were in the islanders' shoes I'd maintain my privacy and do my best to ignore the foreigners in my midst. They've lost so much. Or am I romanticising? Gone the arduous tradition of farming to the mountaintops, yet gone too days spent amid those breathtakingly expansive views of land and sea. All sacrificed to the tourist dollar. Dollars lining the pockets of developers while the ordinary locals see little benefit in wages and conditions. Tourism in England is different. There's so much else going on in the economy. It isn't the be all and end all. Those, like Celestino—sensitive, creative, concerned—see in the development trend an enormous tragedy and they harbour a moiling discontent, one that sooner or later will erupt. It's what drew me to him in the first place, his passion. For him, Manrique's iconic sculptural tribute, Fecundidad, and the accompanying Museo del Campesino, constitute memorials, not venerations of a lifestyle still lived.

I've always known Celestino is staunch and outspoken when it comes to protecting the island's interests. Although at first, I had no idea the extent of his passion, the lengths he would take to expose shady deals, especially when, as they invariably do, those deals impact adversely on the environment. Having worked in the tourism industry my whole adult life and seen first-hand the way the holiday mentality changes people into amoral pleasure seekers, I share his discontent. I have even started to help translate into English some of his reportage and exposés, which he posts on his anti-corruption blog under the pseudonym 'Dana', after he pointed out that the mainstream media pump out pro-tourism propaganda.

'Someone has to get the word out.'

Yes, but why you?

I study the phone in my hand, run a finger over the buttons. What if Fernando is wrong and Celestino isn't going to turn up? The thought that his disappearance has nothing to do with the storm and everything to do with his anti-corruption campaigns begins to insinuate itself into my mind. I should be looking for him but I'm strangely frozen. How dangerous is it to take his stance? I've often heard references to the island's mafia but up until now I've never taken it all that seriously, despite the scandals. That an island so small, with a local population miniscule by global standards, could have the lucrative wherewithal to support the operations of the mafia has always seemed to me ludicrous. If the mafia does exist, it couldn't compare to the real mafia of, say, Russia or Albania.

Only the once did I express this view to Celestino. I expressed it with a laugh, thinking how quaint, but my mirth fell away when I saw the outrage spread across my husband's face. I'm embarrassed thinking about it. Have I underestimated the gravity of the island's shady dealings all along? I've often wondered if his campaigns would put him in danger but he's always reassured me that no one knows who Dana is. But any hacker with an ounce of know-how could discover the identity of a blogger. Celestino is being naïve. What would become of him if those corrupt officials did find out? I can only surmise it wouldn't be pleasant.

The phone is still in my hand. I clasp it as if it alone will bring him back to me. But there is no one else to call.

Richard Parry pops into my mind and I despatch him immediately. An old acquaintance of Celestino's after he purchased several of his large paintings, Richard is a temporary resident who uses his island home to compose his books. Since we married, Celestino has had little to do with the author. Richard no longer seeks him out on market days, and ever since he took offence at not having received an invitation to our wedding, things have been strained. He was at home in Bunton at the time, dealing with his irascible wife Trish, and we saw no point in posting an invitation. Once, I even saw Richard skirt the markets warily, and on another occasion, upon sighting Celestino's stall he about faced and headed in the direction of his home. For an inexplicable reason, Richard chooses to hold Celestino responsible for what he conceives a personal snub, which allows him, conveniently perhaps, to remain on cordial terms with me. Although I suspect his animosity is due to the flop of *Ico's Promise*, a book Richard hoped Celestino would help him research after his friend and local potter, Domingo, moved to Gran Canaria. His hopes were in vain. Whatever the reason for their strained relations, Richard will know nothing of Celestino's whereabouts.

I return the phone to the console. Hoping to locate the spare key to the mill house, I rummage through the bottom kitchen drawer. After some time shunting about tea towels, oven gloves, aprons, plastic bags, boxes of matches and candles, a roll of cling wrap, several cork screws and a never-used rolling pin gifted by my mother, I kneel down and extract the contents item by item, shaking and rattling until I find the key lodged in a small leather pouch. I shove everything back and close the drawer, ignoring the fingers of a rubber glove poking out.

Wasting no time, I thread the mill house key onto my keyring and leave the house.

Facing down the street I hesitate, thinking I might walk. But I might need my car; for what I can't imagine, but I choose to drive instead.

Pulling up outside the mill house I feel subtly changed, as though the key in my hand represents a turning of much more than a lock.

I enter the vestibule half expecting to find Celestino emerging from his studio. I'm met with silence. Paying acute attention to things I normally take for granted, I notice the dirt and grime coating the tiled floor, the scrunched paper in the far corner, and a small bag of rubbish no one has had the presence of mind to take to the bin.

The vestibule leads to an internal patio; visible from where I stand is a stone staircase winding to the upper level. The balustrade is in good condition and looks freshly painted, but the steps are crumbling. Piles of rubble litter the paving at its base. I doubt anyone has ventured up those stairs in a long time.

'Celestino?'

I turn to my left and open the studio door.

A smell of fresh paint hangs in the air. At the flick of a light I see a new work on the easel. Celestino's palette lies beside it on the long bench that lines the near wall. I go over. The paint splodges look dry. A single clean brush, separate from the others stored in old jars, rests next to a dirty rag. He must have stopped working on it sometime yesterday. There's no sign of the commission for the Swedish doctor. Did he take the commission to his house? He must have done. What other explanation is there?

I step away and cast an eye around the room. Rows of paintings are stacked against the far wall. Motes hover in bands of sunlight filtering in through dilapidated shutters. Between the window and the door, another bench, wider but not as long, is covered in jars and tubs of tools, notebooks, art books, an assortment of acrylics and other paints. On the floor are old scraps of timber, a roll of chicken wire, two saw horses, and an array of power tools. Nowhere, not anywhere, do I see his phone.

I recall Kathy's remark and know he didn't just pop up the road. He's vanished. I flick off the light and close the studio door.

'Celestino?'

The door opposite is kept locked. I try the handle but it won't open. I head through to the patio and call again, directing my voice first up the stone stairs and then at the rooms out the back.

No answer.

He'll answer. If he's here, he'll answer. Besides, as far as I know he never wanders about the building. Disappointed, I return to the vestibule and on outside, making sure to lock the door behind me.

Leaving the car safely parked with two wheels on the pavement, I cross Calle la Hoya and round the next corner, passing the small supermarket and entering the tree-lined plaza with its dense laurel leaf canopy. I stop outside the church to call my parents.

My father picks up.

'No news. Other than I can't find him anywhere.'

'Stay calm. Did you call his friends?'

'None of them have seen or heard from him.'

'Where's his car?'

'Not at home or the studio.'

'There'll be a perfectly reasonable explanation, Paula. Remember that.'

'I hope so.'

'What will you do next?'

'Ask around the plaza. Then I'll come back I suppose. How's Gloria?'

'Happy as Larry. Don't fret.'

I'm doing my best.

I hang up and slip my phone in my pocket. The plaza is quiet. Down at the other end, tables, arranged four-deep outside the two cafes, are mostly empty. I make for the second, the one on the corner, the only café Celestino will frequent.

La Cacharra is owned by the Bandala family, originally from Guinate. The Bandalas were fortunate enough to make sufficient pesetas from the sale of their land to the developer of the former Guinate Tropical Park—once home to thousands of exotic birds and other animals—to open a restaurant. La Cacharra has been a success from the start, not only having the best location in the village, but also the best chef. Tío Pepe prided himself on the finest roasted meats and authentic local stews—potajes, lentejas, estofados, or various kinds of stew to the uninitiated—building on the notoriety of old Inez of Calle Cruz de Ferrer, who for decades gave over her home to feed the locals.

The Bandalas make a significant contribution to the community. One Bandala or other can be found on the committees of all of Haría's community groups, from sporting clubs and festivals to the arts. And they're generous with their donations. But never, Celestino has it on good authority, when it comes to filling the coffers of unscrupulous mayors.

Antonio, son of old Tío Pepe, is wiping down the counter when I walk in. He's spritely for his age, although his closely cropped beard is more grey than black, and in the few years I've been here he's thickened at the waist, but nothing can detract from his ebullient charm. His face lights up when he sees me.

'Hola, Paula. ¿Como estas?'

I force a smile in return, wanting to tell him I'm fine, but I must have betrayed my concern as Antonio's own face falls.

'¿Qué pasa?'

'¿Ha visto Celestino?' I say in my clunky Spanish, preparing to concentrate on his response.

'¿Hoy? No.' He shakes his head and says in very clear Spanish, 'Celestino no ha pasado por aquí.'

Somehow, I didn't think he'd been here. Even so, I can't help asking, '¿Estás seguro?'

Antonio is certain. He's been working since they opened that morning. He glances at his watch. Two hours ago.

I persist. Thinking about the dried paint in the studio, I'm more interested in yesterday. '¿Y ayer?' I ask, watching him closely.

'¿Ayer? Yo estaba trabajando todo el día mas o menos en la lluvia, y yo no lo vi.'

I picture Antonio, shunting the chairs and tables under cover, then huddling under the canopy behind the al fresco servery, no doubt wondering why he bothered to open. If he was there all day, as he says, and Celestino did pass by, then he'd have seen him. And he hadn't. Although he did caveat his remark with 'more or less'. If he went inside, out the back to the bathroom or to the kitchen, Celestino might have passed by, or even called in. Unlikely, unless he had a message for someone or he dropped something off or picked something up. A rendezvous. Something so brief it occurred without Antonio's notice. I pull myself up. My thoughts are running off like headless chickens. And I can't think of a single reason why Celestino would do such a thing. It's too out of character. Besides, the other staff will have seen him, I only need inquire and I'll know for certain. And Antonio will surely ask around. It's human nature. Pre-empting the obvious I ask him who was working yesterday.

'Yo y Carmen.'

Seeing my concern, he goes to the kitchen door and calls out. Moments later, Carmen rushes into the restaurant. A strapping woman in her twenties, Carmen is Antonio's second daughter. She's training to be a chef and, he hopes, will one day take over the restaurant. She prides herself on turning traditional cuisine into dishes favoured by the tourists and the locals alike. Since she's taken over the kitchen, the café has outcompeted every other eatery in town.

'Estoy cocinando, Papa,' she says reproachfully, her hands coated in flour.

'Carmen, espera. ¿Ha visto a Celestino?'

'¿Cuándo?'

'Hoy o ayer.'

She hesitates, thinking back. Then she shrugs her shoulders and says, 'No.' She stares at me, puzzled. 'Why?'

Antonio stands beside his daughter. '¿Sí, why?'

'Celestino ha desaparecido.' Disappeared—it sounds even worse in Spanish. Maybe 'disappeared' is the wrong word. I should have said 'missing'. He's missing. It's less dramatic, less emphatic, less ominous somehow. But it's too late, the word is spoken.

Antonio and Carmen exchange glances.

I try to look nonchalant, then I smile and fob off my remark with quips and suppositions. Must have used a barranco as a waterslide and washed up on Graciosa. Probably busy helping some poor farmer clean out his goat shed after a mudslide. It's no use. I'm suddenly acutely aware that my interrogation of the Bandalas means word will spread throughout the village, embellished no doubt with speculations on the state of our marriage, and told-you-so references to the time he spends away from his family at his studio. There's nothing I can do to arrest that flow. I add somewhat lamely, 'I can't find him. I mean, no puedo encontralo.'

Antonio gives me a sympathetic look. '¿Café?' he says, leading me to a table in the far corner. 'Siéntese aquí.' I sit with my back to the wall.

The café has an old and worn feel with tables and chairs of solid wood, a high counter displaying an array of tapas, and glass shelves lining the back bar, filled with bottles of spirits. The walls are covered in brown and blue patterned tiles. Three old men have taken up the table near the entrance. At the next table, a woman in a wide-brimmed hat of vivid red is reading a newspaper. Outside, a middle-aged couple are seated at one of the tables under the trees. An ordinary scene on an ordinary day, yet for me existing in a strange new reality, nothing looks as it did the day before.

Antonio comes over with my coffee and a small pastry. I reach for my purse but he raises his hand and walks away, his attention caught by a party of six entering the café, followed closely behind by two couples. He herds them all to the seating outside. 'But it's windy,' I hear one of the women complain. 'It's better, it's better,' Antonio says in thickly accented English.

One of the men puts an affectionate arm around his partner's waist and gives her a squeeze before she sits down. He takes up the chair opposite then reaches for her hand. Young love? Well, not so young. He has grey hair and she has to be over fifty. But their love has the fresh spontaneity of youth. Were Celestino and I ever like that? All lovey dovey and holding hands? In the days after we met he was kind and considerate and transparently in love, and in those first weeks after I moved to the island we were certainly close and Celestino attentive, yet his is not a demonstrable, ardent kind of love. What has grown between us is more a mellow affection born of respect and an enduring tolerance of each other's differences. Even through the burden of Gloria's quick arrival and the ensuing financial hardship—the sale of my house back in Ipswich paid out the mortgage and the estate agent's fees, little more—our love was never in

47

question. We don't fight and, apart from that awful day when I confronted him over the La Mareta commission, rarely argue. But, there's little togetherness. Gloria takes up most of my attention and Celestino spends most of his time at the studio or upstairs in his corner of our bedroom, immersed in his latest anti-corruption campaign.

There are days I crave his company, his undivided attention, but I've learned to bury the yearning in domestic and motherly routines. I keep telling myself I need an interest of my own, a fulfilling occupation of some kind, but I've no idea what that might be. I do my best to follow the issues associated with the island's tourism but only at a distance. Almost all the in-depth material written on the history and culture of the island is in Spanish and not seeing any role for myself in terms of employment, my enthusiasm has waned. And I'm too full of Gloria's needs to nurture any pursuits of my own.

I drink my coffee in a few large gulps and leave the pastry untouched. I'm about to stand when in walks my neighbour, Shirley, sashaying to the counter in a long-sleeved velour pantsuit of deep purple, a diamante clutch bag in hand. She has an assertive gait for her age—late sixties I surmise—her figure straight-backed and trim. She's a whole head and shoulders shorter than me, and she dyes her short fine hair a smoky blonde. I've never seen her without one of those matching and garish earring and necklace sets adorning her personage. On this occasion, it's a pearl and crystal choker with globular pendants. She's an energetic woman too, the sort with somewhere to go, something to do, someone to meet. A busy body in the literal and metaphoric senses of the word. And despite her age and independent means, she works part-time for a local estate agent, work that suits her personality.

Shirley hasn't noticed me seated in the back corner, and I decide not to attract her attention. Of all the people in the village, she's the last person Celestino will have told of his whereabouts. I find her harmless but Celestino loathes her.

. . .

ONCE, as we were arriving home from a trip to Gran Canaria to show Celestino's family the baby, Shirley pulled up in her Maserati right behind his car, coming to an abrupt stop a few inches from his rear bumper. I was standing on the pavement watching Celestino extract the baby carrier from the back seat. Alarm shot through me. I was about to say something when Shirley said, 'Whoopsie daisy,' and scurried across the road to her house, disappearing inside before Celestino had manoeuvred himself and Gloria out of the car. He was livid.

Inside the kitchen, I put Gloria, asleep in her carrier, on the floor by my feet. Celestino set about making coffee. It was then he told me the trouble Shirley had caused him after she came to Haría in the late 1990s. The trouble started a few years after her arrival, when he was in his early twenties and had just graduated in fine art, and with both parents recently deceased.

'Shirley claimed that the adjoining property boundary extended well into my backyard and that in fact, my shed was illegal and would have to be demolished.' I caught his eye, pointed at Gloria and pressed my fingers to my lips. He lowered his voice. 'She argued for months over the boundary, then came the lawyer's letters and eventually the matter ended up in court. I had to represent myself.'

'How did it go?'

'She won. The site plans for her property did in fact include half of my shed. And the plans for mine were so old and poorly drawn that it didn't matter that the shed in question had existed in that spot for two hundred years. I had to demolish it and move twenty metres of dry stone wall.' He stood with his back to the bench. 'She was victorious.'

'I can imagine.'

'Steer clear of her, Paula. She's dangerous by association. She won that boundary dispute because she was married to Juan Mobad.'

The coffee burbled. He waited a moment before turning off the flame. Then he put two cups on the table and poured.

'He died, didn't he?' I said, taking my cup.

'Good riddance. He was a property-developing shyster implicated in numerous scandals involving the island's mafia.'

'Shirley must miss him.'

Celestino sat down in the chair opposite. 'I'm sure she does. She blames me too. I never liked Mobad. After the boundary dispute, I worked doubly hard to expose his involvement in a corruption scandal.'

'What did he do?'

'Money laundering. He was arrested during a wide scale anti-corruption sweep of the island.'

'Did he stand trial?'

'The cases against the others involved were protracted. Before he was due to stand, Mobad was found at the bottom of El Risco, or rather, bits of him.'

The way he said it seemed callous. Shirley has never recovered from his suicide. If it was in fact suicide. It's impossible to tell. Fourteen kilometres of cliff, all of it remote, much inaccessible; if he'd been pushed, there'd have been no witnesses. After his death, Shirley became exceptionally extroverted, her days brimming with distractions. Once in a private moment she confided that if she didn't keep busy she'd go off the rails.

I wanted to take Celestino's side—I'm as opposed to corruption as the next person—but I felt sorry for Shirley. Behind Celestino's back, I forged a cordial if secret friendship with my neighbour. Besides, we had something in common; having married local men placed us both in a cultural void. We were neither properly local nor properly expat. We were allies, despite the history between Shirley and Celestino. Although I was well aware he never wanted 'that woman' to ever set foot in his house.

Later, as Gloria became a toddler and a handful, I would even, on occasion, ask Shirley to mind Gloria during her afternoon nap, while I dashed to the supermarket in the fishing village of Arrieta.

It's a short drive and the supermarket favourably priced, and well stocked too, unlike those catering for a much smaller clientele in Haría. Grocery shopping is much easier without grabbing hands. I'm cautious never to let the childminding occur when Gloria is awake, in case she lets something slip to her father. Come to think of it, I'm amazed I take the risk and admonish myself over the deception, quickly justifying it to myself along the lines of 'needs must'.

Shirley is facing the window. The men, huddled together at the front table, burst into laughter. I shift my gaze. The woman in the red, wide-brimmed hat lowers her newspaper, revealing a pair of horn-rimmed reading glasses. There is something furtive about her. I catch her eye and she quickly looks away.

While Shirley exchanges some loose change for the brown paper bag Antonio proffers, I think I might seize the opportunity and slip to the bathroom to escape her notice. But instead of turning towards the plaza, Shirley faces into the café.

'I thought I saw you there,' she says loudly and marches over, pulling up a chair. Before she sits she plants a customary kiss in the air beside each of my cheeks and drops a large bunch of keys on the table. One of her earrings, an oversized faux silver hoop, snags on the collar of her velour top. She tilts her head to free it.

'Survive the storm up at Máguez?' she says, searching my face.

'The house is on a rise,' I say lightly.

'Rotten luck it came on little Miss Gloria's birthday. Was she awfully upset?'

'She had a ball, actually.'

'People came then? In that weather?'

'No one came. My father kept her entertained.'

'Good for him! I expect you all rallied. It's what families do.'

It's a strange remark, as though Shirley is voicing envy when she's always maintained she is childless and loving it.

'We did our best, given the circumstances,' I say, not wanting to sound evasive or give her the impression family life is a joy, at the same time rueing that I've already revealed more than I wanted. We might be allies, but I strive to keep my guard in deference to Celestino.

I'm aware I've failed when Shirley says, 'And what circumstances are those?' Quick off the mark, she adds, 'I sense you mean more than just the weather.'

I wring my hands in my lap. 'Celestino didn't show up,' I say bluntly.

'To his own daughter's birthday party! That's outrageous.'

'I'm sure he had good cause.'

'That's as may be but he should at least have made an appearance, come what may.'

Noticing that the woman in the red hat has again lowered her newspaper and seems to be paying close attention to our exchange, I drop my voice.

'All I know is I can't find him.'

'You've been to the house and the studio, naturally.'

'Yes.'

'And you've tried his phone?'

'It's dead.' I shudder as I say it.

Shirley doesn't seem to notice. 'What time did you say he was due at your parents?'

I didn't. 'At two.'

'Two o'clock? Hmm. I thought the party would have been much earlier. You left in the morning, I recall.'

I had no idea I have a nosy neighbour. Or maybe Shirley just happened to have been by her front window at the time.

'Now I'm confused,' Shirley says, leaning forward in her seat. I lean forward as well, preferring to keep the conversation away from curious ears. 'I definitely saw him leave the house between one and two.' She pauses. 'Must have been about one thirty.'

'You did?'

'I'm sure of it. Can't miss the sound of that old bomb of his.'

'Which way was he heading? Do you recall?'

'There's only one way down our street, Paula.'

'But did you see him turn left, or did he head straight into the village?' My thoughts are racing. Left means Máguez, and straight on means his studio, or on down to Arrieta. From there he could have gone anywhere south.

Shirley looks thoughtful. 'Right,' she says, nodding slowly. 'Yes, he definitely turned right.'

'Right? But that's crazy.'

Shirley sits back and shrugs. 'I wouldn't know.'

'In that direction, he could only have been heading up the switchbacks to Teguise, or down to Tabayesco. Either route would have been a nightmare yesterday.'

'Dangerous, true. It's a wonder he didn't get himself killed, but then again, he's a local. Maybe he thinks he's indestructible.'

'Shirley,' I say reproachfully.

'I'm sorry. I didn't mean it. Look, he didn't, or you would have heard by now.'

'Even so. I should check the hospital.' I should have thought to do that before.

'If it'll put your mind at rest.' She sounds vague. She eyes me appraisingly before she goes on. 'I have to say you look dreadful, Paula. He'll turn up. They always do.'

'Who? Who always turns up?' I say with sudden irritation.

'Just a figure of speech.' She furnishes me with a sympathetic smile, collects her bunch of keys and stands. 'Pop round for a coffee later. You look like you could do with some company.'

'I'm staying with my parents,' I mutter. 'While Celestino's missing, I mean. They're looking after Gloria.'

'Bit melodramatic, don't you think?'

'At least this way I only have to worry about one person, not two.'

'Fair enough. Tomorrow then. Promise. You've got me worrying now.'

I don't believe her. I watch her swan out of the café and head off down the plaza. I remain seated, taking in her revelation. Celestino left the house at about one-thirty, she said. He should have been heading for Máguez but Shirley insisted she saw him driving towards the mountain. Why would he go in that direction and at that time? He wouldn't have been heading to Mancha Blanca to deliver that painting to the Swedish doctor at one thirty, for he'd never have made it back to Máguez for Gloria's party, so I suppose I can rule that scenario out. He might have been heading to Kathy and Pedro in Tabayesco, or to Pilar and Miguel in Los Valles, but both couples and their children were meant to be at the party. And both sensibly stayed home in that storm, when the switchbacks and the sweeping bends would have been treacherous. There could have been a landslide. If Celestino headed that way then maybe he was swept off the road and had hurtled down the mountainside, and now he lay broken in a heap at the bottom. Somewhere obscure where no one could see. A large clean up must be underway, the whole island was inundated. They could easily overlook a lone car half buried by silt, rocks and debris.

I grab my pastry, take a bite and return it to the plate. The woman in the red wide-brimmed hat stuffs her newspaper in her large handbag and stands abruptly. She seems young, early thirties maybe, although it's hard to tell. She has on a polka dot, wasp-waisted, wiggle skirt and figure-hugging top, an outfit entirely incongruous with the setting. She belongs in a film. As she walks away her stiletto heels make sharp taps on the floor, faintly audible over the background noise.

Cautious without reason, I wait for the woman to disappear before I leave.

'Gracias, Antonio,' I say, catching his eye on my way out.

I skirt a group of tourists dithering around one of the outdoor tables, and rush down the plaza, annoyed with myself for having left the car parked outside the studio, making a mental note not to do anything like it again, not under current circumstances.

I'm breathless when I reach it. I put the key in the lock with an unsteady hand.

Once seated I pause and make myself wait and catch my breath. The chances are I won't find Celestino's old bomb on its side halfway down the mountainside. I let a few cars pass before starting the car.

Heading for the mountain I take the first right and wend up Calle las Eras, past rows of old farmhouses, some freshly renovated, others old, dilapidated, crumbling. And small black fields, cultivated with maize and potatoes. The sight of the land in use instils in my frazzled mind a moment of normalcy. Further on, and the farmhouses give way to low walls, rendered white. On the high side, a newer-style farmhouse is set amid large cultivated fields, the picón weed-free. It all looks so cared for.

At the next intersection, I turn left and head up and out of the village. Rows of canary palms flank the road for a stretch. Then the road makes its steady incline up towards Peñas del Chache. Here and there picón and silt have spilled onto the tarmac. Otherwise there's little evidence of yesterday's storm. I slow, careful, keeping an eye out for rockfalls on the road ahead, snatching glances at the fields on the low side beside me, just in case, wishing I had a passenger, a second pair of eyes, ones that didn't need to watch the road. I slow even further when I reach the turnoff to Tabayesco, unsure which route I should take first.

I carry straight on towards the mountain. The terrain on the lower slopes is a carpet of green, sprinkled with the pretty pinks, yellows, blues and whites of the wild flowers in springtime bloom. The undamaged crash barriers indicate no one has recently tumbled to their death. In places where the crash barriers are absent, I slip gear down to second and crane my neck, ignoring the car on my tail.

At the first switchback, at the sight of a small rockfall in the cutting, I brake and change down to first, crawling round the curve in case I meet oncoming traffic. In my rear vision mirror I catch the driver in the car behind gesticulating. I ignore him and approach each switchback in the same manner.

My zigzag journey up the mountainside proves uneventful. There's little debris on the road and the crash barriers are all intact.

I pull into the car park of the restaurant Los Helechos, perching on the crest just after the last switchback. The car behind me roars up the road ahead.

The restaurant is closed. The location, one of numerous island lookouts, is especially magnificent for its view of the crags and deep gullies nearby and of the massif and the volcanoes that are the restaurant's namesake. From here I have an almost aerial view of the valle de Temisa, with the tiny village of Tabayesco in the distance. I go over to the railing and look down, scanning below. Nothing.

The last time I stood in this spot was on my wedding day. I was so heavily pregnant we couldn't risk a picnic at bosquecillo, the little wood tucked in the folds of the mountain beside the cliff edge with its panoramic ocean views. Instead, we drove up here for photos and I threw my bouquet into the wind. That day I became Paula Diaz, witnessed only by our few friends, a special day in anyone's life, momentous, and I was ecstatic. Only, we announced the event to our respective families after the fact, ostensibly to avoid a fuss. We agreed it was for the best, but ever since I've harboured secret feelings of rejection, as though as far as his family are concerned, I'm the estranjera who carried his child out of wedlock.

Fluffy clouds, low lying, scud by. The wind is strong, stronger up high. I face into it, letting my hair fly from my face, letting that indifferent wind blow away my memories.

I walk back to my car, realising it would be ridiculous to drive on. If Celestino had been in a car accident, someone would have found him by now. It's hard on this island to disappear. There are few secret clefts and crevices. No dense undergrowth or thick forest. Only the caves and they are inhospitable. Besides, I haven't eaten save for that one bite of pastry and my stomach aches from hunger.

Alone and wretched, as though I've reached the end of my search and face into a void, the passion that I haven't felt for my man in years wells up in me.

I pull out of the car park heading for Máguez, staying in low gears on the descent to save driving down on the brake. Fifteen minutes and I'm opening my parents' front door.

Angela rushes forward as soon as she sees me.

'Any news?'

'I ... I need to...' I can't finish my sentence. Instead, I go straight through to the kitchen to the phone. I pick up the receiver then put it back in the cradle. 'Can I have your phone book?' Angela fetches it and I locate the number I want.

I have to wade through the options menu and then I'm left on hold for what seems like an age. At last a woman answers and I put my query. Another wait and finally the woman says in an authoritative voice that no Celestino Diaz has been admitted in the last two days. She hangs up.

I stare in disbelief at the handset. Perhaps the hospital is swamped with admissions, although I doubt that straight away. It isn't, it couldn't be, because of my accent. I tell myself at least he hasn't come to harm. Or at least it's a little easier to assume he hasn't come to harm. How many hours have passed since Kathy's insinuation that I was overreacting when I mentioned calling the police? Not many. Not nearly enough for them to take me seriously. It's less than twenty-four hours since Celestino disappeared. Or apparently disappeared. A grown man. They would be right to dismiss my inquiry.

'I ought to be getting Gloria home.'

'I'll fetch her.' She goes out to the patio.

Moments later Bill appears with Gloria on his hip. He lets her slide down to the floor. Taking a discerning look at me he says, 'Might be best if you spend another night with us.'

'What if Celestino comes back?'

'If he does, and he finds you not there, then he'll phone here. He's bound to. If you go back you'll never settle. You'll be jumping at every noise.'

'I don't want to be a burden.'

'You will be if you leave, it seems,' Angela says, 'to yourself, I mean. Anyway, your father has set up the cubby house on the patio. He's teaching Gloria to count to twenty.'

'Ten.'

'Twenty.'

'She's one smart little girl,' Bill says. 'Takes after her ...'

'Don't.'

But I relent. The company will make the time pass. Give me a chance to pull myself together. For I'm overreacting, surely? And this reaction isn't helping anyone. It won't influence the outcome whatever that turns out to be.

My self-talk proves of small comfort.

6

SURVIVAL

I SQUINT. SUNRISE BRIGHTENS THE OTHERWISE DINGY ROOM. I SHOULD be grateful I'm awake, but I'm stiff limbed, adding to the darts of pain shooting down my arm. The leg is not much better. I reach for the water bottle, careful to take only a sip, then rummage in the rucksack for the other half of the protein bar I ate last night. Feeling around inside, not wanting to extract Gloria's present, my knuckles press against something in the interior pocket. I realise in a flash it's the document folder. At first, I'm puzzled. Then I cast my mind back. I put it there last week planning to visit Pedro to discuss a strategy for dealing with the situation. Neither of us was keen to hand over the documents—copies of an illegal development plan, emails, transcripts of text message exchanges—to the police. Besides, I wasn't sure we had enough to prove anything, hence the meeting. Only, what with the birthday party, the commission and the imminent storm, our meeting was forgotten, by me at least, and I've been carrying those documents around in the rucksack ever since.

It suddenly occurs to me the oversight has put both Pedro and Paula in even greater danger. If whoever has been sent to recover the documents were to find them, then maybe he would leave, satisfied. Maybe. No chance of that now. A wave of anxiety and self-recrimination washes through me. I'm an idiot.

An idiot who has to be practical.

I heave myself up using my good leg. The dog could be out there, watching, but I have no choice. A puncture wound, and the leg might heal, but the animal tore at my flesh and would have bitten a chunk right off if it hadn't been for my pants. I need to do something with the wound or infection will set in, if it hasn't already. I don't like to think of what was last in that animal's mouth before it bit me.

I scan the beach and the reef through the window cavity. No dog. No guarantee it isn't out there. I grab the plank of wood and hobble outside.

As I head towards the beach I keep an eye on the steps leading up to the street above. The ocean is calmer, the tide low, and I take a few tentative steps on the soft black sand before it dawns on me I can't use the beach if I want to avoid leaving a trail. I walk backwards, obliterating the evidence of my footsteps as I go, then head across the rocky reef to the water's edge.

The going is uneven. I need to walk slowly and watch each step, yet I'm acutely aware of the exposure and keep turning back to scan the village and the ridge behind me. In any one of those windows an eye might be sighting me down the barrel of a gun.

I kneel close to the waterline, not trusting the ocean much either, knowing how easy it would be for me to fall in if a wave takes me by surprise. I release Gloria's scarf, pull up my trouser leg and bathe the wound as methodically and quickly as I am able. I wash out the scarf, then I unzip my fly and release my pee into the ocean, and hobble back to the safety of my hideout. Letting the wound and the scarf dry, I turn my attention to my arm.

It needs a sling. I eye the scraps of fishing net and sift through what's there. I spend the next hour tying together loose ends of the nets, wincing with every tug and pull, fashioning a makeshift triangle as best I can. Thinking ahead to how I'll tie it around my neck, I use a length of thread to measure the distance from my shoulder to elbow, make a mental guess and tie a knot, hoping I've got the sling height right.

Satisfied it's the best it can be, I grab one of Gloria's stray socks I found lurking in the bottom of the rucksack and ram it into my mouth. Biting down hard, I ease my arm into my sling. The pain makes me roar inwardly but I'm convinced I made no audible sound.

The sling is a good fit but pain relief is a long time coming. I distract myself by assessing my supplies. Half a litre of water a day will get me to Wednesday, so that's the day I have to leave. I figure if I hold out until then, whoever is looking for me will assume I'm dead or long gone.

My food supplies match the water. I have two protein bars, two chocolate bars, a small pack of peanuts and some chick pea snacks. If I spread that over two days, and leave early on the third, I should survive, and if I save the nuts, they'll give me enough energy for the walk.

The day drags on. I feel myself weakening by the hour and my state of mind isn't helping. I keep asking myself if all my campaigning is worth it? There has to be a better way, a less dangerous way forward. I've put my loved ones in peril out of my own stalwart drive. It hits me like a hard slap that all these years I've been selfish in my treatment of Paula. I've not respected her enough for who she is, not only as the mother of my child, but a shrewd, capable, caring woman who gave up her life to be with me. She doesn't deserve this. She doesn't deserve to lose her life twice, once when she came to the island, and a second time because of me. Tears well and spill. I brush them away. I need to get a grip. I'll walk back on Wednesday. I'll be there when the commission winner is announced; to celebrate or not, I don't care. I picture Gloria's pretty face, her adorable if impetuous nature, I picture Bill and Angela, who came to be near their only daughter and granddaughter. All of them I am responsible for and I should have stepped up to that responsibility long before now.

7

TOURISM

I DIDN'T SLEEP WELL. GLORIA TOOK UP THE MIDDLE OF THE BED AS IS her wont. She's still flat on her back with her arms spread wide, her right hand grasping one of her rabbit's ears. I was left with a sliver of the mattress. I spent much of the night lying on my side staring into the dark, reminiscing.

I remembered the first time I met Celestino, climbing down the stairs to the subterranean art gallery in a little plaza in Haría, admiring the artworks on display, thinking I might buy something small, approaching the man standing by a small desk with my inquiry to find he was the artist. We chatted. He was amused by my dreadful Spanish. There was a spark. We both felt it. I hadn't wanted to leave. I must have stayed down there a whole hour.

Over dinner that evening, I discovered him to be a deep, ethical and considerate man. I opened my mind to him. I isolated the moment I opened my heart as well. Fell in love, or more likely tripped over and there it was, there *he* was, with arms spread wide ready to catch me. It was early in my third holiday on the island, and I spent most of the rest of my stay with him. Like all holiday romances, our interactions were intoxicating and it was hard to leave. I booked another holiday soon after, and a few months later I was back. The attraction was strong, overwhelming, and when he asked me to spend my life with him, I swooned.

Then common sense kicked in and I returned to my old life in Suffolk, to my job and my home minus my new love. Whenever I recall that time, I see the painting he gifted me, the way I would gaze at it with longing. I wanted to jump on a plane and be with him forever, but it felt like insanity. It was a work colleague, Joe, who finally persuaded me. 'What I wouldn't give to trade places with you,' she said. 'Live in paradise with the man of your dreams? How could you think of turning him down?'

That missing, and the aching, hollowed out feeling that came with it, feels in the recollecting pure and clear. Besides, I'd been in control. It was my decision. When someone goes missing, the sense of loss is different. Anxiety doesn't ache; it grips. Awake beside my daughter, my belly clenches with worry. Every now and then I feel angry with him for putting me through it all. Then I lie still, unable to shake myself free of the anguish, as though through all those years of feeling neglected, I rejected him in retaliation to protect my heart, and now that he is gone I crave a chance to make amends.

As the room turns to grey in the first moments of the day, I slip out of bed and put on the dressing gown Angela gave me to wear: one of Bill's. Knee length, brown, it wraps almost twice around my body and smells of something like Brut. My feet are cold on the tiled floor. I hurry through to the living-room floorboards. At the kitchen end of the room the ceiling ends and a large skylight encloses what was once an open space in the roof. I stand in the patch of sunlit floor and warm my feet, preparing myself for a continuation of the discussion of Celestino's whereabouts that is sure to take place when I join my parents, already moving about in the kitchen.

Bill sits down at the head of the kitchen table as I enter the room, placing his cereal bowl beside a sheaf of printed matter. He seems distracted; his hair, wispy and white and in need of a cut, is uncombed and he's dressed for the day in yesterday's beige polo top and pants. I pull out the chair next to his where a place for me is laid, and help myself to the coffee on the table. Bill shovels a few mouthfuls of his cereal and chews vigorously. Then he stabs the papers with the handle end of his spoon and says, 'This island is going to the dogs.'

'Morning dad.'

'What's happened now?' Angela says in that careworn manner she puts on.

'They're proposing yet another desalination plant.'

'Where?'

I think of the rocky coastline, already built up between Costa Teguise and Puerto del Carmen. And the sprawl of hotels and holiday villas that was once the quaint fishing village of Playa Blanca.

'Arrecife.'

'Oh dear.'

'Not 'oh dear'. It's infuriating. Does Celestino know about this?'

'Bill.'

'Of course, he does,' Bill says, answering his own question. 'He knows as well as I do that this island can't take much more.'

It's always the same conversation: tourism. One way or another, everything on the island revolves around it. Arguably one of the dullest topics of conversation anyone could have, other people's holidays, yet you couldn't step outside your front door and not be affected by it.

'Won't it be wind powered?' I read somewhere of the possibility.

'How many turbines will that be, Paula,' he says, ever the pessimist. 'No, it'll be fuelled by oil, like the rest. More money for the big boys. And that's beside the point. It's not sustainable.'

'More water equals more tourists, you mean,' I say, warming to the topic, my mind welcoming the distraction, the sense of normalcy it provides.

'More water guzzling golf courses, most likely.'

'I dislike the tourism industry here as much as you do,' I say, recalling that time not so long ago when I cleaned holiday lets in Punta Mujeres. 'But there's thirty-five per cent unemployment on the island as it is. What would the people do without it?'

'Tourism is not the answer. You know full well that most jobs in tourism are low paid. And what about the all-inclusives? Tell me how they benefit the rest of the island. As it is, most holidaymakers don't venture beyond their enclaves, and the same goes for the expats, which does nothing or close to nothing to benefit the island's broader economy.'

'We're expats, Bill.'

He ignores his wife. Keeping his gaze fixed on me, he adds, 'Tourists come here to feed off the island. They're parasites, and parasites give nothing back.'

'You can't blame the holidaymakers,' Angela says, pouring Bill a cup of coffee.

He almost snatches it from her hand and sets it down by her bowl. 'Why not?'

'Just eat your breakfast.'

I put my elbows on the table and my face in my hands. Bees dance about amongst the flowers in terracotta tubs on the patio. The toaster releases its catch.

'He shouldn't upset himself,' Angela says, addressing me as she returns to the table with the toast. 'He was up half the night surfing the web.'

'I couldn't sleep,' he says, leaning back in his seat. 'You know, Paula, what's needed here is quality not quantity.'

'Bill, please. You're being a snob.'

'An environmentally and culturally aware sort of tourist,' I say, hoping my comment will ease the tension.

'Or expat.'

'One who cares and contributes.'

'Tourists with a fat wallet, you mean,' Angela says.

'That wouldn't help,' Bill says. 'Money doesn't necessarily result in quality.'

'Just the pretence of it.'

Golf courses, swathes of lush green grass in a desert—it's a hedonistic folly, a travesty, an insult to the land and its people. I have to agree with him. In the final analysis, the island is so small it can barely contain the influx, but I also think the various interested parties manage the situation well. Besides, tourism is a global phenomenon, not one restricted to this rock.

'Any economy that relies so heavily on tourism is fundamentally insecure,' Bill says sagely. 'Pity the old ways are all but gone.'

'It was a hard life though.'

'Mm.'

The subject exhausted, he returns to his cereal bowl. Angela sits opposite me, and proceeds to butter her toast with quick swipes of her knife.

I put some bran flakes and milk in my bowl and shuffle the flakes about, my appetite fading. Cereal from cardboard boxes, milk from the fridge, bread baked and sliced in a bakery, browned in a toaster, life here was never so easy. How must it have been for the farmers' wives of days gone by? Toasting maize on open fires, milling it by hand to produce the island's staple, gofio. Every farmhouse had a molino de mano, a hand mill carved from basalt. Women milling while their men laboured on terraces high on the mountainside, terraces they'd made and then edged with dry stone walls. When the domestic chores were done the women, protected from the wind and the sun by high-domed hats secured with scarves tied tightly beneath their chins, would go and labour alongside their men, planting, weeding, harvesting and partaking in the view. Always the tremendous view. A view that might have made up for the arduous labour. But three, four, five, six hundred metres—it's a long way up and a long way down. Some farmers chose to remain at the mountaintop, building their homes on the crest, or at the edge of the cliff, anywhere the soil was tillable and the mists rolled in. Anywhere the rain fell greatest. It's far from the bucolic idyll of the peasant farmer and not at all the plentiful existence of farmers tilling the flatter, wetter land of Suffolk. Here was hardship on an exceptional scale, and those steadfast Lanzaroteños have to be commended for the numerous techniques and inventions they created to survive.

Those not so steadfast left, or fled, following the migration routes to the Americas, escaping the volcanic eruptions and the droughts that plagued the island. The population remained small, growing little until the 1960s when tourism first took hold, but it wasn't until the last few decades that the tourist industry began to devour the island in its entirety. There are few places to escape to. Some locals, craving time to relax in a place far from the invasion, have re-occupied the once abandoned village of Tenesar, no more than a cluster of rundown buildings fronting the churning ocean of the northwest coast, and surrounded by malpais. Celestino told me about it. Accessed by a gravel road, Tenesar sounds like one of the most inhospitable places I can imagine. I wanted to visit to see for myself but Celestino wouldn't take me. 'Best leave them alone, Paula,' he'd said, honouring the locals' wish for privacy.

I force down the remaining bran flakes and slurp the last dregs of milk in my bowl. Bill pours over his papers. I, too, crave a more sustainable tourism, one not riven by overdevelopment. Especially since that overdevelopment is the result of exploitation and corruption. But I struggle to think of a holiday destination that hasn't fallen foul of those two human weaknesses. It always comes down to short sightedness and greed. Yet Bill isn't exaggerating, despite his tendency to pontificate; on Lanzarote, corruption is a story to match the days of its conquest.

Not long into our relationship, Celestino told me the story of the day a German tourist arrived, fell in love with the island and asked to buy a field of potatoes. Duly purchased, the German then profited from his sale of that field to a construction company wishing to build a hotel. A bunch of local officials soon saw an opportunity for gain. The German had given everyone an idea. Celestino went on to describe how some government officials had their family and friends purchase land from farmers, then arranged for the land to be rezoned so they could sell it on to property developers, this time for a huge profit. It was a scam that corrupted all of those involved, except for the farmer whose land it was. All those involved in the initial purchase, all involved in the rezoning, all who turned a blind eye to it, all who spent the proceeds of the property deals, all those lured by sweet deals, all those with greasy palms, all who knew about it and kept quiet for fear of repercussions, everyone from local government officials and staffers, to the lawyers and their families, the developers and beyond. The corrupt practices of those early initiators metastasised at a tremendous rate. Celestino started campaigning when he

realised no environmental protections written into law were making a
jot of difference and no one ever seemed accountable.

My own reflections about the island always brought me back to
Celestino, as though the two were twinned, like suns. This time I'm
brought back with a lurch. It was Celestino who educated all the
Crays on the island's corruption. It's what binds him and Bill; they're
comrades in arms. Whenever we get together for dinner, after the
food is eaten and Gloria asleep, the two men spend hours mulling
over some dirty deed or other, Celestino telling Bill all he knows
about corrupt practices on the island and Bill wading in with various
scandals in the UK and Europe and the United States. Bill trying to
tell Celestino that Lanzarote is small potatoes by comparison and
Celestino refusing to have it. I suppose male rivalry has to anchor on
something.

'I really need to find him,' I say aloud.

Bill looks up.

'Perhaps you should call the police.' Angela sounds as worried as I
feel.

'It's still too soon for that,' Bill says.

'Forty-eight hours?'

I exchange glances with Angela.

'He's a young, fit, healthy man. And he's a local. There's been a
terrible storm. I expect you'd be fobbed off, Paula. Better to wait a bit
longer, I'd say.'

'Then, do you mind having Gloria? I want to keep looking.'

'Oh, Paula.'

'You go off and do what you feel you need to,' Bill says.

As though she's been summoned, Gloria comes running into the
kitchen in her pyjamas, clutching her toy rabbit by its neck.

'Granddad!' Her eyes are wide and bright as day. She runs around
to the head of the table and leans against him, her little face pressing
against the mound of his belly. Then she steps back and pulls at his
arm. Bill stands and takes her outside.

· · ·

BACK IN HARÍA all looks as I left it yesterday. Walking through the house, standing in each room, I can't shake the sense of unfamiliarity in the objects that surround me, that on Saturday morning were so familiar I hardly took any of it in. Now an empty feeling pervades the place. Climbing the stairs to our bedroom, hearing the familiar creak of the treads, the feeling intensifies.

After a quick scan of the room, I grab a pair of shorts and an old T-shirt thinking after a shower I'll keep busy for a while cleaning Gloria's bedroom; it will ease the anxiety and give me time to decide what to do next.

A shower refreshes me a little and I'm soon back in the kitchen. My gaze settles on the landline and the dull green of the unlit message indicator on the console. The absence of that flashing light reinforces in me a growing despair. I take one look at the cloth and detergent beside the sink. Cleaning a bedroom? —It's something my mother would do. Tea will more likely help me think. I fill the kettle instead.

With mug in hand I go outside and sit beside the tree planted in the centre of the patio. Celestino told me once it was a drago tree. He said it was special but I can't remember why. The bees are in over-drive amongst the lavender, geraniums and herbs in full flower, making the most of the short season. I make a mental note to water the pot plants that will soon be dry, despite Saturday's rain. Again, I feel as though I'm turning into my mother. Angela's first thought always concerns practicalities, serving to assuage her anxiety over one thing or another. Is this a family trait passed down through the female line, manifesting belatedly in me in the face of my own anxi-ety? Yet upon putting down my cup and turning on the hose, setting the spray to a soft drizzle, directing the flow first here then there, watching the leaves bow under the weight of the droplets, the soil in the pots change colour in the wet, the calming effect inherent in tending things that have little chance of disappearing since they are rooted to the spot, doesn't escape my notice.

A quick rap on the front door takes me by surprise. I turn off the hose and hurry to answer it, my heartbeat quickening.

Shirley hovers out on the pavement, all breezy in an oversized silk dress of ocean blue, adorned with a blue pearl necklace and sea horse earrings.

'Come to see how you're faring,' she says, giving me an appraising look as she steps forward to enter. 'Still no sign of him then.'

I let her in and lead her to the patio.

'I'm thinking of calling the police,' I say as I retrieve my tea.

'I don't think Celestino would like it if you did that, to be honest.' She bunches together her lips in one of her stern pouts, the wrinkles on her face deepening, and with a critical sweep of my garb, she adds, 'Get your glad rags on and come with me.'

'With you?' I say doubtfully. 'Where are you going?'

'To lunch in Costa Teguise.'

'It's a bit far.'

'You are joking.'

'Why not Arrieta?' I'm keen not to be distracted for long.

'I'm lunching with Maria.'

'Then I don't want to intrude.'

'You won't be. Come on. It'll give you a break.'

'What if Celestino comes back?'

'We'll only be an hour or two. Paula, I'm sure if he returns he'll be in touch. He'll have known you'd be worrying,' she insists, adding, 'surely,' almost as an afterthought.

'I suppose you're right.'

'Leave a note.'

It's obvious, the moment she says it.

'I won't be long,' I say, caving in.

'No rush. I'll meet you in the plaza in an hour. I've one or two things to do myself.'

Satisfied, Shirley makes her way back down the hallway. I trail behind.

'Hasta luego,' she says, pronouncing the aitch.

I watch her stride back to her house next door.

Lunch in Costa Teguise? Why ever did I agree? But there is no arguing with Shirley. Besides, it might do me good. Yet I can't help feeling disloyal knowing Celestino's opinion of her. And I'm annoyed by it. I'm an independent woman who can make up her own mind about people, and not, most certainly not, the sort of woman who lets her husband choose her friends.

I go up to the bedroom and change into a plain cotton dress and my best sandals. I run a brush through my hair and smear on some clear lip gloss, then take a quick glance in the mirror. I look as good as can be expected. Succumbing to a sudden urge to leave the house, I hurry downstairs to the kitchen. On the hunt for some notepaper I riffle through the pile of assorted books and magazines left on top of the small bookcase. In my quest, I stumble on one of Richard's business cards. I pick it up, take in the self-satisfied face, the copperplate writing detailing his particulars, and with an ironic smile promptly put it back. I find the blank notepaper at the bottom of the stack.

I scribble a short message and leave it on the kitchen table so Celestino cannot fail to find it. Acting before any of my earlier misgivings have a chance to sway me, I collect my shoulder bag, sunglasses and keys and leave the house.

8

RICHARD PARRY

RICHARD RETURNS THE GARDEN BROOM AND THE RAKE TO THE SMALL storeroom at the back of the garage, the patio at last free of silt and grit. Picón, the locals call it, a form of volcanic ash. What a lot of effort. Taking in the lay of his small patch of Lanzarote, it seems to him thoroughly stupid to sink a patio below the height of the garden beds and expect the dry-stone walls to retain it all, whatever the conditions. And so much for a raised bed. His cacti nearly drowned in Saturday's deluge! Still, on the positive side, the water never lasts long here, it seems to just vanish, unlike in parts of his homeland, his blessed Bunton, where he's heard the land has turned to bog and looks set to stay that way until the summer.

He goes inside, deciding he needs to employ a gardener to attend to the weeds that are springing up out of the picón even as he watches. His back simply isn't up to the strain. Sweeping the patio alone has caused a twinge. And twinges put him in poor spirits. To make matters worse, he's at a loss as to how to find a gardener. It occurs to him that his wife, Trish, whom he's left at home in Bunton as he always does, would one way or another have arranged for a chap to come in. Perhaps he'll ask Paula. Yes, Paula is sure to know, or at least know whom to ask. She might even do it herself. Besides, he has another reason to consult her and this gives him the perfect opening.

Paula became his mainstay when she moved to the island—little does she know it—for the demands of churning out another work and finding himself in a persistent hiatus has just about rendered him in solitary confinement.

She's taken the role of Celestino after he proved an impossible and outright obstructive research assistant. Richard only latched on to him after the sudden departure of Domingo, whose fiancée, the dear Ann Salter, miscarried and fled back to the Cotswolds. They were going to call the child Ico, if it had been a girl. An awful tragedy that left Richard at a loose end with his project. Then, he encountered a replacement, another local, and hope returned. But Celestino was always preoccupied with one thing or another, and became tetchy when pressed. The work, *Ico's Promise*, an epic tale of Lanzarote's history, flopped as a result, and his agent, Trent, wanted to know why he didn't visit the archaeological site at El Jable, since that was what a number of astute and better-informed readers had indicated might have set him straight. Celestino never said a thing about El Jable.

He also suffered the ignominy of being confused with another Richard Parry, with one reviewer referring to an earlier work, a work not of his own pen but of this other chap's—from New Zealand, for heaven's sake! It turns out there are two, or at least two other Richard Parry authors, and to save confusion Trent urged Richard to change his name. But what of his previous works? Richard had asked. They couldn't be re-printed in another name; that would be absurd. 'You must find a way of being distinct, Richard.' Then Trent had a moment of inspiration. 'Do you have a middle name?' Richard did, but he was reticent. Trent pressed him. Richard wouldn't divulge it. Then the tone of Trent's voice changed and he started to talk about midlist authors being dropped by their publishers, in droves. Alarmed at the insinuated threat, Richard muttered, 'Alright, alright. It's Harry.' After a short pause, he heard a snicker on the other end of the line. Richard Harry Parry. 'Richard Harry Parry,' Trent said with a distinct chuckle in his voice. There was a long period of silence. Trent broke it with, 'I tell you what. We'll shorten it. Richard H Parry. How's that? I'll get onto your publisher in the morning.'

All of Richard's works were re-printed with new covers featuring the obligatory capital aitch. Richard has felt singled out and picked on ever since.

It was a windy day when, some months later, Richard spotted Paula and Celestino having coffee in the plaza. He was on his way to the library with a new copy of *Ico's Promise* under his arm: a donation. He intended to wave and pass by but Paula called him over. When he sat down at Paula's behest, he put the book face down on the table. Celestino appeared preoccupied with the contents of his satchel.

'How are you, Richard? How's the writing?' Paula said, removing her sunglasses, a welcome act of conviviality as she never liked to take them off.

'Very well thank you, Paula. Where's the little one?'

'Gloria's with her grandparents,' Celestino said without looking up.

'Her grandparents? But I thought...'

'*My* parents, Richard. They've just moved to the island.'

'That must be terrific for you, Paula,' he said, feeling oddly ineffectual.

The wind picked up and blew a napkin across the table. Instinctively, Richard leaned forward to retrieve it and when he sat back he found Celestino eyeing his book. He didn't have a chance to put his elbow down before Celestino reached across and shunted the book his way. He eyed the back cover for what felt like an age then turned the book over and scanned the front.

'Richard H Parry,' he said, aspirating the aitch with a guttural inflexion. 'What is this haitch doing there?'

Richard tried to snatch back the book but Celestino handed it to Paula, who glanced at the cover then up at Richard.

'Yes, Richard. What's with the aitch?'

Richard cringed inwardly.

'Long story. My agent insisted I distinguish myself from the other Richard Parry authors.'

'There are *more* Richard Parry authors?' Celestino said.

Richard offered a carefully crafted explanation. As he got to the part about the mistaken identity, Celestino interrupted with, 'What does it mean, this haitch?'

Richard cringed at Celestino's over-pronunciation and fell silent.

'Come on, Richard. Tell us.' Paula turned in her seat to grin at him squarely.

Trust her to wade in. Humiliation tightened in his chest in anticipation, and he had to quash an urge to stand up and make his excuses.

'Tell us.'

He wouldn't be pressured. He reminded himself that Trish would never tease him like this. He succumbed to an uncommon longing to be back in Bunton.

'You have to, Richard,' Paula said cheekily. 'You can't leave us in suspense.'

He kept his mouth closed.

'Okay, let me guess.' She paused, her grin widening. 'Henry.'

She looked at him closely.

'No? Okay, then what about Horatio?' She spoke the name in an exaggerated fashion.

Celestino sniggered.

'Herbert?'

'No, it isn't Herbert,' he snapped.

Celestino sniggered again.

'Harold then. It has to be Harold.'

'Close,' Richard muttered, suddenly wanting to fall into a crack in the paving.

Celestino and Paula exchanged glances.

'Harry,' Paula said softly. 'Richard Harry Parry.'

'Richard Harry Parry,' Celestino repeated, enunciating each syllable, with that special emphasis on the aitch. His lips spread wide and in moments his body convulsed with laughter. A single tear trickled down his cheek and before long he was clutching his belly. Then he bent over double and all but fell off his chair.

Paula, too, was laughing loudly.

Failing to see what it was that they both found so amusing,

Richard stood up, snatched back his book and marched away, only to collide with the waiter approaching to take his order. The waiter trod on his foot, adding injury to insult and he changed his mind about the library, and made a swift about face and went home.

A SHARP SCIATIC pain grips his calf, shooting through his hip and into his buttocks. There's nothing for it. He has to give up gardening. Focus on his next book, whatever that might be.

He hasn't written a thing since the dreadful reception of *Ico's Promise*. 'A tiresome, confusing narrative.' 'Utterly unconvincing.' Worse: 'I'm looking forward to when this author's writing matures.' He's never been so stung. Upon that string of ghastly reviews, he fell into a slump, re-injured his back and, after being required to change his pen name, all but sulked for most of the following year. From time to time Trent telephoned and urged him to persist. When Richard complained he lacked the inspiration, Trent told him to get himself to Lanzarote and find some. Richard then voiced a vague inclination to write a sequel to the successful Haversack Harvest, a crime novel set near Bunton, but Trent wouldn't hear of it. 'Not another bloody Midsomer Murder wannabe. Go and write something else set on Lanzarote. Stick to crime, yes, it's what you do best, but think setting Richard. *Setting*.'

Richard obeyed, and having arrived on the island in time for Saturday's deluge, he's come up with a promising title: *The Aljibe*.

He even has the inklings of a plot: a body found floating in an underground water tank at the base of a volcano. The aljibe at La Corona would be ideal. A lady sleuth making the discovery, a woman resembling Paula perhaps: petite, fair-haired, pretty. Not as becoming as his beloved Ann Salter—she has small brown eyes, her mouth is a little large for her face, her jawline somewhat square—but she has a certain sparkle about her. An expat eking out a living cleaning holiday lets. Isn't that what Paula was doing the last time he was here?

Poor Paula. She used to have a full-time job in tourism. Her working life gone to waste for the sake of a baby and the love of a man. She'd have fared better holding onto her old job back in

England. At least it was a profession of a sort, even if she had tired of it. She'd thrown away her life on a local, had his child and doomed herself to a life of drudgery. She puts on a brave front but he knows she despises menial work. That time he caught her entering a villa in Punta Mujeres, bucket and mop in hand; she had blushed the deepest of reds and hurried inside, tripping on the doorstep on her way in. He hadn't meant to embarrass her and vowed never to mention it again, but he couldn't help it one night the last time he was on the island, when he found himself in the plaza and spotted the Diaz's at a table supping on a shared bowl of meatballs.

Still annoyed at Celestino's mirth over his middle name, he decided not to join them, but then Paula looked over and waved and Celestino turned around.

'Hola, Harry,' he said, with what had become a standard, overly aspirated aitch.

Anger pinged in Richard's belly as he approached.

'Hello, Celestino,' he said coldly. 'I see you are dining. I'll leave you to it.'

'Taking a break from writing?'

He nodded and forced a smile. He wasn't about to tell them he hadn't written a thing all trip.

'Ah, señor escritor,' Celestino said. 'Your book sales better now you are Harry Parry?'

The anger rose up and took his breath away. 'At least I put food on the table,' he said sarcastically.

'¿Qué?'

'He means he earns money for his work.'

'And my wife doesn't have to char.'

'¿Char?'

Celestino looked to Paula for clarification. A worried look appeared in her face.

'He means clean houses,' she said, briefly lowering her gaze.

Celestino made to stand. Paula reached for his arm.

Seeing the waxing of Celestino's wrath Richard's waned. 'I'll be getting along, I think,' he said and he hurried away, filled with a turbulent mix of loathing, uncertainty and satisfaction.

Clearly, he had hit a nerve. Celestino couldn't possibly make enough out of his pictures to sustain a family. Especially now Richard has not only stopped making purchases, he's started to offload the pictures decorating his house, having struck a deal with a market trader in second-hand goods, undercutting Celestino by a considerable margin and splitting the profits. He has no qualms about it. Besides, it's only a few sketches. Celestino must know it's only the high-end artist who makes an adequate living out of his creations. Just as it is for authors, Richard thinks with a slight jolt.

In the recollecting, he unwittingly invokes his greatest fear: to find himself stuck midlist. He knows he can't afford to produce another fizzer. *The Aljibe* will need to be cracking to recover the ground he's lost, for his critics are sure to harken back to *Ico's Promise*. Which leaves him no choice. Since tourist sites are to be the theme of his book, he needs to consult the expert: Paula.

With renewed determination, he heads for the bathroom to comb his hair. Then he plucks a couple of stray long hairs from his eyebrows and splashes on a little aftershave. Satisfied, he collects his keys from his writing desk and leaves the house.

9

COSTA TEGUISE

STANDING IN THE SHADE OF THE EUCALYPT AT THE CAFÉ END OF THE plaza, I observe a few customers as they make up their minds to take an outdoor table in the warm spring sunshine, or opt for the seating shaded by the laurel trees. On Mondays, the village centre is always quiet, even at the intersection of the roads coming down from the north and the south and the road heading east, where cafes take advantage of the passing trade, and where villagers go about the business of the day, frequenting the supermarket, the florist, the town hall or the hardware store.

I watch with sudden envy an elderly couple in loose clothing, replete with backpacks and walking shoes, as they head off, probably on their way to the cliff. It's where all the walkers go. The views are breath taking, the cliff edge accessible in its entirety to those with a good head for heights.

An old man enters the café across the street, and a young woman in a figure-hugging emerald green dress and matching hat hovers on the narrow pavement at the entrance to the children's playground situated up the hill a short way. She seems familiar. Then I recall the woman in the red, wide-brimmed hat yesterday and wonder if it's her. She looks dressed for a wedding and is paying close attention to the goings on inside the florist opposite.

Perhaps she's waiting for a bouquet. The woman shifts her weight and I look away.

The wind stirs. I catch a waft of the scent of eucalyptus and inhale. Do all eucalypts smell the same? My neighbour in Ipswich had one in her back garden but it was a spindly, sick-looking thing and obviously unhappy with the environment. Too wet, probably. That is one thing I'll never miss, the wet. Despite the travails of my life on the island, I love it and the longer I stay, the less likely I'll fit in if I went back. Yet my existence on the island is dependent on Celestino. Without him, I have means, no income. I'd be forced back to England, back to the cold and the murk and the life of a single mother. What on earth would become of my parents? I feel sick in the imagining. The loss of Celestino is a devastating prospect in every respect, never mind the emotional loss. I never considered myself dependent on him quite so profoundly, but I am.

Shirley seems late. I had assumed she would be on time and wonder what's keeping her. When I left the house, I knew I had half an hour to spare, so I walked up to the crest of the hill that separates the valley of Haría from that of Máguez, stopping where several roads meet in an awkward intersection. And without a second thought I made to walk up a track in a field of picón accessed through a break in a stone wall. It wasn't far to the top but I soon turned back, my sandals the wrong footwear for the terrain. I had to lean a hand against a large stone in the wall, rough to the touch, to remove each of my sandals in turn, shaking them free of gravel. Then I waited for a couple of cars to pass before strolling back down to the plaza.

The woman in the green dress crosses the street and disappears inside the florist's. Is it like Shirley to be late? I have no idea. I consider taking a quick look in the hand-stitched leather shop nearby when I spot Richard, dapper in black, emerging through the trees that fill the plaza. To be polite, I wait. It would look bizarre to suddenly walk off, especially when it's obvious to all that I'm waiting for someone. I haven't seen Richard since the last time he was on the island, which, thinking back was about a year ago, around the time my parents moved to Máguez. A year, and in all that time, I haven't cared to see him again. I'm still feeling stung after he called me a char.

The humiliation was so great I forewent my mop and bucket shortly after.

The British couple I worked for had bought and renovated an old farmhouse on the edge of Punta Mujeres and lived in it for a few years before deciding to sell. They found it impossible to find a buyer in the new economic climate so they let out the farmhouse as a holiday rental, following a well-trodden path. Many foreign homeowners choose to own a square of island paradise and establish a holiday let, and Celestino said they often do so without the local government's knowledge or approval and invariably without paying local taxes. Provide the right conditions and anyone will take advantage, it seems. Lanzarote is not an island for the scrupulous. Is anywhere? Yet the holiday lets provide much low paid casual employment. And just as it is with any migrant group the world over, the Brits prefer to deal with those they know and can trust—their own kind—which means residents like me can find such employment with relative ease. Exceptional ease in my case: Shirley put me on to the job, shoving a flier in my hand one afternoon when we encountered each other at the bank.

After Richard's insult, I only managed one more shift. It was a Tuesday, and a party of vacationers had just departed. I traipsed through the rooms, stripping beds and attending to dollops of this and that stuck fast to walls and floors, to the handprints on the windows, the grime on the stove, the orange juice that had leaked in the fridge, and the hairs in the shower. All that filth and I earned no extra to deal with it. I felt more demoralised with every minute that passed. It didn't take long to make up my mind that I'd rather go hungry than suffer another moment. My decision was sealed when I opened the used toilet paper bin—onsite sewerage treatment on the island doesn't cope with the accoutrements of the toilet—to find streaks of brown and red and a sickly stench so overwhelming I blenched. It took all my resolve to empty it.

Without casual employment, my resentment swelled over Celestino's determination to live off the earnings from his art. It was a resentment I struggled to quell, ashamed to find myself one of those people who put money before creativity. I resolved to adopt the attitude that it was the price paid when relocating to a tiny island off the coast of

Africa. A few weeks later, I managed to climb up a rung of the menial-job ladder. Waitressing is still skivvying, but there is at least some dignity to it.

Sunlight burst through the clouds, dappling the shade in the plaza. Richard stops in his tracks and dips a hand in his pocket as though to make sure he has his wallet. He pats the other and a look of mild relief appears in his face. He's aged. There's a lot more salt in his hair, the peppery threads all but gone. He looks drawn, thinner, and his upright gait is laboured. I raise a smile as he nears, and he reciprocates.

'Hello, Paula.' He comes to a halt and forgoes the customary greeting by pocketing both of his hands. The newspaper under his arm slips down to his elbow. He braces and extracts a hand to grab it before it falls.

'Waiting for someone?' He makes a show of admiring my outfit and glancing around.

'She's late.'

'She?'

'My neighbour.'

'Celestino hard at work then.'

'Survive the storm okay?' I reply quickly.

'Thankfully, yes. And you?'

'Fine.'

'Can I buy you a coffee?'

'She should be here any moment.'

'Then she can join us. We can sit somewhere prominent.'

'Really I...'

'That table's free,' he says, looking over at the rows of mostly empty tables outside Antonio's café. 'Come on.'

His persistence is puzzling. I glance at my watch. It's a quarter past eleven. Maybe Shirley has changed her mind.

I choose a seat facing out towards the street, smoothing down my dress as I sit. Richard pulls out the opposite chair. I wave him aside and indicate the one on my right.

'Yes, of course.' Richard looks nonplussed but he obliges. With inward attention, he places on the table beside him the day's newspaper, folded in half, and he spends a few moments cleaning the lenses of his glasses. He doesn't put them on. Rather, he sets them down carefully so that the rims line up with the paper's title, as if underscoring it: 'Yaiza Mayor Opens Playa Blanca's New All-Inclusive Resort'. There's the usual cheesy grin for the camera. I make no comment, not wanting to get into a discussion about the effect all-inclusives have on the local economy with someone as ill-informed as Richard.

Antonio approaches and welcomes us both with a warm hello and a menu.

'¿Qué tal?' he says, directing his inquiry at me.

'Bien,' I answer, although I don't feel at all good.

'¿Algunas noticias sobre Celestino?'

'Nada,' I say, lowering my gaze, hoping Richard can't understand the question, at once somewhat baffled at the intense privacy I feel in his presence.

Sensing my unease, Antonio says, 'Perdoname,' which only serves to worsen the situation, for Richard is sure to know what begging your pardon means in any language.

'¿Café?'

'Si, gracias. Dos cafecitos.'

'¿Para él?'

'Sí, para él también.'

As Antonio strides away, I turn to Richard. 'You still drink espresso, I take it? I ordered for both of us.'

'Yes, I know. I heard. I can speak Spanish too.'

'Of course.' I cringe inwardly. 'I was forgetting.'

I stop short of explaining that waiting on tables has shown me the complexities of the variations, the accents. I have to work hard at my own fluency to keep up. Interpreting isn't necessarily that straightforward either, and there was one time only last month when an Englishman sat down, all grandiose gestures and false airs, treating me as though I was a backpacker on a long holiday. His mispronounced Spanish when he tried to order tapas had thrown me and I brought out the little salty potatoes instead of the squid he wanted. Flustered, when he then told me to fetch another two chairs because some friends of his were due to arrive any second, I tried to convince him to move to another table. I communicated to him in Spanish, believing that was what he preferred, and yet he couldn't, or wouldn't, understand me. Instead he demanded to speak to the manager and stood up abruptly, spilling a carafe of water on the table. It was a moment of intense chagrin, having to stand there and remain polite to a man I felt like slapping. I was thankful no one I knew was in the restaurant at the time. But I could feel all eyes on me as I went to the kitchen, and could scarcely defend myself when the proprietor, Eileen, sought my version of events.

'I wonder, Paula,' Richard says, interrupting my thoughts. 'You don't happen to know of a good gardener?'

'A gardener? Haría is full of gardeners.'

'For hire, I mean.'

'For your place?'

'I'm finding it hard with my back. Too much bending.'

'Have you tried asking at the supermarkets? They might know of someone. "Un jardinero", or "una jardinera".'

'I can ask.'

'But you might not understand what they tell you in reply?' Or them you, I think but don't say. 'Everyone speaks so rapidly.'

'I thought I'd ask you first.'

'I can't help you, but if I come across anyone, I'll let you know.'

'That would be wonderful.'

Antonio comes with the coffees. He sets them down with deft care, then looks at us both inquiringly.

'Would you like to eat something, Paula,' Richard says.

'I'm about to have lunch.' I hand back my menu to Antonio and draw my cup closer. 'You go ahead, though.'

'I've some cold meat in the fridge,' Richard says, handing back his as well.

'And pumpernickel?' I say, recalling the day I discovered he brought it with him from England.

'Ever the tease.' He laughs lightly then his demeanour changes. 'What's all this about Celestino? Antonio wanted to know if you have any news.'

Damn. I think it best not to reply and we fall into a moment of awkward silence.

Richard breaks it with, 'Pardon me for asking, then.'

I sip my coffee and stare at the street, wishing Shirley would hurry up.

'Paula, I didn't mean to upset you, or to pry. Your private life is your affair.' He fiddles with the spoon in his saucer. 'I've been meaning to get in touch. I hope you don't mind. It's just that I have something to ask you. Something else to ask you.'

'Ask me or ask of me?' I say, keeping my eyes fixed on the street.

'Ask of, I suppose.'

'And what might that be, Richard?'

'My latest work.'

'I thought so.'

'I need your advice.'

'Really? On what?'

'Water storage.'

'I don't know a thing about water storage. You're mistaking me for Ann.' I didn't mean to sound quite that tart.

He ignores my tone, or is oblivious to it.

'Fresh water storage,' he says matter-of-factly. 'Aljibes, actually.'

'Aljibes?' I can't help correcting his pronunciation. He said all-hee-bees. 'What on earth would you want to know? They're nothing more than underground water tanks.'

'The one at La Corona. It's ancient. You're the expert on local historical sites. I was wondering what you knew about that one.'

'I'm not an expert.'

'Of course, you are.'

It's true I know far more than him, although nowhere near as much as I would like. When I moved here, I made it my business to know all about the island in the hope of securing a job in tourism, only to find my language skills were not up to the mark.

'I know little, Richard. Some Conejeros must have spent a long time digging a ruddy great hole and lining it with cement.'

'Is that it? A pity. It's terribly important.'

'I'm sure it is.'

'It's the setting for my latest crime novel. The Aljibe.'

'*The* Aljibe?'

'Whatever is wrong with that title?'

'Sounds like a Western.'

'It does not!'

I can't help taking pleasure in needling his oversensitivity. 'Richard, it should be El Aljibe, at the very least,' I say with a wry smile.

'Whatever you think, Paula. Will you come with me one day this week, or not? To La Corona, I mean.'

'Richard, I can't.'

'You can't,' he repeats flatly.

I refrain from telling him why. If he's trying to make me feel guilty, it isn't working. I sip more of my coffee, tiring of waiting in his company. I begin to consider going home when Shirley corners the plaza. She's changed into a flowing chiffon dress of lurid orange with matching scarf. She stops suddenly, feet apart, hands on hips, making a show of looking around, her manner suggesting that whoever it is she's looking for should be right there. She spots me and strides over.

'Sorry I'm late.' Her hands grip the back of a chair. 'Maria phoned, and then I had to get changed.'

I take in the chandelier earrings and accompanying necklace of fake white gold she has on. Garbed in orange, she looks like a fancy cup cake.

Shirley shifts her gaze to Richard, and putting on a prim voice she says, 'Richard Parry, isn't it?' She proffers her hand. 'I heard you were back.'

'You did?' Richard appears puzzled.

'Richard,' I cut in, 'this is my neighbour, Shirley.'

'I'm not sure we've met,' Richard says, shaking her hand.

'We have. Once or twice, but not formally. How's the writing?'

'Very well, thank you.'

I stare down at my half-drunk coffee. It's the way he says things, so abruptly and defensive. A sudden beep startles me and I look over as a car reverses to let a small truck go by. Celestino flashes into my mind and I'm awash with guilt that I'm not out there searching for him, guilt that quickly shades into irritation. Life goes on. Whatever has happened to him, life has to go on.

Shirley opens her mouth to speak when Richard says, 'How long have you been on the island?'

'Twenty years. I'm practically a local.' She emits a self-deprecating laugh.

I find myself recoiling. It's a reaction I often have to the claim made by expats that the time they've lived on the island earns them the right to a 'local' identity. For with it comes an implicit sense of ownership. Here we are, three Brits living in an island paradise, staking a claim like Bethencourt himself. Little wonder the Lanzaroteños, the real locals, call all the migrants 'estranjeros', which literally means strangers, for strangers we are and will always be, forever outside no matter what we ourselves think, here by invitation and not by divine right. I'm surprised by the strength of how I feel, and the hypocrisy embedded in it, for I know I have to include myself in the condemnation, despite my marriage to Celestino.

Seated in the plaza of the island's ancient capital with two Brits who one way or another epitomise the cultural arrogance I despise, I suffer a sense of collective shame over the numbers of estranjeros who flock to Lanzarote, to all of the Canary Islands, or even to main-land Spain, a nation that undoubtedly has made the whole life-in-the-sun dream possible, easy and enticing.

Shirley steps aside to let Antonio pass by behind her.

'I'm going to steal Paula away from you, Richard, if that's all right. We have a lunch date.'

'Where are you off to?'

'Didn't Paula tell you? Costa Teguise.'

'To the Dicken's Bar?'

'You've been there?' Shirley replies.

'There's a writer's group that meets there, but no I haven't.'

'Surely you've been invited to give a little talk.'

'They wouldn't pay your fee.'

'How did you know that, Paula?' Richard says, a look of astonish-ment appearing in his face.

'To answer your original question, Mr Parry, no, we are not going to the Dickens Bar.' And with that, Shirley makes to walk away.

'Have an enjoyable time, then.'

'We will.'

Richard looks disappointed not to have received an invitation. The man's sense of entitlement beggar's belief. I have never encountered in him such neediness. I almost feel sorry for him as I walk away.

Shirley drives a blue Maserati coupe and she drives it fast. She has to sit on a cushion to see through the windscreen and she's had the foot pedals lengthened. She looks even smaller behind the wheel, child size, and it's as much as I can do to keep from screaming out, alarmed as I am by the proximity of the walls—low stone or the high white-washed walls of the buildings—that whizz by as we pass. It's my first time in Shirley's car and I don't feel at all safe. My eyes won't leave the tarmac. As the car hurtles towards the hairpin at the edge of the plateau, I have to resist gripping my seat. Shirley lunges into the bend, the car leaning hard to the left, and once through, she storms down the straight descent towards the sweeping hairpin at the bottom. I remain quiet. I don't want to break Shirley's concentration until we make it to the Arrieta roundabout a couple of kilometres further on.

It is Shirley who speaks first. Heading across the coastal plain, she says, 'How long have you known Richard?'

I quickly realise Shirley knows little about me beyond the general comments that neighbours make about their lives and the little updates I volunteer concerning Gloria, Bill and Angela. I recall my old neighbour in Ipswich, Carol, the one with the struggling eucalypt, how close we were, and it's with a measure of nostalgia in my heart that I answer. 'He was the first English person I met when I moved here four years ago.'

'Aloof, if you don't mind me saying. Don't you find him aloof?'

'Not really.'

'Stiff then.'

I picture his injured back. 'Yes, stiff. Definitely.' Perhaps his back influences his manner, or is it the other way around? 'He comes to the island to write,' I add.

'Got that. I heard his wife's full on. Have you met her?'

'Trish? No, I haven't.'

It suddenly seems odd he keeps his English wife tucked away at home in Bunton.

'Have you read *Ico's Promise*?' Shirley asks, continuing with the topic. Her acerbic tone leaves me wondering where the conversation is heading.

'Not yet.' I feel bad admitting it.

'Don't bother. It's a travesty. He did the island such a disservice.'

'Surely not.'

Although I can perhaps imagine how. Richard's ability to comprehend the history of the island with any depth or sympathy is limited. He's too quick to judge, to draw conclusions. I'm surprised to find myself defending him.

'You won't be saying that after you've read it.' Shirley says. 'He portrayed Ico as a product of unwarranted lust, a half-breed who promised nothing and gave nothing, and left the island at the mercy of her son, Guadarfia.'

'Guadarfía,' I say correctly, stressing the penultimate syllable.

'If you insist. Richard had it that this Guadarfeeya, as you say, surrendered to the Spanish since they were genetically his own kind. The way Richard tells it, Ico should have failed that smoke test and died. Where on earth did he come up with it? Every danger something like that would put people off coming here.'

'It's only a book,' I say, alarmed at the fast approaching Arrieta roundabout.

'That's as maybe.' She presses down on the brake, coming to an abrupt stop on the white line. 'He's well known. People are easily influenced.'

A stream of traffic flows through from the north. Must be the end of a cave tour, I think, recalling the time I shared that experience with Richard. He spent the whole tour talking to me about his dear sweet Ann.

Shirley taps the steering wheel, waiting for a chance to pull out.

'I don't rate him much as a writer, to be honest. Do you?'

'Haversack Harvest's okay.' I try to come up with something positive to say about the book but my mind goes blank.

Shirley puts her foot down on the accelerator and the Maserati shoots out in front of a red hatchback.

'He has no right to come here and use the island for his own personal gain,' she says. 'There, I've said it.'

'Why ever not?' A writer has to get their inspiration from somewhere. Yet I'm horrified to hear my own thoughts reflected back at me, a view shared by Celestino too; a literary gold digger—that's what he called him. He said he got the term from Domingo.

The moment I have the thought I'm tense. I haven't dwelt on Celestino's whereabouts for perhaps half an hour, and now he's with me, summoned to the forefront of my mind.

On the wider arterial road that connects the northern tip to the capital, Arrecife, Shirley's fast driving is less confronting. Although she doesn't care much for cyclists. As we approach the Costa Teguise turn off, my determination to accommodate my neighbour's driving is given a thorough run for its money as she barrels towards a brace of Lycra-clad men. Determined to frighten, she waits until the last opportunity to slow down, coming up far too close behind and whipping round them with only a whisker to spare.

In Costa Teguise, Shirley's driving changes. She adheres, if barely, to the speed limit, cruising down the main street past numerous low-rise resorts. Is she showing off her Maserati? At least I have a chance to take in the surroundings. The verges in the holiday town are planted up with rows of stout palm trees, many still modest in height, their fronds dancing in the wind. Ever since I first commuted to work here, I have been of the view that the town's urban planning has been executed with a measure of taste and presumably in keeping with the architectural principles of Manrique. It all looks pleasant and neat, a tourist idyll on a desert island, just as Celestino depicted it in his Lanzapoly. Yet here is the location of some of the twenty-seven illegal hotels that are the primary focus of Celestino's wrath. They are too big, too high, too out of keeping with their surroundings and constructed without the necessary permissions. Feeling the force of his chagrin in his absence, it's as though I've entered enemy territory just being here.

My mind flits back to when I worked as a hotel receptionist. Tourists would come in to collect their key and take the opportunity to complain about the concrete skeleton across the road ruining the view from their bedroom window. 'Bloody eyesore,' was the most frequent phrase I heard. Most would note the lack of any workforce on the construction site. And I was then forced to explain that the courts had condemned the building to demolition. Didn't look like that was going to happen any time soon, they'd say, and I would respond with an apologetic smile, saying that at least there wasn't any dust. It was the best I could come up with. Celestino had explained the difficulties particular to the Canary Islands, the result of complex political and legal processes involving the various tiers of government that led to a kind of stalemate and thence inaction, the same complexities that provided the ease of illegal construction in the first place, but I hadn't taken it in sufficiently to offer any comment to disgruntled tourists. Even if I had, I probably wouldn't have bothered.

Before we reach the parade of shops that contains the Dickens Bar, Shirley turns left down Calle la Rosa, and follows it to the end. Redoto's restaurant, aptly named 'El Viento del Mar', stands alone across a promenade: a low, flat-roofed building hugging the rocky shoreline.

Shirley swings into an angle park, giving the brakes a final hard squeeze, causing me to launch forward and slap back against my seat. When she switches off the ignition and the engine dies, I release my seat belt and waste no time opening my door.

The wind is cool but not unpleasant, carrying with it the fresh salty air of the ocean. I wait while Shirley collects a paper bag from the back seat, and together we cross the promenade, dodging a pair of power-walking octogenarians.

The restaurant appears quiet, the outdoor seating area empty. A path fringed with chunks of basalt leads to the entrance set within a stylish paved porch. A staff member in bistro black is placing a sand-wich board to one side. The board advertises the menu del día scribed in bold chalk. The man straightens, and ignoring us, looks up and down the promenade before returning inside. We follow.

We haven't reached the porch when we hear the commotion. 'What on earth,' Shirley says and quickens her pace. I'm close behind, removing my sunglasses on my way in and depositing them in my shoulder bag.

The dining area is large, with rows of tables fanning over to where bi-fold doors open out onto a large terrace. Near the entrance, a small bar set back in the wall leads through to the kitchen. An aroma of garlicky fish infuses the air. Confronted by a barrage of emphatic hollering, we come to a halt at the first table, Shirley standing, feet apart, arms behind her back, one hand gripping her paper bag. Staff are gathered in a huddle beside a pillar near the terrace. Before the gathering, a burly man with a full but closely cropped beard is stabbing the air in the direction of a painting hanging in a prominent position on the side wall behind him.

'¡Dígame!'

No one speaks.

'Which one of you did this?'

His staff appear shocked and bemused. There's a lot of shaking of heads and the raising of open palms.

The offending painting hangs above a deep open fireplace. At first I can't pay it close attention, my eyes dazzled by sunlight streaming through tall windows in the north facing wall, placing the contents of the side wall in relative gloom. I dearly want to don my sunglasses but it seems rude. I direct my gaze at the huddle of men with sudden sympathy. No one deserves to be yelled at like that.

The irate man is blocking my full view of the work. It isn't until I turn my back on the glare and he steps forward to intensify his menace that I can properly take it in.

It's a large, square canvas depicting the smooth and bald mountains of Los Ajaches in the island's south, their slopes descending steeply to the ocean. In the foreground, on a small beach of black sand, is a congregation of what appear to be tall stakes, arranged in some sort of formation. I want to inch closer, but a staff member glances over and the burly man turns.

'Shirley!' he says and his manner changes as though by a flick of a switch, a broad smile spreading across his face. He shoos away the others on Shirley's approach. I follow, rounding the tables to my right to gain a better view of the offending artwork.

The man reaches down and plants a kiss on each of Shirley's cheeks, then he straightens and stares across at me.

'¿Quién es ella?'

'This is my friend, Paula Cray,' she says, using my maiden name. 'Paula, meet Redoto.' She pronounces his name Reedoetoe. I have to suppress a reaction. I have no choice but to greet the man and condone the customary exchange of kisses. At least up close I can better observe him. He has to be in his fifties, judging by the looseness of the skin about his neck, the lines beneath disingenuous eyes, hair thinning about the crown. Average in height and build, he's garbed in a black leather jacket atop expensive-looking trousers. Wafts of something like Armani fill the air around him.

'Whatever is the matter?' Shirley says in a tone of contrived concern.

'Mira.'

He takes Shirley's hand and steers her to the fireplace.

They stand together for the briefest moment. Shirley's reaction is immediate, emphatic, almost mocking.

'It's a fine artwork, Reedoetoe.'

'Is it? Is it?' he says, his distress again rising. 'From a distance perhaps, but look harder, Shirley. You too,' he says to me with an impatient gesture. 'And tell me what you see.'

Shirley makes a show of peering at the artwork then she steps back, still clutching her paper bag.

'I don't understand. What's wrong with it?'

The close proximity allows me to see that the stakes on the little black beach are in fact solar panels, depicted at oblique angles, and fashioned into crucifixes, a pair of panels set on the horizontal serving as wings. I haven't seen the work before or anything like it. He's emulated the naturalistic surrealism of Paul Kuczynski with considerable finesse. I love the work of Paul Kuczynski. Who doesn't?

I know it's his, my husband's; I recognise the mark in the bottom right corner.

At first, I'm thrown by the style, although it comes as no surprise that he's veered in the direction of political satire. I hope the work is not indicative of his La Mareta submission or he won't stand a chance of securing the commission. The location of Celestino's work in Redoto's restaurant slowly sinks in and my mind starts racing. If it is his work, and I'm sure it is, then how did it come to be hanging in a restaurant in Costa Teguise? More's the point, why?

I force upon my face a deadpan expression. Shirley and Redoto seem concerned solely with how the work came to be here. They show no sign of recognising its creator. Thankfully Celestino's new signature is too obscure, having the appearance of an inscription. Celestino told me it says 'guanamene', which means 'seer' in his native tongue. Knowing this, I can't help taking umbrage inwardly when Redoto says, 'The work is offensive. Everything is wrong with it, Shirley. Everything.' He throws up his hands. 'Tell me, who would do such a thing?'

'I have absolutely no idea what you mean, Reedoetoe.'

'And I have absolutely no idea where this thing came from. Someone put it there.'

'And you think it was one of them?' Shirley says, referring to his staff.

'Someone got into my restaurant, removed a painting and replaced it with this.' He flicks a hand in the direction of the work as if to seal his point.

Shirley turns away and puts her paper bag on the nearest table. She shoots me a wry look and I join her.

'Art theft?'

'I wouldn't go that far, Paula,' Shirley says quickly and quietly. 'The original picture was an amateur rendition of his restaurant. Nothing special. Not like this,' she says, nodding at the painting. Raising her voice to a normal level, she addresses Redoto. 'It's bizarre. Normally people steal expensive works of art. They don't generally come in and hang one unbidden. Perhaps it's a gift. Is it your birthday any time soon?'

'It is not my birthday and this is not a gift.' There's a soft growl in his voice.

Shirley doesn't react. 'Do you have any idea how they got in?'

'I have no idea at all. There is no sign of a forced entry.'

'Which is why you are accusing the staff.'

'They all have a key, or access to one.'

'Perhaps someone forgot to lock the door,' I volunteer.

My comment is ignored.

'I don't see the point of it, to be honest,' Shirley says, clasping the back of a chair, more for effect than to steady herself. 'I'd leave it there if I were you. It looks nice.'

'I will not leave it there.'

He's struggling to entertain Shirley's teasing remarks, her frivolity.

'Then sell it,' she says, apparently oblivious to the affect she's having, or indifferent to it. 'It's rather a good painting. Not a work trotted out for the tourist market. A lot of thought's gone into it. I'm sure it would fetch a good price.'

Redoto emits a sharp laugh.

'Will you call the police?' I ask, trying not to sound apprehensive.

'What good would that do?' says Shirley. 'Nothing's been stolen except for that picture. Hang on...' She shoots the artwork an appraising stare, her face breaking into a grin. 'What if someone has stolen this marvellous painting from elsewhere and is trying to implicate you in the theft.'

Redoto doesn't respond.

Absently fiddling with one of her chandelier earrings that has caught in her scarf, Shirley goes on. 'Do you have any enemies, Reedoetoe? Someone with a vendetta?'

Shirley seems to take enormous pleasure in her new role as sleuth. Redoto isn't impressed, but at least she has managed to mitigate his fury with her last comment. He looks thoughtful and is about to respond when a woman's voice calls out with much sarcasm, 'Everyone loves Redoto.'

'Maria,' he murmurs, almost to himself.

We all turn at once to see a woman emerging from behind the bar. She's voluptuous, all curves and cleavage, the mauve dress she has on clinging to her like skin. My own simple cotton dress suddenly feels like a hessian sack.

'I've got what you wanted, Redoto,' she says, walking towards us, hips swaying, high heels clicking on the tiled floor.

'Where is it?'

'In the car.' Her gaze doesn't waver.

'Mujer, give me the keys.' He holds out his hand and yells for Carlos.

The man who placed the sandwich board outside comes rushing through from the kitchen.

Maria's response is measured. She dips a carefully manicured hand into her patent leather handbag and extracts her car keys, holding them up like a taunt.

Redoto snatches them and tosses them at the waiter. 'Get the fish.'

The fish? In his wife's car? My mind races with possibilities, interrupted when in a quick change of manner Redoto addresses me with, 'I'm sorry, Paula, isn't it? Paula this is my wife, Maria.'

Maria gives me a charming smile and extends her hand. The cool touch of her flesh settles on my palm for the briefest moment before Maria pulls her hand away.

Shirley, who took several steps away from the couple during their exchange, approaches and Maria greets her warmly. Redoto watches, his earlier agitation returning.

'Reedoetoe has another restaurant in Puerto Calero,' Shirley says aloud, but addressing me. 'Maria had to do a mercy dash. The supplier forgot to include the prawns.'

I'm reminded of that phone call Shirley said she received from Maria, the cause of her late arrival at the plaza and I'm suddenly aware of the intimacy between the two women. Noting the age gap of some decades, I can't help marvelling at Maria's loyalty, for surely from her point of view, Shirley is just an eccentric old widow. Or perhaps that's a little mean. Obviously, there's the matter of rapport, of shared history and outlook, of solidarity even. Who knows? Perhaps my thoughts are tinged with envy. I've never had a best friend. Not even my old neighbour, Carol, qualified as that. I suddenly want to put as much space between myself and the looming lunch as the island will allow.

'Where are my manners.' Redoto is all stuck-on charm. 'Ladies, come and sit down.' He ushers us to a table nearby and pulls out a chair for his wife. 'What can I get you? On the house.'

Shirley fetches her paper bag and takes up the chair facing the ocean, leaving me the opposite chair with a view of the bar.

'What is that?' Maria says without sitting, her attention on Celestino's painting. 'It's horrible.'

Outrage pings in my belly. I manage to hide it.

'Maria, don't,' Redoto says with a censorious hand, and he walks away before she can utter another word.

'Whatever possessed you?' she says, raising her voice at his back. 'Throwing good money on rubbish.'

'He didn't buy it, Maria,' Shirley says. 'He was given it.'

'Given it?' She sits down with her handbag on her lap. 'By who?'

'He doesn't know.'

'Then why hang it there, where everyone can see it?'

'That's where they left it.'

'They?'

There's no time to offer an answer. Redoto returns with the menus and a bottle of white wine. He pours the wine into three large glasses. Maria waits for him to leave before she speaks again. The momentary diversion is all it takes to change her mood and the painting is forgotten. She smiles winningly and leans back in her seat. 'I bought a little something, Shirley. Couldn't resist it.' And she withdraws from her handbag a velvet jewellery box.

The two women coo adoration over a tiny crucifix suspended on a gold necklace. Then Shirley extracts a gift-wrapped package from her paper bag and hands it to her friend.

Maria gasps, her face alight in anticipation. She rips opened the silver paper like a child, tossing it on the floor and flourishing a silk wrap.

'I bought it in Puerto Calero. I hope you like it.'

Maria beams and kisses her friend and they both agree it's a perfect match with the necklace. They twitter on about the difficulties of finding suitable gifts on the island, bemoan the lack of shops and the annoyance of having to fly to Santa Cruz de Tenerife for anything special.

In what appears to be an effort to include me in the conversation, Maria turns and says, 'Here on my island the old families, they wanted to have it all. Very bad. They blocked everything.'

'Ikea fought for years, didn't they Maria?'

'Years,' Maria repeats grimly.

I'm quick to grasp the allusion. I picture my parents' new furniture with a pang of conscience, wondering what they might have managed to purchase in the pre-Ikea days.

The two women go on to agree that Puerto Calero has been their only salvation. The conversation proves tedious, but at least any lingering concern Maria may have over the painting has vanished. I'm left to the menu and my own private musings. I haven't decided on my choice of dish when the waiter comes to take our order. Maria chooses a seafood platter and a salad to share and hands Carlos the menu, indicating for us to do the same.

I take a gulp of my wine. I feel strangely diminutive. The other two women make small talk until the food arrives. I allow myself a measure of hope that we'll get through the meal without another mention of the painting but Shirley, as tenacious as ever, takes two calamari rings, nibbles briefly at one, then sits back and says, 'We have a mystery on our hands, Maria.'

I have to force myself to eat. It was easier to hide my reactions in the midst of the earlier commotion, but seated round a small table, deflecting Shirley's speculations on means, motive and opportunity, there's almost no avoiding revealing my unease. Thankfully Shirley appears oblivious. For she's taken on the role of a boisterous Miss Marple, running through the likely suspects, focusing on the staff— Carlos, the chef, the kitchen hands—quizzing Maria about their backgrounds. She makes reference to crime novels she's read, every-thing from *Murder on the Orient Express* to *The Number One Ladies Detective Agency*, and by the end of the meal, she's had the entire apparent crime figured out in four different and equally absurd scenarios. Maria is amused. Thankfully neither woman mentions the curious signature of the artist or endeavours to unpack the meaning and significance of the artwork.

Shirley saves her more salacious ideas for the drive home. As she roars her way back to Haría, she decides Redoto must be having an affair and Maria has found out. Or could it be vice versa? —Maria doesn't tell her everything. And what about those crucifixes in the painting? —Funny how Maria never mentioned them. Are they a death threat of some sort? Did she react so strongly to cover her alarm, or her culpability? Or was it Redoto who was reacting wildly to cover his own complicity in a plot to kill his wife?

By the time we reach the village my mind is spinning. I try to contribute, to at least appear to offer an opinion, and I manage to steer Shirley away from her more outrageous speculations. Yet she does have one thing right. She can't figure out how any of her suspects might have laid their hands on such a painting.

I can't either. I can't imagine that painting falling into the hands of anyone associated with Redoto's restaurant. It just isn't possible. There's only one person with ready access to Celestino's work: Celestino.

Only, I've never seen the work before. I'm as certain as I can be that it isn't a work composed years earlier: a commission or a sale. It's a new work, a very recent work, a work crafted in the oils he bought six months before with the proceeds from the sale of a commission in acrylics. I couldn't have known that this is what he intended.

10

LIMPETS

I'M AWAKE IN THE GLOAMING AFTER A NIGHT OF FITFUL SLEEP. THE shoulder will keep but the leg is in a bad way. I can feel the swelling beneath the fabric of my trousers, inflamed, hot and throbbing, signs of infection.

I'm not sure I can hold out another day. My instincts are telling me to stay put but the hole in my stomach is urging me to risk it and head back. Then again, there's food out there in the rock pools. If I wait until low tide and take my weapon, I should come back with a feast of shellfish. A feast!

It's a long and tiresome wait. I nibble on a chocolate bar and sip some of the day's water ration. I keep my eye on the ocean. There's a gentle swell. Boredom soon kicks in. I find a stray pencil and some scraps of paper in the rucksack and doodle little sketch: a pitiless still life replete with upturned table, broken chairs, crates and a bucket. Even in moments such as this, there is art.

Satisfied at last that the time is opportune, I grab hold of my weapon and head off, taking my time, scanning every nook and cranny on my way, pressing against walls at the corners. I picture myself from afar and begin to feel ridiculous. The whole situation is surreal.

Before long I've left the village behind me. Now I'm too exposed.

Paranoia kicks in, all my senses alert, and my heart beats that much faster.

I tell myself to get a grip.

The day is bright and the sun warms my back. The only sound, the waves hitting the rocks. There's no sign of the dog. As I walk I look behind me, ahead, to my left at the cliff. If the dog comes, I'll be prepared. If it's the henchman, I've had it. My best option would be to launch myself into the ocean and drown. Better that than a bullet.

I need to stop thinking like that. The chances are I'll be fine.

I apply myself to the hunt for food. I crouch on my haunches beside rock pool after rock pool, making sure I'm facing the cliff. I divide my attention between dog watch and the shellfish—limpets mostly—and I creep up softly and use a stone to tap them free. Before long, my pockets are full.

I head back, pausing by a clump of spurge. I grab that too; it's edible, although I'm not sure of the taste. The moisture in those fleshy stems will add to my water intake. For a brief moment, I feel like a survivor washed up on a desert island, awaiting rescue from a passing ship.

The sunshine, the waves slapping the rocks, the shimmering blue and the vast expanse of malpais beside me, encrusted with lichen and euphorbia, it's a kind of paradise for those who like open space and isolation. Although the tourists don't come here; few leave the enclaves in the south and east, the island's leeward side, sheltered, where they can enjoy beaches of creamy white sand. Why, with all that, would they come here?

Lanzarote, a playground for pleasure seekers; I like to keep my distance from the madness of it. I've seen what it's done to my people, a violent and radical transformation in a single generation, perhaps two.

The wealthy were quick to seize the opportunity and scramble for advantage, the poor peasant farmers too slow and ignorant to see what was coming. Manrique saw as early as the 1970s, and he tried to pre-empt the tide and mitigate. I admire him for that; the island's hero. Paula thinks I don't, but I do. It's just that we need living heroes, not dead ones; we need to undo the damage that has already been done and prevent further destruction. Manrique cannot campaign from the grave. Memorialising him only serves to make history of the present. Suddenly, we are mourning instead of fighting. And fight we must.

All these thoughts I have as I hobble back to the hut, keeping an eye on the ridge, not only for the dog, but, by chance, a passing tourist.

A laugh, brief and bitter, escapes my lips in a single short burst. Never before have I wished to see a tourist so badly, not even on my market stall on quiet days. Then, I only wanted cash to pay the bills. My life has never depended on a sale. Now my life might depend on a tourist appearing, full stop.

My mind drifts to Paula. Tourism is how I met her. And she was not just any tourist, but a woman working in a tourist information centre. I've always felt a private triumph stealing her from her career and depositing her into my world. But what world is this I've put her in?

As I open the door to the hut, doom descends in my mind, black as night.

11

THE ALJIBE

RICHARD TOSSES HIS PEN ON THE DESK. IT SKITTERS TO REST BESIDE HIS notepad. He takes in the odd angle and nudges it into alignment. The screen of his laptop stares back at him, the cursor arrow pointing at the end of a solitary paragraph, as if in mockery. He takes a slug of his gin and tonic, the second he's had this morning in the hope of stimulating his inspiration. So far, it isn't working.

The Aljibe is to be crime fiction. He has in mind a pretty young tourist out hiking one day, found floating face down in the aljibe at La Corona. Better give her dark hair. Short and curly to distinguish her from his Paula-like sleuth.

Of course, the police are informed and there's an investigation. His Paula would no doubt find the interference intrusive and damn annoying. Trouble is he hasn't a clue about police procedures on the island, or which police force would be in charge—the local, the national, the Guardia Civil? Would they fly chaps in from Gran Canaria? Or Spain? After all, a tiny island with a miniscule population can't have that much serious crime. Most likely they deal with petty theft, the odd break in, traffic offences and drunken British teenagers running amok. To make matters worse, he can't begin to speculate on how skilled or otherwise the officers might be. After *Ico's*

Promise, he isn't about to risk the criticism. Crime fiction fans are sticklers for that sort of accuracy.

He has to find a way of avoiding police involvement without stretching the plausibility boundary. What possible motive can his sleuth-Paula have for concealing the body she's discovered? What does she do with it? Walk away and leave it there? But that would mark the end of the story, not the beginning. She'll have to drag it out and hide it somewhere. Maybe she goes for help and when she returns the body is gone. But who would take it? The killer? It all seems so impossibly contrived.

The laptop screen goes black and his attention diverts to the view of the hill to the east and he finds himself idly counting palm trees.

He rues the day he agreed to set a crime novel on Lanzarote. Trent hasn't a clue about the place and he shouldn't have trusted his judgment. Lanzarote has always seemed to him something of a backwater. Little more than a tourist haven awash with ex-patriots, most of them retired—those who come to escape the tribulations back home; warm the bones, lead a quiet life. The locals are a peaceful law-abiding bunch as well, more interested in earning a decent living out of tourism and putting on a good show, especially at their numerous festivals. There really isn't much about the place to make for good crime. Although he can't be certain that his assessment is accurate; in all the years he's been visiting he hasn't paid much attention to his surroundings, the demands of producing his next book practically tying him to his chair.

One, two, three ... he counts seven palm trees, eight when he stands, fifteen when he goes to the window. Despite his lack of inspiration, he has to admit with its unusual setting and sleepy lifestyle, Haría is the perfect writer's retreat. Although Bunton would have done just as well. Or it might have, if not for the relentless demands of his wife, Trish, who has been less than sympathetic about his literary hiatus.

She's been fretting about money. Making a show of having to cut back. She has even started to invent plots. He would be lying on the couch resting his spine and in she'd glide, filled with delight, coming to a stop at his feet. 'Richard. I think this one is perfect.' He would affect pain, wince and writhe and sigh, but she wouldn't be swayed. 'Hear me out. And don't worry about committing the plot to memory. I've written it all down.' And he was then forced to listen while she launched into some convoluted scenario involving several interconnected families, a bishop, a member of parliament and a smutty scandal, and at least three dead bodies. Means, motive and opportunity, always clichéd or unconvincing, or both. Her latest, involving an entire exhibition of paintings swapped, not with forgeries but with different works of art, and some ludicrous explanation as to who was behind it and why, caused him to rise from the couch with sudden mobility, and head straight to his travel agent to book the first available flight to Arrecife.

Not that he's come up with anything better.

He thinks back over the elements of his current plot. The body in the aljibe has to be a tourist. That much he's sure of. A tourist with a compelling backstory. What is her name? Where does she come from? Why is she out walking in that inhospitable terrain? He can't decide on even the simplest of matters. As for the suspects, he struggles to conjure anyone interesting. Making matters even worse, that pretty young tourist ambling over all that rock and scree at the base of the volcano has fused with the Paula-like sleuth of his imagining, despite the difference in hair colouring. But he can't think of a finer sleuth than Paula: intelligent, moral, introspective; someone who will ponder and puzzle. She has all the key traits. Yet there's something lacking. She doesn't have that additional zing, that singular idiosyncrasy so necessary in a character whose task it is to solve crimes. She is, dare he admit it, a trifle ordinary. Perhaps he should give her a lisp, although that would be annoying, or a wooden leg, but then she'd never discover the body in such a remote location. He thought of dumping her from the narrative and coming up with a more compelling sleuth, but with Paula he felt comfortable. Never mind he can't conceive of a single reason why she'd investigate the crime. She's all he has that gives him a sense of purpose.

Her, the aljibe, and the body.

Which leaves him no choice.

He closes his laptop, and downs his gin and tonic in three

measured gulps, enjoying the bittersweet aftertaste, the slow burn, the delicious expanding of his being as the alcohol courses through him. He takes his tumbler to the kitchen and rinses it under the tap. Then he dries it thoroughly with a tea towel and puts it back in the cupboard. Not wanting Paula to regard him an alcoholic, he brushes his teeth.

Paula and Celestino's house is situated on the other side of the village, making for a pleasant walk on this warm March morning. The air is fresh, the breeze invigorating and, being a Tuesday, there's little traffic about. He takes pleasure in the view of the mountains, the palm trees, the smart white houses with their flat roofs and ancient wooden doors and shutters the same shade of green, the vacant lots filled with wild flowers, the occasional ruin. There is always something about the place to catch the eye. He succumbs to an exquisite sense of belonging to the exotic, so far from the oaks and hollyhocks of home. Sometimes he wonders if his choice to spend the first few months of every year here, at a time when the rains have freshened the landscape, has more to do with the charm of the place, than it does his need for retreat.

He cuts through the plaza and on past the town hall, pausing to admire the colonial façade from the vantage of the plaza opposite, then veering left near the little market set back on the other side of a concreted swale in the road. The swale forms part of a watercourse that passes through the village. Normally bone dry, but there must have been a torrent running through it on Saturday. No evidence remains; there isn't a puddle in sight. He's yet to visit that little market and as he goes on by, he thinks he might take a look on his way back.

About two hundred yards on and he finds himself at the Diaz's front door. He hasn't visited the house before, although he's passed it many times on his rambles about the village: ancient and simple in design, with green shutters on all the windows, open and pinned to the wall. The roof of the tower on the right peaks at a low angle, and a decorative turret, like those found in North Africa, is positioned on the flat roof to the left. Charming. It would make a good feature in a streetscape postcard too, were it not for that ostentatious monstrosity of a house next door, with its oversized windows, grey stone quoining and tiled front yard; a house built with an abundance of cash and a paucity of style.

A tall, bald-headed man with a lumbering gait approaches and Richard makes way on the pavement for him to pass by, his attention drawn to Paula's car parked at an odd angle across the street. Looks as though she's pulled up in haste and plans to be back out in a jiffy. Probably about to take the child to the grandparents. He's lucky he's caught her in. It occurs to him she may think him pushy turning up at her house uninvited to re-state his request. After all, it was only yesterday that she told him emphatically, no. His courage, earlier bolstered by the gin, begins to wane. Is it desperation that compels him to apply his knuckle to her door?

She opens it shortly after the knock.

'Richard,' she says, surprised.

'I'm terribly sorry to bother you, Paula, but I was hoping...' He trails off at the sight of the harried look on her face.

'You better come in,' she says and moves aside.

Stepping inside the dim, cold hallway, the presence of Celestino seeps from the walls; he can almost smell him and half expects his visage to appear in the bright rectangle of light framed by the doorway at the other end. He's slightly overcome and in need of a chair. The thought of forgiving his former friend, finding acceptance in his heart, reaching out for his friendship once more, are all over-shadowed by the humiliation he still clings to. Celestino ridiculed his name. The man, he has to admit, is not only insensitive, he is cruel.

'Where's the lil' 'un?' he says, looking around upon entering the warm and sunny patio, and taking note of the untidiness: clutters of pots, shoved three-deep against the walls, a mature-looking drago tree in its centre too big for the space.

Paula pauses behind him in the doorway. 'Gloria's with her grand-parents.'

'Still?'

'She's better off there,' she says dourly.

'And Celestino?'

'I have absolutely no idea. Café?'

'That would be nice,' he says, thinking they must have had a row.

She leads him into the kitchen and indicates a chair. He sits down. Finding himself facing the wall and unable to watch her without twisting his spine—an action he's learned to avoid—he stands and goes around the table, taking up the chair facing the patio and the small bench that serves as her meal preparation area. Poor Paula. She has no choice but to make do.

Although he has to admit that occupied with cups and the paraphernalia of brewing coffee, she's a pleasure to watch. Dressed in calf-length trousers and a figure hugging blouse, she's svelte and a frisson of desire rises up in him and he relishes it. Of course, he'll never again betray his wife, not after that dalliance with Ann, but he can't help lusting after an attractive woman and he refuses to feel guilty about it.

As the feeling passes he's confronted with her harried demeanour anew. Perhaps there's more going on than that row. For one thing, motherhood doesn't seem to suit her. Neither does the drudgery of housekeeping. Although looking around, she doesn't seem to do much of either. The child practically lives at the grandparents from what he can ascertain, and the house is filthy. Littering the bench are an empty water flagon and a carton of orange juice—also empty judging by its crushed shape—the remnants of a packet of biscuits, and an assortment of dirty glasses stacked by the sink. Trish would never let her house get into such a state.

At the other end of the bench, her telephone console flashes its message light. He wonders why she hasn't checked the message. Things don't seem right to him. Is she depressed? Has Celestino been cruel to her? Richard thinks it possible, but not likely. Then again, the man can be harsh, almost aggressive at times. And there is the Latin temperament to consider. Poor Paula. What she needs is a lift, a diversion, and fortunately he has just the thing.

She has her back to him when he speaks.

'I know you said you weren't able to help with *The Aljibe*,' he says, launching in without preface. 'But I was hoping you'd spare me a little time. It's just that Trent—that's my agent—is nagging me and I've never felt so uninspired.'

'Richard, I...'

'Please don't say no.'

'I put milk in your coffee by mistake,' she says, turning around, cup in hand. 'You will drink it with milk?'

'As long as it isn't much.'

'Just a dash really. I caught myself in the act. See.' She holds the cup beneath his gaze and he stares into the pale brown contents with private disgust.

'That will be fine, thank you,' he says, with all the grace he can muster.

'Sugar?' She takes the cup back to the bench. 'You take sugar too, don't you?'

'Paula.'

'I think I recall you taking two. Is that right?'

She spoons the sugar into his cup and stirs.

'Paula, come and sit down. Please.'

She hands him his cup and leans back against the bench.

'I don't think I'm able to be of much help to you, Richard.'

'You must know something about ancient water storage. You of all people.'

'They dug wells. Just like people the world over. They dug huge holes and lined them with concrete to store water underground. They dug tunnels to access the water galleries. You know all this already, Richard. They dug a lot of ruddy holes.'

'They didn't just dig holes.'

'All right,' she says with a rising inflexion. 'They concreted stretches of land on the sides of volcanoes, or anywhere the land sloped and the run off could be funnelled into a storage tank. They're called 'alcogidas'. It was all about storm water capture. That's the essence of it. There's really nothing much else to say.'

'There must be.'

'Take yourself to La Galería El Aljibe. It's in the Plaza de la Constitucíon outside the ayuntamiento.'

'Why would I want to do that?' he says, thinking to himself sourly that she's getting too confident trotting out her Spanish.

'It'll give you an idea of what they're like on the inside.'

'But it's been done up. I'm after a real aljibe.'

'There's still water under the gallery floor.'

'That isn't what I meant.'

Richard sips his coffee. Feeling the sweet cloying liquid on his tongue he almost blenches. He does his best to hide his reaction. The notion of basing his sleuth on Paula is becoming rapidly less appealing. Even so, he persists.

'The aljibe at La Corona. It must have an access port, a place for water to flow in. I need to know if it's large enough for a body to slip into, or if there's a grille preventing access.'

'Does it matter?'

'It does.'

'Can't you make it up?'

'I daren't.'

'Then you need to go there, Richard.'

'Won't you come?'

'I told you, I'm busy.'

'Busy.'

He refrains from pointing out that her daughter is with her grandparents, she only waits tables on Fridays as far as he knows, and she clearly isn't about to clean the house.

'If you must know,' she says with sudden honesty. 'Celestino's missing.'

'Missing?'

'You're beginning to sound like a parrot, Richard. Yes, missing. I haven't seen him since Saturday morning.'

'It's Tuesday.'

'I'm well aware of that.'

'Have you spoken to the police?'

'Not yet. He's a grown man. I doubt they'd do a lot.'

He looks down at his coffee, at the brown skin forming on the surface. His gaze wanders over the other items on the table: an assortment of pens in a chipped earthenware jar, three placemats, stained, and a square of notepaper. Without his glasses, he has to strain to read the writing, but he can see it is Paula's. Addressed to Celestino. Something about going out. She really ought to see to that phone message.

'Are you looking for him then?'

'I've asked his friends. I've searched the house and the studio and found nothing to indicate foul play. I don't know what to do next.'

'Difficult.'

'You're a detective novelist. What would you do?'

'Hard to say.'

He didn't mean to sound evasive. In fiction, characters solve mysteries by following the clues he, the author, puts in the story. It was contrived. Real life is different. In real life, it takes an exceptional human and a lot of good luck to solve a crime.

'I was thinking of going for a drive. Visit the places where he's known. Art galleries maybe. Ask around.' She eyes him thoughtfully. 'Would you like to come with me?'

'Me?'

'You're doing it again. Yes, you.'

'I'd be of no use.'

'You'd be company.'

'I'm afraid I can't help you, Paula,' he says, suddenly rattled that she won't go with him to La Corona, but she expects him to traipse around the island helping her. Besides, she knows he has a bad back. All that sitting for long periods in a car will do it no good at all. He begins to wonder if she isn't rather selfish.

Leaving his coffee with its congealing brown skin on the table, he stands.

'You're leaving.' She seems taken aback, but he's hardened to her sensibilities.

'All the best with your search, Paula. I daresay I'll see you around.'

He avoids her gaze as he rounds the table. She follows him to the front door.

12

PEDRO

I WOULD HAVE BOOTED RICHARD OUT INTO THE STREET IF I'D BEEN THE booting-out type. Instead I slam the door on him. Never have I known a human being so self-centred. Surely Richard can see I'm wracked with worry? All he can think of is his blasted book. Come to think of it, I'm glad he chose not to accompany me. He'd have been atrocious company, quizzing me on my knowledge of local culture or complaining about his back. And a headache too no doubt, for I'm sure I detected alcohol on his breath; disturbing, so early in the morning. Why did I even suggest it? If he had agreed, I may have been tempted to divulge my concerns about that painting in Redoto's restaurant and the fewer who know about that, the better. Six days until the winner of the La Mareta commission will be announced and reason is getting away from me. I only came home to grab a few things. Leave another note, just in case.

I return to the kitchen and toss the contents of his cup in the sink. A sliver of brown skin slides towards the plughole. I watch it disappear, then attend to the message light on the telephone console that has been flashing since I arrived and I didn't manage to press the button before Richard turned up.

There are two messages, one from Pilar, the other Kathy, each asking for an update and hoping I'm okay. I delete them both. I'll call them later. I ought to talk to Pedro too. As comrade-in-arms he, more than anyone, may have information leading to Celestino's whereabouts; but I baulk at the thought. Besides, I don't have time to interview my husband's friends. It's a lie. I know it's lie. I have plenty of time. Time enough to be consumed by a mix of shame and trepidation, as though talking to his closest ally will bring the notion that my husband has walked out on me to the fore.

I RETURNED from Costa Teguise yesterday with Celestino's painting uppermost in my mind and no idea if its presence in Redoto's restaurant implied he was alive and in hiding somewhere embroiled in subterfuge, or if he was in some sort of danger. Shirley's speculations hadn't helped. In a turmoil I could hardly contain, I bid her a hasty farewell, got in my car and drove straight to Máguez to confide in my parents, the only people I felt I could trust.

I arrived a little after three, bursting with my news, but Gloria bounded to the door with her usual exuberance. Bill and Angela seemed relieved I was back and quickly exited the living room, Bill making for his office, and Angela heading out to the patio. Resigned to Gloria's needs, I sat on the floor with puzzles, with teddy bears and dolls, with crayons and then with picture books. Two hours of undivided attention and I took her through to the second living area at the back of the first and turned on the cartoons hoping for freedom, but Gloria insisted I sit with her. I pretended to watch, one ear cocked to the kitchen where I could hear my mother preparing dinner. A short while later came the spicy smell of frying sausages.

It was six when at last we were seated round the table and I could detail my day. Angela appeared baffled but Bill gripped the situation with his usual tenacity. First, he speculated on how I came to find myself viewing the painting, which was remarkable in itself. I explained that other than Shirley and Maria, no one could have known I would turn up at the restaurant, which I supposed made them prime suspects. But neither woman knew it was Celestino's work, or knew a thing about how it got there. Maria was appalled at the sight of it and Shirley had found the whole situation hilarious, quickly deciding that someone must have been playing a practical joke and that Redoto shouldn't take it seriously. I thought back over Shirley's speculations—the cook did it, one of the waiters, the painting had been stolen and planted in the restaurant to set Redoto up—they were the sorts of scenarios that would have found their way into one of Richard's books, if *Haversack Harvest* were indicative. The more I talked it through, the more it did appear to be some sort of joke. Bill agreed. Which left the matter of the artwork itself.

'Why would anyone put that particular painting in that particular restaurant? That's the question we need to keep in mind,' he said, cutting Gloria's toast into thin strips to dunk in her boiled egg.

The rest of us were dining on the sausages and a creamy mash, not Gloria's favourite. At home, I would have required her to eat what was put in front of her or go hungry. Angela and Bill had other ideas. Ignoring the pleasure she was taking in making an eggy mess on her plate, I tried to think about Bill's question, come up with answers, but my mind clogged up over the thought that Celestino was behind it all.

'Solar panels on a beach,' Bill said, 'Any idea where?'

'The mountains are undoubtedly Los Ajaches.'

'That's a start.'

'You mean it could be a pointed reference?'

'Implying something that the recipient would understand, yes.'

'Which would explain why Redoto was so angry.'

But that was all it explained. Without knowing the context, it was impossible to grasp the precise nature of the message implied by the painting, beyond that it had something to do with the death of solar power.

Angela changed the subject, asking if I minded them taking Gloria to the Aloe Vera farm near Órzola one day in the week. I thanked her with some relief. At least Gloria would be kept enter-tained. With luck, they'd tire her out and she'd be less covetous of my attention when I returned.

Before the conversation could revert back to Celestino I took my plate of almost-finished food to the kitchen sink to make a start on the dishes.

An hour spent attending to Gloria's bedtime and I whittled away the rest of the evening slumped in front of the television doing my best to stay focused on the images on the screen and not those my mind kept wanting to mull over.

STANDING in my own kitchen beyond the reach of the morning sun streaking in from the patio, my mind is a blur of incomprehension. Three days since I last saw Celestino, and the house seems to exude him from every pore. I can only think one step ahead. I go upstairs to pack some clean clothes into a travelling bag, leaving plenty of space for some of Gloria's. Not knowing how long we'll be staying in Máguez, I toss in a few toys and toiletries as well. I give the patio plants a quick water, grab all I need and leave the house.

Once seated behind the steering wheel I can only think of one course of action. I'll check the paintings in the studio in case I missed something vital when I went there on Sunday, and follow up on my search for Celestino as well, which thus far has amounted to little.

I park outside the studio with two wheels on the pavement, leaving no room for a pedestrian to get by. I observe the street with a suspicious eye, noting the vehicles parked here and there, white rental cars mostly, and a black sedan reverse parking further up. There are no people about.

On my way inside, I decide to give the building a thorough search first. It is something a real sleuth would do. And I have to adopt the role, ill-suited as I am.

Forcing myself to tackle the upstairs before I lose my nerve, I head through to the debris-strewn patio. The banister looks secure but I don't touch it, preferring to make my way unaided up the broken stone steps. Trepidation rises with every tread. I've watched too many thrillers. And I can't shake the feeling that I've somehow entered one.

I pause on the landing. The air smells musty. Sunlight shafts in through rotting shutters. Old floorboards are stacked in a corner, those still in place in disrepair. The landing leads to two rooms, one on my right and another on my left. I pick my way across to the right.

I don't enter. The room contains nothing except a single wooden chair, placed off centre. It's a perfect setting for one of those grim interrogation scenes. A hapless man strapped, gagged, beaten. I shudder and quickly cross the landing to the room above Celestino's studio.

Part of the roof in the far corner of the room has collapsed leaving a small section of exposed rafters. Water pooling on the floor beneath has stained the boards. In the centre of the floor rubble has been piled in a heap. I skirt the rubble looking for clues, or what I think might be clues, the sort a real sleuth would stumble on: a discarded receipt, a scrap of torn clothing, track marks in the dirty floor. There's nothing.

Filled with a strange mix of relief and disappointment, I make my way downstairs, across the patio and through to the rooms at the back. There are two, both empty rubble-filled shells. The dirt and the dust appears undisturbed.

On my way through to the front of the building, I hear movement in the empty room opposite the studio. Something shuffling. I stop and listen. A car engine revs in the street. A voice, female, grows louder then fades as a woman passes by the front door. Drawing up courage, I enter the vestibule, the only part of the building in reasonable repair.

The room opposite the studio should be locked. It was locked when I tried the door on Sunday. I try again and to my surprise this time the doorknob turns in my grasp.

The shutters are boarded up, allowing in little light. A large desk takes up the centre of the room, along with an old armchair. Nothing looks disturbed and I'm about to make my exit when a waft of something hits me and I pause and sniff the air. Sitting atop the dank smell of an unaired room is the faint odour of something sweet, aromatic with a hint of musk. Perfume of some sort, male or female I can't tell. Someone else was in the room recently. When? How long do smells like that linger? Minutes, or hours? Whoever it was must have a key. And they forgot to lock the door on their way out. Maybe the person was in that room when I arrived and sneaked out when I was upstairs. It isn't a comforting thought. I remember the mill house is listed for sale. Chances are the agent showed around a prospective buyer. Even the vendor may have swung by, although I'm certain Celestino said he's returned to England for good.

Not exactly reassured by my rationalisations, I open the door to the studio. Celestino never keeps it locked. Perhaps he should. If an intruder has gained entry from the street, he could also have riffled through the artworks. It puzzles me why he's lax about his art when he's paranoid when it comes to his anti-corruption work. I flick on the light and scan the contents of the room.

As far as I can tell nothing has changed, although there's so much clutter it's impossible to be certain. I make my way to the stacks of paintings leaning against the back wall. Most of them I've seen: the smaller ones for the markets, larger pieces for exhibitions. Sifting through, I don't see any new work. I survey the bench then pick up a sketchpad and leaf through the pages. Some of the drawings look like ideas for the La Mareta commission. There is no other work that resembles the solar-panel crucifixion. Yet that work is his, it has to be. And I can tell by the squished tubes that he's been using his new oils. Maybe there are other similar works and they've all been stolen. Perhaps by that recent intruder. It's a discomforting thought. I prefer to think that Celestino has taken them, if they exist. In which case, why on earth doesn't he get in touch?

I'm about to leave when I notice something glinting on the floor underneath his easel. I bend down. It's a necklace. As I reach to pick it up I find the pendant has come free and is lying a few inches away. I recognise the pendant immediately as Celestino's; the stone of polished obsidian I gifted him the holiday we met; Pedro's craftsman-ship evident in the ornate silver clasp that holds the stone in place. A chill wind billows through me. Celestino never goes anywhere without the necklace now hanging between my fingers, broken as though wrenched from his neck.

I quickly dismiss my reaction as the workings of an overwrought mind, and deposit the necklace in my pocket.

There's nothing to be gleaned in the studio. I switch off the light and close the door.

Out in the street the wind tousles my hair. The day has grown bright and clear. I walk to my car keen to retrieve my sunglasses thinking I need the same clarity. Like a hound sniffing out prey, all I can do is follow my instincts and try to keep a grip. I wait for a few vehicles to pass. Observing the street, I note that the white hatchbacks all look the same as before and the black sedan has gone. Straight away I feel half ridiculous for even paying attention, seeing in myself little more than a child playing at being a detective.

Where next? If Celestino is behind all this, then it will have something to do with his anti-corruption efforts, and other than me and my father, the only person who knows of Celestino's campaigns is Pedro. I have no choice. Reticent as I am, I need to speak to him. With a new sense of purpose, I turn on the ignition. Eleven o'clock on a Tuesday seems a good time to find Pedro at home. The car is pointing in the right direction.

I prefer taking the fast route to Tabayesco on the flatter, wider roads of the coastal plain. The road that winds down through the head of the valle de Temisa, while scenic, is narrow and too often cluttered with cyclists. It's a good road for a long walk. Yet after the storm there's sure to be rockfalls and landslides and I want to see, at a closer range than when I stood at the Los Helechos restaurant at the top of the switchbacks, if amongst the debris is an abandoned car. It's an off chance, but at least I can rule it out and it will be one less possibility playing on my mind. For if Celestino did take the mountain road south as Shirley claims, then despite it being insane to have taken that route last Saturday, he may possibly, just possibly, have been going to visit Pedro.

The barren saddles of the Famara massif stretch out eastward like elongated arms, the valle de Temisa forming a steep-sided U. The road snakes around the valley's head, where barrancos have carved out crevices in the folds of the mountain. The terraces extend the full height and length of the saddles, only the most rugged, scree laden areas left untouched. Many of the terraces are abandoned, yet in the flatter areas at the valley's base, farming continues apace.

I take it slow, keeping the car in low gear, stopping now and then to peer down at the squares of black fields and the low-lying scrub, mostly euphorbias and prickly pear. The bends afford a clearer view of the hillside up ahead. When I reach the gullies, I stop to take a longer look around. The road winds on for a kilometre before straightening out somewhat as it courses along the southern saddle to the village of Tabayesco. There's nothing to see. Any rockfalls and landslides have already been attended to and not a car wreck in sight. As I approach the sweeping hairpin at the village edge, a party of cyclists, taking up the whole road, pant their way towards me. I pull over in a lay by to let them pass and meet the stragglers on the next hairpin.

Tabayesco is a hamlet. I take a side road and park outside Kathy and Pedro's. Opening the door, I pause, suddenly in no hurry to go inside. Running through what I plan to say, I don't feel confident I know Pedro all that well. My friendship is with Kathy.

Pedro and Celestino have been friends for about fifteen years, ever since Pedro moved to the island from Madrid and started doing the markets. Kathy, originally from Hampshire, and Celestino, met Pedro on the same day. They all became instant friends. Although I prefer to think of them as comrades since they've all told me on various occasions how their close bond developed over their mutual abhorrence of the resort development that has been taking place on the island since the 1980s.

I sympathise with their view, yet I can't help thinking it a touch parochial. Since when have the powerful in any nation the world over resisted the temptation to profit, personally, out of business deals? Although I'm well aware that this universal trend doesn't negate the specific conditions. A river is a river but each river is unique. There appears to be a business-as-usual mentality to corruption here too, and Celestino has told me often enough that anyone on Lanzarote who dares to seek change is hounded into silence. A shared disapproval of corruption isn't basis enough for shared confidences. Pedro has no reason to trust me except that I'm his friend's wife. I brace myself for my first interrogation.

Simple in design, the main parts of the farmhouse face away from the road in favour of the view of the coast towards Arrieta, the front wall containing a little used entrance door and two small windows. I catch a glimpse of the three daughters, frolicking on a concrete patio at the side. At two, four and six, the girls are full of the high jinks of spring, their squeals carried away on the wind. I round the corner and find Kathy pegging out washing. Kathy wears an open-mouthed smile, and with her thick hair tied back from her face she beams good health and wellbeing. When she meets my gaze, her joyful look gives way to concern. She reaches down and picks up a pink spotted dress. 'No Gloria?' she says, looking past me.

'She's with her grandparents.'

I yield to a rush of guilt. Gloria would have enjoyed the company of the Ramírez family. I might even have left her in their care for a few hours. Given my parents a break. But Gloria is demanding, as any three-year old can be, and a further distraction. No, Gloria is better off where she is.

'Is Pedro home?' I say casually, not wanting to reveal the only purpose of my visit, knowing my question is abrupt, if not rude, customary as it is to wait for and accept the invitation of coffee.

Kathy looks at me strangely. 'He's in his workshop. Would you like me to get him?'

'If you don't mind.'

'No Celestino then.'

'No.'

'This is very rare. He wouldn't disappear. Have you been to the police?'

'I don't think I can.'

'Good. You see ...'

Pedro pokes his head through a pair of drying sheets. Kathy giggles spontaneously.

'Hola, Paula. ¿Qué pasa?'

He's a dishevelled looking man, heavy set, with scruffy hair receding at the temples. A long apron covers an old T-shirt and pants. He comes forward and kisses my cheeks. He smells of stale sweat.

'Can you spare a moment?' I ask.

'Follow me.'

As he turns, anticipation flickers through me. It's only the second time I've been in his workshop since my initial visit when they showed me around. Since then, when I visit I sit with Kathy on the patio outside and watch the children play.

He leads me inside and on through the kitchen, rounding the table in its centre. With a single sweep of my eye, I observe a room that, despite the house being two-hundred years younger than my own, is in much the same condition, with no cupboards to speak of, and a bench too small for meal production. It's Kathy who showed me how to chop vegetables in the palm of my hand, a technique she acquired from Pilar.

A door at the rear opens into a short corridor. At the end, five steps lead down to a glass-panelled door. He holds it open for me to pass through and once I'm inside he lets it go. The door closes of its own accord. I must have looked surprised because he's quick to explain that it's on sprung hinges to allow him to keep an eye on the children without them entering uninvited.

The workshop is lined with wooden benches strewn with an array of hammers of all sizes, awls, clamps, saws and an assortment of pliers. A solid and tall table takes up the centre of the room and an equally solid desk is set to one side. Pedro removes a pile of books and notepads off a stool and invites me to sit down. He leans with his back against the desk and eyes me appraisingly.

'You want to ask me about Celestino. He still hasn't shown up?'

'I'm worried he might be in some sort of trouble.' Even as I speak, caution rushes in from the wings. Can I trust this man?

'Trouble?' he says. 'What are you talking about?' He stares at me, his expression stern.

I hesitate. Not feeling I have much choice, I swallow and go on. 'I was at a restaurant in Costa Teguise yesterday. And the owner was in a fury over a painting that someone had hung in place of another. He was berating the staff when we walked in.'

'We?'

'I went with my neighbour.'

It feels like a confession but he shows no reaction. He must know how much Celestino loathes Shirley. Surely men talk about such things? Maybe he hasn't made the connection. After all, I didn't say, next-door neighbour. I might have been referring to anyone in my street.

Seated on his stool I'm disempowered and dearly want to stand up. His eyes haven't left my face. When I again speak, I note a defensive ring in my voice.

'The owner thought one of his staff must have switched the paintings since there was no sign of a break in.'

'I don't understand.' He frowns. 'What has this got to do with Celestino?'

'It was his painting.'

Pedro shakes his head doubtfully.

'I'm sure of it.'

'Have you seen it before?'

'It carried his signature. The one he's only just started using.'

'In Guanche.'

'You know about the signature?'

He doesn't speak. A troubled look flashes into his face. He turns away and picks up a clamp, twisting the handle of the screw. The squeak sets my teeth on edge.

Losing patience, I say, 'Pedro, please. It could be important.'

He puts down the clamp and crosses his arms over his chest. 'He told me in private, more or less. We were at the markets.'

'More or less? Someone else was there?'

'Only Fernando.'

I pause for a moment, trying to make some sense of the implication and cautioning myself against leaping to premature conclusions. I'll deal with the matter of Fernando later. Right now, I need answers, and they are not forthcoming.

'And this painting,' he says. 'What was it?'

I'm reluctant again, almost protective of my knowledge, as though in the telling I'm giving too much away. He listens as I depict the rendering of Los Ajaches, the little black beach, but when I get to the solar-panel crucifixes he laughs.

'Typical.'

'Really?' I say, resenting his reaction. 'I've never seen anything like it.'

'You haven't known him that long.'

His words sting but I try not to show it.

'It was as if he was trying to make a statement,' I say. 'And it must have worked because the owner was livid.'

'Do you know who he was?'

'Redoto.'

'Redoto Redoto.'

'Just Redoto,' I say drily. 'He didn't give his last name.'

'It's Redoto Redoto. Son of Juan Medina Redoto.'

'How do you know him?'

'Never mind.'

I let it go, realising I need a notepad. Sleuths always carry a notepad.

'Do you know if Celestino was working on a new corruption campaign?'

'Not that I know of.'

'He would have told you.'

'He would.'

I detect an evasive air about him. I make a mental note to write that down as well, the moment I get back to the car.

A silence descends. I can't think of a thing to fill it. My mind is a whirr. He remains leaning against the bench with his arms folded, head bowed slightly, gaze lowered. I thank him for his time. 'De nada,' he says. He doesn't move. Slipping off the stool I regain some control and I manage to admire a partly finished bracelet on my way by, one hand slipping into my trouser pocket and closing around Celestino's broken necklace. I let myself out, the door springing shut behind me.

Kathy and the children are still outside. I forgo her pleasantries and words of sympathy and head straight through the kitchen to the front door, letting myself out into the street.

I've come away none the wiser, save for the little revelation that both Pedro and Fernando knew about Celestino's signature, something I presumed Celestino had told me in confidence. Then again, I might have known he told Pedro. He seems to tell him everything. Pedro was in no doubt that the work is Celestino's. He's almost certainly hiding something too; he was wary, cagey. In all likelihood Celestino divulged to his friend the subject of this new artwork as well, a work he kept hidden from me. And coupled with the physical loss of him is a renewed sense of betrayal, as though I've already lost a vital part of him—if I ever had it. My mind is grim. I feel thoroughly excluded from the important aspects of Celestino's life—his politics, his art—and wonder if I'll ever be included in the intimacy he seems to share with his friends.

I rummage through the contents of my shoulder bag, but I can't find any paper, not even an old receipt. I look in the glove box. Nothing. Still, I don't have that much to remember, although Pedro has certainly left me with plenty to think through.

Along with my misgivings comes a fresh idea and as I turn down the road heading towards the coast, my earlier suppositions that either Celestino put the painting in the restaurant, or he was in some kind of danger, begin to waver. Perhaps it's nothing more than a practical joke. Which rules out Pedro straight away. I can't imagine him doing such a thing, not to anyone. He isn't the type. Besides, as far as I know he doesn't have access to the studio. Which eliminates him as a suspect.

Whereas Fernando does have access. Celestino had another key cut so that for a small fee Fernando can use the studio space on the days when Celestino is at the markets, on the condition that he packs away all his materials and takes them home with him, Celestino not wanting evidence that he's in effect subletting. Fernando works in chalks and pastels, easily transportable, and he has been content to take advantage of the arrangement having no space in his tiny flat for his art.

I stop at the main road intersection and wait for an opportunity to turn left. Cars whip by in both directions intermittently, not providing an adequate break. I reef the handbrake, happy to wait, until a small truck pulls up close behind, indicating right. Feeling pressured, I release the handbrake and nose forward, ready to shoot out once a blue Hyundai has passed by.

Professional jealousy would be the most likely motive. Celestino's works sell more frequently and fetch a higher price. Fernando doesn't like his job at the timple museum but can't live off the proceeds of his art. Yet what will he hope to gain from hanging one of Celestino's paintings in a restaurant in Costa Teguise? It can hardly be to discredit him since no one else knows the identity of the creator.

I come to a halt at the Arrieta roundabout and wait for a stream of cars heading down from the north. The Manrique wind sculpture in the roundabout's centre catches my eye; rendered in burnt orange, it's emblematic of the island's civic pride that pivots on the artist with entrenched reverence. A gap in the flow and I head up the road to Haría, returning to my preoccupation with Fernando.

One time a few years ago, I visited the studio to find Fernando at work instead of Celestino, who'd gone to an art gallery in Arrecife to discuss a forthcoming exhibition. He told me the night before but in my early-motherhood haze I'd forgotten, despite all the complaining he'd subjected me to as we were readying for bed. He was most unhappy about it, DRAT having scuppered his plans to hold his exhibition at the prestigious Casa de la Cultura Agustín de la Hoz, a grand old house containing a number of murals by Manrique. It was a controversial request, the house less a gallery and more a stately home. Celestino was planning his exhibition to coincide with an international conference on fresh-water management and conservation, and had created a series of works that in a somewhat unsubtle manner depicted Playa Blanca's on-going problem with sewerage.

I would have liked to attend the conference. As I lay there in bed waiting for Celestino to turn off the light my mind drifted, the island's culture of water conservation fascinating, the ancient wells, the aljibes and the alcogidas that fed them dotted all about the island evidence of the islanders' ingenuity. In each home would have been a stone water filter. For them, all of those methods amounted to water conservation and management. Tourism meant desalination plants to feed water-wasteful swimming pools and golf courses. Lying on my back with my hands folded beneath my head, I pictured those in attendance in their slick suits. And I imagined Celestino's works on the walls all around them, raw, brutal, confronting. I smiled inwardly. Of course, DRAT wouldn't let him have his way, and he was shunted instead to the Punto de Encuentro con el Arte, where, according to DRAT, works such as his belonged. He was furious. He even huffed in his sleep. After that, in our household, uttering DRAT was tantamount to swearing.

The following morning, when I arrived at the studio, Fernando was there in his stead, taking advantage of his day off to knock out a run of simple island scenes. I saw their appeal the moment I entered the room; volcanoes silhouetted against vivid sunsets in various hues forming a temporary frieze on the bench.

Fernando had his back to me. The unexpected inpouring of natural light from the patio brightened the floor at his feet, causing him to turn, the look of alarm on his face fading when he saw who it was. A short man, no more than me in height, and slight of build, he had a pinched face framed by a goatee beard that served to age him beyond his fifty years.

'I'm sorry,' I said, momentarily confused. 'They're beautiful,' I added, at a loss for something appropriate to say.

'Thank you. They're for a gallery in Puerto del Carmen.' He returned to the work on the easel.

'I didn't know there was a gallery in Puerto del Carmen.'

He didn't answer. I went over for a closer look at the works.

'Is the gallery new?' I said, turning to catch his gaze.

A look of irritation flashed into his face.

'It's an arts and crafts shop. Not an exhibition space. No one consigns to a gallery. Not even Celestino.'

At the time, his resentment took me by surprise, but looking back I have a better understanding of the context for it. Fernando hails from Arrecife. He claims to have been one of Manrique's protégés back in the early 1990s before a terrible car accident stripped Lanzarote of its cultural ambassador and ecological crusader. Fernando was then in his early twenties. He's a self-important man and I don't put much store in his claim that he was a protégé. Many are prone to gross exaggeration when it comes to associations with the famous. Fernando uses his to puff up his artistic abilities. No wonder. Alongside Celestino, who has an exceptional talent of his own, Fernando must feel diminished.

Given Fernando's irascible manner, I marvel at Celestino's loyalty. Since that occasion at the studio I haven't considered Fernando entirely truthful. How vindictive he's capable of being is impossible to gauge. What might have triggered an upsurge of professional jealousy of such magnitude that he would seek to discredit his friend? Surely not the La Mareta commission? Celestino has only just entered. There's no certainty of success. Besides, I have no idea if Fernando knows about it. Considering how he felt about applying, Celestino may have chosen not to tell him. And if Fernando is behind this, then discrediting Celestino might jeopardise his chances, but only if the creator of the work at Redoto's 'El Viento del Mar' is exposed. And even then, only if it could be shown that the creator made the switch. It all seems far-fetched but my suspicions fly off Pedro and land on Fernando like a bird on a passing ship. And I can't decide if my conviction is a comfort. If my husband is the culprit, at least that implies he's alive. If Fernando is behind it, or some other enemy, then what of Celestino?

BACK AT MY parent's house, I walk in on Bill entertaining Gloria with a collage of scenery and animal photos he's cut out of old copies of the National Geographic. One Christmas, a sister-in law gifted a subscription and, despite neither of them having much of an interest, Angela packed them, along with all his other magazines, when they moved here. Bill and Gloria are having a merry old time. By the look of it, not one copy of the National Geographic has escaped the scissors. Gloria, who has her back to me, is absorbed instructing her grandfather as to what parts of a flamingo she wants cutting out. Bill obediently follows her directions. The moment she turns she squeals, 'Look, Mummy!' and holds up a scrappily cut photo of a headless giraffe in one hand, a pair of child-size scissors in the other. I grin and go over to inspect the progress, forcing myself to focus. It takes quite an effort, but for a brief time I feel the stress fall away and I'm at ease. In noticing the change, it's as though I've alerted my anxiety to something it has predetermined I've no right to feel, and the tension returns with force. Feeling somewhat cheated out of that scrap of wellbeing, I inhale and leave Bill and Gloria to it.

My mother is in the kitchen, preparing lunch. Four rolls, each on a plate and split in half ready for the crumbed fish she's frying in a large, flat-bottomed pan. The table is laid, with a bowl of mixed salad in the centre.

'This situation is quite dreadful,' Angela says without preface, as though she's done nothing but fret about it all morning. 'I don't know how you're managing to cope. I'd be in pieces.'

She slides the breaded fish onto the rolls. I step forward to put on their lids.

'Don't press down too hard, Paula.'

There is nothing I can say that won't sound childish. I take the plates to the table and call to the others.

'No sign of him then?' Bill says as he sits down.

I shake my head. Gloria removes the top half of her roll and pulls off the crispy coating of the fish. Before long her plate and the surrounding table are sprinkled with bits of fish and bread.

'Tomato sauce?' Bill says, directing his comment at Angela.

'I think not,' she says, cutting her own roll in half.

We fall into silence, each absorbed with their food.

At Bill's elbow is yesterday's edition of *El Diario de Lanzarote*. Although his command of the language is minimal, he insists the only way to learn is full immersion. The front page is given over to more news about the tropical storm. A burnt-out car has been found at an intersection near Mancha Blanca. My belly lurches. Mancha Blanca? Isn't that where the Swedish doctor, Erik lives? I read on. The police are unable to identify the vehicle's owner or find a trace of the driver, who may have died at the scene. It wasn't unusual, the reporter said, as the heat in a car fire will turn bones to powder. The police are seeking witnesses.

'Have you seen this?' I say, addressing my father.

'What is it?' Bill glances over. 'Ah, yes.'

'I should call the police. It could be Celestino's car.'

'I think you're being paranoid, Paula. Stop jumping at every little thing.'

'But when I went to the studio, the commission for the doctor wasn't there. What if Celestino went to deliver it.'

'In Saturday's weather? Hardly likely.'

I have to agree, and besides, Shirley said she saw Celestino leaving the house at about one-thirty, so wherever he was heading, it was not to Mancha Blanca, for if he went there at that time he would have missed the birthday party. Celestino would not have done that. He just wouldn't.

That gnawing anxiety intensifies. Keen for a distraction, I scan the other articles on the front page. Another headline concerns the demolition of the illegal hotels in Playa Blanca, a story Bill is following with keen interest after considering the volumes of concrete involved.

They're hardly going to ship the stuff to somewhere else, he said the other week. I imagined the expense, the enormous scale of the work involved. In a fanciful moment, I suggested recycling or reusing, but he scoffed away my ideas. You can't demolish those hotels brick by brick. Eyesores, he calls them. And they are. Celestino even created a 'kickback in your favour' Chance card for his Lanzapoly game, providing the acquisition of an illegal hotel for which rent can be gained, along with another Chance card that finds the owner of said hotel guilty of corruption and lands them in jail, and a third which requires payment of a vast demolition sum which generally bankrupts the player.

Preferring not to get into a heated discussion about who is responsible and therefore who should pay for what amounts to an exercise as monolithic as the buildings themselves, I observe Gloria's antics, privately decrying her table manners, certain Angela never let me make such a mess. She's arranged strips of bread and slivers of fish around the edge of her plate and is busy decorating the fish slivers with the bits of salad greens that she's strewn on the table along with a few rounds of tomato. She's consumed by her task and no one stops her. After a while, Angela fetches a cloth to wipe her hands.

'Did he end up entering that competition you mentioned?' she says without preface, directing her question to me.

'Celestino? He did.'

'Only I think I read somewhere they'll be announcing the winner on Monday.'

'Angela, leave it.'

'Well.'

'Angela, you know full well Celestino's disappearance has nothing to do with that painting competition.'

'That's as may be, but he'll need to be here to accept the prize, won't he? Or they'll give it to someone else.' It's her rising inflexion that grates.

I say nothing. Her words are as stodgy to swallow as the fish rolls. Maybe Gloria has the right idea.

It isn't until I've laboured through to the last bite that I'm able to relate the events of my morning. When I get to the part about the necklace, my voice rising on a string of speculations, each dourer than the last, Bill cuts in with, 'Hey, now. Calm down. Sounds like he left in a hurry, that's all. Don't let your imagination run away with you.'

Chastened, I lower my tone and continue with a short account of my conversation with Pedro.

'None the wiser, then,' Bill says.

'I need to talk to Fernando.'

'Are you sure? You're not a detective, Paula,' Angela says. 'If he does have something to do with this, aren't you putting yourself at risk?'

'At risk of what?'

She doesn't respond.

'If you do speak to him, avoid telling him you know about the painting,' Bill says. 'Find some other way of seeing if he had the opportunity. Do you have any idea when the painting turned up at that restaurant?'

A quick reckoning and I surmise it may have been put there anywhere between late Sunday night and sometime Monday morning, before Shirley and I walked in to find Redoto in a state. That was about noon, leaving a period of twelve hours, assuming the restaurant closed late. A pity I can't narrow it down any further.

Casting around for a change of subject, I forego my earlier reticence and gesture at his newspaper. 'Any news?'

'Only the first anniversary of the opening of the underwater sculpture.' He says it with a sneer and I do my best not to sigh. Almost everyone else on the island is rapt that Lanzarote secured the talents of world-renowned British sculptor, Jason deCaires Taylor, and now has a series of life-sized human figures in various poses, submerged twelve metres beneath the ocean, there to create an artificial reef to attract marine life and to make a critical comment on rising sea levels: Thirty-five people in a botanical garden walking towards a gate representing a point of no return. It is novel, ingenious, the artist's brand; the Lanzarote version building on the success of a similar sculpture in Mexico. The sculpture is a draw card, something to add to the buffet of tourist treats. Celestino and Bill are wont to complain that it cost many hundreds of thousands of Euros of public as well as private money; that the negotiations had proceeded behind closed doors and therefore without due public scrutiny; and that the sculpture is located in the heartland of the island's corruption, all reasons why it should never have been allowed to go ahead. I want to scream at them sometimes. What sort of utopian world do they imagine possible on the island, or anywhere else for that matter?

I reach for my water, suddenly thirsty. Bill attends to Gloria who has resumed playing with her food.

In the face of their relentless tirades about how the wealthy are taking over the island and making it theirs, I find myself defending tourism more and more, in spite of my own misgivings that it's out of control. Despite the corruption, Lanzarote strives to maintain and build on its uniqueness, undoubtedly driven by the knowledge that without tourism, the island's economy would wither away. It's a constant battle of competing interests. I understand that DRAT, along with many others in high places, want to attract what they consider to be a better sort of tourist, those who can afford the 5-star resorts. Those who come to the island in their yachts, the sorts of tourists Manrique initially envisaged would be the island's mainstay, and not the regular sort of holidaymaker, the average Brit or German or Swede seeking sun and sand and plenty of booze. I'm torn in all directions just thinking about it, my mind suddenly crowded with a recollection of the day Celestino tossed his copy of *El Diario* across the room in disgust after reading the announcement that the underwater sculpture was to proceed. For Celestino it was an obscenely expensive outrage that had little to do with the environment and everything to do with big money showing off. I tried to defend the project, citing the sculptor's credentials, but Celestino glared at me. 'Might as well toss all that money in the water.' He paused before adding, 'It should be spent on solar power.'

I hear his voice as though he is right here by my side, and I'm reminded of the solar panels in his painting. Solar power crucified, but in the name of what? Although something starts to make more sense.

I take my plate to the sink.

'Do you mind if...'

'Go. Do what you have to do.'

'Oh, Bill.'

I DRIVE MORE QUICKLY than I normally would, first through Máguez and then on through Haría, taking the Peñas del Chache route to Teguise, slowing only at the switchbacks. Once I crest the mountain and the road flattens out I put my foot down again, swerving past two cyclists rounding the sweeping bends down into Los Valles. Why the urgency? I'm not looking forward to confronting Fernando one bit. I have no idea how I'll broach the matter of his whereabouts on Sunday night and Monday morning. It seems somewhat ridiculous to even be trying. I'm not cut out for detective work, yet I don't question the role, far preferable as it is to sitting at home thumb twiddling as the hours slide by. I have to keep busy, even if it means driving first here then there like a wayward goose.

I enter Teguise and turn into Calle Garajonay, parking behind the old church where Celestino likes to have his market stall. A black sedan pulls up at the other end of the near empty car park as I lock the driver's side door. A tourist grabbing what little there is left of the warmth of the day, maybe. My thoughts wander back to the black sedan I saw earlier in the day parked up the street from Celestino's studio. I tell myself not to be ridiculous. I didn't notice I was being followed. Then again, I can't be all that sure. I was in such a hurry to get here.

I make my way down through the warren of cobbled streets that is old Teguise, not taking much notice of the fine old architecture that surrounds me, buildings that on a normal day capture my interest. The village is how I like it, quiet. Most of the shops look closed.

Situated in one of Teguise's grander plazas, the timple museum where Fernando works is housed in the Palacio Spínola. The Spanish colonial building has been beautifully restored; whenever I come here I always admire the decorative panelling of the windows, carved out of ancient wood and stained a dark brown. Even today, their size and complexity catch my eye. I head for the entrance doors, equally impressive, as a party of eight holidaymakers file their way outside.

They seem to be taking an age. I turn around and look back at the plaza, allowing myself a few moments to soak in the almost medieval vibe, wondering if anyone lives behind all the closed shutters, peeking out at the near empty plaza. A tall, wiry-looking man in black leather over dark denim appears and stands in the centre of the plaza as though waiting for someone. With his bald head and dark glasses, he doesn't have the demeanour of a tourist. More that of a local businessman. Teguise attracts an interesting mix of folk. As the man turns in my direction I look away, and seeing the others have moved on, head inside.

My eyes take a few moments to adjust to the dim, the stone floor, high wooden ceiling, and walls of deep red absorbing what little lighting there is. The foyer is empty so I take a few steps in the direction of the main exhibition room. I've never visited the museum before and I stand in awe, gazing at the rectangular room, with its impressive wooden ceiling and polished floorboards, timples and other string instruments housed in glass display cabinets set in two long rows. The room leads on to a second through another set of ornately panelled doors at the end. I'm about to walk through the room when behind me someone makes a discrete cough.

I turn to find a young woman standing beside a small easel. 'El museo está cerrando,' she says. 'Closing,' she adds in English.

My words almost lodge in my throat. 'Puedo hablar con Fernando, por favor.'

The woman looks doubtful.

'Fernando Brena.'

'I'm sorry,' she says, choosing to speak in English. 'I am new here.'

'Fernando works here as curator.'

'Wait a moment.'

The woman disappears through a side door, discretely obscured behind an easel used to display the museum's events. I read the information board without taking in anything on it. I picture Richard strolling through the building, enjoying the elegance, making a show of reading the displays, hands behind his back, all sage and pretentious. I shift from one foot to the other, clasp my own hands behind my back, tilt my head to one side as if in reflection. My neck soon goes stiff and I decide the posture unwise, so I lean against the wall, hoping the red paint won't rub off on my blouse.

Ten minutes pass before the young woman reappears with a colleague in tow, a remarkably sour faced old man.

'I'm sorry, and you are?' he says with a cool stare.

'Paula. Paula Diaz.'

'Do you have an appointment?'

'With Fernando? No. I am a friend. I came to see him, that's all.'

'He isn't here.'

'I see. Do you know when he will return?'

'He no longer works here.'

'Does he have another job?' Masking my disappointment, I smile as if to demonstrate that I know Fernando hated working at the museum. From the little I've experienced of the staff, I'm surprised he stuck it out for the however-many years that he did. I wouldn't have lasted a day, working for that old trout.

'Another job,' he repeats. 'I believe that is the case.'

'And where might that be?'

He looks me up and down. 'You are his friend. Why don't you ask him yourself?' And he walks away.

I drive back to Máguez, humiliated and dispirited by turns. I have no idea where Fernando lives, and now I have no idea where he works.

13

RESPITE

TENESAR FEELS SAFER AT NIGHT. THE NEAR TOTAL DARKNESS, THE SKY lit only by the stars and a sliver of moon, and I assure myself my pursuer, whoever he is, and the dog, whose ever it is, won't be visiting. To some extent, I can relax.

I gaze into the void of starlight and listen to the ocean but fatigue soon sets in again and I retreat behind my barricade.

Huddled in the corner on the cold concrete, I doze. Before long the grey light of dawn lightens the room and I'm on guard again.

My plans to walk back to Mancha Blanca are compromised by the dog bite. The wound is angry and, together with the broken arm, the hunger, the dehydration, I'm too weak to make it. If I'm attacked again, the animal will kill me. But I can't stay here. I have no food save for that packet of peanuts. The water will run out today too.

In a sudden burst of determination, I grab the weapon and leave the sanctuary of the hut and hobble around the village, venturing further this time, on the lookout for houses with some sort of rear entrance.

My search seems in vain. There are few houses accessible via their rear and every back door I try is well and truly locked. Pushing aside the sense of futility that seeps into my being with every footstep, I keep trying, heading up to the larger, better maintained buildings below the cliff.

I walk down a narrow passage between two houses that I failed to notice when I searched the village before and arrive in a concrete driveway. To the right and left are high walls with no point of entry. It occurs to me I could have scaled that wall and broken into the house through the rear, but not in my current state. It's hopeless. I should be conserving energy. I'll need to leave Tenesar in the afternoon, and head back to Erik's house before I am no longer physically able to do so.

Before leaving the driveway, I round the corner and face a garage door. I try the handle, not expecting it to open. But to my astonishment it does and it's empty. In the rear wall, there's a door leading through to the house.

Surely no one has left that open as well?

I turn the handle and a second later I'm standing in the patio of someone's holiday home. I'm incredulous. I can scarcely believe my luck. The door to the house is open as well. Amazement gives way to practical common sense. I hobble back to my hut and grab my things, making sure to leave no trace of my stay. I hobble back as fast as I am able and as I shut the garage door and lock it from the inside, relief washes through me and I almost collapse. The feeling passes and I lock the other door, cross the patio and enter the house.

I find myself in a kitchen. There's fresh water, some cans of food with ring pulls, a carton of juice, another of long life milk, tea, coffee, jars of sugar and cocoa and an unopened packet of crackers. Heaven! The stove is fed by bottled gas. The fridge is switched off. No power, which means no running water. There's a sense no one has been here for a while. They probably shut the house up for the winter and someone forgot to lock the doors on their way out. I look forward to a feast, but first, I head to the bathroom on the hunt for a first aid kit.

There's nothing, not even a plaster. The food might help fight the infection, but it won't be enough.

On my way back to the kitchen I glance out at the patio and a lone drago tree catches my eye. My ancestors would use the sap of that tree as a cure all. Dragon's blood, they call it. With nothing to lose and the possibility of a cure, I search the kitchen and find a cleaver and a plastic container for the sap.

I could do with both arms to wield the cleaver but after a few blows, I manage to break through the skin of the trunk. Sap oozes and I capture what I can and take it back to the kitchen where I find a clean tea towel in a drawer. Then I sit at the table, roll up my trouser leg and gaze at the swollen, mangled flesh. I have no idea how to apply the sap so I smear it all over and wait for it to dry on my skin before wrapping the wound in the tea towel and tying it off with Gloria's scarf. Now, all I can do is hope.

I put a saucepan of milk on the stove and cocoa and sugar in a cup and open a can of tuna. Basic, but I'm surviving. If the dragon's blood works, I'll get out of here. I'll be in Paula's arms in days.

Poor Paula. She must be worried sick.

14

YAIZA

GLORIA HAS TAKEN UP THE GREATER PART OF THE BED AGAIN. I WAKE TO find her splayed out, arms akimbo, one hand as usual gripping her rabbit's ear. The serene look of the sleeping child reveals no sign of the tantrum she threw the previous afternoon.

She was fractious the moment I returned from Teguise frustrated by the lack of progress, realising as I entered my parents' house that I might as well consider myself a single parent, the sooner to get used to my new and lonely future.

'Where's Daddy?' Gloria asked, glowering at me, her large brown eyes filled with hurt. I couldn't contain my own worry a second longer. A single spasm and the tears flowed before I had a chance to hide my face.

Shocked at the sight of me distressed, Gloria ran off to seek comfort in the arms of her grandfather.

Angela stood in the kitchen doorway, helplessly wringing her hands. 'Oh dear,' she said as though admitting guilt, leaving me surmising that the source of Gloria's distress had little to do with her absent father.

Gloria's search was in vain. Bill was at the supermarket and when Angela at last reminded Gloria of his whereabouts, the child screamed and threw herself onto the living room sofa, hurling all the cushions on the floor.

Seeing that look of alarmed consternation distorting Angela's face, I quickly reined myself in and went to soothe Gloria, attempting to bring that screwed up face and those clenched little fists back to calm.

No enticement worked. It wasn't until Bill returned from the shops that the tension in the house eased. A few squares of chocolate and a new toy settled things down but the strain had become palpable in us all.

I turn over on my back. Gloria emits a soft sigh but she doesn't wake. Bill and Angela are taking her to the Aloe Vera farm today: a much-needed distraction.

Unable to face another family breakfast, with Bill's inevitable 'What's the plan for today?' and Angela's anxious naysaying, I leave Gloria asleep in bed, grab the clothes I had on yesterday and a clean change of underwear, and go to take a shower. Once dressed, I tiptoe to the kitchen and scribble a note on a paper napkin. Then I creep back to the bedroom to stuff yesterday's underwear in my shoulder bag, leaving the house without a clue how I'll spend my time. After yesterday the weight of responsibility is heavy on my back, as though it's down to me and me alone to find my husband.

Celestino has been missing for four days and the La Mareta commission will be announced in five. Sometimes I picture him in that upstairs mill-house room, tied to that chair and gagged. Or hiding out in one of the island's caves, knocking out political art and plotting his next move. Lanzarote's very own Banksy, replete with balaclava and greatcoat. Other times I picture him dead.

Back in Haría I find Shirley's car parked across the street from her house. I manoeuvre mine into the space in front. It's odd to see the Maserati left outside. Shirley must be on her way somewhere. Forgotten something and popped back home. Funny how my mind, suspicious, picks over every tiny detail.

A couple on an early morning stroll pass by. For them, it's no doubt a normal day. My envy trails behind them. I wait until they're further down the street before opening the car door.

I cross to the pavement and look back at the two vehicles, the one shiny and new, the other dull, faded, with a few dents in the body.

Pushing wide the front door, I don't expect to find Celestino at home. Instead I face his absence anew and I can't help wondering if something awful really has happened to him. Straight away I refuse to believe it. Then I have no choice but to convince myself that he has planted that painting. If I don't, then what I am left with? I tramp down the hallway and through the patio to the kitchen and toss my shoulder bag and keys on the table, taking more care with my sunglasses. Then I fish out of my pocket Celestino's necklace and put it on the table with the rest. My note explaining my whereabouts is just as I left it. Nothing in the room has been disturbed. The answer phone light is off.

I slump down on a chair, put my elbows on the table and hold my face in my hands. Despite my empty stomach, I'm more nauseous than hungry, the knot in my stomach, now a fixture, matching the ache in my heart.

I don't sit like this for long. Some inner strength causes me to draw myself up. Tells me I need a strategy.

I remove yesterday's underwear from my bag and toss it in the laundry basket in the bathroom. I water the pots in the patio then go to fetch more underwear to tuck in my bag.

It isn't until I've reached halfway up the stairs that I detect the musky aroma of someone's scent. Is it the same scent I smelled yesterday in the old mill? My hand clenches the banister. I force myself to look, bending to peer through the railings at the space under the bed. There's no one there. I climb the rest of the stairs and cast a quick eye about the room then go over to the front window and look down at the street, taking another sniff. The smell seems to have faded. Or I've gotten used to it. But it is still discernible. Just.

Other than my car and Shirley's, the street in the immediate vicinity is empty. Further along, past the intersection, is a black sedan. It has to be the one I saw parked up the road from the studio, the same one that pulled up in the car park in Teguise yesterday. Yet I can't be sure: I didn't note the number plate. What sort of sleuth am I?

A very poor one, I think. From this distance, I'll need binoculars to see that number plate and I'm not game to take a closer look.

I leave the window and cross the room to Celestino's desk. All looks normal. His submission letter remains atop his keyboard. I tug at the drawers. They're still locked. Those folders under the desk look the same as before. Is anything missing? I dare not touch them and besides, even if I do I'll have no idea of the contents. It's with considerable annoyance that I realise I won't be able tell if anything's missing or not. Someone has been up here though; there is no doubting that. And that someone is surely not Celestino, for he never wears aftershave or scent of any sort. As far as I recall, neither do any of his friends.

I head downstairs and into all the rooms checking the windows and then the back door to the garage. It remains bolted on the inside. Whoever it was has managed to gain access without breaking in. Scaled the patio wall maybe? But it's over two metres high, topped with broken shards of old glass and earthenware pots, cemented in place by Celestino after Shirley's boundary dispute. And the base of the wall is littered with pots. It would be impossible to make landfall without disturbing all those plants.

I return to the kitchen and flick on the kettle. Unsure why I'm bothering to boil water for a hot drink I don't want, I flick it off again and lean with my back against the sink. When the phone rings I all but yelp.

I snatch the handset from the console.

'Hola. Who is it?' I didn't mean to sound curt.

'It's Richard.'

He sounds almost apologetic, yet his voice is an intrusion. I rake myself together, summoning all my resolve to seem unflustered.

'Richard, this isn't a good time.'

'Paula, I'm sorry to call like this but I'm at my wit's end. Trent phoned last night seeking a progress report. What on earth could I tell him? I haven't even managed to get to La Corona.'

'Why ever not?'

'It's my back.'

'Your back.'

'I can't take the risk. If anything were to happen, I'd be lying in a ditch.'

'Take your phone.'

'What if there's no reception.'

'Richard, I don't have time for this,' I say, doing my best not to yell.

'Very well, then,' he says and hangs up.

The audacity of the man. He didn't even have the presence of mind to ask me about Celestino. It occurs to me I might have accepted his barely veiled plea. Traipsed with him to the aljibe. At least it would be a distraction. As it is I stare into the void of the day, unsure of my next course of action.

I have to do *something*. Try to track down Fernando maybe. Visit every gallery on the island—there aren't that many—see what he knows. At least it will keep me busy. It doesn't seem to be the best use of my time but what else can I do? I dismiss the idea of paying Redoto a visit straight away, not wanting to draw his suspicion. Perhaps I should try Pedro again. See if I can extract from him more information. He's definitely holding back. And I'd be behaving like a real detective. Isn't that what they do? Follow leads?

I'm about to head off to the galleries in Arrecife when there is a knock at the front door. Hope squeezes my heart and I race to answer it. I have to fight back disappointment when I see Shirley standing squarely on the pavement in a long and flowing kaftan of lurid green over black leggings. She's topped off the outfit with a jade pendant necklace and silver leaf earrings. She steps forward and makes to enter.

'He's not turned up, then,' she says as I lead her through to the kitchen. 'How long's it been?'

'Four days.' I grab Celestino's necklace off the table and slip it into my pocket.

'That long. Sorry, I lose track of time. Must be my age.'

'Coffee?' I ask, putting more water in the kettle.

'I won't.'

I shrug and plonk the kettle unceremoniously back in its tray.

'Don't look so despondent. I've come to invite you out.'

'Again?'

'Why ever not?'

She picks up my note, turns it over then hands it to me. 'Just update this.' She rummages through the pot of pens on the small bookcase and extracts a turquoise marker. 'Here you go,' she says, thrusting it into my hand. 'Use this one. More distinct.'

Feeling mild disgust that Shirley even tried to match the pen colour to her outfit, I scribble out the date and write Wednesday in capital letters. I should have thought to amend the note before. With the pen still in hand, I hesitate, momentarily undecided.

'Come on,' Shirley insists.

Thinking whatever she has in mind must be better than, in all likelihood, a fruitless quest to locate Fernando, I say, 'I need to change.'

Shirley gives me an appraising look. 'Might be an idea. Put on some glad rags and we'll try to have some fun.'

I climb the stairs in twos. The smell of scent has faded. I stand in the middle of the floor not knowing what to do with the necklace. I don't want to take it or leave it. In the end, I tuck it away in a shoebox in the bottom of the wardrobe.

When I return to the kitchen wearing a loose cotton blouse and a fawn skirt, Shirley is sifting through the pile of assorted magazines and books stacked on top of the bookcase beside the pens. Upon my entry, she quickly pulls away with an errant giggle, saying, 'That red spine caught my eye.'

What red spine? I never calculated her to be the type to ferret through other people's things. Suspicion swiftly gives way to self-condemnation: I mustn't let anxiety sway my thoughts. I observe my neighbour, standing there looking sheepish in her lurid green kaftan with her skinny black legs poking out beneath. She looks like a beetle, and a harmless one at that.

I go through to the bathroom to apply some makeup. The mirror reflects back my careworn visage: the dark rings beneath my eyes; the pinched set to my mouth. I apply a light foundation, unable to stop the return of anxious thoughts. My mind rushes to those few times I asked Shirley to mind Gloria while I went to the supermarket in Arrieta. How much snooping can anyone cram into an hour? Rather a lot,

I imagine, with a two-year old asleep on the couch to watch over. An awake Gloria demands almost all the attention. Asleep, none. But, there's nothing of interest to anyone down in the living room. Shirley would have needed to venture up the creaky stairs and risk waking the child. Besides, Celestino keeps his anti-corruption material locked in his desk, hidden even from his wife. As I apply a thin smear of lip balm, I file away my uncharitable speculations in a folder marked 'paranoid'.

I give her a warm smile as I re-enter the kitchen.

'Will I do?'

'Much better. Now, come on.'

She seems impatient to get going but once on the road, Shirley's driving is thankfully slower. She takes care rounding the bends down to Arrieta and holds back when approaching cyclists. Relieved, I settle into my seat. My gaze, freed from the tarmac ahead, takes in the scenery.

'Never a dull moment on this island, eh?' Shirley says as we wait at the Arrieta roundabout.

'I'm sorry?'

'There's always something going on. Something to be done.'

'I suppose so.'

'Maybe you need to get more involved,' she says, pulling into a break in the flow of traffic heading south. 'Roll up your sleeves and muck in.'

'I have a three-year old.' Surely it hardly needed mentioning.

'Gloria has grandparents. And a father.'

That was uncalled for, I think but don't say. Where is this leading?

'It's no good hanging around in Haría all day long,' Shirley says, clearly on a roll with her topic. 'You need to get south. Network with the expats. Find out what's going on and join a few things. You'll have something on every day like me before you know it.'

'I might not want something on every day.' I watch the houses of Tabayesco slip by in the near distance.

'Of course you do. A busy life is a happy life.' She pauses, shooting me an appraising look. 'Anyway, I've just the thing.'

'I thought you might.'

'Don't be like that. Bentor Benicod is running for re-election in Yaiza.'

'As mayor?'

'Naturally. He was a good friend of my husband. I said I'd help him with his campaign.'

She explains that her husband and Bentor grew up together. They lived in the same street, attended the same schools, and shared a passion for wind surfing. I try to picture the two men as boys but my imagination fails me.

We pass the southern foothills and the saddles of the massif with their long and deep valleys, nowhere as fecund as the valle de Temisa. The further south we travel the drier and more barren the terrain, the volcanoes soon drawing my attention. Before long the traffic thickens and we approach the neat cuboid dwellings of Tahiche.

'You'll like Bentor,' Shirley says, pulling into the outside lane on the approach to the turnoff to Arrecife. 'He's a good man.' She relates how Bentor showed much support when her husband was going through his difficulties.

The way she portrays her husband's dirty dealings is bewildering. As if she's erased all culpability from his shoulders. For she must have known what he was up to. She makes Juan Mobad sound like a babe in the woods at the mercy of vindictive anti-business scoundrels looking for a fall guy. She's referring to the journalists, government officials and independent activists campaigning relentlessly for Lanzarote to clean up its act. She doesn't say it, she doesn't need to say it, but the biggest scoundrel in Shirley's mind is Celestino. Little wonder she couldn't care less what happens to him. Maybe Shirley is privately relishing this opportunity to steer me away from my quest to find him. Lunch? Twice in one week? Coming across the expat ally? Shirley probably wouldn't mind if Celestino is gone for good. But that has to be my most ungracious thought yet. I don't like the way my suspicion keeps landing, first here, then there, on my friends and my next-door neighbour, the only people other than my parents whom I can trust. Besides, Shirley is too caught up in her own world to be bothered with a vendetta. She strikes me as the sort of woman who doesn't invest energy in bygones.

It is Celestino who bears the grudge, I think with a sick feeling in my belly.

I do my best to ignore the feeling, making a few comments about how different the vibe of the island is in the south. Then we fall into companionable silence, Shirley concentrating on the road, the traffic around the capital and the airport thicker and always impatient.

The traffic doesn't thin again until we pass the turnoffs to Puerto del Carmen. I spend what remains of the journey taking in the stark landscape, noting how different it is from the north: the arid plains of sandy clay, black where mulched with picón, accented by the volcanoes and the barren peaks of Los Ajaches; and the neat white cubes of houses dotted around, with their plantings of palm trees, cacti and succulents, each a little oasis.

As we near Yaiza the vineyards come into view, with their orderly rows of cinder pit plantings protected by dry stone walls. Vineyards planted right to the edge of the lava plains of Timanfaya. I venture south so infrequently, the unique harnessing of all that basalt visits me like a surprise. Living on the island is all about the lava. The lava and the picón. There's no getting away from it.

There's no getting away either from the enormous effort that has been made by every municipality to temper the impact of the inhospitable terrain through lovingly restoring buildings and lavishing funds on formal street plantings that speak of civic pride. Yaiza is the exemplar of this phenomenon. A village sandwiched between the westernmost peaks of Los Ajaches and the lava of the Timanfaya eruptions that lapped at its northern fringe, Yaiza is all palm trees and raked picón and pure white lines.

'See that,' Shirley says, pointing at a derelict building set on a large block. 'Redoetoe owns that. And the one next door.'

I see another house, in better repair but empty.

'And he's just purchased the ruin behind it. On quite a large block too. See?'

I can't fail to. It would have been a grand home, once.

'How do you know all this?'

Shirley laughs. 'I have my sources.'

'Maria.'

Shirley makes no comment.

'What does he plan to do with all that land?'

'No idea.'

Whatever it is will be grandiose and designed to draw the tourists, the development most likely receiving instant approval. And if he's short of cash, no doubt Redoto could seek capital overseas. I recall Celestino mentioning how foreign investors were lured to the Canaries after the islands were declared an 'investment reserve', resulting in huge corporate tax savings. Investment reserve; the irony doesn't escape my notice. An endangered species in need of protection? —Corporate investment is anything but. I'm in no doubt that whatever Redoto has in mind, he'll profit from it. And the significance of those three properties—historical, archaeological, cultural—will be lost.

Shirley pulls up in a no-parking bay outside the town hall, a stout building set on its own block and fronted by a small plaza. The fronds of sturdy palm trees flap a backbeat for the flags lined up in a row in one corner, there to tell passers-by the location of the power.

Inside, the foyer is chilly. A reception area corralled by a high counter occupies much of the space. Shirley goes straight over and speaks with one of the receptionists, whom she seems to know. I look around. Doors lead off in all directions. There is nowhere to sit. I can't fail to notice several men dressed in plain pants and shirts—the typical garb of the office worker—who've formed a huddle to the left of the entrance doors. I turn away, not wanting to intrude on a private conversation. When I glance back, I see they're staring at a painting. My breath catches in my throat. Even before I can see it, I know what it's likely to be.

I edge to the left until I'm lodged in the corner beside a leafy indoor plant. From this purview, I can see past the men to the painting, albeit at an oblique angle.

Where any visitor might expect to find a portrait of the mayor, current or former, or even the King of Spain, there's a depiction of a volcano in the throes of an eruption, emitting great clouds of ash into the sky. Risking drawing attention, I step forward, keen to study the work. I see in an instant that the ash has fallen into several heaps in the foreground. But it isn't ash. It's mounds of Euro notes. The volcano is spewing money. I don't get a chance to view the signature but I don't need to. I quickly step back again, not daring to look over in the direction of the reception in case the staff behind the counter think me strange.

The onlookers are as perplexed as me. Curious to hear what they're saying, I again edge closer. This time I bow my head and fiddle with the straps of my shoulder bag.

'Benicod won't be happy,' one of them says.

'Maybe we should take it down.'

'What if he wants it there?'

'He'll lose the plot. You know what he's like.'

'Where is he?'

'He should be due at any moment.'

'Someone must have broken in.'

I look up with sudden interest.

'No one broke in,' says an older man sporting a pencil moustache. He frowns disapprovingly at a gathering of tourists milling about outside the entrance doors. I begin rummaging through the contents of my bag.

'An inside job?' a younger man says.

'What else could it be?'

The man with the moustache takes out his glasses and studies the work. 'All I know is it wasn't there last night when I left.'

'What time was that?'

'Late. Nine-thirty, I think.'

'Where's his portrait? Anyone seen it? Maybe we could put it back.'

Seeing the men about to disperse I move out of my corner and head towards the counter. Shirley is already entering a doorway on the far side. She glances back at me and mouths, 'Come on,' then disappears.

I hurry past the receptionists, pushing the door before it closes on its sprung hinges.

A passageway leads to a narrow flight of stairs. Shirley is almost at the top. I run up behind her, gathering to the forefront of my mind enough pretence to affect an unflustered manner. Shirley, thankfully, remains oblivious. She's too preoccupied with her visit.

I'm not relishing the thought of meeting Bentor Benicod, and I can only hope I'll be able to maintain a casual attitude.

Together we enter a well-lit antechamber leading on through a heavy door to the mayor's office. In the antechamber, seated at a small desk, a large middle-aged man bedecked in suit and tie looks at us with cool indifference.

'Can I help you?' he says without warmth.

'Mr Benicod not in?' Shirley says airily.

'He's at a meeting in Arrecife.'

Relief passes through me.

'He said he'd be here,' Shirley says, matching the man's manner.

'He's delayed.'

'Never mind,' Shirley says. 'We've come for the leaflets.'

Leaflets?

The secretary points at a table behind him. On it, piled high, are boxes and leaflet bundles. So this is what Shirley meant by helping Benicod with his campaign. Shirley takes a bundle.

'Grab a couple of those boxes, would you,' she says to me.

The secretary makes no attempt to help. The boxes are heavy. I feel in their weight the purpose of my presence. I'm the mule. And I resent the time I'm wasting when I could, I should be looking for Celestino.

On the way down the stairs, one tread at a time, along with a mounting resentment I mull over how I came to be here on this very day. And not some other day. A normal day when the walls of the foyer displayed nothing but the mayor. My efforts to find Celestino have come to nothing. Yet when my attention is so thoroughly diverted and I'm unable to follow the paintings trail, I manage to be hot on it.

'Come on, slow coach,' Shirley says, waiting at the bottom of the stairwell. When I reach the bottom tread Shirley holds open the door, letting it go as I pass through and crossing the foyer and heading on outside without a backward glance.

On the way through the foyer I notice a man in overalls lifting the offending painting off the wall. I stagger by, pretending to struggle with the weight of my cargo, which isn't too far from the truth, and when I'm close enough I stop and take a sidestep and manage a glance at the bottom corner. The signature is unmistakable.

I ease my way through the entrance doors, narrowly colliding with a woman pushing a pram. Shirley is standing by a palm tree, watching.

'God, I'm hungry,' she says on our way to the car. 'Are you?'

'I am a bit.'

I'm ravenous but prepared to wait until we're heading back to Haría, thinking we might call in somewhere on the way. Shirley has other ideas.

'I know a nice place in Playa Blanca.'

Playa Blanca? I make no comment. I don't feel like entering a tourist den. I'm feeling frayed and over-stimulated as it is, and crave someplace quiet where I can collect my thoughts, but Shirley is not the sort to quibble with. Besides, there'll be an ulterior motive at play, I'm sure of it. I don't have long to discover what it is.

Fifteen minutes later, looking for a place to park, we cruise down the Avenida de Papagayo with its long parade of shops and eateries. It's only the second time I've visited since Celestino refuses to come to the place, and it's with a measure of guilt that I view the streetscapes and decide Playa Blanca isn't an unpleasant place to be at all, although there's rather a lot of it. I half expect to see the word 'illegal' plastered across the facades of the various resorts we pass, but I find it to be just like most of the other towns on the island, neat and clean, with narrow streets filled with white flat-roofed buildings.

Shirley parks outside a good-looking fish restaurant. When I open my door and inhale the aroma of garlicky fish, my mouth waters. I stand on the pavement poised to head straight there, when I'm called back.

Shirley is standing by the boot. I look on in disbelief. All that talk in the car about getting more involved, and here I am about to be seconded to a leaflet drop. If I had even an inkling, I might have asked Shirley to pull over and let me out. Not all that likely given how diffi-cult it may have proven getting home, but I would certainly have preferred to have waited two hours at a bus stop than be co-opted into enabling a mayor, any mayor, but especially a mayor of Yaiza with his campaign.

'It won't take long,' Shirley says, reaching in and extracting the leaflet bundle.

Realising I have no choice, I lean into the boot, pulling one of the boxes forwards.

'And the other one.'

'You expect me to take both?'

'Why not? We'll distribute them faster that way.'

Efficient it might be, but ten paces on and my forearms are already protesting the weight. To make matters worse, Shirley chose a parking spot far from her first port of call. She marches on ahead, her lurid green kaftan blowing in the breeze, the most business-like beetle there ever was. I trudge behind, the boxes heavier with every step. By the time Shirley stops, I'm panting and cursing beneath my breath. We're outside a clothing boutique.

'I'll hold the door,' Shirley says, as though that's all it takes for her to consider herself helpful.

Inside, racks of clothes fill the space. I look around for somewhere to put the boxes. Even the counter is cluttered. I notice an uphol-stered chair in the corner and dump them down on that. Shirley looks askance.

'Hello, my lovely,' she says to a smartly dressed woman who steps out from behind the counter to receive a hug. Judging by her demeanour she must be the owner.

'Hello to you too, my old china,' the woman says in a mocking tone. 'Doing Bentor's dirty work I see.' She eyes me and smiles.

'Nothing dirty about it Marg. You'll be needing these.' And she hands over the leaflet bundle.

'That should do nicely.' She sets the bundle on the counter.

I look on, dismayed.

'Time for a cuppa?'

'Gotta dash, I'm afraid.' She tilts her head at me. 'Have to feed the staff.' They both laugh.

With the politest smile I can manage, I retrieve the boxes and head back through the shop, struggling out the door and waiting for Shirley on the pavement.

Shirley seems acquainted with just about every business on the strip. We go next to a restaurant, depositing half a bundle on the bar, then on to a souvenir shop. We work our way back and forth across the street, the only highlight for me emerging when I have a chance to buy a notepad and a pen in a newsagent's, while my organ grinder parlays with the owner, a brash-sounding Yorkshire-man sporting the deepest of suntans. Each drop point makes the boxes a little lighter but by the end of it I'm exhausted and light-headed, irritation rising in the face of Shirley's blithe manner and her breezy-as-you-please banter.

As we return the empty boxes to the boot of the Maserati, an athletic-looking man decked in knee-length shorts and a brilliant white shirt stops on the pavement in front of the bonnet to admire the car. Seeing us congregating behind the boot, his gaze shifts from the car to me with fresh interest. He catches my gaze as I offload the boxes. The man looks to Shirley and back to me again as though trying to pick the owner. He gives me a cheesy wink and looks poised to come over when Shirley stands back on the curb, all proud in her lurid green dress, and raises the remote high in her hand. The Maserati emits its customary yelp. The man's face falls and he about turns and heads up the street. Nonplussed, I follow Shirley to the restaurant vowing privately I'll only come here again if I have recourse to catch the ferry to Fuerteventura.

The fish restaurant is popular. A spritely waiter finds us a table for two overlooking the street with glimpses of the ocean beyond. The sky is brilliant, the glare intense even behind my sunglasses. This time, Shirley lets me have the better seat.

As I scan the menu I can't help overhearing the conversation carrying on apace on the next table. I try to ignore it but the crisp voices emanating from bubbly faces draw me in.

'Fancy coming all the way here and having to deal with that.'

'Did they manage to find somewhere else to stay?'

'They did, but it was nothing like they'd booked.'

'They should have gone to the police.'

'What can they do? The company was based in Ireland, apparently.'

I lean forward in my seat and make to speak.

'They're talking about holiday scammers,' Shirley says without lowering her voice.

The label completes something that began with the man eyeing off the Maserati, another natural consequence given the initial conditions. I face anew the intractable problem of tourism. The very pleasure sought and the expectation of its fulfilment rendering vulnerable all those who participate.

One of the women on the next table glances over and smiles. She seems about to engage Shirley when the waiter returns to take our order.

'Two fish platters and a bottle of your best white.'

Whatever it is I might have ordered is snatched away. Resigned, I hand the waiter my menu. Shirley leans towards the others and joins in their tirade, gushing empathy, her engagement culminating in a quick riffle through her handbag and the flourishing of several helpful business cards, which she hands over effusing reassurances.

The party leaves as the waiter appears with the wine. Shirley takes a swift gulp and sets down her glass. I do the same. I want to at least appear to be good company but when the food comes I focus on my fish platter, scarcely listening to Shirley's reminiscences of happy days spent in Playa Blanca with her late husband. I zone in and out, hoping I'm smiling in the right places. Fortunately, Shirley is in a garrulous mood. She remains oblivious to my quietude, or is accepting of it, enjoying the free rein she has. On the way home, she launches into a long-winded story about some uncle of hers who sailed to the Cape Verde islands and bought himself a beach.

All the while, my mind drifts back to Celestino's art. How did that painting come to be hanging at the Yaiza town hall? Did Shirley see it? She didn't seem to have taken it in. She went straight over and chatted at reception then trooped on upstairs. That huddle of men would have blocked her view. On our way back outside, the painting was already being removed. She was on a mission, a single-minded purpose, one for which I am suddenly grateful.

How many of these paintings are there? There could be dozens cropping up all over the island. Although if that's the case, surely the media would have hold of it by now. Besides, Celestino won't have managed to produce that many works of political satire. Does the appearance of a second artwork make it unlikely to be a practical joke? It seems too elaborate for that. I hope someone hasn't kidnapped Celestino. Then again, he still remains the most likely candidate, enacting a kind of surreptitious activism. I hold on tightly to the view. It's all the hope I have. 'The Banksy of Lanza'. That would be the headline. Only Banksy has a long history, a reputation, people expected such stunts from him. No one expects it from Celestino. And the more I dwell on the meaning of the two works—the solar panel crucifixes and the money spewing volcano—the more I doubt Celestino's sanity.

How could he be so reckless, so inconsiderate, disappearing only to lurk somewhere on the island, planting paintings? Paintings I've stumbled on through no action of my own. As if Celestino knew Shirley would take me to both places. As if he knew we were friends and as soon as his back was turned we would be off gallivanting. Hardly. As if he knew, too, who Shirley's friends were and when she planned to see them. Assuming that there are only the two paintings.

My reasoning seems absurd and hope slips away. After all, he isn't a rabid nut, the sort of activist who makes poppets to stick pins in. But as soon as I feel reassured Celestino's sanity is intact, my earlier fear that it was him in that incinerated car resurfaces and I'm gripped by a sickening anxiety. Insane and safe, or sane and in danger, or worse, dead—neither scenario provides any sort of solace.

My thoughts dart off, my normally orderly mind unable to cope. And I realise with a small shock that my quick presumptions over Celestino's state of mind also come from a comparison unconsciously made, a comparison to my last partner, Tom Pickles, a paramedic who suffered a nervous breakdown after witnessing one too many car accidents. It happens, I was told in a joint counselling session not long before we split up.

Done with her beach-buying uncle sunning it up on Cape Verde, Shirley proceeds to describe her other family members' entrepreneurial adventures. I strive to be polite but I'm unable to manage more than the briefest of responses, bristling privately in the face of all Shirley's vicarious bragging. By the time Shirley pulls up in the street outside her house, I want nothing more than to lie down and rest my mind.

'You're not in a good way,' Shirley says before I get out of the car.

'I'm sorry I'm not much company. I'm worn out.'

'Tell you what. I'm ducking into Arrecife tomorrow. Why don't you come along?'

'Not more leaflets.'

'I'm popping into the Cabildo,' she says, ignoring my remark. 'Meeting a friend for afternoon tea. But I could drop you off somewhere and we could meet up later. Have an adventure of our own. What do you say?'

I struggle to find a way to decline.

'I'll pick you up at two, then.' Shirley pats my arm. 'He'll turn up. Don't worry.'

'I'm trying.'

I get out of the car and cross the street without a backward glance.

Once inside the house, with a renewed sense of purpose I go straight upstairs to Celestino's desk. I tug at the drawers knowing they are locked and, feeling the resistance, I desist. I pick up the commission letter. If Celestino hasn't returned by Monday, what will I do if he wins? Suddenly the whole of Lanzarote will know he's disappeared.

On the hunt for whatever clues I can find, I sit down and switch on his computer. A few clicks later and I'm staring at his anti-corruption blog. Last time I updated the English version, we were translating a historical piece on the illegal hotels, pulling together all the information to hand. I click on the original Spanish version, much longer than mine, and for once make an effort to understand fully why Celestino is so passionate about those hotels.

I'm quickly buried in expired building permits, fudged technical reports and unauthorised planning approvals. It isn't so much that the developers and local councils are breaking the rules; they're ignoring them completely. I'm not at all surprised about the kickbacks. And it isn't as simple as pointing the finger at the mayors. All sorts of government officials are in on it as well. Many hands at play, and many hundreds of thousands of Euros passing through those hands. But how can they all get away with it?

I picture the times I've seen Celestino scoff at the mention of PIOT, the island's strategic plan meant to protect the environment, saying it's scarcely worth the paper it's written on because the island government has no power to enforce it except through the courts, and even then, all of the various political parties in governance have to endorse that enforcement. His voice is loud in my head. 'And that is hardly likely, is it Paula?' I hear him say. 'When they can't manage to keep a President for more than a year.' He's right here behind me, leaning over my shoulder, pointing at the screen. He always maintains that the courts are partly to blame. 'Would you be worried about committing a crime if you knew it would take years if not decades before your case reached a verdict? Bah! You wouldn't even bother to cover it up.' I can almost feel the weight of his body pressing against my back. I want to turn, to hug that presence, but instead I keep reading. It took five years for the Spanish courts to oblige some municipal mayors to send their dubious hotel permits to the island government and another five to nullify those permits. All up, ten years!

Even after nullification, those hotels still operate. 'Only, do you think they are required to pay any rates?' If the town halls are allowed to operate with impunity, the island government is restricted to act, and the Spanish courts are ineffectual, that only leaves the regional government of the Canary Islands. 'Las Palmas are useless. Worse than useless. They could step in, and they don't. They have the power to make sure PIOT is adhered to, but they won't. They can order the demolitions and they do nothing.' Now, in a fashion, I understand. It's rotten through and through, and while the same sort of rot is everywhere the world over, as universal as air, on an island the size of Lanzarote, a holiday destination coveted by the rich and famous and the ordinary tourist alike, it seems to stink all the more.

I take it all in, feeling his presence grow stronger with every word I read. Suddenly, I can see why nothing is more important to Celestino than saving this island from the developers.

'And it is the people who lose, Paula. The people who pay their taxes. They are the losers. Hundreds of millions of taxpayers' Euros have gone into those illegal projects along with tens of millions in EU grants that now have to be paid back. But what do the people do? They vote, again and again they vote for pro-development parties with known histories of corruptions. Why?'

Yes, why?

I have no answer.

Wanting to kiss his skin, I reach out for his hand, and feel the air.

It's with a new resolve that I grab the manila folders he's left under the desk and open each one in turn. I have no idea what I'm looking for. Two of the folders are filled with press cuttings from campaigns I've translated into English. I set aside the one on the campaign against the Spanish government's granting of drilling rights, a campaign turned success story when the Lanzarote government formed its own action group. Then there's the folder on the political movement, Somos, bulging full. A third folder, unmarked, contains a few press cuttings relating to the illegal hotels in the Yaiza municipality. Nothing more. The folder appears new, yet judging by its shape, has at one time contained much more than just those few cuttings. Recalling that scent I detected in the room I'm immediately suspicious. Whoever entered this bedroom was probably searching for the missing documents and now has them. But what if they were already missing? Or at least not here but at Pedro's? It's possible. They work together. And now I have an excuse to make another visit. I'll tell Pedro about the second painting too, see if he'll open up to me.

I take the file to the kitchen. The answerphone light flashes two new messages. I press the button. Kathy and Pilar again, asking for an update and offering support. I delete them both with a mental promise I'll return their calls soon. Then I update my note and make sure it's prominent on the table, stuff the file in my bag and leave for Máguez.

15

PUZZLING EVIDENCE

GLORIA COMES BOUNDING TO THE DOOR AS I ENTER THE HOUSE. 'HELLO, darling.' I bend down with open arms, kiss her cheeks and sweep back her hair. Pleased to find her in a good mood, I pick her up and carry her through the house.

The kitchen is empty. I deposit my bag and sunglasses on the table. There's movement on the patio and I see Angela on her haunches in her gardening clothes, tending a cactus. Do cacti require that level of maintenance? A sudden churlishness rises up in me. That annoying way she has of keeping occupied with trivial things, a habit that has spilled over from her job as school secretary, her mind filled with myriad little requests and tasks, from a sore knee to a teacher searching for a key to a parent wanting to collect her daughter early. If she stops and reflects she'll probably find herself unfulfilled. It was the same in my own work at the tourist information centre, only the context was different. But I don't have my mother's temperament. I don't need to fill my hours with small occupations. At least, not domestic ones.

Opening the patio door, I recognise the source of my resentment, the attention my mother never gave me, and I pull myself up, resolving to fix the child in me one of these days.

The wind blows Angela's hair hither and thither.

'Stem rot,' she says, without getting up.

'How was the aloe vera farm?'

'Quite interesting. I bought that.' She points behind her to a potted succulent nearby. Tibbles is asleep on his side in the sunshine beside the cubby house.

'And Gloria?'

'Bill kept her amused.'

Gloria is getting heavy. I let her slide down off my hip.

'Mummy, look.' She tugs my arm and I allow myself to be led to the far corner of the patio. Leaning against the high wall is the cut and paste collage Gloria and Bill made, glued to a large board.

'Granddad painted it,' she says proudly.

I realise she means the lacquer.

'We mustn't touch it, Mummy. It's wet.'

I take in the work. Bill has surpassed himself. Out of a concatenation of animal cut outs and bits of scenery emerges the form of a face, a human face with eyes and nose and mouth. Simply executed but it doesn't matter. There's a bit of the artist in us all.

A door claps shut somewhere in the house.

'That'll be Bill back with the shopping.'

Seeing Gloria now occupied stroking Tibbles, I say, 'I'll go.'

Angela squats back down without hesitation.

Heading through the house, I pass Bill loaded up with shopping bags. I go on outside to find he's taken in most of it. All that remains in the boot is a small box of assorted groceries and a carton of juice that must have fallen out of a bag. I prop the juice on top of the box and reach in and pull it towards me. The box is heavy, but not as much as those leaflet boxes I lugged around earlier. A brace of cyclists heading for La Corona draws my attention and I rest the box on the edge of the boot and watch them labour up the long rise.

The wind is fresh but not unpleasant. A film of low cloud to the west dampens the rays of the sinking sun. I observe La Corona, drawn by its presence. There is a natural uniformity to the island's volcanoes, with their smooth conical shapes too steep for an easy climb. Each has its own unique majesty, found mostly in the shape of its crater. La Corona shares with its sisters of Los Helechos, a formidable if spent power, its barren form tempered only by the euphorbias and lichens clinging to its sides.

It occurs to me I ought to try and find a way into the tourism industry. Do my bit to change things from within. Surely my Spanish is good enough by now? I could volunteer. Would they welcome a volunteer? I have no idea. All I do know is Shirley is right; I have to create some meaning for my existence on the island beyond my family.

I pick up the box and elbow the boot shut.

I find Bill emptying the bags and putting the last few tins and jars in the pantry. I set the box down on the table and take up Bill's chair at the end.

'How was the day's detective work?' he says, closing the pantry door. 'Still no sign?'

'No. I mean, well, yes.'

Curious, Bill comes over and draws up a chair. He sits with a forward lean, hands clasped together on the table.

I fiddle with some loose packing tape on the grocery box, nagging it free. 'Shirley invited me to lunch.'

'That was nice of her.'

'Not really. I didn't realise until we got to Yaiza that she planned to use me as her packhorse.'

'Her packhorse?'

'She had me trailing her around delivering leaflets for Bentor Benicod's election campaign.' I press the tape back down and put my hands flat on the table. 'Two boxes full. Lunch came after.'

'The cunning fox,' Bill says with a laugh. 'And I don't suppose you would have been too happy helping out with that campaign either. Benicod is not known for his scruples.'

'There were moments I felt like dropping the boxes in the gutter and walking off. But I didn't want to find myself stuck in Playa Blanca with no easy way home.'

'I'd have been livid. What a waste of your time!'

'Not entirely,' I say, turning my gaze to his face. 'Another painting showed up.'

His reaction is immediate, in his widening eyes and sudden intake of air.

'Another one! Where this time?'

'At the town hall. A number of staffers were puzzling over it when we walked in. Someone replaced Benicod's portrait, apparently.'

'He wasted no time getting his phizog on the wall then.'

I ignore his remark. 'I managed to get close enough to see the signature.'

'Celestino?'

I nod.

'And the painting?'

'A volcano spewing money.'

'Straight to the point then.'

'I don't follow.'

'Paula, it's obvious. Celestino is having a dig at Benicod. That shyster must be raking it in over all the development going on in Playa Blanca.'

'I doubt Celestino would have created that painting specifically to criticise Benicod.'

'I wouldn't put it past him.'

'Besides, you're assuming he put it there. And we don't know that.'

'What did Shirley make of it?'

'She didn't notice. She was preoccupied with the leaflets.'

'Probably for the best. The fewer who know about this, the better. And Benicod?'

'He was out. The staffers arranged for the offending painting to be removed while I was still there. Although I dare say Benicod will be told what happened. After all, it was his portrait that was switched.'

'He'll realise the moment he walks in that his visage is no longer bearing down on the foyer.'

'But what does it all mean, Dad?'

'We need to find a connection between the two men.'

'Redoto and Benicod?'

'Granddad!' Gloria presses her face to the windowed patio door. Bill gives her a winning smile as he goes to open it, leaving me alone with my thoughts.

Even without reading Celestino's blog I know enough about the complicity of business people and politicians to realise the implications. There have been enough scandals over the years in Britain and beyond. You'd need to live in a vacuum not to notice.

I surmise that Benicod was, is, or would be gaining enormous wealth out of some sort of development. The island is better than a gold mine. And with the election imminent, whoever swapped those paintings is trying to besmirch his reputation. But how is that connected to the solar panel crucifixes at Redoto's restaurant? The environmental insinuation is transparent, but that is as far as my reasoning takes me. Were the paintings put there to expose the two men, or simply to ridicule them? My father is right. I need to find out how Redoto and Benicod are connected. I'll ask Shirley tomorrow, for she's known both men for years.

My thoughts arrive back where they started. Celestino has disappeared. Two of his paintings have appeared where they shouldn't have. Shirley aside, there are only two people I know who can further my inquiry: Fernando and Pedro. I need to ascertain if Fernando has had any involvement in the planting of those paintings since he's the only one with a motive and ready access to the studio. Did he rip that necklace off Celestino in a sudden fury? And Pedro is the only one who knows anything about Celestino's anti-corruption campaigns. He might know where the missing documents in that file are. Between them they might throw light on what is proving to be an impossible situation.

It occurs to me I dare not involve the police, not now, not with two of Celestino's paintings involved, not least for fear of jeopardising his chances in the lucrative La Mareta commission. I see straight away my own desperation affecting my choices, and I'm disconcerted by it.

Hearing the laughter through the doors to the patio makes me shrink. Unable to face the others, I take my sunglasses and go through the house to sit out the front where it's quiet. Outside my bedroom window, on a small patch of old concrete crumbling at the edges, are two outdoor chairs and a low table. I position the nearest chair to face La Corona and sit with my back to the island's south, with all of its bustle and ethically dubious ways. Feeling the cleansing wind on my skin, I close my eyes.

16

STALKED

I MUST HAVE FALLEN INTO A DEEP SLEEP. I WAKE UP SUDDENLY, JOLTED out of slumber by a sudden noise. I'm alert in seconds. I strain to listen above the slap and rush of the ocean. I'm sure there was something else. I sit up in the bed, hoping to hear better. I don't.

The canned tuna followed by the cocoa and yesterday, fatigue had consumed me. I couldn't keep myself upright. I took my rucksack and lumbered upstairs and collapsed in the first bed I saw.

With its windows shuttered against the weather, the bedroom feels safe, as safe as it's possible to be here in Tenesar. Now, even hidden away in this little sanctum, I feel under threat. If I peer through the slats, will I be seen? Unlikely, but I won't risk it.

I look around the room. It's a kid's bedroom, a girl's judging by the pink, the pretty stickers plastered to the chest of drawers. My mind drifts momentarily and I think of Gloria, my dear sweet child. I'm jolted back to the present by the scrunch of footsteps.

A single pair of footsteps, heavy, keeping a regular pace.

Where's the dog? Not here, that's certain.

The footsteps come closer and stop. The front door rattles in its frame. He can't know I'm here, surely? But will it open? Did whoever fail to lock the rest leave the front door unlocked too? Why didn't I check? I should have checked. I can't believe I forgot to check. I can scarcely breathe. I'm defenceless. I left my weapon downstairs too.

A pause and then a second rattle, harder, louder this time.

Silence. The door hasn't budged.

More footsteps. Another door further on. He's working his way down the street. He's being thorough, which can mean only one thing; he knows or he's fairly certain I'm here.

Either he's made that assumption based on the dog, or someone saw me escape my car and that same someone saw me head off in this direction. Whichever it is, I can no longer see how I will get out of this place alive.

How far will he take his search? He's assuming I haven't managed to get inside a locked house. Or that I'm stupid enough to leave the door open for him to walk right on in. Which I am. If I'd broken down a door, there'd be evidence. He'll be looking for signs. Or he's looking for somewhere accessible like the fisherman's hut.

I'm there in my mind in a flash. How stupid am I? Did I gather all my things? Did I leave a trace, a wrapper, blood stains, anything to show I was there?

An hour passes before I hear the car drive off. Only then, do I head downstairs with a sick undertow in my guts. He'll come back. The first visit was just a cursory and thwarted search. This second time, he was determined, convinced of my presence. Next time, and there will be a next time, what will he do? If it was me, I'd stake the place out and wait.

17

LA MARETA

RICHARD HAS TAKEN TO PACING. TEN LONG STRIDES ACROSS THE LIVING room, and ten back again if he takes the route across the deep pile rug; fifteen if he goes around the back of the leather lounge. Sometimes he makes a detour into the kitchen, rounding the island bench. His is not a ponderous gait. He pounds frustration into the floor with every footfall. Although he is wont to clasp his hands together behind his back, trying to imagine he's smoking a pipe. Now and then he pauses mid stride, bringing a hand to his chin, or pointing at nothing. It's all affectation but still. He's even started to grind his teeth.

Making his literary hiatus even worse, his visit to the aljibe at La Corona yesterday proved an arduous trek across acres of lava rubble, and when at last he arrived at the base of the volcano he found himself in an exposed, windswept locale. So what someone plastered a great mess of concrete to the slope to funnel storm water runoff underground? —People have been fiddling about with the passage of water the world over since time immemorial. Up close it was not that impressive. He might just as well have relied on a photo. To add to his consternation, the aljibe's access port comprised a rectangular hole large enough for an average size body to enter, which would have suited his literary needs perfectly well were it not for the solid looking metal grille barring access.

That grille has scuppered his plans. His plot is lost. His wayward hiker cannot be found dead in that water tank by his luscious sleuth. Not if he wants to please those critical readers bent on picking holes in the most trivial of circumstances. Whatever happened to poetic licence? If you want a haberdashery between the shoe shop and the bank, then you put one there. After all, he isn't in the business of writing facts. But he can already hear the derision.

Dismayed, and buffeted by the wind, he made his way back to his car in a funk, treading carelessly as he went. Several times he lost his footing, stumbled, and went over on his ankle, not dramatically, but enough to send a twinge right up through his spine.

The spasms started the moment he arrived home.

Dreading the incapacitation should he take to his seat, he started pacing, and he's scarcely stopped pacing since. His physiotherapist back in Bunton advised him on such occasions to walk and walk and so he is, on the flat and stable floor of his living room where he is safe.

Paula might have cautioned him of the dangers. She must have known. Seems she's taken on 'Diaz' not only in name.

Having trekked to the aljibe, he's decided that even had the grille not been there, no one in their right mind or even in their wrong mind would lug a body across that rugged terrain to dump it there. It's a ridiculous idea and he admonishes himself for even considering it. When all anyone around here has to do is choose a spot along the cliff and push. He's been wasting time, and time he does not have.

As for a murder committed at the site, what could possibly be the reason? He keeps coming back to accessibility, or the lack thereof, and exposure, it being visible for miles.

The Aljibe: he came up with the title because he wanted his detective to resemble Paula.

The intrepid Paula.

He stops in his tracks. He should be honest with himself. Has he been harbouring a secret longing for her all these years? Ann's replacement? No, no, that's absurd. It's simply that she makes an interesting character and interesting characters are hard to come by. With her background in tourist information, she has so much potential. He hopes there'll be a way of persuading her to help him, for without the real Paula, the literary Paula refuses to spring to life.

Besides, he needs a new plot. Those abandoned tunnels Ann mentioned one time, dug into the cliff face to get at those water galleries in the mountains, do they reach the source? Paula will know. She's bound to.

Hoping to find her at home, he hurries out of the house and on down the lane to Calle Fajardo. Then he heads down the hill. As he corners the plaza he nearly bumps into the bald-headed man he saw walking past the Diaz residence the last time he went to solicit Paula's assistance. The man looks him up and down before crossing the street and standing at the next corner. Richard walks a few paces and glances back. The man seems to be waiting for someone, although it's an odd place to stand. Perhaps he isn't sure in which direction whoever it is will appear.

Something clicks in Richard's mind. His speculations arrive like a drum roll at the foot of a new idea. Here right before him is a new character and an intriguing one at that. He appears preoccupied, troubled, haunted even. Has he suffered some kind of breakdown? Perhaps his wife has betrayed him, or died, and he's come to this remote part of the island to get away from his tribulations. Enjoy some peace. What does he do? A dentist maybe. Yes, a dentist. Dentistry is known to be a dreadfully high-pressure job. Richard makes a few mental notes of his appearance, taking in the stature, the prominent chin and stern brow, the deep-set eyes, deciding there and then that the man will make the ideal conflicted character.

Satisfied, Richard marches off down the plaza, slowing to a normal pace as he nears the café end, not wanting to appear too excited, his urge to consult Paula stronger than ever.

Perhaps if he offers her something in return, a sweetener, payment, a tour guide fee, something of that sort. After all, she isn't the flowers and chocolates sort of girl. He reaches the café at the end and is about to pop in for a couple of sweet pastries when Paula appears, heading straight for him. What good fortune!

'Paula!' He arranges a pleasant smile on his face. 'How are you?'

'Hello, Richard,' she says cordially.

He supposes it's the best he could hope for.

A loud cheer followed by exuberant applause catches his attention. He glances over at a large party seated at the café. For midweek, the plaza is rather busy and he isn't altogether sure he likes it.

'May I buy you a coffee?' he says out of politeness.

'Are you insisting?'

The impatience in her voice takes him aback. She sounds thoroughly dejected. Although he can't be altogether sure; she hasn't removed her sunglasses.

'I take it Celestino hasn't reappeared,' he says, guessing that must be what is affecting her mood.

'You make him sound like a stain.'

The sharp tone of her reply is unwarranted. 'I'm sorry to cause you any offence,' he says countering hers with a conciliatory tone. 'I meant no harm.'

Privately he decides the woman has more barbs than a stonefish. It is becoming apparent to him that she is most likely the cause of his writer's block. He ought to walk away, but something in her manner makes him stay.

They both hover, looking around. Then in an astonishing turnaround, she says, 'Look, I'm sorry, Richard. I'm worn out. How have you been?' And he finds himself erasing his previous judgement.

'I went to La Corona.'

'And how was that?'

'Not good. I hurt my back.'

'The terrain? You didn't fall?' It's the first show of concern she's graced him with in a long time. He sees in it an opportunity.

'I stumbled. Turned on my ankle. I'm having to do a lot of walking. Stay on my feet.'

'I'm sure you'll make good use of that.'

He emits a short laugh. Seizing the moment, he says, 'Paula, do please consider what I'm about to say.'

'Ask.'

'Ask? No, I'd like to hire you.'

'Hire me?'

'For your expertise. I've given up on the aljibe.' He refrains from telling her why. 'I think a body would be better placed in one of those water tunnels. The ones in the cliff. Only, I need a guide. What with my back.'

'I can't, Richard.'

'Why ever not?'

'I just can't.'

She looks about to cry.

'Then what can you tell me about them? For example, do those tunnels reach the water galleries?'

She manages to recover herself. 'I believe so. But access is probably impossible.'

'You've been there, though?'

'Not yet. Last I heard the main one was closed due to vandals.'

'Damn.'

'Richard, with your back the way it is, you'll never make it. The path is uneven and rocky. And if you do manage to get inside the tunnels you'll just about be crawling along on your hands and knees.'

Richard is crestfallen. It must show on his face, for she follows with, 'There's a lower path though, which might be worth exploring.'

'And why's that?'

'A German man built a house down there. At the bottom of the cliff somewhere near Haría.'

'Someone lives down there!'

'Not any more. He died. But I understand he was quite an eccentric. He built a swimming pool, right at the water's edge.'

'I'd love to see it.'

'You'll need a guide. The path is in disrepair. And you'd need to pick a nice calm day at low tide.'

'All sounds a bit treacherous, Paula.'

'I thought you were looking for somewhere for a body.'

'I am. But it's no good if I can't pay the place a visit. There's the matter of authenticity. I have to make sure I have my facts right.'

A thoughtful look appears in her face. 'You're after somewhere remote, right?'

'Yes, yes, remote.'

'There's a near abandoned fishing village west of Tinajo that might interest you. Tenesar it's called.'

'Sounds perfect!'

In a sudden about turn she says, 'On second thoughts, you mustn't go there. Celestino says it's more or less off limits to tourists. The locals don't want us there.'

Exasperation rises up in his chest and he has to fight to contain it. 'I'm not a tourist,' he says in a low voice. 'This is research.'

'Even so. We, I mean, us Brits, we need to give the locals some privacy. After all, we've practically taken over their whole island as it is.'

'Very well, then, Paula. Have it your way. But I'm desperate. You must know of somewhere, preferably nearby.'

'I tell you what. Go to the mareta in the valle de Temisa. That won't be all that hard to reach. It's secluded and very pretty. Might be just what you are looking for.'

'Sounds fascinating. But won't you take me, Paula? Please.'

'Richard, I'm not a tour guide and I'm too busy. But I can explain where it is and how to reach it. You'll be fine.'

She reaches into her shoulder bag and extracts a notepad and pen. Without further ado, she sketches a rough route, with an X to mark the spot. She rips the paper from her pad with a flourish.

'There,' she says and hands it to him.

He studies the spidery line wending its way to its destination.

'The Mareta,' he says slowly.

'Better than The Aljibe. But it should be La Mareta, Richard. You can't mix up your languages like that. It sounds dreadful.'

She's right. La Mareta has a good ring to it. He thanks her and walks away, already abuzz with ideas for a plot. Paula has come up trumps and he hasn't needed to part with a single Euro, not even for a coffee. She's missed an opportunity, the foolish woman. He might have been the solution to her financial ills. Still, if she wants to give herself away like that, who is he to quibble.

Wasting no time, he hurries back to the house to fetch his car. Fifteen minutes later he's in Famara. Heading for the cliff, he drives around the back of a swathe of bizarre-looking semi-circular holiday lets and, ignoring the rollers breaking along the beach, he follows a low track until it peters out. He leaves his car and continues on foot. It's an inhospitable place, the terrain rocky scrub. The path narrows but is at least in reasonable shape and he feels assured he's agile enough to cope with it. Only, the cliff becomes steeper the further he goes, until he feels it towering above him. And the ocean below churns like a washing machine. He hasn't made it that much further when the wind suddenly picks up. Still, he presses on, the path deteriorating with every step. He thinks he sees the swimming pool up ahead but whatever it is soon disappears from view. He begins to feel dreadfully exposed.

He reaches the landslide Paula mentioned, and is pondering if he dares edge across it when the wind gusts and a king wave pounds the rocks below him, covering him in spray. A rush of blind panic washes through him and he all but loses his nerve. He only just manages to turn back around without losing his footing and slipping to a certain death.

He regains his composure and his resolve on his return to civilisation. After a late and leisurely lunch in Teguise and an examination of Paula's mud map, he drives back to Haría, taking the Tabayesco turn off after the switchbacks, and pulls over at the last ravine where some effort has been made to create a parking area.

He surveys the terrain and although rugged, it's more favourable than anywhere he's recently been. He clambers up what amounts to a goat track and finds the mareta without too much difficulty. But once he's there, it starts to rain. He can scarcely believe his luck. He stands there getting wet, convinced it's only raining in that bit of the valley; he can see the eastern coastline lit by glorious sunshine. It's only a light shower, not much more than drizzle, but it's enough to soak right through the thin shirt he has on. Still, he will prevail. He goes to the edge of the mareta, not much bigger than a swimming pool, and pictures a body floating in the murky water. Face down, as readers of cosy mysteries don't like blood and gore, and he's had to forego his venture into another work of crime after conceding to himself that his knowledge of police procedures on the island is non-existent.

The mareta has been cut into the hillside. Water trickles in from a small pipe emerging out of a hunk of rock. He notices in the far corner a pair of iron gates leading into a tunnel. The gates are open. Keen to escape the rain he walks over and ventures inside.

The ground is damp and rock strewn, the roof little more than head height. It takes a few moments to adjust to the gloom. He wishes he had a torch. He has it in mind to hover at the entrance but a pertinacious wind carries in the rain. Careful where he treads he backs in further. Three steps and he feels something soft against his ankle. He looks down. It's a hat. A woman's hat, wide-brimmed. He reaches down and picks it up. And there, slumped on the ground not a metre from where he stands, he makes out the figure of a woman, seated with her legs straight out in front. It's an odd posture. He's about to say hello when he sees that her head is hanging forwards.

The realisation that she's dead makes him sway. He drops the hat and steadies himself against the wall and inches away. For all the crime novels he's written, he's never seen a dead body. He isn't even curious to take a closer look. Instead, he rushes back outside to the mareta.

Panic slowly gives way to curiosity. There was no blood, none that he could see. It's unlikely she was murdered in situ. More likely the body was dumped. He squints into the mizzle, surveying the bluffs and gullies above. It's too rugged to drag a body, there would be nothing left of it by the time it got here, although someone could have rolled it down from the road at the top. It's a long way though, and completely visible. Which means someone parked down on the Tabayesco road and hauled it up the gully. Whoever it was would have to be strong. And determined. A man. A scoundrel. Maybe he had an accomplice.

And who is this villain? A local perhaps? A tourist? An expat. Someone with an axe to grind. About what and with whom? His wife? A lover? That all sounds sordid. His secretary then. And the victim could be a holidaymaker interfering in his business. Someone who has discovered a secret. Was it an opportunistic murder? An act of impulse? Or an accident, and the culprit was forced to cover it up? A plot begins to manifest. He feels the buzz of characters forming in his imagination.

The weather clears on his descent and he's feeling somewhat assured that he can make the story work when he trips on a rock and loses his footing. Toppling backwards he lands on a bit of soft ground just inches from a jagged boulder.

It takes a few moments to recover from the shock. He picks himself up and scrambles down to his car, wet and sore and convinced he'll be crippled for weeks.

He not only lost his footing, he's lost all affection for his new plot. He should have gone to that abandoned village Paula mentioned. Off limits, she said. Off limits? Since when is anywhere on Lanzarote off limits? Then again, he isn't in the mood for a repeat of his recent experiences. A complete revision of his ideas is called for. He'll have to come up with an altogether different sort of plot.

18

ARRECIFE

I watch Richard head up the plaza and disappear before making my way over to Pedro's café. La Cacharra is alive with patrons; remarkable for a Thursday morning, and almost all the outdoor seating is taken. I spot a free table set to one side of the café entrance, nestling beneath the boughs of a laurel tree, deeply in the shade.

I sit with my back to the restaurant wall and remove my sunglasses, grateful for the solitude. Richard is a draining companion at the best of times but when he's endeavouring to contrive a plot, he's insufferable. At least I managed to provide him with a modicum of inspiration. It continues to amaze me that he knows so little about Lanzarote.

The bustle of the café, the familiarity, the oasis of the plaza with its exotic laurels and eucalypts, there is nowhere on the island to match it. Yaiza speaks to me of a civic pride born of new wealth, Teguise of the wealth accumulated by the Spanish colonists and honourable Lanzaroteños largely through trade with the Americas. In Haría, the ancient capital, I sense a different sort of wealth, that of a relative abundance of water and tillable land. I heard the valley referred to recently as the bohemian north, in reference to the artists and market traders and alternative types living up on this little plateau, drawn by the seclusion, and the softer, greener, though no less dramatic views. Looking around it's a fair assessment.

I catch Antonio's eye as he goes by laden with dirty plates, and he acknowledges me with a quick smile.

It's good to see La Cacharra thriving. There are places on the island that speak not of wealth but of its opposite, poverty, and of the struggle and the hardship that comes with it: suburbs in the hinterland of Arrecife where the housing is cheap and the facilities poor; where unemployment and crime are, for the island, high; where locals, paid a pittance in the tourism industry, struggle to make ends meet; where the bank foreclosure signs speak of a deep resentment fomenting out of sight of the promenades, for it's always a local forced into financial ruin, forced to watch as their home is sold off for cheap to a foreigner.

It hasn't taken four years of living on the island to ascertain the demographics, the inequalities, and the entrenched, systematic, taken for granted corruption that affects the daily lives of every resident in large and small ways. 'Corruption always makes the poor poorer while enriching the rich'. And Celestino is beside me again, with his tape-loop diatribe on the evils of the powerful cartel dictating the island's affairs. But when it comes to corruption, nowhere, and no one, is immune.

Something about the barren landscape seems to make everything stark, as if any impurity will inevitably be flagrantly exposed. This condition isn't merely figurative, it's born out in hard fact, visible to the naked eye. The ruin of an ancient dwelling disappears and appearing in its stead is a large white abode replete with extensive concrete patios. Or a restaurant. Or a swimming pool. Even after the sweeping raids and protracted court cases and the near loss of Lanzarote's biosphere status, illegal constructions are springing up as though from nowhere. Business as usual and nobody bats an eyelid. Except for Celestino and others like him in the so-called bohemian north, those few prepared to take the risk and speak out.

Antonio approaches with my usual espresso.

'¿Algo más?'

I shake my head. Angela cooked a large breakfast; to set me up for a big day, she said. I'm grateful. It was hard to get through but I feel better on a full stomach.

'Celestino?'

I shake my head again, this time despondently. Thursday means four more days until the commission winner will be announced and five days since Celestino disappeared. Five days? I've begun to doubt I'll ever see him again.

As Antonio walks away, a man pushes past behind him and I catch a waft of his scent. Aftershave, presumably, and it's potent, the sort that lingers. Probably expensive. I look after the man with interest; try to recognise in the corpulent figure turning the corner by the bank anyone I know.

My gaze settles on the diners eating late breakfasts and early lunches. I let the hubbub of talk and laughter wash over me like a benevolent wave, and as I stop listening and the wave recedes, I'm flotsam on an empty beach and I feel suddenly set apart. I sip my espresso. It's hot and bitter and suits my mood as the full weight of my problems bears down on me.

I feel guilty, guilty for being here, guilty with no excuses, not even motherhood. I try to tell myself I'm hardly responsible for the corruption but it's no use. Like so many others, I came to the island to escape my humdrum life and Britain's dismal weather. I thought I was moving to paradise. Instead I've encountered hardship and strain, tempered only by the landscape that never fails to exhilarate, and my love for my child and my man.

I don't consider myself a typical British migrant. Is there such a thing? Yet my presence on the island is in some fundamental way the cause of all the overdevelopment. For without tourism, without home-in-the-sun migration, the goings on wouldn't occur. Or would they? Corrupt men and women don't manifest from nowhere. They form a percentage of every population the world over. Worse, others far more powerful than those at the local level, cruise about the planet like great white sharks on the lookout for the next killing field, lured too by tax-haven benefits, and by nations with weak, insubstantial laws and ineffectual governments. After what I've read on Celestino's website, Lanzarote seems well suited. It's this binding of local with international, this twinning of dark power, that those like Celestino find so difficult to arrest. Perhaps that's why I haven't wanted to engage. It's always seemed too hard and too dangerous. And the corruption too ingrained.

Perhaps Lanzarote's story has always been one of tenacious survival, and over recent decades good ambassadors have sought to preserve, and then to restore the island's dignity. The landscape exemplifies power, raw power, the apocalyptic power of the earth and its extraordinary capacity to transcend the devastation. It's as though these two types of extreme power, the one wantonly destructive, the other transformational and restorative, have manifested in the human population too. Then there are those who don't give a fig. I glance around. Do any of these diners care? Or haven't they bothered to pack their values in their suitcase along with their sunscreen? With my background in tourism, it hasn't taken much to realise hedonism is corruption's accomplice.

I feel the strain of caring too much about this small lump of rock, and without any means of making a difference the burden of care crushes my spirit. I have no idea how Celestino keeps up the noble fight. The island seems to bring out the best and the worst in people, and Celestino is too caught up in the battle, driven by a conviction that only by naming and shaming will the corruption end. He must have gotten too close to something. Has he *been* disappeared as a result? Five days have gone by. Five whole days. Long enough for the police to discover a body and knock on my door. I wish I could contact them. Tell them he's missing. Inquire about that burnt out car in Mancha Blanca, but I daren't.

All I can do is keep searching for answers. And hope those answers lead to my husband.

I down the rest of my espresso, leave a Euro by my cup and wave a thank you to Antonio coming out of the café carrying a large platter of tapas. I make it down to the other end of the plaza before I have to don my sunglasses.

Opening the mill house door, I have an inkling something has changed, although there's no evidence of anything different in the vestibule other than a hint of scent hanging in the air. It isn't the same as the one worn by that corpulent man pushing by Antonio at La Cacharra. I'm sure of it. This scent is muskier. Whoever has been here before has come back. Perhaps he's still here. Or she? On Tuesday, when I searched the building I didn't expect to find a body. This time, with a curdling feeling in my belly, I do. My reaction seems inexplicable, save for the influence of Richard and his crime writing. But fear, once lodged, is hard to shake. I take a deep breath as I go inside.

I can see without entering that the studio is unoccupied. There's no light filtering under the door and the windows are always left shuttered. Unless someone is there in the dark. I'm about to go in when impulse takes me and I decide to search the building again first. Establish that it, too, is empty.

On my way through the patio I pick a chunk of rock out of the rubble piled in its centre. It's a precaution, nothing more. I hesitate. Would it be better to search the upstairs first, or head through to the back? Someone could creep up behind me wherever I go. I choose the stairs, picking my way over the cracked and broken treads, steadying my ascent using the wall, avoiding holding the banister rail.

On the landing I picture myself, a light-framed woman in her late thirties dressed in a skirt and blouse, carrying a rock in her hand for self-defence. I feel ridiculous. Whatever would I do with it should the occasion arise? With sudden resolve, I march into each room in turn. Finding them in an identical state as before—nothing moved, nothing disturbed—I head back downstairs.

At the last tread, it occurs to me that the mill house must have an aljibe. Every dwelling in Haría has an aljibe. I berate myself for not thinking of it before. Richard, in his inimitable and unwitting way, has been flagging aljibes for days. So much for being a sleuth. I can't even see what is right in front of me. Dropping the rock in the rubble on my way by, I cross the patio and quickly inspect the other two rooms—both empty, windowless shells—no evidence anywhere of Celestino, or even that the building was once a mill. Then I make for the back door. It's bolted on the inside. I draw across the bolt and the door swings open. I enter a walled yard. Beyond a concreted area, weeds grow in the picón. Scanning the ground, I head around the side of the building towards a pair of high gates. There, half-buried by the picón, I find the access port to the aljibe: a heavy-looking concrete rectangle.

I kneel down and brush away the dirt and the grit, revealing a rolled metal handle. I grip the handle, testing the weight. The lid won't budge. Determined, I stand and bend and pull, bracing my back. It won't give. I straighten and decide not to risk another attempt. What am I expecting to find? —A body face down in the water as if Richard's plot has spilled into real life? My mind is playing games with me. Real detectives follow clues, not impulses. And it's transparent from the dirt and the grit lodged in the cracks that the lid hasn't been opened in years.

I'm not sure if I'm disappointed or relieved. Finding Celestino's body floating in an aljibe would not have been pleasant. Yet it would have provided closure, and heading back inside I confront anew my harried state of mind. I realise with a shock of concern that I've become accustomed to it; I've been feeling anxious for almost a week, long enough for the greater part of me to accommodate it as the new normal.

The scent still lingers in the vestibule. At least, I think it does. Or is it only in my imagination? I try the door opposite the studio and find it locked, confirming my suspicion that someone has visited the mill in the last two days. But that someone could have been Fernando. Maybe he gained access to that room. Found a key somewhere. Taken to wearing aftershave. Anything is possible.

Not knowing what I expect to find, I open the studio door and flick on the light. All appears to be the same. I stand in the doorway, an upwelling of sadness gripping my throat. His sketches, his paints, his brushes, his rags, the whole of him in this one room. Tears prickle and I'm about to leave when I see that his new artwork, previously on the easel, is leaning against the bench. There's another painting on the easel in its stead. The easel is angled away from me so I go over.

I'm staring into the face of the mayor of Yaiza. At least I presume it's him. Bentor Benicod, standing in regal pose before an antique desk. There are flags in the background, propped beside a large window with latticed panes. Benicod has a forthright face, with hard eyes and a prominent jaw; the smile he wears speaks of a smug, patronising manner, of a man with a strong sense of entitlement. The artist has evidently captured him well.

On the floor beside the easel, not visible from the door, two more paintings are leaning against the bench. I haven't seen either of them before and they do not appear to be Celestino's handiwork. One is a lively if tacky expressionist rendering of a restaurant scene. I picture it in Redoto's restaurant. The other is puzzling. That there's a third painting implies another switch. The work is minimalist, a strangely conceptual depiction of a piece of traditional pottery. It is notably distinct from the other two works and I try to imagine where such a painting might be found. Someone with money and a love of modern fine art? Could be anyone. I can only assume that one of Celestino's works is hanging in its place.

A rush of incredulity replaces the trepidation I felt upon entering the mill house. It's impossible to take the matter seriously. Unless he put the works there himself, Celestino is being set up. And if that's the case, and I'm fairly sure it is, then the methods are crude, childish, silly. More a schoolyard prank than anything sinister. Were it not for the fact that Celestino has disappeared I might have laughed.

I have to track down Fernando. If he's behind all this, then maybe he's playing some sort of practical joke. Although Fernando is as dour a man as they come. And what would he hope to gain from it? What would anyone be hoping to gain out of this except to make Celestino out to be an art thief? And a hapless one at that.

Unless Celestino really *is* setting himself up to be a Banksy-style provocateur and has staged the whole thing. I wouldn't put it past him. Only, if that were true, then he is implicating himself, not to the world at large, but to me. For it suddenly occurs to me that whoever put those paintings in his studio meant for me to see them. Perhaps Celestino is trying to tell me something. If he is, the way he's going about it can only be regarded cruel.

Hungry for clarity, I flick off the light and close the studio door.

Cursing myself for leaving the car at home, I put on my sunglasses and make my way back through the village streets as fast as I dare. I want to run, but I don't want the attention that would attract. I walk, trotting along every now and then when there is no one about and I won't be seen.

Back in my kitchen I toss the sunglasses on the table and retrieve from my shoulder bag the list of art galleries with contact numbers that Bill helped me compile the night before. Ignoring the flash of the answer phone light I pick up the handset and make to call the first number. I stop after three digits to play the message. It's only Kathy, asking for an update. With a twinge of disappointment, I press the delete button and return to the first number. My call goes straight to message bank. I hang up. The second number gets me through to a woman who says she doesn't know any Fernando Brena. I try the third, not expecting Fernando to have landed a job at the International Museum of Contemporary Art housed in Arrecife's Castillo de San José, ostensibly the most prestigious gallery on the island. As far as I know, he doesn't have the credentials for such a place.

Seven rings and a man answers. He sounds a little breathless. When I ask to speak with a new employee, Fernando Brena, he becomes confused and says he's never heard of him. Then he tells me to wait and he goes away from the phone.

Five minutes pass before he returns, even more breathless, to tell me that yes, a man by that name has started at the gallery. He can't tell me if Fernando is working today but I quickly thank him and hang up.

I'm out the door in seconds.

The wind blusters from the north, buffeting the car on the rise out of the village. I ease off the accelerator, wanting to feel more in control. It isn't until I reach the sweeping bend at the escarpment that I notice the black sedan in my rear vision mirror. I wish I'd had the courage to note the licence plate when I saw it parked in the street outside the house yesterday. Am I going crazy, adding twos and coming up with odd numbers? Perhaps, but I'm convinced that driver is following me.

I turn right at the Arrieta roundabout.

So does he, but there's nothing unusual about that; most of the traffic from Haría goes south.

Keeping an eye on the rear vision mirror, I follow the road to Tahiche.

He is still behind me, too far back for me to read the licence plate.

I go through the string of roundabouts to Arrecife. He follows.

I take the ring road, heading down to the port. He does as well.

It's a common enough route. No need for alarm. But it makes no difference to the apprehension stirring in me. When I pull up in the car park outside the Castillo de San José, I'm trembling.

The black sedan drives straight by, too fast to get a glimpse of the driver.

I unbuckle my seatbelt and sit back in my seat, the sun through the windscreen hot on my skin. I wait, keeping watch, but no black sedan pulls into the car park. Relieved but still shaken, I grab my shoulder bag and leave the car.

The old fort, part of the island's defences against pirates, is located on the southern edge of Arrecife's docklands, flanked land-side by a swathe of warehouses and light industry. The fort overlooks the docks across a sheltered bay. It's a strange location for an art gallery, and hard to find due to minimal signposting. Visitors coming up from the south either have to fight their way out of Arrecife's confusion of narrow streets, or take the ring road like I did, and make sure they take the right exit at the roundabout and not miss the next left turn. Either way they have to make a special trip, for there is nothing else around to bring them here. The Castillo de San Gabrielle, situated in the heart of Arrecife, would have made a much better location.

Still, enormous effort has been taken to restore the fort. The car park is fringed with rows of palm trees. Flat basalt cobbles break the uniformity of the concourse. A formal garden of raked picón, deco-rated with a smattering of smooth basalt stones and a few boulders, and containing nothing save a row of sedges at the edges, greets visi-tors on their way to the museum entrance. The fort itself, a chunky and stout building of dark grey stone, stands proud on a low promon-tory. Man-sized turrets guard the corners. I pick my way across a pebbled path and a small, hinged bridge, the only passage over the dry and narrow moat several metres below. An attendant confronts me before I take a step inside, pointing behind me at a shipping container converted into a kiosk. 'Billete, por favour.'

'¿Cuanto es?'

'Nueve euros.'

Nine euros. I doubt I have that amount in my purse. I explain to him in Spanish that I've come to speak with Fernando Brena. The man refuses to understand me. He remains in the doorway. I repeat my request. The man looks nonplussed. Behind him, I spot another staff member and try to draw his attention. It's no use.

'Billete, mujer.'

I ignore his addition of 'woman' to the word 'ticket', finding his tone insulting. He's a squat man with a mean face and he begins to look impatient. I tell him I don't want to visit the gallery. I just need to speak with Fernando. A queue forms behind me.

'You have to pay nine euros,' the attendant says in English. 'Over there.'

He *can* speak English.

'I just want to speak with Fernando.'

'He isn't here.'

'Just go and get a ticket, for crying out loud,' a woman behind me says.

'I'm not buying a ticket because I'm not here to see the paintings,' I snap.

'Then get out of the bloody way.'

Defeated, I edge to one side and make my way back through the car park.

'Daft cow,' I hear on the wind.

As I pass the shipping container the man inside beckons me over.

'Can I help you?' he says when I enter.

He's a friendlier, relaxed looking man and in the aftermath of my humiliation I warm to him immediately.

'My name is Paula Diaz. I'm here to speak to Fernando Brena. I'm a friend of his.'

He frowns. 'You can't. He isn't working this morning.'

I groan inwardly. 'When will he be here?'

'This afternoon.'

Then I'll return.

The drive north seems quicker and I'm not trailed by mysterious drivers in black sedans. It isn't until I reach the turnoff for Tabayesco that my earlier anxiety returns with a thump. A black sedan is parked in the bus bay across the road. That has to be the same car. Almost no one on the island drives a black car. It just isn't that safe to merge with the landscape so effectively.

I wait for a break in the traffic and turn up the Tabayesco road. I take it slow, keeping an eye behind me in the rear vision mirror. My mind tilts sideways as the sedan pulls out of the bus bay, makes a U turn and enters the road behind me.

I resist the impulse to put my foot down and maintain a steady pace. The sedan holds back. It's a short stretch to Tabayesco. As I near the hills, the houses tucked away on the low side come into view. Then the road forks. I take the lane to the right and pull over beside a field of prickly pears. The black sedan cruises on up the left fork. With some relief, I carry on, rounding the next bend. Choosing not to park directly outside the Ramírez house, I pull up in a neighbour's driveway, cursing the lack of places to hide on this empty coastal plain. I lock the car, hoping it won't be in anybody's way for a brief time. Satisfied after a good scan about that no one is watching, I head up the street and round the side of the house.

Pedro waves to me through a window and beckons me into the kitchen. He tells me Kathy has taken the girls to Pilar's for lunch.

'It's you I've come to see.'

'Again?' He looks instantly uncertain. 'Still no Celestino?'

'Not a sign,' I say, realising as I speak that isn't exactly true.

'How many days?'

'Five.'

'I'm sorry.'

It seems an odd response.

'Café?' he says, unscrewing a coffee percolator.

I grasp about in my mind for a smooth way to broach the topic. Failing, I launch straight in. 'You work closely with Celestino on his anti-corruption campaigns.'

'You know I do.'

He has his back to me, tapping out old coffee grounds. I wish I could see his face.

'Did he give you any documents relating to the illegal hotels in Yaiza?'

No answer.

'Only, there was a folder among his things. A brand-new folder. I don't normally snoop through his private papers, but under the circumstances...'

'I understand.'

It's all he says.

He fills the bottom half of the percolator with water, sits the perforated basket inside and loads it with fresh coffee, taking his time tamping down the grains with his fingers before screwing on the top.

'The thing is,' I say, hoping he'll turn around, 'the folder doesn't contain much. Just a couple of press cuttings.'

'Maybe that's all he had.'

He lights the stove. The percolator sizzles, briefly.

'It did contain more, judging by its creases.'

'He said nothing about it to me.'

I don't press him. I have no idea whether to believe him. I'm not sure it even matters. All the material I translated into English to post on Celestino's website came from press cuttings. He has other information, official documents and letters and transcripts of text messages, but he never lets me see any of that and he never tells me where it all comes from. The source suddenly seems vital.

At last Pedro turns around. I study his face, the rugged pallor, the dominant brow beneath receding hair, the wide cheekbones, and cool reflective eyes. He remains standing, leaning back against the kitchen bench.

'Where do you get all your information for your campaigns?'

He stares down at the floor.

'It depends. Sometimes through freedom of information.'

'But you must know people with inside knowledge? Whistle-blowers?'

He shrugs. 'Like I said, it depends.'

'Pedro, please. He's been missing five days.'

Something seems to have occurred to him and he begins to look worried. The percolator gurgles. He waits a few seconds before turning off the gas. I say no more while he pours the coffee into cups.

'Sugar?'

'No.' I take the cup he proffers. 'I know Celestino has a source,' I say, lying. 'More than one I expect.'

'Only the one,' he says with unexpected honesty.

'Who?'

'I can't tell you, Paula.'

'But you know, don't you? And you know where Celestino is too.'

'If I did, don't you think I'd tell you?'

I sip my coffee. It's strong and too hot to gulp in one go. Should I tell him I think I'm being followed? Maybe he's seen the black sedan hanging around in Tabayesco. I open my mouth to speak when his phone rings. I can tell by his reaction it's Kathy. I sip more of my coffee. When he hangs up he says, 'I've got to go out. Kathy needs me to go to the shops.'

I put my cup on the table and get up to leave.

'I'm sure he's fine,' Pedro says, showing me out.

I wish I shared his confidence. Perhaps I should have mentioned the broken necklace, but what difference would it make, except to have me appear overly dramatic in Pedro's eyes? As the door closes behind me, I scan up and down the street. No black sedan.

I take the back way to Haría, up through the valley, hoping to avoid another encounter with whoever is following me. The drive proves uneventful and by the time I reach the edge of the village I begin to relax. I swing by the supermarket for bread and goat's cheese, and go home to eat my lunch.

I'm about halfway through the cheese roll, sinking in my teeth to take another large bite when there's a knock at the door. I'm still chewing when I answer it and confront a rather flustered looking Shirley standing on the doorstep in a crumpled-looking off-white smock dress.

'Oh, Paula,' she says and almost pushes her way inside. 'The ruddy car has conked out on me. Today of all days. I'm meant to be meeting my friend Lolita Pluma in a couple of hours.' She takes herself through to the kitchen and makes no effort to disguise her disgust at the state of it. I haven't done the dishes in days.

Before I can finish my mouthful, Shirley says, 'I see you are eating your lunch. You're still planning to go into Arrecife I take it?'

I nod and swallow, remembering vaguely I agreed to accompany Shirley.

'You see, my mechanic has gone on holiday. Mechanics shouldn't have holidays, should they? Whatever next! You wouldn't do me a favour and run me in.'

'Sure.' I reach under the sink for the water flagon and fill one of the glasses left out on the bench. 'I can put you onto a mechanic too.'

'And who might that be?' Shirley sounds doubtful.

'Miguel.' I slosh back the water. 'Honestly, he's terrific.'

'Where's he based?'

'Arrecife.'

'But how will I get the car there?'

'He'll come and fetch it. That's what he did for me,' I say, recalling the day my alternator died coming down the switchbacks. 'And when you need to collect it, just ask and I'll run you in.'

'That's remarkably generous of you, Paula.'

'Not at all. You've done a lot for me, lately. Gives me a chance to show my gratitude. Besides, isn't that what neighbours are for?'

I reach into my shoulder bag for my notepad and grab the turquoise pen Shirley handed me the other day. Then I sift through my phone for Miguel's work number. Shirley hovers, snatching the note the moment I proffer it.

'I'll go and phone him. Miguel, you said?'

'I did.'

'Back in fifteen. Give you a chance to finish that,' she says, eyeing my roll on her way by.

Another few bites and I abandon the roll and down the rest of the water. I only have time to quench the thirsty pot plants and run a comb through my hair before there's another rap on my front door. Moments later I'm heading back to Arrecife with Shirley beside me, small and prim in a red and white striped skirt suit, topped off with red button earrings and matching beaded necklace, a giant red handbag on her lap.

'How do you know Lolita?' I say once we're in open country.

'She works at the Cabildo.'

'As?'

'Director of the Department of Recreation, Art, and Tourism.'

'DRAT.' The acronym rings through me.

'She's hard to pin down,' Shirley says perfunctorily. 'Otherwise I would have cancelled.'

There seems no end to the notable folk Shirley knows. It strikes me just how far apart I am, an ocean's worth of separation in fact from the woman seated by my side.

I drive at a steady pace, slowing to allow oncoming traffic to round a cluster of cyclists. I keep an eye on the cars behind me but no black sedan comes into sight.

'What's wrong with your car?'

'Won't start. That's all I know.'

Shirley grips her oversized handbag with both hands. She's impatient. Twice I catch her tapping a finger on the shiny red leather.

We reach the turn off for Guatiza as an oncoming car screams towards us, swerving into our lane to overtake a white hatchback. I swerve in reaction, averting an accident. I'm about to blame it on a hoon when I see a woman in a large hat behind the wheel. She looks vaguely familiar.

'Stupid mare,' Shirley says. 'She had plenty of room. Shouldn't have overtaken so wide.'

I drive even slower after that, ignoring the fingers tapping in my side vision. All I can think about are the paintings. With Shirley in such a strange mood, I wonder how I'll broach the subject of whether and in what capacity Benicod knows Redoto, and I decide to let it go. I take the ring road, arriving outside the Cabildo with a good ten minutes to spare, and turn into the car park opposite.

'Why are you pulling up here?' Shirley says. 'Plenty of room out the front.'

'You're not meant to park there.'

'And I have to traipse across the roundabout?'

For the first time in our friendship, I give voice to my own irritation. 'I'm driving, so I decide where to park.'

'Have it your way,' Shirley says.

She alights, and holding the passenger side door as if about to fling it shut she bends and peers at me still strapped in my seat.

'Meet me back here in two hours. Lolita's office is easy to find. Just ask at the desk.'

The car shudders on the slam.

I watch her march off past a children's playground, a diminutive woman clutching an oversized handbag, looking a lot like a canvas deck chair.

On the other side of the roundabout the Cabildo sits grandly in its own formal grounds. It's a modern building several stories high, of Spanish colonial style with tall windows set in mustard coloured walls replete with white pilasters. A symbol of the island's newfound wealth. I wait until Shirley has crossed the road and is making her way across the concourse before I set off.

Avoiding the warren of roads in Arrecife, I head back to the ring road, pulling up outside the museum of contemporary art just after two. Before I enter I get straight in my mind what I need to find out. I have to discover Fernando's whereabouts on Saturday night and Sunday morning, the rather large window of opportunity in which the solar panel painting was placed in Redoto's restaurant. And then there's Tuesday night and Wednesday morning, when Bentor Benicod's portrait was switched with a money-spewing volcano. Thinking about it, the matter of opportunity is too broad. Perhaps I should focus on means. How would Fernando have gained access to both Redoto's restaurant and the Yaiza town hall?

I go to the kiosk but it's empty so I head across the basalt cobbles to the old fort. The same idiot attendant is there, bent over and fiddling with his keys. I plan to stride right past him but he must have seen me coming because he straightens and blocks my path. Behind him, I spot Fernando on the far side of the main gallery.

I remove my sunglasses and call out.

Fernando looks over. 'Paula.' His expression changes from one of reflective preoccupation to puzzlement, although I imagine he knows why I'm here after my phone call last Sunday. He walks towards me. 'This is a surprise. Luis said someone had called in.'

The attendant scowls but lets me pass, and I enter a long chamber of heavy stone, more a bunker stretching left and right with a small window recessed in the walls at either end. The bunker has a low rounded arched ceiling and there are stairs heading to chambers above and below. It's an austere setting and the few paintings on display—large pieces of abstract art that appear to me little more than a few strategic smears of paint—look curiously out of place.

I wait until he's close before speaking.

'They told me at the Timple museum that you'd found work at a gallery in Arrecife. I'm glad I found you.' I didn't want to sound too dramatic but there didn't seem much choice. 'Celestino is still missing.'

Fernando looks at me with genuine surprise.

'Is there somewhere we can talk?'

'There's a restaurant downstairs,' he says quickly. 'Follow me.'

The attendant retreats into a small antechamber, more a nook. I slip on my sunglasses, the better to ignore him as I go by.

Fernando leads the way round the side of the fort and down a flight of carved basalt steps that follow the curve of the promontory. The low cliff has been landscaped, with an array of carefully chosen boulders set in a garden of agaves planted in deep picón. Tones of red and orange meet the gaze. Beyond, the lava is rough and gnarly. The ocean, a few metres below, a clear turquoise. The setting speaks of Manrique and when I reach the last step and face an elegant sculpture centred on a patio mosaic of carefully chosen pebbles set in concrete, I can't help marvelling at the lengths taken on the island to preserve the architect's memory.

The main feature of the restaurant is a curved wall of glass. We go inside and Fernando chooses a table in the sun, neatly laid with a black linen tablecloth and matching napkins. We both sit down in wide and deep chairs facing the ocean. The view is so bright I leave on my sunglasses. To the south the marina is pleasing to the eye. The dock to the north with its long row of shipping containers and the occasional crane lending the ocean setting an industrial feel.

Fernando tries to hail a waiter. After a few moments he leaves his seat, muttering something about the service.

I wait, tuning into the murmured conversations emanating from the other side of the room, the occasional cutlery chink. There's a notable absence of cooking smells.

The room behind me is so dimly lit I have to take off my sunglasses when I turn to see where he's gone. I spot him over by a pillar, chatting to a uniformed waiter. Beyond them, groups of two or three sit at square tables that extend to the bar. The place looks expensive. As do the people. No one in the restaurant looks like a regular tourist. A woman glances over and catches my eye. I avert my gaze and sit back around in my seat, replacing my sunglasses.

Perhaps I'm over-sensitive, imbuing the atmosphere with a conspiratorial gloss, but I feel as though I've entered another world, one of private meetings conducted in subdued voices. A hideaway on the edge of the city, somewhere for the rich and powerful to conduct secret deals, where local politicians wine and dine with members of the board and palms are greased with fat wads of cash. Probably some of the very people seated behind me.

Odd that Celestino has never mentioned this restaurant. Perhaps he has no idea the sorts of people who come here. As I sit waiting for Fernando to join me, I hear Celestino's voice in my head, telling me of politico-corporate entanglements, of the lengths the greedy will go to unless they are stopped. Sensing the whispers in the dim behind me, I feel uncomfortable and entirely out of place. Dining with the enemy? It's with a measure of despondence that I think I'll never be an anti-corruption activist. I don't have my husband's courage or his zeal.

It's a view reinforced when I turn around again. Fernando is still in conversation. Behind him, a man appears at the entrance to the men's toilets, making his way to a table near the pillar. Even without removing my sunglasses I recognise him immediately. It's the proud posture, the regal tilt to the head. Bentor Benicod sits down with his back to me as I return my gaze to the panorama outside, my heartbeat quickening.

I'm beginning to think Fernando rude for taking so long. I entertain a paranoid thought or two about him as well, half-anticipating a tap on my shoulder, a curt 'come with me please', and I'll disappear into the bowels of the fort never to be seen again.

At last Fernando comes to the table. 'Sorry about that,' he says without explanation. 'So, you're trying to find Celestino.'

'I'm not having much luck,' I say, swiftly restoring my composure.

'If there's anything I can do.'

'There might be something.'

He seems to freeze.

'Only, I'm not sure what use I'll be,' he says as if he hasn't heard me.

'I'm following a couple of leads.'

'I lost my driver's licence you see. Speeding. My advice to you, Paula, is to keep within the limits. They'll catch you eventually, mark my words.'

I hide my disappointment. 'When did this happen?'

I observe him sitting there all sombre with his goatee beard.

'Last week. I've been catching the bus ever since. Can you imagine!'

His words deflate me. There's no point in pursuing this line of questions any further. Either he's lying or he can't have planted those paintings. Yet there's something supercilious in his manner that makes me wary. His is still the strongest motive. Professional jealousy, I only have to think of a former work colleague to know how deep that goes, how it gnaws away at all that is good in a person.

The waiter arrives and sets down two wire baskets of croquettes along with bowls of dipping sauce arranged on a thin rectangle of basalt. He disappears and returns moments later with plates, a bottle of water and two glasses. I have to marvel at Fernando's audacity. To have placed an order for us both without consulting me; I suspect he acquired it for free.

'I take it you haven't been to the studio,' I say, biting into a croquette. The centre is creamy and delicately flavoured with fish.

'This is the most frustrating aspect of the speeding fiasco,' Fernando says, pouring water into my glass and his. 'Have you seen the timetable for the guaguas to the north?'

'There's quite a few.'

'If you call six a day quite a few.'

'I used to catch the bus all the time.'

I dip the remaining piece of my croquette into the sauce by my elbow. He slugs his water.

'All right I suppose, if you have plenty of time.'

'I found it scenic.'

Finding the exchange increasingly irritating I take another croquette, hoping to hurry things along.

'It wears off after a while.'

'What wears off?'

'The fixation with the views.'

'Hasn't for me.'

He dips a croquette into an oily sauce and leans forward to catch the drips.

'You're a tourist,' he says with his mouth full. 'Or you were.'

'What does that have to do with it?'

'Beauty is your thing.'

'But you paint landscapes,' I say, making little effort to mask my ire. 'Surely a bus ride would be stimulating.'

'I stylise what I already know.'

I recall the last series of paintings he made, a production line of works, all similar and perfect for the tourist trade.

'How are you getting to the Teguise market?'

'I don't have time for the markets these days,' he says, his face filled with hauteur.

The man is insufferable. I reach for the last croquette and move the bowl of sauce closer. It's then that I notice the square of paper centred on the board beneath. It's a photocopy of a newspaper cutting concerning an exhibition upstairs in the gallery: A photographic display of the construction of the Museo Atlántico. The director of DRAT, Lolita Pluma, is quoted announcing the extraordinary honour and privilege it is to have secured a world class sculptor with renowned ecological credentials to produce such an innovative work of art beneath Lanzarote's pristine waters. It's as though my world has folded in on itself. The situation on the island really is as Celestino would have it; held by its neck by a bow tie of pomp and privilege. Fernando, it seems, was now happily ensconced in it all.

I reach for my glass and gulp a few mouthfuls of water. Fernando dabs at his beard with his napkin. I extract my wallet but he stops me with, 'It's taken care of.' I withdraw my keys instead. 'I better go. I'm running late.' With as much grace as I can muster I thank him and bid him a good day.

A fresh wind blows my hair in my face as I head up the basalt steps to my car. I'll be back at the Cabildo in ten minutes, leaving about half an hour to spare before I meet Shirley.

Without bothering to look around for black sedans, I drive straight back to the car park opposite the Cabildo, thinking a walk along the promenade would clear my mind.

Despite the wind the afternoon is sunny and warm. Past the children's playground, I enter a cactus garden fringed with low stone walls. I choose the path beside the ocean. There are few people about. I think I might benefit from the wind on my face but it does nothing for me.

About halfway I stop and lean against the wall, staring out at the surface of all that water, its surface a shimmering blue. I have no idea what to make of Fernando, his evasiveness, his arrogance. Or why Celestino puts up with him. But despite Fernando's jealousy, deep down I doubt he has anything to do with the paintings or Celestino's disappearance. Which leaves me with no suspects and no clues, and an all-consuming desire to scream with frustration into that ocean wind. All I know for sure is that someone has entered the house and the studio. The person in question wore aftershave, or maybe it was perfume, and is possibly the driver of the black sedan. And that whatever is going on is serious enough to warrant such behaviour. Even then, I have to wonder if perhaps I'm imagining things. In the absence of Celestino, the entire situation leaves me fit to burst.

I go on my way, hoping a brisk walk will ground me.

At the end of the garden the promenade curves round Playa Reducto, a small beach of golden sand where the waters are shallow and calm. The beach is empty save for a sand sculptor, dressed only in shorts, at work emulating the eruption of two volcanoes. He's lit a fire in each crater. Rivulets of black pour down the cones of sand. I stop to watch for a few moments. A small gathering forms. I drop a generous euro in the tin on the promenade wall and leave them to it.

Soon there are more people about: couples, young and old, women pushing strollers, old men sitting on the wall, passing the time of day. The atmosphere is unhurried and relaxed. Normally I would have enjoyed the pace, the anonymity, the casual way people go about their day. Instead, when I reach the end of the beach I turn back, not wanting to enter the bustle of the city, the sight of the Grand Hotel blocking access to the next stretch of promenade enough affront to my sensibilities.

I make it back to the Cabildo on time, noting with some cynicism that no expense has been spared by the Lanzarote government to create a sense of civic status; the concourse, a vast expanse of pale stone paving interspersed with formal plantings, has even been edged with a patterned paved footpath.

I cross the concourse and climb a flight of long and wide steps, entering a light and airy foyer that has an atrium in its centre and corridors going off in all directions. The floor is so highly polished, and the walls and the furnishings so rich with gold and chrome, the building seems to radiate its own light.

I approach a discrete reception area to my right and ask for the office of Lolita Pluma. The woman behind the desk requests my name.

'Paula Cray,' I say, suddenly wondering if the name 'Diaz' might raise an alarm.

A brief phone call and the woman directs me down a corridor to a door on the left.

The door opens on my knock, and a tall woman in her fifties, garbed in a cream trouser suit, welcomes me inside.

'Paula Cray, isn't it. I'm Lolita Pluma.'

She proffers her hand. I feel the cold of her skin, observing the friendly veneer of the wealthy and socially adept as Lolita withdraws her hand and steps aside.

The room is large and well lit. Shirley is seated before the desk with her ridiculously large handbag on her lap. She shifts and glances round.

'There you are,' she says.

'Am I late?'

'No, not late. But you'll never guess what's happened.'

A few paces into the room and I see the amusement in Shirley's face.

'Look.'

I follow her gaze. Lolita is standing beside a small artwork no bigger than a sheet of A4 paper. I can't stop the, 'Oh' that comes out of my mouth.

'You recognise this work?' Lolita says, quick off the mark.

'I don't know,' I say, cringing inwardly under the woman's scrutiny.

'I was telling Lolita about the one at Reedoetoe's over lunch. Then we came back here and found this.'

'When was it put here?'

'Well that's the strange part,' Lolita says. 'The previous painting disappeared last night.'

I picture straight away the third painting in Celestino's studio, a minimalist rendering of a piece of traditional pottery. A work befitting its owner.

'But this one only appeared while we were out to lunch.'

'Bizarre. Quite bizarre,' Shirley murmurs.

'Can I take a closer look?'

Lolita moves away, allowing me to study the painting. It's more complex than the others. Cut into a mountainside is a gated holiday resort. Outside the gates stand a gathering of locals with begging bowls. It's another oil painting in the same satirical style as the others. And there is Celestino's signature in the bottom corner. The message of the work is clear. A critical portrayal of an exclusive resort, one that doesn't benefit the locals who have been kicked off their land to make way for it.

But what did this have to do with Lolita Pluma and DRAT? They don't grant building permits.

I notice the spare chair and sit down heavily.

'Whatever's the matter?' Shirley says, reaching forward to put a hand on my arm.

And that is all it takes for my pent-up emotion to overwhelm me. Hot tears sting my face. Before I can stop myself, I blurt to the two women that the work is that of my husband.

Shirley looks astonished. 'It can't be. That isn't possible.'

'That's Celestino's signature,' I say, berating my thoughtless honesty even as I speak. 'I'd recognise it anywhere.'

'Celestino Cray?' Lolita looks puzzled. She turns to Shirley. 'I've never heard of a Celestino Cray. Who is he?'

'Not Cray,' Shirley says. 'She's referring to Celestino Diaz.'

'This is the work of Celestino Diaz?' Lolita says slowly. She frowns.

'And he's missing,' Shirley adds. 'That's why she's so upset.'

'Missing?'

'He's disappeared.' I shudder as I say it.

'How long has he been missing?'

'Five days.'

'Five days! Have you contacted the police?'

'I can't.'

'Why ever not?'

'I don't want to get him into trouble.'

'What's more important, some silly prank or your husband's life?'

'If it is a silly prank.'

'What else could it be?'

'We better go,' Shirley says quickly. 'We've taken up enough of your time.'

She stands abruptly and clasps her enormous bag to her chest.

'Pleased to meet you, Lolita,' I manage, drying my eyes with the back of my hand as I edge towards the door. 'I'm sorry about this.'

'Don't be sorry,' Lolita says with a sympathetic smile. 'You have done nothing wrong.'

Once out the door, Shirley hurries down the corridor, across the foyer and out of the building. I trail her across the concourse.

'I suppose the car is over there,' Shirley says, pointing in the direction of the roundabout.

'I couldn't find anywhere closer,' I say, cringing inwardly at the amount of lying I've been doing lately.

We walk in silence. When we reach my car, Shirley says, 'Where to?'

'Home, I thought.'

'So you don't fancy a jaunt around Arrecife.'

'Not particularly.'

'Very well then, You're the driver.' I press the remote and Shirley yanks open the passenger side door.

It isn't until we're heading up the slipway to the ring road that Shirley speaks her mind.

'You shouldn't have said anything. Not to Lolita.'

I react with alarm to the harsh tone of her voice.

'Because she might call the police?' I say, holding to the right-hand lane despite the belching fumes of the old truck up ahead.

'I doubt she'll do that. But it's one thing admitting your husband is missing and quite another that two of his paintings have turned up in inappropriate places.'

'Three.'

'Three?' Shirley almost shrieks.

I tell her about the painting in the foyer of the Yaiza town hall in the place of Benicod's portrait.

'Bentor would have gone nuts if he'd seen he'd been replaced,' Shirley says.

I emit a short laugh.

Shirley doesn't follow suit. 'Honestly, I don't know how you're putting up with him doing this. Going into hiding without warning to plant paintings about the place. These are all friends of mine, Paula. Old friends. You don't think he's trying to have another dig at me?'

'Shirley, I don't think...' but I let the sentence fade away. I still haven't asked Shirley how Bentor and Redoto know each other, but for now I've lost my chance.

We drive on in silence.

19

MÁGUEZ

THE SUN HAS YET TO DIP BELOW THE MOUNTAINS WHEN I GRIP THE steering wheel with two hands and watch Shirley cross the street and enter her house. As I pull away from the kerb silvery bands of light stream through low cloud clinging to the peaks of the massif, dazzling me through my sunglasses. Minutes later I come to a crunching stop on my parent's gravel drive and release my seatbelt, pausing before I open the door for my heartbeat to slow to normal.

I force my mind on the present, on my shoes crunching on the picón, the stillness of the air now the wind has dropped. The silence wraps around me, intense, timeless, benevolent.

I survey the surroundings, taking in the rise and fall of the massif, the bumps, creases and folds. This valley with its barren rim of mountains and hills cradling the fertile soils that are still farmed here and there with loving care is closer to paradise than anywhere I can imagine. Even as the harrowing situation of the last week holds me in its grip, I can still take time to appreciate my surroundings. Even as the larger part of me remains wracked with worry and confusion. As though the contrast between my inner turmoil and the stillness of the land causes some part of me to reach out for the solace it offers.

As the island yields to the demands of a tourist economy, up here the traditional and timeless ways continue; the farmer next door still weeds his small plot of land with a scythe. His family still plant their neat rows of maize and potatoes and onions by hand, one by one. And while much of the most inaccessible terraces have long been abandoned, the farmers out at Guinate still farm right to the cliff edge. These farmers seem to me now symbolic of the tenacity of the human will to survive, to push necessity to the brink of what is possible.

Fernando is wrong; his take on scenery betrays an artist crippled by a lack of empathy. One uncharitable thought and I can't restrain my analytical thinking. I consider the south of the island, where much of the land is untended or not tillable. Where the land is fertile and suitable for grapes agribusiness has taken over many of the bodegas, with vast sums invested in irrigation and streamlined styles of planting. I consider those areas where the lack of small-scale farming has reached such a crisis that in a bid to draw the locals back to the land the Cabildo are giving away large plots with access to water.

I mentioned the land giveaway to Celestino one time and he scoffed. 'They'll never get the young back on the land.' Maybe he's right. Maybe in the future the land will be tended not by locals but by immigrant British and German back-to-earthers with a passion for dry-land farming and a tolerance of ferocious wind.

I let out a long breath of air and go inside.

The living room is neat and tidy, evidence of Gloria's presence erased by Angela's fastidiousness, the dining table already laid for dinner. The air is infused with the rich smell of roasting pork. I detect her moving about in the kitchen. Following the sound of the television, I tiptoe down the room, entering the second living area given over to visual entertainment. Gloria is sitting upright on a sofa, her eyes glued to the screen. She doesn't acknowledge my presence. The placid way she sits, legs outstretched and hands upturned in her lap, belies her passionate nature. Gloria must be wearing out her grandparents. I vow to leave her with them for only one more day. Just one more day. After that, I think grimly, I'll have to cope as a single parent.

I walk away without disturbing her and go through to the kitchen.

'Hi, Mum.'

'You're back.' Her remark has a judgmental ring.

I see Bill out on the patio, seated in a lounger with his feet up, reading a newspaper. Opening the door, I note the drop in temperature but it is still warm enough to sit. On the table beside him is an empty whisky glass.

'Hello there,' he says cheerily when I enter his field of vision. He puts down his paper and I draw up a chair.

'Time for the day's report,' he says with unsurprising relish. 'Did you track down Fernando?'

'He works at the museum of contemporary art.'

'At the old fort, down by the docks?'

'We had lunch there.'

'I had no idea the place had a restaurant.'

'It's tucked away,' I say, thinking back to the black tablecloths and whispered conversations. 'I did discover he's in the clear. He's lost his driver's licence. He's been getting around on buses all week.'

'That's something, I suppose.'

'Although it doesn't mean he didn't do it. Just that it would have been awfully hard.'

'And farfetched. What would he hope to gain?'

'Maybe nothing. Except the satisfaction of humiliating Celestino.'

'But nobody knows the paintings are his.'

I wince privately.

'Unless Fernando's planning a great reveal,' he says reflectively.

'Possibly. But I expect he's too late.'

'I don't follow.'

I self-censor, not ready to confide my terrible divulgence. 'A third painting has turned up,' I say instead.

'A third!'

'In Lolita Pluma's office at the Cabildo.'

'What were you doing dancing with the enemy?'

'The enemy? She works for DRAT.'

'I know. She's the director, recently appointed. She's a businesswoman with quite a history. Married into one of the island's wealthy families. They say she's as mucky as they come.'

'Who says?'

He looks evasive. 'So far, no allegations have stuck.'

I observe him, the look of triumphant satisfaction on his face. 'How do you know all this?'

'Her name came up in proceedings.'

'The illegal hotels,' I murmur.

He reaches for his glass before realising he's finished the contents and sits back with a soft grunt.

'Dad,' I say with impatience. 'Do you want to hear what happened?'

'All ears.'

'Shirley invited me to go in with her to Arrecife.'

'Nice of her.'

'But then her car wouldn't start so she asked me to run her in.'

'I thought she had a Maserati.'

'Dad,' I say sharply, wondering how many times that whisky glass has received a refill.

'All right. Go on.'

'She had a coffee date with Lolita.'

'Did she?' he says slowly.

'I was going in any way, to speak with Fernando. I collected her afterwards at Lolita's office. That's when I saw the painting.'

I think back to Shirley's foul mood in the car on the way home. The way she marched off without so much as a thank you when I pulled up in our street.

'Whoever is doing this sure does get around,' Bill says.

'The painting was a bit more obvious though. A newly built resort cut into the mountainside and, in the foreground, villagers with begging bowls standing outside the gates.'

Bill chuckles.

'It isn't funny.'

'No. But still.' He pauses. 'Three paintings, three locations, three people.'

'There has to be a connection.'

'A restaurant, a town hall, and an office in the Cabildo.'

'Hmm.'

'Solar power crucifixes on a beach, a money spewing volcano and a gated resort impoverishing the people. I think I need to write this down.' Bill gets up and heads inside, returning moments later with Gloria's drawing pad and a fat red marker.

'So, the crucifixes were in the restaurant, the volcano in Yaiza and the resort at the Cabildo.'

He draws a rough sketch of the paintings and labels them by location.

'And the three victims of this apparent crime: Bentor Benicod, Lolita Pluma and who was the other one?'

'Redoto.'

'Redoto who?'

'I'm not sure. Pedro said he would have to be Redoto Redoto, but I only have his word for that.'

'And he is?'

'Pedro didn't say. But by the tone of his voice I'm surprised you haven't come across him.'

'I'm still very much in the learner's seat when it comes to this island's corruption history.'

Somehow, I doubt it.

'We should probably double check. May I?'

I retrieve his laptop from his office. When I open the lid and stroke the mouse pad the screen lights up and there's his browser with its ten open tabs, all with the words 'corruption' or 'Caso Unión' and the like, in English and also in Spanish. His thoroughness is impressive, yet I'm concerned all at once that he's feeding something of an obsession.

I search listings for Redoto's El Viento del Mar restaurant, but can't find any mention of the owner. I trawl through a raft of websites, phone listings, business listings—nothing.

'Let's leave him for now and focus on the other two,' I say.

We both pour over Bill's mind map.

'What have we got?' he says.

'Just another corrupt property deal.'

'Involving Redoto.'

'Maybe he's fronting the cash.'

'Won't just be him.' Bill folds his hands over his stomach, knitting his fingers and pressing together his thumbs. 'You won't have heard the latest,' he says, and before I have a chance to interrupt he launches into a tirade about the Stratvs bodega. I've heard it all before. A local tycoon developed the site without the necessary permissions, tunnelling into the side of a volcano underneath an existing bodega. The ensuing scandal forced the bodega's closure, much to the disappointment of many a tour operator.

'That fox of a magnate now claims the place is infested with rats and he needs access for pest control. I ask you! I hope the authorities don't fall for that one. He's probably got a stash of cash hidden down there.'

'Dad.'

'Might not be all his. Maybe he needs it to pay off the big boys. You know that hotel of his, Princess Yaiza, is owned by a consortium? I bet the Italians are in on it.'

'The Italians?'

'Mafia, Paula. Our friend doesn't know who he's messing with. Or maybe he does. Those Mafioso types are just using him to serve their own agenda. Lanzarote has a big problem with international capital. Did you know private jets arrive here every day?'

'Dad.'

'Who are these people? I ask you! Holding secret meetings in luxury villas, cruising around the island in convoys of luxury cars with tinted windows. There's huge money pouring into this place and no one knows where it's coming from. And what's to be done when it all goes on behind the scenes with government approval, one way or another.'

He stops to inspect his glass a second time, and finding it empty he makes to stand.

'Dad, there's something else.'

'What is it?' he says, sitting back with a frown.

'The three paintings that were replaced have turned up in Celestino's studio.'

He doesn't reply for a few moments. I wait for the news to sink into his whisky-fogged brain.

'They must have gained access to the mill house,' I say. 'I haven't seen any sign of a forced entry.'

'Isn't the building for sale?'

'It is.'

'Then just about anyone could have got in there on the pretext of wanting to view it.'

'And switched three paintings in the attentive company of an estate agent?'

'Well someone definitely has.'

'And I don't think it's Celestino. Twice I've smelled scent when I've walked in.'

'Scent? What sort of scent?'

'Just scent.'

Bill looks at me blankly and I begin to wonder if there's anything more to be gained from the conversation.

Angela opens the door and the aroma of roasting pork follows her outside. She's carrying a colander of vegetable scraps, which she tosses into a small bin in the corner.

'I keep coming back to the anti-corruption work Celestino is involved in,' I say, persisting regardless. 'Someone wants to discredit him.'

Angela stops on her way back to the kitchen. 'You need a compelling motive,' she says. 'In all good crime stories, there's a solid reason: usually jealousy, revenge or greed.'

'Could be a personal vendetta,' Bill says.

'Or to shut someone up.'

'But we're still no closer to the truth. It's as if we have all the pieces laid out before us and we're too stupid to see it.'

'We need to confirm Redoto's surname,' Bill says.

I pull the laptop closer, aware I was going about the search the wrong way round. I enter 'Redoto Redoto' and a photo of him appears immediately. According to the websites, Redoto is one of Lanzarote's most well-known and highly respected businessmen. He has numerous business interests, including several restaurants. There are photos of him shaking hands with the mayor of Teguise. No mention of his involvement in anything untoward. Whatever Pedro knows is not in the public domain.

I'm about to show Bill the screen when he eases himself up off the lounger.

'I'm famished. Shall we eat?'

I follow him inside, his laptop in one hand, his glass in the other.

LATER, when Gloria is asleep and Bill and Angela have taken her place in front of the television, I wrap a soft blanket around my shoulders and go out to the front garden. I sit down on one of the seats outside my bedroom window and gaze at the conical shapes of the volcanoes, heavy and close set against the night sky. It's easier to gain clarity in the clear cool air, easier to ponder, in the dark.

It's as though a circle has completed, three paintings swapped for the three in the studio. The odd thing is each time I've encountered a painting Shirley has been with me. The fact nags at me and I wonder if I've been premature in my assessment of my neighbour. Although if Shirley is behind this, then her acting skills, and the elaborate nature of her methods, are nothing short of phenomenal. It isn't possible. No one would go to such lengths. Not even someone with a longstanding grudge. Shirley is nothing more than an unwitting conduit leading me to each painting. For how else would I have seen them?

There's only one person other than Shirley who could have known my movements over the last few days: Redoto's wife Maria. It was Maria who invited Shirley to Redoto's. Shirley must have told her she'd invited along her friend. For all I know, Maria might have suggested it. She was genuinely surprised and outraged at the sight of those crucifixes but maybe that was just an act. She even bought herself a necklace sporting a crucifix, as though to mock the situation. She would most likely have known about Shirley's trip to Benicod's office to collect those election leaflets. Those two are as thick as thieves. Maybe Shirley let slip she was meeting Lolita too. If Maria was using Shirley to lead me to those works, then she could have hired the man in the black sedan to ferry them about, make the switches, keep tabs on my movements. It all starts to make sense.

But why?

It has to be revenge. Maybe Shirley was right all along with her salacious remarks about Redoto having an affair. Maybe the woman in question is Lolita. I try to picture them together without success. I also have no idea how Benicod might be involved. Perhaps for some unknown reason Maria wants to humiliate them all. She must have somehow stumbled on Celestino's paintings at the studio and seen in them an opportunity. The more I think about it, the more likely it all seems. It's the best I've come up with so far and if true, it might mean that Maria knows the whereabouts of Celestino.

Maybe he's being held captive. Then again, what would be the point? Did he get in the way? Arrive unexpectedly when Mr Black Sedan came to take his artwork? Defend his paintings and suffer the consequences? So many variables. I could explode from the confusion. How do real sleuths manage to unravel crimes? If any of it is a crime. I don't even have a clear idea about that. If it is, then for all his foibles and insecurities, Richard would have better luck solving it.

Tomorrow will be Friday. Six days without Celestino and in small ways I'm becoming accustomed to his absence. The anxiety I've carried in my heart all week that he will turn up in time for the announcement of the commission winner has transmuted into a gripping impatience. With my arms folded across my belly, I gaze at the night sky, the visibility of the stars muted by the bright streetlights of the village.

20

AN OUTING TO PUERTO CALERO
AND LA QUEMADA

RICHARD NIBBLES AT A SLICE OF PUMPERNICKEL; THE FLAVOUR IS EARTHY, almost rancid, the texture like glue in his mouth. The frustration he's been feeling for days turns to fury with every swallow. He promises himself that one day soon, he'll switch to white bread. He's suffered the loaf long enough. How many years has it been? He reflects back and realises with a shock that half a century has passed since he adopted the habit, a habit born of grief and guilt over his mother's tragic suicide. No one takes their own life because their son won't eat the bread put in front of him. No one. Even if he'd gone into a full-blown tantrum. It's time to let go and move on. Time to move on from a lot of things, in fact. He needs progress and it's hard to come by. The pumpernickel, he decides with a measure of vehemence, is holding him back.

He begins to wonder if his literary efforts to set a crime novel on the island are jinxed. Yesterday, on the way to the police station to report the body, he had it in mind to make the most of the opportunity and see if he might learn a thing or two about police procedure. Instead, his efforts to make himself understood were met with incomprehension and derision. The officers at the main desk seemed determined not to take him seriously. When he produced Paula's mud map in an effort to explain the location, one of them chuckled and winked at his colleague. 'Muerta cuerpa,' Richard repeated. The men just smiled. He was on the verge of giving up when a woman entered, a friendly looking civilian in a long white dress. She stood at the other end of the counter. Richard made one last attempt to get across what he'd seen. The woman interrupted and said one word to the officers. 'Cadávar.' That was all it took to change their expressions. They snatched the mud map, took down Richard's details, and hurried him out the door, muttering something about a traductor. 'They're getting a translator,' the woman called out as he exited the building.

He leaves the remains of his pumpernickel on his plate, and goes to the fridge and pours himself a glass of tonic water. He swills his mouth then gulps down the rest, eager to banish the taste of the pumpernickel. Hoping to calm himself, he marches about the house putting things away. It's to no avail. He's still in a grump when he drives to the plaza, parking outside the supermarket at the end. It's too early for a proper drink—he isn't about to develop that bad habit —so an espresso will have to do. He's feeling soothed by the walk beneath the trees but his mood hardens the instant he sees Paula slumped at a table outside the café at the end. Part of him wants to turn back but she's facing his way and she's already seen him. As he gets closer he sees by her posture how done in she is, although with half of her face hidden behind her sunglasses, he can't be sure. Come to think of it, the poor creature is probably at the end of her wits. And in a remarkable whoosh of feeling that takes him by surprise, his grump gives way to something like pity. He approaches and hovers by her table.

'Still no sign of him?' he says gingerly.

'Nope.'

'And the lil' un'?'

'Gloria's at her grandparents.'

He rests his hands on the back of the vacant chair.

'Mind if I join you?'

'Go right ahead.' She sits up straight and pushes her empty cup to one side. 'How's your back?'

'Improving,' he lies.

A waiter comes over to take Richard's order. Richard glances at Paula but she shakes her head.

'Una café, por favor,' he says.

'With milk.'

'No, thank you.'

He watches the waiter walk away. Then he gazes at his wan companion. She seems to be looking in his direction. He wishes she would take off her sunglasses so he can see her eyes. He lowers his own gaze, suddenly lost for words. An awkward silence grows.

After what feels like a century, she breaks it with, 'Any headway with your book?'

It is the obvious question. He wishes he has a better response for her, but honesty, of a sort, prevails. 'I went to Famara but had to turn back at the landslide,' he says, trying not to inject into his voice the bitterness lurking inside. 'And when I went to the mareta you told me about at Tabayesco, I got drenched.'

'Don't blame me.'

'I wouldn't dream of it,' he says, realising as he speaks that she's probably right; he does blame her.

He goes on to describe his day, leaving out the bit when he was nearly swept away by a king wave, the bit when he found the woman's body, and the bit when he lost his footing and toppled backwards narrowly missing a boulder.

'Maybe you should give up.'

'On the idea of a Paula-inspired sleuth? Never!'

She smiles. It's a strange smile, a little mocking, and it makes him uneasy.

The waiter brings his coffee. He draws the cup and saucer closer to the edge of the table.

'But I've had to give up on that fabulous title you came up with,' he says, trying not to sound spiteful.

'A pity.'

'Yes, a pity.'

He gives his coffee a brief stir and takes a sip, for once enjoying the sharp aromatic flavour. They must have brought in new beans for he doesn't recall espresso in Haría tasting quite this good.

'There is another meaning you might think about,' she says.

She sounds serious so he says, 'Do tell.'

'La Mareta is a building in Costa Teguise. Manrique was commissioned to build it by a King Hussein of Jordan who gifted it to King Carlos of Spain. It was a royal residence for many years. The king entertained the rich and famous there, so I hear. Now it's being opened to the public.'

'Impressive. How do you know so much?'

'I married a local,' she says drily. 'And Celestino has entered a competition for a commission of artworks to be hung there.'

'I hope he gets it.'

'That's generous of you.'

'I'm thinking of you, Paula.'

She looks askance. What on earth has he said now? She really is far too touchy for his liking. What is it about him and touchy women? He seems to attract them. Not a quality he'll be giving his sleuth Paula.

'This building,' he says, persevering. 'You wouldn't care to show me where it is?'

'On a map, sure.'

'Won't you come for a drive?'

She doesn't answer.

He strokes the rim of his saucer. That bald-headed man he saw wandering about the village walks by. Richard admires the cut of his leather jacket. Despite his eagerness to walk fast, he's hampered by a gaggle of teenage girls milling about. An older woman with a little terrier looks set to catch him up. Then the woman pauses to let her dog sniff about the base of a tree trunk. The dog cocks its leg. Richard averts his gaze.

'Come on then,' Paula says unexpectedly.

He hesitates, unsure whether to believe his ears.

'Hurry up, before I change my mind.'

He downs his coffee in one gulp, scalding his mouth.

'I take it your car is at home,' she says, standing.

'It's at the end of the plaza.'

She marches off and he has to trot to catch up.

'Why the change of heart?' he says when they reach his car.

'What do you mean?'

'You've been refusing to come with me for days.'

'I'm sick to death of waiting and of searching. I have no idea how on earth you write crime, Richard. But I tell you, in real life, sleuthing is no joke.'

'Some people love it.'

'Detectives maybe, but I'm not a detective.'

He unlocks the passenger side door and holds it open. She all but falls into the seat.

'Maybe I can help you,' he says once they're on their way. 'From a crime writer's perspective, I mean.'

She makes no comment but she seems amenable so he goes on.

'In fiction, anything can happen. You're only limited by your imagination and what's plausible. Take Celestino's disappearance. A sleuth can make any number of assumptions as to his whereabouts and surmise whether he met with foul play. Then there are the suspects. I like five.'

'Five?'

'That's the standard. Each must have means, motive and opportunity of course, just like in real life. Take the plot I'd been working on in the Mareta.'

'La Mareta.'

'La Mareta then. The plot I did have in mind revolved around a body being found in a mareta. The Tabayesco one, let's say.' An image of the woman in the tunnel flashes in his mind. He dismisses it immediately and continues. 'You, the sleuth, make the discovery. But you end up following false trails. Could be that someone is planting evidence to implicate someone else. Or you and the reader are led to believe one person is the culprit when all along it's the one pointing the finger.'

'Interesting.'

'Now setting is crucial,' he says, warming to his theme. 'As you know, I've been plagued by it. The root cause of my writer's block. But now the juices are flowing and it's thanks to you. I have to say that this building of yours has me thinking I'll focus on the rich and famous. I haven't focused on that group in any of my previous works. Perhaps it's time I try.'

'Richard,' Paula cuts in. 'I forgot to mention. You can't visit La Mareta. It isn't yet open to the public. The renovations are a work in progress. All you'll see is a high wall.'

'What a shame!'

He must have sounded as crestfallen as he feels because she comes back with, 'I'm sorry. Did you think it was already open?'

'Why else would we be going there?'

'It's my fault. My mind is scrambled. I tell you what. If it's the rich and famous you're after, let's go to Puerto Calero.'

'Where's that?'

'Just past Puerto del Carmen.'

'Do you have time?'

'Sure.'

Her turnaround in attitude is remarkable. But he isn't about to challenge it. He heads straight to the Arrecife ring road and takes the dual carriageway past the airport and the tourist strips, thick with traffic in both directions. Once through the sprawling town of Tias, things quieten down and he's able to observe the desert scrub of the coastal plain, a touch green after recent rains, but nothing like the greenery of the north. In his opinion, there isn't much to commend the area to the eye.

He only has to drive another handful of kilometres before reaching the turn off for Puerto Calero, a road that arrows straight to the ocean. Five minutes and two roundabouts later and they're in the village centre. It doesn't look to be much of a place, but just as in Costa Teguise, they've gone all out on tree planting. There are chunky palms trees everywhere. Paula directs him to some angle parking near a set of boom gates, which block vehicular entry to the road beyond. He isn't sure why she's made him park there until he gets out of the car and sees the tall masts of the yachts in the marina below.

They walk past the gates, Paula explaining that the marina was built by a José Calero in the 1980s, and developed into an exclusive community of expensive hotels and large houses. There are designer boutiques and the village even has its own security. Hence the gates.

'The marina attracts the super yachts of the terribly famous,' she says.

'Like who?'

'George Michael. Leonardo DiCaprio.'

'And they are?'

'Oh, Richard. The wealthy come for the marlin and the tuna, or to sail the waters of the Atlantic just for the pleasure of it.'

They keep walking and before long the marina comes into full view. He isn't disappointed. On the clean sapphire waters, boats of all sizes bob about in the wind. A market displaying quality wares occupies a portion of the wide promenade. Set back behind thin-trunked palm trees, a row of restaurants, replete with deep verandas, looks sure to offer fine dining. The people ambling about are smart and civilised. He's immediately at home and is reminded of a time during his *Haversack Harvest* heyday, when he was invited to address a writer's festival and found himself escorted from the airport in a limousine.

They stroll along amicably, admiring the boats, although they quickly discover that neither of them know much about sailing. It's an odd thing to have in common but he's comforted by it.

On their way round the market stalls a delicious aroma of spices and roasting meats wafts by on the breeze and he's suddenly ravenous.

'Lunch?'

He escorts a surprisingly compliant Paula to the first restaurant they come to. He's about to enter when he realises she has no intention of following. Instead she stands at the entrance reading the menu on display and giving the inside a thorough if distant appraisal before wandering off to the one next door. That isn't good enough either. She leads him down to the very end of the promenade, checking each eatery in turn in an identical manner, then she ambles back, pausing again at each one, apparently dissatisfied. By the time they return to where they started, he thinks he'll die of hunger.

She leads him back in the direction of the car, mumbling something about prices, when a restaurant at the end of the marina catches his eye. Set in its own grounds, the two-storey building has all the grandeur of old colonial days, with tall sash windows and verandas on each level.

'Let's go there,' he says.

Paula stops in her tracks. She takes one quick glance at the restaurant and turns to him, an incredulous look appearing in her face. Without a word, she continues walking in the direction of his car.

'Don't be ridiculous,' Richard says, catching her up. 'We have to eat. I'll pay.'

Without waiting for her reply, he marches off, expecting she'll follow. When he reaches the entrance, he senses her behind him.

'A table for two, please,' he says to the maître d', who plucks two menus from his lectern and leads them to a table, laid out with white linen and polished cutlery.

Richard looks forward to a pleasant meal. Once seated, he drinks in the view of the marina then he scans the menu. Flicking through the pages he thinks he might order the goujons of chicken with asparagus and a nice berry jus. Hoping to consult Paula, he looks up to find she's using her menu to bury her face. She must have seen him try to gain her attention because she promptly leans forward, and moving the menu to one side, she hisses, 'Richard, this place is too expensive.'

'Nonsense,' he says, although eyeing the prices, he privately agrees.

She again shields her face with her menu. She's behaving in the most ridiculous manner and Richard worries she's bringing undue attention to their table. A couple seated nearby have already exchanged glances.

He returns to his own menu. A short while later, she moves hers to the other side and reaches forward with her free hand.

'I really think we should leave.'

There's surprising desperation in her voice.

She pauses, eyeing the back of the restaurant behind him. Then she stands up abruptly and rushes to the door. Richard shrugs apologetically at the other diners and follows her outside.

'What was that about?' he says, hurrying to her side as she heads off. 'I told you I would have paid.'

'Twenty euros for tapas!'

He opens his mouth to protest.

'Richard, I brought you to Puerto Calero to show you how the rich and famous holiday on Lanzarote for inspiration for your novel. Personally, I can't stand the place.'

Her explanation is paltry in consideration of the excessively furtive behaviour she just displayed. She reminds him of Trish. Or rather a curious inversion, for his wife would never cast aspersions on a village as fine as Puerto Calero.

'Can we go back now?'

'But I'm hungry.'

'It won't take long to drive to Haría.'

'Paula, I'm famished. I think I'll faint behind the wheel.'

She pauses.

'There's a little fishing village nearby.'

'How far is it?'

'Not far.'

She directs him back to the highway and south towards Yaiza. At the next roundabout, she instructs him to follow the sign to La Quemada, and they are heading for the coast again, leaving Richard wondering why someone hasn't thought to build a coast road to link to two locales. As he nears La Quemada he realises why. The village is small and run down and has little to commend it save for the view of the mountains and the rugged coastline to the south. Caravans litter the hillsides on the village outskirts. The buildings look basic, and the beach is strewn with large pebbles. He can't see why anyone would bother with the place. They drive through the main drag and are soon out the other side. He wants to make a U turn but she has him pull up in a car park and points out a rustic-looking restaurant, set back from the shore and probably family run.

'Why here?' he says reproachfully, eyeing the two pleasant-looking shore side eateries they just passed.

'Trust me,' she says and heads off across the street.

Before he can protest she's greeted the waitress, a plump, round-faced woman in her forties, selected a table on the patio outside, and sat down and ordered the menu of the day and a bottle of beer. Too hungry to care any longer what he eats, he orders the same.

He considers confiding his gruesome discovery at the mareta, weighing up the restraint he's been practicing in deference to her situation and not wanting to cause her alarm, against the literary value in her reaction if he does. He's about to confess when he hears a high-pitched beep and watches Paula extract her phone. She reads the message and puts her phone away without comment. It's then he notices the restaurant door opening, and out strides a middle-aged man, notable for thinning sandy hair combed over a balding pate. Richard recognises him immediately as that irritatingly sycophantic fan, Fred Spice, who accosted him one time at a music concert and has been popping up on the island ever since. He looks ludicrously garish in a red shirt and matching pants, as though he belongs in a carnival. His wife trails behind. Richard bows his head, suddenly wishing for that large menu Paula used to cover her face, but it's no use.

'I don't believe it!' And the pint-sized Brummie comes over to their table.

'Hello, Fred,' Richard says, raising a faint smile as he proffers his hand.

'Aren't you going to introduce us to your lovely lady?'

'Paula, this is Fred Spice and his wife.' He pauses, straining. Failing to recall her name, he says, 'I'm sorry.'

'Margaret.'

They exchange polite greetings. There's a brief moment of silence.

'Working on anything special?' Fred says.

'How's your holiday?' he says in reply.

'We've just done the bodega tour in the hire car.' Fred is beaming. 'Do you mind if we...?' and they both draw up chairs and sit down. 'Fascinating, you know. Got some terrific shots.' He extracts his phone and commences a long ritual of scroll and show, first to Paula, whose plastic smile never wavers, then Richard. 'Almost got a parking ticket pulling up at the camel roundabout though.' He emits a chuckle.

'The camel sculptures?' Paula says.

'On the roundabout, yes. Bloody marvellous what this island gets up to.'

'On Rosa's roundabout.'

'I don't follow.' Fred looks confused.

'That's the name of the businessman who owns a farm there,' she says. 'Going into cheese I believe.'

'You are well informed,' Richard says, genuinely impressed.

'My father mentioned it.'

'We saw it,' says Fred. 'There are goats and sheep and cows. In feedlots mind you. Quite remarkable what he's done there. No expense spared. Those milking cows have their own custom-built shade canopies. You'd need that here,' he adds, turning to his wife who bobs her head in concord.

'I'm not a fan,' Paula says ironically.

'Of Rosa? Why? He throws a lot of money at his ventures. And he's a good employer of the locals. The owner of our favourite tea rooms was telling us all about it only this morning, wasn't he Margaret. Adventurous too. If you want my opinion, I think he's picked on by those jealous of him. Always happens to us entrepreneurial types. Think of Richard Branson.'

'Must I?'

Feeling awkward Richard fumbles with his keys. He dearly wishes Paula wouldn't encourage the man. Fortunately, Spice took that last remark as a rebuke. Then the restaurant door swings open, the waitress coming with their beers.

'We better be going, Margaret. Leave these two to their lunch.'

'Enjoy the rest of your stay,' Paula says.

'We'll make sure of it.'

After they leave, Paula's phone beeps again and she attends to the message. Richard is left with his beer and his thoughts. He refuses to let Fred Spice's intrusion interfere with his flow. Uppermost in his mind is their whistle stop at Puerto Calero and he begins to conjure scenarios to link the marina to the La Mareta building in Costa Teguise. Sleuth Paula, unlike the real Paula, will have no objection to fine dining. She might meet a good-looking yachtsman. Go out on his boat. Maybe they'll head off to Cape Verde together, although that might be better in a sequel.

He drifts in his thoughts, leaving Paula to sulk behind her sunglasses. Since she's slipped back into a recalcitrant mood, when the food arrives he ignores her and occupies himself with his meal.

The entrée of sardines in a tasty vinaigrette, served with bread and dipping sauces, proves surprisingly palatable. The green sauce has certainly been made on the premises. When the main course comes he's equally pleased, the fish fillet grilled with skill, and the fries homemade. He anticipates the usual set custard that any tourist would expect to find on a Spanish special's board, but instead for dessert they both receive a scoop of light-brown ice cream in a metal dish.

He takes a mouthful of the creamy nutty dessert and is pleasantly surprised. He asks Paula if she knows what it is.

'Gofio ice cream,' she says, tucking into hers. 'Gloria's favourite.'

'I've never come across it before.'

'You have to go to the right restaurants.'

'You've been here before?'

'You can get it in Arrieta, too.'

Her phone emits several beeps. She sets down her spoon and reads through the messages.

After a lengthy silence, she takes him by surprise by saying, 'How's Trish?'

'She's fine, as far as I know.'

'Meaning?'

'I haven't spoken to her in a week. She was in a lather about the plumber turning up an hour late. She can't stand it when people are late. And she has a bee in her bonnet about my latest work. Whenever I speak to her she interrogates me then provides me with a blow by blow account of a plot of her own.' He stops talking when he realises Paula is no longer listening, her attention caught by some activity across the road.

Seeing her in such a distracted state, he again feels sorry for her. It can't be easy not knowing where your husband has got to. The waiter comes to clear their table and he asks for the bill. Paula is already standing ready to leave when he pays it.

As they head back to the car she stops as though she's spotted something of interest and her manner changes dramatically. She rushes past the car and corners the bottom of the street. Perhaps she's spotted Celestino. He hurries after her but by the time he reaches the corner she's already standing at the end of a beachfront lane, hands on hips. She has her back to him and there's no one else in sight. Before he has a chance to catch her up she's rushing back towards him.

'Come on,' she says breathlessly on her way past.

Baffled, he follows her back to the car.

Her strange mood persists all the way back to Arrecife. She spends most of the drive pulling at a loose thread on the hem of her shirtsleeve.

As they approach the ring road she says, 'Can you turn off at the next roundabout, please?'

'Where are we going?'

'I'll direct you.'

She navigates him through a quarter of Arrecife he's never had recourse to enter, a sprawling industrial area and adjoining housing estates. Construction is going on all over the place, with all the road works, cranes and dump trucks commensurate with the development. It's an area where rendered walls are left unpainted, where workers having a break sit on the pavement. He can see that the ring road cuts off from the rest of the city from this downbeat looking hinterland, this ghetto.

She has him pull up on the forecourt of the garage.

'What are we doing here?'

'Shirley's car is in for repair.'

'That woman I met the other day?'

'Yes. I've come to collect it.'

'Was that what those messages were about?'

Paula faces him abruptly. 'Thanks for lunch, Richard,' she says, cutting off further enquiry. 'I hope you now have some inspiration for your book.'

'I hope you find Celestino.'

'Thanks.'

He watches the smooth way she manoeuvres herself out of his car, swinging her legs round first, ducking as she leans forward and standing with no need of a hand on the seat's backrest for support. He feels old and stiff in comparison. All the more reason to hurry home and crack on with his new plot. Progress smells sweet, masking the unpleasantness of his present surroundings. He forgets about the real Paula and lets the sleuth Paula consume him. Feeling the intoxicating thrill of a new work at his fingertips, he drives off.

21

TABAYESCO

RICHARD'S CAR DISAPPEARS UNDER THE RING ROAD BRIDGE. I HOPE HE'LL find his way through Arrecife's complex grid of one-way streets and back north without too much hassle. I'm glad I accepted his offer to accompany him. Sighting in the Haría plaza that bald-headed man I'm sure I saw in Teguise the day I went to the timple museum in the hope of encountering Fernando, I thought it a good idea to escape watchful eyes. Richard provided a reprieve of sorts, too. It wasn't until I was in Richard's car that an opportunity to visit Puerto Calero sprang to mind. The adventure wasn't onerous, and for the most part Richard left me to my musings. Perhaps I should show him more respect. Value his insights. He might be inept in some ways, many ways, but he still has talent. It's something he said about false trails and being led astray. That just about sums up the events of the last week.

I spy Shirley's Maserati parked on the forecourt, looking a little dusty but strikingly out of place. This part of Arrecife is representative of the first square on Celestino's Lanzapoly board, the local equivalent of Old Kent Road, whereas Puerto Calero, I think with grim irony, is the equivalent of Mayfair. I scan the commercial buildings and vacant lots, the abundance of trucks and almost total lack of trees, thinking the locale reveals more of the reality of the island than the charming streetscapes of the tourist enclaves. An underbelly area maybe, yet here, like everywhere else on the island, the locals pay their taxes. And all that money is funnelled elsewhere. Not for the poor the wide tree-lined streets and the parks and the promenades. It strikes me that there are two Lanzarotes, an outer face and an inner truth. What would the likes of Fred Spice make of that?

I walk along the forecourt, passing the office entrance and on to the open roller door, removing my sunglasses on my way in. The building is cavernous and grimy. I wrinkle my nose at the smell of the petrol, oil and grease, fumes that have no doubt penetrated every atom of the place.

I notice Miguel beneath a hoist, working on the bowels of a van.

'Hola,' I say as I approach.

He glances over, surprise lighting his face. He downs his wrench and offers his hand, then emits a short laugh as he looks at the grime and the grease and pulls it back.

'Pilar told me,' he says, observing my reaction. 'Still no sign?'

'No.'

'She's tried to contact you. She's been leaving messages.'

'Tell her I'm sorry. I've been searching for him for days.'

I feel awful, knowing that Pilar and Celestino are cousins. I should have returned those calls.

He hovers, looking awkward. I've interrupted his work. It's Friday and he's probably keen to get on.

'The Maserati?'

'Follow me.'

He leads me to a side door and retrieves a set of keys hanging on the back.

'This neighbour of yours,' he says, toying with the remote control.

'What about her?'

'Que raro. I didn't know they made these cars fully automatic. Le sobra dinero pero le falta sentido común.'

I smile. It's true; Shirley does have more money than sense.

'What was wrong with it?'

'A loose connection.'

I take the keys along with the invoice and make my way to the car.

Opening the driver's side door, I wonder how I'll manage to handle the elongated foot pedals without getting into a tangle. I sit down to find the seat has been pushed right back. I adjust it forward a fraction. Then I switch on the ignition and the engine purrs to life.

Driving proves easy, although it isn't until I'm on the road heading north to Arrieta that I'm able to think back over the day.

Richard must believe I'm going slowly nuts, considering how strangely I behaved throughout our little adventure. I certainly didn't anticipate I would stumble on Redoto's other restaurant after trawling the promenade without a glimpse of him or Maria. Although for all I know they spend little time at this second restaurant. Seeing him standing at the bar gesticulating with a glass of wine in hand didn't phase me; we only met once and in all likelihood he wouldn't recognise me, considering how preoccupied he'd been. I could easily have stayed seated and let Richard pay for an expensive lunch. I did consider doing just that when Redoto's companion turned in his seat and I saw him in profile. With his shaven head and his leather jacket he was unmistakable. He appeared unmoved by Redoto's gesticulations. The man just sat there, gazing at the back-bar mirror. I kept my face buried in my menu, as ridiculous as that must have seemed, while I came to terms with his presence in the Haría plaza not two hours before. It took me a few moments to realise he was staring at the reflection of the room, possibly at me. I managed a few more discrete glimpses and when I saw the man walk off, I took my chance and forced Richard out of the restaurant.

Could he be the man in the black sedan? Instinctively I check the rear vision mirror. There's no one behind.

Seeing the turn off for Guatiza up ahead, I flick the indicator. A slip road leads down to a roundabout. I exit at the petrol station, alone on its own corner, and park on the forecourt as far from the bowsers as I can. There are few cars about. Two volcanoes rise out of the coastal plain, one close by, the other partially obscured by the embankment of the main road. No trees. The wind gusts, forcing a sideways lean on the roadside weeds, but I can't feel it buffeting the car. It's a surreal environment in the Maserati, the calm, the silence, and the smell of leather and Shirley's aromatic air freshener.

Have I been betrayed by my instincts or guided by them? Seeing that man talking to Redoto alarmed me but I have no solid justification for that alarm, just a nagging sense of danger. I was taken by surprise, that's all. That he was in Haría hours before means nothing. The island is small. People get around.

Did unexpected discoveries feature in Richard's stories? Is that allowed? Or is it only in real life that a supposed sleuth stumbles on evidence when they least expect it?

Le Quemada was an obvious antidote to Puerto Calero, a quaint, unspoilt village where the locals go to enjoy a holiday. It's a village so special to Celestino he refused to feature it on his Lanzapoly board. I couldn't have known I was leading myself straight towards the location of one of his paintings. It was only on the way back to Richard's car after lunch that I saw the formation of the slopes of Los Ajaches, just as Celestino depicted them in his rendition of a gated resort, and when I went down to the end of the beachside lane and saw the little beach all secluded on the far side of a bluff, a beach of black sand cut off from those of La Quemada at high tide, I knew I'd found the location of his solar panel crucifixes as well. It was one of his favourite places on the island. Back when I was pregnant and the romance in our relationship vibrant, he often talked of taking me there. It was as though through that painting he provided me with a secret message. Wanted me, and me alone to discover the truth. Why didn't I think to go there before?

The message is clear. If accurate, then plans are afoot to build a resort on the southern edge of La Quemada, one that cuts into the mountainside on land protected under the biosphere ruling. And whoever put those paintings in those three locations knows who is involved.

Richard mentioned that crime novels contain five suspects. Well I have four contenders: Fernando, Pedro, Maria and Celestino. Five if I include Shirley. And I still need to eliminate each one. Shirley might have a motive, however weak, but she hasn't the means or the opportunity, not least since she was out to lunch with Lolita when that third painting was planted. I can only assume Maria wants to get back at her husband whom she clearly holds in contempt. That remark of hers as she entered the restaurant in Costa Teguise—everyone loves Redoto—her sarcasm was palpable. She has the disposition and plenty of opportunity. Fernando still has the strongest motive but the loss of his driver's licence throws into doubt his capability. Pedro knows more than he's prepared to say but I can't fathom why he would set out to get his close friend into trouble. Then there's the possibility that Celestino is out there somewhere, engaged in an elaborate attempt to spotlight corruption at its inception, long before the bulldozers destroy a swathe of protected land. If all that is true, then I have to admire his resolve, even his methods, but his timing is abominable. Besides, would he really put me through all the worry for an elaborate ruse, one that so transparently implicates himself? Even if he has, it still doesn't explain those missing documents.

A blue hatchback emerges through the underpass and shoots off in the direction of Guatiza. Tabayesco is not far. If I persist, perhaps this time Pedro will divulge more. I turn on the ignition, release the handbrake and go on my way, choosing the route taken by the blue hatchback, along the old road through Guatiza and Mala.

Guatiza is home to the prickly pear, farmed for its fruit and for the cochineal beetle, the source of the much-coveted dye. On entering the village, I snatch glances at the flat fields of cactus flanking the road, interspersed with farmhouses and villas. At the town centre, with its small supermarket, bus stop and social club, a planting of mature eucalypts, many leaning heavily to the east, line the road. For a while I drive by this odd combination of cactus and eucalypt, set in the picón against the backdrop of the bare mountains, a landscape so strange I almost forget who I am. Then the village gives way to yet more fields of prickly pear, and I see the windmill of the cactus garden up ahead, and I wonder how anything bad could ever happen in such a sublime and tranquil place as this.

Back on the main road I instinctively scan behind me for a black sedan. All the cars I see in the rear vision mirror are white. When I slow at the Tabayesco T-junction the bus bays on both sides of the road are empty. I indicate left and wait, feeling comfortably safe in Shirley's car. After the vigilance I've been practicing for the last few days, I'm grateful for the break.

This time I park right outside the Ramírez house. Both cars are in the driveway. I gently reef the handbrake and unbuckle the seatbelt. With my hand poised on the door handle, the smooth metal cold on my skin, I pause to collect my thoughts. How will I handle this? I welcome the chance to talk to Kathy but not the distraction. It's Pedro I've come to see and with his wife there, probably his daughters as well, it will be all the harder to quiz him a third time. He'll most likely avoid being alone with me. I consider driving away, leaving the interview for another time. I'm not even sure what it is I want to know. Determination takes hold of my thinking and I get out of Shirley's Maserati, a car sure to draw the attention of any on-looking neighbours.

I haven't reached the front door when I hear the cries. I look up and down the street, eye the smattering of houses, someone's washing flapping in the wind. There is no one about. The door is ajar so I push it open.

I hover in the doorway. Beyond the short hallway, the contents of shelves, cupboards and drawers are strewn across the kitchen floor. There are papers and books everywhere, the girls' artworks scattered in amongst the rest. I step cautiously inside and find the girls huddled in a corner of the kitchen, cowering and crying. It looks like they've been told to stay there. And they're terrified.

I go to comfort them.

'Valeria,' I say to the eldest. 'Where's Mummy?'

'In there.' She points without looking. Her face is all blotchy, lips quivering. My heart clenches in my chest and I pause to give the child a quick hug. Then, following the whimpers, I rush through to Pedro's workshop.

The glass-panelled door is wedged open. Kathy is on her knees on the floor, bent over a prostrate Pedro, her arms folded around his chest. His legs are askew, his head slumped sideways, eyes closed. I realise with a flash of horror that in all of my supposed investigations, I wasn't taking seriously the gravity of the danger. If I had, I would have gone to the police.

I approach, giving the couple a wide berth, not wanting to startle Kathy. The moment I enter her line of sight I gently say her name.

Kathy looks up, slow recognition appearing in her face. She releases her grip and pulls away, her blouse smeared with her husband's blood. I edge closer. Blood streams from a single wound in his chest.

I look around for something to cover him and grab the cloth he uses to display his wares at the markets. I don't want to stain that fabric, it seems wrong somehow, but there's nothing else to hand and it isn't a good idea to leave him there for his wife and his children to see.

'Don't,' Kathy says, trying to stop me.

'We must. For the children.'

Kathy sinks down where she sits and howls.

'Kathy,' I say gently, 'Have you called the police?'

'No. We found him. We only just found him.'

I put a hand on her back and feel her tremble.

I have to think quickly.

The eldest child is six, old enough to call the police if she's told what to say. Name. Address. Daddy's dead. I can scarcely bring myself to say it.

I locate a phone in the mess on the kitchen bench and squat on the kitchen floor before the girls.

'Valeria. Can you make a phone call?'

The girl shrinks back.

'Valeria, listen. Mummy can't do it.'

'Why?'

'She's too upset.'

'You do it.'

I hesitate. I wish I could, but then the police would want to know who I am. Picturing the awkward questions that would ensue, I say, 'I can't. Valeria, you have to do it.' I hold out the phone. 'Please.'

Valeria steps forward, leaving her sisters huddled together, whimpering.

'I'll dial the number,' I say reassuringly. 'You ask for the police and an ambulance. And you tell them, tell them your name. Where you live. Tell them daddy's...' I pause. 'Tell them daddy's hurt.'

Valeria nods doubtfully.

'Say, Casa Ramírez, in Tabayesco. Can you say that?'

I have her repeat the message several times.

I dial emergency and hand Valeria the phone. I watch. The child does well. When the call is over, I take the phone and tell her to wait with her sisters. The police will come soon, I say.

I feel cruel walking away. I want to stay and offer comfort but something in me tells me I daren't.

I race from the house to Shirley's car, parked like a beacon. A few inquiries and the police will know I've been here. My hands shake so much I have trouble inserting the key in the driver's side door. Once seated behind the wheel I'm not sure I can drive. But I have to. Not wanting to meet a police car tearing down the road from Haría, I take the back way through the valley, forcing myself to drive slowly, keep my eyes on the tarmac, stay focussed.

I manage to navigate my way out of the village and round the two hairpins before I feel myself collapsing. The need to stop driving grows with every metre I traverse. I spot a small lay by up ahead and pull over.

The sun is low to the west, the head of the valley in shade. I wind down the window and stare and stare, letting the land and the air infuse me. Before me, the valley, with its steep sides coming to an abrupt end at the crags of the mountain is one of my most treasured places on the island. The cyclists know of its beauty, they're sent by resort operators, it's one of the designated routes of the north. And the walkers, unhampered by fences, walkers who know no limits when it comes to exploring the island. Odd thoughts to have at a time of tragedy, incongruous thoughts, yet the cyclists, the walkers, the tourists of all stripes bent on exploring this little bit of land, I suddenly hate them, blame them all for everything, for their hedonism, their selfishness, their ignorance. Tourism has the island in its grip, and someone has committed murder because of it.

If Pedro is dead does that mean Celestino is too? I went to him for answers and now everything that has happened in the last six days has been thrown into the air.

Nothing makes sense.

I've been driving around the island, following lines of inquiry, oblivious to the magnitude of what was surrounding me. Murder. It's beyond comprehension. None of my suspects fit the profile. Not even Fernando. Maria and Shirley lack the strength. It takes a special sort of human to kill. And that didn't look like a frenzied attack. It was a single stab wound executed in cold blood. Does it have anything to do with those paintings? Has the prank backfired? But how did the perpetrator get from those paintings to Pedro? Maybe it has nothing to do with the paintings. There seems only one other thing to link to his death and that is those missing documents. Documents Pedro denied having any knowledge of.

Has the killer been to the studio and the house? I think back. Which day was it I suspected a break in? Tuesday? Soon after, I knew I was being followed by a man in a black sedan. How long has that been going on? And what about that woman in the red wide-brimmed hat who almost ran me off the road? She was almost certainly the same woman who was eavesdropping on my conversation with Shirley in Pedro's café. Does she have anything to do with this? But these are all questions for the police, not me. All I know is that I have to continue as normal. Pretend nothing has happened. Deliver Shirley her car with a broad grin on my face. I turn the key in the ignition.

Easing off the handbrake, a soft squeeze of the accelerator and I'm heading up the lane, rising higher with each bend, and before long I'm rounding the curves at the valley's head. The road takes all my concentration. By the time I reach the intersection at the end of the lane I'm calmer. Keeping an ear open for sounds of sirens—I hear nothing—I drive down into Haría and park across the street from Shirley's house, bracing myself for my pretence.

Shirley opens the door in a bright red muumuu and matching headscarf. She's such a sight I almost burst out laughing.

'There's your car,' I say, gesturing behind me. 'Drives perfectly.'

I hand Shirley the keys and the paperwork.

'Excellent. Come on in.'

'I can't. Thanks all the same. I have to be at work in an hour.'

'Suit yourself.'

Her hospitality rejected, she duly closes the door in my face.

Astonished, I close my own front door behind me and exhale. My unease returns. I check the rooms in turn, sniffing now and then, eyeing books, clothes, papers, anything that could have been disturbed, but it's all exactly as I left it. I derive little comfort; unsure whether or not I'm safe.

In the kitchen, I check my phone messages. There are none. I phone my parents to let them know I'm okay.

'I'm sorry I haven't made it back today,' I tell my mother, without explanation. 'I'll be back late. I have to work.'

There's a long pause.

'Everything okay your end?'

'Everything's fine,' she says. Which means it isn't. That's the tone she uses when things are certainly not fine. I don't dare inquire.

I ring off on the pretext of running late, which is more or less the case. I take a shower, grab my waitressing uniform, and ready for work. My actions are automatic. All I can think of is I don't want to be in the house.

I walk down my street in a haze, my thoughts lingering on Kathy and the children. I can't help picturing them, the police asking questions, an ambulance pulling up. It's all so vivid in my mind, his body lying there, Kathy's bloodied shirt, the children's tears.

By the time I arrive at the plaza I'm numb. I'm barely functioning. I have to concentrate on every step I take. Trust that once inside, my automatic self will manage. I'll be okay as long as nothing exceptional happens.

The restaurant is owned by an Irish couple from Donegal. Donal is warm and friendly and generally demands little of me. Eileen can be fiery and exacting, and after last week's fiasco when that Frenchman pinched my arm and I dropped a plate of fish in his wife's lap I'm keen not to put a foot wrong. Seems a lifetime has gone by since that incident. How trivial it now seems too.

The restaurant is busy. With a smile fixed on my face, I go around, taking orders, and delivering drinks and meals. The hours slide by. Then the door opens and in walks Richard and my legs buckle and I have to cling to the counter hoping no one has noticed.

'Paula,' he says. 'What a lovely surprise.'

He's lying. He knows where I work and when. After spending the best part of the day with me, I wonder what he could possibly want from me now. I show him to a table away from the other diners. He sets down his newspaper as I hand him a menu.

'I'll have a carafe of the house white and the stew,' he says as though he already knows what he wants.

I hear but don't write it down. My gaze is fixed on the newspaper headline: La Mareta Art Prank Scandal.

'Do you mind if I...?' I don't bother to finish my sentence. I take the paper and open it out to read the front page.

The article states that someone has played a practical joke on the three judges of the La Mareta art competition, named as Lolita Pluma, Redoto Redoto and Bentor Benicod. And that artist Celestino Diaz is wanted for questioning by the police.

I grip the back of the vacant chair to steady myself.

'What's the matter, Paula?'

'This article.' I stab the paper with my finger. 'Have you read it?'

'I only just bought the paper.'

'You better take a look.'

He scans the article then looks up at me, puzzled.

'I've been trying to find out about this all week,' I say, keeping my voice low.

'Is that why you've had no time for me?'

'Partly. I started out trying to find Celestino. But these paintings kept turning up and I was occupied with trying to figure out who was behind it all.'

'Celestino?'

'I don't know. If it is him then I think he's lost the plot.'

'Celestino doesn't strike me as the sort who would ever lose the plot. I wish you'd have told me. I might have helped.'

'How could you possibly have helped?'

'I am a crime writer, Paula,' he says with a healthy dollop of pride.

'That's not the same as real life. You said so yourself.'

'Perhaps you're right.'

'I could kick myself. None of this would have come out if I'd kept my mouth shut.'

'I don't follow.'

'I was the one who stupidly told Lolita Pluma that I knew who the artist was. Up until then, no one knew. Celestino's signature was not obvious.'

I feel odd telling him, but the words spill out their own accord. His wince doesn't help. At the sight of it, I'm compelled to offer a defence.

'Lolita didn't seem to mind at the time. She took it as a joke. At least, that's what I thought. I had no idea she was one of the judges. That all of them were the judges.'

Something in my mind clicks into place. I might not have known who the judges were but Shirley would have, surely. So that's what she meant when she said I should have kept quiet.

Richard reaches for my arm. A troubled look appears in his face. He inhales as if to speak, then a group of diners leaving the restaurant catches his attention. I look around to find Eileen observing me with a mix of interest and annoyance.

'Celestino hasn't a hope of winning now,' I say quickly. 'If he's still...' I can't say it. Feeling Eileen's eyes piercing my back, I say, 'Tell me your order again, please.'

This time, I write it down.

22

TYSON

THE MORNING SUN BEAMS THROUGH THE SLATS IN THE SHUTTERS. I MUST have slept but not that well. Not after having spent the whole of Thursday in a state of high alert, anticipating the return of the henchman. I crept about all day, avoided windows, kept an ear out. Even after sunset, I listened.

I leave the comfort of the bed, straightening out the sheets and pillow. Downstairs, I assess my condition. The arm is a mess but there's nothing more I can do about it. Noting a marked improvement in the inflammation around the dog bite, I sneak out to the patio for more drago blood and return to the kitchen to redress the wound.

On my way in, the boom of a king wave sends pulses of shock through me. Still on high alert, I can't shake the fear that's enshrouded me all week. Anything is better than being in hiding, waiting like prey.

Out of the kitchen utensils, I select the knife with the longest blade and sharpen it on the steel I found in a drawer. That and the plank of wood will be my defences. I eat and rest for a few hours and set off in the afternoon.

I have to beat down my own resistance as I leave the house through the front door, shutting it behind me knowing the garage door is now locked and there's no going back.

I walk through the village of abandoned homes and holiday houses bidding a silent farewell to my lonely sanctuary.

Leaving Tenesar behind, facing the lava scree of the land, and again I hope the only vehicle I encounter is a hire car driven by an intrepid tourist. Although seeing me in my bloodied and filthy state holding my weaponry they'll no doubt drive right by.

The exposure is intense. There's nowhere to hide if anyone comes. I'd have to hurry into the lava scree and lie flat. Too late, if a car suddenly appears. I consider walking off the road but the going is too rough, even on two good legs, Besides, it would make little difference. Anyone walking can be seen for miles.

The further I go the more vulnerable I feel; my eyes are everywhere on the lookout for the dog. At least this time, I can protect myself. There's nothing I can do about the henchman. If he finds me, I'm dead.

I put one foot in front of the other and summon my courage. I'm a grown man. I should be able to take care of myself.

I'm on edge, a lone man trudging through stark, rugged wilderness. Each step brings me closer to civilisation. Each step takes me further from my sanctuary.

When I reach the first T-intersection and I know I'm halfway, I start to relax. I turn left and head to Tinajo, following the road that courses by the base of the volcano.

Soon, the lava gives way to fields of black. Passing a lonely winery, I'm convinced the dog will leap out at me any moment, but I turn right to Mancha Blanca and make it past without mishap.

The neat flat fields edged with dry stone walls, the volcanoes scattered on the horizon to the south and the west, the white cubes of the houses up ahead, it's my land and my people and right now it feels like a no-man's land, my personal battlefield and I wish I was anywhere else.

On and on I tramp, looking back every few paces, paranoia rising, pumping through my veins. I'm convinced I'm being stalked.

Worse, the path is now a steady incline all the way and I feel myself weakening with every step. I keep looking ahead, willing myself on, steeling myself not to waste my energy looking behind me.

It's only when I reach the outskirts of the village that a desperate gratitude sweeps through me and I draw comfort from the knowledge that I've almost made it.

I turn down a side street and now I can see Erik's house up ahead. I quicken my pace, eager to enter the safety of his front yard.

I'm about to pass through his front gate when I hear the snarl.

The bite that follows takes me off guard. Sharp pain shoots through me.

The dog has its jaws in the same leg, the same place, re-opening the wound through the tea-towel bandage.

I emit a loud roar and turn, gripping the plank of wood.

The dog clenches its jaw and growls, its teeth a vice bearing down on my flesh. Saliva, pink with my blood drips from the canine's mouth.

I deliver a hard blow, the nails piercing through the skin of its haunches.

I wince in response, the humane side of me not wanting to do the beast harm, but the mongrel doesn't release its grip. Instead it tugs all the harder, turning its head from side to side.

The pain is blinding. I struggle not to lose my balance. I'm convinced those vicious teeth will bite a whole chunk out of my calf.

I hit the animal again and then again and then I hear, 'Hey, Tyson. Come here!'

The dog lets go but doesn't leave my side. It crouches down, bares its teeth and growls.

I look around. I don't see the owner of that high-pitched male voice.

'You okay?' the voice says in English.

Then I see him, or at least his face, craning over the neighbouring wall.

'Is this your dog?' I growl.

'Tyson? Sure is,' he says, all upbeat. 'Best guard dog ever. You need one out here. You never know who might be lurking out there.' His gaze wanders past me at the lava fields and the volcanos.

I'm saved from wielding my knife at this idiot by Erik, who pulls up in his driveway, looking over and honking his horn.

'Would you mind removing your dog?'

'Tyson, come here.'

The dog slinks away and I head over to Erik, unloading groceries from the boot of his car.

23

A CONFESSION

I WAKE TO THE TRILL OF MY PARENT'S TELEPHONE. I'M NOT SURE I SLEPT and it certainly wasn't for long, yet the beginnings of dawn are filtering through the shutters. Gloria is lying on her side of the bed, cuddling her toy rabbit. Keen to answer the phone before it wakes her, I hurry out of bed. When I enter the living room, Bill is already halfway across the room, tying off his dressing gown. He reaches the phone first and picks up the receiver.

'Hello?'

There's a long pause. I hover anxiously. Who would call so early? The police? Knowing they'll catch me at home? But it isn't the police. I know that when a broad smile spreads across my father's face.

'It's for you.'

I take the phone from his outstretched hand and press it to my ear.

'What are you doing at your parents' place?' He sounds hurt and indignant and confused.

My world shimmies. Relief surges through me like the ocean. Bill draws up a chair for me to sit and leaves the kitchen.

'Celestino,' I whisper.

'There's no food in the house,' he says reproachfully.

'Celestino, where have you been?' My voice has grown husky.

'What do you mean? I left you a note.' Again, there's that indignant tone.

'A note?'

'On the table, right here.'

'But.'

'I've read yours,' he says bitterly.

From his tone I can tell he thinks I'm angry with him. He's jumped to a false conclusion in the face of my absence and an empty fridge. But they are hardly indications that I've walked out on my life with him. Then again, thinking of it now, the note is ambiguous: I hope you read this because it means you're back. We're staying at my parent's. Please call. No miss you or love you. Sounds like I think he's walked out on me. I didn't even sign it with a kiss. Even so, his misunderstanding seems trivial, his reaction out of proportion. I begin to feel impatient.

'Celestino,' I say, repeating his name. 'I haven't left you. I've been worried sick. You disappeared, that's all I knew. I didn't see any note. I thought you were...' I let my voice trail off.

He doesn't comment. To fill the silence I say, 'What happened?'

'After you left the studio I got a call from Erik. He was insistent I deliver his painting. I explained it all in my note.'

'There was no note.'

'There was.'

'You have to believe me.'

'And you have to believe me,' he says, the irritation rising in his voice.

'Celestino,' I say, relishing in the new significance his name has taken on, an alive and well husband who could have nothing whatsoever to do with Pedro's murder or the painting fiasco. Yet I'm simultaneously grappling with the danger he is in. The police are looking for him and the man in the black sedan is out there on the prowl.

'I'm going to take a shower,' he says. 'Are you coming home?'

'Celestino, listen to me. Something's wrong,' I say, imbuing my voice with urgency. 'Don't stay at the house.'

'I'm having a shower.'

'Have it here.'

'Paula, I'm exhausted. I've had a rough week. It'll be a lot easier if you come here. When do you think you'll be home?'

I might have known he'd be stubborn. Which leaves me no choice. I glance over at Bill to make sure he's out of earshot. He is. Lowering my voice, I say, 'Pedro's dead.'

'Say that again.'

'Pedro. He's been murdered. Just get here and I'll explain. Promise me you'll come now. It's too dangerous to stay there.'

Even as I speak I know that anyone watching my movements would know where I am, where my family is. But to kill a whole family, a British family at that, would cause a scandal of international proportions. Bumping off a local market trader would only make the local headlines and only for a day. Besides, there's safety in numbers and I've seen no black sedan in Máguez.

When at last he says, 'I'm on my way,' I feel a sudden release of tension. I hold the receiver to my ear until I hear the click. Will he leave immediately? I can only hope he does.

I'm suddenly cold in just my nightshirt. I place back the handset in its console and go to check on Gloria. She's turned onto her back, but she doesn't stir when I tiptoe into the room. I dig around in my travelling bag for some clean clothes and head to the bathroom. In five minutes, I'm dry and dressed and ready. My anticipation grows. I have to force myself not to wait outside. Bill and Angela are moving about in the kitchen. I join them, getting as far as the doorway.

Angela is cracking eggs into a bowl and issuing instructions to Bill as he sets the table. 'Use the other plates. The ones in the dresser.' He dutifully re-stacks those he laid and returns them to the cupboard. He opens the dresser, wisely choosing to seek her approval for which plates, cutlery, even napkins she deems suited to the occasion. Occasion? Angela is behaving as though Celestino's imminent arrival is a cause to celebrate, which of course it is, but not in the fashion of a breakfast party. I suppose it's the only way she knows to show how she feels. Yet from Celestino's point of view the elaborate spread might appear an unwarranted, even unwelcome surprise. But there's no altering the course of the event. They have no idea Pedro is dead and I'm not about to tell them, at least before they've eaten. Besides, the breakfast will reinforce for Celestino the Crays' concern for his absence, the strain we've endured, and thus, I hope, reinforce in his mind the veracity of my claim that I saw no note.

Gloria bounds past me into the room. Bill looks to me before bending down to greet his granddaughter. I give him a discrete shake of the head, not wanting to arouse Gloria's hopes prematurely. I remain in the doorway with an ear cocked to the road outside.

The sizzle of frying sausages, the kettle's hiss, the chatter and the clangs and I retreat to stand near the front door. The wind is strong, moaning through the gaps in the shutters. Several cars drive by. The rumble of a bus. Then I hear a car's engine fade as it approaches and the crunch of tyres on the gravel of the drive. I'm outside in an instant.

I pull the door to behind me, stopping a few paces on, confused. Celestino is easing himself out of Miguel's car, rucksack in one arm, the other arm in a sling. Where's his own car? I watch Miguel through the windscreen. He looks troubled, his face sombre. Then Celestino closes the passenger side door. The wind ruffles his hair. There's at least six days' growth on his face. He stands still, framed by the volcano behind him. As he walks forward, he limps. Miguel starts the engine, gives us both a cursory wave and reverses out of the drive.

'He's in a hurry,' Celestino says.

I wait, unsure how I feel. He drops his rucksack and holds open his one good arm. I move forward, unhurried, strangely uncertain. He seems changed and I can tell the shock of my news has affected him deeply, no doubt compounding whatever has happened to him.

I linger in his embrace. He smells strongly of stale sweat and the ocean.

'I thought I'd lost you,' he says, his breath warm in my ear.

I press against his side, feeling the curves of his flesh, absorbing his strength. I let myself meld. It's the closest we've been in months. Tears prickle as I inwardly vow not to let our togetherness slip away so easily. I love him, as strongly as I did in those first few days of our union.

Our embrace is broken by squeals and the patter of little feet, and Gloria races outside.

'Daddy! Daddy's here!'

Celestino bends down awkwardly and kisses her on both cheeks and hugs her tightly. He closes his eyes and smiles.

'Come on,' he says, standing and grabbing his rucksack. 'Daddy needs a shower.' Then, addressing me, he adds, 'There wasn't any water where I've been staying.'

I walk behind, noting he still has his rucksack, the one he takes with him everywhere.

'Will you manage?' I say, eyeing his arm.

'I'll cope.'

I take a reluctant Gloria back to the kitchen and sit her down at the table next to Bill. Leaving the head of the table free, Angela sits opposite her husband. I sit beside her. Aromatic smells of fresh herbs and spicy sausages and brewed coffee fill the room. I glance at Bill's elbow resting on yesterday's newspaper, the front-page news partially exposed. I inhale to speak but think better of it. Seeing my reaction, Bill turns the paper over. It's become one item on an unspoken agenda, and I know he's eager for an explanation. We wait for Celestino, listening to the pump, the distant sound of running water.

When Celestino appears, wet hair slicked back from a clean-shaven face, all fresh in a clean shirt and pants, he's to me trans-formed. His left arm hangs limply by his side and I can see it's causing him pain.

He exchanges greetings with Bill and then Angela, and draws up the chair at the head of the table.

'Can you help me with this?' he says, handing me the sling. I'm about to try when Angela snatches the fabric and takes over.

Resigned, I pass round the sausages and omelette and Bill pours the coffee.

For a while we're each occupied with our food. Gloria busies herself dunking sausages into the dollop of tomato sauce Bill has centred on her plate, smearing red streaks around the rim. Celestino is about to stop her when I put my hand on his arm.

'Let her be.'

He eyes me doubtfully. I'm the one usually caught up on table manners. I offer an unapologetic shrug.

He appears nonplussed, and bites into the sausage he's stabbed with his fork. 'This is delicious,' he says to Angela, gesturing at the spread and proceeding to eat with the use of one hand.

Angela thanks him, satisfied.

I drink my coffee. In between forkfuls of food, Bill makes Gloria bite sized sandwiches out of segments of omelette and thinly sliced sausage, which she promptly pops in her mouth.

Celestino reaches across the table for more bread. An onlooker might be forgiven for thinking the family are engaged in a convivial if subdued get together, but all of the adults in the room are on edge. To me it's palpable.

Bill breaks the tension when he sets down his knife and fork on his empty plate and says, 'How bad is the arm?'

'Broken.'

'You need to get to a hospital. It'll need re-setting.'

'All in good time.'

'Where have you been?' Angela asks. 'We were worried sick.'

'Holed up in a shack in Tenesar, hiding from an evil dog and the man who ran me off the road.'

'Then it was your car in Mancha Blanca? The one that burned out.' Hurt pings as I realise he chose to deliver that painting in a storm knowing full well he would be late for Gloria's party. How could he even think to do that? 'What happened?' I murmur, unable to look at him.

'The storm had just started and a vehicle, a car I think, slammed into me at an intersection. I only just got out alive. Now, tell me what's been going on here.'

It was half an answer, but I suppose it will have to do, for now. I hesitate, wondering where to start.

Seeing me waver, Bill hands Celestino his copy of the local paper. 'You might as well read this first.'

Celestino opens out the front page. He takes in the photo of his painting of the money-spewing volcano then reads the article.

'Mierda,' he says, pushing the paper away.

I'm glad Angela has yet to learn enough Spanish to understand that particular word although I'm sure she can guess.

'Who would do such a thing?' Angela says.

'More's the point, why?' says Bill.

I don't speak. Bill gives me a puzzled look and I lower my gaze, resisting the impulse to divulge all I know.

'And they're looking for me,' Celestino says. 'The police.' His face has a gloomy set to it. 'And Pedro?'

Gloria slides from her chair and tugs at Celestino's shirt. She starts to whine.

'Not now, Gloria,' he says, pulling away.

Bill inhales and makes to stand but Angela moves her chair back and extends her arm. 'Come on, Gloria. Let's go outside and look at the flowers.'

'Thanks, Mum,' I say, watching Angela and Gloria leave the room.

'Celestino, Bill doesn't know.'

Bill leans forward in his seat. 'Doesn't know what?'

There's no easy way to put it.

'Pedro's been murdered.'

'How?' says Celestino.

'Stabbed.'

'Mierda.'

'When did this happen?' Bill says.

'Yesterday. I didn't have a chance to tell you.' I feel the pressure of both men's gazes on my face. As I inhale to speak, images flash into my mind like movie stills. My bottom lip quivers as I give them voice. 'Kathy and the girls found him on the floor of his workshop. It was awful.'

'Friday afternoon?' Celestino says slowly.

'Yes.'

'Then that was why I managed to get to Erik's house.'

'I don't follow.'

'While I was trudging back from Tenesar, Pedro was being attacked.'

Bill frowns. 'I never would have thought.'

'Thought what?'

'That anyone would commit murder over an art prank. Can't people take a joke on this island.'

I'm sure he didn't mean to sound offhand but that's the way his remark comes across. Celestino ignores him and addresses me. 'How did you find out?'

'I'm not sure why I went round there.' I recall how I stopped at the Guatiza roundabout. 'I'm frightened, Celestino. Why is this happening?'

I can't catch his gaze.

'This has to do with your anti-corruption campaigns, doesn't it?' Bill says.

Celestino nods slowly.

'And all those papers that were missing from one of your files?' I add.

He frowns. 'You've been searching through my papers.'

'I had no idea what had happened to you.' I do my best not to sound shrill. 'Besides, I only looked at the folders on the floor under your desk.'

He seems content to let it go. He's silent for a short while. Then he says, 'They are not missing. I had them with me. Here,' and he leaves the room and returns with a thick sheaf of official looking documents.

'Where did you get all that?' I say, astonished.

He's reluctant to answer. He takes a gulp of his coffee and gazes out the window, stalling.

'Now is not the time for holding back,' Bill says with surprising firmness.

Without shifting his gaze, Celestino says, 'Olora. She's a legal secretary. Works for a lawyer in Arrecife.' He pauses. 'A corrupt lawyer.'

I cave in to a new sense of betrayal. 'I don't understand,' I say as lightly as I can. 'Who is this woman?'

'Relax,' Celestino says, cottoning on to my mood. 'Olora's an old school friend. She's crazy. But she's useful. She sees it as her duty to the island to work for the enemy.'

'And pass on documents.'

'We're building a case.'

Bill raises his hand. 'Don't tell me. Against Redoto Redoto.'

'How do you know?'

He stabs at the newspaper. 'Just a guess.'

A shrewd guess at that. It never occurred to me that those missing papers and the paintings were in any way connected, and I suddenly feel stupid. The whole week I've felt thrown, this way and that, by those ruddy paintings.

Celestino shifts in his seat. 'Redoto's planning to build an illegal eco-resort.'

'Near La Quemada,' I say quietly.

He looks at me strangely. 'What's going on?'

'I'll explain in a moment. I thought Pedro must have had those documents. And whoever killed him must have thought so too. Their place was trashed.'

'Who else knew about the documents?' Bill says.

'No one.'

'That isn't true,' I say. 'Olora did.'

Celestino's face remains firm. 'She'd never betray us. It's all she lives for.'

'Then someone must have found out.'

'Indeed,' Celestino says grimly.

'We need more coffee,' Bill says, getting up.

My mind whooshes back to the mill house and I'm creeping up those patio stairs, picking my way across the landing. I shiver. Celestino reaches for my hand.

'I think someone has been following me,' I say weakly. 'Someone in a black sedan. Oh, Celestino, I think I led him to Pedro's house.'

'Sh. It's not your fault. What happened?'

I describe my week in the briefest way possible. He listens attentively, his frown deepening with every sentence. 'I had no idea who was behind it,' I say, summing up with a growing knowledge that I can't avoid mentioning Shirley much longer. 'I wanted to search for you but I didn't know how, beyond asking your friends. And then when the first painting turned up...'

'On Monday, wasn't it,' Bill says, cutting in from over by the stove. The coffee percolator begins its hiss and gurgle.

I catch Celestino's gaze and hold it, determined to make him understand the facts. 'I only discovered last night that the supposed victims of this crime were the three judges for the La Mareta commission. Until then, it was a mystery.'

He takes a moment, searching my face. Then he stands and goes to the window. I wait. In the background, I hear laughter and music. Angela has switched on the television. Celestino has his back to me. I have no idea what is in his mind. He opens the door and steps outside. The wind tousles his hair. He walks over to the far end and eyes the cut and paste montage Bill made with Gloria's help. He picks it up and carries it inside.

'This shouldn't be left out. It's good. I like the face.'

'Gloria's masterpiece,' Bill says.

'Yours, Dad. Really.'

Celestino leans it against the dresser and sits back down.

'Someone is setting me up,' he says darkly.

There's nothing for it. I have to tell him the whole truth. He'll find out soon enough and it might be easier with Bill present. I brace myself and say, 'It's my fault they know those are your works too. I let it slip to Lolita Pluma.'

'Lolita Pluma! Where in god's name did you meet her?'

'In her office.'

'DRAT.' He all but spits and in a surprising show of annoyance he brings a hand down hard on the table. There's a clatter of crockery. I hope Angela didn't hear it.

'Steady on,' says Bill.

'This is crazy. I'm not understanding how you came to be in her office.'

'I was so overwhelmed,' I say defensively. 'I've been on my guard all week. Shirley told me it was a bad idea,' I blurt, wincing as I say it.

'Shirley?' Celestino swings around to face me, nearly knocking out of Bill's hand the fresh pot of coffee he's carrying to the table.

'Now take it easy, Celestino,' Bill says, putting a hand on his shoulder as he sets down the pot. 'Paula's been tearing her hair out trying to make sense of all this. Shirley was being a good neighbour, I believe.'

'A good neighbour? She can't be trusted.'

After the events of the week, I'm inclined to agree.

'It was Sunday and I'd gone to look for you,' I say by way of explanation. 'I went to Pedro's to see if he'd seen you. Shirley came in as I was leaving.'

'And offered to help.'

'She didn't. She joined me briefly and then left. The next day she called round to see if I was okay and invited me to lunch to take my mind off things.'

'Good for her,' Celestino says sarcastically.

'Celestino, this isn't helping,' Bill cautions.

'The woman is a leech.'

'Your dispute with her is a long time in the past. Ancient history. People change.'

'Not that much.'

'She's my neighbour too,' I snap. 'Or can't I have a life.'

I breathe deeply, shocked by my outburst and regretting it straight away. Yet it has an effect.

'Okay,' Celestino says, backpedalling. 'I'm sorry. This is a lot to take in.'

Bill pours the coffee. A silence descends.

After a short while I break it with, 'That's how I found the first painting.'

'Which one?'

'The solar panels on a beach.'

His smile takes me by surprise. I make a mental note to speak my mind more often. I'm about to continue when Gloria comes running in with Angela not far behind, cradling Tibbles in her arms.

'Daddy,' Gloria says and climbs onto his knee. He winces and leans around her for his coffee. I push it closer.

'We need to go back to Haría,' he says.

'It's safer here,' says Bill.

Celestino turns to his father-in-law. 'Can we leave Gloria?'

'She's been here all week. A little longer won't hurt.'

I catch the expression of forced tolerance on my mother's face as she sets down the cat. I want to tell her it won't be for long and I'm annoyed I even think I have to.

Celestino drains his cup. 'Come on,' he says, setting Gloria down.

I fetch my sunglasses, bag and keys and follow him outside, leaving Bill to explain things to his wife.

24

A MATTER OF LATITUDE

WE DRIVE IN SILENCE, EACH LOST IN OUR OWN THOUGHTS. AS WE approach Haría, I keep a lookout for a black sedan but don't see one. I turn into the lane at the back of the house and park my car in the garage. I try the door then remember it's bolted from the inside. I have to race around to enter the house from the front.

In the kitchen at last, I reach out to Celestino and say, 'I thought you were dead. Or you were tied to a chair somewhere. Or you'd gone into hiding to hatch a mad plot. I didn't know what to think. I was worried sick.'

'And I thought you'd left me. I saw the note on the table instead of mine and that's what I thought.'

'I'd never...'

I draw close. He holds me for a few moments before pulling away.

'We don't have time,' he says, and I know he's right. 'That man who killed Pedro works for Redoto. He won't rest until he finds those documents.'

'Then we shouldn't be here.'

'Agreed. Go and pack some clothes.'

The urgency in his voice jolts me and I run upstairs and throw clothes at random into a suitcase. Opening the wardrobe door, I recall his necklace that I tucked away in a shoebox. I retrieve it and slip it into my trouser pocket. I'm back downstairs in minutes, rummaging through Gloria's things, taking what I can.

I leave the case in the hallway and find Celestino in the kitchen, reading over my note. In a flash, I think to ask a question all but forgotten in the drama.

'Which way did you go when you left for Mancha Blanca?'

'Which way? Arrieta, of course.'

'And what time? Do you remember?'

'Twelve. I got the call not long after you left. I wish I'd phoned you. But I was convinced I'd be back for Gloria's party.'

Unease fills me. Shirley said one thirty. She was adamant about it. Maybe she got the time wrong. But not the direction.

He leaves the kitchen, brushing past me in the doorway and mounting the stairs in twos. He returns with a battered old address book.

'Pass me the phone.'

I hand it to him and leave him alone to make the call.

In the living room, I sit on the second-to-last tread of the stairs and extract his necklace, rolling the stone pendant between my thumb and finger, then idly inspecting the broken clasp. With my breathing shallow, I can hear him speak. Then I hear the soft clunk of the kitchen door latch and his voice fades away.

A quick rap on the front door and I all but leap out of my skin. I'm about to answer it, then hesitate, half expecting the bald-headed man in leather to be standing on the doorstep with a pointed gun. I walk lightly across the room and peer through the window. Shirley is standing out in the street looking absurd in a lemon-yellow silk jumpsuit. Anger ripples through my belly. I go to open the door, not knowing whether to step outside or usher her in.

Shirley presses forward the moment the door is ajar, so I hurry her into the living room.

'Celestino's back,' I hiss.

'That's terrific news,' Shirley says with a wary look and an overly broad grin. She stands there in the middle of the room looking like a fake sun, the yellow pendant earrings she has on resembling moons that come wildly into orbit around her face as she moves. 'You must be so relieved,' she says, her eyes darting about the room. 'Now you can get on with your lives. Has he explained why he swapped the paintings?' She said it like a quip.

'He was in Tenesar the whole time.'

'Is that right?' Shirley says casually.

How can she be so blithe? She might not have known where Celestino went but she's certainly led me astray. To what end? Perhaps she's losing her faculties. Or is she simply malicious, as Celestino would have it? I struggle to hold onto an ounce of loyalty that is vanishing rapidly in her presence.

'Shirley, this is serious. This isn't some stupid prank.'

'Of course not. You've been missing him terribly.'

'That's not the point,' I say with sudden impatience. 'Pedro's been murdered.'

'Who?'

'A friend of ours. A market trader. I found the body, or rather I found his wife and children with the body. He'd been stabbed.'

My final word slices through the atmosphere. A look of fright comes into Shirley's face. She fixes her gaze on the floor, the fake smile she wears wavering about the edges.

'When?'

'Yesterday. I swung by before delivering you your car.'

'I thought something was odd. You were in too much of a hurry. You should have told me.'

'I had to get to work. Besides, why would you need to know?'

Shirley backs away towards the door. Recalling her riffling through that pile of magazines in the kitchen, I move forward and block her exit. I look at her with intense interest. Has Shirley been snooping for those papers? She's friends with the others. How involved is she in their scheme?

'We think whoever killed Pedro thought he was behind those painting swaps,' I say, anticipating a reaction. Of all the little lies I've told this week, it's the most calculating. And it has the desired effect.

A look of alarm appears in Shirley's face. 'I never meant.'

She edges sideways, reaching behind her, feeling for the sofa. She touches the armrest, takes another step and collapses in the seat.

Upon entering the room and seeing her there, Celestino says with a snarl in his voice, 'Never meant what?'

'I only wanted to...' Her voice trails off. She buries her face in her hands. Her earrings jiggle to rest beside her thumbs.

'Celestino, get her a glass of water.' He doesn't look as though he'll move, so I add, 'Please.'

'Shirley,' I say once we're alone. 'How could you!'

'It was just a bit of fun,' she says weakly. 'Seize the day, don't they say.'

'Seize the day! I've been through hell and you just stood by and watched.'

Celestino returns and shoves a glass brimming with water at her, the contents sloshing on her jumpsuit. She takes hold of the glass in both hands and has a few sips.

The room is heavy with her silence. Celestino crosses the floor and turns his gaze to the window.

I back into the corner, as far from them both as it's possible to be. My head spins, the events of the last week demanding fresh evaluation in the light of Shirley's complicity. All of my assumptions and speculations are thrown into chaos. All I know for sure is Celestino is right about our neighbour. Worse, Shirley has played with my distress as a cat would box a toy, worrying, mauling with that strange fascination of the feline species.

We wait. Shirley just sits there.

'Explain yourself, mujer.' There's a bitter growl in his voice I have never before heard.

I watch Shirley cower, but hers is not the reaction of a woman scared. As Shirley shrinks back she sucks in her cheeks and purses her lips. Her eyes darken, and when she raises herself up her demeanour is that of a spite-filled shrew. She takes a large breath and speaks.

'Lolita told me you'd applied for the La Mareta commission,' she says, addressing Celestino. 'That you were in fact set to win.' She turns her gaze to me. Hatred burns in eyes narrowed to slits. 'And I knew what he was like. With all his anti-corruption work.'

'How did you know about that?' Celestino says, shooting me an accusatory look.

'She's a snoop,' I say, hoping that would cover it. I glare at my neighbour.

Shirley shifts to the edge of the seat, pointing a bent finger up to Celestino. 'You won't stop ruining the lives of good people like my husband, will you? How could I let you win knowing what you've been up to?' The hostility in her voice takes me by surprise.

Celestino clenches his jaw. He's demonstrating enormous restraint. I can see the instinct to lash out building in him.

Shirley crouches forward, resting her elbows on her thighs, holding onto her glass with two hands. With her face pointing forwards, she takes on the appearance of a ghoulish banana.

'I got a little drunk one night, and a film I was watching gave me an idea. I knew Gloria's birthday was coming up. It was the perfect time to take those paintings.'

'*My* paintings?'

Shirley pointedly ignores him. Directing her gaze at me, she says, 'At the time I thought any paintings would do the job. But those particular works suited perfectly. I had no idea just how perfect they would be. It was as though he'd painted those works especially for my little prank. I could hardly believe my luck.'

'How did you get in?' Celestino asks.

'She works in real estate.'

Shirley straightens to reach into her pocket, extracting the large bunch of keys she carries around with her. She emits a short and flippant laugh. 'I have access to half the island.'

I don't want to look at her but can't take my eyes off that withered, mean-looking face.

'I hardly think this is funny.'

'You don't like my little ruse?' She gives me a blank, wide-eyed stare, her face quickly contracting back to what I decide is the true Shirley.

'You must have known you'd get found out.'

'Not really. It was all so easy too. I waited for you to leave for the party.' She speaks directly to me as though Celestino isn't present. 'Then I saw him come back and head off in a rush. I thought he was running late. So I went to the studio and took the three paintings. When I came back I noticed that your front door was ajar. He mustn't have closed it.' Her face contorts as if in spasm. 'If you're looking for someone to blame, Paula, then look no further. Call me a weak-willed woman if you must but the temptation was too much.' Then she raises her eyebrows and her shoulders, her face sinking into her neck. She's astonishing to watch. Her earrings have no idea where to put themselves. She looks in that instant almost tragic. 'I couldn't resist going inside. I found the note and I took it.' The note of triumph in her voice is grating. She sits there now all puffed up. I want to throttle her.

I step forward. In a low voice I say, 'You took his note?'

'I know. I'm sorry.' Her face breaks into an apologetic smile. She looks more grotesque than ever. 'But it was enormous fun.'

'At my expense. I never thought you could be so callous.'

'Once I started, I couldn't stop. It became a mission. Redoto was easy. Like I said, I have keys to everywhere. Same with Yaiza. Although Bentor's portrait was a little hard to get out without being seen. I had to pay a friend to help me. Lolita's was even harder. I had to grease the palm of a contact at the Cabildo to remove the original painting.' She gulps her water before going on. 'I planted the original works in Celestino's studio that morning. Then my car broke down. I thought my final gambit would be scuppered. I had to get that third painting hung. So I put it in my shoulder bag and paid the same contact to hang it while we were having tea.'

As Shirley speaks, I run through my own experiences in my mind, astounded at the pretence she maintained throughout. How she kept a straight face while she speculated on possible suspects at Redoto's restaurant, all, it now transpires, for my benefit. How she managed to march right past that money-spewing volcano as though she never saw it. How she pretended to be angry when I let slip to Lolita that Celestino was the artist when she was leading me to make that divulgence all along.

'The only part of the whole escapade I couldn't be sure of was that you'd spill,' she says as though reading my mind. 'I was quite prepared to prod you if I had to, but you did it anyway.'

'I can't believe you'd go to such lengths.'

'It's just a matter of latitude.'

'You mean you wanted to see what you could get away with?'

Shirley shrugs. 'No harm done.'

'Get out!' Celestino roars.

Shirley doesn't move.

'I didn't want you to win!' she shrieks. 'You don't deserve it.'

'Just get out!'

Shirley flinches like a terrified rodent. She all but scuttles from the room. I see her out, resisting slamming the front door behind her. I never want to encounter the woman again. Impossible, considering we're neighbours. To make things worse, she committed no crime, or at least not one the police would bother with, so there'll be little comeuppance.

'Thank goodness you had the presence of mind to take those documents,' I say upon re-entering the living room.

'If I'd left them there,' Celestino says grimly, 'Pedro would be still alive.'

And what about me? I think but don't say. Was it just good luck that I wasn't home when that intruder came by? It isn't something I'm inclined to pursue. It would sound too egotistical.

'Celestino, if Shirley hadn't started her meddling, nothing would have happened to Pedro.'

'You think so? I was run off the road before Shirley started her escapades. Redoto already knew those documents were missing. Olora needs to be more careful.'

'Maybe. But Shirley had me on a wild goose chase. And part of that involved me visiting Pedro, twice. The second time I was followed. If I hadn't been bent on finding out who was behind those paintings, I would have had no reason to question him. I'd have gone to the police. And I should have gone to the police. Instead I was too scared to, in case I inadvertently caused you trouble.'

'You are not to blame, Paula. Don't ever think that you are.'

He reaches for my hand and pulls me to him. His hug is firm and warm. As he loosens his hold he says, 'That woman is poison.'

I step back, holding his gaze.

'I should never have doubted you.'

We stand together, each observing the other, and I sense something has changed. It's as though a weight we never acknowledged was there, something that obstructed our regard for each other, has suddenly vanished.

He looks down at his watch. 'We better go.'

I follow him to the kitchen where he takes hold of the luggage.

'Wait.'

He pauses and I extract the necklace. 'I found it on the floor by your easel.'

He takes it from me and examines the broken clasp. 'So that's where it fell. I was in such a hurry when I got the call from Erik, I must have snagged it on my smock when I took it off.'

He puts it in his shirt pocket and grabs the suitcase. I collect my bag and sunglasses and we go out the back door. Leaving the house, I wonder if I'll ever again feel good about being here. My domestic idyll, such as it is, defiled.

Making my way east in the direction of Arrieta, I take it steady through the village streets. Each dwelling and small field we pass puts a little more distance from the drama, although I know it isn't over yet. I'm not sure where we're heading until he tells me to veer off the main road and swing into the grounds of the police station on the outer reaches of Haría. I park in the car park at the rear.

The police station is a two-storey flat-roofed building with small windows and imposing basalt wall panels. I suppose it was designed to appear like a prison or a fort, the sort of place where people go in and never come out. Celestino unbuckles his seatbelt and reaches behind him, extracting his wallet from the front pocket of his rucksack.

'At least I'll get one thing straight. Erik wanted a receipt. I kept a copy.' He leans across and kisses my cheek. 'Back in a moment.'

Having no choice but to wait in the car guarding the suitcase and the rucksack filled with those documents, I settle back in my seat, ignoring the high wind buffeting the car.

An hour later, I see Celestino in the side mirror, limping hurriedly towards the car. I hold my breath as he opens the passenger side door. Taking in the triumphant look on his face, I exhale.

'Took some explaining,' he says as I back out of the car park. 'But the arm and the dog bite persuaded them.'

'Dog bite!'

'Never mind. They're going around to talk to Shirley now.'

For the first time in a week I feel confident some sort of justice will be served.

'Where to?'

'Tahiche.'

I make a right at the main road and head down to Arrieta, taking the sweeping hairpin at the crest of the saddle with measured care. I wait until we've descended the saddle before asking him exactly where we're going.

'To visit a friend.' The tone in his voice invites no further inquiry so I decide not to pursue it. I can tell he's determined by the set of his jaw.

Ten minutes later he tells me to stop outside a house in Tahiche. It's a two-storey cuboid affair in a street of similar style houses: modern, and fronted by white-rendered walls containing gardens abundant with an array of hardy shrubs and trees in amongst the usual cacti and palms. Celestino grabs his rucksack. This time I go with him.

A bearded man in his fifties opens the door before we knock and welcomes us inside.

'Can I get you something?' he says. 'Café? Beer?'

'No, thank you.' Celestino makes a gesture. 'Javier, mi marida, Paula.'

I remove my sunglasses and we shake hands. I suppose being described as his wife means I have a right to be here.

Celestino follows Javier to a cool, dimly lit living room and they sit together on a leather lounge. I sit in the straight-backed chair I noticed on my way in.

The two men speak rapidly in Spanish, too fast for me to understand. But I glean enough to realise the man, Javier, is a journalist. Celestino hands him the rucksack. The man goes to open it but Celestino waves him not to bother.

'Keep it,' he says in English.

It's as though he's decided to relinquish his anti-corruption campaigns altogether and I'm strangely saddened by the thought. Still, I'm comforted in the knowledge that our lives will be much calmer.

The two men stand and hug and Javier shows us to the door.

'He'll break the story as soon as he can,' Celestino says as we drive away. 'There should be enough material to bring a case against Redoto.'

'And Benicod?'

'I don't know. Olora had nothing on him, nothing concrete. For all I know Redoto's bought half the municipal staff of Yaiza. Could be anyone.'

'It's a matter for the police then.'

'And others. Javier has contacts in the government. They have the ear of a judge.'

'At least this time it will get stopped before it's built.'

'That's why I won't give up,' he says, and I smile inwardly. Any hopes I might have held of a quieter safer life are dashed before they've had a chance to take root, but I no longer want him to stop. More, I want to help him, take an active part in his campaigns. I can't take the place of Pedro but perhaps I can do something else, something to inform the Brits maybe. I realise I haven't, up until now, fully stepped into Celestino's life. It takes courage to do the sort of anti-corruption work that he's dedicated his life to. I once heard that back when he began, anyone who denounced corruption would lose their jobs, receive death threats; their children were attacked, their lives and the lives of their families rendered a living hell. The people have been conditioned through violence and persecution into acquiescence, too scared to rock the boat. Well, I'll risk it. I'll rock a boat or two.

'Won't Javier's life be in danger too?' I say, my thinking returning to the present.

'He's flying to Las Palmas and then on to Madrid.'

'What about us?'

'Once the media get hold of the story, Redoto won't be able to do a thing. The police will have to get involved.'

We drive back to Máguez, agreeing that the best course of action will be to all stay together in the one house, and wait.

25

JUSTICE

'CELESTINO, LOOK AT THIS!'

Paula nearly collides with her father in the doorway. He's clutching his laptop. She moves aside and follows him to the kitchen.

'You all need to see this,' he says.

Paula and Angela crowd round.

'What is it?' I say, taking up a chair.

'There's been another murder.'

Paula reads out the headline. 'Woman's body found by British author'. The story goes on to describe how author Richard Parry discovered the body in the galeria el chafaril, a tunnel beside the mareta in the valle de Temisa. The woman is thought to have been stabbed to death early on Thursday afternoon. The article doesn't disclose her name.

'Where's that?' Angela asks.

'On the way to Tabayesco.'

Bill shunts his laptop across the table. I read the article, disbelief giving way to anguish.

'Olora.'

'The legal secretary?' Paula murmurs. 'How do you know it's her?'

'Scroll down.'

There's a photo of the scene. And the reporter has interviewed Richard, who said he found a large red hat on the ground nearby.

'Could be anyone's,' Paula says doubtfully.

'It's hers.'

CELESTINO GOES TO THE WINDOW. I observe him in three-quarter profile, the lips pressed together, the knitted brow, a single tear making its way down his cheek. A burst of sunshine streams through the skylight and brightens the living room. As if on cue, Gloria appears and runs straight to her father. He picks her up and takes her outside.

I leave them alone and help my parents as they busy about with cereal bowls and toast. The atmosphere is subdued. When the table is laid, Angela calls her son-in-law and her granddaughter back inside.

It's an altogether different breakfast to Saturday's and Celestino can't bring himself to engage with the others.

We gather the last of our things and this time take Gloria with us. The parting feels strange. Watching my parents standing at the door waving us off underscores the drama we've been through. I drive back to Haría, this time parking in the street, boxing in the Maserati.

Once inside the house, Gloria runs to her bedroom. I drop my travelling bag at the foot of the stairs. Celestino sets down the suitcase beside it. Our luggage seems to fill the room.

I follow Celestino to the kitchen. The message light is blinking. We exchange glances.

I press 'speakerphone' and then 'play' and hear a woman's voice I recognise straight away as Lolita Pluma's. There's an obsequious tone to it. She gives a lengthy preamble, which at first makes no sense. Then she offers her congratulations. Celestino has won the commission. A letter of confirmation is in the post. Would he please make himself available for media appearances and attend the DRAT celebratory dinner next week?

The look of incredulity on Celestino's face makes me laugh.

'Congratulations!' I reach for him and plant a warm kiss on his lips.

'Now we can eat,' he says. 'And you can stop working at that restaurant.'

'When the money comes through.' And not a second later.

I picture Lolita making that call while the police hover waiting to take her in for questioning. Suddenly puzzled, I frown and say, 'Lolita Pluma. Why would she be part of that eco-resort scam?'

'She isn't. At least, not as far as I know. Why would she be? She might have known about it, who can say?'

My image of a handcuffed Lolita vanishes. In its place comes the realisation that in all likelihood Shirley had no idea what Redoto was up to after all.

'YOU HAVEN'T TOLD me properly about your week in hell,' Paula says, recovering her composure with a few sharp sniffs.

I sit down at the table. She's right. I owe her an account.

'Café?' she says tentatively.

'Vale.'

I watch as she sets about unscrewing the percolator and rinsing cups.

The room fills with the sound of squeaks and chinks, then the aroma of fresh coffee. It isn't until the coffee is poured and she's taken up the chair beside me that I speak, offering up short sentences, giving the barest account of the accident, Tenesar, the dog, and the man who came looking for me. And of my trek back to Mancha Blanca, the night I spent at Erik's. How I left Gloria's birthday present there by mistake.

'Will you drive me to the hospital this afternoon?'

'Sure, but first, let's go down to the plaza and grab some lunch. We can't celebrate here. There's no food.'

She laughs and her laugh rings in my ears. Paula is the first out the door.

We are just like any other family strolling down the narrow village streets, enjoying the sunshine, anticipating a satisfying lunch. But we are larger than ordinary somehow.

. . .

ANTONIO CRIES out when he sees Celestino. His daughter Carmen comes rushing outside too. There are hugs all round. It's all very public as though the whole village is watching. Perhaps it is. Between us we launch into partial explanations and a narrative quickly grows in the place of the truth, a car accident, a misplaced note, and a rough week in Tenesar with a dog on the prowl take up the centre of it all.

Antonio steers us to a free table beneath the big old laurel tree. He walks away and returns with beers and lemonade. Before long there is tapas and fish and chips to share.

We are settling into our feast when Richard appears, walking briskly down the plaza. He's in a chipper mood, but when he notices us he comes to an abrupt stop.

Realising more than a cheery wave is called for, I stand and remove my sunglasses and issue him a warm smile.

Reassured, if a little tentative, he comes over.

'Delighted to have you back, Celestino,' he says stiffly.

Celestino looks up and offers him a cordial smile. 'It's good to be here.'

Richard looks poised to make his excuses and walk away.

Then Celestino shifts round in his seat in a welcoming gesture. 'Pull up a chair,' he says.

As Richard slowly sits down, Celestino raises his good arm to Antonio and asks for another plate.

'I've already eaten.'

'Pumpernickel?'

'Actually, I've given it up,' he says with certain pride.

A waiter comes with Richard's plate and we all make room for it.

'And another beer,' Celestino says.

I think Richard might try to refuse that as well, but instead, as the waiter walks away he says, 'The lil' un' has grown.'

'Gloria,' Celestino says, reaching out to tousle his daughter's wild black hair.

'Yes, Richard. Gloria. You never say her name.'

'I must remember to do so in future.'

'Promise?'

Richard doesn't respond. 'She's making quite a mess there,' he says. We all observe the array of tapas fringing her plate; chick peas, strips of peppers and fish all arranged in a pattern around a piece of fish. 'She's an artist in the making,' he adds.

'I suppose she is,' I remark, seeing for the first time in my daughter's culinary habits a propensity for art. I make a mental note not to slip back into reprimanding her.

The waiter comes with Richard's beer. He reaches for it and says, 'I hear congratulations are in order.'

So much has happened that at first I'm not sure what he means.

'Thank you,' is all Celestino can bring himself say.

I go on to provide Richard with the briefest possible synopsis of the events of the week, which still proves complex and convoluted, watching my food go cold as I speak. He listens attentively and without interruption. When I stop speaking, a faraway look appears in his face. Celestino eyes him and frowns.

'What is it?'

'Trish.'

'Trish?'

'She's been inventing plots. Her latest involved a painting swap. Sounds awfully similar to what happened to you two, Paula. In hers, the blaggards in question sent their henchman to follow the hapless sleuth. Only, this man noticed another person hanging around, a person acting most suspiciously, an employee, it transpires, turned informant. Not the sort of thing that would happen in real life, but plausible nonetheless.' Satisfied he's established something, for himself at least, he takes a draught of his beer and sits back in his seat.

My mind is flooded with images of red wide-brimmed hats. I don't have a chance to ponder the implications before he goes on.

'And it's given me an idea.'

'Another one?'

'You, the paintings, Trish, the whole kit and caboodle.' His gaze slides from me to Celestino with a measure of uncertainty.

'Your Shirley,' he says slowly.

'She's not our Shirley,' Celestino is quick to retort.

He ignores the remark and Celestino along with it. 'Paula,' he says, looking contrite. 'I'm going to have to replace you. I'm dreadfully sorry and I hope you don't mind. You see; it's just occurred to me that this Shirley woman would make an excellent sleuth. No offence, but she has so much dimension.'

'Dimension.'

'Eccentricity, pizzazz and a devilish attitude.'

'Qué es un hijo de puta.'

I suppress the mirth building inside my chest. A spritely breeze rustles the leaves of the laurel trees. Patches of high cloud race by. Richard swigs his beer then pushes back in his seat.

'It's been lovely, thank you, but I better get on.'

'I'm not offended, Richard,' I say.

'Honestly?'

'Not in the slightest.'

I watch him head off wondering why he chose not to mention his discovery of the body. I can understand Celestino not wanting to mention it, but surely a crime writer would relish in the telling, yet all he's told me about that visit was that he got wet in the rain. It's strange and I make a mental note to ask him next time I see him.

I turn back and observe my little family as though seeing them for the first time. Gloria clasping her lemonade with both hands. Celestino watching on, ready to help her set the glass back down without mishap. Celestino, my talented artist husband, a one-man champion of integrity.

'You created those paintings on purpose,' I say with sudden interest. 'What did you plan to do with them?'

'At the time, nothing. It was a way of letting off steam. But I did want to create a visual documentation of what was going on. I thought I might use them in an exhibition.'

Instead, his creativity, a pure act of good intention in itself, precipitated a cataclysm. That is the way of things; you could never fully know how something would be used, after it is made.

ACKNOWLEDGMENTS

This story was written with the support and encouragement of many who saw value in the work. I am indebted to Patricia Leslie, Michelle Flammell, James Synot, Jasmina Brankovich and Elizabeth Blackthorn for all of their kind words and suggestions. I would like to express my special gratitude to Christy Byrnes for her valuable feedback on an early version of the manuscript.

A very special mention to Vivienne Fisher, who was a tremendous support to me throughout the composition of this book. I did name a character after her, but when this character took on a life of her own, one far removed from the adorable Vivienne I had come to know and cherish, I felt uncomfortable, so I changed my character's name to Shirley. I am saddened that Vivienne never had the chance to read this novel. Her love of Lanzarote matches my own and I will never think of the island again without recalling her.

I travelled to Lanzarote in 2016 to research the story. I am deeply grateful to all who offered me their time freely while I was there. Special thanks to Jerry Lefever for showing me sites of interest and sharing his view of Lanzarote's recent history, and to Nuria Roach Casares and all at The Mix radio show for their ongoing support. My gratitude to Angela Webster for translating in a meeting and providing me with valuable research material, and to the César Manrique Foundation for providing me with an account of their own fight against corruption. I am indebted to Ezequiel Navio Vasseur for his structural overview of Lanzarote's political scene and for his account of the struggle to protect the island's fragile environment. I am grateful to Bettina Bork of Arte de Obra, who gave up her time to talk about her experiences on the island, to No Oil Canarias, whose campaign against the oil giants is ongoing, and to others whom I shall not name, who gave up their time to talk with me about their knowledge of Lanzarote's corruption scandals.

I could not have written this story without Michelle Lovi, publisher at Odyssey Books, who travelled with me to Lanzarote and drove me to all of my meetings. Her willingness to participate in the adventure and accommodate my itinerary is above and beyond anything an author can hope to expect from their publisher. I am eternally grateful.

My sincere thanks to Miika Hannila and the team at Next Chapter publishing for having faith in my writing and nurturing its progress through to publication.

AUTHOR'S NOTE

In researching the background for this novel, I consulted numerous newspaper articles, too many to mention. Anyone wanting a fuller account of Lanzarote's corruption story would do well to read this paper. "Can't control/won't control: opportunities and deterrents for local urban corruption in Lanzarote" García-Quesada, M., Jiménez, F. & Villoria, M. Crime Law Soc Change (2015) 63: 1 https://doi.org/10.1007/s10611-014-9549-z

It is the task of the author of a work of fiction to entertain, not educate. I took what I had learned and created a fanciful and completely fictitious story. No one appearing in *A Matter of Latitude* is based on or even alludes to a real figure, and I have no knowledge of any corruption scandal similar to the one I have portrayed.

I have attempted to offer a fair and balanced portrait of corruption on Lanzarote within the very tight confines of fiction, offering a variety of perspectives. The views of the characters are not my own. I have tried to avoid naming individuals known publicly to have been involved in corruption scandals in deference to those individuals and their families. The truth is always fuzzy and complex. I have adopted a measured and reasonable approach in certain passages of exposition, mindful that I am not judge and jury. There is much that can be said, and there is much that I would have liked to include, but which the story did not permit. For a comprehensive understanding of the facts, the reader must always consult works of non-fiction. I offer this story with all sincerity as a contribution to raising awareness of the vital issue of corruption and its effects on the environment, an issue that affects not just Lanzarote, but the whole world.

CLARISSA'S WARNING

CANARY ISLANDS MYSTERIES BOOK 2

For J.F. Olivares

1

BUYING A DREAM

EVERYONE HAS THEIR PRICE. IT IS MY FATHER'S FAVOURITE SAYING. HE IS a used-car salesman turned property developer. I am neither of those things. But when I read in a local newspaper that the owner of the house of my dreams was intent on demolition I took swift action. I tossed sanity into the Jetstream and, in a single if complicated move, threw my all into saving that house.

In truth, not a house, it was nothing that could be called a home, the building – not much more than sections of stone wall and roof – holding on through its own tenacity, little left to brace against a relentless wind. For the ruin was located not among the folds of green in my home county of Essex, nor in any other quarter of bucolic pasture, but on a flat and dusty plain in desert dry Fuerteventura, an island I had been visiting each year for my annual holiday.

I wasn't entirely devoid of common sense. My ruin was situated in the inland town of Tiscamanita, a safe distance from beach-crazed revellers yet not so far off the beaten track as to be isolated and remote. The island was desolate enough without secreting myself away in one of its many barren and empty valleys. In a well-established village, I would have everything I required for a comfortable life, secure in the knowledge that there were others nearby if I needed them. As a single woman used to living in a bustling English town, one had to think of these things.

The troubles began the moment I decided to act. The former owner of my beloved ruin, the gentleman poised with his wrecking ball, had not been difficult to identify. His name was mentioned in the same newspaper article, the Fuerteventura journalist at pains to detail some of the recent ownership history. The various genealogical details meant nothing to me. I could read Spanish well enough—I've been learning for years—but I had no understanding of Spanish nobility, and I lacked a deep knowledge of Fuerteventura's colonial history. In the age of information technology, when business deals could be conducted remotely with a few mouse clicks and the odd signature here and there, nothing might have been simpler than purchasing a property overseas. There were websites talking prospective buyers through all the legal requirements, pitfalls and traps. Were it not for the fact that the possessor of my coveted dream home resided somewhere in mainland Spain and had he not been bent on using the property for whatever development aspirations he may have held dear, the purchase would have sailed through to completion in a few months.

The first complication was locating the owner's address. Entering the name in a few online searches revealed his business interests. With those scrawled in my notebook, I hired a lawyer to make the initial contact and establish my credentials: I, Claire Bennett of Colchester, a humble bank teller by profession until my fortunes turned on the numbers of a lottery ticket and I found myself astonishingly well-off.

Possessing all that wealth had taken possession of me, given me the will to leap, to take a chance. The greater part of me remained shocked I had the courage to go through with it.

Much to my chagrin, the owner, Señor Mateo Cejas, responded to my inquiry with a cool and firm refusal. The ruin was not for sale. Well, I knew that. The local government, in a fit of guilt over letting so many old buildings fall into ruin, had deemed the dwelling of special interest and already made an offer and it was declined. A full account of the frustrations of various officials and the local community were felt by the writer of the newspaper article who shared their view.

I suspected Señor Cejas opposed the building's transformation into yet another island museum, the restoration of a traditional windmill in Tiscamanita already serving the purpose. Or perhaps he had in mind the construction of holiday lets on the substantial parcel of land. It was the sort of plan my father, Herb Bennett of Bennett and Vine, would have had in mind. Demolish and rebuild. Sell at a premium to investors keen to rent out to holidaymakers; developers couldn't lose. They were an inexorable breed, prepared to play a long game. No doubt Cejas would have waited until the walls collapsed to rubble then the government would have given in and granted a demolition permit. That Cejas may have had a deeper, more complex reason for wanting to erase the structure didn't enter my mind.

My father tried to talk me out of my plans. He took to phoning me in the evenings when he knew I was watching Kevin McCloud, and he would go on and on about how there were a million better uses for my winnings. I would hold the phone away from my ear and let him rant until he ran out of advice.

I was immutable. I had passed by that ruin numerous times on my drives down the island's backroads and grown fascinated by it. I stopped one time and took a photo. Over the years, I had taken an abundance of photos of the ruins littering the island, but I had that one blown up and framed and it hung above the fireplace in my living room. I would stare at it every day, the image becoming for me a focus of wishful thinking, fervent at times, a potent symbol of longing for a different sort of life to the one I was stuck with. Until I won the lottery, that was the nature of my desire.

One very large deposit into my bank account and I was no longer stuck where I was. I had freedom and that freedom entered my life like a lightning bolt, destabilising me to my core. Suddenly, I couldn't imagine doing anything else with my life. Out of all the old dwellings falling to ruins on the island—a combination of lack of interest, strict restoration regulations, apathy and the ease of building with concrete blocks—I had chosen to save that one, like a child with her nose pressed to a sweet-shop cabinet, her pointy finger tapping the glass.

The stubborn Señor Cejas had not come across the likes of Claire Bennett, a woman fixated on a dream, a woman prepared to offer far in excess of the already overly inflated amount offered by the government. Initially, I offered the four hundred thousand Euros they had. It was declined. Four-fifty. Declined. I upped the offer in increments of fifty thousand, the tone of my lawyer's letters to Cejas increasing in indignation, his letters to me in exasperation, until at last we agreed on a sum. Six hundred thousand Euros and I had my grand design.

By the time I received word my offer had been accepted, I had already relinquished my position as clerk at the bank. I resigned the moment I knew I was rich and would never have to work again if I was sensible with my money. It was with considerable relief that I walked out of my branch for the last time, saying goodbye to the only career I had ever known.

For twenty years I had endured that cloistered environment, dealing on a daily basis with deposits and withdrawals, mortgages and loans, and with those incapable of managing their finances, one way or another. I preferred the pre-Internet days when we had to write in passbooks. Even in 2018, there was always one for whom internet banking was unfathomable. Often, they were old, but not always. Or there were those who used telephone banking but couldn't recall their customer reference number or pin, or the answers to any of the security questions they themselves had created, or even the balance in any of their accounts. They would come into the branch to get their account reinstated after it had been suspended. They would rant about that little injustice as though the bank had forced their hands beneath the teller screen and guillotined their fingertips, then they would go on to take an age making a number of simple transactions and I would imagine a steel plate descending with force to cut them off from breathing their disgusting germs through the Perspex.

When that type of customer surveyed the bank staff, they inevitably chose me, kindly Claire, to dump a potent mix of outrage and desperation on, and I would look at them coolly and explain that internet banking was really very easy and it would put them in control of their own banking and they wouldn't need to come out in all weathers and wait in a long queue to do what would take all of two minutes seated comfortably in the warm and the dry with a nice mug of cocoa. Many a time a disgruntled customer argued they were keeping me in a job and I responded inwardly with, I wish you wouldn't, because I didn't want the job. In fact, I loathed it. I had applied twenty years before only because back then it was the late 1990s and Blair was in power after years of economic recession and jobs were hard to come by and finance seemed to be the new god and I, like many others, believed things would only get better. I was fresh out of school and banking was the place to be. But not in Colchester.

Banking was never my dream. The world of finance was all about numbers, whereas I had achieved a good grade in A level English, which I found fascinating, History, which I adored, and General Studies, the latter due to my quiz loving father insisting I went with him every Wednesday to the local pub's trivia night. He would sink a couple of pints of Directors and I would sit on a lemonade and a packet of pork scratchings and I acquired a sizeable array of seemingly irrelevant facts. Highly relevant, they turned out to be, when it came to sitting the General Studies A level, a course cleverly designed to weed out the riff raff from achieving enough high scoring A levels for entry into the most prestigious universities.

When it came time for me to choose a career, my dad shunned all notions of university, especially in the humanities and the arts, describing those courses as dead ends.

There was no mother to argue my case. She passed away in the summer of 1985, when I was seven. I did what any obedient daughter would do in the absence of alternatives, I secured a job at the local bank. On my last day, I handed in my uniforms and went home via the Indian takeaway and the off licence to celebrate.

My house, a humble abode set halfway down a row of drab and poky terraced houses on Lucas Road, sold in a fortnight. As the settlement of the sale and the purchase went through I felt as though I had rubbed Aladdin's lamp and was about to be transported to paradise on a magic carpet.

The only other person with a vested interest in my life is Aunt Clarissa. She is my mother, Ingrid's older sister, a retired psychologist with a predilection for all things occult. She played a vital role in my upbringing after Ingrid died. A robust, no-nonsense woman with an affection for deep colours and aromatic smells, Aunt Clarissa exposed me over the years to Ouija, tarot, palmistry, enneagrams and her mainstay, astrology. I took little interest in any of it, for the occult seemed to me to be built up on spurious associations and make believe. Yet I could not deny that through it, my aunt was uncannily accurate when it came to seeing beneath the surface of people to their deeper, darker motives. I ascribed this talent to her training as a psychologist, but she insisted her perceptions were entirely the result of the occult. Not being one to argue, I took a passive, accepting role in her company, humouring her for the sake of our relationship. When I let her know I had bought a property on Fuerteventura and was about to move to the island, she invited herself over for morning coffee.

I was getting a tray of white chocolate and raspberry muffins out of the oven when the doorbell rang.

'Smells marvellous,' she said as we dodged by packing boxes on our way through to the kitchen, where she perched on a stool.

She was a stout and big-boned woman with thick and wiry hair framing a keen yet welcoming face. Those perspicacious eyes of hers followed me about the room as I attended to the muffins. Then she rummaged in her bag and extracted a sheet of paper protected by a plastic sleeve.

Without wasting much time on pleasantries, she said she had punched my birth details into an online astrology site that calculated relocation charts. The idea being, she said, that the angles of a birth chart can be adjusted to the new location. Indeed, the whole of a person's natal chart can be superimposed on the globe in a series of straight and wavy lines, providing an enormous source of fun and intrigue for astrologers and holidaymakers alike. Clarissa had explained it to me once before. She was a big fan. I was sceptical.

As I poured the coffee and put muffins on plates, Clarissa said, 'I am not sure how to tell you this, but I thought I'd better warn you. In fact, seeing this,' she pointed at my relocated chart, 'I wish you'd told me before you went ahead and bought the place. Has it all gone through?'

'It has.'

'You wouldn't consider selling? No, I suppose not. Silly question.'

Repressing my irritation, I stared at her inquiringly.

'Well, you see, the thing is,' and she pointed at the lines and glyphs, 'relocating to Fuerteventura puts Neptune on your Nadir.'

'And?'

'Well, Neptune also squares your relocated Ascendant. As if that were not caution enough, you have Moon and Saturn both in the twelfth house, the house of sorrows.'

'I meant, what does it all *mean*?'

She lifted her gaze to the ceiling. 'Typical Leo Moon.'

'I'm sorry I have a Leo Moon. Please, tell me.'

'The Neptune placement will leave you open to deception on the home front, at the very least. It really is one of the most difficult placements when it comes to buying a home. Unless you are opening a spiritual retreat, I suppose.'

'Do you really see me doing that?'

'Hardly, but anything is possible.' A glazed look appeared in her face as she went on. 'You'll be open to psychic impressions. With your Moon in the twelfth, this tendency is strengthened. And with Saturn there as well, you'll endure much isolation, aloneness, and you will be exposed to much fear. Beware of hidden enemies.'

I didn't reply. I maintained a bland face as I held back a burst of cynical laughter. Seeing my ears were closed, she didn't pursue it.

As we ate and drank she brought me up to date on her own adventures and little bits of gossip about her friends.

When the muffins were reduced to a few crumbs on our plates, she returned to the topic of my chart. 'I'm sorry to be the harbinger of doom. It might not turn out that bad. Especially if you're careful. On the positive side, you'll learn a lot.'

'Well, that's a comfort.'

'Just be aware that people are not always as they seem.'

'I wasn't born yesterday.'

'Oh, now you're offended.'

I fiddled with my cup. 'I know you mean well, but it's just that everyone is against me. Even the owner, Cejas.'

'What did he say?'

'First he wouldn't sell until I upped the price.' I left out by how much. 'Then he wrote to me personally advising me to do what he had planned and demolish.'

'I wonder why,' she said slowly.

'To build holiday lets, I expect.'

I went and put my empty plate on the draining board and stood with my back to the room to finish my coffee. I felt defensive, ganged up on, my grand design scorned. It was isolating; when I really needed support, none was forthcoming. Seeing my face when I turned, Clarissa slid off her stool and gave me a hug.

'Astrology is not the be all and end all. There really is no telling how it will all unfold. There are always other factors. Be positive. You are following your dream. Not many get a chance to do that.'

Buoyed by her sympathy, I described my renovation plans. I soon became animated and enthusiastic, and she said she could see I was acting on a noble impulse.

'I'll visit when it's done.'

'Not before?'

'I cannot abide building sites. Too unsettling.'

After she left, I continued with the packing and reflected back over her words. Even if she had warned me in time, I would never have put off a major life decision on the basis of an astrological coincidence. Besides, I was acting on my deep appreciation of the island and my desire to save one of its grand houses from complete ruin. And I wouldn't be upping and moving were it not for the lottery win. I didn't dare ask Clarissa the astrological significance of that stroke of luck. I didn't want to know what the stars had to say. My bank balance said enough.

2

ARRIVAL

ONE EARLY MORNING IN MARCH, I WAS SEATED IN THE DEPARTURE lounge at Gatwick airport, all smug and pleased to be leaving the murk that was British weather. Dressed as though for an appointment in plain trousers and a loose-fitting blouse, I was squashed beside a rotund man garbed in shorts and a large white T-shirt, and a fake-tanned and wiry woman smelling strongly of coconut oil. She was decked out in a tight skirt barely reaching her mid-thigh and a match-ing, bosom-revealing top. Both characters were stark reminders of the holiday destination I was heading for. They seemed to know each other, too, and held a conversation across me. I leaned back further in my seat to let them have it, each informing the other of their preferred island locale, the man heading for Gran Tarajal, the woman Morro Jable – both seaside towns in the south. They were the sorts of holidaymakers I had never minded being amongst on previous flights. This time, I felt set apart. With my newly acquired wealth, I had no need to travel economy, but the only upmarket flights to Fuerteventura involved changing planes in Madrid. Still, considering the conditions the budget airlines forced passengers to endure, that hassle might be worth it.

The departure lounge, an enclosure with a deceptively large feel upon first entry, had become claustrophobic as passengers filled all the available seating and crowded around the perimeter of the space. The door to the walkway was closed and there was a marked absence of staff. People were getting restless. The woman next to me on my right was fidgety and the armpits of the man on my left, if my olfactory system was serving me well, had started to hum.

The room breathed a sigh when a woman in a neat suit appeared, and behind her a clean-cut man. They each took their position behind a computer screen and stared blankly into the crowd. People stood up and a queue formed. The woman received a phone call, made eye contact with the person at the front of the queue and boarding began. I sat back. I was assured of my spot on the plane and I decided the least amount of time spent squashed into a narrow, vinyl-covered affair with no leg room the better.

The flow stalled when a woman in ludicrously high heels tried to carry through a shoulder bag the size of a large suitcase. An argument broke out, the woman insisting she take it aboard, the young man insisting it go in the hold. Then others piped up, irritated, and the whole fiasco had the makings of a pub brawl. I felt sorry for the staff. Any job that meant dealing with the public came with its down side.

When the departure area—it could hardly be called a lounge— had all but emptied, I stood and took my place at the end of the queue.

I was travelling with a lightweight canvas tote containing my purse, keys, iPod and wireless headphones along with various official documents permitting me to reside in Fuerteventura, safely ensconced in a thick plastic wallet: my future.

It was hard to know whether the aisle or the window seat was the preferable option. It was certainly not the middle seat, as the airline was determined to cram in as many passengers on the aircraft as was humanly possible, basing the calculation on the general proportions of a slender child of ten. I had plumped for the aisle, despite having to lean aside whenever anyone went by.

How the carrier could justify packing holidaymakers into their aircraft in such a fashion was a matter for considerable speculation but most were happy with the cheap fares and were prepared to put up with it.

I buckled up and extracted my headphones. A four-and a half hour flight meant I could listen to a fair slap of my Cocteau Twins' playlist.

I hadn't always enjoyed the Cocteau Twins. I had never heard of them when my mother had died. Aunt Clarissa told me in my early teens that Ingrid used to listen to the band on her Walkman. She let slip in a wistful moment that a refrain of their single, 'Pearly Dewdrops' Drops', was the last thing my mother heard before she slipped from her mortal coil. Her Walkman had stopped as Elizabeth Fraser was halfway through the first verse.

My mother, Ingrid Wilkinson, was a lot like Aunt Clarissa. Although she had been much more than a dabbler when it came to the mystical side of life. The sisters came from a long line of psychics, scryers and occultists. One of their great grandfathers was a member of the Hermetic Order of the Golden Dawn. One of their grandmothers a Theosophist. The Wilkinson's were of good social stock, among them could be found bankers and wealthy businessmen. How did a woman of Ingrid's background come to marry a used-car salesman from Clapton-on-Sea? The answer lay in my father's exceptional looks and natural magnetism coupled with a compatibility chart indicating they were soul mates. Besides, they met in the flower power years when idealism formed an illusory mist in the minds of the susceptible and my mother believed him when he told her he was an actor. Which, in a fashion, he was.

Clarissa never took to my dad. In a candid moment, she expressed her view that men like Herb Bennett belonged behind bars for all the conning they did. She had never been one to mince her words and had always held the conviction that he had railroaded me into a mediocre career in banking when I was capable of much, much more.

Ingrid had been the dreamy one in the family. Born in 1950, her musical tastes moved from The Beatles' White Album and trippy Grace Slick to the vocal acrobatics of the Cocteau Twins' Elizabeth Fraser via the likes of Tangerine Dream, favouring the electronic side of the 1980s' post-punk era. After her death, my dad was quick to clear out her things, but Aunt Clarissa stepped in to salvage mum's record collection, photos and a scrap book of musical memorabilia.

After discovering the close association between the band and my mother's passing, I wouldn't listen to the Cocteau Twins, even when my dream-pop loving friends at school were raving about the band's latest release. By then I had heard the track my mother had been enjoying at that fated moment and I rejected all the band's output on a point of principle, as though their music in its entirety had caused her demise. I went through my twenties and much of my thirties deaf as a post to the sounds emanating from the band. It took the thirtieth anniversary of my mother's passing to trigger an interest, thanks to a record store assistant who had chosen my entry to put on the offending track, 'Pearly Dewdrops' Drops'.

I stopped, and for the first time in my life actually listened, opening myself up and letting in the sound, and in seconds I was mesmerized. It was a kind of awakening. I used the birthday gift voucher given to me by my aunt and made up the rest to buy everything they had by the Cocteau Twins. Thirty years, and I was cured of my stubborn resistance and I felt closer to my mother than I had in all that time, as though she were with me, bobbing her head beside me, enthralled.

From that moment, the only band my mother and I both appreciated was the Cocteau Twins, and their music was the only way I felt connected to my mother.

The plane taxied then took off, and there I sat, content in my little world of sound, filled with anticipation. I had no idea what sort of life I was flying into.

Liz Fraser accompanied me all the way to Fuerteventura, the mellifluous tones of her voice on 'Aikea Guinea' soaring as the plane descended. We were coasting along the runway as the song ended and I turned off the iPod and returned the headphones to my tote.

I sat up straight with my bag on my lap, keen to disembark before the throng. The moment the plane came to a stop and others shifted and stood, I bolted to the nearest exit, fighting by men pulling cabin luggage from overhead compartments and women pointing their butts into the aisle as they attended to their bits and pieces on their seats.

The runway runs parallel to the ocean and the airport building runs with it. Designed to resemble a hanger, the building is elongated with an elegantly curved roof, walls of glass and lots of skylights. It is an open, light and airy space that gives an impression to the first-time visitor of a climate accustomed to endless sunshine.

Back among the throng, I collected my luggage—two suitcases of modest proportions—and checked in at the car hire booth.

Freedom greeted me as I crossed to the car park. I located my car sheltered under its own corrugated iron awning and I was away on that bright and sunny day in March, heading north on the highway to the capital, Puerto del Rosario, where I had booked an apartment for a month.

Everything appeared as it always had, but I felt markedly different, as though behind me the airport were folding itself up like a deck chair and carrying itself off into storage.

The drive was pleasant enough, the ocean coming into view, and then the capital, a distant sprawl of white cutting into the dry and rugged plain. To my left, on the high side of the highway, I passed a sprawl of unimaginative, cheek-by-jowl dwellings—developers, residents and holidaymakers alike enamoured with the ocean view and the beach, a short distance away. Although the trek with thongs and a towel was made ludicrously difficult by the obstructive presence of the highway. It seemed to me development on the island was in dire need of strict regulation and town planning. Otherwise every square inch of land would be given over to greed and the result would assault the senses.

I was familiar with Puerto del Rosario, enough to know the best areas to stay in. I chose to rent in the capital as the shops, banks, industrial areas, car yards and trades were all close to hand.

My apartment was in a side street off Avenida Juan de Bethencort, named after the Norman knight who had first conquered the islands. A supermarket was a few blocks away and the port itself was about a fifteen-minute stroll; downhill there meant uphill back so I would choose my moment. Calle Barcelona was one of the more established streets, but development in the city had been sporadic, and even here vacant blocks still waited to be filled.

The streets are narrow, the traffic one way, the pavements lacking room for street planting. Buildings are mostly two-storey. The combination hems in the citizenry, somewhat like the streets of Colchester. In all, there are too few trees, a paucity of green, although the council has taken the trouble to squeeze in some foliage here and there, demonstrating an awareness of the need for shade in such a hot and dry climate.

Taking in the city streets, I made a mental note to set to work establishing a proper garden on my property, a garden filled with natives and palm trees, whatever was hardy and drought and wind tolerant.

On impulse, I stocked up at a supermarket I passed, and arrived at my apartment in the middle of the afternoon, pulling up in the designated car space out front. The woman next door was expecting me.

Dolores must have seen me pull up for she came out and greeted me in the street, proffering my keys. Her Spanish was rapid and her accent thick but over the years of visiting the island I had come to anticipate the hurried flow, the nasal tone, the lack of fully enunciated consonants. A brief exchange and Dolores left me to ferry inside my suitcases and groceries.

The apartment was on the ground floor and comprised an open plan living room with a small kitchen tucked in a corner, a double bedroom and bathroom. The furnishings were basic and clean. Once the perishables were in the fridge, I sat back on the couch and put my feet up on the coffee table. I was about to take possession of my stately old ruin. The sense of triumph made me swell to twice my size.

I had no idea what lay ahead of me, other than what I had learned from Kevin McCloud. I had no idea what I would do with my life on the island either, now I was a lady of leisure, but I felt confident some activity would present itself. All that mattered to me was I had arrived and I was brimming with anticipation.

Gazing at the bare white walls of the apartment soon invoked a listless feeling and I was eager to drive to Tiscamanita. I downed a glass of orange juice and made a sandwich of the local cheese and ham and headed out the door.

3

TISCAMANITA

THERE ARE FIVE ROUTES TO TISCAMANITA AND I HAVE TAKEN ALL OF them. The fastest involves heading due west from Puerto del Rosario and cutting a path through Casillas del Ángel before veering south-ward and on through Antigua. The road cuts a straight path across the flat and denuded coastal plain, making a crow's flight to the mountains that rise in the near distance. Away from the arterial road that connects the northern fishing village turned resort town of Corralejo, down to Puerto del Rosario and then on south to Morre Jable, Fuerteventura takes on its true nature, a vast empty expanse of treeless land, farmed in places, decorated with low mountain ranges that define the landscape and give it its beauty. Pleased to leave the city behind me, I was drawn by those barren ranges, their moulded shapes and delicate hues.

Most holidaymakers come for the beaches. Fuerteventura is an island of beaches. To appreciate the interior the beholder needs the artist's palette, an eye able to detect the soft tones of ochre and gold and sienna and pale umber, the hints of pink and copper and bronze. If the beholder thinks of all that as brown, they have no place being on the island. Unless the eye catches the nuances, the heart the fragility of the desert environment, then the observer will only see lifeless plains flanked by lifeless mountains, the sort of land many would conjure in parts of North Africa and the Middle East and deem fit for nothing. The ever-changing subtle colours was one of the features of the island that first captivated me. The traditional architecture a close second. After three holidays, my friends started to ask why I chose not to go somewhere else, after all there was the whole world to see, and I defended my decision by saying I was guaranteed heat and sunshine and, to satisfy their prejudices, gorgeous beaches.

Tiscamanita is a small farming village situated a little south of the island's epicentre, on a sloping plain surrounded by an array of interestingly shaped peaks. The views are three-sixty and splendid. The village itself is not much to speak of. Some effort has been taken with the main square and a few shops struggle on, the hinterland consisting of farmhouses dotted here and there, interspersed with patches of land and half-built houses sitting beside crumbling dry-stone walls or the remains of the walls of some ancient dwelling, evidence that folk still try to make a go of things while many have failed. It's always been a harsh place to be. The odd field is cultivated where once all were. For the most part Tiscamanita has abandoned the traditional way of life and who could blame the farmer for wanting things easier? How does anyone farm land that receives eight inches of rain a year at best? It is brutal.

Yet Tiscamanita was once wealthy by island standards, made rich on the belly juice of a beetle. The little sap sucker drank from the prickly pear and its insides turned a rich red hue, and when crushed, the beetle juice seeped into flesh and fabric making bright red stains that no doubt proved hard to remove. Those discoveries resulted in the late eighteenth century cochineal industry, and the poor farmers were faced with the uncomfortable task of cultivating fields of cactus, which they then had to fight their way through to pick off the beetles. The only positive on the farming side of things was the harvesters remained upright. On the other hand, I was about to discover that the bane of any farmer's life can be found in the bending. There was a lot of money in cochineal, and the bourgeoisie land owners had known it. Lucky devils. They were not the ones who got their hands pricked. Looking around as I drove through the town, evidence of the prickly pear was everywhere, but it didn't look like anyone was farming it, even for jam.

My heart swelled in my chest as I pulled up outside my property. I could scarcely believe I owned the whole half acre. The ruin had been built at the northern end of the block, leaving a sizeable patch of land stretching from the street to the dry-stone wall at the rear. Beyond, dominating the landscape to the northeast and rising up behind some low hills, a volcano sat with its gaping maw and russet flanks. Towards the south-east were the other volcanoes in the chain and due south, a range of serrated-edged peaks in the distance. The Betancuria massif rose to the east, with mountains dotted before it. After four decades cooped in Colchester, the effect on me was one of exhilaration. The wide expanse of arid land elevated my spirits and I dismissed as hocus pocus Aunt Clarissa's worrisome predictions. I took comfort, too, knowing I had a neighbour to either side and one across the street, although there was no sign that anyone was at home in any of those houses.

I walked over to the ruin. The structure was set back from the street and built with much uniformity. The main façade comprised eight boarded-up cavities where once were windows. The cavities were evenly spaced, four above and four below. On the lower level, one of the central cavities was wider than the others and would have contained the front door. In places, the render was crumbling. Some areas were exposed stone. The side walls were uninteresting, containing two bricked-up window cavities on the upper level. At the rear were three small outbuildings, one in good repair although minus its roof.

By rights I needed permission in the form of a key to get into the main building, not that there was a door to open, but I knew a way inside at the rear where there was a gap in a poorly boarded up door-way. I came across the gap on my last visit to the island, on the day I took my prized photo that I had blown up and framed, the photo that had hung in my living room like a lure.

I squeezed through the gap and entered a short passage that led to an internal patio, taking in the interior of the building that I had only seen in online images emailed to me by my lawyer when Señor Cejas was bent on putting me off the purchase. Dilapidation scarcely described the state of disrepair. Some of the interior walls were free-standing. Much of the roof was missing. Stairs to the upper level did not exist, and the balcony that would have run along three of the walls of the internal patio was missing save for a section cantilevered in the western wall and supported by two skinny posts. I didn't dare walk beneath it. I could hear Kevin McCloud's voiceover telling his viewers that, yet again, the owner had bitten off far more than she was able to chew and the cost and time blow outs would be enormous.

Not if I could help it.

I picked my way around. There was evidence of paintwork in some of the rooms, harkening back to more glorious times. Many of the walls had been painted a yellow ochre. A simple frieze decorated the top of some of the walls, straight lines of cobalt blue and black and stencilled flowers in the corners. Different, more earthy colours had been employed in a similar design of straight line borders and simple stencil work in other parts of the house.

There appeared to be four large living areas, a dining room and kitchen, and what was probably a laundry or bathroom. There was no way of accessing the upper level but I imagined a similar arrange-ment of grand rooms and estimated at least six bedrooms. In one of the downstairs rooms the floorboards had been pulled up, revealing the subfloor of bearers and joists.

The whole arrangement of rooms faced the internal patio, which had been divided into two by a partition wall. The wall had a large hole in its centre as though someone hadn't wanted the wall there and bashed through it, and evidence that it was a later addition could be seen in the way it cut off a portion of architrave, and dissected the existing balcony in the west wall.

I stood beside the hole in the partition in what would have been the centre of the patio and absorbed the atmosphere. The wind blew through every crevice of the ruin, moaning and whistling. Other than the wind there was no sound. I couldn't hear a dog bark or a vehicle engine or any other evidence of life beyond the walls. Despite the wind, there were pockets of stillness and the ruin exuded a timeless quality. Embedded in its dilapidated state remained faint echoes of its history, overlaid with sorrow, as though the very stones and ancient timbers mourned their former selves, when they were united as one, strong and proud and true.

The house was rumoured to be two hundred and fifty years old, built by a wealthy family from Tenerife enjoying the riches of their wine exports and later sold to a family of lawyers. I pictured what it may have been, the grandeur of the carved wood and the vaulted ceilings, the balconies, the patio filled with plants and elegant outdoor seating.

I imagined men and women in period dress, all straight backed and God-abiding, going about their daily business in hushed voices. They would have had servants too, to cook and clean. The lady of the house would tend her plants and go to mass. The gentleman would read a book or a newspaper and take trips away on camel-back or donkey to attend to business. They would discuss their concerns over the weather, public health, the harvest, matters of politics and trade. Perhaps they received visitors, the priest, overnight guests. And there would have been children and extended family members. Aunts and uncles and cousins. A surviving grandparent or two.

Outside the walls, the wind would have blown and picked up the dust. The interior of Fuerteventura endures many a sweltering day in summer, and with no trees to shade the rocky land, ambient temperatures rise to infernal heights. I couldn't imagine any of my dainty well-bred family venturing out unless they had to. Not in summer. Instead, they would have taken full advantage of their cloistered life within, enjoying the cool of the internal patio.

A faint odour of animal urine wafting on a breeze brought me back to the present. A dog? Or a cat? The light was fading and I thought it wise to make my way back to my apartment before nightfall. On impulse, I thought to take with me a small piece of my new country estate to mark the occasion. I picked a craggy stone out of the partition wall. It was the size of my hand and the colour of orange ochre and rough to the touch. As I walked away a sudden gust of wind blew through the hole in the wall. It was a preternaturally cold wind for the climate. Goose pimples broke out on my skin. I thought nothing of it.

4

THE BUILDER

BACK IN MY APARTMENT, I GAVE MY ROCKY MEMENTO PRIDE OF PLACE ON the living room's single shelf, between the television and a white, urn-shaped vase, arranging the rock in various positions until I was satisfied it displayed its best face.

Around dinner time, I threw together a cheese omelette and salad. After eating, I soaked in the ambience of the modern, rectangular space, with its clean, streamlined feel.

I felt somewhat stunned. There I sat, having left the only career I had ever known, sold the only house I had ever owned and moved to an island where I had no family or friends, to embark on a major restoration project. Had I taken on too much? It was not a thought I was prepared to give shrift. I was tired from the travelling, that was all, and fatigue was colouring my thoughts. I needed an early night.

I was asleep by nine despite the unfamiliar noises in my new neighbourhood.

The following day I was up, showered and out the door by seven-thirty. Back in Colchester, I had asked the Fuerteventura lawyer in charge of my conveyancing if she knew of a reliable builder. She put me in contact with Mario, who I promptly emailed. We arranged to meet on site that day at nine. I was there at eight, wandering around my land in the morning cool, marking my territory with my footsteps, toying with the idea of buying a campervan instead of a car and parking up in my would-be garden for the duration of the build. I could only imagine what the locals would think of a strange English woman emerging each day from her home on wheels.

Was anyone watching me through the windows of any of the houses I could see? Were they judging me? For there I stood, dressed in beige capris and a loose white blouse, my mane of copper hair held in place with the assistance of a large headscarf, my fair skin and blue eyes unsuited to the terrain, my bank teller shape, larger at the haunches and soft about the belly, a far cry from the wiry muscula-ture needed to till the land. But Claire Bennett of Colchester was no longer a bank clerk. Claire Bennett planned on getting fit, and there was plenty for me to do.

I thought I would begin by creating a garden bed in the corner of the property furthest from the restoration work. Plant some trees and shrubs. Or at least start tidying up the place. There were stones all over the ground and the dry-stone walls at the rear of the block were in disrepair.

A dusty old van pulled up a little after nine. There was a long pause before the driver's side door swung open and a solid, deeply tanned man with short black hair got out. I waved. He looked over and approached. I could see he was a builder at a glance. He had that air of authority as he observed the ruin and he carried a large, battered notebook under one arm.

'Mario,' I said, the moment he was close. I held out my hand.

He didn't match my smile but he gave my hand a firm shake.

'Claire.'

His gaze slid to the ruin. As we walked over, I drew my knowledge of the Spanish language to the forefront of my mind, ready to reel off the building terms I had learned by rote in preparation. But Mario was not the talkative type and he wasn't the least bit interested in my opinion. His eyes were everywhere, making quick assessments of this and that and scribbling in his notebook. Even before we had entered through the crack in the boarded-up window, he was making noises that suggested a negative take on the project.

Inside, his attitude was even worse. Before long, he was shaking his head and sighing and making soft tutting noises. In all, his demeanour began to irritate and I had it in mind to find another builder, for there had to be dozens on the island with the skills to work on a restoration.

After he had poked about in all the downstairs rooms and gazed long and hard at the rafters and beams and what was left of the roof, we stopped in the patio beside the hole in the wall, the only area of the entire structure that felt safe to stand in for any length of time. The building may have been standing for centuries, but there was no telling when something might slip and a whole section tumble on our heads.

'This is a partition wall,' he said, patting the crumbling render and looking at where the wall met the rest of the structure.

'I want it gone, obviously.'

'It is bracing the two walls, there and there,' he said, pointing ahead and behind him.

'It does need to come down.'

'Okay, but we start with that room there.' He gestured at the living room in the north-west corner, the room in the best repair.

'Any reason?'

'We can finish it faster. There is not so much to do.' His eyes bore into me beneath thick, arched eyebrows. 'This will cost a lot of money.'

'I am well aware of that.'

And I have a lot of money, I thought. I didn't say it. I didn't want to give him the impression I could afford more than a basic restoration in case he saw me as an excuse for extravagance.

Despite an urge to look away, I held his gaze.

'When can you start?'

He exhaled and leafed through his notebook, which seemed to double as his diary. The wind gusted and one of the timbers groaned. He looked around in response and we both waited for another groan. It was not forthcoming, but that single sound caused him to close his notebook and say, 'Why don't you demolish and put up something nice and modern?'

I was instantly defensive.

'I love this house,' I said, infusing into my voice a measure of indignation.

He ignored my reaction, or was indifferent to it.

'A new build will be cheaper and faster.' He grew in enthusiasm as he spoke. 'We can re-use the stone. Make it a feature. You will have a very nice house.'

'I don't want a very nice, modern house. Look, Mario, I was told you were the best builder to restore this ruin. Will you do it? Otherwise I will need to find someone else.'

'Of course, I can do it. I just want to be sure it is what you want. I thought I would make an alternative suggestion. This is a lot, I mean a *lot* of work and it will be very expensive. But if you are sure.' He paused as though to allow me time to reconsider. I made no comment.

'Do you want to use it for something?' he inquired.

'I just want to restore it to how it was.'

He puffed out his cheeks as he exhaled. Then he said, 'Do you have architect plans?'

'No, but I want it restored, not changed.'

'You will want some changes, believe me.'

If you say so. Although he was probably right.

'What happens next?'

'I can draw up the plans for you and submit them to council for approval. Then I must find local materials. You cannot use new materials in an old building like this. And I must make a team. You need everyone here, for the roof, the carpentry, the masonry, and then the plumbing and electricity. That is a lot of men.'

'How long will all that take?'

'Three months?'

'Three months!'

'That's fast. I can draw up the plans for you straight away. I have a friend in council who can make the approval process go faster. But I will need a deposit.'

With the situation suddenly looking positive, I said, 'Tell me how much and I will transfer the amount.'

'Okay.'

'You'll get to work on the plans as soon as I pay you?'

'Yes, yes.'

He looked at me expectantly. He seemed keen to leave. I led him outside through the gap in the boarded-up doorway, careful not to snag or soil my nice clothes.

We stood together for a moment. He held out his hand and I was about to take it, but at the sight of the outbuildings I had an idea.

I gave him my winning smile and said, 'Mario, surely you can get started sooner. I mean, isn't there work you can be doing before the council gets involved?'

He looked at me blankly.

'Maybe you can make a start out here,' I said gesturing at the outbuildings.

He seemed resistant. 'Usually the owner wants the house complete before working on the outbuildings.'

'Usually the owner has run out of money by then. I know how it goes. But in my case, that won't happen.' I wondered if I had revealed too much but his manner didn't change.

I went over to the largest outbuilding, the one with no roof. Mario followed. The building consisted of thick stone walls, an opening where a door would have been, and a small high rectangle in the adjacent wall serving as a window. The floor space looked about fifteen feet by twelve, large enough for a studio or workshop of some kind. A pile of stones in the centre was evidence of some sort of interior wall.

'For keeping in the goats,' he said, kicking a pebble and created a puff of dust.

'With a roof, a floor and some render, I could use it for storage.'

'You will have a lot of space in there,' he said, pointing back at the house and then eyeing me with puzzlement.

Did he have to be so resistant?

'You could use it, too,' I said. 'You might want to store tools or bags of cement, maybe.'

'True.'

'When can you start?'

'On this?' He shrugged.

'Tomorrow?'

He laughed. 'I will message you.'

'I want it done straight away, if at all possible,' I said to his back as he walked away.

Watching him get in his van and drive off, I couldn't say I liked Mario. He was evasive, non-comital and a touch inscrutable and I fully expected never to see him again. Aunt Clarissa's warning flashed into my mind and I dismissed it without consideration. I would give Mario a few days to prove himself, and then look for another builder if need be.

5

PACO

I couldn't steal myself away from the block. The sun had a sting to it and I was growing hungry and thirsty, but I wanted to do something on my property, make a small difference to mark the occasion. Thinking I would tidy up, I went back to the outbuilding and picked up the rocks scattered around in the dirt, creating a small pile of them outside. I soon tired. My gloveless hands burned and my back was stiffening from the effort. I hadn't dressed for hard labour and I didn't want to dirty my capris.

I needed gloves, a wheelbarrow, gardening tools and a strategy for re-using all that rock littering my block. I was about to head off back to Puerto del Rosario to a hardware store when I noticed a man standing on the other side of the road, gazing my way. Already, the project had aroused interest, I thought, feeling pleased if a little intruded upon. A neighbour perhaps? Or a nosy holidaymaker? Curious, I walked over.

He crossed the road and we met on the pavement.

'Lovely morning for it,' I said with a cheery grin.

He didn't return my warmth. Hearing I was English, he said in a low and thickly accented voice, 'What are you doing on this land? It is private.'

'The land *is* private,' I said. 'I own it.'

298

He shook his head. 'You cannot. It belongs to the Cejas family.'

'Not any more. They sold it.'

'That's impossible. Not even the government could make them sell.'

'The government were not offering enough.'

He eyed me appraisingly, perhaps a little taken aback, as though I didn't appear to him the type to be rich.

'You're English. And you buy this?' He tilted his head at the ruin. 'What for? A hotel?'

'I bought it to live in it.'

Who the hell does he think he is, treating me with such disdain?

We both looked back at the ruin, all forlorn and dilapidated, its windows and door cavities boarded up, the render crumbling off what walls still stood. I took the opportunity to steal a glance at this abrupt and somewhat rude man who was taking an extreme and perhaps possessive interest in my house. He was tall, over six foot, slim and fit. He had long black hair, tied back in a ponytail, framing a well-proportioned face, with an intelligent turn to the mouth and a fervent glint in his deep-set eyes. The swarthy complexion indicated a Southern European lineage. A local? I placed him in his late-thirties. A satchel—grubby, worn and bulging—hung from his left shoulder.

'A big house, no?' he said in his stilted English. 'You have a husband? Children? A large family?'

I found his prying intrusive.

'Only me.'

'Wow!'

I could detect the judgement in that simple word even in Spanish and he wasn't referring to my marital status. I was awash with guilt, guilt that didn't belong to me, but to expats in general. There were too few affordable dwellings for the locals, while foreigners bought up the housing stock at exorbitant prices and lived out a paradisiacal existence on land that really wasn't theirs. In essence, the trend was a form of colonisation and it was a common complaint in the Spanish social media groups I was in. The key difference in my case, was not many foreigners bought ruins. No matter where you lived, they were notoriously expensive to restore. Not to mention time consuming.

Standing before the tall and mysterious stranger I was made to feel as though I had committed the ultimate cultural transgression. I had no right of ownership. Worse, I sensed he might have thought I was appropriating local history. I should have bought an apartment in Corralejo like everyone else of my sort and left the hinterland well alone, my notion that I was doing the island a public service, dashed.

My second day on the island as a resident and something sour pervaded my being. I hadn't realised how much I wanted my choice to restore a ruin and save it from demolition sanctioned, not until that very moment when it wasn't. I couldn't help seeing the absurdity in the situation too. For what ordinary local could ever afford the expense of the purchase, let alone the building work. Such projects had become the terrain of the rich and the government. This man before me should be thanking, not condemning me.

The wind picked up, catching the ends of my headscarf and using them to slap my face. I brushed the fabric away and shifted my stance. With my back to the building, I gazed up at the stranger and some part of me, call it self-preservation, compelled me to heal the rift forming between us. I did not want animosity from a man I suspected would pop round at whim.

'I'm Claire.' I held out my hand.

He hesitated, took it and said, 'Paco.'

'Pleased to meet you, Paco. Do you live in the village?'

'Tiscamanita? No.'

He didn't supply an alternative. I had no idea how to progress the conversation or how to close it. An awkward moment passed between us. The wind showed no sign of abating. Despite wisps of his own hair whipping across his face, Paco was untroubled by it.

'You have an interest in this house?' I asked, stating the obvious.

He patted his satchel. 'I'm a photographer.' He announced his profession, or hobby, as though it, of itself, were sufficient explanation.

'Then you'll be pleased to know I plan to return the building to its former glory.'

'Ha!' he said with as much sarcasm as it was possible to pack into that short word. 'And then sell it and make a fortune.'

The man, Paco, was driving me crazy with his antagonistic remarks. I did my best not to give him the benefit of seeing my chagrin, keeping my voice cool and firm. 'To live in it, like I said. You've been inside?'

'Many times.'

I thought about offering him another tour but wasn't sure how he would interpret that. In a final effort at assuaging the irascible photographer I said, 'Then perhaps you'd help me. I have been visiting the island every year and I have driven by this ruin many times. But I don't know its history. I'd like to learn everything there is to know. Maybe I'll write it all down and produce a booklet as a keep-sake. That way, whatever I, we, discover will be preserved.'

I had no idea where the idea came from, I hadn't kept so much as a childhood diary in all of my forty years, but his face lit with interest and I felt I had committed myself, through an uncommonly loose tongue, to a project I didn't have the capacity or the inclination to pursue. It was a moment of desperation to appease, but why I felt I needed to go to such considerable lengths to gain Paco's approval, I couldn't fathom. Perhaps some intuitive part of me knew he would play a significant role in the months ahead, or maybe deep down I had decided I needed an ally and since he had a keen interest in my ruin, he fitted the bill. Whatever the motive, I assured him he was welcome to visit any time he wanted and observe the progress.

Reassured, he headed off and left me to tramp about my block, quelling a mix of trepidation and frustration, and an equally strong desire to get on and make an impression on the garden.

6

MOVING ROCKS

Not long after Paco left, I set off for Puerto del Rosario, heading to the hardware store on the town outskirts. There, I bought a shovel and spade, a garden fork and trowel, four pairs of heavy-duty gardening gloves, a watering can and a small wheelbarrow. I had to fold down the back seats to get the wheelbarrow in the car. Mindful of the dirt those tools would bring into the boot, I went back and bought a sheet of thick plastic. I dearly wanted to get back to Tiscamanita but it was nearing lunchtime and my stomach was eating itself.

I drove to my apartment and made a ham and cheese baguette, and poured and large glass of juice. I ate and drank so fast I belched on the last mouthful. Then I changed into a loose t-shirt and shorts and a pair of canvas plimsolls and I was back on my block within a couple of hours.

That afternoon, with gloved hands and a wheelbarrow I managed to clear out all the rocks in the outbuilding, making a heap about ten strides away. I added to the heap with other rocks lying around. I was pleased with the result. The area around the outbuildings looked much tidier. I'd left my mark and it felt like progress.

In the days that followed, I went up to the block and spent a few hours braving the sun and the wind to scour the land clearing rocks, determined to cover every square foot of it. I heaped the rocks into cairns that grew and grew in size until they were visible from a distance.

Now and then I would fully straighten and stretch my back, and take a moment to absorb the curves of the volcano that rose up behind the nearby hills, it's gaping maw evidence of the fiery lava it had spewed long ago, evidence too of the powerful geography of the Canary Islands. It was odd that on Fuerteventura, an island with few volcanoes compared to its sister, Lanzarote, I should have chosen to have one dominating the view from my back yard. The volcano was the first in a chain of four that had spewed lava and ash eastwards, towards the coast. Standing by one of my rock piles, beholding the majesty of that natural killer, I wondered if I had been drawn as much by the setting as the ruin itself.

A week of back-breaking labour out in the sun and I gained a tan and lost some kilos, the waistbands of my trousers noticeably looser. The exposure out on my bare land had put paid to the campervan idea. I contacted the owner of the apartment and booked myself an additional month. Not the most luxurious accommodation, I could have afforded anywhere, but I was still Claire Bennett of Colchester and frugal suited me to my core.

In the evenings, I blocked out the noise of the neighbours with my headphones, and lost myself in the music of the Cocteau Twins. Sometimes, I would think of my mother and wonder what she would have made of the island. I imagined she would have been as enchanted as me. She would have seen the beauty and the subtlety in the stark desert vistas. They would have reminded her of the Persia and Arabia of yesteryear, of Morocco, of desert lands and ancient mysteries, of Sufis and Dervishes with their mystical ways. She would have walked down the streets of Tiscamanita imagining she was on her way to a souk. Clarissa said Ingrid had that sort of imagination. She would be walking down a street lost in another world, a world of her imagining. She had been a danger to herself, Clarissa said. When they were growing up, many times Clarissa had to tell my mother to stop at the kerb as she made to step out across a street. It was a quality she never lost.

On Fuerteventura, Ingrid would have enjoyed the beaches, too. Clarissa told me once Ingrid loved to be beside the sea. I have no recollection of us visiting, but apparently, we went on outings to Clacton-on-Sea. We would build sand castles and enjoy the amusements on the pier and eat sticks of sugary rock. It must have been when I was very small.

Mario contacted me on the Wednesday of that week of hard labour and we talked through the project. He sounded more amenable on the phone and I thought perhaps he had been having a off day when we had met on the block to discuss my proposal. Hearing him bend to my wishes, I softened and paid the deposit. We discussed my ideas and I sent him photos of my hand-drawn sketches. I begged him to draw up the plans as soon as he possibly could and he told me I was fortunate he was having a day off to look after one of his children who was off school. The next day, he sent me screenshots of his drafts. Not wanting to quibble and slow the pace, I agreed to his small alterations and suggestions. He then drew up the final plans which he submitted to council before close of day that Friday.

After that, in the evenings when I tired of listening to music, I poured over my electronic copy of the house plans.

The design was formal. The living room on the north-western corner was a room of about twelve by fifteen feet, accessed via the vestibule that led to the double doors facing the street. Entry to the adjoining room, once the dining room, was from the patio and those two rooms were interconnected. There was a window in the living room, facing west like the front door. The other room was window-less, there being no downstairs window in the north-facing wall. Sensible, as that was the direction of the prevailing wind. On the northeast corner was the kitchen, a room fifteen by eighteen feet. There was no door through to the dining room. Like most rooms in the building, access was via the patio. The two kitchen windows over-looked the volcano. Imagining rinsing a glass at the sink, I began to see through the building's magnificence to the joy of living amid stunning views.

There was a laundry centred in the east wall beside the rear exit.

A bathroom would take up the south-eastern corner. A room identical to the dining room would be a study or library, and on the south-western corner would be a large L-shaped living room. Both rooms had windows facing the garden and the corner room also had windows facing the street.

The entire building was forty-five feet wide and forty-eight feet long, with walls three-feet thick. Upstairs mirrored downstairs in the dimensions of the rooms, and would comprise six bedrooms and two bathrooms, and an area of flat roof for a terrace above the laundry. I chose the best room for my bedroom, the one above the kitchen, with a magnificent view of the volcano.

The internal patio was about twenty-seven by twenty-one feet, large enough to contain the wide balcony that would run along three of the walls, and the aljibe beneath the ground in its centre. The plan was both grand and simple and eminently liveable, a noble-man's home with every thought given to a kind of sub-tropical comfort.

After picturing myself in each room, I studied other restorations online and visualised how my home would be. My mind was buzzing with ideas for linens for drapes, fabric patterns for furnishings and rugs, kitchen designs, lamps and light shades, even and bathroom fittings. Mario warned me I would need to consider every single detail in each of the rooms and it was a good idea to start browsing. The only difficulty I faced was needing to restrict my searches to the island. It was too easy to slip onto websites where the goods were only available in the UK. I didn't want to ship furniture over. I was drawn to vintage styles and the antique furniture traditional to the islands and limited my searches accordingly.

While we waited for council approval, Mario pulled together a small team of labourers to tackle the largest outbuilding, which Mario was calling a barn.

On the first day of the build, I did an early shop at the super-market and spent the morning tidying up the apartment and washing my clothes that had formed a small mountain on my bedroom floor. Listless, I sorted through my suitcase. Buried at the bottom was the framed photo of my ruin that I had brought with me on impulse; a symbol of the reason for my being there. The rest of my possessions would be arriving by ship.

Wanting the photo on display on the one shelf in the entire apartment, I put it between the television and the vase, relocating the rock I had taken from the partition wall to the other end of the shelf, placing it in front of a short row of books held in place by carved-wood bookends. The books included a Spanish-English dictionary and another in Spanish-German, a guide to Fuerteventura in English, an Agatha Christie in Spanish, two romances in what appeared to be Dutch, a hardcover on German Expressionism and a Stephen King in French. I imagined each had been left behind, intentionally or otherwise, by a previous guest. The rock blended nicely with the arrangement. A rock of no particular beauty or significance other than it came from that wall, and already I had imbued it with meaning; the first rock removed from a wall that had for too long divided that ruin, cleaving it into two separate dwellings.

I was about to restore that house to its original unified whole. Thinking about how the partition detracted from the building's integrity, that wall seemed to me a transgression and the sooner it was gone, the better.

I picked up the rock and turned it over in my hand. It had six distinct faces in amongst the little craters and outgrowths. I traced a finger over the surface, felt the weight of it—about half a pound—and returned it to the shelf, sitting it down on its largest flattest surface, pointing a prominent bulge to the front. That way the rock took on the shape of a broad and flattened head and I could pick out eyes, a nose and lips from all the indentations and protuberances, as I used to as a child with my mother's floral-patterned curtains.

Done with domesticities, I deposited in a thin canvas bag what had become my customary ham and cheese baguette, along with two oranges and a litre of water, and set off for Tiscamanita. I doubted the workmen would want me there but I needed to witness the occasion.

In the narrow streets of Puerto del Rosario, I hadn't noticed the dust haze, but out in open country, there it was, reducing visibility, the mountains no longer distinct, the horizon behind me fuzzy. The temperature was rising steadily as the air blew in from the east. It was a calima, a Saharan dust storm. I had no idea how long it would last or how intense it would be, but when I pulled up outside my property in front of a row of cars and vans and opened the car door, my English self was brutalised by weather conditions that made sense of any apparel that covered the body head to toe, including, no particularly the face. I had endured my share of calimas and they varied in intensity, but that day conditions were especially bad and, I thought, unseasonal.

The other vehicles were facing the other way to me. The men must have all come up from the south. I didn't know whether to leave my window open a crack to let out the heat or keep it closed to keep out the dust. I left it shut and snatched my lunch bag off the backseat.

Signs of the build were everywhere, in tools and wheelbarrows, voices, and sharp repetitive dings of hammer on chisel. Timber was stacked near the rock pile I had created beside the barn. Although it was a rock pile no longer. My neat and tidy arrangement had been flattened, the rocks scattered. I quelled my dismay, all my hard labour for nothing.

Mario and I had agreed on a pitched roof. In the searing heat and the dust and the wind, four men—I counted four—were at work repairing and capping the stone walls in preparation. I was ignored, but one of the men must have said something to Mario, because he looked around and seeing me standing by the side wall of the house, he came over.

'You did all this?' he said, not bothering with even a hello, waving a disparaging hand at my rock pile.

'I wanted to help.'

'Help? You have made an easy job hard. Those rocks inside the barn had fallen off the walls. They would have been better left where they were and not mixed up with all the other rocks. Now the men are having to hunt for each rock, thanks to your pile.'

'I had no idea,' I said defensively, succumbing to a sudden rush of humiliation. I did my best to repress it. How dare he address me with such impatience, such rudeness!

'Please, Claire,' he said in a sudden change of manner, 'you must leave the work to us.' He reached for my hand and pressed it between both of his, a gesture that was as much conciliatory as it was patronising and I snatched my hand away. The turnaround had me wondering at the truth of Clarissa's metaphysical warning. I had no idea where I stood with this man. Yet I knew he was right; I needed to leave well alone. They were the experts, me, the owner, clearly the ignoramus.

'Are they already capping the wall?' I said, anxious to display my scant technical knowledge and progress the conversation past that juncture.

'There was not much to be done to some sections.'

I took a step forward. He stepped to his left and stood squarely before me, blocking my path. I craned to see past him. He emitted a humourless laugh as he stepped aside but he had made it clear in the most blatant manner he didn't want me approaching the men. He was advancing far beyond what I would have considered appropriate behaviour, even if he was mucking around. Besides, his eyes and his words were serious. He would brook no interference from me.

'Mario,' I said, smiling to soften the tension. 'This is an important day for me. I will leave the men to work, but first I would like to take some photographs, if that's okay.'

I didn't wait for a reply. I marched by him, phone to the ready.

The men all looked over at once, stared briefly at the crazy Englishwoman lining up a shot with her phone, then continued working. As I neared the barn I overheard their chatter. They assumed I understood no Spanish or that the wind would carry away their voices. Both were true to some extent, I had to strain to hear and interpret their thick accents.

'Who is she?'

'The owner,' said a man in a white shirt. 'Mario says she wants to restore the main house.'

There was a ripple of dark laughter. I pretended not to notice.

'I'm not working on that,' a short man in a dirty fawn shirt gestured behind him.

'Me neither.'

'Glad to hear it. You would be mad to,' said a third man.

'Mario will have to bring in men from Lanzarote.'

'He'll find workers here,' the white-shirted man said. He seemed to have authority over the others.

'You think so? Foreigners maybe. No local will work on it.'

'True. They'd have to be crazy.' He spat on the ground.

I took three discrete photos and walked away. My mind raced. Whatever did they mean? Had I heard them correctly? I began to doubt I had.

Mario exited the opening in the boarded-up doorway. I put away my phone and joined him.

'Any news on the house plans?'

'In one week?' He laughed. I didn't laugh with him. 'When this is done, we will start.'

'Those men just said they won't work on the house.'

'Take no notice of them. There are plenty of men I can use.'

So, I did hear them right.

'But they are saying no local will either. I don't understand. What is wrong with my house?'

'Relax. It is just superstition and local gossip.'

He walked away before I could inquire further. I was left nonplussed. Superstition meant ghosts, paranormal activity, a curse powerful enough to stop rational, hardworking men from earning a good wage on a major project. Something had to be very wrong with my ruin to cause that reaction. Perhaps it explained why no one had restored it before, why Cejas wanted it demolished. He had wished me good luck. It sounded like I was going to need it. Aunt Clarissa's warning sprang to mind again but I shooed it away. The relocation chart she had created pertained to the whole of the island, not just my block.

I hung around for a few moments longer to take a slug of my water. The baguette, tucked in my thin canvas bag all this time and steadily getting warmer was, I decided, inedible. If I wanted packed lunches, I needed to invest in a cooler bag. The men kept glancing over at me. Realising my presence was slowing the pace, I went back to my car.

Opening the door on a furnace and scalding my hands on the steering wheel that had taken the brunt of the sun, I realised why all the other vehicles were facing the other way. I had a lot of acclima-tising ahead of me.

I turned on the radio for the drive back to Puerto del Rosario to drown out my scrambled thoughts. Above all, I refused to heed the voice within that was busy assessing the inaugural day of the build as portentous. The coincidence of the calima hadn't helped. The trouble was, those workmen knew something I didn't and while Mario fobbed off their fears, part of me couldn't. It was the part of me formed by Ingrid and Clarissa, one at odds with my rational bank-teller self. I chose not believe in ghosts or the supernatural or in Clarissa's scrying, but those men clearly did and I remained unsettled by it.

The car indicated an outdoor temperature of thirty-five degrees and there was a lot of day left for the temperature to rise further. In the past, locals would have stayed indoors, closed all the shutters on the windows and rode out the easterly, ready to sweep up the dust once the wind turned. I had washing drying outside, a bathroom window open, and the sooner I followed in those sensible traditions the better.

I pulled up outside the apartment with my equanimity partially restored. It remained that way for a full two minutes. Then, I entered the apartment and saw that the rock I had so carefully positioned on the shelf in front of the books, was lying on the floor.

How the hell did it end up there?

I raced for explanations to soothe my alarmed mind. Had it fallen? No, it couldn't have. How was that even possible? It was resting on its natural base from which it could not have toppled. The floor tiles were not chipped, and had it fallen or even been dropped, surely there would have been a chip. Had someone been in my apartment? Dolores? The owner? An intruder? Why would any of them put that rock on the floor? Yet that had to be the answer. Maybe they had come with a child who saw the rock and picked it up and examined it. Yes, that is what had happened.

I looked around for other evidence that someone had been inside while I was out, but there was none. Clarissa's omen shot to the fore-front of my mind, but she had said nothing about ghosts and I refused to put store in a poltergeist. Preferring to avoid a recurrence, I put the rock in a kitchen cupboard, well-hidden at the back behind a stack of plates.

It took a cold beer and a bowl of ice cream to settle my thoughts. Then I brought in the washing and closed the bathroom window and set about saving on my hard drive the photos I had taken of my outbuilding.

Later, I wrote my first entry in my notebook, pleased to at last be using the pretty, folio sized hard cover I had found in a local bookstore. I called my first entry, Day One. It was not an easy entry to scribe. I had wanted the day to be joyous and celebratory and I had come away with a trough full of negativity. My build sat beneath a cloud of doom. I described the calima, Mario, the men, the good progress and even my faux pas with the rock piles. I saw no need to mention the partition-wall rock in my living room.

7

BETANCURIA

THE CALIMA LASTED ANOTHER THREE DAYS. I REMAINED INDOORS FOR the duration, reading the Agatha Christie in Spanish translation that had been left on the single shelf, and when I tired of that I listened to music through my headphones. I steered clear of the Cocteau Twins, choosing Fela Kuti and Angelique Kidgo, upbeat music with a happy, exhilarating vibe, from artists with roots not too far from the Canary Islands. A boyfriend – Simon, I think it was – had put me onto them one time.

When the Kidgo album came to an end, I sent my father and aunt each a short email informing them the building works had begun. Neither replied, at least not soon enough. I found myself checking my inbox intermittently, craving human interaction, even at an electronic distance. Alone in my tiny apartment as I rode out the dust storm, listening to the laughter and clatter of my neighbours through sound-porous walls, I stared into my immediate future wondering how I would fare for much longer with no friends and little meaningful human contact. But I wasn't about to let a spot of isolation bother me. The answer was simple. I would keep busy. My friendless state wouldn't last forever. I had always been good at the self-pep talk. Perhaps it is an attribute that comes with the single life.

On the Friday of that week, I drove to Tiscamanita and parked outside my property on the opposite side of the road, with a direct sightline to the barn. Binoculars would have been handy, but I could see at a distance that the timbers had begun to go up on the roof and the doorway had a new lintel. Four men meant fast progress. The barn was small and in much less disrepair than the main house. It was a pleasing sight but I didn't hang about. The moment one of the men spotted me in my car, I turned on the ignition and drove off.

Keen to learn more about the history of the house, I pulled up in the main street of Tiscamanita near a small café that had 'local' stamped all over it. Before I went in, I stood on the pavement and surveyed the surrounds, realising as I did that in all the time I had driven through the village, I had never bothered to stop and visit the shops and cafés.

The businesses in the village centre comprised a bakery, a butcher, a small grocery store, a hairdresser, two cafés and a restaurant all huddled around the church and plaza. Enough to service the local population and nothing more. With a population of about five hundred, you couldn't expect much by way of facilities. Yet the village was doing little to appeal to the passing holidaymaker. The potential was there; the village was cut in two by the Antigua-Tuineje road and home to a restored windmill, Los Molinos, that had been turned into one of the island's numerous museums. Although, the windmill was situated on the edge of the village and holidaymakers would no doubt be on their way to the next tourist site. It would probably take a lot to make them stop awhile, much more than a bit of village titivation.

Sadly, Tiscamanita had an atmosphere of decline. Shop premises were vacant. Many of the farms abandoned. There was not enough to attract people, nothing around to keep people. Most of the foreigners favoured the coast and who could blame them, and the locals who remained probably enjoyed their quiet lifestyle while their offspring left in search of work and excitement.

It was with a sense of unease that I approached the café, wondering how I would be received, this blow-in from Colchester, a cashed-up new resident keen to establish herself amongst the locals.

At least I was able to communicate in the language. Surely that would invoke a positive response.

I had chosen to live in Tiscamanita in part because situated there I could disassociate myself from the rest of my cohort, the Brits, or at least, so I thought. Standing on the pavement observing the quietude, my assumptions seemed unrealistic. I didn't know a thing about the village or its people, save for what I could see with my own eyes and a few paragraphs I had come across online. I was, and I suspected would be for a long long time, an outsider.

I entered the café, foregoing the outdoor seating in favour of a table by the window. It was too early for lunchtime trade. Two men in work gear ambled in not long after I sat down. They made their purchases and went on their way, leaving me the only patron. I scanned the menu written on three small boards hanging on the wall behind the counter. There was to be no table service. I got up and approached the woman standing by the tapas bar and ordered a coffee. Thinking to please her with my custom I also ordered a slice of the tortilla on display. She seemed pleasant enough: dumpy, middle aged and proud. I guessed she was the owner.

I resumed my seat and when she came over with my order, I gave her my warm bank-teller smile and asked if the café was hers. When she nodded warily, I let my smile broaden and, holding her gaze I said, 'Then we are neighbours.'

The woman appeared taken aback, no doubt thinking, not another English migrant buying up the real estate. She opened her mouth to speak and changed her mind.

Seeing she was about to walk away, I shifted round in my seat. 'I've bought the Cejas house. In Calle Cabrera.'

A curious look came into the woman's face, part wonder, part hesitation, part fear.

'Casa Baraso?' she said slowly. 'I heard someone had bought that. It was you?'

'Casa Baraso? Was that the original owner?'

The property had been in the Cejas family for many generations and I had presumed they were the original owners. I had not come across a Baraso.

'Señor Baraso never owned the house,' she said, taking a small step closer. 'He lived there for many years. He was a government official from Tenerife.'

I thought back to that article I had read, the one that had piqued my interest in purchasing the house. I felt certain there had been no mention of a Baraso. Perhaps it was local knowledge, or I simply hadn't taken in the information. I wondered how I would go about investigating the man. A library? A historical society? I should start by quizzing the café owner.

I opened my mouth to speak when two women entered and greeted the owner in loud voices. They all headed to the counter together and I had clearly lost my chance. I attended to my omelette, enjoying the faint garlicky flavour, and sipped my coffee, which was average. As I ate I could feel the eyes of the women on my back. They had lowered their voices but I knew they were talking about the house. I heard 'Cejas' and 'Baraso' clear as a bell. I wanted to ask more questions, especially about Señor Baraso, and I also wanted to ask the café owner if she knew the reason for my labourers' refusal to be involved in the restoration, but confronting three local women at once felt daunting. Small village gossip and the knowledge that I was being judged had already caused me to retreat somewhat. It was a defence. Whenever I felt threatened, I retreated into the clam shell I had created as a child to protect myself from hurt. Right then it was a shrinking back that served to reinforce a sense that my new life would not be as easy a ride as I had thought.

I finished my tortilla and coffee and waited for the two women to either sit down or leave—they left—before approaching the counter to pay. I tried to catch the woman's eye, but she showed no interest in talking to me. I thanked her and as I was leaving I told her the tortilla was delicious, which clearly pleased her but she remained impassive.

After the interior gloom the sudden brightness of the day, glaring off the café's whitewashed walls, stung my eyes. A a cool reception in the café, and despite the oven heat that blasted me when I opened the car door, I was relieved to get going.

With the men on the building site preventing my presence on my property and the whole day to fill, I decided on a whim to drive to

Betancuria, the island's original capital, taking the southern route via Pájara to enjoy the sweeping bends up through the mountains. I would behave like a holidaymaker, I thought, and take my time. I even stopped at the designated lookout to admire the view of the mountains.

Betancuria nestles in a small basin of a valley, surrounded on all sides by low mountains with their smooth, almost sensual curves, the massif undulating like a scrunched and ruffled blanket. Elevated, and situated on the western coast, the old town tends to be cooler than the rest of the island. That day, it certainly felt more refined to me, too, with its narrow streets zigzagging up the valley slopes, flanked by charmingly restored buildings. There was a sense of opulence to the village centre, the island's showpiece. Manicured and immaculate, attention had been paid to every detail.

The island's conqueror, Jean Bétancourt, had chosen Betancuria to be the capital not for its ambience, but for the protection it afforded from piratical attack. Its sheltered position did not prevent the town from being razed by pirates in 1593, an event that fascinated even as the violence of it repelled me.

I pulled up in the main street, lucky to find a place to park outside the church. Fuerteventura, I thought wryly as I got out of my car, was known not only for its beaches. Although it had taken a good few visits before I stumbled on the island's art.

La Iglesia Santa María de Betancuria is undoubtedly the finest example, a church that dominates the old capital. It is a magnificent edifice by all accounts. Baroque in style, it has arched windows set high in its brilliant white walls, a stout tower and stone quoining. The church shouts to all around. There is no escaping the faith that ruled here.

The structure is cut into the hillside. A large paved plaza, containing several stone seats and an arrangement of formal plantings, provides holidaymakers and locals a chance to soak in the atmosphere. Entry to the church is through carved wooden doors set in a rounded arch capped with an intricately carved pediment. I passed by a family who were preparing to head off to the gift shop and made my way into the cool.

The church interior exudes majestic religiosity, with its vaulted ceilings and impressive altarpieces made all the more striking beside the stark white of the walls.

Ignoring a few holidaymakers milling about, I went into the sacristy to stare up at the coffering. I had visited this church every holiday since the day I wandered inside to see what all the fuss was about, after overhearing two women enthusing.

The sacristy ceiling was enough to cause a crick neck in even the most cynical of observers. Each square contains a uniform pattern of rosettes and foliage painted in rich tones of gold and red and green.

When my neck felt stiff and sore, I studied the paintings. Then, I returned to the nave and sat at the end of a pew, my gaze fixed on one of the smaller altarpieces, rendered in the same rich colours. A statue of the Immaculate Virgin Mary stood in its own recess flanked by pilasters. My eye was drawn first here, then there, by all the intricate details. Such a piece of art was surely enough to lure even the non-religious into the church. You almost felt an impulse to worship.

I had never understood that impulse. Neither side of my family were devotees of any faith. My father is a materialist to his core, and my mother's side are dyed-in-the-wool occultists. Little wonder that to me, religion was brainwash, designed to force obedience in return for vague and unsatisfactory explanations of human suffering and spurious promises of an afterlife. Too often religion was used to control and oppress. When the Canary Islands were conquered, natives were forced to relinquish their own belief system and adopt Catholicism. If they didn't, they would die. For centuries thereafter, churches were built and congregations went to mass and took communion and learned to do what they were told. Stifling. The best that could be said was it left a legacy of fine old art.

People wandered in and out. In no hurry to move, I remained seated, absorbing the results of so much wealth and power. An inner peace infused me, but it was to be a peace short-lived. For it occurred to me in an unwelcome surge that I had bought into the island's colonial history. For I had fallen for a nobleman's house, not one owned by a humble farmer. Did that mean I had delusions of grandeur? Me, Claire Bennett, a humble bank teller from Colchester, the owner of a mansion by island standards. The realisation made me feel uncomfortable in my own skin. What did I imagine I was going to do in such a grand house once it was restored? That photographer, Paco, was right. I needed a husband, children, people to fill six bedrooms. Perhaps I should rent out rooms or otherwise turn a profit from it, but nothing of the sort held any appeal. I wanted my home all to myself, although sitting in that big old church, the prospect suddenly seemed absurd. It was as though I had been pierced by a pin that deflated my hot air balloon of fantastical, grand-design desire.

Shaken, I left the church and sat in the plaza, watching the sight-seers ambling back and forth. I had been on the island two weeks. I had had little chance to enjoy my wealth, although the sense of freedom it gave was liberating. I was consumed with anticipation over the build. For yet again I knew I had not addressed one fundamental and ghastly question: Had I done the right thing moving to Tisca-manita? Shouldn't I have bought a villa on the coast?

Aunt Clarissa leaped into my mind, reminding me for the umpteenth time of all those astrological lines criss-crossing Fuerteventura. This time, I paused for thought. What was it she had said about Neptune and the twelfth house? Whatever it was, I doubted the relevance and my rational self waded in with an answer. There are times when bridges are burned and there is no going back. I had six-hundred-thousand-euros invested in that ruin and I was not about to buckle. Besides, I had no past to go back to. The only way was forwards. It might not prove an easy progression, but it was one that had to be made.

After a while my pep talk worked and my positive mind-set returned. On the hunt for a good place for lunch, I left the church and went for a walk down first one, then another of the narrow, paved streets.

I chose an eatery near the cultural centre, drawn by the old wine barrels serving as tables outside. Finding the restaurant full, I sat at a table by the door and ordered the menu of the day and a bottle of beer. I soaked in the din, the clatter, the delicious cooking smells. What better reason did I need to be here?

A vegetable soup came first and I tucked in, not realising I was famished until that first mouthful of rich stock enlivened my taste buds.

I was scraping the last of the soup from my bowl when a figure entered the bar. I looked up to find Paco staring at me. How odd.

'We meet again,' he said, hovering behind the vacant chair.

I raised a smile. 'Are you keeping well?'

He gestured at the table and, seeing my nod of encouragement, he pulled out the chair and sat down.

'How goes the restoration?'

'I'm having a barn renovated first. The men were working on it today when I drove by. I think it's going well.'

'I saw them too. Why are they not fixing the house?'

'You went by my property?' I said, feeling intruded upon, almost spied on, even as I knew that feeling was silly.

'I often take a detour,' he said, as though driving by my ruin was a daily occurrence. 'I'm a photographer.'

'You told me.' I held his gaze, expecting more.

'I like to monitor the old houses, make sure nothing bad happens to them.'

I was not convinced but his explanation would have to do. There didn't seem anything to say in response.

'What brings you up here?' he asked.

'What brings *you* up here?'

'I'm visiting a friend.'

'And I'm enjoying being a holidaymaker for a day.'

He smiled. It was a warm smile and I returned it with one of my own. The awkwardness between us eased. Paco hailed a waiter and ordered a beer.

'Why are you especially interested in my house?' I said, hoping for an honest answer.

This time, he was forthcoming, no, more than forthcoming; his eyes were ablaze and his face filled with wonder. 'A woman, an Englishwoman visited there many years ago. It is she who I am fascinated with.'

'Who was she?'

'Her name is Olivia Stone. You may have heard of her.'

'No, I do not believe I have encountered any Olivia Stone.'

'Then you must buy her books,' he said, leaning forward in his seat.

'She was a writer?'

'Of travel diaries. She wrote a very famous book about the islands.'

'I can't say I've come across it.'

'In the 1880s. A long time ago to you, perhaps. She came to Fuerteventura and stayed in a number of houses in the villages. Yours was one of them.'

'Wow, I'm impressed,' I said, not quite believing a single word he was saying.

'You should be impressed. She was a very special lady.'

I wanted to find out more about the mysterious woman, but my main course arrived along with Paco's beer, and after the waiter had cleared away my soup bowl, I beheld a generous sized dish of goat stew with whole potatoes and a garnish of parsley. The aroma made me salivate. I hesitated.

'Eat. Eat,' he said, gesturing at my food.

Chewing the first mouthful, I decided it was the most delicious goat stew I had ever tasted. Paco sipped his beer and watched.

'Are you not hungry?' I asked between mouthfuls, uncomfortable under his gaze.

'I've just eaten.'

Something caught his eye and he swung around and stood up, waving at a woman appearing through a side entrance.

'Until another time,' he said as he walked away.

I swallowed and raised my fork by way of goodbye, watching him leave and feeling his absence.

BACK IN PUERTO DEL ROSARIO I swung by the local bookstore but they did not have a copy of anything by Olivia Stone. The assistant hadn't even heard of her.

I returned to my apartment and looked up the author online. It took several searches before I found it. *Tenerife and Its Six Satellites: Volume II* was available from several international bookstores. It was a peculiar feeling punching in my details and giving my current address.

8

TEARS

It was Saturday. After writing a brief note in my notebook on the progress of the barn, as seen from my car window, I spent the morning creating a spreadsheet. I devised budgets for fixtures and fittings, the kitchen and bathroom suites, and furniture. Immersed in numbers and itemising each aspect of the interior gave me a sense of control and put me at ease after the turbulence of the day before. I needed to restore a sense of normalcy and crunching numbers was the best way I could think of to do it.

During my online travels to various homewares and hardware stores, I had downloaded brochures and price lists and taken screenshots of others to give me an idea. My Essex roots cautioned me against cost blowouts. I would adopt a style that allowed for the occasional piece of stunning furniture yet wouldn't diminish my bank balance. I decided against antique in favour of rustic and locally made wherever possible. I would have plenty of time to collect what I wanted.

Even with my frugal approach I was amazed at the size of the final figure. One curtain rod might only be ten euros but multiply that by the number of windows and costs soon start to run into the hundreds, even thousands. Power points and light switches were even worse. I had to keep reminding myself I could afford it. Adjusting to being a multi-millionaire after watching the pennies for decades was not easy. My banking background didn't help either. I automatically looked for savings.

Before I closed my laptop, I entered 'Olivia Stone travel author' in the search engine to see what came up other than her Canary Islands' book. I soon discovered she was the wife of a barrister, John Matthias Stone, and her book was presented to Queen Victoria. She was well-connected then, a society lady perhaps, and she was the author of an earlier work, *Norway in June*. She lived in an era of curiosity and exploration. She must have been one of those robust British women given to travelling to far-flung climbs. I could picture her, a rational dresser, big-boned with hefty thighs and a strident, forthright look about her.

I clicked on a few more websites and finding little more, my interest waned. I would wait and read the book for myself. I had enough going on without getting side-tracked researching a woman who may or may not have stayed in my house for a night or two.

I lunched on yet another ham and cheese baguette, this time with slices of tomato. I really ought to broaden my culinary habits, I told myself, as crumbs scattered across the counter.

Builders do not work weekends. With the afternoon ahead of me, I filled my water bottle and grabbed my car keys thinking I would check on progress. The drive had already become second nature and I was outside my block in half an hour without noticing how I got there.

No other car was parked in the street. Having yet to meet a neighbour, I was starting to wonder if all of the surrounding properties were empty. Otherwise, why had no one put in an appearance? Surely, they would be dying of curiosity by now?

The first change I noticed onsite was the complete absence of my rock pile near the barn. That, and all the roof timbers were on. On closer inspection, the walls had been capped with mortar and a top plate, and two evenly spaced beams spanned the width of the building. I couldn't be sure as I had no idea how long a job like this would take, but it appeared the men were working at breakneck speed. Adding to the pace of the works, when Mario had emailed me his full quote for the barn, he explained that the timber was left over from another job which was why it had arrived on site so fast. Not that it appeared I had been given any sort of discount. The hip roof would be clad in the traditional curved clay roof tiles which had also arrived. Presumably Mario had a stock of them ready to hand as well.

Mario might have thought me crazy to insist work started on that small barn, but once it was weather tight and lockable, I could use it for storage. My possessions would be arriving from the UK in about two months and, meagre as they were, I still had nowhere to store them at my tiny apartment.

I approached the main house with trepidation. I hadn't been inside since that time with Mario. Whenever I thought of the state of the ruin I felt anxious. I had a gnawing feeling the walls would fall before the council approved the plans.

The gap in the boarded-up doorway was bigger; a bottom section of the plywood had been snapped off. I ducked through and, keen not to stand in rooms with any overhead timbers, hurried through to the patio.

Nothing had changed. Not even the weeds had grown. I stood facing the direction of the street and observed the remaining section of the balcony, a balcony that would have provided access to the upper rooms, and I noticed how the partition wall cut the balcony in two, to prevent anyone upstairs from walking around the internal perimeter of the building. On the side where I stood, the timber was weathered and there looked to be evidence of borers.

Gingerly, I walked around, studying the walls more closely than before. Where the plaster had come away, the construction method was evident. The cornerstones were carved basalt blocks, the rest of the wall made up of large rocks wedged in place, much smaller stones and pebbles filling the gaps. Vertical cracks ran down the lengths of both gable ends at the northern section of the ruin, confirming my fear that if something wasn't done soon, the whole structure would collapse.

As though to reinforce my thought one of the timbers groaned in a room on my right. I heard a scuttle, and the flapping of wings as a bird flew down to investigate my presence.

On my last visit, I hadn't ventured through the hole in the wall. I bent and stepped through, noticing as I did a curious drop in temperature, as though the southern side of the building received less sun and attracted more wind. Yet the opposite was true.

The southern internal wall was in a dreadful state of repair. There was little roof left, no second level flooring and portions of the internal walls had fallen. Others were crumbling. The patio had been all but stripped of its balcony. Out of the two portions of the ruin, the south side was the most dilapidated and forlorn. Unlike the northern half, which groaned and threatened collapse, the southern had already done so. There was not much left to tumble.

Wanting to at least feel the thrill of ownership and gain a realistic sense of what I had taken on, I found a flat patch of rubble-free ground near the partition and sat down, cross-legged. I adjusted the buckle of a sandal that was digging into the ankle of my other foot. Then I straightened my blouse.

As soon as I was comfortable and still, a strange, trance-like mood overcame me. I was not one for meditating but I had taken relaxation classes once and I experienced the same heady tranquillity.

Instead of reflecting on the present circumstances of the ruin, I was drawn back to its past. I felt as though I was paying my respects to the previous owners, to all that had ever happened there. I found myself imagining the home's former glory. I pictured a pond and perhaps a fountain in the patio centre, and beneath the balcony stands of plants positioned in the corners and beside every post. I imagined doors opening onto a salon or a dining room, the stairs ascending. I sensed the stillness, and I could almost hear the acoustics.

Then I heard Elizabeth Fraser's voice reverberating around the walls, the music of the Cocteau Twins filling the atmosphere with ethereal beauty, a sense of godliness in sound, my ruin the equivalent of a cathedral. I was filled with a strong sense of well-being mixed with euphoria. Any doubts I had over the enormity of the project absented themselves and I was entirely mesmerised.

My trance deepened and it was then I saw my mother tiptoeing down the stairs in a long white dress. I was shocked to see her in this alien setting, shocked I was even able to picture her in this fashion. Yet there I gazed, at her locks of honey hair flowing, her face so serene, her eyes alight with wonder. Fascinated and transfixed, I watched as her hand slid down the banister.

She wasn't real. As her feet touched the paving of the patio, I lost her and in her absence an upsurge of grief overwhelmed me. Through the lens of my anguish, I saw the restoration as a homage to the mother I scarcely knew.

Tears tumbled from my eyes and streaked down my cheeks. My throat ached. I shuddered under a weight pressing down on my chest. Soon I was gasping for air, bending over where I sat, my hands clawing at the weeds around me, ripping out stems and leaves, reaching out and yanking at roots.

The emotion faded as fast as it had come and I was left feeling empty and stunned. The anguish, more the intensity of it, had been unexpected. I hadn't cried over my mother's death since the funeral and I only cried then because everyone else was. I had no idea I held within me unexpressed grief. For thirty years I had gone through life accommodating her absence, missing her, wondering what my life might have been like with her in it, but never once grieving for her as though I had been hollowed out.

Perhaps it was a mistake to listen to the Cocteau Twins so much. My imagination was becoming overactive. I had inadvertently invoked an opening deep within and I was disconcerted by it. I didn't want the restoration to carry a stamp of personal religiosity. I was not restoring the ruin to create a memorial to my mother. I wanted a home to live in.

I got to my feet and breathed deeply and wiped my eyes with the back of my hands. Somewhere in my handbag I had a tissue.

Eager for a sense of space around me, I ducked through the hole in the partition and headed back outside. This time I didn't dare take a rock home with me.

9

PUERTO DEL ROSARIO

I AWOKE LATE THE NEXT DAY. IT WAS SUNDAY AND THE NEIGHBOURHOOD was quiet. I opened the bedroom blind to find cloud obliterating the normally garish sunlight.

The cloud thickened and by lunchtime it was raining, not heavily, but enough to keep me indoors. My mood mirrored the weather and I succumbed to an attack of the doldrums. I skulked around the apartment like a caged animal, picturing my lonely life in a restored ruin, mistress of troubled memories. I was bored, tender and disturbed by turns. My grief had been unleashed and looked set to tramp about inside me with a will of its own. My doubts returned. I was taking on too much. I had no right to restore that ruin and should never have bought it. What would I do with myself when I had? I would be doomed to rattle around in my great big house and go slowly mad from loneliness, haunted by my own mother. I began to question what I was even doing on the island. I couldn't bring myself to listen to the Cocteau Twins for fear of stirring up my grief even more, so I played the Gorrilaz hoping they would cheer me up.

They didn't.

My miserable and fragmented state was so out of character, I didn't recognise myself. Eventually, I applied my listless mind to studying Spanish, looking up to watch raindrops trickle down the kitchen window pane as though they were my own tears.

Only once did I open the kitchen cupboard to make sure the rock was still there tucked at the back behind the plates. It was.

Monday the weather had returned to its normal fine and sunny self. I took advantage of the fresh, dry air and, with my notebook in my bag, headed out on foot to see if I could discover from public records something of the history of my house.

I strode down Avenida Juan de Bethencourt until it fed into Calle León y Castille. Both roads enjoyed a central reservation planted with established trees, including palm trees. Puerto del Rosario's efforts at beautification centred in the harbourside locale. My spirits lifted a little in the beholding. It was the tourist in me coming to the fore. I wanted everywhere on the island to look like Betancuria, although Puerto del Rosario was never meant to be a holidaymaker destination. An old fishing port once known as Puerto de Cabras (Goats Port), the capital was the island's commercial and municipal hub and that was it.

I have always found it a shame not more of the villages and towns of Fuerteventura have retained their quaintness. Yet pockets of olde worlde charm can be found, in La Oliva, Tuineje and Pájara, towns I have visited on numerous occasions to enjoy an amble in their sheltered, tree-filled plazas, and a nice lunch.

The ordinary and uninspiring surroundings of the city gave way to grandeur on the next block where the municipal council, a stately building, formal in design, faced the equally stately looking town hall. Both faced the same plaza that was dominated, not by government authority, but by an old church: Parroquia de Nuestra Señora de Rosario.

The plaza was elegantly laid out and paved, but lacked shade.

As if to complete the symbols of power, new and old, all that officialdom was accompanied by a number of banks. I found it striking that power and influence and money should all be huddled together like that, showing off their stature. Yet, why wouldn't they? It was more surprising that in all the time I worked for a bank branch in Colchester, I never once questioned or even acknowledged the same sort of clustering. Acutely aware of my own wealth, I had become self-conscious and therefore more conscious of the wealth around me, yet I would remain an outsider when it came to that level of privilege. I would never have power or influence. I didn't even want it. I would remain humble Claire Bennett forevermore. Unlike whoever built my ruin, who certainly had power, or influence, or both.

Wandering around the perimeter of the plaza, I found an even greater irony. Should a citizen commit a transgression, the police department was tacked on behind the town hall and I noticed the courthouse up behind the church. Every aspect of institutional power, then, was concentrated in that small area. It was probably happenstance, I thought, making excuses, and I supposed it would be convenient for the staff. And for me. If I was to discover the truth about the previous owners of my house, it would be amongst those edifices.

I went first to the town hall but was shunted to the municipal council where the titles of all the island's properties were held. The assistant at the enquiries desk greeted me in English. I explained my request and produced my identification and details of my property purchase. The assistant, an impassive, middle-aged man, walked away.

I had a long wait in that cool and austere interior. Behind me, a queue formed. I felt inclined to step aside, but no other assistant appeared so I stayed where I was.

The man returned with a folder, muttering something about lawyers and questioning to himself why mine hadn't shown me the details. I responded, in my best Spanish, telling him it was because I hadn't asked. His manner changed instantly and he turned a document around for me to read, pointing to the relevant details with a pen.

The newspaper article was accurate, he said.

I sensed restlessness in the queue but the assistant appeared in no hurry and since he clearly wasn't about to trust me with the file, I read as fast as I was able.

The original owner was a Don Gonzalez, a wealthy man who owned a vineyard in Tenerife. He built the house in 1770. What he hoped to gain by living in Tiscamanita, heaven only knew. Perhaps he was an absentee owner of that Tenerife vineyard, a don who resided in Spain and, being a beach-loving type, he chose Fuerteventura for his holiday home. In *Tiscamanita*? Oh, well. Perhaps he saw potential in cochineal. I read on. In 1870, his descendants, for whatever reason, sold the premises to the Cejas family. Upon the death of Señor Juan Cejas in 1895, the property fell into the hands of his daughter, a Doña Antonia Cejas and his nephew, Santiago Cejas. That must have been when the wall went up.

The article told me nothing more. I scribbled down all the details, thanked the assistant and took my notes to the municipal library, a short walk down Calle Primero de Mayo.

The library is housed in a modern building facing a cultural centre and concert hall, in what serves as Puerto del Rosario's artistic hub. Despite the separation of culture from institutional power, I like the compartmentalising of the little city in this fashion. It makes practical sense. On that day of my quest, I especially liked that I could walk to all I needed.

Inside, the library was light and airy, and on the upper level much use had been made of tubular railing painted primary-school yellow. I went straight to the information desk with my query and was directed by a helpful assistant in clearly enunciated English to a selection of local history books. I thanked her in Spanish and we exchanged glances and laughed softly together. She was young, perhaps no more than twenty-five, and her attitude was accommodating and, I thought, refreshingly cosmopolitan.

I went and pulled every book on local history from the shelf and stacked them on a table nearby. I trawled the indexes on the hunt for Don Gonzalez and Señor Cejas. I found no mention of Gonzalez. He couldn't have made any sort of impression here or involved himself in local politics or culture. The house may have been an indulgence, a folly, even a way of sinking his wealth into rock and mortar. Maybe he was a reclusive type and wanted to hide. Or the records detailing him were lost. I did find a short paragraph on Cejas in a book on the history of Tuineje.

From what I could glean, the Cejas family were a distant and lesser arm of one of Spain's noble dynasties, and had derived much wealth from the cochineal beetle. Remembering the owner of the café in Tiscamanita referring to my house as Casa Baraso, I went back through all the indexes. I could find no mention of anyone with that surname. Having no idea when he lived in the house, I looked no further.

I hadn't discovered much, but browsing those volumes aroused my interest in the history of Fuerteventura, so I decided to hang around and have an explore.

I picked up a book entitled *Arte, Sociedad y Poder: Casa de los Coroneles* which had been published in 2009 by the Canary Islands government. My Spanish would be stretched to the hilt in the comprehending, but after my recent observations of how power liked to cluster together and look after itself, I thought it appropriate I took some time to understand the history. I felt guilty that in all my years of holidaying, I had never once taken the trouble to really know the place. Owning a ruin had changed that and was fast putting paid to my ignorance.

The book concerned the reign of colonels that began in the early eighteenth century. The rule was dynastic, all the colonels coming from the same family, the Cabrera Bethéncourts. Primarily, the volume concerned a grand house in La Oliva, Casa de los Coroneles, once the home of the much-feared Colonel Augustín de Cabrera Bethéncourt Dumpierrez. A preamble in the book provided a short history of life in Fuerteventura during the eighteenth and nineteenth centuries, which included the first hundred-year background story to my house.

From what I could glean, both the local bourgeoisie and the Spanish nobility held onto their wealth through intermarrying and bequeathing all to the first bon son, as the aristocracy the world over tended to do. Initially the rich, the Señores, lived up around Betancuria where the soil was fertile. That, I already knew. For two hundred years after its conquest, the island population was organised into militias under the command of the Lord's elected captain. Then, in 1708 under the Borbon dynasty, the age of the colonels began, and for the next one hundred and sixty-two years, up until the year Cejas bought my ruin in 1870, judicial and military power lay in the hands of a single colonel answerable only to the Spanish King. No other local authority or lord had any sway. So much power concentrated in one man, and since his overlord was the Spanish King who was far, far away, the colonel could do whatever he wanted. The church was no help. The bishops were in cahoots.

There had been seven colonels in all, and my house was built during the rule of the most famous, the brutal and greedy Augustín Cabrera who took up the post in 1766 when he was just twenty-three and he ruled for forty-four years. He was also at various times during his term as colonel: alderman, judge and chief constable of the court of the Inquisition. He became rich through taking out lawsuits against landowners who lacked the means to defend themselves, in order to take possession of their properties. He sounded like an absolute tyrant.

I had often tried to imagine what life might have been like for the locals before tourism took hold. I had visited many of the museums and pictured the subsistence farming life, primitive and simple, and inventive. I saw the windmills, marvelled over kitchen items and farm utensils and the water filters. The simple peasantry. Their goats. I saw old photos of oxen ploughing the fields and camels loaded with hay, and the curious domed grain stores the farmers built. Then there were the churches, one in every village, indicating a population devoted to Catholicism. I knew that religion had crushed the native's indigenous faith. I knew the island had been sparsely populated and I knew that the island's primary exports had been orchilla and barilla and much later, cochineal, along with grains when it rained enough for a surplus. I also knew Fuerteventura was looked down upon as the poor relation by its superior island neighbours, especially Tenerife. In all, I had built up a romantic image of peasantry battling the elements and it had aroused in me a desire to champion the underdog.

I also knew about the famous Winter house down in Cofete on the island's mountainous southern tip, home of a German engineer with close connections to Spain and Fuerteventura. Everyone who came to the island ended up knowing about Casa Winter. Gustav Winter had the house built in the late 1930s in a remote and inaccessible part of the island, and the house went on to be the source of much speculation and conspiracy theories associated with the Nazis. I had not visited Cofete, as I had no interest in wild beaches pounded by the Atlantic and there was nothing down there other than the mountainous terrain ending, on the western coast, in a long cliff.

Before I had entered the municipal library, I had felt armed with all I needed to know about the island. There didn't seem much to it. After all, how could there be, the place was that small. I had no idea I was holding onto a one-sided and partial understanding. What I had never taken the trouble to entertain before I bought my ruin was the domination of the peasantry by Spanish nobility and a local bourgeoisie. It was as though a veil was lifting. First Betancuria and now here. I wasn't sure what to make of any of it, other than it made me uncomfortable and, worse, uneasy.

I put down the book. Not given to wandering around stately homes, I had yet to visit the Casa de los Coroneles, but I decided I must, if only to see what sort of life the rich had led, while the poor battled it out with the elements. I would take a trip out to La Oliva sometime.

Claire Bennett from Colchester might be about to do the island a good turn in restoring one of the old homes of the local bourgeoisie, and I still felt it was important to do so, but I sensed I would be elevating the history of the oppressors, something that had been nagging at me since I sat in the church in Betancuria. For while that colonel and his cronies had gotten fat, misery confronted many a peasant farmer faced with drought and disease. It seemed bizarre that such opulence as was evident in the churches and stately homes could be derived from a land so difficult to live off.

I filled a couple of pages of my notebook with general information and took photos of old photographs and left the library with my head full of facts. After stopping for lunch at a local café, I trudged back to my apartment. The walk was uphill all the way.

10

OLIVIA STONE

My inquiries at the government office and the library had provided a taste of the history of my ruin but I was no closer to finding out about Señor Baraso, or why the locals referred to my house as Casa Baraso. The Olivia Stone wouldn't arrive any time soon and it felt like my investigations in Puerto del Rosario had come to a halt. I spent the rest of the week browsing through furniture stores, kitchen and bathroom showrooms, and car yards—I needed to purchase my own vehicle and lose the rental—whiling away the time. I replied to an email from my father with a brief update and sent a longer email to Aunt Clarissa, tailored to suit. By the following Saturday I had had my fill of hanging around Puerto del Rosario.

As the sunlight warmed the street and the air in the city heated up, I packed my gardening tools in the car boot and took myself off to a garden centre in Tefía which, according to their website, carried a wide range of drought and wind tolerant plants.

Tefía is situated on an elevated plain towards the island's remote north-eastern edge. The plain is windswept, stark and too exposed for comfort. The mountains at that northern end of the island are as moulded and as rugged as everywhere else. The tones pale, chalkier-looking in the gullies. In all, the locale is a backwater, if an island as small as Fuerteventura could have such a thing.

I exited the village and found the garden centre, accessed via a short stretch of dirt road. I parked facing north to avoid the worst of the sun on the windscreen, left the window open a crack, and crunched my across the gravel and on inside.

It was soothing browsing rows of plants. I enjoyed the green. A quiet contentment filled me as I wandered up and down. I found plant shopping infinitely preferable to the sterile environment of furniture and hardware stores. Although I faced the same problem. I had no idea what to buy.

Cacti and palms seemed the obvious choices but I fancied a different sort of look. I had been told the municipal council would provide up to forty free plants a year to every householder in an effort to green up the island, but I was yet to tap into that scheme. I settled on three drago trees, five aloe vera plants, ten tubes of a hardy-looking clumping grass and a few pots of a succulent ground cover. Not particularly adventurous choices, but they were all labelled hardy and drought and wind tolerant and they would need to be. I was planting up the far back corner of my block, well away from the build. It was an exposed spot and whatever I put there might well get forgotten.

The drive from Tefía to Tiscamanita took me back through the flat plain fringed by mountains, a plain that seemed to go on forever, although I was soon facing the Betancuria massif and heading down through Antigua. Half an hour and I was mounting the kerb outside my house, pleased I had cleared the block of rocks.

I parked a sensible distance from the area I planned to garden, pushing open the car door on a blast of wind. Eleven o'clock, and the sun had a bite to it. I reached in for my cotton scarf to wrap around my head. No doubt I looked strange, my head and neck covered in a scarf, my eyes behind dark glasses. I really needed one of those large hats the women used to wear.

With plant pots at my feet, my hands in gardening gloves, my garden fork and spade leaning against my wheelbarrow, I felt as far from bank-teller Claire as it was possible to be. My garden in Colchester—north-facing and grim—had consisted of a small paved rectangle decorated with a few straggly pot plants. A hanging basket beside the south-facing front door I maintained for show. Now, garbed in loose pants and a long-sleeved shirt, my head and neck shrouded in a scarf I wasn't sure who I was, this woman standing alone on an acre of land overlooking a volcano, about to dig holes and plant a garden.

Mistress of a ruin?

I looked back at the sad structure, and at my barn with its newly tiled roof. Standing on my own land, poised to dig my first hole and pop in a plant, I felt empowered and deflated all at once. I was alone. I had no one with whom to share any of my experiences. No mother, a father who took no interest—not that he would have been anything other than a bother, with endless reproaches and told-you-so looks— and no Aunt Clarissa, although she would have been at a loss in this wild, inhospitable environment. She favoured her creature comforts, did my dear old aunt. Besides, she was too old to help. As for my friends at the bank, they had started emailing me enthusiastically and were lining up to visit. I began to view the lot of them as free-loaders after a cheap holiday and I made a mental note to distance myself from each and every one of them. Which left a hole inside of me. I had been on the island one month and in that time I had made no friends on the island. Not one.

I shook off my maudlin thoughts, reminding myself that when visitors did come, I wanted to show them something I was proud of. I set to, choosing a spot a good six feet from the dry-stone wall and commenced digging.

The soil was dry, the progress slow. The only positives the paucity of weeds and the presence of a layer of volcanic gravel, which I shunted aside as I prepared a hole. How deep did the hole need to be? How wide? I knew that the plant must not sit proud of the soil that surrounds it, but what about the ground beneath? Didn't that need to be loose too? Or could I let the roots tough things out down there? Ten fork stabs later and finding the digging too hard, I compromised.

I planted a drago and stepped back to admire my efforts. The little plant looked lonely so I persevered with another hole about three yards from the first. The ground proved softer. Determination took hold and I got into a rhythm. When the third drago was in the ground

I downed tools and went to the small supermarket for snacks and a drink, both for me and my plants, coming away with five ten-litre water containers.

Having to ferry water in that fashion seemed ridiculous and I could have done with a garden tap, but that idea belonged in England where plumbing was everywhere and it rained. Out here, water was precious. Each house has its own underground water tank. Thinking about how often those plants would need a drink, I decided I had better go easy on the gardening or I would feel like a water bearer.

I kept digging and planting, taking short breaks to slug water or eat potato crisps and fruit, grateful the smaller plants needed smaller holes. I put the grasses along the front edge of my triangular garden bed, and the aloe veras I spaced out beside the walls. I staggered the ground covers in between the dragos. It was three o'clock when I finished. By then, the sun was ferocious. I was beginning to feel faint and desperate for shade.

I stood back for a moment. Before I set about watering in the plants I whipped off my scarf and doused my hair and face in the bottled water, putting the scarf back on to catch the drips and trap the wet cool.

With the gardening finished I left my tools and wandered around the block, observing the house next door, all enclosed behind a dense prickly pear hedge, and the one on the north side, with its long and high wall behind which I heard no sign of life, not a whisper or a cry or a barking dog. The old farmhouse across the street was clearly another ruin behind its weathered facade, and further up, the front windows of another farmhouse were shuttered. No one drove by as the street led nowhere other than to more ruins. I couldn't have chosen a lonelier spot. When I reached my restored barn, I opened the new and unpainted door and peered inside but there was nothing to see other than the crisscross of beams of the roof and the new window set high in the back wall. The cement floor was yet to be laid.

I was about to return to my car to pack up when a dusty old four-wheel drive slowed and stopped outside my block. I recognised the car as Paco's.

Seeing me, he strode over, adjusting the strap of his battered-looking satchel. I wasn't sure how to greet him having only met him twice, but he decided for me by leaning down and offering me his cheek.

'Good progress,' he said, nodding at the barn.

We strolled past the ruin and I showed him around. He looked inside and up at the roof.

'When do they start on the house?' he asked.

'I don't know.'

I wasn't sure what else to say. I didn't want to go into an explanation of council permits. 'I ordered the Olivia Stone book,' I said, eager, perhaps a little too eager to keep the conversation going.

'You can probably get a pdf online.'

'I prefer paper. Besides, there's no rush.'

'Maybe not. She visited Tiscamanita.'

'You told me.'

'I did?' He appeared puzzled, as though he couldn't fully recall our conversation in Betancuria. To cover his embarrassment he added, 'She stayed in Don Marcial Velázquez Curbelo's house.'

'And he was?'

'The older brother of the man whose street we're in.'

His gaze slid to the view behind me, of my little garden. Seizing on his interest, I led the way. As we walked over I said, 'Calle Manuel Velázquez Cabrera,' I enunciated every syllable. 'Who was he?' I asked with sudden interest.

'A lawyer who championed the causes of Fuerteventura and Lanzarote.'

'Impressive.'

'His brother, Marcial, was a cultured and literary man who impressed Olivia Stone with his wit and intelligence. She probably read his newspaper.'

'He produced a newspaper?'

'El Eco de Tiscamanita.'

'How marvellous! Is it still going?'

'Hardly.' His tone was not disparaging, although perhaps a little mocking. He was difficult to read. We stopped near my tools.

'Wow, you have been a busy woman!'

'It's a start,' I said with modesty.

'Why here in this corner?'

'It's safe from the build.'

'Ah, yes, of course.'

I should have let the conversation end there, but I was curious about this Olivia Stone woman.

'You think she could read Spanish then?'

'Definitely. Maybe. A little.' He sounded vague.

Not wanting the topic of conversation to fizzle before it got fully underway, I said with much enthusiasm, 'She sounds like a remarkable woman.'

'She was a lot more than that,' he said, his tone strangely serious. He turned his gaze back to my face. 'She disappeared, you know. There is no record of her death and no one heard of her after she published her book.'

'Surely, they did.' I didn't mean to sound dismissive. It was a habitual response I had picked up as a bank teller. I cautioned myself to lose the tendency quick smart. Keen to re-establish my earlier interest, I added, 'What else do you know about her?'

'She was born in Ireland and married an English barrister. They lived in London and moved in high social circles.' As I had suspected, he had turned cold on me again.

I grinned, hoping to win him over.

'Where did you acquire all this information?'

'From a biography published in a highly regarded magazine. It came with references.' He sounded proud. I sensed my smile had had the desired effect. He went on. 'The writer of the article suggests, and I believe, that she came to live here in the Canary Islands. There was a mention of a Stone, singular, arriving on the Wazzan in Tenerife in the November of 1895.'

'And you think it was her.'

'Has to be.'

'But people would have known about her then. People living on Tenerife.'

'Not if she came here.'

'To Fuerteventura?'

'To Tiscamanita.'

'But you have no evidence.' I paused. 'I'm sorry, I didn't mean to sound rude. Maybe you do have evidence. Do you?'

'The article says she named her house in Dover, 'Fuerteventura'.'

I paused. *Was that it?* All my efforts at placating the guy only to discover Paco really was nuts.

'But that does not mean she came to Tiscamanita,' I said gently, my impatience rising. 'Besides, what happened to her husband?'

'He re-married in 1900.'

'Then she died.'

'Or they got divorced.'

'People didn't get divorced back then.'

'Maybe she just took off.'

'And abandoned her marriage? Did she have children?'

'Three boys.'

'There you are then. She wouldn't have left them.'

'They would have been teenagers. And a right pack of ratbags if they were anything like their father.'

'You can't say that. You don't know him.'

'The article has a photo of him. I will bring it to you next time and show you. He looks like a pig of a man.'

'Even so, there would have been a scandal. A woman of her standing, it would have been all over the newspapers.'

The wind gusted, plastering my trousers and shirt to my skin. I turned my back on the brunt of it. An empty plant pot fell on its side and rolled a short distance, coming to rest beside the wheelbarrow.

Paco waited for the wind to calm down before continuing with his theory. 'All I know is the evidence stacks up. There is no death certificate, no death notice in any newspaper, nothing at all to record her death. And there is no record of a divorce either. Not according to the article, which was written by a scholar from the University of La Laguna.'

'Okay, so she disappeared. Maybe she came to Fuerteventura, but why Tiscmananita?'

'The answer is simple. Once you read her travel diary you will see.

She enjoyed the company of Marcial very much.' He paused. 'Maybe they had an affair.'

Was he serious?

'Maybe they did,' I said, deciding to humour him.

He pointed past me and said in a low voice. 'Right there, under your roof.'

'But this was Señor Cejas' house.'

'Just because Cejas owned it doesn't mean he lived in it.' He looked at his watch. 'Fancy a beer? You look like you need one.'

I laughed. It was a relief to mark an end to the conversation with a social invitation. 'I just need to pack up.'

'I'll meet you in the café opposite the church in Antigua.'

'The one at the end of the plaza?'

'You know it?'

'Café Rosa. Yes, I do.'

He turned, hesitated, then put down his satchel to help me pack away my tools. Then I watched him walk back to his car, puzzling over this strange man with an even stranger obsession, who might possibly become my first friend on the island.

11

ANTIGUA

I WAS SWEATY AND STICKY AND MY FACE BURNED HOT DESPITE THE SCARF and sunglasses. And I was as excited as a child anticipating cake. I saw Antigua up ahead. Paco made a left at the road leading to the town hall. I followed. The café was on the right, just past the police station.

The area around the plaza benefited from a dense planting of stout Canary palms. We both managed to find a park in some shade and entered the café together, Paco choosing a table in the corner by the window.

Spanish pop music played in the background. A young couple in shorts and T-shirts came in, gave the café a quick scan and, seeing the interior empty save for us and the local men and families at the back tables, walked straight back out again having evidently changed their minds or not seen who they were looking for.

'Beer?' Paco asked.

'I'm famished,' I said, picking up the menu on the table.

'They do a good goat stew.'

The man behind the counter came over and greeted Paco. They chatted in rapid Spanish I was too tired to absorb. Paco slowed his speech and ordered a plate of the stew and two beers.

'Aren't you eating?'

The man hesitated and we both looked at Paco, who patted his belly and shook his head.

'On me,' I said. He maintained a resistant look. 'Please, it's no fun eating alone.' I didn't wait for his reply. 'Make that two,' I said, and scanning the tapas menu I added, 'and give me the tomatoes and the olives.'

I handed him my menu. He grinned, clearly amused I had taken control.

'Anything more?' He directed his question at Paco, who had shifted his gaze to the window.

There was an awkward pause.

'That's all thanks,' I said to cover it.

The man walked away.

'I didn't mean to embarrass you,' I said, leaning forward.

'I'm not embarrassed.'

I didn't believe him.

'You know the waiter?'

'That's Juan, my mother's cousin's son. This café is his.'

I never considered myself socially awkward but there was something about the way Paco chose to converse, how I chose to converse with him, that felt stilted. I suddenly had to ask myself what to say as a follow up remark to his last. 'Are you from Antigua?' I knew I was jumping to conclusions, that he probably wasn't.

'Triquivijate.'

Another small village on the way from Antigua to Puerto del Rosario. Unlike Tiscamanita, the village is set back off the main road and receives no through traffic. It was a sort-after area with new subdivisions and luxury homes.

'Do your family own a farm?' It was the obvious question.

'Did. We grew prickly pear like everyone else.'

'And now?'

He shrugged. 'My parents live in Puerto del Rosario. My mother works at Costco and my father in an auto repair shop.'

'What about you?'

'I work in a restaurant in Caleta de Fuste.'

A waiter, then? A waiter in a restaurant?

'Is that where you live as well?'

'Too many holidaymakers there for me. I rent a small flat in Puerto del Rosario, near the beach.'

Paco's relative, Juan, came over with the beers and tapas, along with a basket of bread, and we occupied ourselves stabbing quarters of tomato drizzled with olive oil, and munching olives. I glanced out the window at the quiet street, thinking it odd that, just as in the past there were two Fuerteventuras, the peasants and their feudal overlords, today there are also two, here and the one on the eastern coastline dedicated to tourism where locals are forced into low-paid menial jobs as they yearn to hold onto a quieter, less foreigner-dominated existence. I felt a ping of awkward shame in the thinking. Then people like me come along and invade the hinterland. The island had already been sacrificed to the tourist dollar and I had no idea the effect that would have long term, but I doubted it would be good. Especially if nobody bothered to restore the old buildings. With the loss of the original architecture comes a loss of culture, a loss of identity. Despite my ethnicity—I couldn't help who I was—I shared Paco's interest, his determination to preserve what was left. Even if my house was the former residence of a fat cat. I wondered if Paco would see it that way. What *did* he think of me? He must warm to me, or why invite me out. He clearly wasn't as lonely as I was.

I guzzled my beer. The bitter fizz quenched a thirst I didn't realise I had. My face burned and my shoulders were beginning to ache from the hard labour of the day. Paco had gone quiet again. A photographer working in a restaurant? He was undoubtedly passionate but I had no idea the standard of his creative output. It seemed the only personal topic left to discuss and I pounced on the chance to discover more about this new and reticent friend.

I tried to catch his gaze as I spoke. 'Are you able to sell or publish your photos?'

He swallowed what he was chewing and chased it with a mouthful of beer before he spoke.

'In newspapers and magazines, yes. I'm working on an exhibition.' He hesitated and then added with a touch of irony, 'The restaurant where I work sells my postcards.'

'I don't suppose it all puts much food on the table.' I instantly wished I hadn't said that. I had probably offended him. I saw in a sudden rush that the comments I made as Claire Bennett the bank teller were no longer appropriate now I was rich.

'It isn't about the money,' he said. 'I take photos to capture the beauty of this island. Every passing moment of it, night and day.'

'Do you photograph the other islands?'

'When I can afford to travel. I want to visit El Hierro. Have you been? No? It is small and dramatic, the top of the volcano rising up from the ocean. There are no beaches there. But the views are breath taking.'

'I am not good with heights.'

He studied my face. 'You get used to it.'

I wasn't sure I would. England was comparatively flat, and I had never been any good up a tall building, let alone a mountain top or the edge of a cliff. Even at the lookout on the Pájara-Betancuria Road I'd had to stand well back from the edge to take in the mountains and the ocean far below.

The goat stew came and the conversation slid away as we each took our fork and spoon and dove in. The meat was tender, the flavours robust, the sauce thick and filling. I dunked in what was left of the bread. Paco looked over at his cousin and in a moment more bread came, and two more beers.

'Do you miss home?' he said eventually.

I felt instantly uncomfortable. 'Here is home,' I replied, hoping I didn't seem churlish.

'No family in England?'

'A father and an aunt.'

'That is all?'

'Yes.'

'That is sad.'

'Not sad. Just how it is.'

'And your mother?' he asked pinning me with his gaze.

'She died when I was seven.'

'A tragedy,' he said, smiling at me with sympathy. 'You miss her.'

I felt too uncomfortable to respond. 'And you?' I said instead. 'Brothers? Sisters?'

'Three brothers living here, and one sister in Gran Canaria. She's married with three boys.'

'Are your brothers married?'

'All married. All with children.'

'And you?' As the words exited my mouth I froze inwardly and was disconcerted by my reaction.

'Me?' He laughed. 'I have no one.' He looked sad for a moment. I thought something must have happened. A tragedy of the heart. Thankfully he didn't inquire of my love life, which was non-existent. I had gone on dates, tried out a few boyfriends – Simon was the longest – but none were my type. Who was my type? No one had broken my heart and I was accustomed to the single-person lifestyle. I had never felt I needed a man to complete me.

We were soon done with the stew. Paco set down his cutlery, glanced at his watch and sat back in his seat. Sensing the end to our time together, I murmured the name that had been playing at the fringes of my mind through the whole meal.

'Baraso.'

'Sorry?'

'My house is known locally as Casa Baraso. A señor Baraso lived there apparently.'

'Yes, I know. Baraso lived there for some time until his death in 1862.'

'Who was he?'

'A friend of Don Gonzalez's great grandson. Don Pablo Baraso Medina Rodriguez Bethéncourt.'

'What a mouthful. A nobleman then.'

I took a serviette and searched my bag for a pen. Amused, Paco reached in his satchel and handed me his. He repeated the name as I wrote.

'He had a wife and four daughters,' he told me. 'They all died in a yellow fever epidemic.'

I kept writing.

'Thirty years or so before you say Olivia Stone lived there?'

'She would have had the house to herself.'

'Maybe. Maybe Cejas never lived there. But when Cejas died he left the house to two lots of family and they had that partition wall put in. That would have been in 1895, around the time you say Olivia Stone stayed there. And that daughter and nephew must have lived in the house. Otherwise, what would have been the point of the wall?'

He considered my analysis without comment. I went on, insistent. 'It would have been a horrendous domestic situation, don't you think? They clearly didn't want to co-habit and perhaps even despised each other. They ruined the house with that wall.'

I sat back in my seat and waited for his reply which was not immediately forthcoming.

'They probably didn't care,' he said eventually. 'They were mainlanders and they were rich. To them, it was just a stupid little house on a stupid little island.'

I was surprised at his bitterness.

'Even so,' I said, determined not to let the topic go, 'I doubt Olivia Stone would have condoned that arrangement for one second.'

'She must have. Or maybe that wall was put up after she left. We don't know when the wall was built.'

'But surely, she could have stayed in any house in the area, more or less?'

Was I starting to believe his crazy story? He may have proof, however scant, and by her own account she did visit Tiscamanita and make a friend of Marcial, but I had no idea where he lived, although it was certainly not my house.

'You need to understand that she disappeared,' Paco said, shifting forward and resting his elbows on the table, holding my gaze, his eyes filled with intrigue. 'Desconocida. My theory is she lived in your house as a recluse. If she'd stayed anywhere else, with Marcial for example, then everyone would have known. There would have been a record. In Casa Baraso, shut up with only a maid, the villagers would have had no idea she was there.'

I couldn't quash the irritation rising in me. Paco was jumping to conclusions like a card-carrying conspiracy theorist. Casa Baraso was *not* Casa Winter.

'They must have known,' I retorted. 'The maid would have gossiped. What are you saying? That she arrived in the night and never left the house?'

All he said was, 'Yes.'

'And no one came? No one saw? She never even appeared in an open window?'

Paco didn't answer. I handed him back his pen and he dropped it in his satchel.

I pictured the size of my house, the enclosed patio, and speculated that it was possible Olivia Stone hid there. Not likely, but possible. Although, not for long, not for years and years.

My thoughts halted. The workmen believed the house was cursed and a curse could mean only one thing – something terrible and tragic had happened there. Maybe Olivia Stone died there and her ghost was trapped for some reason. Not that I believed in ghosts, not for one second, but Aunt Clarissa said the spirits of the dead became trapped on the earthly plane due to their intense emotions. In her case guilt, probably, if she had abandoned her sons. No, the whole scenario was just plain silly.

Not wanting to embarrass Paco, when his cousin came to take our plates I followed him to the counter and waited by the till.

When I turned back to the table, Paco was standing and putting his satchel over his head. I succumbed to a twinge of disappointment and regret. Had I blown a chance of friendship over my quarrelsome comments?

'Thank you for the food,' he said when I joined him to leave.

'It was nothing.'

I offered him a smile. Relief washed through me as he reciprocated.

'Are you returning to Puerto del Rosario?'

I had no idea why he asked, other than to make casual conversation.

'I thought I would head back to the house.'

'Mind if I join you? I'd like to take some more photos.'

'Sure.'

We had left Tiscamanita strangers, and returned as friends of a sort. I wasn't sure what Paco thought of me, but he was the only person I had had lunch with on the island and I wasn't about to pass up the opportunity of developing our friendship further.

He parked behind me. Together we headed around the back of the ruin and squeezed through the boarded-up doorway. Paco took out his camera and lined up a shot and then another. I watched, quiet, trailing him around. Eventually, he stopped and we stood by the partition wall. Every time I entered the ruin, that wall felt like the safest place to be. Yet it also felt wrong, impacting the integrity of the house, preventing it from expressing its glory, its true self. When Paco returned his camera to his satchel, I turned to him and said, 'Most days I can't believe I have taken on this project.'

'It will take years to complete.'

I hoped not.

'But at least it's going to be saved,' I said, absent-mindedly picking up a loose rock in the partition wall.

As if in response, our conversation was cut short by a protracted screech and boom. My heart responded with a boom of its own.

A plume of dust indicated the location. We went and peered tentatively in through a doorway in the northern end to find a small section of an internal wall had collapsed.

12

TUINEJE

D<small>AWN MADE ITS PRESENCE FELT THROUGH THE BLINDS</small>. D<small>ECIDING THERE</small> was no point remaining horizontal despite the early hour, I lumbered out of bed, stiff from yesterday. I had scarcely slept. At the forefront of my mind, stuck on replay, was an image of the wall falling. How much wall had I lost? I didn't know. It may only have been a square foot but in the darkness that square magnified tenfold until I was buried beneath a great pile of rocks and rubble.

I showered and dressed and ate a simple breakfast of fruit and toast. The moment it was decent to do so, I phoned Mario. I hoped he wasn't religious because it was Sunday.

He answered on the third ring. I tried to keep the tone of my voice measured as I explained the collapse, but by the end of my explanation I was frantic.

'We must talk to the council at once, Mario. This is urgent. The whole house might fall before they make up their minds to approve the restoration.'

'They've only had the plans three weeks.'

'Can't something be done?'

Mario told me to meet him at the council in Tuineje the next day at ten.

I was gripped by anxiety for the whole day. It was the longest twenty-four hours of my life. I flew around the apartment, tidying up and folding clothes and doing the dishes. I put on a load of washing and even mopped the floor in a vain attempt at self-distraction. I tried to read, and failed. After lunch, I went over my spreadsheet of costings but found that only made my anxiety worse. I went for a long walk down to the port and back, hoping to tire myself out. I listened to Blur, to Enya, even to Van Morrison, but my mind would not be still.

I awoke Monday on the break of dawn, determined to look smart for the appointment. I coiffed my hair and put on some light makeup, choosing a formal suit to wear. I propped a leather, document case – it was empty – under my arm and looked in the mirror. There was only one word to describe how I looked: official. I had turned back into my bank-teller self.

The quickest route to Tuineje was via Tiscamanita, a thirty-minute drive. I set off at a quarter past nine to allow plenty of time for contingencies, pulling up in the car park opposite the town hall in time to see Mario emerge from the side of the building. He must have parked around the back.

The town hall was a modern building painted terracotta red, with small and low windows evenly spaced along the two visible sides, and a second storey set back from the street. Situated on a corner, the front façade of the lower level comprised a concave arc. The entrance was tucked in the deepest part of the curve. Access was via a small concourse. The effect of the design was one of authority and officialdom on the one hand, and a welcoming openness on the other. Hope prickled as I crossed the road and made for the entrance doors, entering a spacious foyer. I saw Mario talking to a man behind the inquiries desk and joined him.

The man hesitated mid-sentence and glanced at me. I could tell by the reaction in his eyes that my garb had created the right impression.

'This is Claire Bennett,' Mario said, turning to welcome my presence.

'Claire,' the man proffered his hand. 'I'm Raul. I understand you are worried about your ruin falling down.' He gave me a sympathetic smile.

Not wanting to come across the stereotypical hysterical female, I thought better of telling him I could have been killed had I been standing in the wrong spot. 'The house is vulnerable,' I said, setting down my document case. 'Building needs to start right away.'

'Yes, we know. The previous owner wanted to demolish it.' He smiled. It was a wry smile. Were the council disappointed not to have made a successful purchase? Did they resent me? Or were they pleased someone, anyone was taking the trouble to fix up that ruin?

'I want to save the house,' said, 'but I am frightened we'll be too late.'

The man nodded and flicked through the pages of a file open before him. I spotted the house plans and the original versions of letters I had been sent.

'Your application is under consideration. These things take time. There is a process.' He shifted his gaze to Mario. 'You have explained this to her?'

'Can't things be expedited?' I enunciated the word, having learned it only that morning. 'Surely there has to be a way to make this happen faster? It's an emergency.'

Mario reinforced my remark with a brief, 'She's right.'

'Wait here,' Raul said, closing the file and heading off through a door with it under his arm.

Mario explained in a low whisper—not that there was anyone to overhear—that he was hopeful something would be done to speed things up. Before long, an older man in a white shirt came striding out, file in hand.

'Mario, Claire,' he said, proffering his hand to us both. 'You understand, there is a normal process that must be followed.'

'We know.' Mario spoke for us both.

The man opened the file and flicked through the paperwork, stopping at the plans. He studied them as though it was the first time he had ever seen house plans, pouring over every single drawing. It had to be a pretence. Without looking up, he said, 'Since you are making no changes to the original structure of the building, I am happy to say that we can grant you interim approval to make the building safe.'

'That's fantastic,' I said.

The man lifted his gaze to my face. 'For a fee of two thousand euros.'

I nearly fell through the floor. Daylight robbery, as my father would say. What sort of fee was this? Authentic? Or the greasy palm kind? I was pinned by both men's gazes.

'Very well,' I said, 'How do I pay?'

The man left the file and walked away, and before long Raul returned to attend to the payment. We were exiting the town hall fifteen minutes later.

'Thank you, Mario.'

He kept walking, turning to say, 'I will order the scaffolding and find the men. We'll start work straight away. Don't worry, no more of your house will fall.'

I watched him head off round the side of the town hall.

On my way back to Puerto del Rosario, I stopped off at the café in Tiscamanita. I thought it an opportunity to verify Paco's claim that the whole Baraso family had died there of yellow fever. Opening the door, I was relieved to find the café empty and the same woman behind the counter. This time, I walked straight up to her and held out my hand.

'I'm Claire,' I said warmly. 'Since you will be my regular café, I thought it would be good to introduce myself.' Even as I spoke, I felt ridiculous announcing myself like that.

Hesitant, the woman took my hand.

'Has the work started?' she asked.

'Not yet, but it is about to.'

She gave me a doubtful look.

'Who is working on it? Nobody here will go near it. You were lucky to get that barn fixed up.'

Someone has been down my street then, since she knows about the barn.

'Mario doesn't seem to think there will be a problem.'

'Mario Ferrero? It is good you have him. He'll find workers for you.

He speaks good English, and German as well. He'll find you foreigners.'

Despite her cool manner, she didn't seem averse to me. Maybe she didn't want to lose my custom.

'I'll have a white coffee and a slice of your tortilla,' I said, keen to steer the subject away from the house for a moment. I didn't want to barrel in with my inquiry, in case she thought me intrusive.

I took the table by the window and when she came over, I couldn't wait any longer. 'I hope you don't mind me asking, but I am trying to find out more about Señor Baraso.'

She was instantly cautious.

'Yes?' she said slowly.

'A friend told me he had a wife and four daughters.'

'That's correct.'

'And they all died in a yellow fever epidemic.'

'Who told you that?'

'Paco.'

'Paco?'

'He's a photographer from Triquivijate.'

'I know Paco.' She laughed. 'He thinks he knows everything.' She laughed again. It seemed a good-humoured laugh, but I sensed she was covering something.

I was about to probe further when a mother came in with a pram and two small children.

The woman glanced at the family. 'He knows the official version,' she said quickly. 'That is what everyone else will tell you, too.'

She hurried to the counter and soon there was chatter and laughter and no sign of it stopping and certainly no chance for me to ask what she meant by her last remark.

13

PROGRESS

MARIO WAS TRUE TO HIS WORD. A WEEK LATER, HE PHONED TO SAY THE scaffolding had arrived on site. I took the opportunity to thank him, conveying my appreciation of his efforts. We chatted briefly about the weather and I assured him I would stay away and not interfere with the build. He told me I would be more than welcome to visit any time I wanted. There was no sign of the hostile and obstructive Mario I first encountered.

Our relationship had changed the day after we went to Tuineje to visit the council, when he sent me the invoice for the barn restoration and, seeing he had chosen to charge me half-price after all for the roof timbers he had acquired from another job, I paid the invoice without a quibble. He then phoned to thank me. On a sudden impulse, I offered him a handsome bonus in exchange for expediting the build and he said he would try to have the structure completed to lock up in six months. From that moment, our exchanges had gone from cautious ambivalence to cordiality and good humour.

For me, the arrival of the scaffolding meant the day was of tremendous significance. I slipped my phone in my bag, thinking to seize Mario's open invitation.

Earlier, I had been bent on distracting myself from anxieties over the build and the mysterious history of my once grand house; I had planned to drive down to Morro Jable on the island's southern tip and go for a swim in the calm waters, taking advantage of a time of year when the holidaymakers were fewer and it was possible to enjoy a patch of ocean all to myself. It was an hour and a half's drive, but well worth the effort; the beach down there was superb and the day forecast to be a hot one. Already dressed in a T-shirt and shorts, I dashed out to my car, threw my beach bag on the back seat and headed off, taking a detour to Tiscamanita. It was a route I had become so accustomed to, I didn't notice the scenery, except to acknowledge it was there.

Cars and small trucks were parked bumper to bumper outside my property and beyond, save for a space that served as a driveway for trucks. I was relieved to see the workmen had the good grace not to use my land as a parking lot as I came to a halt at the end of the row of vehicles. Killing the engine meant killing the air con. I opened the door on the heat and went over to survey the scene. I was keen for shade but finding none, I stood back beside a giant rock dump located where my much smaller rock pile had been.

Delight filled me as I took in the progress. The front and side walls were enclosed in scaffolding and the men were assembling the various lengths of metal tubing along the back. Seeing me standing around, Mario ended a conversation he was having with one of the workers and came over.

'The men are fast,' I said, shaking his hand. 'I'm not recognising any from the barn restoration.'

'Those men were no good. They refused to work on the house.'

I already knew why and I didn't want to hear it a second time.

'Where are these men from?' None of them looked Spanish, from what I could tell.

'They are from all over the island. Two are from Lanzarote. We have English, Scottish, Irish, German, Dutch, Belgian and Swede. They're good men. Hardworking and skilled.'

'And not superstitious,' I said with a laugh.

He laughed as well, but it wasn't a happy laugh. He glanced back at the build. One of the men was trying to get his attention.

'I have to get back.'

'Is it okay if I stay and watch for a while?'

'Sure. Just don't go inside. You stand out here, you understand? You don't have a hard hat.'

I did as I was told. Giving the activity a wide berth, I wandered around. On the northern side the men were ferrying up rocks for the repairs to the rear gable-end wall.

Other than that northern section, the roof was hipped which meant the walls ended flat. Where the roof was intact, men were re-pointing the wall. Roof tiles were being removed with great care in preparation for repairs to the roof timbers. Boarded-up windows were being braced, as were door cavities. Mario had explained some of the methods they would be employing, including inserting steel ties to stitch together the vertical cracks in the gable ends before filling the gaps with stones and lime mortar.

On the south side of the building, which was in the greatest state of disrepair, sections of wall would need to be almost entirely rebuilt. All the existing internal and external plaster would be preserved. Sections of the wall where the plaster had come away would be repointed for additional solidity. All the timber would be re-used and Mario planned to use timbers from a demolition on Gran Canaria. From what I could see, the primary focus was stabilising the existing structure. I had no idea how many men were working inside the building, but I counted fifteen men engaged in various activities around the exterior. I poked my head in the barn to find the concrete had been laid.

The masonry, the noise, the dust, the stolen glances at me in my T-shirt and shorts, and I soon realised my property was no place for me to be. Before I headed off, I strode over to my little garden of dragos and aloe vera. I had forgotten to bring them water but they were said to be hardy and showed no signs of distress. There was no growth evident either, but it was much too soon for that.

There was no growth in the land beyond my block's perimeter either. At one time it had been cultivated but was now fallow. The field sloped to the low, barren hills. The volcano and the distant mountains drew my eye. There were days I looked out at that arid landscape and wondered why I hadn't settled for somewhere lush and green. Somewhere close to Colchester, to my father and Aunt Clarissa. No words could explain the attraction of a landscape so dry, a landscape that had been drawing intrepid Brits for decades despite holding no immediately obvious, greener-grass appeal.

I turned back to the street and looked around. All the activity on site, and not one neighbour had come to watch. Back in Colchester, when I had romanticised the restoration, I pictured a small group of retired men, or a couple of grandmothers, stopping by for a gander, inviting me into their houses for updates, bestowing on me their gushes of gratitude, grasping my hand in theirs telling me how pleased they were that someone was at last caring for the house. Instead, not one person stopped by.

It was almost midday by the time I left the site, entering my furnace of a car to head down to Morro Jable with my bathers and towel. The drive was pleasant, the mountains rising up from the plain, some near, others far, always present, always bare, like giant statues watching.

Once through Costa Calma, the landscape changed to undulations of sandy desert, sprinkled with round lumps of spurge, clinging on, the terrain resembling pale skin suffering a terrible case of scabby pox. Ahead, slipping in and out of view, was the Jandia massif.

The drive was shorter than had I come from Puerto del Rosario; an hour and I was heading down the main drag of Morro Jable. On the high side were the hotels, some of seven storeys, concrete and glass monoliths testament to the holiday idyll that was Fuerteventura, each apartment looking out at that expanse of sapphire and all that golden sand on my left.

Morro Jable had been squashed between the ocean and the Jandia mountains at the heel end of a long and narrow foot of land some one or two miles wide. The town stretched inland into a deep and narrow valley, stopping where it became impossible to build. The mountains sheltered the town from the strong north-westers, making the climate much warmer than that of the island's north.

Before arriving at the town centre, I took a left and pulled up at the end of a short street beside a beach-side café that had outdoor seating sheltered beneath large umbrellas. Keen for a swim, I forewent the delicious garlicky smells emanating from the kitchen and marched across the sand to the shore. The tide was out. The sand was warm underfoot, and it went on and on for maybe a hundred metres, the widest stretch of sand on one of the longest beaches on the island; little wonder holidaymakers made their way south.

I dumped my bag, unfurled my towel and removed my T-shirt and shorts as I looked around. The southern end of the beach was framed by a low rocky cliff and at that end, the beach narrowed. In the other direction, the breadth of sand widened. In the near distance, a light-house stood at the head of the beach at the point where the land curved to the north. Beyond was more sand.

Feeling the sun scalding my skin, I wasted no time heading into the ocean.

The water was warm and calm. I swam to the lighthouse and back, enjoying the push of the small waves, the gentle rise and fall. I might not want to mingle with holidaymakers, but I sure was able to enjoy what they did, what they saved up for every year. It was paradise. I bobbed about in the water a while longer, swimming and treading water until my arms and legs were tired.

Back on the beach, I dried off, wrapped the towel around my waist and pulled on my T-shirt. I gathered the rest of my things and headed to the café, suddenly famished.

I chose a table overlooking the beach and ordered the paella and a bottle of sparkling water. Taking in the empty chair opposite, I thought of Paco and our meal in Antigua. What did he make of Morro Jable? Did he enjoy the beach? Swim? When we next met, I would ask.

As expected, the food came almost straight away, the paella already cooked and ready to serve. I ate quickly, watching those around me leave their tables and saunter off or approach and sit down. It was all convivial but I felt no sense of belonging. The effects of too much sun had given me a headache. I extracted my notebook and jotted down the progress of the build while things were still fresh in my mind. Then, I ordered an iced coffee and sat back in the shade of the umbrella, content to let the afternoon drift by.

On the way back to Puerto del Rosario I played my favourite

Cocteau Twins' album, *Heaven or Las Vegas,* and enjoyed the waves of contentment that swept through me, affirming in my heart and mind that I had done the right thing moving to the island. For some peculiar reason, or perhaps not so peculiar, that music made me feel expansive, and being on the island had a similar effect. In me, if no one else, the two, the music and the land, fused into one whole state of transcendent wonder.

My euphoria dissipated, my buoyant mood barrelling out of me on the heels of choking fear, when I opened the door to my apartment and almost tripped over the rock.

14

A LETTER FROM CLARISSA

I COULDN'T CROSS THE THRESHOLD. I STOOD IN THE NARROW STRIP OF front yard with the busy street behind me, staring down at the offending rock centred on a tile on its largest face with its craggy rear end pointing at me. The positioning was precise, thought through, planned. The rock had not rolled out of a closed cupboard and bumped its way across the floor tiles from the kitchen to the front door. It wasn't possible.

Behind me, a group of teenagers walked by, chatting and laughing.

Summoning what little courage I had, I stepped inside and closed the door. Shutting out the street felt final, as though inside the apartment existed an alternate reality, one I wanted no part of. I rounded the rock with caution, half expecting the cold hard lump to rise up and hurl itself at my head with sudden force, cracking open my skull.

Nothing happened. I went through to the kitchen and found the cupboard door closed. All looked normal. Nothing else in the apartment had been relocated. I extracted the beach towel from my bag and draped it over the back of a chair and went around opening windows to let in the fresh air. Then I went around closing them again, not wanting to make entry easy for whoever had been in here.

I craved a shower to wash off the salt, but I would feel too exposed and vulnerable knowing someone had been in the flat and moved that rock. Someone who had easy access to the apartment. Another part of me remained spooked. That was the part of me that drew me to the front door, that had me pick up the rock and set it down beside the trunk of a dracaena at the far end of the tiny patch of garden.

Taking no chances, I locked the front door behind me and went straight to the shower before I changed my mind, peeling off my bathers and stepping into the tepid spray.

Having no intention of going out again, I stayed in my bathrobe and tramped about the kitchen pouring juice and making a snack, normal tasks at the end of what should have been a normal day, no, much more than a normal day, a day to celebrate, the renovations at last proceeding.

I was on my way back to the fridge with the carton of juice when I paused. Could those renovations have anything to do with that moving rock? It was an uncomfortable thought, something Aunt Clarissa would speculate on in one of her mystical moments. I was determined to adhere to my original hypothesis. Someone had been in my apartment and that someone was a practical joker who had set out to frighten me.

I wasn't about to let them win, whoever they were. I needed a powerful distraction. The bonks and muffled voices coming through from the apartments to either side of me afforded little comfort. I considered playing music, but I didn't want to listen to music through my laptop's tinny speaker and putting on headphones would isolate me. I needed people close, even if they were a wall apart, even if one of them might be creeping into my apartment when I was absent.

I opened my laptop to an email from Clarissa. Hope stirred. I thought perhaps she would change her mind and visit, but instead, after a string of reassuring platitudes—Rome wasn't built in a day, patience was never your strong suit—the dear old thing launched into a chatty blow-by-blow account of her recent ghost tour escapade.

She had gone to an abbey in Suffolk that hadn't been occupied since the 1950s and had narrowly escaped demolition. Clarissa ended her sentence with a string of exclamation marks. Like mine, was the implication. The abbey was now being restored—more exclamation marks—and the estate included stables, basements and a cellar. The tour guides came with the usual gear: thermal cameras, voice recorders and an EMF meter to detect electromagnetic fields. The guides used stereotypical divination and summoning techniques including dowsing rods, a séance and a crystal ball. 'I was up all night,' Clarissa wrote, 'and despite my best efforts, I didn't detect a thing.' Neither, by her account, had anyone else. Clarissa had to ask herself if it had been worth the money. Those tours weren't cheap. The tour guides had played their parts well enough but the participants—who were there for the thrills—created so much psychic interference they had scared away whatever ghosts might have been there.

I read her account with indifference. Clarissa went on a ghost tour every few months, ostensibly to check out the guide's authenticity and to see, or rather feel for herself if any supernatural entities lurked in any of those supposedly haunted houses. Mostly, she admitted, it was a gimmick, like a parlour game. Cheap thrills, although on reflection, not so cheap.

Clarissa went on to reiterate caution against invoking the lower astral plane. Those tour guides were putting themselves at risk, she said. The participants were mostly too thick skinned to be affected. The entire fad was bringing paranormal sensitivity into disrepute and charlatans abounded, just as they had back in the late 1800s, at the time of the Fox sisters' rappings which led to a burgeoning of interest in the occult, especially in Spiritualism which purported to provide loved ones with access to their dead.

I had heard it all before. Aunt Clarissa's version of a holiday was a ghost tour. Before I wrote a reply, I did a quick search of the Olivia Stone article Paco had mentioned and found it without much difficulty. Reading it through, I could see that Paco had been accurate in his references. Olivia Stone had, to the best of the author's knowledge, disappeared, and there was a '*Stone*' mentioned by a Tenerife newspaper as having arrived on the 'Wazzan' steamship in 1895. The article also stated that Olivia Stone's house near Dover was named *Fuerteventura*. It was strange that no death certificate had been found and there was no record of a divorce mentioned in the article. More's the point, there couldn't have been a death notice or obituary written, or at least not in a major newspaper, one the academic researcher would have found. Perhaps Paco's reasoning was not so fanciful after all.

The article contained a photograph of both Olivia Stone and her husband, John. I studied each in turn.

The photo of Olivia was nothing like the robust Rational Dresser I had imagined. She was a slender, refined looking woman in her thirties, intelligent, introspective, deep perhaps. Her hair, dark and wiry, was brushed back from her face. She had demur eyes and a small mouth. Her manner was not shy and neither was it feminine. She looked haunted, unhappy, possibly of delicate health. Her style of dress—a flowing mid-calf gown tasselled at the short-sleeved cuffs and hem, and matching cape—denoted a woman who was practical and independent and free thinking, not a woman given to makeup or jewellery. Her outfit appeared a touch oriental, and as though to reinforce the style she was seated by a large, decorated urn from which grew a tall plant with feathery foliage.

Her husband was just as Paco had described him, a forthright-looking man seated on some wooden steps, proud with his white, coat-hanger moustache. He was garbed in a suit and tie and matching hat, neither formal or casual. His manner exuded authority and dominance. Perhaps Paco was right; John Stone had been a tyrant and Olivia had fled.

Yet the notion that she had come to Fuerteventura, to Tiscamanita, to my very house, seemed farfetched.

I sat back and glanced around the apartment. As soon as I looked at the front door I pictured the rock sitting outside and my anxiety flooded back. Not wanting my mind to fixate there, I set about translating the entire Olivia Stone piece, including all the references, so that I could send the information to Clarissa who, I thought, would love a fresh genealogical quest. She was a member of an online ancestry site and if anyone were able to uncover the truth about Olivia Mary Stone, it would be my aunt.

For the most part, the article discussed the importance of her book and the genealogy of her husband, John Frederic Matthias Harris Stone.

Translating was painstaking work, and it took me the whole of that evening and part of the following day. In the short breaks I found myself taking in what was, after all, a chore, I followed my interest and searched through all the old newspaper articles I could find online pertaining to my subject. I discovered Olivia Stone's book had made quite a splash in the media and that she had returned to the islands in 1889 and again in 1891, to make revisions to the original work. One newspaper referred to the swarms of holidaymakers flitting to Tenerife after the publication of Olivia's book. And there was a short reference quoting how she regretted what she had started, the islands already transforming into a holiday destination, threatening to destroy local culture.

Ironic, then, that the woman whose words had triggered that influx rued the day she ever wrote them down.

I imagined her in my house, hiding from the world, from her beastly husband, missing her sons—they would have been teenagers by then—and receiving Marcial, her only visitor. Were they lovers? Which room had they used for their trysts? There would have been no partition then; Olivia would have enjoyed the whole patio. She would have sipped tea and read her favourite novels and when night fell, she would have stepped outside to admire the stars. It was surprisingly easy to picture her in my house. As though she belonged there, hidden away. I wondered what had really happened to her. More than anything, I looked forward to reading her book.

15

THE BUILDING SITE

IT WAS WITH TREPIDATION THAT I OPENED THE FRONT DOOR TO MY apartment the following morning to find the rock was where I had left it. Relieved, I stepped out in the early morning cool and knocked on Dolores' door. She was surprised to see me and took a moment to recognise my face. I asked her if she had been in my house, or if she had seen or knew of anyone who had. I didn't mention the rock but I said I thought I had had an intruder, twice. She said she had no spare key and she had not seen anyone enter. She told me to contact the agent, who would ask the owner, who lived in Gran Canaria. She looked bemused, shook her head and mentioned the police. I thanked her for her trouble and asked her to keep an eye out. She said she would and I thanked her and returned to my apartment, giving the rock a sideways glance on my way inside.

I didn't want to appear to Mario, to the tradesmen, and especially to myself one of those fussing owners in a home renovation show, anxious for progress by the half hour, preoccupied with details large and small, but I couldn't face staying in the apartment and my body couldn't take another day at the beach.

My compulsion to be on site was endorsed by Mario, who phoned as I was getting ready to leave for Tiscamanita. He wanted me to swing by the hardware store in Puerto del Rosario and pick up ten bags of lime that the delivery guy failed to load on the truck.

I was happy to oblige, pulling up at the store having swung by a bakery for sweet treats for the men, hoping the offering would endear me to them.

I discovered ten bags of lime was sufficient weight to lower the back of my small rental, and I had to slip the gearstick into third on the inclines. The whole journey to Tiscamanita I had to reassure myself that 250 kilos was equivalent of two obese passengers in the back seat. I vowed to buy a robust vehicle at the earliest opportunity. When I arrived at the building site, I didn't dare mount the kerb.

Seeing me pull up, Mario hailed a guy to fetch a wheelbarrow and I stood by watching the back of my car rise in increments as he went back and forth.

I closed the boot and fetched the selection of pastries from the passenger seat and wandered over to where Mario had headed. He was talking to a tall guy in a singlet and baseball cap, on back to front. I instantly summed him up as cocksure.

Seeing me, Mario stopped talking and beckoned me closer.

'Claire, let me introduce Helmud. He's site manager.' The man made to offer his hand, glanced down at his dirt-encrusted skin and laughed. He was tall, blond and sinewy. His eyes exuded a kindly, warm-hearted nature and I was forced to revise my initial assessment. Beside him, Mario appeared serious and weighed-down with worries.

'We're planning a strategy,' he said. 'You might want to listen.'

'The north side of the building is almost intact,' Helmud said to me. 'I propose continuing to restore the rooms in that section, top and bottom, and re-build the walls on the south side before we pull down the partition wall.'

'I don't have a problem with that,' I said.

'It means no water,' said Mario. 'The aljibe is below the patio and the wall cuts right across it.'

'Why would anyone build the wall right there, then? It seems crazy.'

'Access was on the south side,' Helmud said, ignoring my remark.

'But the aljibe is old and needs to be repaired and cleaned before it can be used.'

'We can't get down there, Claire. It isn't safe with that wall sitting above. The weight of the stone is immense.'

'Fair enough,' I said. I didn't understand why they were making a deal of the aljibe, except that it would be my water supply, the dwelling rendered uninhabitable without it, at least by modern standards. Or perhaps they were thinking of my little garden.

'You won't have access to the upper level except via a ladder, not for a long time,' Helmud explained. 'But you will have two finished rooms downstairs that will be completely self-contained.'

'You wanted a room for storage,' Mario said. 'It would be ideal.' He turned to Helmud, 'She was intending to use the little barn.' They exchanged smiles before Mario said, addressing me, 'We've taken over that space.'

I looked over my shoulder at the barn. Following my gaze Helmud told me one end was crammed full of recycled windows and doors, leaving just enough space for the generator.

'How soon will those downstairs rooms be ready?' I asked.

'A few weeks. There won't be power, and the walls will need painting,' Helmud said.

'But the rooms will be usable for storage,' added Mario.

It meant somewhere for my possessions when they arrived from England and I could start buying furniture. Premature perhaps, but it would give me something to do.

I thanked the men and handed Mario the bag of pastries. 'For the workers,' I said, 'To show my appreciation. I hope there are enough.'

'Thank you. They'll like that. I'll hand them around later.'

I went and poked my head inside the back doorway – no longer boarded up – and took a few steps inside to find the scaffolding erected around the internal perimeter and an army of men tackling every corner of the build. It was a pleasing sight and I could see my offer to Mario of a bonus if he could get the building to lock-up in six months had stimulated a frenzy of activity. Seeing all those men, I knew there would not be enough pastries to go around.

The stone masons on the south side were engaged in the

painstaking work of re-using the fallen stones to repair the walls. The outer wall was being tackled to a degree, but the main focus was around a front section of wall that had portions freestanding at the upper level. On the north side, the vertical cracks were slowly disappearing, the tiles were all off the roof and repairs to the roof timbers looked underway. New timbers were going into the subfloor where needed, and four men were navigating into place a heavy beam spanning the width between the exterior and interior walls. Downstairs, in the kitchen two men were building stone piers to underpin the subfloor. In all, the restoration was well underway.

Outside, beyond the scaffolding, more materials were being brought on site. There were stacks of timbers for bearers, joists, floorboards and lintels, along with two cement mixers and power tools of all descriptions, including an array of saws, powered by the generator.

Every man wore a tool belt. Amid the hammering, sawing, barrowing and the whine of power tools, there was much talk in a variety of languages, and I wondered if the men were working in their various national groups.

Forgetting my promise to take care on the building site, I went back inside to examine progress on the two, soon-to-be-usable rooms. I soon heard a shout and looked up. Helmud was standing on the scaffolding. He tapped his hard hat and pointed at my head. I gave him a coy, apologetic look and left.

Watching progress at a safe distance, I pictured that moment when I would move in and a sense of satisfaction filled me. All thoughts of mysterious curses and moving rock artefacts had faded away. A fleeting memory of how I had sat in the patio and cried over my mother threatened to invade my equanimity and I shooed it off.

Seeing me still standing around at a loose end, Mario approached and said, 'Tonight, you have some homework. I want you to confirm where you want all the lights, light switches and power points.' He ignored my groan. 'Especially in those two soon-to-be-finished rooms. I can arrange the electrician to rough in that section and then we can start plastering.'

My offer of a bonus aside, I wanted to ask why he was keen to have the build proceed at a breakneck pace. Did he have a backlog of other projects? Or was he in financial straits? He was too anxious, more on edge than ever, and I kept catching him looking at the structure with something like fear in his face. I dearly wanted to know the source.

My question was answered at least in part by the haze developing on the eastern horizon. Another calima was on its way.

I headed back to Puerto del Rosario with the dust haze edging closer. The cooling trade winds were abating, the air temperature rising and in hours Fuerteventura would be blanketed in Saharan dust. I had been told in the past a calima was a rare event in May but in recent years the dust storms had become more frequent, more intense and lasted a lot longer. Perhaps this one would pass over in a day. I wondered how I would cope on calima days in my new home with its patio open to the elements, when opening a door to the outside meant inviting in the dust.

I swung by the supermarket for more groceries and it was midday when I carried my shopping to the front door of my apartment. On my way inside, I shot a glance at the narrow garden. The rock was still exactly where I had placed it.

After lunching on slices of chorizo, tomato and local cheese, I laid the house plans on the table and, room by room, confirmed where I wanted the power points and light switches. At first it was easy. A light switch at each end of the vestibule and a light in the centre of its ceiling. After that, each room became harder, the bathrooms and kitchen worst of all. I had to preconceive the arrangement of furnishings for every room in the house. The entire process made worse by the awareness that I could have power wherever I wanted, no expense spared. It would have been much simpler were I only able to afford a single power point in each room. The process took the whole afternoon and I was exhausted by the end of it.

The dust haze cleared quickly and by the following morning the sky was clear. Mario would be wanting the house plans, but before I went to Tiscamanita I wanted to return to the garden centre in Tefia. Even though more gardening would result in more watering, it meant I had an excuse to be on site.

Keen to make an early start, straight after eating a breakfast of cold tortilla and toasted baguette, I filled the ten-litre water containers and loaded them into the boot along with my gardening tools and headed off.

At the garden centre, I bought three more drago trees and five more aloe vera plants, along with twenty tubes of various kinds of succulents. A cautious selection, but a voice in my head urged me to err on the side of uniformity.

Not wanting to start a precedent, I parked in the street and ferried my tools and plants to my little corner of the garden under the watchful gaze of the workmen.

The building work going on behind me as I laboured made me feel strange and self-conscious. I spent the afternoon tilling the ground and digging holes and watering in plants, extending twofold the existing garden bed, all the while striving to ignore the activities on the build. Whenever I stood and straightened my back I glanced over and observed the men at work on the southern wall, pleased to see progress being made, even if the going was slow. Rebuilding stone walls was a mammoth job when they were almost three feet thick. That amounted to a lot of stone. Whenever my gaze was returned by a curious worker taking a short break, I turned and bent down again and continued planting. At lunchtime, I went to the little super-market for snacks. I didn't interact with the men other than to hand Mario the plans when he turned up for a short while.

The separation between Claire, the owner gardener, and that army of builders, along with the perception that I was not as welcome as Mario might believe, reinforced a growing sense of isolation. That creeping loneliness returned and grew larger inside me as the after-noon wore on.

I kept my eye out for Paco, who I hoped would call in, but he didn't appear. I regretted not asking for his phone number. It would have been nice to have a coffee or lunch with the only friend I had on the island, even if he was a little crazy with his Olivia Stone obsession.

When all the plants were in the ground and watered, I packed up my gardening gear and loaded the boot of my car, keeping my gaze down as the workmen drifted off the site and drove away in their dusty vans. It was clear I would need to find other ways of keeping occupied while the building was in progress, or I would have the entire property planted up.

As I pulled away from the kerb I thought I might try my hand at fixing the fallen sections of the dry-stone wall at the rear. Although I would only do that on weekends for fear I would be a laughing stock. Better still, I could pay an expert and find a more fitting occupation. Otherwise, boredom and impatience would send me doolally no matter how fast the progress of the build.

The following day, I bought a car, more than a car, a workhorse, a robust four-wheel drive to make ferrying water and bags of lime and tools and the wheelbarrow easier. Relinquishing the rental felt symbolic of my permanence on the island. To reinforce my status, I registered with a local doctor and dentist and enrolled in an upper-intermediate language course starting in early September. To further fill my days, I vowed to make a point of visiting markets and attending festivals, whatever was going on. I must participate, I told myself, if I was to feel I belonged and create a life for myself beyond the build.

16

THE CURSE

THREE WEEKS INTO THE RESTORATION, MARIO PHONED TO ASK ME TO swing by the builders supplies yard, on the pretext that another delivery was short on the load. I discovered the truth when I arrived on site with more bags of lime.

Seeing my car pull up, he hurried over and told me through my open window before I even had a chance to turn off the engine and pop the boot, that there was trouble amongst the men. One of the stone masons, Cliff, had left his tool belt hidden in a section of wall the previous night, only visible from up high on the scaffolding. When he turned up for work that morning he found his tool belt on the ground, leaning against the partition wall as though propped there on purpose.

With the ignition keys in one hand and my bag in the other, I studied Mario's face, noting the fear in his eyes. He stood back from the car, head bowed, pinching the bridge of his nose.

'Cliff's accusing the others,' he said. 'They all deny it, of course.'

'A practical joke?'

'Probably kids. There's a lot of unemployment among the young. Maybe a school kid. You could ask the neighbours.' He looked at me imploringly.

'What neighbours?'

'Isn't there someone next door?'

'I've never seen anyone.'

'Strange.'

'But I'll ask in the café. The owner seems to know everything going on around here.'

'At least nothing was broken and nothing is missing,' he said, making to walk away.

'Just relocated,' I said as my skin broke out in goose bumps.

He stopped and turned back. 'That's right. *Moved.*'

From tucked away in the cavity of a wall two levels of scaffolding up, to resting on the ground against that partition wall, the incident was too similar to the rock that had moved in my apartment, twice. I wasn't about to tell Mario about that rock, but I wondered if something else, something of the same nature hadn't already happened to him and he was as reluctant as I to share.

I began to think I understood the reason behind Mario's haste. His was not a race against time to secure a bonus, or because he had a backlog of other jobs; he was trying to beat the supposed curse with speed. Mario knew that every day that passed without an occurrence of anything strange and inexplicable was a blessing. For he, too, believed in the curse of Casa Baraso, or was at least wary.

I scrambled to rationalise. Clearly someone was unhappy with the restoration, and wanted to intimidate me and cause disharmony among the workers. That someone had access to my apartment. It had been the conveyancer who had put me onto the estate agent, who I had yet to contact about the matter. Were they in cahoots? Or was all this the meddling of Cejas?

I left Mario to organise the bags of lime and went over to where the men were huddled. Some were returning to their various spots on the build, leaving the stone mason still arguing with his mate. They were both tall and deeply tanned. The man I assumed to be Cliff was the older of the two. He had a larger, heftier frame, and he was sporting a goatee beard and a small paunch. The younger man had bleached blond hair and striking blue eyes. As I grew nearer they lowered their voices.

'Hey, Cliff,' I said, putting on my bank teller's face, the one I used on belligerent customers. 'Mario has filled me in. We think it was kids okay, just kids coming on site after dark. I'm going to ask around, see if there are any known trouble makers in town.'

The older man, Cliff, hesitated, and I watched as his ire diffused.

I went on. 'Thankfully nothing was taken or damaged. It seems whoever did this had no intention of causing anything but mischief. I suggest we all put the matter behind us and get on with our jobs, if that's okay. The weather is only going to get hotter.'

I had no idea what the temperature had to do with the progress of the build but I needed to round off my little speech with something. It did the trick. Cliff thanked me in a thick Yorkshire accent for the pastries I had brought the other day and headed off up the scaffolding. The other guy followed.

I had a quick look around before telling Mario I thought Cliff would settle down; and then I headed back to Puerto del Rosario, fighting off my own misgivings.

Two days later, Mario texted me again for more bags of lime. The request had become a euphemism for trouble and I almost didn't bother swinging by the builder's yard. I pulled up to find Cliff yelling and waving his arms about, and Mario placating. I hurried out of the car and marched over.

The men gathered round went quiet. Even my presence settled things down without me needing to speak.

'It's happened again,' Mario said addressing me, his face more worried than before.

'Same as last time?'

'Pretty much.'

'Take your tools home, Cliff. For Christ's sake,' one of the guys said.

'Yeah, no one should be leaving their tools here.'

'I didn't think anyone would be so stupid as to do it again,' Cliff muttered, eyeing the others with suspicion.

I stepped forward and put my hands on my hips. 'I told you, it's probably kids.'

'Probably?' Cliff paused. 'You don't know for sure. Have you asked around like you said you would?' He paused, eying me critically. I looked away. 'No, I didn't think so.'

'I was planning on doing that today. In fact, I'm on my way there right now. If I hadn't been called on site to help diffuse your temper, I would already have the information you require.'

The men were as shocked as I at the manner in which I spoke those words. All those years working at the bank having to be polite and restrained no matter what idiot was standing on the other side of the Perspex, and a new freedom surged forth. At the back of my mind was the need to persuade all the guys to keep working on the build. Even if I found out nothing about a wayward teenager, I considered inventing one, just to keep the men from getting spooked.

Thinking we had reached a stalemate, I handed Mario my car keys and told him the bags of lime he wanted were in the boot. With one final glare at the men, I marched off up the street.

The front door to my neighbour's house was right on the pavement, midway along a whitewashed wall. I knocked and waited. Nothing, not even a rustle or a squeak. I knocked harder. Still no reply or any movement inside. I continued on past a vacant field to the next house and hammered my knuckles on the door. No one came to the door. All I got for my trouble was a dog yapping somewhere inside. I crossed over and was about to try another house when I began to feel ridiculous and stopped in my tracks.

I was in two minds whether to approach the woman at the café with my query as it would only arouse local gossip, but I had promised Cliff. I spent the short walk conjuring a ruse to discover what I wanted to know without invoking too much suspicion.

As I went in I realised I first had to make a purchase. The woman ran a business, not a drop-in centre. Finding myself the only customer, I ordered a freshly squeezed orange juice and another slice of her tortilla. She probably thought me the most unadventurous woman when it came to food so I also had some of her fish in vinaigrette and I ordered a coffee as an afterthought. She was more than happy to fill my order.

I sat at my usual table by the window. The loud grind of the juicer, the comforting bonks and clangs and chinks, and I wanted to stay seated for an hour or more to unwind.

'You didn't tell me your name,' I said when she brought over my food and drink.

'Gloria,' she said matter-of-factly.

'That's a pretty name,' I said, hoping to coax her into opening up.

'Thank you.'

She smoothed down her apron and stood back. She waited, although she didn't seem in a chatty mood. I knew if any of her local customers came in she would be all rapid talk interspersed with convivial laughter.

'Gloria,' I said, keeping her there with her name. 'I was wondering, what do the young people do in the village? Once they finish school, I mean. Is there much work around?'

'They leave,' she said with a sigh. 'Especially the boys.'

'Where do they go?'

'Puerto del Rosario, but most go to Gran Canaria or Tenerife or the mainland.'

'That's sad.'

'It is.'

'I wondered why I haven't seen any young people about.'

She folded her arms across her chest and tilted her head to the side, watching me closely as she spoke. 'That's because there aren't many families living here anymore. And the nearest high school is in Gran Tarajal.'

'At least you don't get all the usual problems. Vandalism, graffiti, break ins.'

'We get none of that here.' Now she sounded proud.

'Which makes Tiscamanita the perfect village.' I grinned at her and she gave me a strange look as if to convey she found me slightly unhinged.

I let her walk away. It seemed unlikely that any teenager was prowling about. A homeless person, maybe. Or someone from Tuineje? That village was only a few kilometres down the road. Yet as I pondered my latest thoughts they seemed increasingly unlikely.

I would have liked to ask Paco, who was sure to have an answer, but I had no means of contacting him and he hadn't shown up at the block. I was beginning to believe I had been abandoned, and wondered what I had done to put him off. Catching myself in the midst of my thoughts, I realised I had formed an attachment to him.

I drank the juice, ate the fish and followed on with the tortilla. By the end I wasn't sure I had got the sequence right. When I knocked back the last of the coffee and it was all sloshing about in my belly, I felt I might be in for a spot of indigestion.

I didn't return to the building site, preferring to let Cliff stew. I went back to the apartment and cogitated over the thought that Cejas was meddling in the build. I had no way of proving it was him, but the more convinced I grew that he was behind the relocation of the rock and tools, the more resolved I became to take action.

A week later it happened again. Mario dispensed with his lime-bag ruse and texted me to say I had better get up there fast.

I was out the door in a flash. When I arrived, Mario rushed over like a schoolkid ratting to his teacher. He explained the wheelbarrows Cliff had leaned against a wall to drain and dry he found slung on the ground on their sides.

The men were gathered over by the barn. No one was working and an air of unease pervaded the group. In all likelihood, word of the curse had gone around and met with caution if not trepidation among the men.

'Could be a dog,' one of them was saying.

'Or the wind.'

'You need to secure the site,' a burly Scotsman said to Mario. 'If you don't, there's no telling what will happen next.'

The others agreed.

'Mario,' I said. 'I tried to ask the neighbours. There doesn't seem to be anyone living in any of these houses. I called in at the café and the owner said there are hardly any young people in the village and never any crime.'

'This wasn't a crime, though,' Mario said quickly.

'We had an intruder,' said the burly man. 'That's trespass.'

'You don't know that.'

'It's pretty obvious, don't you think?'

378

'Mario,' Cliff said with sudden conviction. 'I can't work here anymore. Someone's got a vendetta against me.'

'Please, don't go,' I said.

'I'm sorry, but that's three times something of mine has been moved. It hasn't happened to the others. Maybe if I go, the prankster will stop.'

As Cliff packed up his tools and left the site, the other men grew uneasy. Leaving Mario and I standing by the cement mixers, they all drifted back to their various jobs but the mood was subdued. Mario looked more worried than the rest of them put together.

'I tell you what,' I said once we were alone. 'Let's meet here tonight after dark and see if anyone turns up.'

'You think someone will?'

'Someone must be doing this, surely?' I said. 'In fact, I am almost certain I know what is going on.'

'If you say so.' He sounded doubtful. Again, I sensed he was holding something back.

'It wasn't a dog that moved Cliff's tool belt, that much I do know,' I said, my rational self coming to the fore.

'Even so.'

'I'll be here at nine,' I said with determination I hadn't realised I had until I said it. 'Please say you'll join me.'

'I'll try.'

He didn't sound keen.

17

THE NIGHT WATCH

IN JUNE, THE SUN SETS AROUND NINE, THE LIGHT QUICKLY FADING. THE villages below the Betancuria massif sink into the gloaming about an hour before, missing out on the glorious sunsets over the ocean that the west coast enjoys. Save for one or two notable exceptions there is not much along that west coast other than cliffs, rocky coves and caves, and the wild beaches of Cofete in the far south. Fuerteventura looks firmly at the sunrise, at Africa beyond the horizon, most inhabitants clustered in towns dotted along the eastern coast. Driving at night down the lonely backroads of Fuerteventura for the first time, with only the distant lights of the occasional farmhouse for company, brought home to me the seclusion of much of the island. Away from the inland villages with their houses shuttered against the darkness, beyond the reach of the streetlights, there was nothing, just the road curving across the empty plain and over the foothills of the mountains. In daylight the terrain was stark, at night it was bleak, the dark reinforcing the desolate landscape. It was with relief that I approached the familiarity of Tiscamanita.

I slowed and turned left and headed down my street. Initially, the way was lit by the electric street lanterns that were attached to each power pole, but two poles on, and the lights were blown and no one had thought to report the matter to the council and have them replaced. My house, beyond a small curve, was rendered in almost complete darkness.

There was no vehicle in sight. Mario was yet to arrive. I pulled up on the opposite side of the road and switched off the headlights, leaving the car to idle while I let my eyes adjust. I could make out the volcano, silhouetted against the starlit sky. There was no moon and I had no idea if there would be. That was something Aunt Clarissa would have known without a doubt, and I could have done with her company on my lonely night watch. I could have benefited from anyone's company and dearly hoped Mario would join me as agreed.

I thought about remaining where I was, then realised no one would approach if they saw the car, so I turned on the headlights and drove across the road, mounting the kerb, and taxiing over my land and parking around the back of the barn where I thought I would be safely out of sight. Thinking to make my exit easier, I backed in towards the wall, so that the car's nose was pointing at the volcano.

I killed the lights and the engine, confident I couldn't be seen. Although, situated where I was, Mario would have no idea I was there either. If I heard his car, any car, then I would send him a text. I thought for a second. There wouldn't be time to fumble about composing a text. I took out my phone and wrote a draft, ready to send. I set the phone down on the passenger seat within easy reach. There was nothing to do but sit back and stare into the void. Facing the wrong way with the barn obliterating my view, I was unable to see in either wing mirror if anyone was walking down the street or, worse, across my block. I was blind. The best I could do was open the window and keep an ear out for movement. No one could walk on my land without making crunching footfalls. They would also need a torch, and I would see any kind of light, even from my obscure post.

For how long did I plan to sit and wait like this? All night? There would come a point when it would be past a criminal's bedtime, surely? Besides, the relocation of a tool belt and the tipping over of a wheelbarrow or two—those were not the acts of criminals. There was a prankster at work, a kid, maybe with a mate.

I waited, letting a soft breeze stroke my face. About half an hour passed. Half an hour of crushing boredom. I couldn't read or play music. I just sat.

Another ten minutes and the waiting was all too much. I couldn't stay cooped in the car a moment longer. I grabbed my phone and eased myself out of the driver's seat as quietly as I could, not that I thought I would disturb anyone. There was no light on in the house next door which confirmed my suspicion that whoever lived there had gone away. I made a mental note to knock on the front door of the neighbour with the yapping dog and introduce myself before too much longer. Then again, they hadn't bothered to introduce themselves to me, so maybe not.

The night was windless. I used the light of the stars to pick my way around the side of the barn and on towards the house. Every footfall sounded to my ears like a crash of cymbals. I thought I was doing well until I stubbed my toe on something hard, and had to resort to using the torch on my phone.

Instinct made me pick up a rock.

There was no sign of life, other than me, and I felt acutely conscious of my own visibility now that the sharp beam of the phone lit my way.

I peered at the illuminated patches of ground, at the piles of timber and stones, and the upended wheelbarrows leaning against the wall where one of the remaining stone masons had left them. I shone the light up into the scaffolding. There was no one up there, not that I could see that far, and I wasn't about to climb a ladder and find out if anyone lurked up there. I stepped through the back doorway and pointed the phone at the interior. I felt like a prowler. The state of disrepair and the chaos of construction were overwhelming captured in the narrow beam of light. Every feature took on a ghoulish hyper-reality spotlighted against the dark.

I stuck fast to the northern half of the house, shining the light into the kitchen. There was no one in there.

I noticed a new lintel above the dining-room door. There was no one in that room either, or the adjoining room. Summoning courage, I crossed the patio and shone the light through the hole in the partition wall. There was nothing to see other than areas of new wall.

I had to gather my wits to step through the hole and check more closely on the downstairs rooms on the south side of the build.

I crept around, shining the torch in each room. Nothing.

Before I left I paused on the spot where I had cried over my mother. I still hadn't thought through what could possibly have caused that peculiar trance state culminating in that strange vision. I began to feel weird in the recollecting and quickly went back through the hole in the partition.

My curiosity sated, I re-assessed the wisdom of my night watch. It seemed I was entirely alone, but what was I to do there? Crouch down somewhere and wait? I was hardly going to tackle someone, and they would have the advantage of being able to back me into any corner of the build. Unease trickled through my veins. I was too vulnerable, too exposed. Where the hell was Mario? I felt a sudden compulsion for the safety of my car.

I was about to turn back when I heard movement behind me. I froze. The sound of soft footsteps, a rustle. I rushed over to the dining room and hid in the doorway. My breath caught in my throat. I killed the phone light and peered round.

The darkness was thick, but I made out a shape moving close to the ground. That was no human. I hit the torch button and directed the beam at the patio entrance. There, huddled with its tail between its leg, was a scrawny, terrified dog. We locked gazes. I raised the rock and made to throw it as I emitted a low growl. The dog hesitated, not ready to give up its position. I raised the rock higher and growled louder, taking a step forward. The pathetic thing let out a soft whimper and scampered away. I threw the rock after it to reinforce my point, and picked up another in case the beast came back. It was only a half-starved mongrel, but my heart was pounding like a jack hammer.

At least I knew one thing; the dog had mostly likely tipped over the wheelbarrows. I doubted it had found Cliff's tool bag and relocated it downstairs, twice, but I was beginning to wonder if Cliff had made up that story to scare the others. Or he was absent-minded and had left his tool bag down on the patio floor. My theories did not account for the strange relocation of the rock in my apartment, but perhaps the two were not connected, but merely coincidental.

I headed back to my car, picking my way past the rubble and stacks of timber. About halfway, I again felt too exposed. After doing a scan for the dog, I killed the light and waited for my eyes to adjust. I heard another dog bark in the distance, then nothing, not a whisper. I looked up. The stars were bright in the sky. There was still no moon. Perhaps it was a new moon.

I took a few steps and a few more, and then I stopped. The barn was about ten paces ahead. Beside it, were two other outbuildings, once storerooms of some kind, both without roofs, their walls at waist height in places. I had no idea where that dog went but I pictured it crouched inside one of the buildings, ready to pounce. I gripped the rock, raised to the ready.

There was nothing for it but to keep going.

I took a few more paces, my footsteps crunching on the gravel. They were much too loud. Between footfalls I thought I heard movement, behind me again. I froze. Was the dog stalking me? Should I bolt?

In my side vision, I caught a flash of light. I turned. There it was again, a pin point of sharp red, darting up from inside the house, rising above the back wall and veering to the horizontal before fading away.

I couldn't move. Panic held me in its grasp. I stared into the blackness, my mind scrambling to make sense of what I had seen. A firework? It resembled a cigarette glow. Had someone thrown a cigarette? But there was no one in there. Besides, how can a cigarette tossed in the air suddenly veer off like that? Especially without the help of even a breath of wind. I began to doubt my perception. All I knew was if someone was in there and I had missed them, I had to move, fast.

I turned and was about to switch on my phone light when another pin point of light shone brightly, ahead of me this time, coming from inside the smallest outbuilding. The light was blue, and as I stared, transfixed, it headed straight for me. I opened my mouth, prepared to scream. But the dot of luminescence moved faster than any sound that could come out of me. It bounced off my chest and darted up into the night sky and zoomed off, zigzagging like a dizzy insect.

Perhaps that was what it was, an insect, but I was not convinced.

Terrified, I ran back to my car. My body shook. I fumbled for the door and bashed my hip on the steering wheel as I got in. I wound the window up and locked the doors. My hands scrambled with the seat belt and then with locating the ignition. I turned the key, threw the gearstick into first and drove off my block as fast as I dare. Whoever or whatever that was, I wasn't about to hang around for more.

18

NO PLACE TO STAY

A<small>FTER THE TERROR ON THE BUILDING SITE</small>, <small>ARRIVING BACK AT THE</small> apartment didn't offer me the solace I needed. My only comfort was seeing the rock where I had put it in the narrow slip of garden.

Hoping to numb my senses, I downed two large glasses of red wine in quick succession. In a mildly soporific haze, I played 'Aikea Guinea', needing Elizabeth Fraser's voice to fill my head and block out the flashback images of darting lights. The trouble was, hearing her voice instantly reminded me of my mother, which had never troubled me before but now it did.

Sleep, when it came, was fitful and interspersed with long periods lying awake with my mind spinning like a whirligig. I was hot, too, which didn't help. And I was annoyed with myself for keeping the windows shut, for it meant I had to endure the warm and stuffy air, but I lacked the courage to throw them open, lest some rock-moving stranger crept in.

At the first sign of daylight, I got up, my skin sticky with sweat. I dove in the shower then nibbled on a muesli bar for breakfast. I felt no inclination to return to the build. I sent Mario a text asking after his whereabouts the night before and while I waited for a reply, I checked my emails.

There was nothing from my father. I hadn't heard from him in

over a fortnight. I pictured him engaged in some high-powered property deal, the way he would pace the floor with his phone pressed to
his ear, the alcohol he consumed too early in the day strong on his
breath. I recalled the way he would disappear all Saturday to play
golf, leaving me, in my early teens with the house to clean. I
wondered sometimes if he had treated me as a replacement for his
deceased wife. Someone to do his cooking and iron his shirts. On
those Saturday chore-mornings, I only ever made a half-hearted
effort. Clarissa did the rest. Until one occasion when she yelled at him
for putting too much on his only daughter. After that, he hired a
cleaner.

Did my mother really cook and clean? I had no image of her ever
having done so. She struck me as the lackadaisical type, or perhaps
not. Perhaps, being more ethereal and dreamy, she left things unfin-
ished while she wandered off on some whim. Was that true or had I
been told or left that impression? Who *was* she? The only connection
we had was a love of the Cocteau Twins. When it came to remembering, my mother and the band were fused and there was little that got
past that fusion, it loomed so large in my psyche. It had started to
bother me that I couldn't access deeper, more intimate memories.
Memories of ice-creams and sandcastles on the beach, of birthday
cakes and blowing out candles, of presents at Christmas, of hugs and
kisses and tears. Instead, all I had was a feeling, an inchoate longing
for some sort of union with my deceased mother that was aroused in
me whenever I heard Elizabeth Fraser sing, one that had creepily
manifested in that vision of her by the partition.

Clarissa replied to my last email saying she was sorry she hadn't
had time to look into Olivia Stone due to a string of medical appoint-
ments—nothing to worry over, just the dentist, an annual medical
and an eye test. Blood pressure a little high, but there were pills for
that.

Disappointed, I closed my laptop. I checked my phone but there
was no reply from Mario. The sounds in the street and the adjoining
apartments had become familiar – children readying for school,
parents for work. I drew comfort from the sounds, the everyday just a
wall away, but it seemed bizarre to be in the middle of all that

normality, while in the apartment I was enshrouded in a dark mystery. The partition wall rock, Cliff's tools and wheelbarrows, the moving dot of light—maybe the villagers were right and Casa Baraso was cursed, haunted by spirits bound to the earth by tragedy. I considered inviting Clarissa's ghost-hunting pals for a bit of occult detection, but quickly dismissed the idea as farcical.

Besides, there was no need. I already had the answers. The lights were insects. The dog, scrawny as it was, knocked over the wheelbarrows, no doubt scavenging for crusts left by untidy workmen. Cliff was responsible for his own tool box, and the relocated rock I put down to Cejas. The curse of Casa Baraso indeed!

But my mind drifted, lured by a nagging unease. What of Olivia Stone? Had she really lived in my house? Died there? Was her ghost bent on spooking anyone who dared to alter the way things were with that house?

What am I thinking? I don't believe in ghosts!

I pictured Olivia Stone in her finery, all demure and introspective, and for a fleeting moment I saw my mother, Ingrid, in her stead. It was unsettling, two deceased women merging like that. What was happening to me, to my mind, to my uncommonly over-active imagination? Whatever it was, I didn't like it one bit.

Ingrid, Olivia, the Barasos, I was immersed by tragedy, mystery and death. Aunt Clarissa had not mentioned I would be plunged into matters of a preternatural order when she had mentioned all those planetary lines crisscrossing over Fuerteventura on my astrological global map. Secrets and deception, yes. Illusion perhaps. But not ghosts.

I reassessed the events and my rational explanations. The only factor puzzling me was the same kind of occurrence had taken place at two separate locations. Was that really coincidence? If a supernatural entity *was* at work—and I didn't want to entertain it, let alone believe it for one more second—then the spirit would need to be able to travel. In the back seat of my car? Ridiculous! Ghosts, as far as I was aware, did not travel. Still, I needed to be sure. I typed a quick email to Clarissa, seeking clarification.

I re-considered those lights. Admittedly, they were just plain weird. Insects? I had heard of insects shining lights, fireflies, lightning bugs. I wanted to believe they were insects but an internet search soon revealed no such insects were found on the island. Even so, there had to be a rational explanation. When I saw the first light I was prepared to believe it was a cigarette, although how anyone could make it move in the fashion it did was beyond me. The second light was blue, and it had come straight for me before zooming off into the night. It must have been some kind of trickery. Someone had been there. Just because I didn't see them, doesn't mean they were not present. There was a lot of the building and surrounds I hadn't checked. If not, if I had not been alone, then who was doing this? Who would want to go to all this trouble to scare me? How had they even known I would be there? Those were questions I could not answer.

What had haunted me all last night and left me feeling haggard, I managed to at least partially explain away. At least in theory. I tried to think of alternative theories and I considered seeking proof that I was right about any one of my hypotheses, but I didn't know where to start. I kept telling myself my explanations were reasonable and sensible, and I was planning on holding onto them with or without proof. They made me feel calmer and more in control.

I began to think about the day ahead and what I might do to fill it.

The ringtone of my phone exploded into my reverie. Startled, I read the screen. I didn't recognise the caller. When I answered, a woman spoke to me in rapid Spanish. She sounded nervous, apologetic. I asked her to slow down and start again.

The second time, as she explained herself, the horrible truth set in. It was the estate agent. The owners were giving me two weeks' notice to quit. They gave no reason other than the apartment would not be available after that. I asked if there was anything else on her books, but the woman said there was nothing, because it was June.

I had no idea how true her last remark would prove to be until I sat down and searched online for an alternative. July and August were peak holiday months but June was popular, too, as the weather was a touch cooler, and the island was booked solid. There was nothing to be had from Corralejo to Morro Jable. I searched every booking agent and several more obscure sites, some probably bogus. I thought of trying for a long-term rental but there was nothing to be had. I began to despair. I re-considered my campervan option, but even the idea of living in the confined space of a campervan made me feel exposed and claustrophobic all at once. When it came to my domestic arrangements, I needed space around me. Lots of it. The sense of uncluttered space was what had drawn me, deep down, to the island and to my ruin. I was not about to let myself be caged.

What would I do? Stay on another island? Go back to Britain? Neither held appeal, not least because one way or another, Mario benefited from having me around and I needed to keep an eye on the building site after hours.

My musings were interrupted by a knock at the front door. I leapt up from my seat to answer it. A postman handed me a parcel and asked me to sign for it. I closed the door and tore off the paper packaging. As anticipated, it was the Olivia Stone book, the second volume of her *Tenerife and its Six Satellites*. Happy to have my attention grabbed by this mysterious woman, I leafed through the front-end pages and studied the illustrations, before jumping straight to her account of Fuerteventura.

19

FUERTEVENTURA OF OLD

Olivia Stone devoted the penultimate three chapters of her travel diary to Fuerteventura, amounting to about sixty pages, a small portion of the thick volume, most of which was given over to Gran Canaria. In the opening paragraph of the Fuerteventura section, she described her arrival in Corralejo and I was confronted with a very different Corralejo to the one I knew.

I had heard holidaymakers comment that the town wasn't what it was back in the 1980s, but Olivia Stone forced me to picture what the place would have been like a hundred years before that. Every resident of Corralejo, then a tiny 'cluster of huts', came to watch a sailing boat drop anchor in the harbour. 'Not a multitude', Olivia said. A smattering then, of bemused and curious villagers wondering who was aboard. Among the onlookers was Don Victor Acosta, who was to be Olivia and her husband John's host. He was there with two camels and a donkey. It turned out the Stones were to spend a lot of time riding camels on the island, for it appeared the main mode of transport, other than feet. Donkeys were mentioned, but no horses.

Two paragraphs in and I could see why Paco was enamoured with the woman and her book. The way she portrayed Corralejo and its people, the simple beauty of the calm waters of the bay, the volcanic islet of Lobos and the mountains of Lanzarote beyond, hers was a portrait locked in time, a primary source depicting a group of islands about to undergo a rapid transformation.

Olivia's observations were plainly and concisely stated and it was easy to race on through the text, but I noticed I needed to go back over vignettes and even single sentences a number of times to absorb the fullness of what was being said.

Olivia was acutely aware of the poverty she witnessed all around her. The villagers she encountered had nothing but the bare necessities and eked out a very simple existence. Living alongside them were the rich, for there appeared to be little if nothing in between, and it was with the rich that the Stone's stayed, having arranged by correspondence various hosts prior to their arrival.

The Stones, I thought, were well-connected. I gained the sense that they were residing with the local intellectual set after looking up a Don Gregorio Chil y Narajano, and discovering he was an academic from Gran Canaria with an interest in natural history and anthropology. He seems to have introduced the Stones to his connections on Fuerteventura.

It was obvious Olivia enjoyed her stay and was taken by the landscape. She referred to the wind that blew across the plains, to the mountains and the volcanoes and the views, to the churches and the methods of farming, including the beehive grain stacks I had seen photos of, and the sorts of implements I had seen in museums.

Her journey took her to La Oliva, then on to Puerto del Rosario, then known as Puerto Cabras. From there the couple headed inland again, to Antigua, and up to Betancuria, making the arduous journey down the massif to Pájara before turning north a fraction and arriving at Tiscamanita, where they stayed until they journeyed to Gran Tarajal to board their next vessel and leave the island.

I took particular interest in what the author had to say about my village. She used the word 'straggling', aptly describing the arrangement of farms arranged around the village centre. She observed the rich red soil, the cinders used for mulch, the depressions in the plain where water would pool and provide oases after rain, and the glimpses of the ocean caught between chains of rugged mountains. Her words were my reality, so little had changed in the landscape.

The year she arrived it hadn't rained on the island for seven years. People were starving. Many fled to the other islands and beyond. I wondered want the Spanish government had done to help, but I already had the answer, knowing their reputation: nothing.

That she spoke Spanish was no longer in doubt, for she mentioned the strain of concentrating for hours on the conversation of others. It was a mental strain I was all too familiar with.

They did indeed stay with Don Marcial Velázquez, as Paco had said, and enjoyed their time with Marcial, his mother and his sister. Olivia was impressed by Marcial's collection of books and his knowledge of politics, history and geography, and in the same brief sentence she revealed her own predilections and intellectual refinement. She described Marcial's house as one storey.

There was no mention of her even walking by my house, let alone going inside.

I flicked back through the pages. Earlier, when they had been staying in La Oliva, she mentioned passing a quaint grey building that was two stories in height and I realised she was most likely referring to the colonel's house – Casa de los Coroneles. By then, the age of the colonels was over.

As a whole, the Fuerteventura she described bore little resemblance to the island I knew and loved, except for the landscape. The old way of life was long gone. All that remained could only be found in the museums. For people like Paco, Olivia's travel diary was a eulogy and I could see why. I supposed a lot of the world was swallowed up, one way or another, and old cultures lost, deemed worthless or unimportant by developers, men like my father, who, when all was said and done, could not have cared less.

I read and re-read Olivia Stone's book and copied some descriptions in my notebook. Following up on Paco's claim that she had absconded to Tiscamanita, I hunted for clues that she was an unhappy woman trapped in a bad marriage, dipping into the chapters on Lanzarote and Gran Canaria, but there was no indication of the sort. Olivia rarely mentioned her husband, other than to acknowledge his presence.

It was with bitter irony that at the end of the day I returned to my search for accommodation and, finding the island chock-a-block, I imagined camping under the stars, or sleeping in my car, as I had heard others resorting to. Those who, like me, refused to be defeated. If Olivia Stone, a less than robust woman by her own account, could manage to ride a camel in the searing heat and blasting winds, I could manage a little discomfort, surely?

Another thought occurred to me. There were two rooms almost completed in my house. If I could manage to persuade Mario to make them habitable, I could stay there even without power or plumbing. At least it would be a proper roof over my head and it would be a lot better than sleeping in my car. Having someone on site at night would add security, too, not that I thought any was needed. I refused to give sway to the notion of a curse, or let Cejas, a dog or those bizarre darting lights put me off camping out in my own home. Besides, I would have to live there eventually.

I suspected it would have been something Olivia Stone might have done. Not willingly, but she would have put up with it.

20

THEORIES TESTED

I PHONED MARIO THE NEXT MORNING, AS EARLY AS I DARE, AND ASKED as politely and indifferently as I was able what caused him not to turn up at the property the other night. I thought we had agreed, I said. He sounded apologetic as he launched into a tedious explanation involving a prior engagement he had forgotten about, and how he had to rush out the door almost the moment he arrived home and left his phone on the kitchen bench by mistake. The scenario he painted sounded plausible but I did not believe one iota of it. Frustrated and a little let down, I cut in, swiftly changing the course of the conversation with, 'Have the workmen finished plastering those two rooms?'

There was a moment of silence in which he processed my question and answered in the affirmative.

'Good, because I am going to have to move on site.'

'What?! Why? You have an apartment!' Thankfully my phone was on speaker or I would have burst an eardrum.

'Sadly, the owner wants me out,' I said softly, not allowing his hysterical tone to influence my own. 'I cannot find an alternative.' I described my online efforts of the day before in a measured voice. 'I don't feel I have much choice. Other than to leave the island for the summer.'

'Okay, okay. No, don't do that,' he said, calming down. 'Progress will be much slower without you around. When do you need to move?'

'Two weeks.'

I heard him exhale.

'You won't like it.' He referred to the noise, the dust and the lack of privacy, power and water.

'There's a generator.'

'That's only for the cement mixers and power tools.'

'You mean, I can't use it?'

'No.'

'Why?'

'Because you would need to run it all night for a fridge and there'd be noise complaints.'

It was my turn to react and I all but gasped. Who was there in my street to complain about noise?

'And the men won't like it,' he added.

That, I could understand. There would at the very least be the matter of an extension cord running from the barn all the way into my rooms. As my mind scrambled to assimilate the lack of power, I told him I would find a way to deal with all the difficulties and I would keep looking for an alternative. Meanwhile, at least having me around at night would keep away intruders. He relented, but not before telling me I should paint the rooms first.

'Me?'

'My men are not painters. I can't get a painter in until all the work is finished. Painters always come in last.'

'Can't you make an exception?'

'I have my reputation to consider. The painters don't like it and neither do the others. Can you paint?'

Of course, I could paint. What self-respecting owner of a mid-terrace home in Colchester didn't know one end of a paintbrush from another? Although I had to admit privately that I had only tackled the bathroom in an Easter break, a small bedroom in another, and all I did was paint over what was already there. Still, I had watched enough DIY shows to know the dos and don'ts and when I was tackling the bedroom, Clarissa showed me how to use a roller without making paint spatters, how to spread the paint evenly and achieve a brushstroke-free finish, and how to feather and cut in. She said she had learned from a professional when she was having her extension built and her painter fell sick; she had needed the room completed in time for a party.

I consulted my Spanish-English dictionary and jotted down the essential language and went to the hardware store. I took the advice of a helpful assistant and bought three six-litre tins of white paint, a roller and tray, an extension pole, masking tape, a paint brush for cutting in, drop sheets, a small step ladder and a painter's platform. Loading up my Hyundai SUV workhorse, I realised I had nothing suitable to wear. I swung by a cheap clothing store for slacks and a loose t-shirt, using their changing room to swap outfits.

Seeing me arrive with my gear, some of the workmen smiled at me, others grinned, although some of those grins were probably jeers and inwardly the men were rolling eyes. Mario must have told them. I responded in kind, vowing to ignore them all and set to work.

On my way in, I found a carpenter hanging the dining room door. He ignored me as I passed by with an arm full of drop sheets and entered the living room via the vestibule. The walls were grey plaster. The window with its curved seats and wooden shutters, and a sturdy wooden door, matched the exposed beams of the ceiling. The floor-boards were yet to be sanded. I ferried in the rest of my gear, feeling like an oddball and as far from a team member as it was possible to be.

As I was spreading out the drop sheets, Helmud entered the room. With a quick sweep of his eye, he took in the paraphernalia of the painter and proceeded to issue me with instructions. He told me how to use the roller without making spatters. He demonstrated how to hold a paint brush and how to cut in. I watched in silence, noticing a look of surprised approval at my purchase of a rat's tail brush. 'Good brand, this,' he said. I was then treated to instructions on the use of a step ladder and platform and how best to stir paint. I smiled into his face and thanked him for his tips. I didn't mention Clarissa or my own prior efforts. I didn't say that I had a steady hand and I was plan-ning to do a good job. I knew he would be back to check on me, over and again. He was a man, I thought, and men like to explain things. Some men, most men, all men? I had no idea. Still, I was grateful for the extension cord and the light he brought in.

What Helmud did not tell me and I had to find out for myself was how taxing painting would be, up and down ladders, stirring, pouring and brushing and rolling on paint, all the while taking care not to let it spatter. Yet I couldn't stop; seeing the grey turn white was satisfying and the process rhythmic, almost hypnotic and compulsive, and much to my surprise I was enjoying the process.

The render absorbed most of the first coat. Cutting in was easy in the corners and there was no skirting board to deal with—Mario had advised me to paint almost to the floorboards—but around the beams was a lot more challenging. I didn't want paint smears on my timber. Taping up the edges of all those beams meant stretching tall with my arms above my head. Yet I refused to ask for help.

As anticipated, Helmud kept a watchful eye on my progress, poking his head in the door from time to time. Seeing me reaching up and painstakingly cut in along the edge of a beam, he told me not to worry too much as they would need to be sanded and then oiled. That was when I realised those beams had my name on them too. 'Oiling with what?' I asked. When I next got down off the ladder I put sandpaper and linseed oil on my shopping list saved in Notes in my phone.

Ten-foot ceilings meant a lot of paint. I managed two coats of the first room before I finished for the day. By then, my wrist was aching, I had a headache and I felt dizzy from the fumes.

The following morning, I awoke with a stiff neck and shoulders. Undeterred, I set off for the building site early, getting there before the men, already at work giving the second room its first coat before I heard the usual hammering and footsteps and talk. This time, I put on my headphones and played Stereophonics and stayed lost in a musical world oblivious to the cacophony going on all around me.

On the third day, Helmud showed me how to sand and oil the old timber beams and lintels. This time, his instructions were welcome. I taped up my fresh paintwork thinking maybe I should have approached the tasks in reverse order.

I didn't take to the sanding or the linseed smell, but I did enjoy watching the colour of the timber darken. As the day wore on, the strain on my shoulders and neck had me deciding I needed to locate a masseur.

The doors and window required the same treatment. At least all that sanding and oiling was at body height. I had to wait three days between coats and apply a top coat containing varnish to stop the timber turning dull.

Next, Helmud arranged a floor sander and a man to go with it. I used that day to buy furniture, arranging delivery on the day I needed to move in. In the meantime, it was down to me, on my hands and knees, to seal the floor.

Eyebrows raised when the delivery men turned up with a bed, a chest of drawers, a table and chairs, a free-standing two-door cupboard, and two small and comfy arm chairs. All of it practical and none of it antique. Thinking hard about my needs, I bought a two-ring camping stove and gas bottle, saucepans, crockery, cutlery and utensils, a carrier bag full of candles, a lighter and ten boxes of matches.

Working out how I would get by with no plumbing, I arranged the delivery of a second portaloo, as I had no intention of using the men's. I had it put on the other side of the nearest outbuilding. Theirs was over by the barn. Recalling a scene in one of those survival television shows, I cleared an area inside that outbuilding where the walls were above head height and laid a square of pavers to serve as a base for the large plastic bowl and bucket I would use as a makeshift shower. Helmud helped me put a large water container on a low platform made of a couple of planks and some concrete blocks.

The other device I bought off a German guy in Tetir, was a solar battery and two small panels that came with props that I could angle at the sun. He gave me a demonstration and I took some notes, and I rigged up the panels behind my portaloo, well away from the build. It meant carrying the battery back and forth but it would be worth it.

I was busy arranging my things in preparation for my first night when Paco appeared. I saw him through the living-room window, which I had left open to air the room. I rushed out to greet him, his appearance a welcome surprise.

I hadn't seen him since we had lunch in Antigua about two months before and had given up hope of ever seeing him again. As he took in the scaffolding and the frenetic pace of the build, he explained he had been to El Hierro and then gone on to La Gomera and La Palma, in fact all of the islands to take photos for a travel brochure and website.

'It was unexpected. I couldn't pass it up.'

'A terrific opportunity, by the sound of it,' I said, Paco rocketing up in my estimation. 'I wouldn't have passed it up either. Your employers in Caleta de Fuste didn't mind?'

His eyes filled with amusement. 'The owners of the restaurant are my mother's sister and her husband, and no, they were fine with it.'

It was with a twinge of envy that I marvelled at the close-knit family network he was part of and wondered if all the families on the island were the same.

I covered my reaction with, 'Make sure you show me when it all comes out.' Seeing the men down tools for a morning break and gather over by the barn, I added, 'Come in and have a look at what's been happening.'

He glanced at the men whose eyes had no doubt gravitated to the English woman and her friend. Under their scrutiny, Paco appeared uncomfortable. 'Are you sure?'

'It's my house, Paco. Not theirs. Come.'

He followed me into the building and we stopped in the patio to look around. I turned and waited. He had extracted his camera and was taking photos of every little detail on both sides of the partition, murmuring to himself. He crouched on his haunches for a better angle of whatever had caught his eye, and I observed the pull of his pants around his butt, the way his ponytail trailed down his back, the thickness of his forearms, my gaze lingering on the tanned skin, the masculine hair. I found myself admiring the masculinity of him altogether and quickly looked at something else.

'Paco,' I said, sensing we were losing time and heading for the vestibule.

As he entered my new living space his jaw dropped.

'This is incredible.'

'You like my efforts?' Pride swelled in my chest.

'You?'

'I painted the walls and oiled the beams and varnished the floor. All me.'

'Wow!' He eyed the furniture. 'You are living here?'

'I had to leave the apartment. They wanted me out.'

'Bastards. Did they give a reason?'

'No.'

'That's because they know they can get more money charging someone else a daily rate.'

'Really?'

'It's holiday season.'

I wasn't convinced although I had no alternative explanation. I didn't want to argue with him. There seemed nothing else to say, nothing either of us was prepared to say. A pressure built.

Then, in a moment of courage he said, 'I came to invite you to lunch.'

'It's a bit early,' I said much too quickly, cringing inwardly at my knee jerk lack of grace.

He looked disappointed and I wasn't surprised.

'Where are you thinking of going?' I smiled up at him to atone for my lack of consideration.

'Pájara.'

'I need a few minutes to get changed.'

I showed him to the door and closed the window, putting myself in near-total darkness. My eyes soon adjusted and I changed out of my scruffy pants and t-shirt and pumps in favour of a colourful beach dress and sandals. A quick brush of my voluminous hair and I was done.

When I exited my rooms, Paco was taking yet more photos and the men were making their way back up the scaffolding and to their various stations around the build. Gazes shot back and forth. Dressed as though for a date, I was pleased to hurry away.

The day was heating up and there wasn't much of a breeze. I

walked with Paco to his car. It seemed natural to travel with him, even though I was foregoing the luxury of my brand-new Hyundai for his dusty old bomb. I hadn't been a passenger in a car since Aunt Clarissa drove me to the station one time when my Vauxhall was in for a service, and never on the island. For once, I could fully take in the scenery, the mountain chains, the skyline, the sweeping plains. It was over too soon, a ten-minute drive and we had arrived.

Pájara is one of my favourite inland towns. Situated at the southern end of the Betancuria massif, it has a quaint, historical vibe with a beautiful plaza in its centre filled with established trees and pretty hedgerows. The plaza is dominated by the modern town hall building and the old church, Nuestra Señora de la Regla, famous for its Aztec-style carvings. Paco parked in a side street and we strolled to a restaurant facing the plaza. Sitting by a window afforded a pleasant, side-on view of the church's façade.

I had visited the church on my last holiday. I much admired the Aztec feel of the stonework on the pediment above the entrance and, inside, the magnificent floor to ceiling altarpieces, intricately painted, predominantly in red and gold. The church was completed about seventy years before my house, and the vaulted ceilings were made of the same carved wood.

While my attention was drawn to the sightseers ambling about in the plaza, Paco studied his menu. Behind us, the café was filling. The atmosphere felt relaxed and convivial. The hiss of frying and the rich cooking smells I had come to expect aroused my appetite.

'What would you like?' he said, interrupting my reverie.

My eyes landed on the mixed tapas platter and I suggested we share it.

He looked back at the bar and a young woman came over and took our order, Paco adding two beers. We sat for a short while in companionable silence. He seemed preoccupied, or momentarily lost in thought. I considered confiding recent events, particularly the strange lights I had seen darting about, but decided against it. I didn't want spooky preoccupations to spoil our lunch. I wanted nothing more than to enjoy the local food surrounded by people, and especially to enjoy the company at my table.

When the food came he grew chatty, sharing stories from his childhood growing up on his family farm in Triquivijate, and of the large gatherings, the feasts and fiestas. I listened, attentive and fascinated, while envious of his large family network. He sounded especially fond of his mother. Hearing him praise her, I wished I could remember mine. I was saddened that I had managed to erase whatever recollections there might had been. I hadn't a clue what to do about it. Perhaps it was too late and nothing would ever be retrieved.

When we were done soaking up tapas juices with crusty bread, Paco fished out his camera and showed me the photos he had taken on his trip, the camera passing back and forth between us as he explained the sequences of shots. Those he had taken of El Hierro were impressive. The sense of elevation at the island's peak, and the great expanse of cliff that embraced a littoral where the land was cultivated and a town and some farmhouses were dotted about. 'Frontera,' he said, pointing out the town itself. What an exceptional place to find yourself, facing the Atlantic to the west with a great cliff rising up behind you. I wasn't sure I would feel comfortable with so much elemental power all around me. Paco had taken shots of the special wood at the mountain top and others of ribbons of houses hugging narrow lanes that wended down steep-sided ravines. Views typical of the other islands, as I discovered viewing his photos of La Gomera. When Paco described the journey he had made from the port to the west side of that island, the road clinging to steep mountainsides, the hairpin bends and plummeting views down into ravines and to the ocean, my palms broke out in a cold sweat.

His shots of La Palma were even more breath taking. He had taken dozens looking down from a purview above the clouds at the shimmering ocean far below.

'It's two-thousand five hundred metres at the peak,' he said.

'Is that the Canary Island's highest?'

'No. Mount Teide on Tenerife is.'

'How high's that?'

'Close to four thousand.'

I had never been to Tenerife. I tried to imagine being four kilometres up a mountain, and instantly preferred the low-level vistas of

Fuerteventura. But it occurred to me as Paco described his trip that the islanders had no problem with altitude, and were quite prepared to terrace steep mountain slopes to make use of fertile soils, chasing whatever rainfall there was to be had. Where there was height there was water.

He handed me the camera again to view a photo of El Tablado, and I was gazing at a track meandering up through a hamlet and carefully farmed fields situated on what could only be described a razorback, because the land fell away dramatically to either side. The fields on the plateau were lush and green and the mountainsides all around forested, reinforcing my thinking about harvesting the rain. I couldn't see any way to access the locale other than by following the track up into the mountains.

'The plateau ends in a cliff,' he said, reinforcing my observation as he pointed at the next photo, this time of the end of the little plateau where a sheer drop looked down on forever.

I swiped forward anticipating more of the same and saw instead photos of my house. They were the ones he had just taken. I flicked through them and was about to hand back the camera when a photo of the partition wall caught my eye, or rather a dark shape seated in the hole. I thought for a moment the shape might have been that stray dog or, on closer inspection one of the workmen crouching down, but the dark figure was neither man or dog. It was something else, something inexplicable.

'What is it?' Paco said, holding out his hand for the camera.

I passed it back and he stared at the image. The expression on his face darkened.

'It's Olivia Stone,' he said slowly. His face wore a wry smile.

I wanted to tell him not to be ridiculous.

'Let me look again.'

The camera passed between us several times before he put it away in his satchel.

The figure did look human, hunched down beside the wall, but the shape of the clothes was vintage, the outline resembling a woman garbed in a long and sleeved dress, a hat with a wide brim tied closely around her face. Who was she and what was she doing there? Or was

Paco right? Could Olivia Stone have lived in my house and taken to haunting it?

On impulse, I asked if we could exchange phone numbers. 'Saves you turning up and having a wasted journey,' I said, although that was hardly likely and hardly my motive. He remained my only friend and despite his apparent obsession with Olivia Stone I found I liked him more and more. He was attractive in a rugged, bohemian kind of way and I admired his passion for his islands. He had earned my esteem too, for his recent travel assignment. He really wasn't some loser serving beers in his family's restaurant. I had never seen him that way, but I imagined that was how my father would picture him, and even Aunt Clarissa, who had no time for wastrels.

He told me his number. I entered it in my phone and sent him a text, watching him save me to contacts. The act bound us somehow, even casually, and I felt reassured.

21

FIRST NIGHT

WHEN PACO DROPPED ME BACK AT THE BUILDING SITE, THE WORKMEN were packing up and leaving. Concerned something had gone awry, I said my goodbyes and rushed over, approaching one of the stone masons, who explained Helmud had given them the rest of the afternoon off to enjoy the festival in Tuineje. The mason looked at me with interest and wanted to know if I would be going, but I said I preferred settling into my new home. A look of amused incredulity appeared in his face. I ignored it.

As soon as I was alone I changed out of my dress and went and tried out the portaloo, which wasn't as bad an experience as I thought it might have been. I exited the plastic capsule and wandered around the block, soaking in the expanse of view and affirming I belonged there, on the island, in Tiscamanita and right there on my half acre of land. The locals would respect me in the end for restoring one of their great houses. I could become a patron of ruins. Not a saint, a real living patron rescuing abandoned dwellings, their saviour. I could start with the ones in my street. There were enough of them to absorb a decade or two of my time. It was a noble if fleeting thought.

I returned to my quarters for the wide-brimmed hat I purchased in Puerto del Rosario one time, securing the ties under my chin. With my head and neck and face shaded, I pottered about tending and watering my plants. I selected some large stones from a nearby rock pile to edge the garden bed. Then I made an effort at rebuilding a small section of the collapsed dry-stone wall, telling myself whoever had built the wall couldn't have done a good job since it had collapsed in so many places, and I couldn't possibly do a worse job, especially as I took a lot of care positioning my rocks so that they fitted into each other more or less. It was an assumption that kept me going and from which I drew some satisfaction. The work was slow and peaceful, and it was good to be outdoors feeling useful.

Now and then I lifted my gaze to the volcano and sat and stared. Whenever I raised my head, there it was, dominating the landscape and I asked myself who else I knew that had a volcano for a view. No one.

The robust sun was on the wane when I headed inside. After stepping over bits of timber too heavy to shift with my foot, I set about shoving all the moveable obstructions in the patio out of my way, keen for a clear path to the ablutions. Living on a building site, I was fast discovering, presented numerous hazards in the dark.

I had taken the living room as my bedroom. Access was via the vestibule. The window overlooking the street opened out beneath the scaffolding. I planned on keeping the window closed to seal off the room from dust. I had arranged the bed against the wall facing the door. Two bedside tables completed the furniture along that wall, along with a chair in the corner to sling my clothes. I had centred a chest of drawers in the length of wall behind the door. A suitcase, half-closed on the floor, contained clothes that needed to be hung. I had thought of buying a free-standing wardrobe but preferred to keep my things covered as much as possible. I had even taken up a local tradition and bought a large clear plastic cover to serve as a dust sheet for my bed, to throw on during the day when the men were at work.

The dining room was mostly empty, save for a table and chairs in its centre and a low, two-door cupboard beside a length of benchtop on trestles that I planned to use for a makeshift kitchen. Four large water bottles sat on the floor. The two small armchairs I purchased for comfort completed the furnishings.

There was no door separating the two rooms. I had asked Mario to leave the double doorway open, although standing in that cavernous space I could see that at night in bed I might feel exposed. Too late to change what I had decided in a moment of haste, and besides, when the rooms were filled and used for what they were designed, the opening would be desirable. Even so, I made a mental note to think through every future decision carefully, approaching it from all angles. When it comes to a build, decisions are hard if not impossible to undo.

The sun had yet to set, but inside with the doors closed the rooms were black as night. I went about lighting candles, chunky church candles each in its own saucer. The effect of all the light gently flickering gave the space an ethereal, moody feel.

For dinner, I made a tuna salad baguette and sat at the table, my attention absorbed by the candle in front of me guttering and fizzing then settling into a steady flame.

Establishing a routine I considered sensible, I filled a beaker and readied my toothbrush and went outside, keen to brush my teeth before nightfall. Then I brought in the solar battery.

Dashing to the portaloo for a midnight pee held no appeal whatsoever. Neither did my solution. I took the plastic bucket I had been using to water the garden and found a broken piece of plywood on the rubbish pile to use as a lid. My chamber pot, and I revisited my campervan idea one more time as I set it down in the far corner of the dining room.

Shut in my chamber for the night I was alert to every sound. No one would know I was alone in these two rooms, although they might see my car parked by the barn. If an intruder did chance by, then they would be sure to open one or other of the doors into my makeshift home. Which left me no choice. Careful not to damage my newly sealed floor, I shunted an armchair hard up against the dining room door as a deterrent. In my bedroom, I propped a chair so that the backrest was under the handle, as I had seen done in films.

To obliterate the silence that crowded in on me, I paired my laptop to my new sound bar that I had purchased on one of my numerous shopping trips, plugged the sound bar into my new solar battery and played the Cocteau Twins' *Treasure*, softly at first, then realising the acoustics offered a new sensory experience, I turned the volume up a little louder, and a little louder still. There were too many flat surfaces for sound perfection, but as I listened I knew Elizabeth Fraser's soprano voice belonged in my house. Her vocalisations soared, the distinct tones came alive, and the mood of the guitars, with their dreamy, wistful tones, opened in me that familiar if inchoate yearning that quickly transformed into a wide-eyed melancholy.

It was a moment of imprudence and I knew I should turn it off, play something else. Instead, I sat on my bed and opened myself up to the music and as the second half of 'Donimo' kicked in I was filled with aching loneliness. Cut off from the world by the walls of the house, cut off from the island by my newness, cut off from my roots and my family, I was bereft of all that I once had and it was a peculiar feeling, poignant, an emptiness needing to be filled.

The Cocteau Twins were interior music, to be played in castles and cathedrals, contained spaces, not lost on the wind, although somehow the sounds mirrored the emptiness outside too. Yet the music was discordant, out of place, for it was another wilderness it spoke of, another wild, rugged landscape, a Scottish one. Here, if I was to truly belong here, I needed to engage with the local music, maybe something akin to the Cocteau Twins, some musical group who would open up in me, the listener, the same longing.

Treasure came to an end and I put on *Heaven or Las Vegas*. All thought evaporated when Elizabeth sang the first verse of 'Iceblink Luck'. I hadn't anticipated what the music would summon in me to fill the hollowness I had succumbed to despite my, or maybe because of my heightened state. One sort of loss was a conduit for another and I began to ache for my mother. My throat constricted as though a heavy lump was lodged there and hot tears burst from my eyes and formed rivers down my cheeks. I was locked in to every vocal rise and fall as though the agony of losing my mother swayed along in synchronicity. What was happening to me? As if in answer, the void in me soon filled with memory.

A memory of a number 13 bus.

A bus that ploughed through a pedestrian crossing. The driver too slow to react.

She had fallen on her face directly in front of the passenger-side wheel. The bus served as a municipal steam roller. Her shopping bag, filled with overripe tomatoes, fell under the front wheel along with her, creating a god-awful mess of tomato juice and bits of vegetable skin and pip, all mixed in with mum's blood and skin and flesh. The combination of vegetable matter and my mother seemed thicker and much more obvious on the white stripes on the zebra crossing.

A horrific scene for onlookers and particularly for one onlooker, me.

Having seen the bus, I was still on the kerb. I had felt unsure the bus would stop. I was seven years old and I had more of a sixth sense than my mother. To be precise, I was exactly seven years old because the Number 13 bus hit my mother at thirteen minutes past one in the afternoon of the thirteen of July, which just happened to be my birthday. My mum had bought the tomatoes to make Gazpacho soup. My favourite.

The remembering was all too much, as was the guilt. My mother set off that day to buy the ingredients for her only daughter's favourite soup, a woman so lost in the music she listened to she failed to turn her head and see that great lump of metal hurtling towards her.

I had blocked out the horror of that day, the congealing mass of red on the white stripes of the zebra crossing.

The only vestige of the trauma I was aware of was I never cared to celebrate my birthday. My father and Aunt Clarissa had tried to lure me with cake and candles, and brightly wrapped gifts and trips to the seaside, but I retreated inside myself, stuck on a smile and laboured through the hours, numb.

I had always fought against the memory of that horrific day, my birthday, but it was there, I was there, forcing my way now through 'Pearly Dewdrops' Drops' as though my ears were my mother's and I was inside her head as the shock of that bus shattered all that she was.

I stood up, I walked around the room with its huge shuttered window and carved wooden door and beams, and it was as though inside this chamber I had summoned the grief, hot grief, and finally granted it permission to exit.

The crying went on and on.

I hugged my arms around me and paced the room, caving and crouching every so often. When I thought it was finally waning, some poignant melody would kick in and trigger more tears. Yet I couldn't replace the Cocteau Twins with anything else. It would have been disloyal to a memory.

Eventually, I put on *Victorialand*. The tempo, slower and gentler, allowed my feelings to settle and be still. Before long, the battery ran out of charge and the music came to a sudden halt. I was thrust into silence.

Tears of grieving locked away for over thirty years had to end sometime, and after three whole albums of music, I was spent. My eyes burned. There was a small mountain of soggy tissues by my bed. I moistened a clean tissue and dabbed at my tear-stained face and my hot puffy eyes. There I sat, shocked by the outpouring as reason took control.

I told myself I had spent too long almost entirely alone, under considerable strain and uncertainty, and enduring some significant set-backs. That it was natural that so much stress had triggered the memory I had been repressing for so long. That I needed to practice self-care and not allow myself to reach such a peak when triggers would set off an avalanche of pain. I found a sorry-looking block of dark chocolate in my bag and ate the whole lot.

There was nothing else to do except read. I opened the Olivia Stone, which already had pride of place on my bedside table, and started at the beginning of her journey to the eastern Canary Islands, sinking into her easy style as she described the day she disembarked at Las Palmas, steering my eyes back to her words when my mind drifted elsewhere.

She made the same kinds of observations as she had of Fuerteventura, only her point of entry onto Gran Canaria was not that of a tiny fishing village but of an established town with a small port, roads and houses. Upon her arrival in 1883 there were no hotels in the capital, but tourism already had a foothold and the Stones were far from the only English couple to appreciate the island. Hotels were poised to open or be built. Unlike the single-room fishing huts of Corralejo, Olivia described established streets flanked by grand, three-storey buildings. John Stone had sketched a fountain in one.

The descriptions were vivid. Hers was a travel diary to get lost in, and in two pages I had almost forgotten my grief. Two pages more and I was drifting to sleep.

I put down the book and went about blowing out the candles, saving the one by my bed until last. I had one last look around, blew out the flame and settled beneath the covers thinking a good long sleep was in order.

It wasn't to be. The moment the light had gone I was hypersensitive to sound. The town was as quiet as death. All I could hear was the wind whistling where it could. There was no barking dog. I heard a car engine, faint in the distance. I thought I caught the crackle and pop of fireworks as Tuineje enjoyed its celebrations. The sense of others out in the streets a few miles away did nothing to calm my unease. I had never before suffered from night terrors, but alone in the dark I felt nervous. I reached for my phone and opened the toolbox for the torch, ready to turn it on if need be. There was little else I could do. I lay on my back and drifted.

I must have fallen into a deep sleep for when I awoke daylight was squeezing through the cracks in the window shutters. A sense of well-being infused me. I had spent my first night in my new home, never mind it was a building site and never mind I had cried my eyes out. I lit a candle and lay still for a while, pondering the day ahead.

When I sat up and looked around, fear jolted through me, a sensation quickly followed by anger.

The chair that I had propped under the door handle was lying on its side on the floor. I got out of bed and picked up the chair, setting it down on its four legs against the wall.

I went into the dining room and found the armchair I had rammed up hard against that door, pushed away at an angle. The dining room door was ajar. Why hadn't the sounds of all that moving furniture woken me?

Someone had been on site, there could be no doubt about it. That someone had entered my bedroom as I slept. A reveller from the festival, perhaps? One of the workmen? A prankster? How many of them had there been and why had I not woken?

As the full realisation sunk in that I had lain vulnerable in my slumber while an intruder had crept into my room, a sickening dread seeped into my awareness. I was too unnerved to even wash. After scanning about to find nothing stolen or disturbed, I dressed quickly, downed a glass of water and pocketed an apple. Clearly my efforts at security hadn't worked. There was only one solution I could think of. Bolts. I would go to the hardware store in Puerto del Rosario and buy bolts for the top and bottom of both doors and for the window. Barrel bolts. Big ones. I grabbed my keys and purse and headed off.

It was Saturday and the store was busy with handymen. I explained my needs to the same assistant who had sold me the paint, and arrived back at the house kitted with bolts and a cordless drill. I managed to partially charge the battery before losing patience and setting to work.

I would not be defeated by that joker.

22

BAD LUCK

A SQUEEZE OF THE POWER DRILL AND I HAD THE LAST SCREW IN PLACE at the bottom of the dining room door. Pleased with my efforts, I packed the drill in its plastic carry case. Mario would no doubt be dismayed by the holes I had drilled into that ancient wood but my personal safety was paramount.

I went and stood in the doorway to the vestibule. It was not going to be pleasant camping at the house, even during the day, even on a weekend when I had the place to myself. What I had previously taken in at a glance now I absorbed in detail, the overwhelming scale of the restoration affecting every corner of the building. I had no idea how long it would take but even with an army of men on the job—minus Cliff—I couldn't see the project completed in six months. They had been at work about two months and in that time, despite having two habitable rooms, the rest looked a long way from finished.

The door to the vestibule was centred in a two-foot thickness of wall, on my side freshly painted white, on the other, old render and stone. The double front door was being restored offsite and the cavity remained boarded up. The wall facing me across the once prettily tiled floor was in a poor state, with large patches of crumbling render. The beams had been replaced in the ceiling but no floorboards had been laid and I could see up to the roof, itself in disrepair. At the patio end of the vestibule would be a door with transom window above. It was a low priority, but it would complete the house, creating an airlock between the patio and the street.

I went back inside and shut the door and fastened the bolts top and bottom, two satisfying clunks of security. Reassured I would be safe, I unfastened them, fetched the battery and went and hooked it back up to the solar, then grabbed my laptop and charger and walked to the café. Halfway up the street I spotted a stray dog in a field, watching me. The same dog? This one looked bigger, stronger, healthier. Probably not a stray. It didn't approach.

In the café, I felt adventurous and ordered an array of tapas, along with grilled fish and chips and a glass of orange juice, no doubt pleasing Gloria with my order, who sprang into action as I walked away. There were a few diners in and others having coffees, but fortunately the table I was after was free. I spotted it the other day. There was a power point close by. Since the solar battery would not work with the laptop battery – something that had almost stopped me buying the solar kit – I had no choice but to find other options. I went and asked Gloria if it was okay to charge my laptop and she nodded agreement from behind the counter.

There was a message from my father wishing me well and hoping the restoration was getting along. Clarissa sent her apologies for not having time for the Olivia Stone research as yet. She was busy attending to the arrangements for the funeral of another friend who had passed away suddenly and had no family to speak of. At least, none that cared terribly much. Her and her friends at the Spiritualist church had given poor old Dorothea a proper send off. Not one relative made an appearance. Astonishing. But yes, she said, ghosts do travel. Why do I ask?

I tucked away that last piece of information in a mental file marked doubtful. My money was still on Cejas.

Leaving my laptop to charge, I tucked into the tapas Gloria had set down at my elbow, enjoying the bursts of vinegary fish, the garlicky mushrooms, the sweet tang of tomatoes. As I ate I tuned into the conversation at the next table that had suddenly risen in volume and I was alerted to the word 'curse'. I couldn't make out what they were discussing as their Spanish accent was different and they spoke so fast. One of the party shot me a sideways stare and I had to look down at my plate to avoid meeting it. Were they talking about my house? Surely not. Surely, they were talking about something else.

Gloria came with my fish and took away the tapas. I was uncommonly hungry, which I put down to the catharsis of the night before and the lack of a proper breakfast. That, and the food was well cooked and the chips, of course, moreish. By the end of the meal I was feeling too full to drink my juice. I extracted my notebook and wrote down a few impressions about building dry-stone walls and the strength of the sun and some minor observations of the build. I refused to log my own emotions or the strange goings on. I wanted my notebook to report nothing other than the nuts and bolts of the restoration and how good it was to have two rooms already completed.

The laptop was sitting at about fifty per cent charged. I sat back and waited. Before long, the café emptied and Gloria cleared the tables around me and came back to wipe them down. When she looked finished I beckoned her over, thinking to use that conversation I overheard to raise the topic of the curse on my house.

She laughed. 'They couldn't have been. They were from La Gomera. They were discussing a local legend. The Curse of Lauringea.'

'Lauringea? Who was he?' I asked, watching her fiddle with the cloth in her hand.

'She. It's an ancient curse and it has nothing to do with your house.'

'Do you know it? I'd love to hear it, if you have time.'

She glanced at the door. Seeing no one was about to enter, she put down the cloth, drew up a chair and said, 'Alright, I will tell you. Legend has it Lauringea was an indigenous farmer's wife who was seduced when she was young by the ruler of Fuerteventura, Don Pedro Fernandez of Saavedra. A right womaniser, he was and she ended up having his illegitimate child. One of many, I should imagine.'

'He sounds like a real creep.'

'He was,' she said with a quick glance at the door. 'Then one day when Lauringea's son was a man, he tried to defend the honour of a young maiden who was being seduced against her will. The seducer was none other than one of Don Pedro's legitimate sons.'

'Must be genetic,' I said. 'You know, womanising.'

She laughed. 'I don't know, maybe it is.'

There was a pause and I realised she may have lost her thread.

'Sorry, I interrupted. Please, go on.'

She took a breath. 'Well, of course right then Don Pedro appeared. Seeing what was going on he killed the man who was trying to defend the poor maiden's virtue. Lauringea was horrified. She cried out to Don Pedro that he had killed his own son. I have no idea what he made of that.'

'What happened?'

'She was grief-stricken and also furious. She called on the Guanche gods and placed a curse on the whole of Fuerteventura for being under the rule of such a man as Don Pedro. An east wind blew and brought the calima and the flowers shrivelled and all the grasses dried to a crisp.'

'That truly is fascinating.' I meant it.

'That curse is five hundred years old,' she said, now all talkative. 'The curse on your house is different. It isn't really a curse but people see it that way. That is what they believe and, I promise you, with good reason.'

'But why?'

'For the last hundred and fifty years, ever since the Barasos lived and died in your house, something bad has happened to those who have tried to live there.'

'Like what?' I said, sceptical.

'I know of three examples. There was the Rivas family who had five children who all died of influenza in the one season.'

'That's sad.'

'Then there was the gentleman farmer, Juan Perera, who lived there with his family. They had to move after he lost his fortune due to a bad harvest.'

'That could happen to anyone,' I said, knowing I should have held my tongue.

'Not in a year of good rain when everyone else was enjoying abundance.'

'Fair enough,' I said, although I was not convinced.

'Then there was Concha Delgado, a mother of two, who died in childbirth.'

'Sorry to question, but wouldn't that have happened anyway?'

She stood up and made light finger stabs on the table.

'Perhaps, but every single person who has lived in that house has had bad luck. Over the years, people stopped wanting to have anything to do with the place. They don't like the feeling there.'

'What feeling?' I said, looking up at her, genuinely puzzled. I had never felt any kind of 'feeling'.

She picked up her cloth and proceeded to fold it into squares. Her manner had become a touch agitated. She held my gaze. 'An unpleasant one. I have been told one of the maids who worked there heard voices.'

'Voices!'

'Ghosts. And things moved.' She looked away and I sensed she regretted that last comment. A look of concern came into her face. 'I wasn't going to tell you. I'm not sure I believe all of it but that is what I was told. Things moved.'

The door opened and an elderly couple in shorts and sunhats strolled in. Gloria rushed away, leaving me to absorb what she had said. Her last comment reverberated in my mind. *Things moved.* But it was gossip, all of it, no one had lived there for over a century. The witnesses were long dead. What remained was hearsay and tittle tattle.

Once my lap top and phone had charged, I left the café and wandered up the street and bought supplies from the supermarket. A different assistant served me. I introduced myself but he already seemed to know who I was.

With a bag of groceries in each hand and my laptop weighing down my shoulder bag, I trudged back to the building site, the vigorous sun determined to scald whatever bare skin it could find.

There was still a long way until sunset. I toyed with spending time repairing the dry-stone wall, but thought better of it. I was spending too much time out in the sun, far more than was healthy for my fair skin. Instead, I put away the shopping and went for a drive to Ajuy on the west coast, where the ocean breeze would be strong.

Thirty minutes, I had joined the holidaymakers enjoying the beach, the surf and the outdoor dining of a tiny fishing village given over to restaurants. I sat in the shade and whiled away a few hours with Olivia Stone and an iced coffee.

It was close to six when I parked behind the barn. The air felt no cooler, the sun no kinder, but it was surely weakening. I changed into gardening clothes and ferried water over to quench the thirst of all those plants in my garden that were looking worn out from the day. Then I attacked the wall. I knew my skills were abysmal but at least the rocks were where they belonged and not strewn along the back perimeter of my block where I planned to create a border of small trees and shrubs.

Ideas for a garden were growing in my mind. I would close in the garden with a high wall running beside the pavement, leaving space on the other side of the house for a driveway and, eventually, a garage. I fancied a pergola outside the south-facing windows. I would grow wind tolerant plants in exposed areas and in sheltered spots, vegetables and tender plants. I had been reading up about gardening on the island, and observed the choices of others by peering into any gardens I passed whenever the opportunity arose. A lot could be done with the fertile soil, that was obvious.

As the sun disappeared behind the mountains, I fetched the battery and went inside. Not wanting to drain what little power the battery held—I already knew I had been sold a lemon—I lit the candles, poured a glass of wine and continued reading. Before daylight disappeared altogether, I took my first bucket shower, cleaned my teeth and brought in the chamber pot. Then, I bolted myself in for the night and returned to Olivia Stone and her travels in Gran Canaria.

I was enjoying the narrative more and more. Her observations were informative and practical, from the day's weather to the condition of the soil and the plants that grew. When she described the preponderance of superstitious beliefs and practices amongst the

locals, even in the larger towns and the capital, Las Palmas, she did so
with much scepticism, clearly incredulous that in the age of science
such beliefs were still adhered to. Although she was at pains to
mention that the same sorts of superstitious beliefs abounded in
England. I had found an ally in Olivia Stone. She was a true rational-
ist, a woman who did not believe in ghosts, the supernatural or the
evil eye. In the company of that intrepid explorer I felt comfortable,
settled and contented. At ten, I blew out the candles and went to
sleep.

SHE WAS REACHING FOR ME. I couldn't see her but I knew who she was.
Her hand was smeared with fresh blood. I hesitated, watching. I
wanted to reach out and touch that blood-smeared hand and pull it
towards me, but I was repulsed by it all at once. Around us, all was
thick black. I held out my hand. Hers protruded further out of the
black, clawing for me, parting the darkness that began to fade around
her. Then a light went on and she was staring at me with eyes that
held no life. Her head hung back. The rest of her was mangled.

I awoke, startled, sweating, immersed in a slick of fear. The room
was black, the same black as the dream. I fumbled for my phone. It
was almost morning. I lit a candle and sat up in bed, dazed. The first
rational thought I had was I needed a proper window, not those
wooden shutters that let in no light. That may have been the tradition
but I needed some glass. The dining room had no window at all.

I would talk to Mario.

I sat for a while in my own pool of light. The dream was still with
me, a haunting. I had never dreamed of my mother before, and never
in such vivid horror. I couldn't recall ever having a nightmare. It was
as though moving to Fuerteventura had stirred up in me inner
demons that had been lying dormant, waiting for their chance to
unfurl.

I threw off the covers and put on a loose bathrobe. I went around
lighting the other candles, something that felt like a ritual all of
its own.

As I went over to the chest of drawers, fresh terror shot through me, a single drum beat.

The bolts were slid back.

Sometime in the night someone had entered my room and opened those bolts.

The dining room bolts were the same.

Not only were the bolts slid back but the door was ajar.

It wasn't possible. There was no natural explanation. I felt for a single moment like Jonathon Creek trying to figure out how the trickery might have been achieved.

I couldn't face the possibility of a supernatural force in my house.

A poltergeist?

Who?

My mother? She was certainly now haunting my dreams.

Olivia Stone? She didn't seem the type to haunt.

The Baraso family? But why? They had died of yellow fever. A tragedy, true, but that wouldn't explain a motive for haunting.

Aunt Clarissa always maintained ghosts were trapped on the earthly plane through intense emotions. Through trauma. Sudden death, suicide, that sort of thing.

What about Gloria's comment about the maid who claimed things in Casa Baraso moved? Should I take that seriously? If true, then the culprit could not have been my mother unless she was trying to frighten me into leaving the house well alone in order to protect me from other spirits.

What about the rock in my apartment that had moved twice? Was that my mother warning me too? Was I meant to draw comfort from that? Why didn't she, they, whoever it was want me to live in Casa Baraso?

What about that image of the woman in the patio that Paco had captured on film. She was not my mother. Could she be Olivia Stone? Maybe she was worried I knew her true whereabouts after she disappeared and she didn't want to be discovered, even in death.

No.

It was all rubbish, codswallop, cock and bull and I would not entertain one single element of any of it.

Someone must have got in through the window.

23

EL COTILLO

Dawn brought fresh fear.

I threw open both doors to let in all the light there was to be had. Candlelight flickered in the moving air. The light inside remained dim, the dining room entrance shielded by the scaffolding. Steeling myself, I took a candle to the solitary window and placed it on the curved seat. An examination of the window shutters revealed what I already suspected. The bolts were drawn shut and there was no sign of a forced entry. Whoever had entered was clever, skilled, an expert. They had managed with considerable stealth to slide the bolts open, enter my bedroom, close the bolts, throw open the door bolts and exit through the dining room door all without waking me and for no other reason than to scare me out of my wits.

Cejas? Had to be. No one else had a motive. Although the culprit could be any prankster wanting to intimidate an Englishwoman bent on restoring a ruin. Some kind of activism perhaps. Someone with a deranged attachment to the ruin and a hatred of foreigners. Someone mentally unstable, rabid, paranoid, insane. How far would they go? It occurred to me that the perpetrator had been inside my room in my absence, seen the progress, studied the window fastenings and figured out a silent way of gaining access. They knew I was living on site and that I had installed bolts. They were watching, closely. It had to be a neighbour, someone nearby, someone who saw me return from the hardware store with the bolts. What about that assistant. I had told her what I wanted them for. That might have provoked gossip and speculation. Fallen on the wrong ears. It all seemed convoluted and outlandish, but my reasoning was a lot less outlandish than the alternative. A ghost.

I grabbed a towel and my toiletries, shuffled my feet in flip flops and went outside. My eyes were everywhere. For all I knew my stalker was right there in the building. Filled with reluctance I poked my head through the hole in the partition wall. There was no one with their back pressed against the wall, no one I could see in any of the downstairs rooms, although I didn't have a line of sight to every nook and cranny. I forced myself through the hole and walked over to peer into each of the south facing rooms. Empty, as anticipated. I went back through the hole and headed on outside, glancing in the kitchen on my way by. No one was there.

Needing to make absolutely certain I had no company, I placed my towel and toiletries on a large rock and returned to the patio to climb the ladder at the end of the interior scaffolding. Walking along the makeshift balcony and entering the upstairs rooms, an inexplicable sadness washed through me. I thought of my mother as I looked around for triggers, wondering if something I had seen had set me off. The vaulted ceiling? The vast windows looking out over the volcano? The decorative paintwork on the patches of old wall? None of it reminded me of my mother. The rooms along the north side were all empty and there was no evidence of an intruder that I could see. Not that I would have been able to pick the difference with so much activity on site.

I stood for a while looking down at the patio with its curious partition that destroyed the magnificence of the building. From that elevation, I could take in the state of the ruin in a single sweep. The house was gargantuan, the work involved in rebuilding the southern side enormous. What have I taken on? In one spot I was able to see past my house and down the street. A critical scan of the surrounding properties with their shuttered windows and absent inhabitants yielded nothing, and it was with a mix of frustration and defiance that

I went downstairs, collected my things and made my way to my makeshift shower.

Crouching in the plastic bowl drizzling cold water tentatively over first one patch of naked flesh then another, shivering, I hurried through the motions as fast as I was able. Intruder or no intruder, I doubted I would get used to al fresco, bucket and bowl showers and made a mental note to tell Mario to prioritize the plumbing.

I ate fruit for breakfast. Seated in the dining room, I tried to imagine what it would be like when the patio was filled with plants and how pleasant it would be to sit inside a dark room away from the glare and the harshness of the summer sun. It was no use. My sensibilities would not adjust to the experience of a windowless room. No room should be a cave. I latched on to the matter, which was fast becoming a bug bear and the sooner glass panes were inserted in what was currently my bedroom, the better.

Even with a proper window, neither of those rooms I would occupy once the house was fully restored. They were too gloomy. I could see myself enjoying the south side where the windows I had included in the plans would look out over my garden.

The workmen would not be on site until the following day. While the morning was still cool I inspected my plants. The drago trees and aloe veras were standing proud and strong, the grasses seemed happy and the ground covers and succulents determined to thrive. I pulled out a few weeds then went and put a few more rocks on my wall. The view of the volcano and the mountains drew me as ever it did, the yellow and red ochres, the near total absence of green. Beholding the desert-like setting, it was hard to imagine the events of the previous nights, impossible to believe that anything could disturb the magnificent energy of the island.

Out in the open away from the house, I was prepared to contemplate the supernatural explanation, if provisionally and if only to dismiss it altogether. For surely that tenacious wind that blew and blew would sweep the spirits away? The sun blazed brilliantly, withering all but the most robust beneath its glare. Didn't ghosts lurk in dark, secluded places? Were they not the stuff of dank castles and ivy-festooned mansions deep in the woods? Places where the air was still and the energies trapped. Ponds and swamps and wells. Not here on Fuerteventura. Or was I buying into stereotypes, making assumptions based on gothic novels and haunted house films. There was no rationalising away the possibility along those lines. Besides, I had those two gloomy rooms in there. Yet I refused to entertain the idea of a spirit world that interfered with the real world. What I did know was I had no idea how I would sleep every night not knowing what next would occur.

The empty street, the closed-up houses, the lack of any living neighbour or a passer-by added to my misgivings. Not even the emaciated dog had returned. The absence of life down my street was little short of weird. Were the villagers hiding from me? Was that it? Too scared to interact in case the curse of Casa Baraso fell on them. Were folk still that superstitious? Perhaps they were. After all, Mario couldn't hire locals from anywhere on the island to work on my house. Instead of curious or nosy neighbours, I had fearful ones keeping their distance as though I had the plague.

I heard the rumble of a car engine in the distance and paused, listening. The sound drew nearer and to my relief and delight, Paco pulled up in his dusty old bomb. I waved and hurried over and we met by the southern wall of the house.

He leaned down and kissed my cheeks.

'I didn't expect to see you so early on a Sunday morning,' I said, smiling into his face, overjoyed to see him, knowing my exuberance mingled with relief.

'I wanted to catch you before you headed off somewhere.'

'I thought you would be working,' I said, my mind too slow for the pace of the conversation.

'Even a photographer gets a day off. It's Sunday. Come with me to the beach.'

'You like the beach?'

'What self-respecting majo doesn't like the beach?'

'It did occur to me to go for a swim,' I lied, delighted by the suggestion, 'but Morro Jable will be full of tourists. I thought of Gran Tarajal but that will be the same. Corralejo even worse.'

'Why go east? It will be too hot. I'm going to El Cotillo. Fewer tourists and it catches the ocean breeze. Claire, today is going to be very hot. I have come to rescue you from Tiscamanita.'

A dart of something I didn't recognise whizzed through me. 'El Cotillo. Yes, of course.' I paused, hesitant. 'Come inside for a minute.'

'That's okay.' He raised his camera that was an extension of his arm. 'I'll wait here for you.'

'Please, I have something to show you.'

He followed me around the back.

'Much cooler in here,' he remarked as we entered the dining room. 'Make sure you shut it up and it will trap the cool and be nice when you get home.' As he drew the door to, his gaze drifted to the bolts.

'That's what I wanted to show you.'

He inspected them more closely.

'You put these on?'

'I did.'

'Good job. But why bolts? You are locking yourself in?'

'I felt I had to. I woke up yesterday to find someone had opened the doors while I slept. Or I should say pushed open.'

'Pushed?'

I felt embarrassed admitting my fear but went on. 'I couldn't sleep for thinking about a possible intruder so I half barricaded myself in with chairs. When I woke one chair was lying on its side, the other was pushed away and the dining room door was ajar. I thought if I put bolts on the doors then that would prevent a recurrence.'

'Did it?'

'I wish. This morning the bolts were drawn and the dining room door was open. And don't say Olivia Stone. Please. I think someone got in through the window and let themselves out.'

'Possible.' He went over to inspect the window. I remained where I was, taking in my unmade bed, the clothes lying around.

'How could someone get in here?' he said, opening the shutter and closing it and drawing the bolt. 'You had locked the window, right?'

'I thought I had.' I hesitated, my memory hazy. Perhaps that was it; I had forgotten to lock the window. I didn't know whether to feel relieved I definitely didn't have a ghost or alarmed I definitely had an intruder. 'I don't know,' I said. 'Maybe I hadn't. Maybe they got in anyway, found a way to slide the bolt across.'

'That would have to be some magic trick. Maybe your intruder is an escapologist.'

'I know.' I cringed. 'I was thinking there might be someone like that around here. A prankster.'

'Unlikely.'

'Not as unlikely as a ghost.'

'Why do you deny it? I told you the house is haunted.'

'By the Barasos.'

He let out a soft grunt. 'By Olivia Stone.'

'You can't know that.'

'A photograph does not lie. And you saw it yourself. A woman sitting in the patio.'

I gave up. There was no point arguing with him. When it came to Olivia Stone, he was intractable. I stuffed bathers, a towel, a sunhat, sunscreen and a water bottle in my beach bag, along with a cotton sundress. 'Shall we take my car?' I asked, thinking he had already driven up from Puerto del Rosario, and besides, my air con was fierce.

'Sure.'

I closed both doors and he followed me to the back of the barn.

'Wow,' he said, seeing my Hyundai for the first time. 'Is it new?'

'I needed something to ferry building supplies.'

He laughed. 'My car would be better for that.'

I resisted offering my agreement.

Seated behind the wheel, inhaling the brand-new car smell, I felt my confidence returning. There was something about being behind the wheel of a large and brand-new car that made me feel grander, stronger, more confident somehow. I manoeuvred off the block and headed off.

El Cotillo was situated on the north-western tip of the island, accessed on the back roads past Tefia and on through La Oliva and Lajares. An hour's drive and we had covered half the length of the island and I was crawling down the village streets until I found a place to park.

Paco was happy for me to take charge. He seemed amused that I knew the area so well. I told him I had booked a holiday here one time and enjoyed it so much, I scarcely left the village to venture elsewhere. I must have eaten in every restaurant from El Cotillo to Lajaras.

I slipped into an indulgent mood, treating us both to an iced coffee in a café overlooking the harbour, using the opportunity to change into my sundress, with bathers beneath, in the facilities. Paco was all happy banter. I found him entertaining. He had a ready supply of amusing tales and a storehouse of knowledge about the islands.

Not wanting to miss the opportunity of the high tide we saw on our way into the village, we went back to the car and I took us up to my favourite beach, one of several where the reef protects swimmers from the force of the ocean.

With the creamy sand between our toes, we slipped out of our outer apparel like two excited children and dumped it all where we stood and ran to the shoreline, entering the cool, shallow water. Feeling the gentle push and pull, inhaling the salty ocean air, I emitted a pleasurable sigh. Paco splashed me, teasing. I splashed him back and we laughed, momentarily drawing the attention of the others in the water. Then, mindful of the rocks, we swam together the length and breadth of the enclosed bay, not stopping until we were both too exhausted to swim another stroke.

Never in my whole life had I enjoyed a swim at the beach more than that time with Paco. We fell into the pleasure of the experience as though we had been doing it all our lives, together, as friends or siblings, or as lovers. My thinking took me no further.

We dried off in the freshening wind and strolled back to my car. I drove into the village and took Paco to my favourite restaurant for lunch, tucked down a narrow lane away from the main drag.

Over tapas and grilled fish washed down with cooling beer, our senses mellow from the exercise, we chatted some more about the island and what it meant to locals and holidaymakers alike.

'I think the main thing is it's safe here,' I said, summing up. 'The average Brit or German or Swede gets the sunshine of North Africa without the ferocity of the climate and the hassles that come with interacting with markedly different cultures. Most holidaymakers who come here want nothing more than the beach.'

'Yet here I am, a photographer, a farmer's son, working in a restaurant. I embody the entire paradox of tourism.'

'And here am I, a bank teller made rich by chance and all I want to do is make things better. Is that so bad?'

We locked gazes.

'Most rich people don't care. They are selfish.'

'I'm not.'

'You are not used to it.'

He was right. I wasn't. I hadn't a clue. I was running on passion and dreams.

'Tell me about your family,' he said, changing the subject.

'My family? Nothing to tell.'

'There is. You know all about mine. Maybe you will meet them some day. I will take you to Caleta de Fuste and you can meet Ana and Julio.'

There was that feeling again as though there was something in the air between us. Was this friendship, or something more? I popped another chip in my mouth, stalling.

Paco persisted. 'Your father, what does he do?'

I cringed inwardly. 'Property developer.'

He didn't show a reaction.

'Is he rich?'

'No, not really. He hasn't been that lucky and he doesn't have the backing of big money.'

'What's he like? Are you close to him?'

'He isn't that kind of guy. Growing up, I hardly saw him. He was either working or out playing golf.'

'Who brought you up?'

'Aunt Clarissa. She is my mother's older sister. A psychologist.'

'Interesting.'

'You would like her. I think you share similar interests. She believes in ghosts and that sort of thing.'

'I am liking her already.'

I related her latest ghost-tour tale and he laughed.

'She's very down-to-earth otherwise,' I said. 'Practical.'

'And your mother? Was she practical?'

Something in me froze. It had been a very long time since anyone had asked me about my mother. I ignored the feeling and offered him an answer. 'Not that I recall. She was a dreamer. Clarissa and Ingrid come from a long line of occultists. Clarissa has traced the trait back through many generations.' I paused to look out the window at the ocean, the sky, the people. 'I think Ingrid didn't belong in the real world. She didn't make much of an impression, at least not on me. I hardly remember her.'

'When did you lose her?'

'I was seven.'

'Seven.'

'Yes.'

'Then you would have a lot of memories of before then. But you have forgotten them. You wanted to erase the memory of your mother. It would have been easier that way.'

He stared at me, expectantly. Under that interested and compassionate gaze I couldn't hold back. What was the point of holding back? Better to let things flow. I gave him a full account of the accident. I told him in a clinical, blow by blow fashion. When I got to the part about the squashed tomatoes he inhaled and reached forward to touch my arm.

An electric current shot through me as though in answer to my earlier puzzlement. This man invited me here because he wanted more than friendship. How could I not have spotted his intentions before? Am I so dim-witted, so inexperienced not to know when a man has designs on me? I let him hold my hand across the table. He gave it a squeeze before leaning back to attract the attention of a nearby waiter.

'We need ice cream,' he said to me. 'What flavour? Chocolate? Caramel? Vanilla? We'll have all three.' He looked up at the waiter. 'And two brandies, doubles, and two espressos.'

'I have to drive.'

'We must stay for the sunset.'

'The sunset?' But that was hours away. I didn't say it.

He grinned. 'Plenty of time to relax and enjoy the day. Besides, the ice cream is better with brandy.'

He was right. We poured the alcohol and the coffee on the ice cream and luxuriated in his version of an affogato. Neither of us was in a hurry to leave. We spooned our intoxicating desserts slowly and caught each other's gazes and offered shy smiles. The conversation meandered, covering what books we liked, what films, and what we thought of the world. Neither of us mentioned Olivia Stone. After a while we slipped into companionable silence.

'There's an exhibition at the tower,' Paco said eventually.

'That sounds marvellous.'

I stood on the pretext of needing the loo and paid at the bar. When I returned, Paco was scrolling through photos on his camera. Seeing me, he stood and we walked outside, squinting into the glare.

'You needn't have paid.'

'I wanted to.'

'Well, thank you.'

The breeze had strengthened, cooling the temperature of an otherwise scorching day. I imagined back in Tiscamanita it was forty degrees.

Torre de El Tostón was a short walk away and it was pleasant to stroll down the promenade, past the little harbour with its restaurants brimming with patrons, the hubbub of Sunday dining, and on across flat, gritty land to the low promontory on which stood a stout, stone edifice constructed to defend the island from attack. We walked up a short flight of stone steps and across a gangplank and entered the fort.

Hanging from the bare rock walls of the small, bunker-style interior were a series of landscapes. Expecting traditional works geared for the tourist trade, I didn't anticipate the vibrancy and originality of the pieces. My impulse was to buy one but I didn't want to embarrass Paco with my wealth. I chose instead to take note of the artist's name. Buying paintings represented a whole new level of shopping, one I had no experience in. It occurred to me Paco would make the ideal companion and advisor and I made a mental note to remember that.

We wandered over to the edge of the promontory to take in the view, watching as others scrambled down to the rocky ledge below. To the south, the creamy sand of the surf beach met the low cliffs, with the Betancuria massif in the distance. The setting was sublime and we stood together in appreciation as the wind pressed our clothes to our skin.

As we strolled back to the village, crunching our way over the gravely terrain, Paco took my hand. It was the most romantic gesture in the most idyllic of settings and I savoured the sensation of his flesh, hot and firm, against mine. Any stray thoughts lingering on the fringes of my mind of the build and the strange disturbances evaporated.

We went down to the harbour wall to admire the little fishing boats. Then we found another café and had a second iced coffee.

Deciding we were again too hot, we took ourselves off for another swim, and then lay on the beach in the late afternoon sun. One more swim and we were ready to visit a fourth café to share a paella. Never, had I enjoyed the company of a man so much. I didn't want the day to end.

By the time the sun sank low on the horizon and the sky glowed crimson, we were standing alone on the beach and Paco had his arm around my shoulder, and as the colours faded and the sky to the east deepened to indigo, we kissed.

24

AN INTERLUDE

CALLE MANUEL VELÁZQUEZ CABRERA WAS AS DESOLATE AS EVER. NO people. No cars. It was as though life in the village ended at the intersection, the last street light marking the end of civilisation. When I reached my block, I mounted the kerb and parked behind the barn.

After our deliciously pleasant day in El Cotillo, the arrival was a let-down. As I unbuckled my seat belt, I wasn't sure what to do next, invite Paco in or thank him for the day and bid him farewell.

He walked me to the house and we stopped beneath the scaffolding. The night was warm, all that stone radiating the heat of the day. The wind, blowing from the northeast, wrapped itself around the building, moaning, whistling through cracks. Plastic flapped, a plank somewhere above thumped lightly then stopped. Then the wind pulled back, leaving the building alone for a moment and all was quiet. Deciding I was not ready to face the night on my own I invited him in.

We used our phone torches to light the way, Paco pausing by the hole in the partition to shine his light into the other half of the patio, then standing back and shining the light at the hole itself, presumably at where he had taken the photo that had captured the image of a woman crouching.

Both doors to my rooms were closed. The air was cooler inside, if stuffy. I went in and lit the candles. Everything was as I had left it, bed unmade, a few dirty plates and cups piled on the makeshift bench.

Paco came up behind me. I turned and gestured at the table and invited him to sit and offered him wine.

'A nightcap.'

I poured two glasses of a Lanzarote red and joined him.

'Will you be okay sleeping here tonight?' he said, taking his glass.

'I have the Cocteau Twins for company.'

'Who?'

'Here.' I reached for my laptop and headphones and played him 'Iceblink Luck'. The expression on his face changed from curiosity to wonder. I waited for the track to end before speaking.

'What do you think?'

'Astonishing.'

'You like them?'

'Where are they from?'

'Scotland. Now I'm here, I think I need to find some local music to listen to.'

'You would like Luis Morera. He's from La Palma. He's the islands' greatest musical talent.'

I made a note of the name, not quite believing I would. Or was that prejudiced of me? He returned the headphones to his ears. He appeared to enjoy the next track. Listening to the spill, I felt excluded from the pleasure. I waited. I took a sip of my wine. It was piquant, robust. I thought of rioja, of tempranillo, of how Spanish wine travelled, finding its way on the supermarket shelves the world over. I reached and tapped his arm. He slid the headphones down to wrap around his neck.

'Have you ever been overseas?' I asked.

'I've just got back.'

'I meant, beyond the islands.'

'Barcelona, that's all.'

'And you?'

'Only here.'

'You would like Barcelona.'

'I'm sure.'

He smiled and returned my headphones to his ears and continued listening. The expression on his face was one of wondrous pleasure. Either he was determined to enjoy the music, putting on a good show to keep himself in my good books, or he really liked it.

Just then, I wanted to show him Colchester. He might like it there. Feeling the desire, I realised I had become closer to him than I might have found comfortable in other circumstances, this quirky photographer with a passion for Olivia Stone.

What was it with him and his fixation? Perhaps he was taken by her image, she might be attractive to a man like him, but that was unfair and belittling. A man like Paco didn't harbour a fetish for a dead woman. I was being absurd. Besides, I could see she reflected back to the islands a version of themselves now lost. That was justification enough for his admiration. So successful was her book that after its publication, tourism, on Tenerife at least, began in earnest among the wealthier classes. More steam ships were put on. Hotels opened. And on it went.

I drank more of my wine and kept watching him listening to my music. Now and then he would look at me and smile before his gaze slid away and he lost himself to the sound.

Through Paco, through Olivia Stone, I was receiving an unexpected education, a sort of induction into the ancient way of life of the islanders, in much greater detail than a museum could provide. Olivia Stone's narrative was lived experience. She was showing me how distinct the islands were from the land of their Spanish colonialists. I had never seen the islands that way before. I had always considered them a geographically convenient outpost of Spain, with year-round perfect weather and stunning landscapes. Somehow, when Paco was around, I ended up dwelling on Olivia Stone. I supposed she was my point of entry into the truth about the island.

The album was nearing its end. I didn't want Paco to leave but I had no clear idea how to make him stay. I replenished our glasses and sat back. He removed my headphones and took a slow sip. He was the one who brought up the haunting.

'You might need to do an exorcism. I know of a priest who does that sort of thing.'

'An exorcism?'

He nodded. 'You would be doing Olivia a favour. Setting her free.'

Why did he have to ruin the moment with this rubbish? I wanted to say don't be ridiculous. Instead, I kept sipping my wine.

He glanced around, his gaze lingering in the corners. 'This place has a definite vibe. Can't you feel it?'

'You are imagining things,' I said quickly, recalling Gloria mentioning the same. 'The place feels strange because it's a building site. That's all.'

'If you say so.'

I struggled to suppress a yawn that rose from nowhere, concerned it would give the wrong impression.

He looked uncertain for a moment. Then, as though making up his mind, he drained his glass. 'I better go. You need your sleep. Will you be all right on your own?'

'I should be fine. I'll lock myself in.'

'That didn't work last time.'

Part of me wanted to plead with him to stay but I resisted, not wanting to complicate what was developing between us out of fear. He was making to stand when the living-room door opened and slammed shut of its own volition. Startled, I let out a small yelp. He grabbed the table and leaned forward.

'That, whatever that was, well, it wasn't possible, was it?'

'The wind,' I said helplessly.

He stood and headed for the door.

'Paco, don't go.'

He came back and put a hand on my shoulder. 'I'm not going to. Don't worry.'

'Thank you.'

'I just need to ...' He trailed off.

'Me, too.'

I took a beaker of water and my toothbrush and went out into the dark, lighting my way with my phone. I didn't bother bringing back the battery. When I returned, Paco went and did the same, using the new toothbrush I proffered. It was still in its packet.

While he was gone I straightened the bed and pulled off my dress.

I hesitated, not sure what else to take off and what to put on, when he re-entered the room. He took one glance at me in my underwear, and went and bolted both doors, checked the window shutters and blew out all the candles save the ones beside the bed. Then he came around to where I was standing.

'Come,' he said, and we lay down together on top of the covers.

My skin was warm from a day in the sun, and salty too. I thought I would need to make a trip to a launderette before long. What a stupid topic to enter my head, given the situation.

My domestic musings were interrupted by the softest touch as his hand reached for mine.

I responded in kind and he turned on his side and brushed my hair from my face.

'You are very beautiful,' he said. 'May I?' And he leaned and reached for my mouth with his.

I yielded, tingling with anticipation and sudden yearning, opening up to him as he caressed the skin of my arm. He was tentative, slow, as was I as I touched him, although I was soon aflame, eager to sate a hunger for too long buried. Our kisses grew passionate, our flesh soon naked, and we wrapped our limbs up in each other, pressed together our torsos, our heat combining. Before long, we were a furnace, hot, wet and panting.

When at last we both lay back in the afterglow, breathless, I laughed.

'What's funny?'

'Not funny. Blissful.'

'Good.'

He blew out his candle and I mine and we lay in the darkness, holding hands. A million questions passed through my mind. Who was Paco, really? A good man? Bad? Was he sincere with his affections, or was he a womaniser and I another conquest, a chalk line on his doorframe filled with chalk lines? What did he want from me? My love? My wealth?

I only knew one thing. I had been seduced. Two things, because it had felt delicious.

25

SEÑOR BARASO

THE WARMTH OF PACO'S BODY BESIDE ME AND THE STEADY BREATH OF his slumber put a seal on my decision to restore the ruin. It was as though out tryst signified some sort of deeper approval of my being here. I had no idea if he would form part of my future life on the island, if what was happening between us had any future to it at all, or if it was an interlude. In many ways, I would have preferred the companionship of female friends who would have filled out my life without any danger of a romantic complication. In a curious fashion, for the present, Paco reinforced my isolation.

It was still night. My bladder nagged to be emptied. I knew he was asleep but I wasn't about to pee in a bucket, not even at the far end of the other room. I grabbed my phone, fumbled about for my bathrobe and flip flops, and unbolted the dining room door as softly as I could.

He didn't stir.

Heading out through the patio, passing the hole in the partition wall that had come to symbolise the haunting, I felt more confident, knowing I had another living presence, a benevolent one, nearby. Yet my unease remained. Out in the backyard, I shone the torch around as I walked. Amid the chaos of the build I felt only an inkling of ownership of the land I trod. I was yet to make the place my own. More than anything, I felt like an intruder. Maybe Cejas was right and

438

the ruin should have been demolished. Or maybe I should have taken Mario's advice and built a new house out of the old.

Exiting the portaloo, I paused to take in the night. The wind had dropped. The moon, a crescent of milky light, hovered about the volcano. Stars were visible in the firmament beyond its reach. I stared into the heavens, impressed by the magnitude of stars, their patterns, their brilliance. In Colchester, I could have been forgiven for not knowing they existed. I could scarcely recall ever seeing the evening star. Perhaps I hadn't been paying attention.

Feeling the strain in my neck I returned my gaze to ground level and took in the building, reluctant to enter despite, or perhaps because Paco was there.

I glanced at the outbuildings and then behind me at the volcano. As I turned back a flash of light caught my eye. I pinned my gaze to where it had come from and saw, emerging as if from nowhere, a brilliant dot of red light hovering above the patio. I watched it rise up suddenly, dart back down and up again, then make a frenzied, erratic dance like a crazed fly. The light shot up into the sky and disappeared. Had to be an insect, really, it did. Or maybe I was hallucinating and going slowly mad. Whatever the cause, it was weird and I hurried back inside, closed and bolted the door and slid into bed.

Paco stirred but didn't wake. I lay in the dark, eyes closed, mind racing. I refused to believe in the supernatural. Haunted houses do not exist. There is no such thing as ghosts. I thought if I sat up, if I stayed awake, I would discover who was opening those bolts. A better idea occurred to me and I slipped out of bed, grabbed a broom, a chair and some plastic containers and quietly made an arrangement of obstacles in front of the shutters. If anyone did manage to open that particular bolt, they would make a racket getting in and we would be certain to wake up. Satisfied, I slid back into bed, assured of more sleep.

I awoke to a gentle stroking sensation on my cheek. I slowly emerged from slumber realising it was Paco. The room was dark but a chink of light was visible under the door.

'You were busy in the night,' Paco laughed, shining his phone light at the window and pointing to my little fortifications.

I saw they were still as I had left them, as best as I could recall. I gave Paco a brief account of my nocturnal interlude, excluding the strange darting light. I didn't want to give him yet more fuel for his supernatural theories.

'And when you came back in, you bolted the dining room door?'

'I did.'

'Are you sure?'

'Certain.' Why would he doubt me?

'Well, it's open now.'

'That's impossible,' I said, diving out of bed to take a look.

He laughed. His laugh had me wondering if he was the one who had opened that door. I only had his word for it. Surely, he wouldn't be so cruel? Maybe not cruel, but capable of taking action, any action to prove his point.

As though to reinforce my suspicion, he said, 'I told you, Olivia Stone doesn't want her true whereabouts discovered and will stop at nothing to keep you from telling the world where she went when she abandoned her family.'

We locked gazes. I was naked, acutely aware of the fall of my breasts, the curve of my belly, my bushy mons. He was already fully clothed.

'If it's her,' I said, snatching my bathrobe off the floor in a moment of coyness.

'It's her. That photo proves it.'

'That could be anyone.'

'If you insist. But you do need to banish her if you want to live here.'

'Or live with her tricks, as my aunt Clarissa would say. Get to know what she really wants.'

He smiled at me and planted a kiss on my cheek.

'Wise woman, your aunt. Now, I need to go do some things. You'll be alright on your own?'

'Of course.'

Despite my irritation, I wanted to ask when I would see him again but it seemed possessive. I had to fight back a gnawing desperation watching him head out the door, not sure if he would give me the protection I suddenly craved.

Seeing the time—it was six—I grabbed my toiletries and a towel and rushed to my provisional shower. Once clean and dressed, I went and packed away the solar panels and battery, storing them under a plastic tarpaulin in the third outbuilding, planning to leave them there until I decided whether they would ever be any use. Then I bundled up towels, sheets, clothes and bathers into a large bag to take to the laundromat, grabbed my laptop and charger and set off on my way to the café for breakfast. As I drove off the block, the first of the workmen were arriving.

Other than washing my clothes, I had no idea how I would spend the day, or any day Monday to Friday with the build in progress, but I would just have to make it up as I went along.

I parked outside the café and marched inside with my laptop and chargers, determined this time to get a full answer from Gloria to the question of Casa Baraso. She had been holding something back each time we had spoken. I was sure of it.

There was a flurry of custom soon after I arrived and patrons hovered behind me. I ordered coffee and orange juice and toast and scrambled eggs and sat at my preferred table, the one with the power point. The moment I sat down I put my laptop on charge. With nothing to do but wait for Gloria, I checked my emails on my phone and watched the clientele come and go.

By the time she brought my coffee, the café had returned to its usual lull and I asked her who lived in the vicinity of my house. She said the houses opposite were bank repossessions, the stone building beside me was a holiday home that was mostly empty, and closest to me on the north side lived an old couple who were almost totally deaf. Further up my street most of the houses were either holiday lets or holiday homes left empty by their Spanish owners. Two or three were deceased estates. Altogether, that explained why I felt so alone in my street.

She rushed away to see to my eggs. Before long I heard the grind of the juicer. When she came with both, she said, 'I added some cheese. I hope you don't mind.'

I smiled up at her. 'I prefer them with cheese.'

Satisfied, she left me to eat.

I took my time over my breakfast. The laptop had charged by the time I had finished the toast. I plugged in my phone and ordered another coffee, awaiting another moment when the café was empty.

When Gloria came to clear a nearby table, I broached the topic without any preface. 'Did you know I am having to sleep at the house now?'

'Yes.' She put down the plates she was holding and came over. 'How are you finding it?'

'Strange. Comfortable enough in the two rooms, but strange.'

'Are doors opening by themselves?' she asked tentatively.

'How did you know?'

A worried look appeared in her face.

'Tell me, please. What are people saying?'

'You want to know what really happened at Casa Baraso?'

At last! I nodded, all ears.

'Then I will tell you. But you won't like it. Baraso was not a good man. He was brutal. He brought his wife and four daughters from Tenerife so he could terrorise them, hidden away in that house.'

'How do you know this?'

'My great grandmother was born in 1890, and her grandmother was twenty-three when the Baraso family died. She was their maid. She said they did not die of yellow fever. The truth was covered up. She saw the blood, the knife, the stab wounds. He'd smothered the girls in their beds, killed his wife and then himself.'

I gasped. 'But how did all that get covered up?'

'He was from an important family. They were well-connected. They paid my relative to keep quiet. And eight years later the house was sold. In fact, it took a whole eight years to sell it. Cejas didn't know a thing, being from the mainland, and it sold for cheap. No one has been able to live there since. Not for a hundred and fifty years. People have stayed there, but they have never stayed long and they always suffer some misfortune or other. I am afraid the same will happen to you.'

I took in her words, stunned by the awful revelation. A brutal murder suicide, *in my home*. I felt queasy and a little faint. Perhaps the Cejas who sold me the house had heard the rumour, discovered its veracity and wanted to demolish the house to erase the memory. Is it possible demolition would have solved the problem? Or would the spirits of those listless dead haunt the very ground where the house had stood? I caught myself as my thoughts strayed into realms I staunchly refused to give any credence. Ghosts! Yet dismissing the idea of a haunted house did not eradicate the bare truth, four girls and their mother were murdered there. I was not sure I wanted to set foot on my own property ever again.

Seeing the expression on my face, Gloria said, 'I should not have told you.'

'I would have found out, eventually.'

'Maybe. Just be careful, Claire. Very careful.'

I told her I would. As she walked away to serve a customer, I replayed her words, picturing the scene, wondering which of the bedrooms each of them had slept in. Four daughters and a wife meant probably all of them. A murder in every upstairs room. Images of that brutal attack ran through my mind like photos of a crime scene. I unplugged the charger and packed up my things. When Gloria came over to my table, I gave her a twenty euro note and told her to keep the change. I couldn't get out of Tiscamanita fast enough.

ESCALATION

I DROVE TO PUERTO DEL ROSARIO WITH BLUR PLAYING LOUD THROUGH the car speakers, refusing to give in to thoughts of the Baraso family and the horrors that had taken place in my house. At the laundromat in Avenida Juan de Bethencourt, I sat and waited for the wash cycle and then the dry cycle. I could have wandered up the street or crossed the road to visit the café opposite for a coffee, but instead, I tuned in to the steady drone of the machines, the heavy scent of washing powder and the brightly lit, industrial vibe. I lost myself to a shop full of appliances. There was something soothing about the normalcy, the domesticity, the basic humanity of washing clothes that I latched onto. Anything, so as not to have to think through Gloria's divulgences.

With my clothes and sheets folded and smelling like a field of flowers, I drove up the coast to the tiny village of Puerto Lajas and parked beside the little chapel at the end of the main street. The beach was sheltered but lacked the creamy sands of El Cotillo or Morro Jable. Here, the sand was basalt-brown and pebble strewn, the locale less developed, and there were less holidaymakers about as a result. Although it was clear they were missing out on an inviting location. A reef protected the bay and although the waters were deeper than the lagoons of El Cotillo, they looked safe to swim in. Small fishing boats, anchored offshore, bobbed about in the protected waters. I went over to the waterline and stared into the blurred horizon, comparing the azure of the sky to the azure of the ocean, listening to the gentle slap of the waves, the cries of fun and laughter carried on the wind.

What had I come to this island for? To live a hermit's life in a house disturbed by its own past? To be a pleasure seeker, tanning and swimming and eating in restaurants? Provide free holiday accommodation for my supposed friends? Or had I come here to be seduced by a local? I needed an occupation, that much was becoming clear, and plans for my house once it was restored, but I could think about neither. Maybe the Spanish course due to start in a couple of months would at least result in some friends and possibly even a fresh sense of purpose.

I was listless again, and troubled. The sun burned my skin and even in the brilliant light I couldn't shake a sinister, creeping sensation oozing through me as my thoughts settled on Baraso, who had murdered his four children and his wife and then killed himself. Gloria had been adamant and I had no reason not to believe her. It was hard to process. The heinous crime was ancient but that didn't change the knowledge that it had happened. I doubted it would have made much difference if it had taken place only last year. The fact remained that people, children had been slaughtered in my house. I found that hard to assimilate. The chances had always been high that deaths had occurred inside those walls over the centuries but a death from illness or ageing was part of the normal flow of life. Murder was different. It was brutal, sudden, shocking and I was disturbed by it. I couldn't recall ever being as disturbed by a sudden death, other than my mother's. I supposed that was why I was reacting strongly to the Baraso killings. I had intimate knowledge of the trauma of violent death, after having witnessed my mother's accident. Had I inadvertently been attracted to, obsessed by and then consequently driven to purchase Casa Baraso due to my own unconscious trauma? Did life work like that? Or was it all coincidental?

Maybe Olivia Stone had been drawn to the house for the same reason. The energy would have resonated. Only, she had escaped one bad domestic situation to land in the echoes of another, exemplifying what could have happened to her had she stayed with her husband. If Paco's version of reality was true.

It was nearing lunchtime and the smells wafting from the beach-side restaurant were appetising. I wandered over and as I entered I was ushered by a friendly waiter to a vacant table halfway along a wall decorated with guitars. The interior had a homely feel with a green-painted floor. The lower portion of the walls were painted the same shade of green, meeting yellow ochre at waist height. Rustic, and the colours leant an earthy feel to the interior, the colour of green always a welcome touch on an island bereft of it. The tables were covered with brown and white check table cloths. I had taken the chair with my back to the kitchen and I looked out at the al fresco seating, the palm trees, the beach and ocean beyond. I ordered a coffee and soaked up the atmosphere. Paradise. It was unequivocal. As other diners wandered in for lunch, I hailed the waiter and ordered tapas of quartered tomatoes, seasoned with oil and herbs and slices of garlic, followed by paella. Pure indulgence, and since I was in a position to eat out on a daily basis, perhaps I would continue to do so. My way of supporting the local economy.

Over the last months, I had become accustomed to my own company but seeing couples all around me, my thoughts drifted to Paco and I wondered even if I would ever see him again, let alone be with him as his girlfriend or partner. They were painful doubts and my recent discoveries about the house made me want him to be with me always. I cautioned myself not to rush into a relationship with someone I hardly knew based on my fear. I cautioned myself not to want him simply because I was idle, bored, impatient and desirous of distractions. If I wanted to be with him, it needed to be for a solid reason, and that reason would be because I loved and admired him.

If all I wanted was a companion and a protector I should get a dog.

I arrived back at the build as the men were packing up. I left my car in the street, scanned for progress but saw none and headed round the back and into the patio. Mario was standing by the hole in the partition wall, talking to Helmud. He waved when he saw me and beckoned me over.

'I'm glad you're here,' he said in a serious tone. 'We need to talk.'

'Oh, yes?'

He hesitated. It was Helmud who broke the news. 'The partition wall needs to come down.'

'Wow! Already?'

'Progress is fast when you have this many men. Today, the kitchen windows went in. That lintel,' he pointed over my right shoulder, 'and the upstairs rooms on the north side are ready for the plasterers.'

'That's excellent news.'

'Only, we need to start work on the balcony. And we can't do that until the wall is down.'

'I'll be glad when that's gone,' I said, already imagining the sense of space. 'It's an eyesore, and it means the aljibe can be fixed.'

'All that, and much more. But...'

'There's a but?'

The two men exchanged glances and then both looked at me at once.

'It will make it very difficult for you being here,' Mario said.

'It won't be possible,' Helmud reinforced.

'Because of the dust.'

They were beginning to sound like Tweedledum and Tweedledee.

'A lot of dust,' Helmud went on. 'There will be rubble and rocks everywhere. The works on the balcony will be taking place right outside the doors to your rooms.'

'And you can't enter through the front door yet, as those doors are still being made.'

'We'll seal up the doors to protect your things, but you won't have access.'

'Is there anywhere you can stay?' Mario said.

They both looked at me expectantly. Then Helmud said to Mario, 'Maybe she can visit another island. Gran Canaria or Tenerife.'

'True. If she can get a flight.'

They started walking away in the direction of the back doorway. I followed, listening.

'There'll be flights, surely?' said Helmud. 'She's only one person.'

'For tomorrow? Maybe.'

Tomorrow?

'Well, she has to go somewhere, and as she says, there is no accommodation on the island.'

'A tent?'

'That is possible.'

'For how long?' I said, interrupting, preferring to be included in the conversation and not referred to as a 'she'.

'Until Friday,' Mario said.

Helmud looked doubtful. 'At least.'

'They should have the worst of the mess cleared up by then.'

'But what about the balcony? She'll need a hard hat just to go to her portaloo.'

'This is true.'

'I'll pack up and be gone by tomorrow morning.'

'Thank you, Claire,' said Mario, visibly relieved.

'No problem.'

Although it was a problem. A big one. It felt like being ousted. I had only been living on site one weekend and I wished they had told me before. Helmud must have known. All that work preparing those two rooms and I got to sleep in them for just three nights. My mind raced over my options. I pictured myself sleeping at the airport awaiting the first available flight off the island, bound for anywhere.

I was about to head inside when I caught sight of Paco's old bomb pulling up in front of Mario's clean blue Renault. Relieved, I went over and met him on the pavement. My concern showed on my face, in my manner altogether.

'What's up?' he said, kissing my cheeks.

'You won't believe it,' I muttered, leading him around the front of the building and down the north side, away from Mario and Helmud who were still talking as they ambled to their cars. 'I have to move out, or at least not sleep here for at least a week.' I explained about the partition wall.

'It will be good to see it gone.'

'They were suggesting I fly somewhere, or buy a tent.'

'A tent! You will not buy a tent. And you will not fly somewhere.'

'Then what will I do?' I asked, a little peeved at being told what to do again.

'You will live with me.'

'I couldn't,' I whispered. I was stunned, a little thrilled and extremely apprehensive all at once.

'Why not?' He sounded offended.

I hesitated. Would there be room for me in his flat in Puerto del Rosario which was bound to be small, very small? I wanted to ask how many bedrooms he had, although the question instantly felt ridiculous after yesterday.

'If you're sure.'

'Why would I not be sure?' He looked at me intently. 'It will be safer.'

'Yes, it will be safer.' I thought of telling him Gloria's version of what happened to the Baraso family, but I did not want to add any weight to his ghost theories.

Paco watered the plants while I packed. In under two hours I was back in Puerto del Rosario, this time in Calle Canalejas, in an apartment above an empty shop.

The apartment was two streets back from the promenade and the beach and a bunch of restaurants. The locale was lively, noisy, more vibrant than Calle Barcelona. Inside, a spacious, open-plan living area led through to a single bedroom. I saw at a glance Paco kept the place tidy. Had we not already shared my bed I would have eyed the deep and comfy-looking sofa with relief and plotted my next move, no doubt leaving the island on the first available flight. As I watched Paco deposit my suitcase at the end of his bed, I shrank inwardly in resignation. I had been catapulted into a domestic situation I was not ready for. Paco, in contrast, appeared fine with the arrangement, more than fine. Satisfied.

· · ·

FIVE DAYS TURNED into five weeks as the men demolished the partition and worked on the balcony and aljibe. When Paco was working, I whiled away the days wandering around the harbour, swimming or walking on the little beach, dining out, and dining in when Paco chose to cook. He was a good cook. He seemed to enjoy sharing his space with me, too, forever keeping me entertained. He even took me out on his photographic trips and introduced me to his parents and other family members – all who looked much the same as Paco – as his companion, the English woman restoring Casa Baraso. They all, each and every one of them, eyed me with real interest, and a hint of expectation. What else had he told them about me?

One evening we talked about my idea for a booklet and sat together selecting suitable photos out of the scores he had taken. I had never written anything like it in my life, but I thought I would mimic something similar I had found in a bookshop. It shouldn't prove too difficult, I thought, since I had no intention of getting it published. He was the one who suggested I should include a small chapter on Olivia Stone. I thought the idea absurd since there was no evidence she even stepped foot in my house, but I humoured him.

The next day he took me to another house she had stayed in, situated on the corner of Calle Ruiz de Alda and Calle Leon y Castille, close to the port and only a block down from the plaza surrounded by the town hall and government buildings. It was a house I had passed many times on my way down to the port and never noticed.

We went down the side street and stood together on an opposite corner. Paco told me the house had been owned by José Galán Sánchez and his wife, Benigna Pérez Alonso, who ran it as a small hotel. Olivia Stone offers a full paragraph description of its curious layout and windowless rooms. I took my copy of her book with me and compared what she wrote with what I could see from various angles and it was surely the right house. Only, it stood in complete disrepair, another ruin, this time right in the heart of the island's capital. For a horrible moment, I thought I had bought the wrong house. Then again, I would not have enjoyed living so close to the thick of things. Yet the dwelling was not alone in having been left to ruin.

There were many ancient buildings dotted around, dating back well over a hundred years and probably closer to two hundred years old. The former hotel would have made a good café or small arts centre and could even be transformed into a small museum commemorating that auspicious visit of Olivia Stone.

'I wish I could save all these old buildings, Paco.'

'It's not your responsibility.'

'True.'

'But it is a nice thought, Claire.'

On the way back to his apartment, taking the circuitous route along the promenade, we linked arms and enjoyed the breeze coming off the ocean. In no hurry to return to the confines of the apartment, I suggested we go for a coffee somewhere.

We went to our usual and sat outside. As we watched the world of Puerto del Rosario go by, a funny little man sporting an I Love Fuerteventura t-shirt sat down at the next table with his wife – who was wearing an identical t-shirt – and assorted bags. He had a loud voice and spoke in a thick brummy accent.

'I don't know, Fred,' the woman said, 'the one on the corner looked cleaner.'

'Did you see their prices? I think we made a mistake coming this far south. Should have stuck to Corralejo.'

'But it was you who wanted to see Casa Winter, not me.'

'Worth it though.' The man called Fred chuckled. 'And who would have thought we would bump into Richard!'

'Richard Parry does tend to pop up everywhere we go, I've noticed.'

'Not everywhere, Margaret. Don't exaggerate.'

'He said he was researching another book.'

'I'm still struggling through his last.'

'Are you going off him, then?'

'Oh, no. But every author has their off moment. And I didn't quite understand his last...'

And so it went on. Holiday banter between an old married couple. After rummaging through their bags for a few moments, they left, having evidently changed their minds. I watched them walk away then saw they'd left behind a bookmark. Curious, I went and picked it up.

It was a novel called La Mareta by Richard H Parry. I put the bookmark in my bag, thinking I'd look him up sometime.

Back at the flat, Paco edited some photos at the dining table and I lounged on the sofa and read Olivia Stone. I could find nothing wrong with our cohabiting, we seemed to have fallen in with each other's routines with ease, yet watching him work I knew it couldn't last. Not least, with me in the flat, there was an acute lack of space. I sensed, too, that the situation was unnatural and somehow wrong. Yet, returning to the build felt like splitting up and I had to censure my heart.

In the days that followed I told myself over and again I couldn't stay.

One morning over breakfast, I finally summoned my courage and told Paco leaping into living together so soon was the wrong way to go about starting a relationship, even though it felt natural and harmonious and fine, and that if we as a couple was what we both wanted, the future would tell. I had taken all that talk from a film I had seen.

Paco was visibly disappointed.

I reached for his hand.

'I need to spend tonight alone. Please try to understand. I need to live in my house alone and not be terrified. Otherwise, I will never live there, or I will want you to live there, only because I am too scared to be there by myself.'

It made logical sense even though it felt awful and I knew Paco took it as a rejection.

ON THAT DAY of my return, I pulled up at four in the afternoon to find all hell had broken loose on the building site.

The water truck was leaving, but an ambulance was pulling up in its stead.

Helmud saw me and came over.

'It's a carpenter. He's been injured.'

'Is it serious?' I asked, rushing to where the carpenter was lying on the ground of the internal patio, writhing and groaning.

Helmud followed. 'Could be. He was up a ladder when that short length of rafter swung away from the wall and hit him on the back of the head. He fell and cracked his arm on a rock. He's lucky to be alive.'

The offending rafter, which had sat in situ for hundreds of years, was situated on the south side of the partition, the last remaining rafter of the balcony hanging from the east wall about halfway along. The way Helmud described the accident, the rafter had taken a swipe at the poor carpenter. How was that even possible?

Everyone was wondering the same, and the men were clearly spooked. They shifted about, heads low, muttering under their breath to each other. I ferried in my things, not looking forward to when they all went home.

When they did, I was able to properly look around.

In five weeks, the men had cleared almost all of the rocks in the patio and built the balcony on the north and west side. It was deeper than I had imagined, with stairs running up beside the west wall, accessed at ground level near the vestibule leading to the front door. The men had re-rendered the aljibe, too, and upstairs on the north side, the plastering was finished and the bedrooms were ready for the painters. The front door was in, and work had begun on concreting the stretches of patio beneath the balcony, leaving the centre to be paved. I had a clear, rubble free run to the back door. The kitchen and laundry remained grey, empty shells.

On the south side, the walls were complete and beams tied them together at the start of the first storey. Some of the roof rafters were in place. Casa Baraso was soon to be Casa Bennett and I allowed myself feelings of pride. When all was said and done, nothing could detract from the magnificence of the house and I wasn't going to let ghosts spoil things for me. That was my resolve and I hoped I could maintain it.

I went through all the rituals I had established the last time I slept on site. I walked over to my little garden and examined my plants. I took in the view I loved. As the sun dipped below the jagged mountain ridge, I had a bucket shower to wash off the salt from my last swim at the beach in Puerto del Rosario, brushed my teeth and organised my portable latrine before locking myself in for the night. I put on the Cocteau Twins' *The Moon and The Melodies*, dined on canned tuna and a mixed salad, and settled back to read a Stephen King in Spanish. I was missing Paco, but I refused to give in to sentimentality. Above all, I refused to be dependent on a man.

It was only when I blew out the last candle that the knowledge of the violent deaths of the Baraso family came tumbling back to the forefront of my mind. Alone in the house at night, it was hard to shake off the belief that the place was haunted. The gruesome scene of the murder suicide replayed itself over and again and it took me a long time to fall asleep.

I awoke to the sound of whimpering. It was coming from the other room. I thought it was a dog at first, but as I listened I realised it sounded more like a child. Unnerved, I turned over and lit the bedside candle and looked at my phone. It was two o'clock. I wanted to use the phone torch but I discovered my battery was almost out of charge. I'd forgotten to charge it at Paco's. Instead, I took the candle and headed in the direction of the sound.

It was hard to place. I wandered around in the dining room and whenever I thought I was close, the sound seemed to come from somewhere else, as though the source was determined to remain forever out of reach. After a complete tour of the room, I knew there was nothing to see and no one was there. The sound must be coming from outside.

I went to the door to check the bolts. They were drawn closed. As I stood, pondering my next move, trying to decide if I felt brave enough to go out to the patio, the air grew preternaturally cold, so cold, it felt as though I had stepped into a freezer. I shivered. In that moment, the whimpering stopped. Then the candle sputtered and went out.

Terrified, I stepped backwards. The room was instantly warm again. It dawned on me, standing there in nothing but my panties, that I had to find my way back to bed in the dark. As I took slow, tentative steps, I vowed from then on, I would never let my phone run out of charge.

I couldn't sleep. For the rest of the night, I lay on my back, rigid with fear, thinking of sleeping in my car but unable to act on the impulse. For the first time, I faced the sickening realisation that Paco and Clarissa and Gloria were right, there were such things as ghosts and my house was haunted.

27

CASA CORONELES

My head felt thick, fuzzy and dull from lack of sleep, yet still, I was on edge. A dog bark, a gust of wind, every creak and rustle sent a ripple of panic through me. One thought kept returning over and again. If the whimpering were a child, it must be one of Baraso's daughters. Not my mother, not Olivia Stone, but a Baraso and a child. Perhaps it was harmless but I was not reassured. I had no defences against a ghost.

It was the realisation that prompted me to get up, open the doors and let in some light. August, and the morning sun had already set in with determination. I went about my usual ablution routine, keen to leave the building site before the men arrived.

When I was washed and dressed, I wandered the site. The aljibe meant water, but with no power I would have to use a bucket on a rope. The access port was covered with a square of wood, held in place by a rock. I imagined Helmut had arranged for a proper hinged lid of some kind to be installed in the future.

Much of the focus was on the front rooms in the southern corner, where the upper level looked about ready to receive its floor. Outside, beneath the scaffolding the façade of the house had begun to take on its former glory, with the insertion of the downstairs windows. I was keen to inhabit more rooms, but Mario had already explained the kitchen and bathrooms would be fitted last, and that it was better to wait for the painters to do their job before moving into the upstairs.

I took my usual breakfast in the café, forking into Gloria's tortilla as I went back over the terror of the night before. In the harsh light of day, I could almost convince myself I had been dreaming, but I knew I hadn't. I couldn't help linking the whimpering and the ice cold to that rafter that had taken a swipe at the carpenter. A violent child seeking revenge on her awful father? It occurred to me living at Casa Baraso could prove not only spooky, but dangerous.

During a lull in the morning rush, Gloria came over and inquired if I was sleeping at the house again.

I set down my fork. 'I couldn't stay in Puerto del Rosario forever,' I said, offering nothing further. She might have known I had been staying with Paco but I wasn't about to confirm it. She didn't ask.

'How is the carpenter?' she said with concern.

'You know?'

'Word travels fast. I saw the ambulance.'

'I'll find out more today. It was an accident.'

She shook her head emphatically. 'No accident. This is why men won't work on your house.'

'But it was a ruin. No one has done any work there for about a hundred years.'

'That is not true. Cejas started work on the renovations about twenty years ago.'

'They didn't do much.'

'They didn't. But that is why there is a hole in the partition.'

Ah, so it was Cejas who did that. something awful must have happened. More than one incident. Enough to cause him to abandon the project and decide to demolish.

'Did you know the wall has come down?'

She seemed to shudder. 'The ghosts of Casa Baraso won't like that.'

'What do you mean?' I said, having had the same thought as she.

'No sooner had Cejas' men smashed through the wall, than one of them was hit on the head by a rock that no one threw. A length of timber fell on another as he walked under the balcony, and part of another wall fell as the third man was walking by.'

Then my theory was confirmed.

'All of those events *could* have physical explanations,' I said slowly.

We locked gazes. Neither of us believed they had.

'Those men were not superstitious,' she said. 'They had scorned the rumours. Then they experienced for themselves the power of the spirits that haunt Casa Baraso. You are lucky to be alive. That's what everyone is saying. That carpenter is also lucky to be alive.'

She wasn't exaggerating. I watched her walk away, deciding I needed to take action to protect myself. I needed to get rid of that belligerent ghost.

As I waited for my phone to charge, I checked my emails. There was a short note from my father and another email from Clarissa. She made no mention of Olivia Stone. Disappointed, I reminded her. Then I closed the lap top and considered my options for the day. Recalling Olivia Stone had passed by Casa Coroneles and noted the building in her travel diary, I thought I would visit. Perhaps I might glean ideas for décor. At least it was something to do on a hot day and inside should be cool.

SET back on a sweeping gravel concourse, Casa Coroneles observes La Oliva in the near distance and a few volcanoes to the north and, despite the massif behind and the perfect cone of a volcano to the east, the building dominates the landscape. Stout crenelated towers at the corners and the uniformity of design give off an air of authority and military dominance, the building essentially a fortress. In the façade, eight large windows—those on the first storey with Juliette balconies— are arranged one atop another to either side of a grand entrance. Shuttered windows in the side walls complete the look. The windows and doors are constructed of carved wood. A close inspection will reveal the detail.

The interior patio was much larger and grander than mine, with deep balconies overlooking a stand of palm trees. Inside, the deep salmon-pink tones of the walls set off the timbers of the vaulted ceilings, windows and floors. The rooms were given over to a museum-style display, with large portraits arranged beside printed explanations. Empty room by empty room the visitor was taken on a historical journey of the reign of the colonels in what amounted to a lot of reading. Much of the information was a repetition of the book I had skim read in the library in Puerto del Rosario, the day I was researching Casa Baraso. Even so, I read every word, at once repelled by the glorification of what amounted to a rule of terror.

The colonels were a dynasty known for their opulence and the museum reinforced that grandeur even as it educated. Just like all aristocracy, the dynasty married to accumulate wealth and property. Since the colonel oversaw military rule and also functioned as the island administrator, he had absolute power and could do whatever he wanted. The bishops were complicit, leaving ordinary people with nowhere to turn. In effect, Fuerteventura, a tiny island with a miniscule population, endured one hundred and fifty years of ruthless dictatorship, endorsed by the throne of Spain. The rich fed off abundant harvests in times of rain, harvests exported for profit. None of that profit was poured back into the island to benefit the people.

I came away from Casa de los Coroneles unsettled. I knew the British were no better when it came to dominating other cultures, but I was saddened that Fuerteventura should have endured such oppression when as far as I knew the other islands had not.

Since I was there, I went for lunch in a café in La Oliva. While I waited for my order, I texted Paco, hoping he would reply straight away but he didn't. Was he upset with me? Of course, he was. Ten minutes passed. When the waiter came with my meal, my phone beeped. I swiped the screen. Paco said he was busy, sorry, and he would see me on his next day off. Which was when? I chose not to answer. He was definitely hurt, then. I was hurting, too. More than anything, I had put myself in a position of defenceless vulnerability. I wasn't sure I could spend another night alone in my house, only I had to, or I would never live there.

I recalled Clarissa talking about banishing spells. What had seemed ludicrous nonsense now took on the appearance of sanity and necessity. I searched online and upon various instructions I went and bought two kilos of salt from a supermarket and then drove to Lajares, where I knew of a new-age shop, for a bunch of dried sage. I still had a few hours to while away. I wandered around Lajares and went back to La Oliva, lingering in shops and in the church where it was cool. At about four, I headed back to Tiscamanita, calling in at the garden centre in Tefía for a browse.

Back at the house, when the last of the workmen had left, I set about my ritual. I poured salt in the corners and entryways of my rooms. I lit the sage and waved it around as I walked the perimeter of the space. I created my own mantra, politely asking the ghost to leave. Finding myself engaging in banishing spells, I scoffed at myself, even as I knew the seriousness of living in a haunted house with a grumpy ghost.

Satisfied I had done what I could, when it came time to sleep, I blew out the last candle with a small measure of assurance that all would be well.

I awoke in the thick black of night to the sound of something scraping across the floor. My breath caught in my throat. At first, I thought the sound was coming from one of my rooms, but I soon realised the scraping was right above my head. My heart was pounding. A few mores scrapes, a sudden bang, then all went quiet. Who was up there? And what could they possibly be dragging across the floor?

I struck a match with trembling hands. The sound seemed deafening. I lit a candle and then another. I murmured my mantra and lit the sage. The smell was pungent, but better that than the presence of an unwelcome spirit. How long till daylight? I checked my phone. Two hours. Two hours sitting up in bed, hugging my knees, too scared to move, waiting, hearing acute. As if the ghost was satisfied now I was awake and terrified, it made no further sound.

My rational mind slowly kicked in and made my situation even worse. In this instance, I didn't know for sure if it was a ghost. If it wasn't, then I had a prowler. Which was worse? I had bolted the doors. I was sure I had bolted the doors. Were they still bolted? I forced a look. Yes, they were. Then the prowler couldn't get in. If it was a prowler. The ghost would have no problem opening those bolts. Around and around my mind went until I was made dizzy and nauseous. I found myself wishing one of those brutal colonels were around to dispose of the torment.

28

STRONG EMOTIONS

By sunrise, I was angry. Angry that my one grand venture, my big statement in the world, such as it was, had been marred by the supernatural. I drew back the bolts and threw open the doors and let the light shine in. I donned a shift and some flip flops and went out to the patio. Before I lost my nerve, I marched up the balcony stairs and entered the room above my bed. The floorboards were rough and the walls unpainted. Some of the original paintwork had been saved on patches of old render. The vaulted ceiling was magnificent and reminded me of Casa Coroneles. I momentarily lost myself to its potential before my anger at my supernatural intruder rose up in me again. No one and nothing was going to scare me into leaving that splendour.

In the room were two saw horses and a step ladder and nothing else. I had no idea if one of the saw horses had been moved but I was relieved to find objects that could account for the sound I heard in the night. I might have thought I had a living human intruder, but that idea no longer tallied with other events no matter how much my rational mind wanted it too, not since the whimpering and the pool of cold air. I had to face facts even if they were metaphysical. I had a poltergeist, a child, and an angry one at that.

I showered and dressed and readied for the day, packing my

bathers and a towel and making sure I left before the workmen arrived. In the café, I placed my usual order of coffee and tortilla to a nonplussed Gloria who no doubt saw the fatigue and irritation in my eyes, and received from me a gruff and harried demeanour, which was not like me at all.

I sat at my usual table and plugged in my laptop. Gloria came over with my order and I made a space for the plate and cup in front of me without looking up or thanking her.

'Is everything alright?'

She sounded tentative, and her question alerted me to my rudeness.

'Gloria,' I sighed, at last meeting her gaze, 'That ghost is persistent. I'll give it that.'

I told her I was woken by the sound of scraping on the floor above me and had spent the rest of the night awake.

She reached for my arm. 'You be careful, Claire.' She seemed about to say more when some of the workmen from my build came in the café. I gave them a courteous nod as they walked by. Gloria went back behind the counter.

I took a bite of the tortilla and slurped my coffee. When I opened my emails, I was surprised to find one from Clarissa. Seeing its length, I relished in the possibility of a distraction. She had at last found time to research Olivia Stone. Scanning her email, I saw she had been thorough, too. I read with interest, grateful for something to occupy my mind.

She said Olivia Stone was born Olivia Mary Hartrick in 1857, one of five children of Reverend Edward John Hartrick and Mary Macauley Dobbs. She couldn't find out anything about the Dobbs, but she said the Hartricks were descended from German Palatines, those Protestant refugees from neighbouring Germanic states who had escaped to Palatinate to rebuild their lives, only to again flee from persecution, this time sent to Ireland by Queen Anne in the early 1700s. They would have been on their way to America, Clarissa said, but Queen Anne's coffers ran dry. I had no idea who the Palatines were and I was not sure it mattered much, not to me, except that I was impressed by Clarissa's efforts and it was interesting to have a little context.

I read on, hungry for the information that mattered: Olivia's death.

Olivia married John Frederic Matthias Stone (b 1853, Bath) in 1878 and they had three sons. I knew that already, from the article Paco put me on to. Clarissa went on to provide more detail. John Stone was a barrister who participated in the social life of the moment, founding The Camera Club in 1885 and The Caravan Club in 1907. It was easy to see who was the driving force behind the couple's travels. Although it was Olivia who had a talent with words. She was one of several notable travel writers of her day, having penned the highly regarded *Norway in June* which was published in 1882.

Clarissa said the Stones had a great affection for the Canary Islands, not only embarking on a thorough six-month tour in 1883, but returning in 1889 and 1891 to conduct research for future editions of the book. Again, these were facts I already knew and I read with mounting impatience, unsure if I was about to be told anything significant.

They had lived in London, then moved to or had a second residence in St Margaret's at Cliffe near Dover, in a house they named 'Lanzarote'. She had highlighted the word in yellow.

Lanzarote? I paused. Not 'Fuerteventura'?

Paco told me she had named her home after his island. He had gleaned that information from that article he talked of, the article I had painstakingly translated for Clarissa. I kept reading. Clarissa had been thorough in her fact checking. She said the house was probably situated right beside the beach in St Margaret's Bay, since a hotel of the same name had been bombed in WWII, and the local historical society commented that the hotel had been created out of two adjoining private villas. Noel Coward had a residence further along the beach. Sounded like somewhere the Stones would live. It had to be their home. There would not have been two homes called 'Lanzarote' in St Margaret's.

When John Stone re-married in 1900 to Lillie Wellbeloved, he was listed as a widower. Discovering this, led Clarissa on the hunt for

Olivia's death. She said she found it after several attempts, the location somewhat of a surprise since there was no connection to the county of Bedford that she could glean.

Olivia Stone died on 11 March 1897 in Priory Street in Bedford. The cause of death was a rupture of an aneurism of the aortic arch. She had died, Clarissa said, quite suddenly while taking a walk down a street in the heart of Bedford, very near St Paul's Church. Her husband did not appear on the death certificate. She was either walking alone, or with a companion, a Mrs Blanche Adams who was listed as present at her death. Her age was stated as 40. Clarissa went on to explain that her death would have been sudden and painless, and that it was unusual for a woman of her age to die of such a thing. She probably had an underlying condition, most likely genetic. That was the end of the email. Clarissa even provided copies of the relevant evidence.

I searched online for the misleading article that had caused Paco to make false assumptions and build a fantasy about his beloved Olivia Stone, and sat back gazing at that one photo of her. It was easy to see how Paco had conjured his story. She looked wan and wistful, almost ghostly in that loose fitting, short-sleeved dress fringed with tassels. A designer interpretation of a peasant dress of some kind. Her eyes were deep set and filled with longing and her hair, thick and wiry, was cut short and lacked style. In all, she looked like the sort of woman who would abscond and live a secret life on the island of her dreams. She also looked both determined and melancholic, even a touch sickly. Or perhaps my new knowledge was colouring my perception.

A mix of disappointment and outrage welled up in me. At first at Paco, who had insisted his erroneous facts were true and built up a ridiculous fantasy on their basis, but then at both the researcher and the author who had composed the article. How could they have got this crucial information wrong? Was it simply that the death certificate had not been entered into any online database from parish records? Or did the researcher not bother to look that hard? Surely they must have? Perhaps the language barrier had proven a research impediment. Whatever the reason, they had not found the death certificate and had hinted at the conclusion that Olivia may not have died in England. The arrival of a person by the name of Stone on the 'Wazzan' in 1895 was something of a red herring.

The second error was understandable, if annoying. I knew how easy it was to make a mistake when citing a record. A two can become a seven in a pen stroke. Although it was rather astonishing as I could see the census listing with my own eyes. I had a dozen excuses, for in every other respect, the researcher and the journalist who wrote the article had been meticulous. Yet the note that the house had been called 'Fuerteventura' plainly wasn't true.

The consequences for Paco were not pleasant. He had been deceived, basing his suppositions on false foundations. Out of all the islands, it was Lanzarote Olivia loved, not Fuerteventura. How sad, for him, and for the island.

At least now I knew without a doubt that Olivia Stone was not haunting Casa Baraso. She probably never even set foot in the house. She may not even have walked by.

I wondered how I would broach the matter to Paco. How would he react to the truth? Wanting to clear the air as soon as I could, I sent him a text. Told him I really needed to see him. It was urgent. He replied straight away saying his shift ended at five and he would come over.

I replied to Clarissa's email, thanking her for her findings and going on to describe the haunting of the past two nights. I mentioned the whimpering, the cold pools of air, the scraping, and the carpenter whacked on the head by a rafter. I told her I had resorted to banishing spells.

I ordered more coffee and by way of distraction I jotted down in my notebook the latest progress on the building site and then scrolled through websites looking at kitchen designs. As I was about to close the tabs I noticed another email had arrived in my inbox. It was from Clarissa. All she said was as long as the situation does not escalate, I should be able to deal with it using the methods I described. Escalate? Things were already violent enough. Whatever did she mean? I had no idea. What I did know was my mind was firmly back on the supernatural and I wanted to be as far from Tiscamanita as it was possible to be without leaving the island. I had two choices. I could drive to Corralejo, the island's tourist mecca, or head south.

Not fancying mingling with a throng of holidaymakers, I chose south and headed down to Jandia, all the way to the island's southern tip. The road turned to dirt not long after the resort town of Morro Jable, and wended its way some distance above the ocean along the rocky and barren mountainside. The going was slow, the views opening up along the way captivating. I was far from the only vehicle making the journey, and for a long stretch I was accompanied by those heading to or returning from Cofete and Casa Winter and the wild beaches below the Jandia massif. Past the turnoff, the traffic thinned to almost nothing. Empty beaches dotted along the coastline attracted the intrepid, those prepared to scramble down low cliffs. Beyond the massif the land flattened out, the landscape at the southern end of the island dominated by a single volcano. I headed for the lighthouse. Before it, before the land narrowed to form an elongated tongue, tucked beside a sheltered, tidal beach was a cluster of fishing huts with a campsite attached. A secluded resort for those preferring isolation, a real escape, somewhere for the locals to go perhaps, somewhere away from the hubbub elsewhere.

For the rest of us, the lighthouse was the main attraction. Situated on a paved concourse at the end of the tongue was a stout tower built of basalt, one of the oldest lighthouses in the Canary Islands. The tower had been built to form part of a formal building with a flat roof and tall arched windows: the keeper's cottage. What a life of solitude those keepers would have endured!

Beside the cottage was a smaller building, the same in style and given over to a small café. Some outdoor seating and even a wind-break in the form of a Perspex screen had been erected for the comfort of spectators. And people sat and gazed at the ocean, mesmerised.

Keen for a closer view, I went over to the edge of the low cliff, dodging a few others meandering about. What drew the sightseers to this end-of-earth spot was the meeting of the waters east and west. A strong current pressed against the southwestern side of the tongue and where it met the waters to the east, the waves rippled and I sensed the force of those mingling forces beneath the surface. Treacherous and for swimmers, deadly. I stood until I was tired of standing, then I sat until I was tired of sitting. I didn't tire of the view. There was something about being on the edge of things, something about setting, the rocky land where almost nothing grew, with the mountains of Jandia rising behind, and all that ocean. Like everyone else, I found it hard to pull myself away. For a whole hour, haunted houses did not enter my mind.

Not ready to leave, I went inside the main cottage that had been converted into a museum in the same fashion as Casa Coroneles, with a few artefacts and numerous information boards explaining the history. Each room was painted a different colour and portrayed a different theme. I meandered around the rooms not taking much in, and eventually went back to my car.

On the way back up the coast, I stopped at Morro Jable for a swim. It was good to be in the water despite the preponderance holiday-makers who were noisy and idiotic. I ate a pleasant lunch at my favoured beachside café and then I drove inland, crossing the island's narrow waist to La Pared – a town largely given over to surfers – then I tracked my way up to Páraja on a backroad through the mountains. A dawdle around the town and I was back in Tiscamanita close to five.

When Paco pulled up outside my property, I no longer had the heart to disabuse him of his Olivia Stone fantasy. The risk to our relationship, fragile as it was, was too great. Seeing him all tentative and concerned, I weakened. I needed him by my side. I could not face another night of terror alone in that house.

We hugged and kissed and I sensed his relief. 'What's happened?' he said in my ear.

I pulled back and recounted the events of the last two nights, the whimpering, the cold pool of air, the scraping sound of something being dragged across the floor above my head and then I described the carpenter's accident. Paco saw the salt on his way into my rooms, and he couldn't help but smell the sage.

'What *is* that?' he said, sniffing.

'I read somewhere that burning sage banishes ghosts and salt keeps them at bay.' I laughed to cover my embarrassment.

Paco looked serious. 'Olivia Stone would not wish to cause anyone harm. I could never imagine her trying to kill someone.'

'I think it might be someone else,' I said gently, biting back my urge to divulge all. Instead I recounted Gloria's testimony of the Baraso family, and how señor Baraso had murdered his entire family before killing himself.

As he listened, Paco shook his head. 'They died of yellow fever. That's what everyone says.'

'I think that was the story put about to cover the truth.'

He didn't speak. I hoped he wasn't going to be stubborn. I went on, needing him to believe me. 'Gloria has first-hand accounts handed down through her family, and I am convinced she's telling the truth.'

'First-hand?'

'Her grandmother's grandmother, no less, who used to work for the Barasos as their maid.'

'But *murder suicide*?' His mouth hung open a little. He looked shocked.

'It would explain a lot.'

I waited for him to process the information. A silence grew between us. He broke it with, 'I appreciate what you are trying to do, Claire. But you can't be here alone. Not until this is dealt with.'

I had no idea how I would ever deal with that ghost. If salt and sage and little mantras were not going to banish it, what would? Or should I be thinking of who? A priest?

All I knew for certain was we had returned to coupledom. Our togetherness was as natural as breathing, the rapport undeniable, and it felt right to be with Paco, even if we had been forced together by a ghost. Even for someone as cautious as me.

Seeing him there all concerned for my welfare, I realised I had been fighting against being with Paco not out of a sense of propriety in terms of how a relationship should unfold, but out of a deep-seated fear of entanglement. I could trace that fear all the way back to the zebra crossing and that awful moment when I witnessed my mother's death. It wasn't hard. There was little in between other than the monotony of my work at the bank, the predictable interactions with my father and aunt Clarissa, and a few failed attempts at having a boyfriend.

I had never lived with any of those men. I hadn't wanted to. They hadn't attracted me that way. None of them were right for me. Although perhaps I hadn't been right for them.

I found it hard to be open and emotionally available and I could not abide an emotionally needy man. Oddly, I had managed to attract that type over and again. Until now. Paco was different. He kept his reserve. He didn't have temper tantrums, displayed no jealousy or possessiveness and even handled rejection well. I suppose I had put him through his paces, inadvertently but still, testing him without realising that was what I was doing.

We shared a plate of canned tuna salad and a bottle of wine. I described my day down in Jandia and he said he'd take me to the other lighthouse near Gran Tarajal. I was about to say I had already visited but I caught myself in time. After all, I hadn't been there with him, and after our day in El Cotillo, I knew he brought something magical to my experiences of the island. I asked how he had spent his day, and he recounted a funny scene in the restaurant where he worked, involving a very loud and very drunk couple so sunburnt they looked like lobsters. The staff had a running joke at their expense in the kitchen out the back.

'The chef was saying he should find a large pot to boil them in and we were choosing ingredients. It was really very funny.'

I laughed and yawned all at once. He took my hand. We took turns in the bathroom, made love and slept curled in each other's arms. On the ghostly front, that night was quiet.

29

AN UNEVENTFUL MONTH

For the rest of August and the whole of September, I stayed with Paco through the week and we spent weekends at mine. We settled into a routine of companionship.

As part of my campaign to forge a life with friends on the island, I attended the Spanish class I enrolled in back in April, held in a room at the local library and run by a native Spanish speaker who was fluent in English. Her name was Sofia. She had long black hair, warm eyes and an expressive mouth. I took to her immediately. As for the other students, they proved a prickly bunch of highly competitive expats. There was a lot of jostling for position both with regard to who spoke the best Spanish and who was closer to Sofia. I found the interactions, the asides and jibes and pointed if jocular barbs tedious. I was there to learn and after one session I had given up any wish I held of making friends. After finding I had nothing in common with any of the cohort, I had to quell my disappointment and force myself to attend.

My position was made even harder once the others discovered I was restoring Casa Baraso. Sofia was the one who told the class. In the introductions, I had simply announced I was renovating a ruin, for which I received many eye rolls and comments about local builders. It was during the second session that Sofia asked me, in Spanish, if I was the new owner of Casa Baraso. Honesty prevailed, there being no point in denying it, and one of the other students overheard and before long everyone was gasping and carrying on like there was no tomorrow. What was bothering all of them was that I was rich. Somehow, they all knew I had won the lottery. I could hardly believe it. Back in the apartment, I discussed the matter with Paco, and between us we managed to surmise that it was the estate agent who had spread the word that an Englishwoman who had won the lottery was restoring a ruin not even the local government were able to buy off the previous owner. Gossip. And my word, did it spread fast. I was famous without realising and without knowing barely a soul on the island. Incredible.

At least the classes gave Paco and I something else to talk about. We had taken to conversing in both our native tongues in rotation, a habit that benefited us both.

I tried hard not to mention Olivia Stone and if she came up, I changed the subject. The pressure of the withholding was hard, it felt like a betrayal, but I didn't know Paco well enough yet to calculate how he would react and I didn't want the truth to jeopardise what we had. It would most likely trigger our first row.

At Casa Bennett, I had begun to believe my banishing spells were working and the haunting was over.

Despite the heat the men continued to work hard. I suspected both Mario and Helmud were pushing them, anxious to complete works as fast as possible, in case there was another incident and the workmen downed tools and left.

All the windows were in, all the doors hung, and the painters had finished the upstairs of the north wing and the exterior walls of that half of the build. The floors were sanded and sealed. A week later, and the scaffolding came down on the northern external wall and sections of the east and west walls as well. Carpenters had erected the timbers for the balcony awning on that half of the patio. Corrugated iron would protect the balcony from rain and Helmud had suggested I insulate and sheet beneath to absorb the radiant heat. Having spent one entire summer on the island, that sounded like a good idea.

On the south side, the roof reconstruction was slow due to the vaulted ceiling, but the floors were laid and the downstairs walls rendered and the balcony was under construction.

The last week of September I received delivery of three four poster beds, along with wardrobes and tallboys, filling the rooms above the dining and living rooms and kitchen. I took the room over the kitchen as my own. It had an ensuite – or it would have – and a spectacular view of the volcano. I arranged for my possessions that had been in storage for months to be delivered and I was eager to make my home my own.

Mario and Helmud took my presence in their stride but I knew the workmen preferred me not to be around. Until then, I had obliged by leaving the site early every Monday with Paco and avoiding turning up through the week, but now I was insisting on subverting the order of things by moving in my things and by having a kitchen and the plumbing installed, and there was a little friction and a few grumbles. I was not about to give in. Besides, it couldn't be helped. The two halves of the build, at distinct stages of restoration, with one almost complete and the other a work in progress, created an odd situation.

Mario relented and arranged for a plumber to install the ensuite and a downstairs toilet and connect the property to the mains sewage. In anticipation, I bought a pump for the aljibe.

Sewage coincided with the kitchen installation. I chose an ultramodern, glossy white look with polished concrete bench tops. All the appliances were steel. The room was a large rectangle with the window centred in the longer wall facing east, which determined the location of the sink. On the shorter, north wall, were the stove and fridge. A breakfast bar formed the third arm of a U, leaving about half the room spare. I bought stools for the breakfast bar and an oval dining table and chairs, all in a polished ebony, allowing room for a matching wooden rocking chair in the near corner. Whoever sat there could observe the whole kitchen as well as a portion of the patio beneath the balcony.

Unpacking my crockery and putting appliances in cupboards and drawers had to be the most satisfying of feelings. My past, decades of it, had found its way into my future and I was pleased with the blending.

Life at Casa Bennett just kept getting better. The day the electrician came – a demure and petite man called Simon – I was singing inside. I took a keen interest as he connected the power and wired the power points on the usable side of the house. He put the kitchen on a separate circuit, the oven on one of its own, and all the lights and power points of the living and dining room along with the bedrooms above, on a third. He created another circuit for the laundry, a grey rendered shell, and the patio lighting. No more generator. It took Simon three days and I used that time to accumulate light shades and desk lamps and occasional tables to put them on.

The day the power was connected to the mains, I raced back to Puerto del Rosario bursting with delight to find Paco had news of his own. He had received another assignment, this time for a prestigious geographic magazine. He would be away three weeks and had to leave immediately. We went out to dinner to celebrate.

So full of joy at my own red-letter day, I didn't give his absence a second thought, other than I knew I would miss him. He wanted me to stay at his in his absence but I had much to occupy me on the build and the ghost appeared to have gone for good.

The first evening of power was heaven. I was overjoyed. I could read by a beside lamp, charge my phone and laptop, and go up and down the balcony stairs without a torch.

I stood at my bedroom window watching the sky darken behind the volcano as the sun set. The sense of space gifted by the view was exhilarating, expansive. Contemporary Fuerteventura shaded into an eighteenth century version beneath my gaze, to a time when the farms were going concerns, when Tiscamanita was a centre of activity. The mill, the wells and the simple lifestyle was an idyll. It was a time when superstition abounded. When I thought of all those churches in every little village, I was reminded of the division between rich and poor, the Spanish inquisition and the era of the colonels, throughout all of it the church was abiding towards those in power.

My house afforded a sense of dominance over the surroundings and I couldn't help remembering it represented the lives the nobility and the bourgeoisie enjoyed as they imposed themselves on an impoverished and compliant poor. After considering all of that, it was easier to gaze at the present, at the legacy, at the ruins dotted all around Tiscamanita. I wanted to resolve the past and the present but I couldn't. It wasn't my place.

I headed downstairs in the gloaming, flicking on the kitchen light as I entered the room. It was a defining moment, the brilliance of all the shiny white dazzling enough for sunglasses and I chuckled to myself. The room was a triumph. Modernity housed in ancient walls. It worked. I poured a glass of chilled white wine to celebrate and threw together a cold chicken salad. When I had chomped my way through the mountain of lettuce on my plate, I went and sat back in my rocking chair to listen to *Treasure* through my sound bar, enjoying the way the Cocteau Twins filled the space as though they, too, had been craving room to expand and breathe.

Following the rise and fall of the vocals, my head brimmed with joy in the knowledge that whatever I did with my life on the island, I was going to delight in my home.

When the album finished I sat in silence wondering what to play next. It was then that the air around me went suddenly incredibly cold. I shivered. I wanted to rub the bare skin on my arms but I dare not move. I stared straight ahead at my shiny white kitchen. Would this ghost child reveal herself to me? Is that what was about to happen? Could I handle it if she did? Maybe not.

I scarcely had time to inhale when the lights, my beloved lights that had only been burning for a few hours, went out. An outage? Temporary? The room was still freezing which meant the ghost was still around.

I couldn't sit in the dark. Plunged into blackness with no phone in reach I was disoriented. I needed light but I waited.

Nothing changed.

I stood and walked tentatively in the direction of the kitchen bench, feeling my way. Two steps and two more steps and when I thought I was about halfway something lunged at me from behind. I stumbled forwards and crashed my left hip into the bench. Terror rang through me. I groped about on the polished concrete bench for my phone. There was a bar stool at my side. I shunted to the left. I knew I had left it there somewhere.

As my hand found the phone, the cold dissipated and the lights came on. I looked around. There was no one in the room. I went out and switched on the patio light hoping to catch a figure scampering off, something corporeal, but there was no sign of anyone. I thought maybe I had been too slow. My rational mind seemed to me then pathetic, scrambling to explain the event away any way it could so I didn't have to feel the terror.

I knew I wouldn't sleep. I wanted to leave, get far away but the impulse made me angry. I was entitled to occupy my own house, my big and beautiful house. If that ghost was going to be territorial, well, so was I.

There were no bolts on my bedroom door, so I stayed downstairs, planning to bolt myself inside the living room which still contained my old bed. Leaving nothing to chance, I put obstacles under the window. I sprinkled another trail of salt around the whole perimeter of the room, repeating my banishing mantra as I went.

I left a light on in the dining room, carefully removed the plastic dust cover and got into the bed fully clothed, drawing the covers up to my chin. Despite my precautions, fear kept a hold and I knew I would be awake all night.

I found myself trying to think like a ghost. If I had scared my victim out of her wits, if I had made her freeze, deprived her of light and pushed her hard from behind, hard enough to make her tumble, what would I do next? Would I go and put my feet up somewhere, satisfied? Would I take pleasure in the terror I had invoked? Or would I plan my next move? Do ghosts think or do they act spontaneously? I soon found it wasn't possible to think like a ghost. All I knew was I had been physically assaulted, that this entity could not only blow out candles, turn off lights, make the temperature of a room plummet, slide bolts, open and close doors, move rocks, send timber flying and whimper, it could make *real physical contact*. This was a ghost with dogged intent, a ghost with malice in its heart, a ghost prepared to leave the place of its haunting to frighten the owner wherever she might be. This was one determined spirit and I had few defences.

At least the salt seemed to work. I spent hours sitting up hugging my knees, interspersed with periods lying down and tossing and turning. Nothing weird happened. There was no scraping of furniture, no doors slamming. Nothing. All I heard was some light rain. It didn't last long. The moment I saw daylight, I went and had a shower.

The roof tilers arrived as I was heading to the kitchen for strong coffee and breakfast. I heard vehicles pull up and conversations, then footsteps up the scaffolding outside. It was barely dawn. Then Helmud poked his head in the kitchen door and greeted me, saying there was more rain forecast and they wanted to get the roof on before it came.

I remained on site and spent the morning sorting out my things and cleaning rooms. I ignored the workmen and they ignored me. There were far fewer men on site; the stone masons were long gone, and the other tradesmen too. I didn't care to interact with the roof tilers who seemed to me a raucous bunch of larrikins.

In need of a change of atmosphere, after lunch and more coffee, I drove down to Gran Tarajal for a swim. Billowing cloud filled the sky but there was no rain in it as yet, as far as I could tell. I spent the whole afternoon doing laps in the ocean and walking on the sand.

The tilers were still there when I returned home at six. I spent an hour in the kitchen, reading. The slam of a car door and a few revving engines told me the men were knocking off. It was then seven. I watched the cloud thickening over the volcano as I prepared a salad and, not wanting to leave the kitchen after I had eaten, I settled in the rocking chair and streamed Dolores Claiborne on my laptop.

When the film ended and I was sitting in the quiet of the house contemplating whether I thought Dolores was justified in doing the things she had, I sensed my otherworldly companion would soon start its nocturnal activities. It was only a matter of time.

As though in tune with the thoughts running through my mind, my laptop screen went black. Then I realised it was the power saving kicked in. I was about to get up and close the lid when the kitchen lights flickered. A step ahead of my supernatural foe, I had my phone torch to the ready. When the lights went out I switched on the phone's sharp beam. It was a brief moment of triumph. I had outfoxed a ghost.

My smug satisfaction did not last long. The room turned to ice in an instant. I was alert, tense, waiting, listening.

Nothing could have prepared me for the cold hands that gripped my throat. The sensation was real, thumbs against my neck bones, fingers curling tight, pressing hard against my larynx. I gagged and gasped for breath. Alarm filled me, blinding. I was suffocating. I had an impulse to scream but I had no voice.

I struggled to get free. I lunged forward in my seat but it made no difference. I dropped my phone in my lap and reached to pull away the hands that were determined to lead me to my death – *but there were no hands. Only air.*

Panic bolted through me. I was being strangled. The pain was excruciating. I couldn't breathe in or out. Blood boomed in my head in synch with my racing heart.

I couldn't peel away those murderous fingers. I was surely at the point of death. In a final terror-fuelled effort, I jumped up off the rocking chair.

The hands slid away, as did my phone, falling face down on its torchlight. The room went black. The air remained ice cold. *It wasn't over.*

I panted, each intake of air laboured. I clutched my neck, disoriented. I wanted to run, flee the house, but I couldn't see. I had no idea which direction to take or where the next attack was coming from. *I can't just stand here.*

But the moment I took a step forward I was shoved from behind. I stumbled and regained my balance and was shoved again, harder this time. I lurched forward and stumbled to my knees. I heard a crack. Was that a kneecap?

Too vulnerable on the floor, I recovered my stance. I reached out and felt the wall and stood with my back to it. Then I screamed in a voice hoarse and rasping, and in that scream, I told that ghost to leave me the fuck alone.

All returned to normal in an instant. The room grew warm and the lights came on. My laptop sat on the table where I'd left it. The fridge whirred. The dishes were in the sink. It was almost as though nothing had happened. I saw my phone on the floor behind me. A chair was askew. That was all the evidence of the attack, that and my throbbing throat.

I picked my phone off the floor and used the camera as a mirror to see myself. The red marks around my neck was all the confirmation I needed that I had not imagined that attack. I knew in that moment that ghosts were capable of hands-on physical harm.

I was accommodating my new awareness and examining the finger marks on my neck, when the whimpering started. Not more haunting! The sound was coming from the patio. I had no intention of following that sound but I needed to get out of the house and there was only one way out of the kitchen, and that meant walking out to the patio and through the passageway to the back door.

The whimpering carried on, the sound moving, fading and then getting louder. For a while the sound came from the doorway and when it did the kitchen lights flickered. I thought of shutting myself in the kitchen but what would be the point? Ghosts could move through walls and there was just no telling if I would be attacked again.

As if to confirm my thinking, upstairs a door slammed. I jumped, startled. That was all the motivation I needed. I grabbed my purse, phone and car keys, waited for the whimpering to fade and ran out the kitchen with my heart hammering in my chest. I didn't stop to look around. I went straight through to the back door, scrambling for the handle.

I didn't close the door behind me. I just ran. I ran holding my phone up to light my way. I ran straight to my car, pressed the remote and fumbled my way into the driver's seat.

I was shaking so hard my teeth were chattering. I inserted the key in the ignition but I had nowhere to go other than Paco's, and knew I was in no state to drive. Instead, I locked myself in. Surely, out in the open I would be safer. Surely the ghost won't attack me out here?

The sky had cleared. I sat for a long time staring at the stars, watching the moon rise up over the volcano. I gradually grew calmer.

I must have dozed. Sometime in the night I awoke. It was teeming with rain.

Before I opened my eyes, I knew I wasn't alone. Call it a sixth sense. I didn't want to look. I wanted to keep my eyes shut and will whatever it was away. But I did open them and I saw, outside my window, a face. It was a woman's face and she was staring at me. At first, I thought she was my mother. Then I saw her long black dress and I knew who it was. Señora Baraso. Had to be. She looked pale, desperate, terrified. Yet no part of her was wet.

She pressed her bone-dry hands against the glass. I shook my head. I mouthed to her, no. She seemed crestfallen. She hurried off, into the outbuilding where I used to take my showers.

After that, I didn't sleep. I began to wonder if I had dreamed that face as I scrambled to regain a sense of normality, but I hadn't. All I knew was I had two ghosts, a child and its mother. Which one had strangled me?

It was with sickening certainty that I realised it was neither.

30

HUNTING FOR GRAVES

WITH DAYLIGHT CAME A TORMENTED CALM, A HEAD FUZZY FROM LACK of sleep and a body stiff in places it shouldn't be: neck, hip, small of back and one ankle.

I shifted and sat up straight. The windscreen was fogged. Using my arm, I swiped away the mist on the side window. The rain had gone, the ground was damp and there were small puddles here and there. Before I got out of the car, I studied my neck in the rear vision mirror. The bruising was plain to see.

My first thought was that I would pack up and stay at Paco's. But that would mean defeat. Whoever those ghosts were they had no right to occupy my home. I held on to the practicalities and a strong impulse to protect my home, taking umbrage at the potential damage to my person and my property that a bad-tempered ghost could achieve. I had been pushed from behind and strangled. What next? Would, could a ghost really kill me?

I extricated myself from the car and marched into my house and on upstairs for a shower. It was easy to be defiant and territorial in daylight. Once clean and dressed, I straightened out my rooms and closed all the doors, leaving through the back door as the workmen were arriving. Heading behind the barn, I could only hope I had become the only target of the spooky shenanigans and none of those men would come to harm.

I drove up the street and parked opposite the café beneath a shade tree. The village was quiet. The church, the centrepiece of the village with its high white walls, its lack of windows, looked inwards, at itself and its god, warding off evil forces, a fortress of faith. I had no faith. I no longer had much confidence in banishing rituals either. I did the only thing that constituted faith. I called Clarissa.

'How are you, my dear?' Her voice alone brought peace.

'I'm not interrupting?'

'Not at all. The funeral was yesterday.'

A jolt passed through me. Whose funeral? I didn't like to ask. 'Did it go okay?' was all I could think to say.

'Low key. Dear old thing was ninety-five, so not too many tears.'

I hesitated. But this was not a time for chit chat. 'I wanted to ask. I'm having more trouble at the house.' I filled her in on the latest happenings. 'I had no idea ghosts could cause humans physical harm in a hands-on way. I thought they would pass right through us, so to speak. Things are getting out of hand.'

'I did wonder if things would escalate. They usually do when violence is involved.'

'It tried to strangle me,' I said, my voice wavering as I relived the horror.

'He,' Claire. 'That would have been Baraso himself.'

'You think Gloria's version of what happened there is true?' I had related the full story to Clarissa in an email.

'These latest events prove it. As in life, so in death.'

'What about the whimpering child? The woman Paco photographed?'

'Sounds like you have at least three spirits trapped there.'

'*Three*.'

'At least. Could be the whole family.'

'I need them gone,' I said with an air of desperation.

'Difficult.'

'There must be something I can do. The banishing spells are not working.'

'You can try the ten tips of Madame Boulanger.' She sounded doubtful.

'I'll try anything.'

'On second thoughts, you are already employing the basics. Exorcism is a last resort.'

'Exorcism!' I glanced at the church. My mind reeled with images of priests and strange rituals.

'It isn't as dramatic as you think. I've witnessed several. Poltergeists don't only inhabit ancient ruins, Claire. Even your regular two up, two down can contain a cantankerous ghost or two. They seem to attach themselves to teenage girls or others experiencing turbulent emotions of their own.'

I didn't speak. We both knew the grief I had harboured in me.

'Where are they buried?' Clarissa asked.

'I have no idea.'

'Ah, then you should find their graves.'

'What will that achieve?'

'Claire, usually with these things, people just want to be heard and understood. Acknowledged is some way. Laid to rest, so to speak.'

A grave hunt? It couldn't hurt and at least gave me a strategy, even a possible solution. I thanked her and said my goodbyes.

Gloria beamed a smile at me as I entered the café, and gestured for me to sit down. I wondered what could be making her so pleased to see me as I took up my preferred table, although I no longer had need of the power point. She brought over my usual coffee and tortilla. After setting down my cutlery she took a step back, hovering.

'Another lovely sunny day,' I said, beaming up at her, a smile behind which all I could think of were cemeteries. 'The rain was good, too.'

'It was.' She hesitated and inhaled to say more. 'Tell me, Claire, what do you plan on doing with your big house?'

It was the same question, every time, and I was surprised she hadn't asked before.

'I don't know yet,' I said, which was the truth.

'You should come to Maria's computer class in Tuineje,' she blurted and I realised that despite her forthright manner, deep down she was shy. Or maybe wary, of me, of what I represented. I hesitated, holding her gaze with interest. There she stood, all expectant and enthusiastic and unsure in her neat and clean apron protecting her blouse and skirt. 'It's for mature, rural women,' she went on, pointing at my laptop. 'We need to learn all this technology or we will be left behind.'

'I already know how to use it, though.' Even as I spoke I wished I could have come up with something appreciative to say instead. Fortunately, she wasn't about to be deterred.

'This is why I ask. There are ten of us. You will make many friends.' She told me they met every Saturday morning at eleven o'clock at the library. 'Will you come?'

'I would be delighted. Thank you.' I made a note in my phone calendar as she stood over me. I held up my entry for her to see. 'There you are, my phone won't let me forget.'

We both laughed. A door had unexpectedly opened, the welcome mat displayed. I had gained entry into the everyday life of local rural women. The invitation marked a turning point. No more Spanish classes. An opportunity to participate in the local community? Nothing could have brought me greater joy. I knew it was rare and it felt almost like a reward for my loyalty to her business.

When Gloria went to serve another customer, I opened my laptop and searched for all the cemeteries in the area. I targeted Tuineje and Gran Tarajal to the south, and to the north, Casillas del Ángel, Tetir, the old cemetery in La Oliva and two in Puerto del Rosario.

When the café emptied, Gloria rushed over, a look of concern on her face.

'I have to ask. What is wrong with your neck? And your voice? You sound husky.' She made a rasping sound of her own, in case I didn't understand.

I didn't want to tell her. I knew once I did the news would spread around the village. Yet the evidence was there and how else would I explain the marks.

'Something strangled me last night. I think it was trying to kill me.'

'You mean, a ghost!'

'I managed to get free,' I said, trying to downplay the drama. 'And thankfully, I'm alive.'

'I told you it is not safe to stay in that house.' Gloria looked frantic.

'You are right. But I have to. I can't let those ghosts win.'

'Don't sleep there again, Claire.' She reached for my hand. 'Please.'

'I'll be fine, Gloria. Really.'

She released her grip and I took back my hand thinking I should have worn a scarf and pretended I was sick with a cold.

I paid my bill and set off to spend the day wandering inside walled cemeteries reading headstones. To begin with, I headed to Gran Tarajal and on to Tuineje. In each cemetery, there were a far larger number of niche stones, typically arranged in rows four high flanking lanes filled with flowers. Niche upon niche, headstone upon headstone, and nowhere yielded a single Baraso. Most of the cemeteries contained recent burials and I wished I had been more thorough back at the café, and narrowed my search to only those cemeteries containing old graves. I wasn't to know and besides, I wanted to be certain and see for myself. Relying on the internet was not always advisable.

Entering the cemetery in Casillas del Ángel I felt more optimistic. At least I was surrounded by old graves, many dating back to the nineteenth century. Niches lined the perimeter wall and other, internal walls. Paths meandered around graves set in pink gravel. The dead, as always, were sheltered from the wind and away from the gawping gazes of the living.

The cemetery at La Oliva was old, too, and contained the grave of the last of the colonels, Cristóbal Manrique de Lara Cabrera, replete with a large statue of an angel, looking down as though to bless where he lay. The locals, I presumed, would have been glad to see the back of him.

I saved the cemetery near the port in Puerto del Rosario for last. The cemetery was close to Paco's apartment and situated on what was essentially a roundabout that adjoined another, making for a noisy and frenetic environment for those old souls buried there. A wander around the graves yielded nothing. There were no Barasos buried there. If the family had been buried in unmarked graves I had little to no chance of finding them, other than by searching local archives. Disheartened and exhausted, I called into a café Paco and I frequented and ate a late lunch.

While I forked a paella, I did a quick internet search for information on the old cemeteries. The first arresting piece of information I discovered was that the graves in the cemetery I had visited last had been desecrated, skulls removed for satanic rituals held in some abandoned houses near Caleta de Fuste. What was it with people? Had any of those skulls belonged to a Baraso? I dearly hoped not, for I feared walking into that dark terrain.

Upon further research, I discovered that the older graves might also be found within church walls. Intramural graves were only for the rich and powerful, people of honour, although Señor Baraso, while undoubtedly a wealthy man, had not been a local dignitary, rendering intramural burial unlikely. Besides, in the late eighteenth century new legislation required the creation of municipal cemeteries within which to bury the dead, in an attempt to stamp out the medieval practice of intramural burials, not least due to the stench of decomposing corpses in shallow graves and concerns for the health of the living.

I thought of visiting all the churches in the vicinity of Tiscamanita, but decided to leave it for another day. Perhaps the remains of Baraso and his family had been returned to Tenerife for burial there. Defeated, I went back to Tiscamanita and called in to ask Gloria what she knew. Thankfully, the café was empty when I walked in, and I made my inquiry without any preface.

A shadow passed across her face.

'I really couldn't say.'

'I've looked in the cemeteries all over the island and there is no sign of any Baraso. I am thinking their corpses were taken back to Tenerife. Did that sort of thing happen?'

'I really don't know. No one said.'

Was she holding back on me? Or merely worried for my safety? I left thinking maybe that is all the family wanted, after all. To be found.

I returned home as the workmen were leaving. I should have gone to Paco's as I had earlier thought to do, but courage and defiance quelled my misgivings. I tended my garden, added a few stones to the back wall and wandered around the block.

A strange peace descended. At sunset, the sky blazed red. I felt the wind. It was warm and coming from the east. A calima was on its way. I went inside and threw together some dinner out of some cheese and the raggedy salad vegetables in the fridge and I struggled through it while I watched an episode of Black Books.

It wasn't until night fell that I began to feel that all too familiar fear. To assuage it before it claimed me, I doused the perimeter of my upstairs bedroom with salt. I did the same with the kitchen. I put a bead of salt across each of the doorways. I walked from room to room, repeating my mantra over and again. I smudged the entire building, even venturing up the scaffolding to smudge the rooms that remained bare stone. I resolved that the instant anything happened, I would yell at the ghost to leave me alone. It was my last defence and it had seemed to work before. It would be a battle of wills and I had better win.

All I could do was hope. Worn out from the day, I took myself upstairs to bed, choosing to leave the light on in the ensuite, for the sense of safety it afforded. I lay in the semi-darkness and slowly drifted to sleep.

31

A CASE OF INFLUENZA

I AWOKE DISORIENTED AFTER A FULL NIGHT OF SLEEP. EMERGING OUT OF slumber, I found I was heavy and weak and my throat burned. Maybe I was dehydrated after yesterday's cemetery tour, or I was still hoarse and my throat inflamed from the strangulation. Whatever the cause, I felt terrible.

The room was dim. Threads of grey broke through the blinds and I noticed a strip of light under the ensuite door. I sat up, ignoring the head spin. I had left that door open. I know I did. Now, it was closed. Fear bounded in, my unwanted companion.

Alert to every sound, I switched on the bedside lamp and scrutinised the room. Nothing had been disturbed. The door to the balcony was closed. I got up and flung open the enuite door and examined the room. All appeared normal.

I slipped on a bathrobe and a pair of mules and went and stood on the balcony, scanning the patio below. Two wheelbarrows were propped against the southern wall just as the workmen had left them. I went down to the kitchen, scanning for signs of change but there was no evidence of things having moved about in the night. Other than that ensuite door, my banishing efforts must have worked, at least for now.

Dawn broke in long red streaks, silhouetting the volcano. The calima had arrived. Perhaps it was just the dust irritating my throat, compounding the strangulation. But then, why did I feel so awful?

It was Saturday. At least there would be no workmen to interrupt me. I made tea and took it with me as I wandered around the building. I had asked the painters to re-create the decorative frieze in the front corner room downstairs. Standing in the doorway, I stopped thinking about ghosts and imagined my furniture arranged in the space, the light flooding in through the south-facing windows. My home would be splendid, fit to feature in one of those glossy magazines. Paco could take the photos. I would sit, first here, then there, describing how it felt to have restored an ancient home and brought it back to its glory days.

I hummed to myself as I made breakfast of fruit and yogurt. I took a shower and, without thinking, I donned an old t-shirt and slacks, and went to tend my garden. I was on my knees putting a rock on the back wall, aware of its weight, when I became overly aware of my arm muscles aching from the strain. I then grew aware of the heat and the dust. What was I doing out here? When my phone sprang to life, I yelped.

It was Paco. He said had taken some terrific shots of Alegranza.

'I miss you.'

'And I miss you,' I replied huskily.

'What's with your throat?'

'I think I'm getting sick,' I said, at last admitting to myself that all my aches and pains were symptoms of a bad cold.

'You know what to do. Plenty of fluids. Stay warm. Rest. There's a pharmacist two blocks from the apartment, in Calle Dr. Fleming.'

'I'm at home.'

There was a long pause as he assimilated the news. Then, 'Claire, what are you doing there? You must go and stay in the apartment. I don't like to think of you at Casa Baraso all alone. What if something happens?'

'I'll be okay. I slept well last night. Things were uneventful.'

'That might not always be the case. You know from before. That ghost is unpredictable. There's no telling what it might do next. Promise me.'

'I promise.'

'You do not sound much like someone who is promising.'

'Paco, please. I don't have the energy.'

'Which is why you must drive to Puerto del Rosario where there are people who can look after you. Where you will be safe. Where...'

The line dropped out. I tried returning his call but the reception had gone. I took my weary body inside, made myself some more tea and checked my emails.

I had received an unexpected email from my father. He wanted to know when I was coming home for a visit. I replied, asking him when he planned on coming to the island to see what I have been up to. Touché.

As if our wavelengths were in synch, an email arrived from Clarissa saying she was booking a flight to Fuerteventura for Christmas. I answered straight away saying I couldn't wait. Her visit gave me a date to work towards. I wanted her to see my home restored, scaffolding-free, and fully painted.

I changed out of my gardening clothes and readied to wander up to the café before realising I had no need to leave the house. Although by mid-morning, my throat was raging and I knew the weakness, the aching, the touch of fever and the sore throat were signs of influenza. Wasting no time, I drove to the pharmacist in Tuineje for various cold and flu remedies, tissues and pain killers. I visited the supermarket next door, stocking up on fresh produce, yogurt, custard, ready-made soups, whatever would slip down easily. Eyeing the others pushing their trolleys, I thought back to who I might have come into contact with in the last few days, someone who had coughed or sneezed in my proximity. Someone from Australia or New Zealand or Chile or Argentina who had brought the virus with them from their winter. It was impossible to know. I had passed by scores of tourists on my travels.

By lunchtime my throat was so sore I could barely swallow. All I could do was try to stay comfortable and ride the virus out.

For a while, I sat in the rocking chair and tried to read. Outside, the wind blew and blew. I got up and looked out the kitchen window. The air was thick with dust. I shut the kitchen door and carried on reading. When turning the pages became too hard I made a cup of soup and took myself, my phone, the meds and a pitcher of water upstairs to my bedroom. And that was where I planned to stay.

The virus proved vicious. I spent the rest of the weekend with my chest on fire, aching from head to toe. I was hot and cold all at once. For long periods, I sank into semi-delirium, half awake, half asleep, too ill to move a muscle, burning up and shivering.

In my delirium, I called out for my mother. I experienced memories, not of the accident, but dim memories of birthdays and beaches. The memories were hazy, just fragments – a pretty dress, a sunny day, laughter, a hug – but they were mine and I held onto them for solace and I tried to replay them, keen to recall them, keen for more.

I hugged myself and cried. Paco was right; I should be in Puerto del Rosario, but I had left it too late. I was incapable of going anywhere.

Now and then, I dragged myself to the bathroom, and once or twice I made it downstairs for food and water. Most of time, I had no idea of the time, or even if it was day or night.

I saw each of the children first. Ghostly apparitions of girls of varying ages dressed in dated frocks. I thought I might have been hallucinating. I was too ill to feel scared of them. Standing by my bed, they looked forlorn, haunted, withdrawn, heads bowed. The eldest three avoided my gaze. They seemed shy. But not that shy since they wanted me to see them.

The youngest was more confident. She locked gazes with me as she sucked her thumb and whimpered. She brought chill air with her. Yet I didn't feel frightened in her presence either. I was consumed by sadness. Nothing more.

The mother had a cowering, imploring look about her. I recognised her as the woman in the photo Paco had taken of the patio, the same woman who had appeared at my car window. She seemed to want to communicate. She reached out to me, as though to pull my hand, but I couldn't get up.

Seeing I wasn't moving she grew agitated, wringing her hands. A door slammed somewhere in the house and then I heard footsteps, heavy and slow, climbing the stairs.

The woman vanished. The next instant the ghost of Señor Baraso stood over me, staring into my face, his own riven with anger. He had an intimidating look about him. As he hovered I took in the set to his jaw, his moustache and unkempt hair. The temperature of the room dropped dramatically. Only then did I react, pulling the covers up under my chin, shifting my body to the other side of the bed.

A piercing scream echoed around the house. Baraso turned away and disappeared. I didn't imagine he would be gone for long.

Footsteps clomped down the stairs. There was a long pause in which I sat up in bed, wondering what I should do. I coughed, violently, over and again, then sneezed and groaned.

More screams, childlike and high-ptiched screams that went on and on. I ought to have issued a scream of my own but when I tried I found I had no voice.

The screams turned into yells and a commotion of activity started, involving running, lots of running between rooms.

Was I imagining all this?

The bedside lamp did not come on when I pressed the switch. I groped around among tissues and bottles and blister packs for my phone. When my hand touched the cool glass screen, I exhaled in relief. In its torchlight, I swung out of bed and slipped on my bathrobe and mules.

Outside my room, the commotion was escalating. There were bonks that made the floorboards tremble. The clatter of china as a tray was carried by someone with an unsteady hand. I opened the door, thinking I would be better off in another part of the house.

I went and stood on the balcony and shone the torch around. The patio was empty. The ghosts were not making themselves visible. Then the woman appeared right beside me. I jumped, startled. She stepped forward and tugged at my arm. I resisted, pulling away. She gave up and leaned against the railing pointing down at a spot in the patio, then she looked back over at me and our eyes met. I shone the torch at her face. She didn't squint. She was trying to communicate something with those eyes.

She then walked away. I followed her with my torchlight. I heard footsteps on the stairs. Shining the light at the patio, I watched her cross. She stopped in the centre near where the hole in the partition wall had been, and where the ground had been left thus far untouched. She pointed at the ground at her feet and then looked up at me, her demeanour changing from anguish to purposeful intent.

I saw it then, the reason for the distress, and I knew without needing an explanation what I had to do to bring the haunting to an end. The youngest child had started her whimpering. The sound was coming from the top of the balcony stairs. I walked towards the sound, shivering as the air grew cold. I sensed her sisters nearby. I could feel their distress. Would any of them try to stop me? I wasn't sure. Perhaps there wasn't a consensus amongst them. Maybe some wanted me to follow their mother's wishes and others did not, preferring another hundred years of haunting.

My feet felt leaden and I was burning up, but I kept walking. Gripping the rail and taking it a tread at a time, I descended the stairs. I expected a shove but none came. Not one of my paranormal companions stopped me heading outside to the barn and returning with a garden fork and shovel.

Where had Señor Baraso got to?

I had little strength but a frantic will consumed me. I was sick, yes very sick, but I was even more tired of the haunting. I ought to have been terrified but I wasn't. I tried the lights and found the power was back on. Making the most of the illumination, I switched on all the patio lights. Then I went to the spot Señora Baraso had indicated and I plunged the fork into the ground with all the strength I had.

A few hard stabs and the surface soil was loose enough to shovel. I used the fork to loosen some more. I forked and I shovelled, aiming for a hole about a yard wide. Any larger, and I would run out of stamina.

The going was hard but I persisted, alternating between tools. Every two shovels I had to break for a short rest. Now and then I had to stop for a good long cough. I was aching and feverish but determination had a hold of me and I was not going to stop.

The going became easier once I had shovelled down about two feet and I found I was removing not subsoil but topsoil. Someone had been here before me.

My digging became more urgent. At one point, my fork stabbed something hard. I shovelled around and found there was a large boulder situated at the edge near the aljibe. I avoided the boulder as I dug.

Down and down I dug. Before long, I had to step into the hole and shovel the dirt out from the centre. Then I attacked the sides. Eventually, after digging and resting and digging and resting the spade hit something soft.

I put down the shovel and knelt down on both knees, brushing away the soil with my bare hands.

My fingers touched cloth. I leaned down further and used both hands to pull at the fabric. A few firm tugs and it gave way.

The cloth served as wrapping. Gingerly, I unfolded it. I sensed by the weight and feel what it was and when at last the cloth fell away, I gazed, horrified and satisfied all at once. It was a skull. A small skull. The skull of a child. My hands were shaking. I quickly wrapped it back up and placed it down carefully beside the hole. My own bones ached as I stood.

I stepped out of the hole. I needed to think things through and act, act fast, but I was caught up in a strange mix of immobilising terror and morbid fascination. My head swam. I felt faint and unsteady. I was burning up.

I needed to phone someone. Paco? The police? I looked around for my phone. I saw it beside the fork on the other side of the hole. I was about to go and grab it when all went black.

It took me a while to process that it was still night and the lights had gone out. I had unearthed the dead in the dark. Not the best plan. Maybe it would be daylight soon. Would that make a difference?

The air temperature plummeted. I knew in a flash that Baraso was back.

The next second I felt a thump on my shoulders and I lurched forwards. Another thump and I stumbled and fell into the hole of bones.

Dread sped through me. I scrambled to get out. Hearing the crunch and rattle of the bones beneath me I knew I had fallen on top of the grave, the grave with six bodies buried, and my first thought was I did not want to break any of those bones.

I manoeuvred myself with care, placing a hand here a foot there, hoping to avoid causing more damage. I was almost on all fours. Before I could get my body in a position from which to stand, I was kicked in the face from above.

Hard boot met with soft cheek, and then with ear and with chin, and I keeled to protect my face. My body took the form of a turtle. It was not the ideal position, I soon found, as the boot landed on my back in the area of my kidney, sending sharp pain right through me.

There was a long pause. I panted and cowered. I thought the attack might be over. If it was, I had to get out of the hole.

I rose slowly, cautious, and eased myself up. My head swam. I was sweating. I sat down heavily at the edge of the hole, thinking I should stand and leave the patio as fast as I was able. But I couldn't see. The darkness was thick. I desperately needed my phone. I started to scramble for it in the dirt around me. All I felt were small stones.

My heart was galloping but my body cooled enough for me to realise I was still in an icy pool of air.

There was a scream. A long, piercing scream and it sounded close. I wanted to leap up. I had to leap up. I had to at least try to get out of the house. As I drew my legs up and out of the hole, cold hands gripped my throat.

The pressure on my throat was strong. I reached up with my hands and clutched at nothing. I struggled to get free but he was too strong. I could scarcely breathe. My heart felt it was about to explode in my chest. My neck was on fire and throbbed all at once.

Desperation shaded into panic. He was going to kill me. I was dying and there was nothing I could do to stop it. I writhed but I had little strength.

I felt myself drifting, fading, slipping, falling.

I passed out.

32

RECOVERY

ALARM SHOT THROUGH ME WHEN I AWOKE TO FIND ANOTHER FACE hovering over me. Who was it this time? Slowly I saw that it was Paco gazing down at me, smiling, a look of relief in his eyes. He was holding my hand. He leaned down and kissed my cheek.

'Thank god,' he murmured.

Yes, I thought, thank god, the universe, whoever, but where was I?

I looked around at the sterile white of a modern hospital room, at the drip stand by my side. Why was I here?

Memories returned, gradual at first, then in a gush and I was back in the grave I had unearthed in my patio, a grave of old bones, a grave I had dug for myself. I remembered digging, falling, no, being pushed in. Strangled. Then, nothing. All was blank. Had I been lying in that grave all night?

I couldn't have been unconscious for long. The flu still had me in its grip. My throat felt like someone had gone at it with sandpaper. My neck throbbed. Swallowing was agony. I moved and winced.

'You broke an arm,' he said.

I did? How? I must have fallen on that boulder.

'I saw a ghost.' My voice croaked and was barely audible. 'So many ghosts.'

'Sh. Not now. You're safe. Olivia Stone was protecting you, I think.'

I groaned.

A look of concern appeared in his face. 'What is it?'

'Not Olivia Stone,' I rasped.

He seemed puzzled. We stayed together like that, with me lying on my back and him beside me, neither of us speaking. Eventually, I whispered, 'Who found me?'

'I did. The trip was shortened. I went to my apartment and found you weren't there so I drove to the house. It was before dawn, but I thought I would surprise you. Only, it was me who was surprised.'

Later, when I had gained some strength and felt able to sit up, I told Paco in short phrases the information I had been holding back for months. I owed him the truth. He listened with patience to my circuitous preamble, trying to make me stop for the sake of my throat, but I wouldn't. I told him it was important. Then, I came out with the first of my hard facts.

'Olivia Stone died in Bedford in 1897. I have a copy of the death certificate.'

A look of disbelief came into his face. Then he seemed confused.

'Then she was not a recluse living in Casa Baraso.'

'No, she wasn't.'

'That does not mean she didn't stay in that house.'

'There is no record of her ever having stayed there.'

'But the Stones returned to the islands twice on follow up research trips. They may have stayed at your house then. After all, they were friends with Marcial Cabrera of Tiscamanita and they called their home "Fuerteventura".'

I cringed. It was easier telling Paco about her death. 'They didn't. Paco, they called their house "Lanzarote". I should have told you when I found out. I can prove I am right. Aunt Clarissa did all the research.'

He looked crestfallen.

'Then that article was wrong,' he said slowly.

'I'm so sorry, but she never came to live here. She stayed in England with her husband and their three sons and she died at forty. Where's my phone?'

He passed it to me. A few swipes and taps and I showed him the

Census entry and death certificate. It didn't take him long to assimi-late the information. I thought he would have railed against the truth, but I had misjudged him. First, he scoffed at himself for believing the article and not fact checking. That was when I saw he wasn't as attached to his fantasy as I had imagined. The only elephant in the room was the one I had put there.

Then he laughed and said, 'It was fun while it lasted, I guess.'

'I don't follow,' I said coolly.

He cringed. 'I never really thought Olivia Stone had lived in your house. I just made it up to tease you.'

'You did what!' I coughed, wincing at the pain that shot through my throat.

'Take it easy,' he said. I settled back on my pillows and he went on. 'At first, I wanted to toy with you a little. Then I wanted to entice you. Without that story, you would not have bothered finding out about Olivia Stone, or her book. You bought into my theory and kept asking questions and I could hardly turn around and tell you I had made it all up. You would have thought I was nuts and I would have blown my ruse.'

'But you *did* have me thinking you were nuts.'

'The joke is on me, then. I didn't mean for it to get this far. After I took that photo of the woman in the partition, I had even started to wonder if I was right after all. I'm sorry, Claire, I never realised you were taking me as seriously as all this.' He gestured with my phone before putting it down on the bedside table.

'I am a serious person.'

'That I am discovering.' He smiled at me. 'And bull-headed.'

As a nurse entered the room, Paco kissed me goodbye and said he would be back to take me home.

The following afternoon, I returned to Casa Bennett, to a giant hole in the patio and a mountain of dirt beside it. There were men everywhere, packing up for the day. Seeing me arrive, Helmud came and told me the remains had been taken away for investigation and then they would be buried in Tenerife, where the family came from.

Paco already knew.

He had cut out all the press articles and I read them while he made chicken soup, glancing up now and then to watch him prepare it, marvelling at him marvelling at my kitchen. He was a delight to watch.

Later, Paco opened his laptop and paired it to my sound bar. He told me to listen as he put on a band called Taburiente. The music sounded as dated as the Cocteau Twins and I loved it. The vocals soared, the melodies were moving and evocative and I enjoyed knowing I was listening to local music for a change. The songs made me imagine the islands, the culture and traditions.

When the album ended I realised I hadn't told him the other news I had been holding back for months.

'I never did tell you about the weird lights I saw.'

He looked up. 'Lights?'

'That night when I came here to see if there was an intruder. After that guy, Cliff, had his tools relocated. I was about to leave when this weird light rose up out of the patio and started darting about. That one was red. Another light, blue this time, rose up out of the outbuilding I used for my rustic shower room. That light was crazy, zigzagging all over the place. It even bounced off my chest before zooming up to the sky.'

'That was months ago,' he said reproachfully. 'You were still renting that apartment. Why didn't you tell me?'

'It happened again. While you were asleep downstairs. Our first night together, it was.'

He looked at me with genuine regard. 'Astonishing.'

'What's astonishing?'

'That you, a foreigner, should have seen those lights.'

'What do you mean?' I said doubtfully.

'It's a local myth called The Light of Mafasca.'

'Another of your tall tales?'

'This one is real. Or at least, many say so. You can read up about it if you like.'

'Tell me.'

I waited while he gathered his thoughts.

'Legend has it, a group of shepherds were walking home after a long day in the mountains. Tired and hungry, they agreed to rest and make a fire and roast the ram they had killed that day. As they were collecting wood, one of the shepherds found a large wooden cross hidden behind a bush. He knew someone had died in that place.

'Now, firewood was hard to find, so as night fell, the shepherds decided to take advantage of the cross to feed their little fire, hoping to fill their bellies and get warm.

'When the flames had devoured most of the cross, a tiny light, little more than a spark, sprang from the fire and began to move among the shepherds. At first, they were puzzled. Then they were terrified. The light leapt around from one shepherd to another, as though it had a life of its own. And they realised it was the light of the soul of the person buried behind the bush. By taking the cross and setting it on fire, those men had disturbed that soul's slumber, destroying the only memory still linking the soul to the human world.'

'Are you saying those lights I saw were the lights of those ghosts?'

'Maybe. Or maybe they were the lights of an ancient soul buried on your property long before your house was built.'

'What happened to the shepherds?'

'They bolted in terror. Ever since, that restless soul, taking the form of this spark of light, appears to travellers passing through unpopulated areas around Antigua on dark and clear nights. Legend has it the light is bright and always has a strong colour – blue, yellow, green or red—and is similar to a cigarette alight in the dark. Sometimes, the light can reach a large size before returning to its usual small point. Everyone who has seen it says the light moves in an intelligent way as if it were conscious. It can stay still, or accelerate, all of a sudden.'

'So, it had nothing to do with the ghosts of the Baraso family.'

'No, other than that it might have been trying to warn you.'

I let it go. I wanted to allow Paco his metaphysical fantasies in the same way that I wanted Clarissa to have hers. After all, I could not quibble with them when I knew that the spirit world existed and if the terror of recent months had taught me anything, it was that.

Besides, I had made up my mind that I wanted Paco in my life as a fixture.

I was hesitant asking him to move in with me in case it dented his male ego, but a week later, when he told me the lease on his apartment would not be renewed, the owners preferring the temptation of the lucrative holiday let, I begged him to come and stay at mine. 'Until you find something else,' I said, but we both knew that was never going to happen.

Over breakfast the next day, we discussed the house and what I planned doing with it in the future. I still had no idea. 'Make use of as much of the space as you want,' I told him. To my ears, the remark sounded flippant.

He was tentative.

'Please,' I added.

'I can make use of your two dark rooms downstairs.'

'I thought photography was all digital these days.'

He laughed. 'I would love to have a dark room. And a studio.'

'Then consider those rooms yours.'

'Are you sure?'

'I cannot think of a better use for them.'

'That only leaves five vacant bedrooms.'

'I am not opening this house up to paying guests,' I said, all uppity and defiant. 'Besides, it will be good to have a couple of spare rooms for visitors.'

'Leaving three rooms spare.'

'A sewing room. A writing room. A painting room.'

'Are you serious?'

'Hell, I don't know. I don't see myself sewing or writing or painting but those are the sorts of things people do with rooms.'

'Or hold séances.'

'Séances! You are joking.'

'You are a medium. You just don't want to acknowledge it.'

I rebelled against the word, the concepts, the occult altogether. Yet he was right. Those ghosts had all communicated with me in the end. But I would not want to put myself at such risk and I certainly wasn't about to host ghost tours in my own home.

· · ·

My arm was out of plaster when Clarissa arrived for Christmas. The broken radius was still giving me twinges, especially when I drove, but otherwise I was fine. The first thing she said when I met her at the airport was that I looked like a skeleton. I had lost two whole dress sizes since moving to Fuerteventura, but it took her a few moments to realise the implications of what she had said and we both laughed about it on the way to Tiscamanita.

She adored the house the moment I slowed to mount the kerb and pointed out the various features. By then, all the scaffolding had been removed, the building fully restored and painted and all that was left to do was erect a garage and work on the garden. Paco had finished repairing the wall at the back and we had begun marking out garden beds and planting up the areas around the house and barn. I had decided to leave the other two outbuildings for the time being, as relics of a long and disturbing history. They looked quaint now we were using them as infrastructure to shelter herbs and vegetables and fruit trees.

'I wasn't expecting it to be green,' she said, taking in the scenery as I showed her around.

'Sometimes it is. We've had some rain.'

'I can see why you wanted to come here. This is magnificent.'

'I'm glad you think so.'

We entered through the back door and, starting with the upstairs, I showed Clarissa around the house. She cooed as she entered each of the rooms, taking on all the details of the décor and furnishings.

'You have done a grand job, Claire, you really have.'

I swelled with pride.

'This room is yours,' I said. I'd installed her in the bedroom above the main living room. It was light-filled and looked out over the garden.

She swept her arms wide and said, 'So much space! You may have trouble getting your guests to leave if you put them in here.'

'You are welcome to be here for as long as you want.'

'That isn't what I was intimating, but I will surely be enticed to come back.'

It was a remark that made me glow inside. I led her downstairs.

'What's in here?' she said, approaching the original dining room.

'Paco's studio.'

'Better not enter, then,' she said with a chuckle. I took her through to the south-facing living room and as we sat down, Paco sung out from the patio.

'We're in here,' I called.

Clarissa stood and faced the door, her demeanour filled with anticipation. I watched them both closely as they greeted each other and I was relieved to see sparkling eyes and looks of real appreciation. Paco came over and kissed me as well.

'Wine?'

He withdrew from the room, appearing moments later with two glasses and a bottle of Lanzarote white.

'Are you not joining us?' Clarissa said, looking into his face as she took the glass he proffered.

'There are the groceries to unpack and the food to prepare.'

She shot me a look of amused surprise and I met it with a grin.

'You have him well trained, then,' Clarissa said once we were alone.

'He just does it.'

We sat back in our seats and soaked in the festive atmosphere. I'd bought a small Christmas tree and created a festive centrepiece for the marble coffee table. Garbed in a rich red skirt suit with matching scarf, Clarissa added to the sense of yuletide cheer. She ran her hand down the arm of her chair, admiring the fabric – it was a gold damask. She asked me how I was spending my days now the ruin was restored and I told her of my Saturdays at the library in Tuineje, where I sat chatting with ten others about computers and smart phones and other technology in a class designed to help rural women get to grips with the modern age.

'You could probably run the course,' Clarissa said.

'But I wouldn't want to. I'm having far too much fun getting to know everyone.'

We exchanged smiles. I had formed an especially close bond with Gloria, who enjoyed showing me off as the woman who had banished the Barasos. I was something of a local celebrity, although I had done nothing other than almost get myself killed.

The conversation drifted to my father, who we both agreed would never change, and on to my account of the tribulations of restoring a ruin, finally halting at the inevitable topic of the haunting.

'The thing that I ask myself is, why me? Why was I drawn to this house and why did all those ghosts appear to me?'

'That is a lot of whys and requires unpacking. To start with, you brought with you the anguish over the loss of your mother.'

'I never knew how much her loss affected me,' I said quietly.

'It was how you lost her.'

'I know.'

'And your unresolved grief connected you, made you a conduit for the anguish of the spirits.'

It made sense. Even my own reason couldn't argue with her remark. I didn't have a reply. I now had few memories of my childhood when my mother was alive. I could only hope more would return, one day.

She took a sip of her wine and gave me a sideways stare. Her face darkened.

'I did try to warn you when I read the astrocartography.'

'You never mentioned a thing about the spirit world.'

'I didn't want to scare you. And besides, you wouldn't have believed me.'

'I believe you now.'

She nodded sagely. 'You are a natural. I always knew it.'

'Paco says the same.'

'He's a good man.'

'You've only just met him.'

'I can tell.'

She probably could.

'We're producing a booklet on the story of this house,' I volunteered, explaining that it would be a keepsake, nothing more.

'It would interest a lot of people,' she said. 'You should think about a print run.'

Typical Clarissa. I supposed she thought I would include the details of the ghosts. She would be telling me to host ghost tours next. Thankfully, there were no ghosts in Casa Bennett, not any more, not since the bones had been relocated.

I wondered which one of the Barasos had moved my rocky memento, from the shelf to the floor, and from the kitchen cupboard to the front door. The mother, had to be. She had been trying to warn me, even protect me.

What about my own mother? Where was she – earthbound, or free?

The setting sun threw shafts of warm light into the room. I topped up our glasses and we sipped our wine and sat quietly in admiration. When it was dark enough, I went and switched on the lights. Clarissa changed the mood by getting up unexpectedly and walking out the door. Curious, I followed.

When I got to the doorway she was creeping across the patio.

Paco came out from the kitchen and we exchanged glances. I shrugged and followed her. He joined me.

By the time we reached the vestibule she had pushed open the living-room door. Paco was about to follow but I put out an arm.

Before long, she exited and stood at the bottom of the stairs. Her face wore a curious expression, part wonder, part astonishment.

'Those are the two rooms you inhabited when you first moved on site?' she asked me.

'Yes,' I said slowly. 'Why do you ask?'

She gave us both a devilish grin and said, 'We've got company.'

ACKNOWLEDGMENTS

I am enormously grateful to J F Olivares, a photographer and artist indigenous to Fuerteventura who I became friends with when I was first researching this novel and whose photos, links and stories of his island, along with our mutual affection for travel writer, Olivia Stone, proved a major source of inspiration. I share with Juan an enduring passion for the precious island of Fuerteventura, where long ago I almost lived. Through Juan's generosity and enthusiasm, I have been able to reclaim lost memories and capture something of the essence of an island that is too often known only for its idyllic beaches.

My sincere thanks to Miika Hannila and the team at Next Chapter publishing for having faith in my writing and nurturing its progress through to publication.

In my Canary Island series, I write from the perspective of tourists and British migrants (expats) but I always include a local character or two and I do my best within the confines of fiction to help raise awareness of the islands' special history, culture and environment.

Some historical notes: I would like to thank Susan Middleton and the 1841-1939 Beyond Genealogy Discussion Group of Facebook for helping me research Victorian travel writer Olivia Mary Stone. I am also grateful to Daniel García Pulido for his biographical article of Olivia Stone in La Prensa del Domingo, El Día, which can be accessed here - http://eldia.es/laprensa/wp-content/uploads/2015/02/20150215laprensa.pdf

There is a rule of thumb in fiction, it goes like this – If you want there to be a bakery between the butcher and the greengrocer, put one there. I've transplanted a magnificent building in La Oliva, Casa del Inglés, changed its dimensions and situated it in Tiscamanita. I kept the dividing wall, as it proved a major source of inspiration. The wall was built to separate the building in half as part of an inheritance. I also borrowed the fact that the owner of Casa del Inglés was reluctant to sell the ruin to local government.

A PRISON IN THE SUN

CANARY ISLANDS MYSTERIES BOOK 3

For Chris Roy

And in memory of Octavio Garcia, a former prisoner of Colonia Agrícola Penitenciaria in Tefía, Fuerteventura, who campaigned for justice and whose testimony enabled the terrible story of this concentration camp to be known.

AUTHOR NOTE

I wrote *A Prison in the Sun* to honour and remember all those men imprisoned under General Franco's regime because they were gay. On Fuerteventura, where this story is set, prison conditions were brutal and likened to a concentration camp. To the best of my knowledge, nothing substantial about this prison has been written in English. All of my research I conducted in Spanish. In 2008 the story of the prison broke after professor Miguel Ángel Sosa Machín interviewed prison survivor, Octavia Garcia. I have known of the prison's existence since 1989, when I lived in Lanzarote and my close friends from the island told me what went on there.

I have purposefully juxtaposed life in the prison with that of the present day, counterpointing the gravity of the prisoners' situation with a touch of bathos in the main narrative, striving not only for balance, but also to entice reflection on who we were, who we are, and where we want to be.

A Prison in the Sun is my fourth Canary Islands' novel and was written in keeping with that narrative style.

I offer the following story in all sincerity.

PART I

1

THE FARMHOUSE

THE FARMHOUSE HAD WALLS THREE FEET THICK, A STAUNCH REMINDER of what it took to live around there and what I refused to get used to: the wind, the dust, the heat, the excoriating sun. I've been on the island two and a half weeks, and I am still not sure what attracts visitors to that locale. The island itself, I can understand. Winter sun, beaches galore, plenty of space and a safe, laid-back atmosphere. It's the Canary Islands' tourist mecca of Fuerteventura. Most of the tourists are corralled in enclaves along the east coast. There, on that barren plain where the ocean views are cut off by hills, and a range of mountains separates the inhabitants from the more populated areas, there cannot be described as anything other than inhospitable. Yet there people dwell; the holiday let, the last of a smattering of farmhouses that calls itself a village: Tefia.

My island getaway.

A rational choice at the time I booked. A Friday, as I recall, and a dreary English afternoon in June, the sun struggling to send its light through layers and layers of cloud. In my cramped one-bedroom flat, ignoring the windows fogging and the radio that the tenant below insisted on playing all day and half the night, I surveyed the island onscreen and considered my criteria. I wanted no beach, no people, no noise, no distractions. A list of negatives, true, but I had enough mayhem going on inside me without suffering the usual gamut of holiday amusements. I wanted a retreat, and I was booking a holiday for good reason. I was booking a holiday to straighten myself out.

When I studied the photos of the holiday let, the numerous small and neatly furnished rooms that appeared to be arranged around an internal patio, the shuttered casements, the beam ceilings, the four-poster bed and claw-foot bath, I thought I had stumbled on the perfect accommodation, if a little large for one person. Views of tawny mountains beneath brilliant skies drew me too. I overlooked the obvious fact that such a photograph would not convey the harsh-ness of a landscape. In all, I didn't give the matter another thought. Impatient, I booked the flights and accommodation in under an hour and went out in the dismal rain to buy a new suitcase and a bottle of Sancerre to celebrate.

A week later I boarded the plane, endured the plastic seats and the crush of bodies in the cabin and, five hours later, collected a hire car at the airport. Fuerteventura greeted me with thirty-five-degree summer heat. I had to locate the car somewhere in a glare of metal and tarmac as I broke out in a sudden sweat.

I extracted the mud map I had drawn on a paper serviette back at Gatwick airport – consisting of three spidery lines and a couple of intersections – and used that rather than GPS to navigate my way the twenty miles to Tefía.

Beyond the bustle of the coastal strip, the island bared its authentic self. For the duration of the drive, through nothing but dry earth and rock and low barren mountains, I allowed in a curious fascination, the larger part of me remaining disturbed by the strange desert landscape.

A final bend and I headed north across a plain, following the line of the mountains to the east. When I saw the Tefía sign, I slowed, knowing my accommodation was close, keeping an eye out for the cottage, spotting its drive.

Stationary at last, I opened the car door on a light breeze. The temperature was not much cooler up on the plain. Looking back the way I'd come, I noticed a haze on the eastern horizon. Dust? I had read something on one of the tourist websites about the Saharan dust.

The farmhouse was stout and quaint, with a flat roof and small, multi-paned windows positioned randomly in walls protected by verandas. There was no house on the other side of the drive, and behind the farmhouse was a field. Other houses were scattered about haphazardly.

I hefted my luggage out of the boot, found the keys under the doormat and let myself in.

The interior was cool, the air freshened with a flowery perfume. I dumped my suitcase and rucksack in the first room I entered and explored the layout of the place – rooms leading on to others, the occasional dead end – ending up in the kitchen where a hamper had been left out on the bench.

Curious, I unpacked the goodies, only to find that everything came in pairs, including two flutes for the champagne. At the sight of the holiday accoutrements of coupledom, a disconsolate hand fisted my insides. I headed to the main bedroom to find two chocolates centred on the coverlet of the four-poster bed. Love hearts in pink wrapping. By now the fist had reached my throat, and I let out a whimper and couldn't hold back a rush of tears.

I'm a man not given to emotion and I made every effort to curb the flow, but I admit it felt good to cry a little, or even a lot. I guess I hadn't faced up to my aloneness until it was so caringly thrust in my face.

The hamper kept me in provisions for the first two days of my stay. The thoughtful owners were not to know how relieved I was not to have to leave the farmhouse. I wanted to venture out and explore my surroundings, but I had arrived with a backlog of work and needed to rid myself of the burden as fast as possible.

I'm a freelance ghostwriter– not my chosen career, if such a job can be called a career. I knock out memoirs, finish novels, write articles, create blog and website content – non-fiction pieces on health and diet, top tips and travel pieces – and even the occasional short story. The last won the author a prize. I give other people voices, help them to communicate whatever they need to say. I work for small businesses and corporations and writers with more wealth than ability. On some level, it is satisfying work and I am proud to say I make a decent living out of it, but at that moment when I arrived in Fuerteventura, I had begun to feel stale.

I had an article to write for a fitness website, five blog posts to compose for various companies – the sorts of posts I churn out with ease, making for a half-decent hourly rate – and a short story to complete for a woman who couldn't conjure an ending. And I could see why – she was white and British and had crossed the cultural-appropriation line by choosing to be an indigenous Australian. Worse, she was writing in the first person, a culturally sensitive move, and she had entered dangerous post-Shriver territory. I felt uncomfortable maintaining the pretence she had created, but she was paying handsomely, and I could always do with the cash and besides, no one would know of my involvement. My name would not appear anywhere on the finished piece.

Being a ghost has some advantages.

The work kept me indoors staring at my laptop. I was so caught up in the backlog, I barely took my eyes off the screen. I might as well have been back in my crummy flat in West London.

On the second day, as the hours slid by, irritation gnawed at me. I had saved the short story till last and I found myself trudging through Australian desert scrub in the searing heat, acutely aware of a similar landscape outside my front door, sweating as the day grew hotter, reminding myself the protagonist would probably not be suffering as I was, probably not feeling sticky and irritable; she was probably entirely at ease as the sun blazed down, but what would I know? Do indigenous Australians get sunburnt? Do indigenous Australians suffer heatstroke? The Internet didn't seem to know. I felt rude, possibly racist even asking.

I managed to insert the paragraphs the draft had been lacking and polish the ending which had lacked pizzazz, but when I hit Save and then Send, I reminded myself freelancing was not what I had come here for and I needed to set up some boundaries, ignore the ghost-writing jobs filling my Inbox.

I had booked a three-month stay because I thought that would be ample time to write something in my own right. No better way to smooth out the battle scars of life and find inner peace than compose a book-length work of fiction in monastic isolation far away from one's regular life.

The writer's retreat.

Most writers on retreat already have a clear idea of what they plan to work on. I did not. I knew what the novel would not concern. I would not draw on my own experiences, recent or from my child-hood. I was emphatic about that. I would leave self-cannibalisation to others. Neither would I delve into the genres. I would compose something literary, contemporary, with a hint of history. I wasn't thinking about sales or prizes. I wanted the satisfaction of seeing my own name on the cover. I wanted to call myself an author.

My problem, therefore, was that of the blank page. I lacked inspiration and had no idea where to look to find it. All I knew was that I would not find that inspiration inside of me. I had nothing in my makeup that would form the basis of a good story, period.

I spent the rest of the day pacing around the farmhouse, standing in the various rooms, trying to imagine who had lived there. A large family. Farmers. Traditional people. Boring. The afternoon faded into evening and I hadn't so much as conjured a character.

Early the following morning, finding I had eaten the entire contents of the hamper, I ventured into the village, taking advantage of the relative cool of the day. The walk took me past a few shabby-looking dwellings – white cuboids with shuttered windows, austere, no frills – the bulk of the village spread higgledy-piggledy to either side of the arterial road.

The shop was located at the other end of the village, set back from the road opposite a bus shelter. Inside, the shelves were surprisingly well-stocked. I bought local bread, cheese, tomatoes, onions, garlic and eggs, along with a length of chorizo, two tins of tuna and three bottles of a promising-sounding red. The woman who served me was friendly, and I gave her my warmest smile. A benevolent soul, her broad face beamed into mine, but I was unable to understand a thing she said. I extracted my wallet and held out what I thought was near enough the correct amount. She took the notes to the till drawer and then placed a few coins in my palm. Gracias, I said, no doubt appallingly. De nada. Then, 'See you later', which she delivered in a staccato monotone, and I could tell we shared the same handicap.

In the time it had taken to shop, the sun had gathered its forces and now had a bite to it. On the walk back to the house, all of five minutes, I was buffeted along by a bossy breeze.

The mountains held my attention. I vaguely enjoyed picking out the various shades of pale brown.

In Fuerteventura, the eye has no choice but to attune to the colour brown and discern the nuances. Perhaps we are predisposed to find beauty wherever we can, but it would be stretching the concept to describe the landscape around Tefía beautiful. It was anything but. 'Desolate' best labels the place. and I was relieved to find myself back at the farmhouse, which already felt like a sanctuary against the elements.

Surveying my meagre purchases, realising they would get me past lunch and possibly dinner but little further, and knowing I didn't plan on popping up to the local shop every day, I decided to do a proper grocery shop that afternoon. After all, I thought, I had a hire car and planned on using it.

I found Internet reception up at Tefía excellent. I jumped online and had no trouble locating a decent-sized supermarket. I had two options to choose from. I could head north to Lajares or south to Antigua, either route an easy drive through open country. I chose the southern route as it was a good deal shorter. After lunching on a baguette filled with cheese, tuna and thick slices of onion and tomato, a combination that proved tricky to eat, I wrote a comprehensive shopping list. I thought through all my needs and wants, and wrote them down in discrete groupings: dry goods, tins, deli, meats, frozen and fresh veg.

I'm one of those house husbands accustomed to the grocery shop. I'm not a browser and I do not dilly dally. I like to be in and out in the fastest possible time. It is something of a sport with me. A game. I have never resorted to a stopwatch, I wouldn't take it that far, but it brings out my competitive side, and I am proud to think how efficient I am. The only challenge I faced this time was the language. I needed to get past the basic level of my free, online language course if I was to be anything other than mute when it came to communicating with the natives.

The drive proved more pleasing than anticipated. There are some fetching vistas along the way heading south, and the barren landscape did begin to hold some appeal, if only through the sheer sameness of it. Round every bend, more bone-dry fields and barren mountains. And the mountains stole the attention yet again. None of them are all that high, but their shapes are visible in their entirety, there being nothing growing on their flanks. That day, I found there was something absorbing about them on an aesthetic level, and I felt the faint stirrings of the muse. Although I would need a lot more inspiration than a landscape could provide, no matter how inhospitable or starkly magnificent, before I could even begin to think about writing a novel.

In Antigua, the supermarket was easy to find. I was in and out in under half an hour with a boot load. As I opened the driver's side door I knew that next time, I would have that half hour reduced to twenty minutes; I would write my shopping list in the order of the aisles.

I felt triumphant on the drive home. I didn't even mind the heat.

There is something comforting about a well-stocked fridge and pantry, the thought that there is no need to leave the house. Liberating, too, leaving me free to think over important matters. Above all, if I went out, I wanted it to be for something pleasurable, something interesting. Not for a chore.

With the groceries all put away, I stared into the hours of nothing ahead and wondered how I would fill the time. I felt like talking to someone, but in those first days of my stay I refrained from letting Jackie and the kids or even my best friend, Angela, know my superb connectivity, preferring to let them think I had adopted a hermit style of existence and had committed myself to silence. Let them wonder how I was faring. Let them all miss me.

As I wandered from room to room, I began to relish the solitude. It was refreshing having space around me, both inside the house and out on the plain, space that acted as a salve. I sat down in one room then another, spending a sufficient period out in the internal patio as was good for my health. I must have occupied every seat in the place by the end of the afternoon, and I deposited something of mine – a book, a magazine, a device – in every room, carefully centred on a table or poised on the arm of a chair.

That evening, the sunset was tremendous. Bands of deep crimson swept across the sky, distracting me as I prepared a chorizo and pasta bake. When the dish was in the oven, I poured a large glass of red and then stood at the kitchen window and sipped the wine as I watched the changing colours, the deepening, the fading into night.

I took much pleasure later that evening gazing at the stars. The sky was especially clear, and after spotting the firmament in the portion afforded by the patio, I went and stood outdoors and soaked in the twinkling pinpricks in their various arrangements, a reminder of the wonders of the universe unknown to us in daylight. Eventually, I felt sleepy and took myself to bed.

The bedroom, with its four-poster bed centred against the eastern wall, was the defining feature of the farmhouse. The décor was pleasing, blocks of strong colour, no frills, no lace. In those early days of my stay, I enjoyed being in that room. I had never slept in a four-poster before, and I went to sleep each night feeling like a king.

The next day, I awoke at sunrise. I sat up in bed and then went and gazed out the window. I found the view nothing to speak of save for a lonely windmill perched on a rise in the mid-distance. A stout affair, probably not in use, its blades appearing still in the wind. It being the only feature of interest beyond the farmhouse walls, my gaze remained drawn, and I pressed my face against the glass as though to get closer.

My curiosity grew stronger, and I felt compelled to unearth the windmill's secrets. What was its story? It must have one. A story tied to the ancient history of the island and local farming practices. Not exactly fuel for any sort of story I might compose, but then again, I shouldn't prejudge. Besides, there was no telling what I might find there that might stimulate inspiration – a fallen handkerchief, a dropped wallet, the chip of some artefact, anything at all that would provoke that inner spark.

Having reasoned things through, I determined to venture forth across the dusty plain and investigate.

2

THE WINDMILL

I WAS A MAN ON A MISSION. MY FIRST REAL EXPLORATION OF WHAT THE island had to offer and despite the short distance, the walk to the windmill felt like an expedition. I needed to be prepared. Above all, I need sustenance.

After diving into a tub of strawberry yoghurt, I scoffed a bowl of cold pasta bake, leftovers from the night before. Then I washed up the spoons and the bowl and left them to drain, took a cool shower and donned joggers, shorts and a t-shirt. Tourist attire. I couldn't help but be aware of how white my skin looked. I gazed in horror in the bedroom mirror at two spindly legs and a pair of flaccid arms poking out the limb holes of my apparel. I was carrying much too much flesh around my middle. Flesh that was covered by my t-shirt but not obscured.

I sucked in my paunch with self-disgust. I had let myself go. Middle-age spread had arrived far too early. I was a heart attack in the making, gurney material, destined for an early grave. Too many nights watching Netflix while downing red wine. Wake up to yourself, Trevor Moore!

Worse, I hadn't got laid in how long? A year? More like two, and little wonder. I was a porker.

After making the bed, which I was unable to leave in disarray, I shoved my feet into a pair of plimsolls and headed off armed with only a water bottle, determined to make the most of the vast, empty outdoors.

The pavement was narrow, but at least there was one. The wind came up behind me, cool on my skin, nudging me along. The sun, still low to the east, had as yet no sting. It was pleasant going, the trajectory a touch downhill, and as I went along, I admired the rugged terrain and the mountains to the south, indistinct in the dust haze.

The pavement ran out at the intersection, where remnants of another windmill had been restored and decorated the landscape, serving as a sort of monument. After standing on the corner, noting how the main road disappeared as it neared the mountains on the southern horizon, I took the road west, which was sealed for a stretch before turning to grit.

Some of that grit found its way into my plimsolls, which made for unpleasant going. In an effort to distract myself from the discomfort, I shifted my focus back onto the surroundings, telling myself that somewhere amid the scree and the scrub might be a source of inspiration for a novel, if only my imagination would find it.

I focused hard on the details. The fields to either side of the track were strewn with small rocks, and the soil had a pinkish tinge to it. I wasn't sure if that was a trick of the light because, in the heat of the day, taken as a whole, the soil had a creamy look. In all, there were too few trees.

The walk took about fifteen minutes. I passed a farmhouse in ruins and paused to take it in, but the crumbling abode failed to provoke even a spark of enthusiasm from my parsimonious muse. Just past the ruin, the track took a sharp turn to the left and, up ahead, set in a swathe of gravel in this most desolate of landscapes, was my destination.

The windmill, a stout affair constructed from large brown stones and pointed with thick, pale-cream mortar, stood proud on its gritty concourse. The six sails, comprising dark-wood shutters, were motionless. The domed roof of the windmill, made of the same dark wood, formed an austere cap. At the rear, the tail pole was anchored to the ground minus the capstan wheel. A simple arrangement of rocks along with a dry-stone wall surrounded the windmill's base and completed the restoration.

Looking around, I supposed the landscaping was one way of clearing the ground of unwanted rock. Even so, without any foliage to speak of – at all – the place felt as though the workmen had packed up and left after hammering in the last nail, and the local government had signed off on the project as a good-enough job done. Perhaps the authorities thought no one passing through Tefía would bother coming out here, I thought, not even to see the windmill, the island no doubt having bigger and better windmills elsewhere.

I walked around the base then climbed the steps that led up to a locked door. There was nothing to see other than a glimpse of ocean to the west. I paused and soaked in the small portion of blue, enjoying the sense it gave of being on an island. Inland, amid all the dry, it was easy to forget the ocean was there.

Before I left, I sat on the stone steps of the windmill and emptied my plimsolls. Not that there was much point. Three steps were enough to shuffle in some more. I took a slug from my water bottle and had one last look around.

In the distance to the south was a farmhouse, and immediately to the north, leading off from the swathe of gravel surrounding the windmill, a drive led to some sort of compound. The owners had made an effort at beautification; flanking the drive were rows of infant palm trees set in garden beds of deep black gravel and edged with large stones. Those beds were a mark of significance, as though an indication of a place of eminence, one incongruous with everything else around. At the end of one of the rows of palms was a sign.

I went over and found an explanation of the ins and outs of the windmill. Turned out in bygone years, this dry-as-dust land produced enough grain to warrant a mill. Incredible. Then again, of course, there would have been enough grain, ample grain, or the windmill would not have been built. It was self-evident.

The sun began to heat the skin on my face and head and neck, and I decided I better return to the farmhouse. Until that moment when I started making my way back, I hadn't realised the entire walk to the windmill had been downhill. The return, I found to my chagrin, was, therefore, uphill, and now I faced into the blustery wind as well and the going was much harder.

My stride soon became a trudge, and the wind seemed to delight in my struggle and strengthened and blew in my face, pushing up hard against me in intermittent bursts. My pleasant morning stroll took on the proportions of a marathon. By the time I arrived back at the farmhouse, I was sweating and panting, and my legs ached.

I went and stood in the internal patio where I pulled off my plimsolls, depositing the grit at the base of a potted plant. I was ashamed of myself. Two years of divorce litigation misery and I hadn't so much as walked to the local shops not a hundred yards from my tired little London flat. I was a man broken, and my body was a shambles. I had always taken for granted my fitness, my muscle tone, my relative youth. To find myself gasping for air like an old man was abhorrent in the extreme.

After downing two glasses of water in quick succession, I took a long cool shower, returning to the patio with my laptop, determined to find the nearest gym.

I was distracted by my inbox. Scanning the messages, I wished I hadn't bothered when I saw the email.

I am not the sort of man others may imagine when they think of a downtrodden wretch, but just then, that was how I felt. I have always considered myself even in temperament, not quick to anger, observant and detached, unlike the more involved and emotional types that seem to gravitate towards me like iron filings in need of a magnet to cling to. Life, in the form of a wife, can destabilise a man's composure on the inside where others cannot see, rendering a smoothly functioning machine a decrepit mess of contorted metal. She had turned me into a heap of junk.

She, being my ex-wife Jackie. Jackie pushed me, pushed us, pushed all of our little nuclear family off a cliff, and we landed on a rocky beach facing a thrashing ocean, gazing up at the halcyon days of our former domestic life. She couldn't help it, and I do not blame her, these things happen after all, but the fallout as we clambered back up that cliff to safety, was more than any of us had anticipated. As if that were not bad enough, she had me scaling a different cliff.

What could she possibly want from me now? Money? Surely not.

I didn't want to look. I put the email in the folder labelled, "pending".

Jackie and I had been married for more than twenty years. It was twenty years, two months and five days in fact when she called time out. What ensued was a further two years of torment, more or less, for I had trained myself to be imprecise when it came to the duration of the divorce, not caring to quantify the arguments, the hurt, the anguish and the loss as we fought over the house and the kids. Two years and at last we reached a settlement, and I naturally found myself with a lot less than I had anticipated.

After perusing my options, involving relocating to some far-flung county where the roads were too narrow, the weather worse than anywhere, and a visit to the supermarket an expedition, I put in an offer on a tiny cottage in the Norfolk Broads.

The cottage was a long way from London, where Jackie and the kids were determined to remain, but at least the new abode was close to my publisher friend, Angela, who had been my closest ally since primary school.

Close we undoubtedly were, but for a long time, too long maybe, Angela and I had maintained our friendship via Skype and the occasional real-life catchup.

After the separation, Angela became my mainstay. I generally Skyped her once a week. It was the only time I took in the man I'd become, my once pleasingly aquiline face gaunt, eyes sunken, lips turned down. A small and depressing square of me and a large image of her, all round-faced and cheery-eyed.

During the entire divorce episode, Angela insisted I was having a mid-life crisis. The term had me feeling like a cliché. In those last weeks before I flew to Fuerteventura, she made a point of telling me my shortcomings, too. I've been putting on weight – I knew that – I need a haircut – I was cultivating the bedraggled look – and, if she saw me wearing that worn-thin Jimi Hendrix t-shirt one more time, she'd make the three-hour drive from Norfolk and rip it off my back. She bought it for my eighteenth.

Angela was the sort of woman who strode through life. Always smart in her black trousers and figure-hugging tops, she brimmed self-assurance. She was who she was, and she was unapologetic about it. Her hair was never kempt. She wore no makeup. Her wife, Juliette, wore the skirts.

I was at their wedding, one of quite a few straight men in attendance who felt strangely threatened, a reaction summed up by an acquaintance, Simon, a commissioning editor at Hedgehog Pie Press who whispered to me in a drunken slur, 'If this same-sex marriage catches on, we'll be redundant.' I laughed to be polite, but in that instant, I saw that my own unease had the same source. I left Simon to quaff champagne and dish his inappropriate banter elsewhere, and found a quiet corner of the village hall in which to regain my equanimity.

Jackie had announced she wanted a divorce over breakfast that same morning, as she was salting her boiled egg. The harsh words dropped like stones in my cereal bowl.

'We don't have anything in common anymore.'

'What makes you say that?'

She paused, eggy spoon mid-air. 'I've been thinking for a long time that our relationship is past its use-by. Don't you think we're in a rut?'

'No, I don't, as it happens.'

She wasn't listening. 'The kids are almost grown up so now is a good time.'

'It is?'

She went all reflective at that point. I began to think she was reading from a script she had written and rehearsed. 'I think we married too young. We've grown apart.'

'We have tons in common.'

'Look, Trevor, I need to rediscover myself.'

It became clear she was not going to brook my defensive remarks. Our marriage, as far as she was concerned, was over. She had all the platitudes. But the truth was she had found Megan, desire had sparked, and she wanted to explore that side of her sexuality. Feeling the need to confess the cold, hard facts, if only to make certain there would be no salvaging what we had, she said, 'I've always been bi, you know that. But this is different. Megan is the one. With her, I can truly be me.'

Jackie could be ruthless with her honesty. It was why she was good at her job. She was a human resources manager. Thanks to her substantial income, I had been able to pursue my own career, although I wasn't sure I'd give ghostwriting such high status.

Not long after Angela and Juliette's wedding, we split up, or rather, Jackie asked me to move out so Megan could move in. She announced that plan along with a sack full of rationalisations when she was suitably fortified by a large glass of Rioja.

I obliged, ever the peacemaker. It wasn't until the solicitors waded in with advice that the wrangling started and the acrimony flared.

Holed-up in a crummy London flat, my frustrations with my ghostly writing existence grew. They soon became the main topic of conversation when I talked with Angela. I want my name on the cover, for once. Then write the damn contents, she would say matter-of-factly. But what would I write?

It was Angela's suggestion that I should book a getaway. By then the lease on my flat was up, and I wasn't due to take possession of my new home for another three months. Jackie and Megan were deep in wedding plans, and the children, Ian and Felicity, were too busy with their own late-teen lives to take much notice.

Where would I go? Shetland? Don't be ridiculous. Nowhere tropical, I told her, I don't do humidity. Have you tried the Canaries? I don't want crowds. Then try Fuerteventura. What's there? Beaches mainly. I don't do beaches. What do you do? Isolation. Then I've found just the place. And she sent me the link to the farmhouse in Tefía on Skype.

Angela was of the opinion I had unresolved issues buried deep in my psyche. Angela would say that. She was one of those women a little bit older and a whole lot wiser than the men she knew. Ran a small press from her home in Norwich. She had forty authors on her books and acted as a kind of benevolent matriarch, smoothing out their concerns with advice and suggestions and oodles of sympathy. When they started to get uppity, she insisted the best way to progress as an author was to write another book, which they then dutifully did, and the anxiety over the lack of sales of the last one waned. Angela then breathed a sigh of relief, and everyone was happy, for a while. Worked every time, she said. Angela thought I should do the same and write a book. She told me she would consider publishing what I came up with. She would even help me knock the manuscript into shape, should I manage to produce one. She said that writing a novel would help me come to terms with my inner demons and move on.

What inner demons?

Which I suppose was partly why I had no intention of reaching within myself to come up with ideas for a plot. That, and I already knew she was wrong; there was nothing in me that I had not already resolved. I had long before dealt with what in essence defined me as a human being: my difference.

3

CHILDHOOD

It was Aunty Iris who said I was different. I grew up with that sense of otherness superimposed on my psyche by my overbearing relative, singled out from the rest of the household in our detached house in Heene Way – a leafy street in the well-to-do end of West Worthing, Sussex – after my father ran off with the woman next door. The family seemed to want someone to blame. I couldn't understand why I was chosen, other than that I was the only male remaining in the house. All I knew was I went from being a happy and innocent little boy to an unhappy child saddled with observing the tortured emotions of others.

My mother was beside herself. She was a god-abiding Catholic who refused her husband a divorce. Consumed by shame, she took no solace in mass or confession or the sympathies of her priest. Instead, she took to drinking heavily, and when she wasn't drinking, she would sit in a chair and stare blankly at a wall. All the family photographs had been removed. My sister, Marnie, who was thirteen when the terrible betrayal took place, started scouring her forearms with blades of various kinds and decided she no longer needed to eat, habits that alarmed Aunty Iris, who had moved in to help.

I couldn't see that Iris helped at all save for attending to the household chores. Along with the sickly-sweet air freshener she sprayed everywhere, she infused the already turbulent atmosphere with her own hysteria, for she was a touch histrionic, was Iris.

I did what any sensible boy my age would do. I retreated to my room. It was the only course of action available to me since I was not the type to run away. Ensconced in the smallest bedroom in the house, I buried my mind in books and comics and, on days when it wasn't raining and I felt a need for fresh air, I would skulk around in the back garden or ride my bike up and down the streets of my neighbourhood.

I was a regular boy, neither shy nor extrovert, and the only difference I could see between me and the family I had the misfortune to live among, was that I did not thrash about or bleed or shrink or wail or sulk or stagger.

I've always disliked extremes: extreme heat, extreme cold, and especially wild displays of emotion. My preference for evenness extends to my environment. I like my land undulating, my ocean calm, my surroundings neat and smooth. Even at nine years old, I made my bed every morning and kept my room tidy. I arranged my books in order of size on a single bookshelf. On the shelf above, arranged in neat clusters, my vintage cars were displayed. My father had gifted them to me, but I never played with them. My chess set, dominoes, draughts and Monopoly were stacked neatly on the bottom shelf next to my piggy bank.

I preferred to visit my friends' houses, rather than have them enter mine, for fear they would encounter my mother or Aunty Iris or my sister in a state, or they would turn my bedroom into one through boisterous play. Aunty Iris was fond of telling me I was too much of a loner and should invite boys over. To appease her, I would invite my best friend, Vince, round from time to time, but mostly I went to his.

A wily and perspicacious child, Vince lived in the next street, and I had known him since my first day at school. Vince was my confidant, and he summed up my domestic circumstances beautifully one time when we were about thirteen, by saying that I was the scapegoat. I think we were learning about the world wars in History, and he applied the term to me. I considered his remark at some length, carrying it home with me and cogitating as I observed the attitudes of the women in the house, how they chose to ignore me, or jibe me, or pick holes in me, and by the end of that day, I had decided that Vince was correct in his assessment. I was indeed the scapegoat.

From that point on, his home became my home. I found his parents warm and inviting. I would spend as much of my waking life in Vince's bedroom as my own.

When boyhood gave way to hormones and our hair grew in our armpits and our groins, that other part of my anatomy grew of its own volition at the slightest spark and demanded release of its own unique kind. Once, while we were shut in Vince's bedroom, he unfurled a sexy magazine, and we lay on our bellies on his bed and leafed through the pages. After some time ogling, Vince pushed me over onto my back and when he looked down at me, his gaze fixed on the growth in my trousers. Without another word, he unzipped my fly and, before I could stop him, he reached in and tugged. I was delirious in an instant, and in the very next, my newly realised manhood exploded in a sudden gush.

After that Vince's explorations grew bolder. He would unfurl his member – his was much larger than mine – and encourage me to unfurl mine and we would have wanking contests, shooting our loads into the waste paper bin.

It was all just boyish fun. Neither of us questioned what we did. On the contrary, we sniggered and joked and drew lewd pictures and shared our fantasies.

A year later, our voices broke, and Vince fell in love with a girl called Amy, and our wanking days were over. I completed school with high grades in English and History and went on to study at the University of Sussex in Brighton. I lived at home throughout the three years of my degree, but I was never there. Vince had by then married Amy, and I was dating her best friend, who would become my wife, Jackie.

4

THE GYM

I CLOSED THE EMAIL TAB AND FORCED MY ATTENTION ON MY surroundings, taking note of the patio with its arrangement of potted plants and wrought-iron furniture and wall décor. Charming surroundings, and there was nothing to be gained from reliving the past. The same memories, along with the same feelings, resurfaced like unwanted and long-buried garbage dug up by a spirited garden fork aroused into action by a wandering mind.

After a short while, I returned to the matter in hand: my fitness, or lack thereof. Locating the nearest gym was the easy part. I found a suitable establishment in Puerto del Rosario, situated near the port, down a side street not far from the main drag. Even navigating my way into the heart of the island capital was not as onerous as I thought it might have been, but the moment I stepped down to basement level, walked inside the premises, and took in the machines and the weights and the men decked in shorts and singlets – all of them tanned and toned – I felt like hightailing it back to Tefia.

Determination won out. Garbed in board shorts and the baggiest t-shirt I had packed, I headed to the counter, paid the session rate and set to, thinking I would try out a few machines after a long hard pedal on the exercise bike.

I mounted the bike nearest the entrance door and furthest from every other male on the premises, adjusted the seat and fiddled with the settings until my feet could manage to pedal with relative ease. Despite the mirrors which doubled if not trebled the gazes flitting my way, I managed to ignore the others in the room as I panted and sweated and strained for a whole ten kilometres. I dismounted, took a sweep of the room and headed to the machines nearby, which looked devoted to the lower half of the anatomy.

My decision to remain anonymous and private was tested when I struggled to change the weight setting on the leg press. I thought I heard laughter above the sound system and kept my head down in case I discovered my suspicions confirmed, and that laughter really was directed at me.

A staff member saw my battle and came over, introducing himself in English as Luis, the gym's personal trainer. He had a friendly face, an ebullient manner and a confronting way of standing that little bit too close. 'No te preocupes,' he said, slipping back into Spanish as he pulled out the pin and thrust it into a lower weight load. Then he looked me up and down and added with a broad grin, 'Pero, tú necesitas el sol.' He said his words slowly and separately and pointed at my skin to make sure I understood. Yes, yes, I know, I am as white as bleached linen, don't remind me.

He switched to English to suggest he devise me a fitness program. He must have been watching me the whole time.

'It is the best way to get fit fast. No injuries,' he said, still all smiles.

With him standing so close as I waited to mount the machine, I felt somewhat coerced into agreeing. 'Although, I am not sure there is any point. I am only here on holiday.'

'For how long you stay?'

'Three months.'

'You will be strong in that time. And lose that,' he added with a short laugh, pointing at my belly.

Humiliation rose. I harboured doubts as to whether I would lose my paunch in three short months, but Luis was right. It was obvious to me and no doubt to everyone else in the gym that I hadn't a clue what I was doing.

I pulled away from the machine and said, 'Okay. That would be great.'

First, he showed me around, introducing me to the machines like they were his old friends. He went on to devise a fitness program based on my embarrassingly weak efforts, taking me to first one machine, then another, and making me do a few reps at various weight loads while issuing me with instructions as to how best to position my body and what postures to avoid. I struggled to take it all in and hoped he would be including his advice in the plan.

Luis' tour proved a workout in itself, and I was done in by the end of it. A remarkably chatty fellow – I did wonder if he had taken some drug. As we stood at the counter where I paid his fee, Luis asked me what I was doing on the island and where I was staying.

Ever honest, I told him I was renting a farmhouse in Tefía. It was the village name that caused a shadow to pass across his face. Why that look?

'Tefía?' he said doubtfully.

'I wanted a place far away from the tourist strip,' I said, instantly defensive. Then I sighed. 'But it is desolate up there. Do you know it?'

'I know Tefía,' he said with dark irony. 'Everyone knows Tefía.'

'That sounds like a warning,' I said with a laugh, inwardly brushing off his remark.

'Not a warning,' he said. 'The village has a terrible history.'

I began to take an interest in what he had to say and was keen to know more. Terrible histories make for terrific stories.

'How so?' I asked.

'Have you been to the windmill?'

The windmill!

'As a matter of fact, I was there only this morning,' I said, a grin spreading across my face.

Luis remained dark and grim.

'Then you must know,' he said, looking down at the counter between us.

'Know what?' I said, puzzled. 'It is just a windmill. There is nothing dark about it.'

'Not the windmill, the hostel next to it.'

Hostel? What hostel? Surely, he didn't mean whatever building was up that well-maintained drive?

'You can't miss it,' he said. 'The entrance is right next to the windmill.'

His words seeped into me. I had evidently failed to realise the drive led to a public building. What sort of hostel was it and what had gone on there? Luis looked poised to give me the full history when someone walked in from outside. Luis' gaze darted to the clock on the wall and, with a quick apology, he went to attend to his appointment.

I drove back to Tefía, my muscles tight and aching. I was in need of a refreshing beer and a snack of some sort, but I headed straight to the windmill and on up the short drive to the hostel, pulling up at the end before a pair of high iron gates which were closed.

The compound was walled, but I was able to peer through a crack in the gates to some low, ochre-coloured buildings and an observatory dome. Then I walked back past my car, and when I turned, I saw that the wall was only high at the entrance. I mounted the low stone wall that enclosed the drive and walked a short distance along the compound's perimeter. I felt strangely self-conscious and hoped I wasn't being watched.

Inside the compound, beyond a planting of giant cacti in a raised gravel bed, on the other side of a small parking area, the arrangement of buildings around a quadrangle had a definite military feel. I assumed the structure served as some sort of army or air base. The atmosphere was not exactly pleasant, although there was nothing about the complex to invoke fear, no snarling dogs, no smashed windows or signs of dilapidation. No one appeared either, and there was no sound or any sign of human life. I noticed two sculpted rocks of black stone. They looked a little like headstones or a memorial of some sort. Whatever was inscribed faced the other way.

I carried on until I found a gap in the wall, entering a swathe of black gravel and passing a recreational field used for sports. Beyond the field, to the northwest, there was a farmhouse inside a stone wall and surrounded by trees. Appeared to be a separate dwelling. I kept well away from it, crunching my way across the gravel to the rear of the compound. The land fell away to the northeast, ending in a row of three small, cuboid buildings, each little bigger than a single room. The buildings were in disrepair. Looked like no one had been down to attend to them in a long while. A cold chill wafted through me despite the heat. I didn't fancy walking down to take a closer look.

I headed back the way I had come, thinking the compound had clearly undergone a change of purpose. What sort of hostel was it, and why locate it all the way out here? More's the point, what was so bad about the place to cause that reaction in Luis? I wasn't about to find out by snooping around. I emptied my shoes of grit, got in my car and drove home.

After quenching a raging thirst and staving off a voracious hunger, I returned to my laptop out to the patio and sat in the sun to brown my legs. A few keywords and I had a bunch of tabs open on images, videos, blogs and newspaper articles on the hostel. Not one of them in English.

My Spanish was rubbish and even with an online translator, I struggled to comprehend what I was reading. Yet I could find nothing, not one article in my native tongue, so I persevered.

I soon realised Luis was referring to a prison, not the youth hostel that El Albergue has now become, the government having taken over the building for educational purposes.

Originally a military airbase, the compound was turned into a prison to house political prisoners and criminals some time after General Franco came to power. From 1954, as the result of a law making homosexuality illegal under a vagrancy act, gay men were incarcerated at the hostel, then a prison farm, for up to three years. From what I could glean, conditions were abominable. Young men of eighty-seven kilos were reduced to almost half that in five months. The label "concentration camp" seemed hardly an understatement.

Little wonder I hadn't liked the feel of the place. Those men must have been imprisoned in that row of small huts behind the main compound. From what I could gather, about twelve men would have been crammed in each. An image of Vince hovering over me with wild intent flashed into my mind, and I shuddered.

One of the newspaper articles was the obituary of a former inmate. A gay activist campaigning for some sort of restitution; he had died only last month. It all sounded harrowing and sad and ugly and not at all what I had come to Fuerteventura to engage with.

It wasn't that I lacked empathy. I just didn't want to be burdened with the tribulations of others some seventy years past, when I had barely begun to recover from my own.

Then again, that prison might be a source of inspiration for a novel, and I would do well to stop and consider it. What sort of story would I tell? Had something similar already been done? What would I be able to make of harrowing events locked away in the past? Me, who could not stand to dwell on heavy emotions and hardship. I wanted to compose something interesting and topical, true, but not dark and gloomy. Besides, the topic of same-sex preference remained a sore point after Jackie and the divorce.

An uncomfortable fire brought me back to the here and now. I had lost track of time, and my thighs felt as though they were frying in the sun. I got up and took the laptop indoors.

Sure enough, I paid dearly for that hour or two of research, the burning deepening as the afternoon wore on, and by dinnertime, I was tempted to use the pack of frozen peas I had bought in Antigua as a cold pack. Had I packed the Savlon?

Fortunately, I had, and I rubbed a liberal amount into each thigh. The cream eased the pain but not the heat that radiated from my baked skin.

That night, I had to sleep with the covers off.

5

A SKYPE CALL

I HAD ONLY JUST FINISHED PATTING SAVLON ONTO MY RED AND SORE thighs after a cool morning shower, when my laptop signalled a Skype call. Garbed in boxer shorts and an old t-shirt, I rushed out of the en suite bathroom, through my bedroom and straight into the smallest living room, where I had left my laptop.

It was Angela.

Seeing her grinning face peering past mine, felt like an intrusion in the extreme. I knew she was just curious to see glimpses of where I was staying, but I almost cut the call. An overreaction on my part – after all, she had found this farmhouse for me – but my muscles were stiff and aching from the gym, and my skin smarted from the sunburn, and altogether I was not in the best of moods.

'Hey there, you. Aren't you going to show me around?'

She wouldn't stop peering past me. I forced myself to soften.

'Okay, you win.'

I unplugged the laptop and took her on a circuit through the house, going from room to room, each interconnecting to the next around the central patio, except the living room facing the street, which was accessed via the square hall; the kitchen, which led off from the same little hall; the main bathroom, accessed via a second square hall on the south side; and my bedroom, which was reached via the larger of the three living rooms.

As I went, I pointed the webcam at features of interest – the wrought iron wall décor in the patio, the granite benchtop in the kitchen, the thickness of the walls, the claw-footed bath in the main bathroom, and the four-poster bed, neatly made, naturally – and at last she told me to stop.

'You're making me dizzy,' she laughed.

I felt dizzy, too.

'How are things in gloomy Norwich?' I asked.

'Same as ever. I've just signed a new author.'

'Anyone I know?'

'Doubt it. He's got quite a backlist. A crime novelist. Richard H. Parry.'

'Never heard of him.'

'Didn't expect you would. Crime writers are a dime a dozen and he is no Ruth Rendell, but still. I have you to thank for me taking him on, oddly.'

'Oh?'

'He has a house on Lanzarote where he writes, and he has taken to writing novels set there. One of them flopped and he's been struggling to regain his former standing, which is why I've picked him up.'

'A bit risky, if he's on the decline.'

'Maybe. But I have a feeling he still has a few corkers in him. Which brings me to you.'

'It does?' I was hoping she wasn't about to suggest I meet the guy.

'You two should meet. Shared interest and all that.'

I groaned inwardly as I maintained a bland expression, which she could no doubt see straight through.

'Any luck coming up with a story?' she said, changing tack.

'I've only been here five days.'

'Okay, then what *have* you been doing?'

I recounted my trip to the windmill, told her she would be pleased to know I had started at the gym and that I was sporting a bad case of sunburn.

'Where?' she asked, not seeing sunburn on my face.

'My thighs,' I said grimly. 'I got caught up in some research out on the patio, and I forgot the time. I was wearing shorts.'

She needn't have laughed quite so heartily.

'I have found something of interest,' I said, keen to distract her. 'Right by the windmill, there's a youth hostel. Seems schools use it for camps. It's a former air base once used as a prison.'

'Sounds intriguing.'

Her vague tone, in fact the phrase altogether, was her way of saying, how dull.

'Angela, listen up. That prison used to house gay men incarcerated during Franco's regime. I've been reading up about it. Or trying to. They are calling it a concentration camp.'

Now I had her. She leaned forward, lips parted, eyes wide. There was a brief pause.

'Well?'

'Well?'

'Don't stop there!'

'That is all I know. I only found out yesterday. It was how I got sunburnt. I was engrossed trying to translate all the details.'

'There's nothing in English?'

'Not that I can find.'

'Pity. I was going to ask you for a link.'

She stared at me and I stared right back, daring her to say it.

'Pretty obvious, don't you think?'

'Forget it.'

'Aw, come on. You were looking for a book idea and now you have one.'

'I'm not writing a book about that. No. Thank. You.'

'Why ever not?'

Did she really have to ask me that? We both knew how I felt about Jackie's betrayal. It was a sensitive area and Angela really should have known better.

'Because, I'm not gay,' I said sourly.

'Why would that even matter?'

'You know what the critics are like. As a straight, white man, my options are constrained.'

'Rubbish! Take no notice of all that crap about cultural appropriation. Spanish people are white in any case and you are a man with certain ambiguities.'

'Angela, leave it.'

'I don't think I will. This is a literary treasure you have stumbled on.'

'You think so? To be honest, the topic doesn't inspire me.'

'Stop being precious.'

'Stop being blunt.'

Angela threw up her hands.

'Have it your way. With that attitude, good luck finding inspiration. What was that place called? A hostel, did you say...?'

The line cut out, or she ended the call. Either way, I didn't much care. I closed the laptop and readied for the gym.

6

LUIS

IT WAS MARKEDLY WARMER ON THE EAST COAST OF THE ISLAND, AND THE buildings huddled on the narrow streets of Puerto del Rosario trapped that heat. As I stepped out of my air-conditioned car, the hot air hit me as though I had flung open the door of a kiln. I hurried to the gym thinking there must be something wrong with me as most Brits hanker for that kind of weather. As I pushed open the door, another worry gripped me, and I paused, self-conscious. Feeling the heat rush in and the cool rush out, I made a decisive move, hoping the muted lighting would obscure the redness of my thighs.

A quick scan around and I saw the room was almost empty, and no one seemed to have taken any notice of my entry.

I went to the counter and paid the single session rate to an older, wizened-looking guy who eyed me with cool indifference. Refusing to be fazed by his attitude, I made my way steadfastly to the treadmills, steppers and bikes. Luis, standing next to one of the weight machines, looked over and gave me his pumped up and ridiculously radiant smile. I held up his fitness plan in acknowledgement.

The exercise bike was harder going, my muscles complaining they were tired from yesterday. The larger part of me wanted to dismount and change the settings, but my pride wouldn't let me, and I pressed on, using the ordeal to purge my mind of thoughts of Angela and that hostel, panting and sweating until I had reached Luis' target of exactly twelve kilometres. Satisfied I was able to push through the pain barrier, I dismounted and took a slug from my water bottle. With my blood pumping through my veins, and sweat trickling down my back, I strode over to the military press.

My workout took a sharp downward turn, thanks to whoever had used the press before me. Must have been a hulk. It was as much as I could do to change the weights on the barbell. I had to grit my teeth and squeeze in my flaccid belly as I heaved the metal plates, one by one, off each end of the bar and stagger over to where the others were stacked. I could feel the eyes of the guys on me as I struggled. I couldn't recall the last time I had felt so humiliated. From the moment I'd arrived in Fuerteventura, my masculinity had been bound up in my physical strength, my appearance, matters I had not given much credence ever before in my life. It had become important, too important to me maybe, to feel fit and strong and able to withstand the harsh environment I found myself in. It was as though my life depended on it, yet really, it was just my pride, my battered sense of self.

I struggled my way through the prescribed four sets of ten reps, at the modest weight Luis had advised, until the muscles in my shoulders and upper arms burned. Luis had mentioned something about the deltoids, and I presumed they were inflamed. When I lowered the barbell for the last time and reached for my towel, my elbow whacked my thigh and my sunburn flared in reaction, adding to the woes.

Still, I soldiered on.

Next was the lateral raise machine. Luis told me to drop-set from the highest weight I could manage, which I knew wouldn't be much. Whoever had been here before me was made of steel, the pin thrust between the two lowest weight bars. I extracted the pin and inserted it about halfway up the stack. Then I sat on the seat, felt some damp cool meet my thighs and got up and placed my towel down to serve as a barrier to my predecessor's sweat. Then I held my arms at right angles, clenched my fists and attempted to raise my elbows to the height of my shoulders. The pads pressing against my upper arms didn't budge even a fraction. My old friend humiliation sparked up as I leaned over to reset the weight load.

Four sets of twenty raises were the instructions. My arms did not want to know after half a set. I pressed on, gritting my teeth, refusing to give in to the burn. By the fourth set, I only managed four raises, and I again hoped no one was watching as I left the machine, six reps short, a dismal failure in my own eyes.

The front raises were even worse. A five-kilo dumbbell in each hand, I raised my arms straight out to the horizontal and back down to my sides. Up, down, up, down, and I could feel the strain in my wrists, forearms and elbows up to my shoulders. By the third set, the muscles in my arms, such as they were, flipped out in a chorus of pain. I had never experienced agony like it. Luis was cruel, I decided. There had to be malice in his soul to create a fitness plan clearly designed to kill me.

The seated dumbbell shoulder press was no better. The only positive was I got to sit. The exercise was much the same as the military press, and by now, every muscle in my upper arms and shoulders was angry and sore and complaining.

And I still had another five kilometres to pedal on the exercise bike! I noted on his fitness plan, Luis euphemistically called my final ordeal a "cool-down". I all but slumped over the handlebars, sweat-soaked and beaten. It wasn't until I was two kilometres in and the endorphin charge that came with hard exercise sped through my veins, that I was able to feel a small sense of achievement and well-being. I pedalled as hard as I was able, right to the finish, dismounting panting and soaking wet, bang on the five-kilometre mark.

With my heart rate still elevated, I approached Luis – who had replaced the old guy at the counter – and thanked him between short bursts of breath for his fitness plan.

'De nada,' he said warmly, grinning his sparkling grin into my face.

'See you tomorrow, then,' I said, making to walk away.

'Wait.'

I turned back.

'If you are coming every day, you should buy a membership.'

'I won't be needing one,' I said rather quickly, reacting to the hard sell.

He looked crestfallen. Ignoring his reaction, I adjusted the bag on my shoulder and was about to walk away again when he said, 'There's a weekly discount.' He paused. 'Or you can sign up for a month if you want.'

Why the persistence? Was he on a commission? Or was the gym that desperate for my money?

'Alright then,' I said, suddenly seeing sense in his suggestions. 'I'll take a month.'

Then a leaflet advertising a special offer on a three-month membership caught my eye.

'Make that three.'

He seemed delighted. As I extracted my wallet, and he organised my membership card, I wondered again if business was bad, but judging by the number of patrons that were here the day before and the central location, I doubted it. Maybe he was a genuinely nice guy who was pleased to see a decidedly white and podgy Englishman make a commitment to get himself in shape. Then I decided Luis was one of those gym-fit men who took fitness a little bit too seriously. I observed his physique, the taut muscles, the flat belly and, of course, the natural Latin tan. He was undeniably attractive. I was not in the habit of noticing other men, but I noticed him, right then and there, and in a way that surprised me.

As he handed me my card, he gestured at my legs, which I had thought were hidden behind the counter, and said, 'You have been too much in the sun, no?'

I cringed inwardly as I emitted a flippant laugh. 'I forgot the time.'

He didn't laugh with me. Instead, he looked serious. 'Be careful,' he said. His eyes bored into mine as though he was trying to see into my core. I was disconcerted by it.

I walked away before he could engage me in further conversation. As I headed out the door, my mind flitted back again to Vince.

7

A TRIP TO THE BEACH

THE FOLLOWING MORNING, I WOKE UP IN A TANGLE OF DAMP SHEETS. AS I extricated my thighs, I felt a smear of cool stickiness, and a slow realisation came over me. A wet dream. I hadn't had a wet dream since I was eighteen. Wet dreams ended for me once I was happily having it away with Jackie.

A wet dream.

The horror of the occurrence permeated my being. Had my loneliness and frustration sunk to these depths?

Filled with self-disgust, I yanked the sheets off the bed and put them in the wash. In the shower, I soaped the sticky mess off me. The stiffness of my shoulders and thighs and calves became apparent as I dried off. It occurred to me I should have stretched those muscles after my workout. Luis hadn't mentioned stretching, probably because he considered the need self-evident. I made a mental note to do so next time.

While I waited for the wash cycle to do its job, I gave the kitchen a once-over with cloth, broom and mop, and then I took a mug of coffee and a bowl of cereal out to the patio. Positioning a chair in the shade, I jumped on my laptop to catch up with the day's affairs.

The first thing I checked was the weather. It was going to be another stinker. That put paid to a morning walk. Eager to get out of the farmhouse and continue on my quest for ideas for a novel which I thought had to be lurking on the island somewhere, I studied a map of the island and found the nearest beach. It was at a village called Puertito de Los Molinos, which according to an online translator literally meant tiny port of mills. The village was situated on the coast due west of Tefia, accessed, if I took a short cut, via the track that went past the windmill. From there, the road coursed its way across the plain, past a cluster of farms and on to the coast. The journey was about five kilometres. I would be there in about ten minutes.

Before I closed my laptop, I had a quick glance at my emails. Nothing more from Jackie, and nothing from the kids. After deleting all the usual promotions and social media notifications, I found there was little left other than a short note from Angela asking if I had heard the news. What news? I clicked on the accompanying link and, as my eyes fell on the headline, my chest tightened; the word "short-list" was all I needed to know, and I was transported back to three months before, when one of my clients, a wealthy heiress who fancied herself a novelist and went by the name of Ms Sandra Flint, had been longlisted for a major literary prize. I had nearly choked on my Wheaties. This time, I swallowed what was left of the cereal in my cheek pouches and rinsed my mouth with a slurp of coffee. Certain I had averted a repetition of a near-death experience, I scrolled down. There were five titles and one of them belonged to Sandra Flint. I told myself I should be happy for her, but I was anything but. All I could feel was a toxic mix of outrage and contempt, stirred with a wand of self-pity.

Two years ago, Flint had commissioned my help with a novel she was struggling to complete. That was the brief she had given. All I was required to do, she'd said, was finish the last chapter and polish the rest. We agreed on my fee and I took on the job despite my misgivings after getting caught before, when one of my assignments won the author a prize. I should have known better than to take on a whole novel, but I needed the cash.

Turned out the final chapter was the least of the author's problems. I ended up doing a complete re-write, tweaking the plot, developing themes, inserting crucial backstory and peppering up the antagonist. In all, I felt as though I had composed the whole damn novel by the end of it, and then, to my chagrin, Ms Flint refused to credit me with having contributed so much as a comma.

Resentment coiled up in me as I deleted Angela's email. Now, Flint stood to win a major prize while I languished in the land of the unacknowledged. I closed the laptop, downed my coffee – revoltingly tepid – in three large gulps and went and snatched my phone and car keys off the kitchen bench. A quick rummage in the bedroom for swimmers and a towel, and I was out the door and heading to the beach.

I took it slow on the dirt road past the windmill, not wanting to kick up too much dust, not that there was anyone around to breathe it in. There was something stark and lonely about that windmill with its shutter sails and its stonework all restored, standing in the middle of nowhere beside a military base-cum-prison, now turned youth hostel. It seemed to me a forgotten place, private almost, not anywhere the authorities were keen visitors would bother with. The dirt track carried on a stretch and at the next intersection, I was pleased to get back on the tarmac.

Driving past a cluster of farms I had seen on the map, I had to strain to imagine the island after rain, when plants grew fast, soaking up the warmth and the sun, producing enough to warrant tilling the soil here, when for the rest of the time there was little to do other than watch all the green wither to a crisp, and the ground return to its barren state. Judging by the small number of farms I had seen on the island, most of the land was not worth the effort.

The road swept down beside a dry and narrow river bed, then made a beeline for the ocean. In a matter of moments, I had arrived at the tiny port, nothing more than a cluster of cuboid fishing huts strung along in a haphazard arrangement at the head of the beach.

The huts were painted white, the edges of their walls trimmed with thin bands of colour. The village, cradled by a low cliff rising up behind, looked out at the expanse of sapphire ocean, dazzling beneath a blue sky. The land beyond the village reached further west a short distance before heading north, sheltering the little bay from the ocean current that drove against that coast. Taking in the scene,

Fuerteventura suddenly made a whole lot more sense as a place to escape to. Even sitting in my car looking for somewhere to park, I could tell that here in this sheltered bay, it was as though the rest of the world did not exist. Although it did, and the presence of other cars parked at the head of the beach underscored that fact.

Before the road crossed the dry stream bed, I pulled up in a small parking area. Alongside the causeway was an arched footbridge. I grabbed my things and crossed the bridge, pausing at the crest like a proper tourist to gaze at the smooth, weathered rocks below. It did rain here, that was clear and, judging by the erosion when the rain came, it rushed out to sea in a great torrent.

The village was sheltered from the prevailing wind that charged across the inland plains, and, on a day like this when the air was still, the little rocky bay baked. I left the bridge in favour of the beach.

It was still early and there were few people about. I skirted the restaurant strategically situated at the head of the beach, passed by the warning sign cautioning visitors against swimming due to the strong currents, and made for the water, disappointed I had to scramble across a wide band of large pebbles to get to the sand. Still, an inconvenience for me probably meant coastal protection, and who was I to start re-arranging the landscape in my mind to attain some kind of contrived perfection. All that mattered was that the water was calm, the waves not too high.

It looked like the tide was on its way out, revealing creamy-white sand slowly drying in the sunshine. I pulled my t-shirt over my head, dumped my things on a large pebble and made for the water, suppressing a gasp as my toes registered the cool, then my ankles, my calves, my knees, my thighs, almost to my belly.

The gradient was slight. I was past the break-line before I stood at waist height. The waves were only about a foot high but they pushed me forward, and I could feel the suck of the tide as the water pulled back after each break.

All too soon, the sun felt hot on my skin. I turned to face the incoming waves and wondered if the water was safe enough. I ventured some breaststroke for a short stretch then made my way back and stood more or less where I had before. Even in the short time I had been in the water, people had arrived, and I kept one eye on my things as I studied the village and the cliff, trying to picture the lives of those who lived here, or stayed here. No sign of any mill.

The cliff comprised a few layers of ancient lava coating the sandstone beneath. With all of its crevasses and nooks and crannies, it held numerous secrets, and my imagination wandered, searching for possible stories. I knew that whatever I came up with would have to surpass my best work so far, my shortlisted book, owned to its last full stop by Sandra bloody Flint.

I spotted a string of ruins on the crest of the cliff to the north, and instantly I saw that Puertito was a perfect smugglers' cove. I began to conjure a scenario, my muse aroused as I watched ramblers wander the cliff edge to either side of the village.

The next thing I knew I was being thrust forward by a wave breaking against my back, and I lost my balance and fell into the wash. The adrenalin rush was instant, and I scrambled to my feet and waded back to dry land before another wave caught me unawares.

My concentration was broken and by the time I got to my towel, I decided I wasn't about to write a novel about drug smugglers in Fuerteventura. If that theme hadn't already been done here, it had been amply elsewhere. Besides, just because I was staying here didn't mean I had to write something set here. I would leave that sort of project to the likes of Richard H. Parry who Angela mentioned, had a house on Lanzarote, and steer my imagination away from this desert island and its unpredictable ocean.

I found a reasonably dry spot to lie down on the sand and let the sun do its work drying and tanning my skin, other than my sunburnt thighs which I covered with my t-shirt. It wasn't long before I had had enough sun and went for a wander.

Close up, the village was quaint if scruffy. The main attraction seemed to be a shrine that had been positioned on a raised bed of stone and gravel. The shrine consisted of a rounded arch, some two metres deep, decorated at the back by a frieze of scallop shells and topped by a wooden crucifix, its windowed front watching over the ocean as though to bless the fishermen and keep them safe.

The shrine was a stark reminder of the treacherous ocean,

although I doubted devotion to God would have made a jot of differ-ence. Having being brought up Catholic, I wasn't even sure God existed. I didn't want to think about it. Instead, I sat on one of the carved stone seats behind the shrine and tried to make up my mind about Puertito de los Molinos and whether or not I liked the place enough to come back.

Food would help me decide if it was worth my while returning to my local beach. No doubt just to get dumped by another wave, I thought, giving way to a sudden rush of self-loathing.

There appeared to be two eateries, one at each end of the village and both up on a bit of a rise. The far one looked rustic and bohemian and closed. I chose the one near the river and closer to my car. The covered outdoor area overlooking the water was a definite draw, and there was already a couple seated at one of the tables.

I thought it too early for lunch, yet as I was choosing a table, I noticed a couple seated in a nearby corner, dive into plates of grilled fish, potatoes and salad, arranged in neat rows on oval plates. The smell made my belly rumble. When the waiter came, frugality held sway, and I ordered a coffee and some of the local goat's cheese.

By now the temperature had soared. Scarcely a breeze came off the ocean. It was cooler in the shade of the canopy but the coffee brought me out in a hot sweat, and the cheese was salty. In all, by the time I returned to my car, I had a raging thirst.

Back at the farmhouse, I went straight out to the washing line, unpegged the sheets and re-made the bed, putting a seal on my sticky embarrassment. Only then did I down a cold beer and prepare some early lunch.

With a tinned tuna baguette filling my belly, I opened out one of the loungers stored in the laundry, slathered my thighs in sunscreen and, leaving the rest of me unprotected, sat in the patio to continue browning myself in the sun. But the heat soon made me dopey, and I started to doze. Irritated by my languor and aware of the danger of severe sunburn, I got up and went back indoors. With the whole afternoon to kill and nothing at all to entertain myself, I donned my gym gear and headed off to the city for more punishment.

Puerto del Rosario was a furnace. I couldn't recall having ever experienced heat like it. Then again, I really couldn't tell. I was radiating my own heat from tip to toe, and the concrete and tarmac of the street were not helping. Armed with my fitness plan, I was out of my car and inside the air-conditioned gym in the space of three breaths, my eyes adjusting to the dim as I succumbed to a head spin.

The feeling soon passed, and I scanned the gym, noticing a very different crowd, comprising serious weight lifters, all of them heavy-set men. You could almost smell the testosterone, the animal masculinity in the room.

It was with some relief that I saw Luis behind the counter. I caught his eye, and he gave me his broad smile. I didn't derive much reassurance from his friendliness, but I also knew that I had as much right to use the gym as those others, and all I needed to do was apply myself to my own routine and avoid eye contact as I went from machine to machine. The loud music would drown out any laughter should they find me a source of amusement, and they were all Spanish-speaking locals, judging by their appearance, which meant I would not understand any ridicule, should there be any. Really, I had no need to feel self-conscious or worse, intimidated. I ignored the lot of them while I pedalled the requisite ten kilometres going nowhere.

It was chest day. When I got to the bench press, Luis came over, and we stood at each end of the barbell.

'Leave the fifteen kilos on the bar,' he said, removing a ten-kilo disc from his end. I did the same. That left thirty kilos plus the barbell itself which was five. I could have sworn he had written down thirty kilos altogether but I wasn't about to quibble.

'You were busy this morning?' he asked as I lay my torso down on the padded vinyl.

'I went to Puertito de Los Molinos.' I glanced up at him and found myself staring into his crotch. I averted my gaze.

'Ah, very good,' he said with approval in his voice. 'Did you visit the caves?'

What caves? Missing sites of significance seemed to be becoming a habit of mine and I kicked myself for being in such a rush out the farmhouse door that morning before fully checking up on the locale online, and for leaving the village before I had had a good look around. 'I didn't get a chance,' I said, pretending I knew all about those caves.

'Next time, but you must go at a very low tide. Sometimes the low tide is not so low.'

'As I discovered,' I lied, hoping Luis wasn't about to ask me exactly what time I was there, and that he lacked an encyclopaedic knowledge of local tides.

'Also make sure you allow plenty of time to explore.'

'I will.'

'And take a torch.'

A torch? I recalled the people I had spotted as I was leaving the little port, like ants scouting the cliffs to the north and south, and I made a mental note to take appropriate footwear too.

I reached my hands up to take the barbell as Luis lifted it off the rack. He stood over me poised to assist if the weight proved too much for my arms. I thought the exercise was meant to work different muscles from shoulder day but I couldn't differentiate and it only took a couple of reps for every muscle in my shoulders and arms to shout at me to stop. But how could I with Luis hovering over me with his crotch not inches from my forehead?

Five sets of five reps later, and I almost caved in to the agony.

When at last Luis took the barbell and placed it on the rack, I felt relieved to no longer have his body with its surprisingly prominent crotch bulge – which on reflection must have been due to the angle I was observing it from – bearing over me like that, a symbol of masculinity, masculinity in short supply in my veins.

As I sat up, Luis left me to my own devices and wandered over to a group of men hovering at the back of the gym.

The four sets of twenty table pec flies might not have been too bad had my muscles not already received a thrashing. The inclined dumbbell press might have been fine as well. I lightened the weight load for each, having realised Luis had probably set every weight a touch too heavy for my capabilities. I had to adjust to a lighter load on the decline machine press as well. Luis had told me to keep pushing on the handlebars until I couldn't manage another rep. That moment occurred all too soon.

For the duration of my workout, I kept my gaze away from the others in the gym, but I could feel theirs on me. I had to be the weakest man in there by a long stretch. Knowing how hot it was outside, part of me wanted to remain where I was, but the psychological oppression of all those hulks far outweighed the physical oppression of the heat, and after my mandatory five-kilometre cool down, I forwent the need to stretch, gave Luis a casual wave and left.

8

A SURPRISING DISCOVERY

I WAS STILL FUZZY WITH SLEEP AS I OPENED MY EYES TO GREET DAWN'S soft light. I rolled over, a tentative move, and stared at the ceiling, my body tight all over. One calf muscle threatened to cramp. I should have stretched the day before, if not at the gym then at least when I had arrived home. Instead, I had downed a bottle of wine as I completed three ghost-writing jobs, cooked up a chorizo and pasta bake and then kicked back to watch Netflix. I threw off my sheet – thankfully dry – and jumped in the shower.

Over a bacon butty breakfast, I checked the local weather. The heat wave was set to continue. The forecast on one weather site predicted the mid-thirties and, if the day before was anything to go by, the temperature would reach even higher in late-afternoon. Inland, even up on the windswept plain of Tefía, was nowhere to be. The island was enduring a dust haze too, with the wind blowing from the southeast infusing the air with the Sahara. There was nothing for it but another trip to the beach and, after a quick search of the tides, I knew where I was heading. I was out the door in under half an hour.

The sky at Puertito de Los Molinos appeared a touch clearer, at least looking out over the ocean, and standing at the shoreline on the creamy white sand, I thought I detected a waft of cooling breeze off the near flat water.

Seemed everyone here had checked the tides like I had, found it to be especially low right at this very moment and come to take advantage. There was a cluster of pleasure-seekers milling about on the wet sand and in the shallows over by the cliff face, one couple even making it the three hundred metres to the caves.

I wasted no time shuffling off my flip flops and dumping my t-shirt and towel on the sand near the pebbles fringing the beach. I wasn't sure whether to wear or remove my sunglasses so I kept them on. I tucked my keys in the secure pocket in my swimmers and with phone in hand, I splashed through the shallows to the cliff.

The water was at times ankle-deep, and I had to go in up to almost mid-calf to walk behind the revellers who were having a hoot mucking about in the rock pools beside a low ledge, and in the nooks and crannies of the gnarly lava cliff.

I kept an uncertain eye on the water as I waded in deeper still, going in up to my knees as I passed by a depression in the cliff face and then rounded a rocky protuberance. Little wonder the more fearful stayed closer to the main beach. The further I went, the more disconcerting the feeling that the tide would suddenly turn or a huge wave would appear from nowhere, like it had the day before. I carried on walking, reassuring myself that I had checked and double-checked. According to the predictions, the low tide was due to occur in about five minutes, allowing me ample time to explore the cave.

The water on the final stretch below the cliff was shallow, and the seabed strewn with large boulders. I slowed my pace, enjoying the moment, stopping to take a few photos.

As I approached the cave, the couple I had seen from the main beach had started making their way back. The woman greeted me and said something rapidly in Spanish I couldn't understand, but I nodded and grinned as though I did. She shrugged and carried on, chatting to her companion; about what, I hadn't a clue. Besides, my attention was well and truly grabbed by the sight up ahead.

In front of me was an arch of lava and, at its base, areas of pink rock. As I neared the arch, the water deepened to form a turquoise pool that was surrounded by seaweed-coated boulders. I waded in, sinking to waist height as I crossed. The water was warm and still, and I wanted to luxuriate for a while, but decided to save that experience for later.

I waded out of the water and entered the cave. I was walking on hard if damp sand. Small waves lapped against my toes. I carried on a few paces, approaching the darkness, at first blinded by the contrast. My eyes slowly adjusted, and I saw up ahead another arch of rock, the sand heading back deep inside beneath a wide domed roof.

Just inside the cave, another rock pool was tucked behind the main arch, and the water swirled around, caressing the sand. I turned, and for a moment, I stood facing out, gazing at the sapphire ocean and milky blue sky. It was surreal and enchanting, and I had to pull my eyes away, keen to explore the interior.

Fascinated by the cave itself with all of its shapes and colours, I wandered into the further reaches, entering a tunnel little more than head height. I ducked, just in case. Before long, the light faded altogether, and I turned on my phone's torch. The sand was cool and a touch damp beneath my feet. Remembering something Luis had said, I stopped to listen to the ocean, which sounded louder as the waves broke against the rocky cliff.

A sudden boom, and I stopped in my tracks. That wave was too big and too close for comfort. I was instantly claustrophobic. How far would the water reach as the tide came in? Not wanting to find out, I turned around and raced back.

I had almost entered the main chamber when something caught my eye, something not made of rock, protruding on a high ledge. I thought at first it was an animal, or even a body, but I soon saw it was a rucksack. I recalled the couple I had passed and decided it must belong to them. I was in two minds whether to leave it there or take it with me when another wave crashed against the cliff base.

I snatched the rucksack off the ledge and, finding it much heavier than I expected, I let it swing to the ground. There wasn't time to look inside.

I entered the main chamber to find the wavelets that had been lapping at the rock pool now creeping into the cave in long sweeps. Beyond the cave, larger waves were rolling in, one after another. They were not high, but they sure were travelling fast. The tide seemed in an awful rush. In my naivety, I had thought the low tide would last at least a couple of hours, but clearly I was wrong. Of course I was wrong. The tide would only be at its nadir for a single moment and after that it would on its way back to high. It was clear to me now that the woman I passed had been trying to warn me of this very fact.

I raced to the cave mouth. Puertito de los Molinos appeared a distant haven cut off from me by the invading ocean. I saw the couple had already disappeared and, scanning the ocean along the cliff base, nobody else was anywhere to be seen.

There was nothing for it but to head back as fast as I could. Staving off raw panic, I shoved my phone in the rucksack and heaved it up above my head, forcing my tight shoulder and arm muscles to obey my will. I waded through the rock pool, now much deeper than before, and as soon as I reached the other side and the water was only calf-deep I lowered the rucksack to my chest and broke into a sprint.

That depth didn't last long.

Where the water had been knee-deep it was now up to my mid-thigh. Eyeing those resolute waves surging for me, I had to resist an urge to retrieve my phone, dump the rucksack and make a swim for it. Otherwise, there was every chance a king wave would slam me into the cliff.

I hadn't waded much further before my thighs and calves started complaining. Curse that gym! Three hundred metres was beginning to feel like a thousand. The current was against me, wanting to drag me south. I pressed on as fast as I was able, but the main beach didn't seem to be getting any closer.

I looked for ways to scale the cliff, thinking that might be my best option, but I was no rock climber, and I would probably only manage to scramble up a fraction, and then I would be stuck, clinging on to the gnarly rock as the tide rose and getting covered in spray, only to then slip and fall in and hit my head and be swept away by that vicious current.

My arms had begun to complain from the effort of raising the rucksack up to save the contents from getting wet. I was a ball of knotty aches and pains, every part of me resisting the effort of wading through the churning water. I kept going, straining against the tide and the current pushing against me, trying to blinker my vision, trying not to give in to the panic threatening to consume me each time a wave surged past.

When I reached the stretch where the water had been mid-calf, I was wading in water above my knees. I wanted to inch closer to the cliff where the water was a touch shallower, but there was a risk that the surge of the backwash would create enough turbulence to knock me off my feet.

As the wash of a larger wave headed for me, I forced the rucksack high above my head and braced myself, feet astride, resisting the surge. Watching the wave crash against the cliff, terror gripped me. If I didn't get a move on, I would be one of those statistics that warranted the warning sign on the beach.

I strained forward, urging my legs to work harder, determined to make it back to shore. Even with a steely resolve only adrenalin can instil, each stride was an effort. The tide was against me in every sense. As I neared the end of the cliff and the beach was enticingly close, the waves gathered their strength as though hell-bent on smashing me into the rocky face. I resisted with all my might, turning side on with the rucksack high above my head. Then I braced ready for the backwash as the surging water hit a ledge that was soon to be submerged. As the ocean pulled back, ready for its next slam, I waded on, unnervingly close to the break line.

My ordeal came to an abrupt end as I rounded the end of the cliff and waded to the shallows of the beach. I half-anticipated a round of applause, but no one was taking any notice. Sunbathers were either lying on their towels on the sand immediately below the band of pebbles, or perching on that band, having somehow found a comfortable spot.

Out of the water, my legs turned to jelly. I made it to my towel, now dangerously close to the encroaching tide, and managed to don my t-shirt and slip my feet into my flip flops. I found a spot to sit on the beach away from the others and recovered myself. I had a sudden craving for chocolate.

Soon, I became too hot. The sun was fierce, and I badly needed to get into some shade. Thinking I first had to find the owner of the rucksack, I fished out my mobile and, with a cursory glance at the rucksack contents – all I saw was a towel – I forced myself up on my feet.

I approached a couple nearby who were sitting up, enjoying the sun on their faces. I held up the rucksack and asked if it was theirs. They shook their heads. Next, I went over to three women lying on their bellies, roasting their back halves in the midday sun. I had no idea of their nationality, so I asked in my own native tongue. They replied – after gazing up at me, puzzled – in heavy accents I took to be Spanish, that they knew nothing about any rucksack.

I carried on, approaching families, single men, in fact, every single person on the beach at that time. None of them claimed ownership of the rucksack or had seen anyone with it or anything similar. All I got for my troubles were a lot of vacant shrugs.

What a bunch of unobservant cretins!

Hoping to find in the restaurant the couple I had passed at the caves, I picked my way across the pebbles then up a flight of stone steps, entering the outdoor seating area. There I scanned the clientele and circulated the tables. I received the same negative and bemused reactions, along with a lot of furtive stares and whispered exchanges which I caught in my side vision.

Defeated, I was about to head off home, when a large woman in an ill-fitting blouse told me to try the other restaurant.

'It looks closed,' I said.

'Not closed. You go,' she insisted.

I didn't take to being bossed about. In defiance, I felt like heading in the direction of my car for a cold shower and a beer at home, but a sense that I would regret not trying everything to locate the owner propelled me on through the village of ten small huts.

In the thick heat of noon, with the sun searing my back and a fishy odour assaulting my nostrils, I began to feel nauseous and faint.

At the end of the beach, I hefted myself up the two flights of stone steps that led to the restaurant. By the time I entered the deep rustic veranda of that distinctly Bohemian eatery, I was ready to collapse into one of its cheap-looking sofas.

From what I could see, the dining was all outdoors beneath rustic pergolas. One section had swathes of brightly coloured cloth, draped perhaps to resemble a Bedouin tent and held in place beneath a haphazard crisscross of beams that shaded the space between two cuboid huts. The back wall was the cliff itself. The father in me assessed the restaurant unsafe for children. A single rope hanging between low posts was all that stopped diners from tumbling over the edge. Jackie would have had a fit. Yet the restaurant was in a prime location overlooking the beach and the ocean and the cliff, and there seemed nothing to do other than kick back, enjoy the atmosphere and eat. And plenty were. Despite the dubious safety standards, beneath various sections of canopy, seated before an open-air cooking area that could scarcely be called a kitchen, an array of happy diners occupied every table. The chef, if he could be called that, was at work creating a paella in a huge dish over an open fire. He was a burly, bearded man in a t-shirt, apron and a baseball cap, cutting a most eccentric figure.

Ignoring his gaze which had locked with mine the moment I noticed him, I went around with the rucksack, receiving the same shaking heads and looks of confused puzzlement I anticipated. Finally, I arrived at a table where a man and a woman were enjoying drinks and the view.

The man was thin, swarthy, with thick dark hair tied back in a ponytail at the nape of his neck. The woman had copper hair and a fresh, English appearance. There was an expensive-looking camera on the table. Tourists. Had to be. I held up the rucksack and repeated my inquiry.

'Does this by any chance belong to you?'

They both stared up at me at once, then the woman looked me up and down. By then, I was used to the apparent rejection of my question, me, my being altogether. I must have appeared as defeated as I felt. The man opened his mouth to speak when the woman said, 'You look like you need to sit down.'

The man's gaze returned to my face. He said something in Spanish. She replied. Then she said, 'Draw up a chair.'

'I'm not disturbing your lunch?'

'We were just leaving,' the woman said. 'You can have our table. Looks like you need it.'

I pulled out the spare chair and sat down, placing the rucksack on the floor between my feet. Bereft of its owner, I felt oddly like its guardian.

'I'm Claire,' the woman said with a broad smile, 'and this is Paco.'

'Trevor.'

She tilted her face at me, all inquisitive and interested. I felt strangely awkward.

'On holiday?'

'Sort of. I'm renting a farmhouse in Tefia for three months.'

'Escaping, then.'

I laughed. 'You could say that. I'm a writer.'

'Impressive.'

'Where in Tefia?' the man, Paco, asked.

'Heading from this direction, the third house on the left.'

A look of recognition appeared in Paco's face as though he knew the property well.

'And you?' I asked.

'We live in one of the inland villages.'

'Which one?'

'Tiscamanita.' The way Paco said the word gave an impression of ownership and I sensed he was a local.

'We restored a ruin,' Claire said with pride.

'*You* restored a ruin,' Paco said quickly.

She emitted an awkward laugh. 'Paco is a photographer,' she said to me. She reached into her purse and extracted a business card. Sliding the card across the table in my direction, she said, 'We have converted a corner of the house into a one-bedroom apartment. Self-contained. Private entrance.'

'Thanks, but...'

'With a spectacular view of a volcano.'

'He already has a place, Claire.'

She glanced out at the ocean. 'He might want to come to the island again or stay longer this time. You never know.' She turned her head, her gaze settling on my face.

'Indeed, I don't,' I said, pocketing the card.

'I hope you find the owner,' Paco said, looking down at the ruck-sack at my feet as he stood.

They said goodbye and wished me luck. I watched them walk away, then went over to the chef as I had seen others do, and ordered a plate of his paella and a beer.

While I waited for my order, I checked the tide times on my phone and discovered I had been right – nothing wrong with my powers of observation or my memory – just my understanding of tides. There was almost a two-metre difference between low and high tide, depending on the day, and that amounted to a lot of water. The beach gradient being slight, it stood to reason the tide would rush in the way it had, stopped on the beach only by that bank of pebbles.

Why hadn't I stopped and thought about what that woman exiting the cave had been trying to tell me? As I considered my answer, I came face to face with a quality in my nature I hadn't truly acknowledged before. I was too quick, too impulsive, too eager to prove – to a gym instructor, for goodness sake – that I was not an ignorant fool. I had taken in at a glance the new information about tides and assumed I had acquired some sort of deep knowledge. I saw now that my assessment was a form of arrogance. After all, even if I had considered what that woman had been saying, I probably wouldn't have taken much notice. Was I always so quick to assume that I was right?

The arrival of my beer distracted me from my thoughts. The paella that came soon after was delicious. The view and the entire experience of that rustic café proved a salve for an otherwise confronting morning.

9

A MOMENT OF CONSCIENCE

WITH ITS USUAL CUNNING, THE SAVAGE SUMMER SUN HAD DONE ITS worst to my skin, the effects not felt until later, until I was back at the farmhouse after my ordeal, the burn developing like a photograph, radiating its fiery heat in the dark of the windowless room where I sat for an hour sipping beer. My skin stung the most on my shoulders, nose, forehead and scalp, those areas of my body that had borne the brunt of the infernal blaze, while my legs, submerged in water for a good deal of time, were still white save for my already sunburned thighs. I also sported two irregularly shaped white discs around my eyes. I looked like a panda. So much for sunscreen. Adding to my woes, I was fast developing a pounding headache that painkillers failed to touch. I felt nauseous, I had a raging thirst, and I radiated heat like a blast furnace.

I had planned to visit the gym later in the afternoon, but in my condition, I was fit only for quiet times in darkened rooms with soft furnishings. I couldn't frown, I couldn't squint, and I certainly couldn't smile. When I did, I paid the price.

I drained a second bottle of San Miguel and went and stood in the shower, letting the cool water soothe my skin. I stood there for a goodly while. Ten minutes had passed before I was patting myself dry and carefully dabbing my skin with dollops of Savlon. Dressed only in boxer shorts, I dragged my poor, smarting body to the kitchen where the rucksack, the cause of my agony, sat on the bench.

Seeing it there, I rued the moment I made that decision in the cave to bring it with me. I should have left well alone, or followed a tiny voice inside that suggested the moment I had exited the ocean that returning to my car, or at the very least, heading for the shade provided by the main restaurant, were good ideas. If I had taken my own advice, much of my sunburn would not have been so severe. Instead, I had roasted like a beast on a spit while strangers on the beach slowly gave their answers as to whether or not they were, or knew of the owner of the offending item.

I should have given up after it became apparent that no one knew anything about it. But that part of my brain that likes to leave no stone unturned, made me approach every single person on the beach.

In point of fact, I ought to have gone straight to the police there and then, handed the ruddy thing in and been done with it. Let them find the owner.

I should have done all of that, but I hadn't. And there the rucksack sat, ownerless, in my kitchen.

I could, I should still go to the police. But I was in no fit state to drive.

Should, ought, should. Bollocks to an inner monologue filled with guilt and self-recriminations! It was about time I summoned some positivity into my life.

I unzipped the main pocket and was about to extract the contents when caution kicked in. Was it wise to tamper with what might be evidence? Shouldn't I at least be wearing gloves?

I found a pair of rubber gloves in a drawer. They were still in their packet. I ripped the plastic open, extracted a glove and inserted a hand. The rubber was tight and pulled at my skin. I hadn't thought my hands were sunburn tender until that moment. Must have caught the sun when I was carrying the rucksack up above the water.

I had to tug and tug to get my fingers partway into the finger holes and gave up trying to put the glove on properly when each digit was about halfway.

One glove would do.

Gingerly, I extracted the contents of the rucksack item by item and laid them out across the bench. A beach towel, rolled up like a sausage, brightly coloured, damp and smelling of the ocean. A pair of tattered plimsolls minus their laces. The soles were worn and the canvas stained. They had certainly seen better days. A journal with a plain blue cover, brand new and devoid of even a scribble. My attention was drawn to the bulging front pouch. A pair of shorts and a t-shirt were crammed into the small space. Both were old and faded. Little more than rags. The t-shirt had a hole near the hem. The pockets of the shorts were empty. I found a bottle of sunscreen in one side pocket and a mobile phone in the other. The only other item filling the bottom of the rucksack's main compartment and too large to extract with my one gloved hand, was a bundle of what felt like piles of paper wrapped in some old cloth. I pulled on the second glove as best I could and then eased the package out of the rucksack and opened the cloth.

My jaw fell open. There before my eyes were bundles of cash secured with rubber bands and stacked in five neat piles. I picked up one of the top bundles and riffled through the notes. They were all fifty euros and a rough guess told me there were twenty in that bundle. That was a thousand euros. How many bundles in a pile? I ran my finger up the pile nearest me and counted ten bundles. That meant fifty bundles altogether. If they each contained a thousand euros, then I was staring at fifty thousand euros.

Fifty thousand euros!

I was unsteady on my feet. My eyes filled with greed as my mind whirled with possibilities. A car. Pay off the mortgage. Book another holiday. Anything at all.

Leaving the cash sitting there, I patted down the rucksack, delved into every pocket, double and triple checked, tipped the rucksack upside-down and gave it a vigorous shake, but there was nothing else to be found.

My hands were sweating inside the rubber gloves. I peeled them off and let my skin breathe while I gathered my thoughts.

That cash belonged to someone, and I had no right to keep it. Or rather, to appease my conscience, I needed to at least try to identify the owner.

The clothes and towel were not telling me much. The only identification was that phone. I switched it on and was surprised when I could swipe straight to the home screen. Not screen locked then. With strange anticipation, I went into messages. Empty. Phone log. Nothing. Social media apps. Not activated. I went into contacts and found two phone numbers, both mobiles and both unnamed. I hesitated. Should I try calling those numbers? It seemed the most direct way of finding out what was going on. But a small, cautionary voice inside stopped me.

I had the presence of mind to switch off the phone's power to save the battery. Then I surveyed the contents of the rucksack one more time. Aside from the cash, the items were those of a regular beach lover, someone who had already gone for a swim – the damp towel – and fancied another. The plimsolls conjured a young holidaymaker, a surfer maybe. Someone who had scored a cheap flight. Someone who liked to holiday off the beaten track. The lack of a water bottle suggested the individual – male, judging by the shorts – had not planned to stay long, but then no one would, not in that cave.

The money put a different complexion on things and a number of thoughts galloped through my mind all at once. Uppermost, whoever the rucksack belonged to would go back to the cave to fetch it. It occurred to me in an isolated thought that the ledge where the rucksack had been hidden must have been above the waterline even in the highest of tides. The sand had been dry there, as far as I could recall. Perhaps the rucksack hadn't been there that long, and I had somehow managed to miss the owner altogether as the tide raced in, even as I stood on the beach approaching every single person there. For no one in their right mind would have swum in the other direction. From what I had seen on maps, the coastline consisted of a long stretch of cliff.

Did the rucksack really belong to that couple I had passed as I approached the cave? Thinking back, the man had appeared agitated. Was that why the woman wanted me to turn back? In case I found the rucksack? Nothing to do with the tide at all? But if that was the case, why disappear from Puertito? Why not wait around for me to appear, empty-handed or laden?

The much larger question was why would anyone want to hide a rucksack full of cash. Obviously, because it was dodgy money, stolen maybe, or the proceeds of crime. Drug money? Had to be. Whoever had hidden the rucksack knew someone was or would be on to them, and they needed to hide the money in the most unlikely of places while they headed off to attend to something else.

What a bizarre hiding place!

Unless they really needed it totally out of the way and utterly inaccessible.

In all likelihood, someone else would be on the hunt for that cash and motor mouth me had approached everyone on the beach and in both of the restaurants, flaunting that rucksack to all and sundry.

Alarm raced through me. Someone might have recognised the rucksack, pretended not to so as not to attract attention, and then followed me back here.

I went straight to the window and peered out through the net curtains up and down the road. There was no one about, no suspicious car parked anywhere nearby.

But that didn't mean I was in the clear. Word would go around. I would be the gossip of the day for all those I had approached, an idiot English tourist with someone's lost rucksack.

My suspicions landed on that couple in the Bohemian restaurant, Paco and Claire; they had been rather too quick to give up their table and leave. They were the most likely suspects simply because they were the ones who took the keenest interest in me. Everyone else had expressed indifference. Not them. They invited me to join them. And I had fallen for their trap and told them exactly where I was staying.

Yet why give me their business card? If they were in any way implicated, wouldn't they rather hide their own identities, not flaunt them? Maybe Claire thought to lure me to their place in order to do heaven only knew what to me. After all, she did seem rather keen to lure me to Tiscamanita. I pictured the couple, all self-assured and relaxed, and told myself I was being paranoid. That couple had exuded a mix of indifference and mild concern. They lacked the air of the criminal. There was nothing shifty about either of them. In all, they were not the criminal type.

Then again, you never could tell.

Considering all the various implications of my situation, it appeared I was left with no choice. I had to drive to the nearest police station and hand in the rucksack. The longer I hung on to it, the worse for me it would be. I pulled on the gloves, wrapped up the cash and then I began returning the contents to the side pockets.

As I picked up the cash bundle, I hesitated. There was more to this than met the eye, and I was making a string of baseless assumptions. The truth would reveal itself if I waited. If anyone pounded on my door, I could act dumb or hand over the cash. Or I could simply hide the rucksack and pretend I had handed it in to the police and then make a run for it after whoever it was had left.

Whatever I chose to do, one thing was certain, while doubt and suspicions replaced hard truth, I couldn't spend a single euro of that cash.

10

UNCERTAINTY

I WOKE TANGLED IN THE SHEETS AGAIN. TO MY GREAT RELIEF, THEY WERE dry, but I was sporting one almighty erection, and I badly needed to pee.

Drifting into my mind were wisps of a dream, translucent images of nubile flesh, barely defined.

A party was going on all around me. I was standing beside a swimming pool. Scantily clad revellers cavorting. Heavy metal played in the background. Laughter rose. Then a man appeared in the water. He gazed up at me and smiled. He pinned me with his gaze as he hefted himself out of the pool. He was naked. His member glistened. Suddenly, it was all I could see. I knew the man to be Vince.

I disentangled myself and went to the bathroom to deal with the awkward situation of a rock-hard penis and a bursting-full bladder. My balls were aching, and I needed to urinate. The balls took precedence.

As I washed my hands, I mused over why Vince should suddenly be popping up out of my unconscious and into my dreams. Those furtive days of frenzied tugging were well and truly in the past. Back then, neither of us had ever discussed being gay, and in the whole time I was married to Jackie I never once felt desire for a man. I had to admit the tendency must have been lurking in me, if weakly, or I would never have let Vince handle my cock with only the mildest alarm and revulsion. Surely a purely heterosexual man would have socked Vince in the face the moment his fingers landed on their member. To me, his soft boy hands were titillating in the extreme. My sexuality felt ambiguous in the recollecting. Yet I still had no desire for, or attraction to, a man, not even in my imagination. So, what was filtering up? Did it mean anything? Or was it just the trickster playing games with me during this most vulnerable phase of my life?

In the shower, I put my nocturnal disturbances down to frayed nerves and too much excitement and put an end to further speculation. My time in Fuerteventura was meant to be a relaxing retreat. Admittedly, I had been on the island for only one week, and I couldn't hope to have unwound and settled into a routine in that time, certainly not one conducive to composing fiction, yet I remained far removed from the stresses of my ordinary life, and I was feeling more relaxed than I had been back in England. My physical transformation had already begun, too. All that pedalling and hefting at the gym hadn't changed my physique, but the effort was starting to generate feelings of wellbeing, even if my body was sore, top to toe.

And what a week it had been! First, the disturbing discovery that a local youth hostel had once functioned as a prison that incarcerated gay men, a matter that had been nagging at the fringes of my mind since Angela suggested I write about it. Now that awful history, only a short walk from my bedroom window, had been eclipsed by a present-day drama unravelling before me, right from the moment I found the rucksack. It appeared life had plans for me on this island, plans that did not involve rest and relaxation. It seemed as though I had been co-opted as a character in some sort of saga which I wished *was* fiction so I didn't have to endure the anxiety that came with it.

I stood before the bathroom mirror and inspected the sunburn. My skin was crimson and making up its mind whether to tan or peel. My nose had already decided. Whatever I chose to do with the day, I had to stay out of the sun, or at least cover my burnt bits. I dabbed on Savlon and followed with a liberal dollop of the moisturiser I had acquired from Jackie. Stepping out of the bathroom, I smelled vaguely antiseptic and florally scented.

Over a breakfast of toasted sourdough topped with thick slices of tomato and goat's cheese, the whole drizzled with olive oil, I checked my inbox, at last braving the "Pending" folder and opening the email from Jackie.

Two short sentences and she was wishing me a happy trip. That was it. Should I reply? Thank her? But then she would reply to mine, expecting updates. She would end up demanding a full account of my stay to satisfy her curiosity. Given the circumstances, the least said the better. I deleted the email. If she was curious, let her stew.

Amongst the usual junk, there were three short writing assignments: A fitness company wanted more content for their website, a blogger wanted an article on men's health, and the last was a request for ten top tips for hikers. I imagined a possible Tip Ten: If you see a lone rucksack on your hike, leave it where it is.

All were good payers. I went against my earlier decision not to take on more assignments and accepted them each in turn. I made a pot of coffee and set to work.

It was midday before I stopped to prepare lunch. I was halfway through dicing salad vegetables, my knife poised over a cucumber, when my laptop emitted its Skype trill.

Angela. Had to be.

I wanted to ignore her, but the ring was too demanding. Knife in hand, I was thrown into a moment of confusion. I needed to finish preparing my salad or it would ruin. If I told her to call me back, she would want to know why. Besides, it would be her lunch break, too.

I put down the knife and went to answer the call, rushing to the little dining room where I had set up my work station and hitting the accept button. Angela instantly appeared onscreen. I smiled at her even though she couldn't see me; I had left my webcam switched off. Without video, at least she couldn't laugh at my sunburnt face.

'Poor connection,' I said before she asked.

'Hi, Trevor. How are you doing?'

'I'm great,' I lied.

'Thrilled to hear it.'

I carried the laptop to the kitchen bench and continued chopping, as quietly as I could, the knife making rhythmic thwacks on the chopping board.

'What's that god-awful sound?'

'Sorry.'

I took to slicing slowly, easing the knife down as it hit the board. I had moved on to a carrot.

'How's the writing?' she said.

'I just completed three assignments.'

'That's not what I meant.'

'A man's gotta eat.'

It was true, my meagre savings would not last forever.

Angela ran a hand through her hair.

'You really should consider writing about that prison.'

'No.'

I thrust the blade down hard on the last segment of carrot. Must have sounded dreadful her end, but Angela made no comment. There was a moment of silence. Then she said, 'Don't sound so emphatic. You are the perfect writer for it.'

I wasn't. I knew full well I wasn't. I had enough turmoil going on inside me, and the last thing I needed was to embody gay characters, especially those incarcerated in a concentration camp. It would be too much.

'What about that Richard H. Parry?' I said dismissively. 'Give it to him.'

Into my salad went artichoke hearts and a roasted whole red pepper which I tore with my fingers.

'He doesn't have your cultural sensitivity,' Angela said. 'He is too old-school to do justice to the theme.'

'Of a prison camp?'

'Of gender preference.'

I tossed the salad around in the bowl and doused the lot in an olive oil dressing and left it on the bench, taking the laptop and Angela back to the dining table.

'And I know all about it?' I said, installing much sarcasm into my voice as I sat down. 'Well, I don't.'

'Trevor, you do.'

'Not this again. Leave it alone, Angela. I'm straight.'

'As straight as a banana.'

Irritated, I brushed a speck of dust from the bottom corner of the screen that had been annoying me the entire call. There was a long pause, then she shrieked, 'What happened to your face!'

A ripple of shocked humiliation went through me. Damn my fumble fingers! She was staring straight at me, tears already rolling down her cheeks.

Caught off guard, I blurted out the whole story of my ordeal at Puertito de Los Molinos, including the bit about not taking into account the tidal range, an oversight that led me to the false belief I had ample time to return to the main beach.

'Trevor,' she gasped when I finished speaking, 'this one you simply must write.'

'I can't. I'm living it, Angela, and it's, well, terrifying.'

'All you need do is hand the rucksack in to the police then make up a story of what would have happened if you hadn't.'

'You mean if I kept the cash?'

'Surely your imagination can run to that?'

'Not while the rucksack is sitting on my bench.'

'Of course not. It's making you too anxious.' She glanced at her office door. 'Gotta dash.' The screen went blank before I could say goodbye.

Angela was right, as usual. I needed to hand in the rucksack.

At least she hadn't mentioned Sandra Flint and her undeserved shortlisting. Then again, the work did deserve it, I thought with sudden pride. That shortlist was mine, and I should at least allow myself a little satisfaction even if any prize money would be denied me.

I retrieved my salad from the kitchen and munched my way through to the last morsel as I scrolled through images of Fuerteventura. When I got bored with photos of sunshine and sand, I located the nearest police station.

Stalling the inevitable, I washed up, dried and put away, my eyes flitting to the rucksack still on the bench. After folding the tea towel over the oven door, I fetched my sunglasses and hat and then I slid the rucksack off the bench and slung it over my shoulder, realising before it landed on my scalded skin that I should not have done that. I stifled a yell, eased the bag off my shoulder and let it fall to the floor.

It took a few moments for the pain to subside. I dared not rub the skin, which instinct compelled me to do.

Outside, it was another furnace of a day. I rushed to my car and opened all the doors, including the boot, to let out the heat. As I stood, waiting with the rucksack at my feet, a car drove by, slowed, did a U-turn then stopped outside my house. The muscles in my gut constricted. There was no time to run inside. No time to jump in my car and drive off. All I could do was look casual and wait.

There was a long pause while whoever was in that car made up their mind to get out. Maybe they were loading a gun.

At last, the passenger door opened.

It was Paco and Claire.

11

PACO AND CLAIRE

'Are you going out?' Claire said, all smiles as she approached, her copper hair piled high on her head, her sunglasses wedged in the mass. 'Cars get so hot here left in the sun. I bet you can't touch the steering wheel.'

I emitted an awkward laugh that sounded more like a grunt.

Paco wandered past me and on down the short drive. I had no idea what might have drawn his interest. The property looked out over the back blocks of the village, and there was nothing much to see of interest or beauty. He stood with his back to us, as though surveying the landscape, but it occurred to me his behaviour was simply a pretence. Taking him in, he seemed uncomfortable, restless as though eager to get going.

Oblivious, or perhaps indifferent to his demeanour, Claire pointed at the rucksack at my feet.

'Still not found the owner?'

'I, um, was taking it to the police.'

'The police? What on earth for? Why not put it back where you found it if it is troubling you that much?'

'The cave is very hard to get to,' Paco said, joining Claire, whose gaze never left my face. She must have noticed my panda-look, but she made no comment. I found her discretion endearing.

'We watched you struggle back as the tide came in,' she said. Her face creased as she grinned. 'You were amazing. I'd have freaked.'

I was taken aback and didn't take kindly to having been their midday entertainment. 'You never said.'

'We didn't want to embarrass you.'

Well, you have now. 'What brings you to Tefia?' I asked lightly, keen to change the subject.

'We were heading to the garden centre, and then we saw you.'

'We stopped on impulse,' Paco said. 'Claire's idea.'

There was a long pause. I wasn't sure how to fill it, then social etiquette broke through my anxiety, and I found myself inviting them inside and giving them a tour.

'You don't find the traffic disturbs your writing?' Claire said as she noticed the road through the front room window, only about three metres away.

The farmhouse was ancient, and I thought the road had been built a long time after. Four steps leading down from the pavement to the front veranda meant vibrations from passing vehicles could be felt in that front room.

'I am rarely in this part of the house and there is never much traffic,' I said. 'I'm not writing much in any case. I don't seem to have the inspiration.'

She turned back to the room and gave me a sympathetic look. 'Not with your skin. That's pretty bad sunburn. What are you putting on it?'

'Savlon.'

'Aloe Vera is best.'

Claire was beginning to remind me of Angela, of Jackie, of all the women I knew who seemed to know everything and took pleasure in dishing up advice.

I led the couple through to the bathroom with its claw-foot bath and from there to the second living room.

Paco, who had thus far not been talkative, said, 'It isn't his sunburn that's affecting him, Claire. It's this place.'

Claire shot him a puzzled look.

'Not the farmhouse,' he said quickly as we carried on with the tour. 'The area. Tefía has a strange energy.'

'You think so?' I said with interest. I was inclined to agree with him.

'I know so. There has been a lot of tragedy here.'

I was about to ask him what he meant, but he had gone straight into my bedroom. I had no choice but to follow. First, he inspected the four-poster bed. I hid my embarrassment over the crumpled sheets that I had inadvertently forgotten to straighten, my mind flashing back to my erotic dream and the outcome I was forced to enact. Then, to my relief, he went and stood by the window. Claire, the more considerate of the two, remained in the doorway.

'The prison?' I said, thinking he must have been referring to the hostel. 'I heard about that. I've walked to the windmill a couple of times.'

'That place was a labour camp.' He pointed out the window, not that the camp was visible. 'The men worked in the fields all around here, breaking rocks and building walls. You would have seen them from here, like scrawny, half-starved ants.'

No one spoke. I began to rail against the thought of all those poor men suffering just beyond my doorstep not that long ago, and for what? Their sexuality? It seemed an unconscionable injustice. I was born just a few years after General Franco died, and I had only ever known Spain as a democracy. But the dictatorship was all too recent, and, of course, I had read Hemingway and Orwell and seen pictures of Picasso's *Guernica*. That Franco had also persecuted gay men seemed almost par for the course, but it didn't change the iniquity, the horror of it. We all knew about Hitler and what the Nazi's did to minority groups. No one I knew had ever given a thought to what had happened under Franco.

'Claire,' Paco said. 'Those prisoners saw the lights of Mafaso.'

I had no idea what he meant. He chose not to fill me in. Claire said, addressing me, 'It's an ancient myth. Although maybe not a myth. I have seen them, too.'

'Really?'

'Small darts of light,' Paco said, fixing his gaze on my face. 'They are from the souls of disturbed graves.' He turned to the window. A poignant tone infused his next words. 'I think the other tragedy has added to the dark energy here.'

'What other tragedy?' Claire looked at him inquiringly.

He let his gaze slide away and muttered, 'I don't like to talk about it.'

Then why even mention it?

'Tell us,' Claire said. Her tone was authoritative. In a flash, she again reminded me of Jackie. It was disconcerting. Although she was nothing like Jackie, in appearance or manner. For a ghastly second, I thought I might be turning into a misogynist, tarring all women with the same brush.

Paco appeared untroubled by her manner. He stayed by the window and spoke in a grim voice. 'In 1972 the area witnessed a terrible event. Thirteen parachutists died in those fields, and many more were injured.'

'What happened?' Claire said, a look of concern appearing in her face.

'It was during a military exercise. Some idiot commander ordered a mass jump. I think ninety men jumped. The wind was so strong, it dragged the men harnessed in their parachutes for three kilometres across the plain. Many men were smashed against stone walls. Others were slammed into fig trees. They say there was so much blood. The whole island was traumatised.'

'I never knew.'

'You haven't lived here that long. I'll take you to the monument if you want. They put it in the middle of a field behind the windmill. Access is on foot. Only the locals know it is there.'

Well hidden, then, rather like the prison.

Paco said, 'At the time, they supressed the news.'

'Sounds like they are still supressing it.'

'I'm not surprised,' I said.

'Why?' They both turned to me.

'The military would have been ashamed.'

'Ashamed?' Paco said, pausing to reflect. 'Yes, probably that is the right word. Can you imagine the carnage?' Paco turned his back to the window and looked at us both in turn. 'There were no ambulances here back then. The villagers used their own cars to take the wounded to the hospital. Others were taken in taxis. A tiny hospital with few doctors and nurses to cope. They had no blood, no plasma – they had to put the men in order of seriousness. Some were evacuated to Las Palmas.'

'How do you know so much about it?' Claire asked.

'I lost an uncle on my father's side, and an aunt on my mother's side was a nurse.'

'I'm so sorry.' She walked past me and joined him by the window, placing an arm around him.

I was stunned. I couldn't speak.

'If you are looking for inspiration for a novel,' he said grimly, 'now you have it.'

'I couldn't possibly write about something so horrific.'

'Why not? People need to know about these things.'

'I was hoping to write about something more convivial.'

'Like what?'

'To be honest, I have no idea. I can't seem to muster my creativity.'

'No wonder. The trauma here on this land would suck it out of you.' Paco made a curious gurgling sound with his mouth.

'You should cut things short here and come and stay with us,' Claire said almost urgently.

I was grateful for the slight change of subject and used it to vacate the room. They trailed behind me through to the kitchen where I had dumped the rucksack on the bench.

'He won't get a refund,' Paco said, apparently not keen on her offer.

'Then he can stay with us for free!' It was a magnanimous gesture, and I could see she meant it.

'As you wish,' Paco said. He didn't seem to share her enthusiasm.

I felt more awkward than ever, but Claire wasn't about to let it drop. It seemed when it came to such matters, she wore the trousers.

'The poor man is stuck up here with no company, wandering around aimlessly on this godforsaken plain. There is no telling where he will end up.' She glanced at the bench. 'Or how many more ruck-sacks he'll find.'

We all laughed, and the atmosphere grew less tense.

'I really don't know what to do with the blasted thing?' I said, wishing even as I spoke that I had said nothing.

'What's in it?' Claire asked.

Paco picked it up. I was instantly on my guard.

'Feels heavy.'

'Gold? Jewellery?'

They exchanged playful glances.

'Definitely suspicious.'

'If you must know,' I said, making a grab for the rucksack in a sudden rush, 'it's full of cash.' I instantly regretted my loose tongue.

'Wow!' Paco said, releasing his grasp. 'Then, you can't go to the police!'

'Why ever not?'

'Many reasons.'

'Such as?'

'Think about it. What will it achieve?'

'It's evidence.'

'Of what?'

'I don't know.'

'Look, it is hardly lost property. No one forgets that amount of cash.'

'But if I keep it, whoever it belongs to will be after me.'

'Only if they know you have it.'

'Paco,' Claire said. 'He did ask everyone in Puertito that day.'

'Which is why I want to hand it in.'

'If you hand it in, you will make yourself even more vulnerable. They will still be after the rucksack. Better you have it. Then if they find you, you can at least give it to them.'

'Paco's right. If you say you handed it in, they won't believe you.'

'He'd be that scared, they probably would.'

I had no idea how to respond. Did I look like that much of a coward?

'All I am saying is what idiot hands that much cash in to the police?'

Claire turned to me with that warm smile she was fond of putting on. 'Even more reason to stay with us.'

'I'll think about it,' I said, suddenly filled with mistrust.

Paco eyed me strangely. 'Don't think too long.'

'Paco's right. Offer's open. Whenever you're ready.'

Paco glanced at his watch. 'We better be going, Claire.'

'I haven't offered you a drink,' I said, relieved to see them go.

'Another time.'

Claire turned to me with a wink. 'Good luck.'

I saw them out and watched them drive away. Then I went back inside and marched from room to room locating the best hiding place. I ended up shoving the rucksack in the back of my wardrobe.

Paranoia took a stronger hold on me with every passing minute of that day. I grew sensitive to noise. A car slowed, and I was by the front window in a flash, back to the wall, peering out.

This was no way to spend a holiday. I had to get a grip.

There was only one way I knew of to inject normalcy into my situation. I wrote a shopping list in the order of the aisles and, forcing myself to leave the rucksack unattended, headed to Antigua, endeavouring to feel like, or at least appear like an ordinary guy.

Pushing my trolley around, I couldn't understand why the other shoppers kept stealing amused glances my way. Then I realised I wasn't wearing my sunglasses.

12

MUSCLE STRAIN

I SCARCELY SLEPT. THE WARM MILK AND HERBAL SLEEPING PILLS I HAD taken the night before made no difference. All night, my thoughts were in the wardrobe with that rucksack.

The only good thing about the start to the day was my sunburn had eased, my skin markedly less tender. My nose was a touch blotchy where the old skin had peeled and my shoulders were beginning to follow suit, but the heat and the agony had faded. Getting out of the shower and seeing the reflection of my face with its panda eyes in the bathroom mirror, I wished I had some of Jackie's brown eyeshadow and vowed to tan my whole face at the earliest opportunity. Thinking back, I found it odd Paco and Claire had chosen to take no notice of my face. Perhaps they were simply being polite.

Back in my bedroom, I dressed then made the bed, folding and smoothing down the top sheet, and tucking it into the mattress and making sure the pillows and quilt were aligned neatly. I wasn't about to risk another visitor barging into my bedroom to confront an unmade bed. Besides, I always made my bed. It was just that one occasion when I hadn't, and I was punished for it with a Paco invasion as though, on some subtle level, he had been intent on shaming me. Or was I being overly neurotic? It felt like no accident that he should raise the topic of the prison right there where I had been having erotic dreams, erotic dreams involving men. Or had I raised the topic? Claire? I couldn't recall.

I made my way through to the kitchen. As I poured cereal and milk into a bowl, an insistent wind whistled through the gaps in the windows and door frames. The sound sliced through me. I wondered how the generations of folk who had resided in this old farmhouse put up with the sound. It interfered with what little concentration I had. I was disturbed enough by the hostel, the parachutists who fell to their gruesome deaths, and the rucksack. I really didn't need that continuous whistle grating on my nerves as well.

I filled the kettle and scooped coffee into the plunger and mulled over my plans for the day. I really ought to start pulling together ideas for a novel. Angela was right; I had terrific material to draw on after my experience in the cave. Yet Paco was also right; Tefia was not a location conducive to creative inspiration, especially since I was not given to explore the topic of trauma or the theme of brutality. As for the rucksack, I wanted to obliterate from my memory the ordeal surrounding its discovery and worried the damn thing was set to bring me further difficulties as I dealt with its presence in my wardrobe.

There was nothing for it but to let the novel issue ride. After breakfast, I spent the morning writing content for the Iron Force Fitness Centre website. A spot of lunch and I filled the afternoon composing a Top Fifty Non-Fiction Books of the Year post for a prominent literary blog whose regular writer had fallen ill with influenza.

By late afternoon, I was restless. A whole day cooped up indoors and my body craved exercise. The gym was the obvious place and, if I went soon, I might avoid those serious bodybuilders who seemed to occupy the gym during the day. In their absence, I would feel less self-conscious. I was sure no one would notice my sunburn in the muted lighting. Such was the reasoning which propelled me out the door.

At six, I was pulling up outside the gym, enjoying the buzz on the inner-city street, inhaling the fish and garlic cooking smells emanating from nearby restaurants and, pushing open the door on the interior cool, absorbing the loud upbeat music, the black and chrome and the faint odour of male sweat.

There were about ten men in the room. Luis was nowhere to be seen, so I hopped on an exercise bike and did the required ten kilometres at the required tension as per my fitness plan.

I had rack pulls, assisted chin ups, table rows and the rear deltoid machine ahead of me. The machines were lined up in a section of the gym that might as well have had a sign above it announcing "back day here". Luckily for me, the behemoth doing his back routine was already working on his delts. No one else seemed about to use those particular machines. The men were evenly spread around the other areas, focusing on legs or arms or shoulders or chests. As long as I didn't look in their direction or in the mirrors, I figured they would take no notice of me.

The behemoth, a gruff-looking man with deep-set eyes and wide lips, was the same height as me, but we were hardly of comparable strength. At the rack pull machine, I faced the same difficulty removing the metal discs – twenty kilos each side, this time – and cursed the hulk for not having the presence of mind to consider who came after him.

Once I had a mere thirty kilos at each end of the bar, I adopted the dead lift pose Luis had shown me – feet under hips, grip at shoulder width, back arched and hips back to engage the hamstrings – and I adopted a hook grip, one hand under and one hand over the bar. With my head forward, I lifted the bar by straightening hips and knees, and pulled my shoulders back as I completed the move.

Luis told me to start at five reps of sixty kilos, and increase in increments of ten kilos, aiming for a hundred. Sixty was easy, seventy that much harder, and eighty felt like my limit. I should have listened to my body and stopped there. Instead, like an automaton, I followed Luis's plan and added another disc at each end of the bell bar.

I lifted, and nothing happened.

I lifted again, and the bar didn't budge.

I tried again and felt something give in my back.

Shaken, I let go of the bar, eyed the weights at each end in disgust and stood back. I swore Luis had set me up for ridicule, convinced I detected mirth rippling around the room. I looked around. No sign of Luis, and not one of those men came over to see if I was all right. I pinned my gaze to the floor, took a few paces then tentatively swung around from my hips. My back seemed fine.

I went and sat at the lat pull down machine, taking a few moments to recover from my latest humiliation. Luis had told me the exercise worked the whole back. I gripped the bar and pulled down in a moment of frustration and self-contempt. Nothing happened other than a sudden ping in my right shoulder. I had forgotten to adjust the weight pin which was no doubt set to suit the strength of the behemoth.

I was an idiot. I could have done with my personal trainer at my side, but Luis was obviously busy elsewhere.

I eased myself off the seat and pulled the pin – which I found set at an astonishing hundred and thirty kilograms – and inserted it at sixty.

Ten reps and I went to the assisted chin up machine, setting the weight high to make it easy on myself. Eight reps and I was back on the lat pull downs.

Four super sets later and, suddenly grateful for Luis's absence and hoping none of the others was watching, I re-adjusted the pins in each machine to lighten the load. My reaction to my own furtive act was almost a reflex, borne of shame. But I didn't want to be more of a laughing stock than I already was.

The four sets of twelve table rows proved doable at the lighter weight, despite a nagging pain in my shoulder. All I had left was the rear delt machine.

Careful to set the pin at the desired weight, I leaned forward on the seat, gripped the bars and pulled my arms back as far as they would go. In a final surge of determination not to look like a weakling, I yanked on the bars and gave the reps everything I had. It was only when I eased myself off the machine after the last rep that I knew I had injured a muscle in my shoulder.

Ignoring the pain, I returned to the exercise bike.

Only then, when I was pedalling the final kilometres of my work-out, did Luis appear, entering the gym through the back office. He caught my gaze in the mirror and issued his beaming grin. As he came over, I winced in response to a sudden dart of pain. My shoulder was threatening to seize.

'Hey, are you okay?' he said with much concern in his voice.

'I think I just strained a muscle,' I said between breaths.

'Back day?'

'How did you know?'

'You want to get some ice on that right away. Come with me.'

I forwent the last kilometre, eased myself off the bike and followed him over to the sofa by the main counter. He went out the back and returned with an ice pack. As he placed the pack on my shoulder, he stared into my face. I was instantly reminded of my panda-eyed appearance and expected him to break out into laughter any second.

He didn't. Instead, he said, 'Stay there,' and he went to attend to another client.

I did as I was told. The sofa faced the doors to the street and I watched the blue of the evening sky give way to tinges of pink as sunset drew near. I had no idea how long I was meant to sit there, but I needed pain killers at the very least if I was to make it back to Tefía.

The gym was filling with heavyset men who all seemed to know each other. They milled about over by the rack pull machine. Regulars. The behemoth – who I surmised had been discreetly observing me during my whole workout – came and sat down beside me. I had to quell a strong urge to stand up and walk away.

I wasn't expecting him to speak English and almost jumped when he said, 'Can I take a look?'

It took the briefest moment to realise he was referring to my shoulder. In that tiny fraction of time, a cavalcade of paranoid thoughts bolted through me.

Always the cooperative type, I removed the icepack. He then placed his bear-sized hand on my shoulder and commenced kneading my flesh. His fingers were hot and hard and worked into the muscle. Despite the additional pain, I experienced immense relief. I almost groaned and an unexpected glow rose up through my loins. I was back in Vince's bedroom in an instant. What the...?

The man took his hand away and told me not to bother with the icepack. He remained where he was, uncomfortably close. He said, 'You want to take something for this?'

'I think I need to.'

I was presuming he would fetch some paracetamol, maybe laced with codeine, but instead he invited me to follow him to the men's.

The men's!

Surely he wasn't planning to seduce me? If he was, I wouldn't stand a chance. There would be no contesting him. He would over-power me in an instant and I, with my ambivalence and strange desires, would no doubt be biddable and offer no resistance. I was appalled at myself for even thinking along those lines. Yet despite all my misgivings, when he stood, so did I, and as he headed off, I obeyed like a pup, walking behind him, noting the tautness of his butt, the rolling gait and the shoulders twice as wide as the rest of him.

Once the door had closed behind us, he said, 'There are drugs you can take that help build muscle and lose some of that.' He stabbed his finger into my paunch. I recoiled as my old companion, shame, infused me. The behemoth didn't fancy me then, that much was clear, not me with my podgy gut.

'Steroids?' I asked.

I had never considered taking steroids.

'I can give you a Tren/Test combo now and these, for later.' He handed me a bottle of pills.

'And these are?'

'Clenbuterol. And don't worry. They're not steroids. They burn fat. Take one only in the morning. Any later and you won't sleep.'

I opened the bottle and counted about fourteen pills.

'How much will this set me back?'

He frowned. 'Depends how hard you train.'

'No, sorry, I meant what is the cost?'

'The cost? Fifty euros.'

'That's extortionate,' I said before I could stop myself.

He shrugged and waited, his face expressionless.

'And what about the other thing you said?'

'The Tren?'

'The Tren. How do I take that?'

'I can inject you now if you want.' He looked at me expectantly.

There was something about being injected with illegal substances in the toilets of a gym that caused me to feel sneaky and excited even as I baulked at the very idea. It occurred to me in a dizzying instant that this might prove to be the very inspiration I was looking for to write a novel. I would put myself through a course of the illegal steroids for the purposes of research. Think of it as an essential experience. An author needed to strive for authenticity, after all.

'How long will the Tren last?' I said.

'A week.'

'The cost?'

'Fifty euros.'

I exhaled loudly.

'If you buy the Clen, then I give you two weeks of Tren for fifty. That good?'

I hesitated.

He shrugged and smiled.

'And I give you some Test as well.'

My conscience stepped in with words of caution. I knew it was illegal to take steroids in this form. I could have gone to a pharmacist and purchased the legal versions. But I doubted their efficacy, and I just wanted to get fit fast and look halfway decent as a man. Maximise my potential, so to speak. What price fitness? I pulled out my wallet and handed him the cash. I stood back as he prepared the syringes.

I had no idea what to expect. I had never taken steroids before and anticipated a sort of recreational drug high. That euphoria didn't happen and the pain in my shoulder was just the same as well. On his way out, the guy tossed me a couple of pills in a blister pack. I saw they were the painkillers I had been hoping for and swallowed them down.

The next moment I felt a tickle in my chest and started coughing. No, not coughing, hacking my guts up. I doubled over, heaving and struggling to inhale.

What the fuck!

Terror charged through my veins.

I was going to die.

I was definitely going to die.

I didn't die.

The cough went as fast as it came, and I knew then the cause was one of those steroids that guy had stuck in me. What other side effects did I face? I wasn't about to wait in the gym toilets to find out.

I slung my gym bag over my good shoulder and strode through the premises, dodging by the equipment and avoiding the gazes of the fit and muscle-bound men I passed. Out in the street, my shoulder flared up again. I thought the painkillers would take maybe an hour to kick in. I headed straight for the café on the corner.

Inside, the place was empty. Judging by the number of un-cleared tables, everyone had just left. A tired old man appeared behind the counter and eyed me inquiringly. I ordered an orange juice and some tapas and sat at a table by the counter that was less strewn with half-eaten food and cups than everywhere else.

Beside me, I noticed a small table littered with an array of magazines and the day's newspapers. I wasn't expecting anything in English, but my gaze settled on words I could understand, and I reached over.

I didn't read further than the front page. Under a photo of a tiny beach beneath a cliff was the headline: Body Discovered Washed Up on Remote Beach in Betancuria Rural Park.

The body of a young man was discovered the day before by some hikers on a remote beach about halfway between Puertito de Los Molinos and Ajuy. The report went on to discuss the strong ocean currents and the perils that can befall the unsuspecting. The man was said to be in his mid-twenties and born on the island. His name had not been released, as the death was subject to police inquiries. There would need to be an investigation into the cause of the tragedy, but the authorities assumed it was an accident.

I was stunned. That young man could have been anyone, but what if he had been the owner of the rucksack? I paused. Then the money was now mine. Finders keepers. That was the thought that caused me to set the newspaper down and retreat into a private fantasy, of a boat or a holiday home, a swimming pool, a fancy car, whatever it was that fifty thousand euros would buy.

As I sat, enthralled by my new-found wealth, the codeine kicked in, adding its own weak buzz to my euphoria. The old man brought my order. I slurped the juice and munched my way through the pickled fish, and after paying for my fare, I headed out the door into a fading sunset.

13

SANDRA FLINT

I AWOKE THE NEXT MORNING IN ASTONISHING DISCOMFORT. I HADN'T known such vice-like pain since I relocated a wardrobe from one bedroom to another at Jackie's behest. It would look better by the front room window, she'd said. No, not said, insisted.

Now I felt crippled. As I eased myself out of bed, yet again I reminded myself of the need to stretch all the muscles I was hell bent on strengthening. If I didn't, before long I would be stiffer than tensile steel.

Finally on my feet, I fished out from the wardrobe's top shelf a clean shirt and some shorts, stoically ignoring the rucksack. I had no idea what I was going to do with that cash, but at least the paranoia that was wont to rise up in me periodically had begun to wane since I convinced myself the likelihood of the stash belonging to the deceased swimmer was high, coupled with the fact that, if anyone I had approached at the beach had had any inkling of the contents, they would have hammered on my door by now.

No one had arrived on my doorstep other than Paco and Claire, and that had been pure chance. The only issue I had on the moral front was whether I really had the right to keep the money, or if I should hand it in, but since I continued to adhere to my supposition that the owner was now dead, I decided I might as well choose the former option. A small voice within cautioned me to wait before I took out a bundle and started spending, at least until I found out who that poor soul was and if there had been any foul play at work in his demise, and for once I took heed.

Besides, I had other matters to deal with. My shoulder nagged at me both physically and mentally. I was determined to loosen the tension and, after downing two anti-inflammatory pain killers, I began with a hot shower. That experiment lasted all of half a minute before my skin started complaining, the sunburn still not healed.

I adjusted the taps to a temperature a touch above lukewarm and after rinsing the rest of me, I patted myself dry and went through my moisturiser ritual.

Ravenous after yesterday's effort at the gym, I treated myself to a full English breakfast, not skimping on the fat, not caring if all those calories deposited yet more blubber around my midriff. After sinking an orange juice and a large mug of brewed coffee, I felt fit enough for the day, my limbs all the better after movement, other than my shoulder which resisted every motion. Maybe I needed to call in at a pharmacist and purchase some sort of ointment for that muscle, but whatever I chose would have to be sunburn safe, which added some complexity to the situation.

I could of course put up with the pain, something I chose to do after exploring the other options online. Only then did I recall the pills that guy had sold me the evening before. I rummaged in my gym bag and found them at the bottom. Clenbuterol. A fat burner, he'd said. I swallowed one as I opened my laptop and before I had a chance to look up the effects, I saw an email had entered my inbox. It was from Angela, letting me know in a single pointed sentence she had inside knowledge Sandra Flint was tipped to win the literary prize.

Win!

Outrage spun through me at the injustice. She was set to win fifty thousand pounds. Stuck up old trout! It was an enormous sum, and I felt like emailing her expressing my chagrin and suggesting she should at least consider splitting the prize money with me if Angela was proved right. Then again, it wasn't worth my trouble. I knew she wouldn't part with her winnings. I needed to forget about it and get on with my day. Above all, I needed inspiration for my own novel and so far, I had none.

I took stock. Angela was right, plenty had happened to me in the short time I had been here. I chanced to find myself situated in an area haunted by terror and horror, but I had already decided those tragedies were better left as memorials, at least by me. More, those were topics meant for some local author to pick up on. If literary types were in short supply on the island, then a Spaniard. There were plenty of Spanish authors of a high calibre, too. Any one of them would do a much finer job of handling the tragedy of the parachutists or the heinous cruelty of the so-called hostel than I could with my paucity of local or regional knowledge.

As for the rucksack, basing a novel around that was a silly idea. Not least, I would be implicating myself, one way or another. Besides, whatever I wrote would need to be stunning, and you couldn't get stunning out of a rucksack full of cash. In the land of crime fiction, it was trite. Frustration gnawed at me. I was capable of being short-listed, for heaven's sake! I had it in me to win the Booker. Surely I could find a good story? If I couldn't, then I should write nothing. I would not be a hack author or even a mid-list author. I needed to be of a certain calibre, or I would remain who I was, a ghost.

I got up and wandered around. The farmhouse was starting to get to me with its warren of small rooms. I felt penned in, despite the ample space overall. I grew more irritable by the minute. The wandering became pacing and the pacing stomping until I could not stand to be indoors a moment longer. I felt like hurling something, anything at a wall, just for the hell of it, just to hear the sound of things breaking, shattering.

This new pent-up me came as a shock. Was I having some sort of breakdown? No, I was just overwrought. That was all. I had been through far too much, and I needed to relax, unwind, go for long walks, find somewhere nice to read, meditate. Or use the hire car, go for a drive, explore. Anything other than stay in the house on this traumatised plain, a location which seemed to magnify my frustrations.

I opened a map of the island and chose a place to visit. I fancied checking out the old villages in the island's interior, and my eyes landed on Casillas del Ángel, which was the closest to Tefía and seemed as good a place as any to make a start. I was out the door and on my way with fresh eagerness, sensing as I buckled my seat belt, that the best way to find inspiration was to go looking for it, and maybe, just maybe, this day would be the day I found what I was searching for.

I reached my destination in five minutes, instantly disappointed. I really had no idea what I was expecting, but the charm of the place was lost on me. As I looked around the main square, it was the mountains in the distance that grabbed my attention. Always the barren mountains, wherever you looked.

There was nothing much to the village itself. As far as I could see, the main feature was the church in its centre. Casting my eye around, I decided there was little else to do but examine the building.

I trudged past a couple of weather-beaten old men in shabby clothes and hats having a yarn in the shade of a tree, and then I stopped in my tracks, caught up in a curious thought. Should I, could I write a travel fiction novel based around a broken character on a spiritual quest of some kind? I let the idea percolate in the further reaches of my mind and directed my gaze to the object of interest.

The church was notably small compared to the churches I had known back home and didn't look like much from the outside. Other than the contrast between the white side walls and the dark basalt of the façade, there was little to commend it.

I began to go off my latest literary impulse. I have never been one for visiting churches, having grown up with and rejected my family's Catholic faith. Aunty Iris and my sisters, having failed to keep all that Biblical nonsense rammed down my throat, chose to disown me from then on. Yet I was curious now. The old men were strolling away. There was no one else about. Finding the door unlocked, I slipped inside.

There was no denying the splendour that greeted my gaze or the ethereal atmosphere that infused the nave. I couldn't help but be impressed by the intricate wooden ceiling high above or the ornate altarpiece rendered in red and gold.

I went and sat at the end of the rear pew, and as I felt the polished wood beneath my fingertips and inhaled the cool air that smelled faintly of incense, memories filtered into my mind, memories of other times I had sat in a pew, listening to the priest, waiting to take communion. Before long, I felt consumed by a choking claustrophobia. My heart raced and I started to pant as memories of confession tumbled into my mind, blown in by a cruel and vicious gust, and I was forced to relive the shame I felt as I awaited my turn, the shame over my escapades with Vince, the shame I held close and never revealed to anyone, not even the priest.

That lack of honesty in confession I saw in hindsight as the true cause of my moral crisis, a moral crisis that had remained deeply buried and unexamined all my adult life. Shame was the root cause of me rejecting the faith and not, as I had always supposed, my choice of a Protestant for a wife. After all, if I had held an unwavering faith, Jackie would have been required to rear the children as Catholics. Instead, I was perfectly content to let our marriage cause a schism between me and my weird and dysfunctional family of origin.

That shame now had me in its grip. I struggled to slow my breathing as panic started to take hold, and I couldn't remain seated in that pew a moment longer. All but gasping for air, I rushed out of the church, colliding with a stray fly on its way in. The sudden bump of insect on man sent a jolt through me. Annoyed at myself for jumping at the slightest thing, I waved the fly away, and as my hand swished across my face. I glanced in the direction I had seen the two old men. Thankfully they had disappeared. I made straight for my car, vowing never to set foot in Casillas del Ángel again.

There was only one way to fill my days on the island. I drove back to the farmhouse, headed straight to the kitchen and, despite my lack of hunger and thinking I would need the energy boost, wolfed down some leftover lasagne cold from the fridge. Then I donned my gym gear and set off for the city.

14

GAZING AT PECS

Two kilometres of pedalling and the sting in the sore shoulder muscle eclipsed the searing agony in my quads. But I was not about to change the bike's setting, which I had increased a notch from yesterday as indicated on my fitness plan, even though my calves burned and the towel around my neck, there to catch the drips of sweat, was making me hot and uncomfortable. The mirror in front of me reflected back a gasping wretch, flush-faced beneath his tan. Everything about my body, my pedalling, my efforts altogether shouted "weak".

So much for the steroids.

As for my weight, the only thing lighter about my person was my wallet. I pulled in my gut, set my jaw and concentrated on pedalling.

I couldn't help noticing that the guy next to me, who seemed to be doing the Tour de France, had perfect form. He didn't wobble about like a flaccid lettuce leaf. His movements were angular, rhythmic. I tried to copy his posture for the last kilometre, but my efforts did not compare well. When I slid from the seat, my legs had set themselves in pedal position and it was an effort getting clear of the bike.

I had noticed a guy the other day doing a quad stretch and, recalling what he had done, I bent my knee, reached for the ankle and pulled. I could feel the stretch immediately and I couldn't pull far. I held on for as long as I could, but I started to lose my balance. I swapped legs and bent the other knee and reached down. As I gripped my ankle and pulled, my shoulder yelled out in pain and I had to stop.

My corporeal transformation had hit a new low. Every muscle in me resisted more exertion. The lasagne I had stuffed myself with earlier sat heavy in my belly, not to mention the full English I had had for breakfast. I had the beginnings of a stitch. I had to suppress the urge to emit a belch as the trapped gas sent darts of pain through my stomach, and there was every chance I would be doubled over in the throes of acute indigestion at any moment.

At least it was leg day, and my circuit didn't appear to interfere with anyone else's in the gym. Most were on the upper body machines. The mix of clientele was different, too. There were even two women – one doing sit ups, the other on a fitness ball – and the atmosphere seemed a touch friendlier.

After reading through the day's fitness plan, I began with the leg press. Luis had told me to try as heavy a weight load as my legs would take. I was to do three sets of eight reps, then halve the weight and do three sets of twenty. Thinking about those instructions, I decided the critical factor was that initial weight. Luis thought I could manage twice my body weight, so I set the machine at two hundred kilos.

The first few reps were easy, but as I had been finding with each of my other designated days, each rep got that little bit harder and each set harder still. Halving the weight and doing twenty reps started off fine, but by the end, I was gritting my teeth and pushing with all my might, not because I lacked the strength to push that weight, but my quads were way too tight. They wouldn't stop protesting they had had enough and it was time to pack up and go home. My glutes were feeling it too.

I sat for a few moments, recovering. Luis was assisting one of the women. The music blared. Guys wandered in, and others went home. There was little conversation. As usual, I appeared to be the only tourist, the athletic cyclist having left after his marathon cycle, the two women undoubtedly Spanish, and all the others swarthy local types. Some of the men I began to recognise as regulars. I couldn't help wondering what they all did for a living, since mid-week mornings were normally a time normal people went to their normal jobs. Clearly, these men did not work in offices or in retail or in any other regular sort of job I could think of. Other than factory shift work and hospitality, I couldn't think what they might do for income.

I watched the guy on the bench press. I hadn't come across him before. He was dressed in tight black Lycra, and the definition of his upper arms and shoulders captured my gaze, the way each muscle tensed and flexed, the bulging, the rippling beneath shiny tanned skin.

Realising I was staring for an inappropriate length of time, I ripped away my gaze and stared at the floor, already knowing when it came to muscle definition, I never had any. Nature had bestowed me with a slender frame, narrow and a touch barrel-chested. I would be lanky but for the paunch. My knees were knobbly. Fat hid poor muscle tone. When I squeezed my pecs, curved bands of sinew did not protrude beneath my skin.

The guy ended his set and worked on the other arm. Now the mirror captured the bulge of his manhood, and my gaze was drawn in astonished fascination. Did he have a whole salami down there? I blinked and averted my gaze, taking in the other areas of the gym, anywhere but that particular appendage which thrust me back into Vince's bedroom.

What was the sudden preoccupation with men's bodies, their cocks? Idle curiosity? Pent-up sexual frustration after having had no sex with anyone since I moved out of the marital home? Or was Angela right about me? Was I gay? But that didn't make sense because I felt no love towards other men, and I had no desire to take any of them to bed. Truth was, the thought of sex with a man repelled me, real sex or even the sort of sex I had engaged in with Vince. Or maybe I was repelled because I hadn't met the right man yet, a man I could desire, even fall in love with.

Did other men think like this? Or was it only me? Was I alone in taking more than a passing interest in my own gender? Did other men admire each other's bodies? Perhaps it was normal, after all. I stole glances around the room, judged the directions of various pairs of eyes and decided on balance that yes, they did. But not in overtly covetous ways. More like envy or competitiveness. The sorts of masculine traits as old as time. The gym akin to a gladiator's pit, a place where raw masculine power was the order of the day, and you couldn't help but observe it, be intrigued by it, obsessed even. Yes, all in all, I was normal.

The association had me back to pondering the various shades of sexuality and that it was as perfectly natural to be attracted to the same sex as it was to the opposite sex. To want to be the opposite sex. To not want sex at all. To be in one way or another queer. I had no problem with any of it. Angela, an out-and-out lesbian, had decided long ago that my sexuality was ambiguous. Jackie had acted on her lesbian leanings. It occurred to me, I owed her some respect for her decisiveness, her courage, even though the betrayal still twisted my guts.

Yet when I weighed everything up – the memories of Vince, the wet dream, my fickle gaze, the existential guilt injected into my veins by the Catholic church, even my choice to come to a gym to get fit and not partake in some other, less sensual, open-air activity – it all amounted to a whopping question mark as large and hard as Mr Salami over there on the bench press.

Luis walked past me with a brief hello, and I was shaken out of my speculations. Besides, I had rested long enough. Before my legs locked, I eased myself off the leg press. Next, I tackled the leg extension machine, applying the same number of sets and reps. As heavy as I could manage, Luis had written down. I set the weight at fifty kilos, half what the guy before me had used. Even that weight proved too much after the first set, but I was determined not to fail and squeezed the last two reps out of each of the following sets.

By now my quads were on fire, and various other leg muscles were making themselves known to me as though for the first time. It was an awakening and not entirely unpleasant, but I knew I would pay for the workout later. I was not looking forward to yet another stiff and sore afternoon.

The hip thrust and leg curl machines were also free. Luis had demonstrated the moves I had to make. Leaning my shoulders on the backrest with my feet and rear on the mat, I held a five-kilo dumbbell at the top of each thigh and proceeded to do the required reps of upward thrusts of my pelvis, excruciatingly aware as I did that I was no Mr Salami.

Between each set, I had to jump over to the other machine, lie on my front and do twenty prone leg curls. It was a punishing workout. As I staggered over for the penultimate exercise, I was inwardly cursing Luis. Four sets of ten on the hack squat machine and I could barely stand. Two sets of forty reps of standing calf raises and, when I extricated my shoulders from the machine's pads and tried to walk away, it took every cell of me not to wobble. I wasn't sure my legs were capable of getting me home in my car.

All that, and Luis wanted to finish me off with another five kilometres on the exercise bike. He had to be joking. Yet a plan was a plan, and I had to stick to it. If I didn't, I would be racked with guilt the whole afternoon. I would be five kilometres short. That thought would rattle around in my brain and take a whole bottle of red to eradicate. I knew it would. Even now the thought made me queasy.

I was heading over to the bike where I had left my bag when that drug-dealing behemoth rushed in. I started pedalling, groaning quietly as I observed the goings-on behind me in the mirror. The guy approached the front counter and whispered something to Luis who then stood back in shock.

I looked away and kept pedalling.

Then the music was turned down and everyone looked over to find out what was going on. The guy, a hundred and fifty kilos of solid muscle with a neck like a tree trunk, announced to the gym in a loud voice, 'Juan está muerto.'

A gasp echoed around the room. I stopped pedalling. No one spoke. No one moved. All eyes fell on one man.

A weight clinked.

'Muerto?' someone said.

Dead? Had to be. Obviously someone they all knew. Luis came out from behind the counter and made a short statement. That broke the tension, and suddenly there were tears and cries and a lot of hugging. The music came back on shortly after, and I resumed my pedalling until I had reached the designated five clicks.

Dismounting the bike, I had the presence of mind to attempt some stretches, mimicking those I had seen the other guys do and holding them for a decent length of time. I had no idea what I was doing and gave up after a few minutes, vowing to look online for some tips. Why, come to think of it, had I never been asked to ghost-write ten top tips for stretches? I'd been required to write about a vast array of topics I knew nothing about but never stretches. Curious.

When I had at last finished my session, I went to join Luis over by the drinks fridge.

'That guy, Juan, what happened?' I asked casually.

He put his hands on his hips and exhaled. 'Juan was the man washed up on the beach the other day.'

The words hit me like punches.

'You knew him?'

'We all did. He was a regular here. Juan Pablo Medina. Son of Miguel Medina. His uncle, Mario, is over there.' He gestured behind him with a tilt of his head.

My knees felt weak. 'How awful.'

'It is a very bad day.'

The raw emotion in the room shaded into outrage and anger. There was suddenly a lot of shouting as an argument seemed to have broken out.

'What's going on?'

Luis hesitated. He looked worried, evasive. 'Better you don't know.'

There was a break in the music, and I caught some words. I knew enough Spanish to make out "accidente" and "asesinato" and I had seen enough Hispanic films to recognise the word "murder" in that language. *Murder?* The men were convinced that the young man's death was no accident, and judging by their manner, they were spoiling for retribution.

On the drive home, Luis's last remark lodged in my head. *Better you don't know.* That remark made me inexplicably nervous. Whatever could he mean?

15

SHOULD I STAY OR SHOULD I GO?

The whole drive back to Tefía, I was consumed by speculations and ominous implications. Why had Juan Pablo Medina, the swimmer washed up on that remote beach, stashed the cash in that cave? For he must have done, surely? The logistics added up.

I had assumed the dead man was a tourist, someone unfamiliar with the treacherous current, a man with very poor knowledge of tides and most definitely not a local. Juan's nationality put a different complexion on the affair. Had he been planning on coming back for the rucksack, or did he put it in the cave for someone else to collect? Whose money was it, and where did it come from? None of it would matter quite as much were it not for the fact that his relatives trained at my gym. Did any of them know about the money? What if they did? What if the intended recipient or loser of that cash was Juan's uncle or one of those other beefcakes? I shuddered. If that was the case and it got back to them that I had found the rucksack, then I would be in deep trouble. Maybe I should switch gyms, but that would look suspicious since I had already bought a three-month membership. Besides, Luis knew I was staying in Tefía. In fact, he had my exact address. It was a sickening thought.

What the hell had I gotten myself into?

Calm, I had to stay calm. But I was anything but calm. Sweat was beading on my brow despite the air conditioning blowing cold air on my face. My hands slipped on the steering wheel. My heart was sprinting, and I kept needing to inhale sharp bursts of air.

By the time I pulled up in the farmhouse drive, I was a tight ball of nervous energy. I approached the front door convinced I shouldn't stay another night in the place. It wasn't safe. I should take up Paco and Claire's offer, and go to Tiscamanita. I would be better off there, in hiding.

The moment I stepped inside, I ran to the kitchen, found the business card Claire had given me and dialled the number. She answered on the third ring.

After a cursory greeting, I asked her if her offer was still open.

'Yes, you can stay. But can you give us a few days?'

She sounded flustered.

'You don't seem certain. If it's any trouble...'

'No trouble. Only, there's been a tragedy.'

'I'm sorry.' Not more bad news. What was it with this island?

'I suppose stuck up there in Tefía you won't know,' she said. 'A body has washed up on a beach.'

My insides lurched.

'I did hear about that,' I said, injecting into my voice a measure of calm indifference.

'It's Paco's cousin,' she said. 'The family are distraught.'

I could scarcely believe my ears. Was everyone related to everyone else on this island? Were they that inter-bred? No, that was unfair. Just a coincidence, bad luck or fate and besides, Catholics had large families, as did farmers.

I offered my condolences and told Claire I would be in touch. The familial connection threw my staying at Paco and Claire's into doubt. What if they really were involved in the rucksack affair, and the invitation to stay at their place was just a ruse, a trap, a handy way to lure me and steal back the cash? What then would they do to me? Yet if they were involved, then why didn't they just take the rucksack from me back in Puertito de Los Molinos? Maybe they didn't realise it was *the* rucksack. No, that was just plain silly. What were the chances of two rucksacks being stashed in that cave? – close to none.

On second thoughts, they hadn't needed to claim the rucksack there and then. Not after I had told them where I was staying. Besides, someone may have been watching. That was why they waited and then turned up at the farmhouse as though by chance when they were sure the coast was clear. Their confidence was astounding, their assurance that I wouldn't in the interim have bolted with the cash. Then again, I didn't look like a guy who would do that, and they were awfully keen to put me off going to the police. They had probably been lying in wait the whole time, and when they saw me about to get in my car that day, they made their move.

The more I thought about it, the more convinced I became that they were involved, which began to make me feel very reluctant to stay at theirs and a whole lot better about returning to the gym.

It was lunchtime. Not feeling that hungry but thinking I should probably eat, I made myself a green salad, and then I went through my options. I had three. I could stay put, risk going to Paco and Claire's or leave the island, with or without the cash. If I took the money I was effectively stealing. There was every chance I would be stopped at customs this end, or that I should stay and slowly start spending the cash and even deposit quantities in my English bank account, small enough not to arouse suspicion. But I resisted that idea. The money was not mine to spend.

I had reached an internal stalemate. Jackie always said if in doubt do nothing. I had never until that moment considered her wise, but given the perplexing situation I was in, her life mantra applied in full.

But, I wasn't enamoured with the idea. For one thing, there was little to nothing for me to do to occupy myself up on this godforsaken plain where the wind blew and blew. Little wonder Tefía remained a backwater where few lived and little new building occurred. The village did not invite tourists. There wasn't even much of a café. The little supermarket must survive on a wing and a prayer. Claire mentioned a garden centre, but I had no idea where it was or even if it existed and even if I did, what would I want with it.

I reminded myself that it was Angela who had encouraged me to book this holiday. Left to my own devices I would never have chosen this place. The isolation appealed but not the history. Although Angela wasn't to know Tefía was situated on a plain where men had died gruesome deaths. Men ordered to jump from a plane in a violent wind and plummet to a certain death. Men who were penned like animals by night and forced to work like slaves by day on this inhospitable plain.

My thoughts faltered at the base of a mountain of self-doubt. Here I was, with my own self-inflicted agonies of sunburn and muscle strain, complaining inwardly I lacked inspiration when really, all I was after was personal glory, a chance to shine. Did any of those men ever have a chance to shine? Should I, could I offer them that chance through my words and immortalise them between the covers of a novel? Was that my purpose? I had never before considered I might have a purpose other than to benefit other writers and businesses through my words. Nothing more humbling than being a ghostwriter, perpetually in the shadows. My entire quest for inspiration had been about me and my own light and a desire to prove to myself and the world that I, too, could have a novel published and maybe even win a literary prize. It was all ego, wasn't it? What if I wrote a novel as a service to others, to help preserve their memory? It was the sort of thing historical fiction writers were into. I didn't feel I belonged to that cohort. But there was contemporary fiction too, and I definitely belonged in that group. And all those writers took on some social or political or moral issue or event. They were often journalists, people of that ilk. They took an interest in what was going on around them. As did I.

Angela was right. I should write a novel about that prison. If I was clever, I could bring in the story of parachutists as well. Although I would not want to overload the narrative with too many themes. Better stick to the prison.

But the moment my mind landed back there and I began to affirm the prison as my literary focus, resistance welled up in me. On the one hand, I would be walking through the mud of cultural appropriation, and on the other, I would have to research the topic in Spanish and then force myself imaginatively into those huts and out breaking rocks on the plain. I was capable of doing all that, even though the tasks were onerous, but I felt blocked. Something in me screamed out in opposition, and I couldn't get past whatever that was. I didn't even want to.

As I shelved the very idea of tackling the prison theme, I wondered if it served as a signpost, a symbol of some kind that might generate fresh ideas, ones that had nothing to do with the island. Perhaps if I could attach some personal meaning, some significance to my being here.

I could only think of one. Tefía was haunted by events and circumstances that had been caused by the authorities, specifically the military. The prison had been run by a military priest – and the guards, to all intents and purposes, were soldiers – and it had been a military commander who had ordered those poor parachutists to jump. The military theme extended to my own circumstances in the form of my father, who had been a sergeant in the army.

My thinking halted. I had come full circle. Perhaps this was why I felt so keen to block out the truth of my surroundings. My father. I had tried to tell myself those dark memories belonged to the people of Fuerteventura and to the Canary Islands. And not to the likes of me. But they did. They belonged to me completely through the lens of my father who had damaged me, damaged my whole family through his wayward lust and caused me to seek solace in Vince.

I held that thought for some time. It was something of a revelation and came with tremendous explanatory power. Little wonder I didn't like it here. When all was said and done, Paco was right, the energy of the place was too disturbing for the muse. I had zero inspiration, and I never would. Whenever I looked out the window at the rocky plain, I saw misery and death. I still had misgivings regarding Paco and Claire, but their place might well be the better option.

A sudden cramp in my calf catapulted me out of my reverie. I got up from my chair and walked around to loosen the muscle before it got any worse. Once the muscle had calmed down, I found a how-to website on stretches and followed the instructions. Thirty seconds was the ideal time length, so I set the stopwatch on my phone. My muscles resisted and then gave a little one by one and I could feel the benefits. There was such a thing as good pain, I decided, and a small amount of discomfort during stretches was that sort of pain. Although my shoulder proved uncooperative and responded to my tentative stretches with a muscle spasm. I spent the rest of the day completing short ghost-writing assignments and downing painkillers.

16

A WORRYING TWIST

The following day I was to focus on my arms at the gym and Luis had me booked in for a PT session to monitor my form. I thought to cancel, given the tenderness of my shoulder, but I had paid a hefty price for the steroids and the gym fee, and I would not be defeated. Arms are not shoulders, I told myself. The session was scheduled in the afternoon at four, the only slot he had free, and with the whole day to fill, I knew I had to get out of Tefía.

The day was forecast to be a touch cooler than it had been. I studied the map. El Cotillo on the island's northwest tip caught my eye. I thought I would head there for lunch then track back and explore some of the inland villages, veering east and driving down to Puerto del Rosario in time for the gym.

Finding myself without an appetite, I skipped breakfast and, after whizzing about the warren of poky rooms with broom and duster, I set off at ten.

It was my first time north and, as the road carved a course between the low mountains, I tried to picture the landscape green. I couldn't. Was it ever green? Surely, after rain, there would be green. As it was, the rugged terrain assaulted my senses and, driving into the endless brown emptiness, I began to crave my new home in Norfolk, with its tall trees and lush green fields and quaint old cottages. Here was stark, brutal, uncompromising. Some might love it, but the desert environment wasn't for me.

I had never cared for brown in any shade or tone, not since my school days and the uniform of brown blazer and matching trousers I had to wear. Not to mention those brown jumpers Aunty Iris insisted on knitting me, year on year. Tight-fitting woollen jumpers with crew necks that threatened to guillotine my ears whenever I yanked them over my head. She created brown vests too, vee-neck with complex patterns on the front. Iris was vintage 1940s, caught in a time warp. Her shrewish face, all bunched and mean, would bend over her needles that clicked and clacked all day and night. My sister, Marnie, complained her jumpers were too small, and she would pull at the cuffs. My mother would tell her it was because her aunty's tension was too taut. Taut tension described Aunty Iris to a tee.

An hour later, the ocean came into view like a blessing, and I was soon driving down through the warren of narrow streets of El Cotillo looking for a place to park.

The village was much larger than Puertito de los Molinos, the old fishing huts surrounding the harbour fringed with a conglomeration of apartments and small businesses. El Cotillo was a more pleasant, vibrant village than Puertito, too, although it had the same cuboid houses and crooked streets.

I pulled up in front of a small truck on the northern outskirts and wandered over to the beach. The sea breeze was pleasantly cool, and the tide was up, or so it seemed. The beach was an arc of golden sand. Swathes of basalt rock extended out into the ocean to form a reef that sheltered the bay in its entirety, creating what amounted to a series of lagoons. There were few people on the sand, the holidaymakers already in the water. I contemplated going for a swim – the calm waters inside the reef looked most inviting – but I didn't want salty skin at my gym session later, and there was no guarantee I would find anywhere to rinse off the salt. Instead, after strolling up and down the strand, soaking in the atmosphere, I wandered back through the village streets looking for the best place to eat.

The eateries all looked and smelled inviting. The narrow, cobbled streets around the small harbour had been given over to pedestrians, and the entire setting spoke of yesteryear. Absorbing the chilled atmosphere, I began to feel a lot better about being on the island.

After much perusing, I chose a small restaurant overlooking the water, sat at one of the tables on the wide terrace and ordered grilled fish with potatoes and salad – the traditional island fare that seemed to be cooked very well and came with piquant sauces.

While waiting for my food, I observed the little fishing boats sheltering from the ocean, the coastline stretching south into the distance, the mountains and the sea cliff and the vast expanse of blue, the chatter of tourists young and old, the occasional bursts of laughter, it all had a soothing effect on my mood. And when the waiter came with a laden plate, I thought at last my holiday-retreat had truly begun.

I observed the waiter as he walked away and greeted some new diners. He was young and handsome with moody eyes and a cheeky smile. He looked fit, too. When he turned away, my gaze lingered on his butt, well-defined beneath snug trousers. I averted my gaze as he walked away, glancing at the others seated around me, hoping I hadn't drawn attention to myself by staring too long.

Suddenly awkward, I attended to the food on my plate, which proved to be as delicious as it smelled. I wasn't exactly hungry, but it was too good to waste. I lingered a short while, but with nothing to do and no one to talk to, when the waiter returned I asked for the bill.

As I headed back through the village to my car, dodging tourists determined to walk straight into me and noting the businesses that were hungry for their cash, I experienced a sudden reversal in my opinion of El Cotillo and decided I preferred Puertito for its innocence from tourism.

I was out of El Cotillo and heading on my way, pondering what other pleasures were in store, when a string of four-wheel drives belted towards me, all of them straying a fraction onto my side of the road. I slowed and hugged the verge, the wheels crunching on grit, and I hooted my horn and waved my fist as the last of them passed me by.

Tossers!

I slowed on the approach to Lajares, which had clearly sold itself to the beast, with boutique stores and cafes strung along the main drag and restored farmhouses and stylish new builds dotting the hinterland. There appeared no sites of interest, so I kept driving, heading east, crossing a flat plain littered with volcanoes that protruded stoutly out of the ground in all directions. The land was farmed, but as far as I could tell, nothing grew in summer.

When I came to an intersection, I took the La Oliva road south and cruised through Villaverde and on through more farmland. I was considering my options when I reached La Oliva and about to find a place to park, when I suddenly, urgently needed to use the toilet. I was furious with the impulse. I had wanted to explore the town, but I refused to chance the public facilities, if there were any. Sabotaged, I clenched my buttocks and headed back to the farmhouse.

Trust my bowels to force me back to Tefia. Duly relieved, I still had an hour or more to kill before I needed to drive to the gym. I looked on the map again and decided to check out the museum on the southern edge of the village, situated just past the turnoff to the windmill.

The museum was a site of interest that I had been passing and ignoring all week. I found it was well conceived, too. Set in neatly landscaped gardens of gravel, paving and small garden beds, a cluster of restored farmhouses and outbuildings contained all the tools and implements of the ancient life of the peasants and their overlords. Demonstrations were going on in some of the barns – a woman baking bread, one making clay pots, one on a loom and another basket-weaving. In the grand house, no one was doing a thing.

Were the local farmers peasants? Was it fair to call them that? Or was it insulting? I could call the locals resilient, hardy, tenacious, or perhaps desperate fools who had known no different. When had they stopped their ancient ways?

A bigger question haunted me. It had been bothering me since I arrived on the island. Where were the trees? Had there ever been trees or had the landscape always been so barren? What sort of trees grew here, if any, and what happened to them all? Plants grew here, you could see that in the gardens of homeowners – Brits or Germans,

I bet – and in the carefully tilled fields waiting for the next burst of rain.

A quick Internet search on my phone using Spanish words for tree, culture and history and I found a scholarly article, in Spanish, on the story of the island's trees.

I was able to glean from the words and the photos that the whole island was once covered in trees and shrubs, thicker in the ravines and hollows, tougher, drought-resistant varieties covering the mountains. On north-facing mountain slopes, there had been thick forests. There had grown native pine trees, laurels and palm trees. The moment humans arrived, the article's opening paragraph said, a long, slow process of deforestation occurred, until the whole island was denuded. How sad. I saved the article to look at later in more depth.

I looked around at the rock and the soil with fresh awareness and was immediately reminded of Sandra Flint's shortlisted book, with its central theme of deforestation of the highlands of Scotland. I had had a lot of fun researching the issue. It was the main reason I took on the assignment. Flint's efforts may have lacked literary prowess, but I admired her choice of topic. I was facing the same deforestation issue here, but I couldn't write another book on the story of trees and deforestation. It would be too tedious and depressing.

If I was looking for inspiration for a new work, then perhaps I needed to stop looking around and dig deeper into myself after all. I shooed away that idea as fast as it came. Above all, I needed to land on originality, and I didn't feel the least bit original. All the best fiction I had read recently had an edge to it, the author's passion leaping from the page. What those authors wrote about meant something to them, and they wanted the reader to know it, to feel it. Authors wanted to share with the world fresh perspectives, ones that had for too long not been considered, or were overlooked. Sometimes it was an alternative to the bugbear of the times: white male privilege.

I was white, male and privileged but I didn't feel it. I wasn't sure what masculinity really meant. I put my lack of knowledge down to growing up in a house of women after my father, a man I scarcely recalled, had left. I was forced to bear a punishing femininity, all that dark Lilith-powered rage directed at me, the only male in the house. All I had back then for male company was Vince.

My adult friends had all been women too. For almost two decades I had been the house husband doing the school drop off and pick up. Jackie had worn the trousers. I wore the apron. She earned the cash, and I cooked, cleaned and pottered in the house. If I wrote about all of that, wrote from that perspective, I would come across as precious or pretentious, and even if I majored in the desperation I had sometimes felt, it would be seen by the wider community as self-indulgence. I, after all, had never had it so good and had no right to complain about my lot, absolutely no right at all.

Scrapping all that, when it came to whatever might be of interest lurking on the inside of me, I was left with nothing. I was in a creative void.

Manhood sucked if a man couldn't be a man.

The hour soon passed, and I headed to Puerto del Rosario, pulling up outside the gym at a quarter to four. Luis greeted me with a wave as I entered. I went straight to the exercise bike and did the required ten kilometres. As I eased myself off the seat, he came over and watched me do the hammer curls.

After the first set, he commented on my technique, told me to pull my shoulders back and lock my elbows, not to lean forward and sway, and not to swing the weights or perform the reps too fast.

'That's it,' he said, moving my shoulders back and pushing my elbows into my waist. As I studied my form in the mirror I caught the gaze of a bulldozer of a man on the other side of the gym who had been taking a sneaky look at me. He quickly looked away, but I saw his wry smile as he turned his face to the wall. Asshole.

Consumed by an indignant rage, I managed the other three sets of ten reps without too much strain.

Luis was in a serious and non-communicative mood. His sole focus was on my form. Next, he had me on the bicep curl machine – which wasn't too onerous – followed by table triceps pushdowns super-setted with eight reps of overhead triceps extensions using a dumbbell, which were. He had me doing all those exercises, correcting my form on each, and he watched me attentively as I forced my way through the required number of reps. As much as my arms and especially my poor shoulder would have loved a reprieve, neither I nor Luis was about to let them have one. The twinges, the pings, the burns, the aches – I pushed through all the discomfort knowing that, with Luis beside me, I had become the object of intense scrutiny, and I would not countenance failure under his gaze. Quite the opposite. I wanted to excel, to prove to him how good I was, or rather, how much potential to be good I had.

'You are doing well,' was all the encouragement he offered.

After that, I still had four sets of ten skull crushers combined with as many triceps dips as I could manage. I didn't understand the logic of so much emphasis on triceps but I wasn't about to argue. Despite the searing agony, I found overall that arm day proved far less onerous than any of the other body-area days. Although I wasn't sure I could judge. Maybe the steroids were working. Or I was getting stronger. Or I was simply getting used to the pain.

I thanked Luis for his time and jumped back on the bike for the cooldown.

Two kilometres in, and my guts went into spasm. Something was definitely amiss with my bowels. I held on until the five kilometres were done then, knowing I would never make it back to Tefía in time, I dashed to the men's before I left the gym. I chose the cleaner of the two cubicles, the one with a decent amount of toilet paper. As I lowered my pants and released my anal sphincter, emitting a sudden gush of smelly waste, the toilet room door squeaked open and someone entered. They were in conversation with someone else, presumably on their phone. The exchange sounded heated, at least from this end. As I waited, toilet paper in hand, for the peristalsis to settle, I listened, curious to see how much Spanish I could make out.

The words "la merca" and "el químico" and "el laboratorio" along with 'Dónde está el dinero?' stood out and had me joining the dots. Merchandise? A chemist and a lab? The money? That man could only be talking about one thing – a drug deal gone wrong.

My hand hovered over the cistern. As soon as I pressed the button, I would need to exit the stall, but I wasn't keen on emerging to face whoever was out there.

All went silent. Did whoever it was know I was in here? They must, since the door was closed, or maybe they hadn't noticed the cubicle door was locked. Then again, no one talks about drug-deal business in a public lavatory before checking to make sure no one else was listening. Besides, it stank in here, a smell that must have pervaded the entire toilet area.

I held my breath.

The silence continued.

Nothing happened.

I knew someone was still out there as I had heard no squeak of the toilet room door. It felt like a stalemate. But I couldn't wait forever. The cubicle was small, and I was beginning to feel claustrophobic. On a small upsurge of confidence, I flushed and unlatched the cubicle door.

I came out to face Juan's uncle, Mario, a heavy-set man with a grey-bristle beard and tattoos. He eyed me with suspicion, and I quickly looked away. Or perhaps his expression was one of disgust since he moved away from the sink to make room for me to wash my hands.

I had no choice. Under his watchful gaze, I pumped the soap bottle, turned on the hot tap and gave my hands a thorough scrub. There were no paper towels. I shoved my dripping hands under the air dryer for a brief blast and then yanked open the door only to collide with Mario's associate, the drug-dealing behemoth, who stood back then changed his mind and pushed past me to enter, acknowledging me with a dismissive grunt.

A chill ripped through me. I broke out in a cold sweat. My pulse started racing and my vision blurred. My reality shrank to what was immediately in front of me. I was jittery. It was as much as I could do not to cascade into a full-blown panic attack. I rushed over to the bikes to retrieve my bag. My bowels contracted anew, but I took no notice. I couldn't get out of the gym fast enough.

17

THE MONEY'S SECRET

ALL EYES WERE ON MY BACK AS I PUSHED OPEN THE ENTRANCE DOOR. I could feel the gazes boring into me. I was as ever the only man of English-extraction in the building and invariably the others stared, but this time I found the attention menacing. Out on the pavement, breathing the salty sea air, imbibing the liberation of the space around me, I might have let go of my fear, but the gym door swung open and out came the nameless drug-peddling associate of Juan's uncle. As he walked up behind me, I thought any moment I would feel a shove on my back, and I would be launched face-first into the gutter, but instead he strode on down the street, stopping beside a small, red hatchback.

I hurried over to my car. I didn't wait for the heat to exit the interior before I got in, and I ignored the sting of the hot steering wheel as I rammed the key into the ignition. A quick manoeuvre in reverse and I was heading up the street on my way out of the city, gulping air and exhaling hard, trying to slow my heart rate.

The sight of the red hatchback pulling away from the kerb made my guts roll over. My bowels threatened a sudden release. I wanted to put my foot down, but I had a green sedan in front of me and besides, Puerto del Rosario's streets were not cut out for high-speed getaways and it would only draw attention.

The behemoth followed me all the way up Calle Juan de Bethencourt, but that wasn't unusual. Everyone leaving the city went that way. I felt sure to lose him at the ring road roundabout.

It was when I took the La Oliva turnoff – heading to Tefía via Tetir – and glanced in the rear-view mirror to find the red hatchback do the same that a fresh wave of raw panic washed through me.

I was being followed.

I scrambled to rationalise.

The guy might not even know it's me in this little white car. He's probably just going home. He probably lives in La Asomada or Los Estancos or in Tetir itself. There are houses dotted all over, and he could live in any one of them. It was no use. He was stuck fast behind me.

The further I went, the more certain I grew that he was on my tail. Why? If he wanted to know where I lived, he only needed to ask Luis. Then again, that was confidential information, and Luis did seem to be a decent, rule-abiding sort.

I drove through Tetir, making every effort to keep to the speed limit, watching the hatchback in the rear-view mirror, hoping, willing the behemoth to turn off.

He didn't.

At the village edge, I pressed the accelerator. The mountains loomed up ahead. The only grace in an otherwise terrifying situation was the behemoth didn't tailgate. He hung back, cruised along, a nightmare. We passed through more small villages and each time, I held my breath hoping he would indicate, slow, turn off or park.

Tamariche?

No.

La Matilla?

No.

The turnoff for Tindaya?

No.

My palms slid on the steering wheel. My pulse boomed in my head, and I felt faint and nauseous.

There was only one village up ahead: Tefía.

I kept going.

He kept going.

He maintained the same distance behind me, casual as you please.

At the entrance to the village, I slowed. I kept an eye on the rear-view mirror, hoping and not hoping he would turn off. If he lived in Tefía, I didn't want to be anywhere near the place and if he kept going, he would see where I was staying; I had no choice other than to pull into my drive since the farmhouse was situated on the main road. I couldn't bring myself to do it. Instead I carried on, and drove to the dirt-road turnoff which led to the windmill. I breathed a sigh when he remained on the main road and disappeared.

I had lost him.

The dirt road was narrow and allowed little room for a three-point turn. I kept going and arrived at the gravel concourse before the windmill, where I turned around, pulled over and killed the engine. Sitting there in that lonely spot on the windswept plain, feeling the car interior heat up under the rays of the violent sun, I became acutely aware of the hostel down the tree-lined drive to my left, an awareness that reinforced the feelings of terror I had succumbed to since I emptied my bowels in the toilet at the gym.

How did I end up here, of all places? I could have driven anywhere, turned off the main road at any intersection I had passed. Instead, I had brought myself face-to-face with the horrors of this plain. The idiot that I was, I didn't think to turn off later for Puertito de Los Molinos. If I had, I could have given the behemoth the impression I was heading to the beach. For all I knew, he might have taken that turn off and be heading here using the other route to the windmill, due to appear at any moment in a cloud of dust.

Alarmed, I fired up the engine, threw the gearstick into reverse and with a deft manoeuvre, I headed backwards up the hostel drive, braking before the car hit the gates. The car wasn't completely hidden from view, but I felt less exposed as I could no longer be seen from the Puertito road. I sat, waiting. Ten minutes passed, and there was no sign of a red hatchback.

I was in the clear, at least for now. I didn't feel all that confident driving home, yet I couldn't remain where I was, already sweaty and tired and hungry and beginning to cook in the car. I got out, stepped into the raised garden and climbed over the driveway wall, and then headed off around the outside of the compound, following the eastern perimeter where I was guaranteed not to encounter a living soul.

Seeing no gap anywhere, I clambered over the wall and crunched my way down the hill to the three rectangular huts. The prisoners' huts. Some effort had been made to screen those huts from the main compound with a dense planting of shrubs and trees. As though to block out the history.

The sun, low in the western sky, was hot on my back. No thought entered my head as I approached the whitewashed walls of the flat-roofed cells: three stone boxes, rectangular, with a single wooden door at one end and a wider cavity at the other that must have served as another door. It occurred to me the buildings had been built as barns for animals. I walked around the back to find two high windows set high in the rear wall, the shutters closed.

My first impression was the lack of light inside. That, and the cells would have baked in the heat in summer. As I pictured twelve men squashed into each room, as I stared back up at the military compound, as I looked around at the rocky plain and the barren mountains, I could think of no worse place to be imprisoned. Of course, there were plenty of examples worldwide of such hellholes situated in extreme locations – after all, humanity did like to major in cruelty to its own – but I was standing right here beside this partic-ular example, an example too few knew about, and I couldn't help but feel its significance. Touching a cell wall with its flaking paint, I could almost feel the energy of the men in there, smell their bodies, sense their despair.

I had never regarded myself as sensitive and least of all psychic, but standing beside those cells on the narrow concrete path strewn with dust and pebbles and overhung with half-dead weeds, I was consumed by a disturbing sadness and a sickening discomfort all at once. From the moment I had set foot in Tefia, I had been clouded with doubts and speculations regarding my own sexuality, and what a luxury that was. The men in those cells never had any such indulgence. How much had changed in sixty years! Or had it? The zeitgeist had changed enough to allow the likes of me to toy with what for those men would have been an agony, a curse.

As I pulled away and trudged up the hill to the compound, I wanted to rip out all those shrubs screening this awful truth and erect a sign pointing all the youth who stayed at the hostel down the hill to experience what I just had.

I mounted the perimeter wall and hurried to my car, keen to leave the locale. Feeling as I did, I could only imagine what it would be like if I were to attempt a novel based on that prison. Never mind cultural appropriation. I would be plunged into creative purgatory.

Back at the farmhouse, my own difficulties resurfaced. I knew I could have no clear idea if that behemoth had been following me, but the chances were high. Whatever the case, I needed to act and act fast. Besides, now Juan's uncle would know I was staying in Tefia, and it wouldn't take long to find out where. I needed to leave the farmhouse, and I needed to waste no time doing that. All things considered, I could think of nothing more appealing than getting off that plain.

Having made the decision, I flew around the farmhouse packing up my things, making sure to remember the bottle of Clenbuterol. I snatched a few perishables from the fridge, leaving the rest thinking I might return for them tomorrow. If I felt brave enough.

I had the presence of mind to stuff the rucksack in my suitcase, using a large plastic bag for my surplus clothes. I didn't stop to think until the car was loaded and I was on my way again. This time, I pulled up at the eco-museum to make the call to Claire.

'Trevor. How's it going?' She sounded hesitant, surprised.

'Is this a bad time?' I asked, remembering my manners.

'No, no. Go ahead.'

'Only, I could do with staying at yours tonight.'

'So soon? I thought we agreed to wait a few days.'

'Something has come up.' My mind raced on, scrambling for an excuse.

'May I ask what?'

'Rats.' I cringed. There was every chance no rat had ever set down its tiny feet on the island.

'Rats!'

She sounded genuinely shocked. I held my breath. There was nothing for it, so I went on.

'The place is infested. I honestly don't know where they've come from.'

'The island has had a bit of a rat problem.' There was a long pause. 'You can't stay there, so you best come.' She didn't sound too happy about it.

'Are you sure? Are you there now? I can be there in under an hour. Will that be alright?'

'Sure.'

'Thank you so much. You've saved my bacon.'

'No bother. The flat is already prepared.' She hung up.

I opened Maps on my phone and checked out the route. It was simple enough. Head south through Antigua and keep going. On entering Tiscamanita, turn left, and Paco and Claire's was halfway down on the right.

More flat, rock-strewn plains, more naked mountains, and I was crawling down Calle Manuel Velázquez Cabrera about half an hour later. It wasn't possible to miss the house. After the usual array of old and new cuboid abodes and a smattering of ruins, there it stood, grand as a mansion set back on its own large block, replete with massive shuttered windows in Spanish colonial style and a terracotta tiled roof. The front door belonged to a castle.

I pulled up in the street opposite, hoping I would later be directed to the garage at the side or at least to the adjoining carport, but there were already cars parked there. Then again, what were the chances of the behemoth or Juan's uncle driving down this street? Close to zero. I got out of my car, crossed the street and pushed open a gate centred in a low stretch of rendered stone wall. The wall rose to two metres where it aligned with the southern corner of the house and met with a perpendicular wall of similar height, screening the side garden from the street. Privacy.

Ten paces through a neat arrangement of succulents in black

gravel and I hammered on the door wondering if anyone would hear me and thinking a bell pull in order. I thought I heard a dog barking somewhere inside. Eventually, I heard footsteps and the door opened, revealing a welcoming if somewhat distracted Claire. There was no sign of Paco.

I thought I would be ushered inside, but without a word she stepped out and drew the door closed behind her as though keen to obscure the interior from my view; then she led me to the southern corner of the house where a white-painted door in the high, white-washed wall – barely visible at a glance – led through to a sheltered patio. We crossed the patio to another door in a wall set at right angles to the main house: my quarters.

'We added an extension to the original back corner,' she said, throwing open the door and stepping inside. 'I hope you like it,' she added, showing me around.

To the left of a square living room – furnished with ultra-modern, ultra-plain furniture, the predominant colour pale grey – was an equally square kitchen. White granite bench tops and stainless-steel appliances had been arranged in the far corner. The centre of the room was occupied by a round table and four chairs in keeping with the living-room furnishings. A wooden staircase set against the near wall led up to a large, square bedroom. Below the vaulted, wood-panelled ceiling, the bedroom furniture appeared to have come out of the same Ikea catalogue. The contrast of new and old seemed to work, although I wondered why they had not chosen to go vintage.

I went over to the window which looked out over the rear garden and the fields beyond. The standout feature was a volcano, staunch and spent with its decapitated cone. I noted the small desk positioned under the window, perfect for a writer.

'The bathroom is through here,' Claire said, and I followed her down a short passage. A door on the left led to the bathroom. At the end of the passage, another door led out to a private roof patio. We stood outside for a brief moment. I remarked on the view.

'We have the same outlook in our bedroom,' she said. 'And in the kitchen.'

Impressive.

We headed back downstairs. Claire was plainly preoccupied, and the smile she wore was weak. Perhaps Paco was stricken with grief or consoling those who were. Or both. And Claire had to step into a carer role. Or they were caught up with the funeral arrangements. A sudden death like that of a young lad couldn't be easy. I felt bad for imposing.

'I'll show you around later,' she said. 'Do you have everything you need?'

'I do.'

'Then make yourself at home.'

She held up a key, then put it on the kitchen bench. I thanked her and followed her back across the patio. She was about to enter the main house through a glass door when she turned and said, 'Make sure you close and bolt that gate when you are done.'

'Sure,' I said, and I would have barricaded it too if she had wanted.

I ferried in my things, lugged my suitcase up the stairs and slung it on the bed. Not wanting to be caught with the rucksack, I went and locked myself in before unpacking.

In the spacious, if confined space of the one-bedroom apartment, I felt a touch less vulnerable and considerably more secretive than I had up in Tefía. I was taken back to my childhood, doing sneaky things in my bedroom while my sister, mother and aunt went about the rest of the house, calling out and yelling at each other. I opened the suitcase and yanked out the rucksack and left it on the bed while I attended to my clothes. When the suitcase and my other bags were empty, I made to return the rucksack to the suitcase when curiosity got the better of me, and I sat on the bed and opened the rucksack, emptied it and checked through all the pockets again in case I had missed something. Finding nothing, I switched on the phone. There were two missed calls that must have come in not long after I had switched the phone off. Neither call was from one of the two stored numbers, and it was a withheld number, too. I turned off the phone again to save the battery.

Next, I took out the money and unwrapped the cloth to examine the bills. It was a luxury even to behold such a vast sum. Temptation fluttered in my belly, but I resisted extracting even one note.

I was about to fold it all back up when some paper caught my eye. It had been placed in the middle of the bundles of cash. I extracted the paper and found it was ten sheets of foolscap folded in half and half again. On each side of the ten sheets was the smallest, most compact writing I had ever come across. My editorial eye estimated a thousand words on each side of a page, amounting to twenty thousand words all up.

A novella? I had no idea if the writing was fact or fiction. It could be anything; the writing was in Spanish. What I did know was whoever had hidden those pages had done so for a reason. Those words were important, as important as that cash. More so, perhaps. Maybe whatever was written had some sort of value, or the words were private or libellous or scandalous in some way.

Leaving the pages on my pillow, I re-packed the rucksack, plonked it in the suitcase and shoved the booty under my bed.

My heartbeat quickened, this time not out of fear.

18

A TRANSLATION

My first thought was to ask Claire to translate the pages, or at least the first few sentences. It didn't take long for me to dismiss the idea. Those words belonged to Paco's relative. Then again, they might not be his. Like me, he might not have known those pages had been shoved in amongst the cash. Come to think of it, there was no proof the rucksack even belonged to him. Paco and Claire didn't seem to think so, or surely they would have said something by now. Regardless of all my suppositions, I could not tell my hosts about this latest find. Not until I knew what the words said. I couldn't tell anyone for that matter. Not even, or especially not Angela. I would risk losing control. And I wanted control, at least temporarily, at least until I found out what revelations those pages contained.

If these were the words of a dead man washed up on a beach, words that had been wedged in a stash of cash hidden in a sea cave, then the chances were high no one else knew of their existence. If anyone did, the words would be of no use to me, the new owner, except as a keepsake. Or, if the pages proved valuable, said new owner, me, would be obliged to declare the source.

The writing was probably rubbish, the ramblings of an angst-filled young man tormented by guilt and fear, mentally unstable, reckless, foolish, about to break his mother's heart. The sort of writing that belonged in a private diary and not unleashed on the world, as far too many were wont to do these days.

Then again, I could be wrong. I could be staring at literary treasure. It was possible I was staring at paper far more valuable than the cash it was buried in.

Out of the plethora of online translation tools, I searched for the best that came free. I chose one that seemed classy and made a lot of grand claims about itself. Not that I believed the hype. It was the sort of blurb I trotted out for companies every week.

Aware of the potential shortcomings and the tendency to offer a word for word literal translation, I typed in the first sentence of the tiny spidery prose – which was short – and then added the next. The translation came out in a reasonably coherent fashion. I pasted the English version into a new document. Word by word, phrase by phrase, sentence by sentence, I soon had about three hundred words of text.

As anticipated, the translation was for the most part literal, but even so, I could tell the writing was both heartfelt and perhaps even inspired. I would need to cross-reference some of the words using an online Spanish-English dictionary, but overall, I found the text workable. If I were to craft that prose, polish it, if I mimicked the emerging style yet elevated it with my own literary flair, I might even have discovered a real gem.

An obvious question began playing on my mind. What was this story about? That, I couldn't tell. All I knew was the prose had a narrative style and carried the flavour of memoir.

A rap on the door below broke my concentration. I hid the pages under my pillow and closed my laptop before heading down in the dim of the evening light to answer it. I hadn't realised it was that late.

Opening the door, I found Claire pulling out a weed between the pavers on the patio. Behind her, the house spilled bright light through the glass-panelled doors. To the southwest, the remains of the sunset – tones of a deepening red – were rapidly fading to black. Aware of my presence, Claire straightened, tossing the weeds into the garden.

'We thought you would like some dinner.'

I wasn't the least bit hungry. To be polite, I followed her

through the patio doors into a large, formal sitting room. The décor was elegant, the furnishings vintage-looking and comfortable. Claire crossed the room where another door led to an internal patio.

I stopped and looked around, impressed. A balcony ran along three of the walls, shading the rooms beneath. An awning over the balcony shaded the upstairs rooms. In the patio centre, was a raised bed filled with leafy plants. A rich meaty smell infused the air.

Paco appeared in a far doorway and greeted me with the semblance of a smile and a tilt of his head. For a reason that was inexplicable, he didn't seem to like me. At least, that was the impression he gave. Claire joined him, and I wandered over, soaking up the grand historic atmosphere.

Beneath its grandiosity, the house had a definite vibe I couldn't quite place. I put it down to the age of the building and my over-wrought mind, yet as I rounded the stand of plants, I couldn't help looking over my shoulder, as though to catch someone coming up behind me.

When I looked back, Paco was gazing at me intently. 'See, Claire. I told you,' he said.

Told her what?

She didn't answer. A string of paranoid thoughts raced through my mind. Paco was still staring at me.

'I keep telling Claire we still have a ghost, but she refuses to believe me. You felt it, didn't you.'

'Take no notice,' Claire said to me, and she turned and walked into the kitchen. Paco followed, and I did the same.

The kitchen, in contrast to the rest of the house I had seen, was ultra-modern with shiny appliances. Paco poured me a glass of white wine, and Claire invited me to sit at the table, laid with attractive plates and fine cutlery and napkins. I wondered if they had gone to all this trouble just for me. Or perhaps it was just a regular meal for them.

'How are you settling in?' Claire asked, sitting on a stool at the breakfast bar. 'Cosier than the farmhouse?'

'I prefer it.'

'A better atmosphere here,' Paco said, and I was reminded of his earlier remark about the ghost and then his comments about Tefía.

I couldn't exactly agree after crossing the patio, but to be polite, I raised my glass. 'Sure is.'

They both smiled and sipped their wine. An undercurrent of tension resurfaced for a moment. The strained silence was broken by the light and hurried tapping of claws on concrete and marble and a dog, a large hound with enormous ears, came bounding in and headed straight for me. Not being a dog lover, I braced and held out my arms to keep the thing at bay.

'Come here,' Claire said sharply. The dog obeyed. She patted the thing with much affection and told it to sit. It was then I noticed a large fluffy rug covering a padded bed in the back corner of the room. The dog's bed.

'Not a dog lover, then.'

'Jackie, my wife, always wanted a dog. But I'm allergic.' It was the simplest of lies.

'That's a pity.' Her next sentence she directed at her pet. 'Zeus, go to your bed.'

The dog, Zeus, obeyed. Zeus? Claire was a serious dog lover, then.

'He's a handsome, um, animal.' I almost said "beast".

'A rescue dog,' Paco said. 'We've given him a home.'

'There are a lot of strays on the island. Abandoned pets.'

Claire looked over at her canine progeny. Thank goodness I never let Jackie, or Ian and Felicity for that matter, pester me into getting one. The hamster was bad enough.

'Good of you to take him,' I offered, keeping the conversation on track. It seemed easier than another awkward silence. I received no reply. I took a gulp of my wine. Claire did the same.

'We were wondering what you did with the rucksack,' she said, idly brushing a strand of her hair from her face.

I had wondered when that topic would come up. I braced myself as I sipped my wine, forcing a bland expression on my face as I said, 'I handed it in.' I offered a cringe by way of reinforcing the truth of my statement, but I didn't anticipate the reaction that followed.

'You did what!' Paco yelled. Zeus reared up in alarm. Claire gave the pet some words of reassurance and told him to lie down.

Paco was shaking his head in disgust. He lowered his voice and said, 'You're crazy.'

Claire shot Paco a censorious look before turning to me with a pleasant and decidedly false smile on her face.

'And you told them where you found it?'

I thought fast. 'No,' I said. 'Casillas del Ángel. Under a pew in the church.'

'Why lie?'

'Instinct.'

'Probably best.'

There was an elephant in the room. I could feel it. And I decided my previous conclusion was wrong. Like me, Paco and Claire also assumed the rucksack had belonged to Juan. They must think that. It came down to basic logistics.

'What did the police say?' Claire said, keeping her tone light.

'Not a lot.'

What choice did I have other than to be evasive? I had never been in a Canary Islands' police station in my life. I had no idea if the officers even spoke English. I watched her take a sip of her wine as my palms broke out in a sweat. I kept staring. I had to keep my eyes from darting around the room. I hoped she didn't pursue the matter.

Paco took one look at me, scowled and turned away to fiddle about with things over by the stove.

'Better he did hand it in,' Claire said to Paco. 'It will be better for Juan.'

'I'm sorry?' I said, all innocence, seizing on the chance to push the conversation in another direction. 'I don't follow.'

'We think that rucksack you found belonged to Juan.'

'Really!' I made myself look shocked.

'He must have gotten himself into some big trouble.'

'Typical,' Paco muttered.

I gasped and covered my mouth. When I had two pairs of eyes fixed on my face, I moved my hand away and said, 'Then that cash really belongs to the family. I mean, to you. I am so sorry. I had no idea.'

'It's alright. We would have done the same.'

'Would we?' Paco said grimly.

'Drop it.'

An awkward silence descended, masked by Paco, who brought the food to the table for us to help ourselves. I expected Zeus to leap out of his bed, but he remained where he was, nose twitching, watchful.

'Smells incredible,' I said enthusiastically, not the least bit hungry.

'Paco is an amazing cook.'

The food eased the mood in the room, helped along by my demonstrative reactions to the flavours – a robust goat stew served with an elaborate salad and spicy potatoes. I occupied myself with eating, despite having no appetite. I had the impression they wanted me to lead the conversation, yet I was too preoccupied with the secrets hidden in my apartment to come up with a topic.

'You've caught the sun again,' Claire said eventually, drawing together her knife and fork on her plate. She had hardly eaten a thing.

I laughed and held out an arm. 'Doing my best.'

Paco showed no reaction. He didn't even look my way.

'We're not brilliant company tonight,' Claire said with an apologetic smile. 'Paco's cousin...'

The reminder sent a jolt through me, and I dearly hoped they were not about to return to the topic of the rucksack. Paco raised the topic of the rats instead, but Claire was quick to demonstrate her disapproval with a sudden intake of breath as if to say rats was not a topic for the dinner table. My mind raced through scenarios, and I knew I had better come up with a plausible fabrication involving an email to the owner and consequent eradication. And I would need to contact island pest control to see how such an eradication would occur. Poison? Traps? I rued the moment I had come up with that lie and wished I had had the presence of mind to invent another cause for my sudden evacuation of the Tefía farmhouse.

Paco drained his glass then wiped up the gravy on his plate with a hunk of white bread. Claire sat and watched. Behind her, Zeus sat up and began to look expectant. I polished off the last of my stew and drank my wine and when they started to clear away the plates, I seized the opportunity to take my leave.

Alone in my quarters, I took the manuscript, opened my laptop and arranged myself comfortably on the bed. Keen to forget about the whopping lie I had just told, I translated another two hundred words, not paying much attention to the translation the website offered as I copied and pasted, ending on the word "marica".

The translator had interpreted the word as "sissy", but the narrator would hardly refer to himself as that. I went on a Spanish-English dictionary and discovered the more usual meaning: gay.

I leaned back against the pillows. The narrator was gay? I took a closer look at the translated sentences. Was this memoir? When was it set? The writing so far gave no hint of time or place, but judging by the way the last paragraph was written, I knew the story had to involve a gay protagonist.

The revelation launched me into a spin. Ever since I had come to the island I had been tortured by my own sexuality. And now this? As though life, fate, the universe was rubbing my nose in something I dearly wanted to run away from.

What could I possibly do with this document? I was straight, despite my teenage dalliance. I was not repressed or in denial, despite my wayward gaze. Angela was wrong about me. Only, given the story unfolding before me, it would be better for me if she wasn't. If I was gay, then I could write a book with a gay protagonist without fear of any backlash. But as a straight man, a *straight white* man? I could hear the chorus of derision. I would be crucified by the critics. Sure, I had read James Baldwin. I could pull off a female protagonist, not a prob-lem. But pretending to be gay, in the first person? I would feel like a fraud. Then again, what right did the thought police have to crush my creativity? Didn't gay men write about straight men? Of course they must. The whole world wasn't gay. There was nothing for it. I decided I would transcend identity politics and press on, drawn as I was by this mysterious text. The opportunity it presented was much too good to pass up.

My eyes grew tired, and my head began to ache, but I refused to stop until I came to the end of the first page. Then I read over the words again and again, fixed the grammar, checked up on the meaning of certain phrases that had come out in the translation in a peculiar fashion, added some flourishes of my own here and there, and then some polish. It was three in the morning when I hit the save button, closed my laptop and readied for bed.

19

THE FAULT IS NOT MY OWN

SHALL WE SIT? YES, DEAR FRIEND, LET US SIT. LET US SIT WHERE THE thermals rise and face where the sun will set. Let us rest awhile, you and I, entwined in a curious intimacy of bird and man.

Look to where the ocean meets the sky. There, on the horizon of all that can be known with the naked eye, see the pale haze. Where on other days, clear days, the eye will observe a line separating the two hues of blue, one a watery reflection of the other.

Blue, the result of the sun that illumes the world and gives it life.

My eyes behold blue beauty but that solar orb of blazing fire cannot penetrate the black that exists in this husk that is me. A void has grown in the place of life. I'm hollowed out of whatever had once filled me, and now I have only memory to pour back into that dark chamber, memory of what used to exist before it was wrenched away.

Can you see that? Or what do you behold? Do you see into me, my raven companion? Do you want to see into me? Should I let your black-feathered body penetrate my black soul? Or should I resist that final temptation?

I have no answer to satisfy your expectant eye. Perhaps I must set myself a task so that you can truly see into me. Reconstruct myself with all that I was. There was plenty of me, I can assure you of that. I would make a grand story, as grand as another, grander maybe, a soaring tale of adventure and aspiration. Shall I give myself permission to dramatize, add colour where colour is needed, invent a title for myself, leave you, dear raven, on a cliff hanger, leave you wanting more, of me, of my story?

There ought to be more, a sequel, maybe three, for I am young, twenty-seven, ready to re-enter the life I once knew.

The Prodigal Son returns! Aha, if only that were so. I fear the door will forever remain closed as it would on a leper. If it opens even a crack in a moment of intense curiosity, in the next fraction of a second, it will slam back in my face.

My name is José Ramos. My name is José Ramos and I once held a desire to be a journalist. My name is José Ramos, son of a lawyer. I am José Ramos from the ancient town of La Laguna, the middle child of three. I am dutiful, obedient, shy, eager, optimistic, craven and God-abiding José. At least, I once was all those things. I was on the dashing side of looks, too. Yes, I am José Ramos, the sinner. José Ramos, carrying a sickness for which there is no cure. I am José Ramos, and I am gay.

Did I shout all that? No, I only thought it. The raven hears me without my speech. My dark companion, all beady, curious, attentive.

I will tell you then, bird, since you clearly want to know. I'll make my outpourings a story for future generations. An autobiography of a young man. A portrait. Perhaps a young man a touch like the one Joyce created. A young man writing a book as honest and telling as any Hemingway. *For Whom The Bell Tolls*? It is tolling for me.

You may look at me with that cynical eye, dear raven, but please stay. You are my only friend.

You may wonder what will propel me forwards or backwards to my fate. Your feet are on the earth, but your wings will let you fly. My feet are dangling off a cliff, a drop of some fifteen hundred feet, and here at last, I have come, facing west, and somewhere beyond the milky horizon is the island of my birth, Tenerife.

I am due to return if I want, but for what? There is no life for me in La Laguna. There is no career to be had, no interest to pursue.

Oh, raven, such a depressing tale as this is scarcely worth telling! Yet I exist, and while I do I have a voice, I should, I must tell this tale.

Are you listening now raven? Can you spare the time as I embellish the story of me?

Perhaps I should reinvent myself, become the protagonist José. Who would know if I did? Only me. I have absolute freedom. I can lose myself to my imagination and do as I please, but what sort of deceit would that be? Besides, I'm not sure I'm capable of fabrication or fantasy. It would do the world no good. I am a journalist at heart, not a poet, and while both deal in presentations of truth, one seeks facts, the other imagery. Here is my story, then, to add to the fabric of truth a single tired and frayed tassel.

20

A WAKE

I awoke hot and sweating. The sun blazed through the eastward window. I got up, opened the casement and closed the external shutters, conveniently fastened to the wall by spring-loaded latches. After shutting the windows, I pulled down the blind, throwing the room into near total darkness. The sudden change was too much. Disoriented, I groped around for my underpants.

My eyes adjusted and I sat up in bed, wondering what time it was. I heard voices outside and went out to my rooftop patio to find Paco and Claire in the rear garden. They didn't see me. They looked busy, each attending to something or other, and I decided not to disturb them by calling out. Zeus was sniffing around. He hadn't noticed me. He cocked his leg to water the perimeter wall, and I averted my gaze. At the northern end of the garden, I noted a restored barn, no larger than a single garage, along with two smaller outbuildings, still in ruins, their interiors planted with what appeared to be tomatoes. A lot of work had gone into this place, a lot of love and care, and it was obvious the couple derived much pleasure from their abode.

Secluded from the street by the high stone wall and the house and the garage, the whole of the garden faced open fields and hills and that one vast volcano, all reddish-brown and open-mouthed. The view was mesmerising and more appealing than the Tefía plain, more sheltered with the mountains all around. I would have preferred a sea view, but I guess you can't have everything. Besides, the mood here was made intimate by the lack of ocean blue. I sat on the cool concrete, hidden from view, and absorbed the new surroundings. Flickers of inspiration sent ripples from the edges of my awareness and I felt that inward pull, that familiar drawing within that was the muse.

I recalled the words I translated and then re-wrote the night before. I pictured the young man sitting with his feet dangling off the edge of a cliff. A young man talking to a raven. I wondered where that cliff was. A habitat for ravens? Or had he borrowed the bird to use as a motif? Was he situated somewhere real or imaginary? The story was definitely set on a Canary Island, for José had mentioned Tenerife.

He was obviously a very troubled young man and literary, too, with references to Joyce and Hemingway. I had to help him with the reference to *For Whom the Bell Tolls*, but I felt justified. Sometimes an idea needs a little expansion. And he was gay. That in itself made the story more compelling, more intriguing. In the warm morning light, I felt at peace with the issue of the gay protagonist. It occurred to me if the author of those words was also gay and that author turned out to be Paco's cousin, then did Paco know Juan was gay? There were a few leaps in my reasoning, but it might be worth finding out. I wondered how I would go about it.

Zeus cocked an ear and looked over in my direction. I anticipated a loud bark any moment. Feeling my skin begin to burn, I went inside and had a shower.

With no intention of leaving the apartment all day, I donned a t-shirt and shorts and went downstairs and sifted through the food I had brought with me from the farmhouse. There was enough to make an omelette and the stale bread would do for toast.

A juice, a coffee and a Clen tablet later, I wrote a shopping list for the supermarket in Antigua; probably not the closest, but I knew where everything was. And I wanted to self-cater. Grim dinners in the main house were not ideal. I would live the hermit's life in Tiscamanita. With the air of the writer-at-work, I would excuse myself from any invitations Claire might throw at me.

Feeling self-conscious in clothes more suited for the bedroom or the beach and not the supermarket, I ran upstairs and changed into long pants and a buttoned shirt. I was out and back in under an hour, putting away the groceries, when there was fast rap on the apartment door.

This time, it was Paco, dressed in a charcoal-grey suit. He had one arm raised, leaning against the doorframe. I took a step back, somewhat confronted by his looming presence.

'We thought you should know the funeral is today.'

At first, I was confused. Then realising who he meant, unease rippled through me.

'I'm awfully sorry,' I said. I didn't mean it, but there was nothing else to say.

'Claire forgot to tell you last night,' he went on. 'I thought she had so I didn't mention it.'

'That's alright.'

He relaxed his arm, let it fall to his side.

'We're having the reception here afterwards. You are welcome to attend.'

I hid my reaction. 'I don't want to intrude,' I said lightly.

'You won't be.'

He moved away from the doorframe and headed across the patio and disappeared.

A reception? That meant the family and friends, including the uncle at the gym, would descend on Paco and Claire's. This scuppered my plans for a quiet day in. Better for me if I wasn't around. Pity I forgot to ask when it was all taking place.

Funerals, as far as I knew, occurred during the day, and Paco was certainly garbed for the ceremony. Stood to reason, they were about to head off. The island was small. I calculated an hour's drive to anywhere, tops. The event itself would take how long? An hour? Then an hour to get back. I checked the time on my phone. It was eleven. My rough estimate of three hours if Paco and Claire were leaving now, meant the reception would begin at two. If I came back at five it should all be over.

That made six whole hours I needed to be away. Where would I go? Not the gym, I knew that much. I wasn't ready to face Luis and the others. My body thought otherwise, muscles wanting the punishment they had resented before. But shoulder day could wait.

I was about to grab my keys off the kitchen bench when the thought of leaving all that cash hidden in the suitcase under the bed triggered a rush of paranoia. I couldn't leave it there, not while the doyens of organised crime milled about in the house and no doubt out on the patio. Yet I could hardly take it with me. I wasn't about to drive around the island with fifty-thousand euros in the boot.

The dilemma brought me out in a sweat. My heart rate began galloping like a spooked horse. I reminded myself that no one knew the rucksack was here. Paco and Claire thought I had handed it in to the police and besides, my sixth sense told me they wouldn't mention it to anyone, at least not at the funeral. It was reasonable to assume they wouldn't want Juan's name besmirched in death. They also wouldn't want it known that they knew a thing about the rucksack.

I hung around inside, listening for sounds of movement in the main house, but I could hear nothing. I went out to the patio and glanced in the windows. There was no one about. Then I wandered around the back to find the garden empty. On the pretext of asking Claire if she needed me to get anything from the shops, I stepped inside the house and poked my head into the kitchen. Trays of glass-ware and stacks of plates filled the breakfast bar. Platters were ready to receive whatever nibbles were stored in the fridge. One was piled with cakes and covered in cling film. There was no sign of anyone and when I called out, I got no reply.

They had gone. Part of me fancied a bit of a poke around in all those rooms, but I curbed the urge and returned to my quarters and readied myself for the afternoon.

Armed only with my laptop and Juan's memoir – if that was what it was – I headed off without a clue where I was heading.

At the intersection in the centre of Tiscamanita, I was in two minds whether to turn left or right. Left meant Tuineje and the southern villages, and right meant Antigua and beyond. I could drive to Puerto del Rosario, but to do what? I didn't feel like a day out anywhere. I wanted to be alone, and it occurred to me the funeral made it safe to return to the farmhouse. On my way by, I called in at the Antigua supermarket for some lunch supplies. The checkout assistant recognised me from earlier that day and said something in Spanish and grinned. I grinned back and said nothing. What was the point? We couldn't communicate.

Driving across the Tefía plain, that feeling of desolation rose up in me, and I recalled Paco's depiction of the awful military accident. As the windmill came into view, I was reminded of the hostel beside it, picturing those low military-style buildings, the quadrangle, and the two plaques – discreetly located out of the way – which I had seen in a photo, plaques erected in memory of the men, the gay men who had served time in those three sun-baked cells.

Auschwitz, Alcatraz, Guantanamo, Evin, I conjured all the ghastly prisons and camps I had heard of, and now Tefía – yet it felt distasteful to compare and besides, the scale of the inhumanity varied in each case. The hostel was tiny and only housed about thirty-six prisoners at a time. But evil was evil wherever it was found, and numbers did not weigh in the scales of justice. Paco was right. There could be no denying the Tefía plain was one of those dark places where memories lived on, imbuing the landscape with their unique kind of haunting.

I was almost relieved to pull up in the farmhouse drive so I could block out the worst.

It felt odd entering the familiarity of all those small, low-ceilinged rooms, rooms now bereft of my belongings. Keen to set to work, I deposited the groceries on the bench and in the fridge, and slunk to the patio with my laptop, shunting one of the chairs into the shade.

The online translator spat out the next few sentences of miniscule writing, and I busied myself giving the language some shape. Seemed to be a passage about a man extracting water from an ancient well. Where was this story set? Africa? India? Somewhere that still practiced primitive traditions, somewhere impoverished. Historical fiction maybe? The writing was disconnected from the passages that came before, although the prose remained in the first person and carried a similar tone. I could not be certain as this was a translation, and there was a marked break in continuity, but I got the sense the protagonist remained the same. The young man sitting on the cliff was narrating the tale of his life. I inserted his name into a sentence to concretise that fact.

I carried on, phrase by phrase, sentence by sentence, correcting and titivating as I went, until my belly rumbled, and I broke for a very late lunch, leaving the text on the screen.

———

THE SUN SEARED MY BACK, scalding the open wounds left by the guard's lash. Flies buzzed around my head. Some bit. I leaned against the beam and pushed, pushed like a donkey, or like a camel, pushed the beam that drove the wheel that turned the cogs that winched the buckets of water. I was an animal. That was what they thought of me. The cog clicked – click, click – and the guard sat in the only shade there was, a lone palm in a field of rock. I leaned into the beam, pushed hard, pushed consistently. The wheel turned, and the sun glared into my face. The wind was hot, my sweat gone as fast as I produced it. Bitter resentment filled my heart. I, José, animal.

We were all animals here. Mistreated animals. If not me, then Jorge or Ruben or Manuel or Rafael – my friends – or any of the other men who would have to push this beam, push and push, each footfall heavy on the gritty ground.

The guard scratched his crotch with his free hand, the other grasped the barrel of his rifle. Across his lap, the lash.

Behind the guard, some distance away, a villager awaited her turn beside her camel, watching. Who was she? Which house was hers? Could she smell me? Did she, like the others, think me no better than the animal she restrained? Worse, unclean?

Men filed by and deposited empty buckets and collected the full ones to take back to the compound. I avoided their gazes, and they avoided mine. None of us was keen to stir the wrath of the guard.

Thirst built, my mouth as parched as the earth I trod. It was a thirst not slaked by the water I pumped, water strongly tainted by salt.

What did the girl use the water for? She must filter it if she drank it.

I maintained the rhythm, keening, my muscles in my arms and legs clenching in dull pain, each footfall an effort. And as fatigue washed through me, I steeled myself, in case I slipped and fell on the gravelly earth. I did not relish giving that guard another excuse to lash my back.

The girl looked content to wait. Maybe, like me, she had no choice. How old was she? Had her mother sent her? Did she have sisters? A brother? A sibling like me? But not like me – no, no – not a shameful outcast, a young man unable to control the deviant beast inside.

———

I RESUMED my seat at my patio workstation and read over the paragraphs. My immediate thought was, poor bloke. A prisoner? Slave, more like. Getting lashed like that and forced to trudge around and around like a camel or a mule, all the while being gawped at by some village girl. It was all horribly depressing, and I wasn't sure I wanted to continue with the translation. The writing might be gold, but it might just as well be fool's gold. Then again, maybe not, I thought as my mind started joining the dots.

If the narrator was the same man, the same *gay* man, and in this latest scene, he refers to drawing water from a well in a field of rock, then there could be little doubt the story was about the hostel. Or rather, the concentration camp. I couldn't be absolutely certain, and I might well be leaping to conclusions. I felt weird just thinking about it, and I wasn't sure I wanted to continue. I wasn't sure I wanted to take on the translation if it was about to lead me into those depths.

The farmhouse, Tefía, the entire holiday retreat was beginning to feel like a curse, as though I was being punished for something that had nothing whatsoever to do with me. As though I had been branded somehow, required by God or fate to take on a project that was my idea of a writer's hell. The farmhouse and its proximity to the hostel, my chance discovery of the rucksack, and those pages hidden in the stash – what a convoluted set of circumstances. And, I noted with wry irony, I was directed to the hostel and that cave by Luis. If it hadn't been for my buff-looking, beaming personal trainer, acting as fate or God's instrument, I wouldn't be in this quandary.

The only mistake I made was deciding to get fit.

Maybe that was the story I should tell, or something like it, and not the story contained in those pages. I should tuck them back where I found them and go and hand in the rucksack like I pretended I had, and be done with the entire affair. Fate can go find another sucker.

Even so, I wasn't quite ready to delete my efforts. I hit save, closed the document, and made a tiny mark on the page of Spanish to denote my place in case I decided to go back to it. Then, I folded up the draft.

It was getting on for four o'clock. I tidied the kitchen, leaving the remains of the macaroni cheese I had made for lunch in the fridge along with what was left of the cauliflower I had steamed to go with it. Simple fare, but tasty. Long-life milk, cheese, eggs, half a loaf of stale bread – I would return here if I felt confident enough or if things at Paco and Claire's grew any weirder.

Before I left, I watered the plants in the patio. Then I wandered into my old bedroom with its four-poster bed and stood at the window and looked out at the plain, at the windmill in the distance, at the low mountains scattered around.

In minutes, I was pulling up outside the windmill, eyeing the driveway to the hostel with cool hostility, feeling I had plenty of time on my hands, curious to discover the parachutist monument Paco had mentioned.

There was a dirt track, little more than a scratch in the ground, leading around the front of the old military air base, on past a house and from there into a flat and open field. Less a field, more a swathe of grit and stone. When I spotted what looked like the monument off in the near distance, I left the car on the track and picked my way to the centre of the field.

Aligned in a row inside a walled rectangle of gravel were three monuments, one a boulder with an inscription of the names of those who had lost their lives mounted on a plaque on its face, another a sculpture of an angel – Dios Victoria – covered in a shroud. More

647

boulders and a large crucifix completed the monument. Situated as it was with not even a road sign to point the way, the memorial indicated a private tragedy. The effect was powerful and deeply private, and I felt I had no right to stand on the rectangle of gravel, a gawping tourist.

On the journey back to Tiscamanita, I took a second detour through the village of Llanos de la Concepción and then on up to Valle de Santa Inés, where I pulled over to look back at the view of the mountains I had glimpsed in the rear-view mirror. With plenty of time to kill, I stood by the roadside, feeling the wind on my face, beholding the naked earth that was Fuerteventura. The view was a sculpture, like that of a naked body. I wondered if the island would ever again be clothed in trees. It really was so astonishingly dry. Perhaps another monument was needed, one in memory of all those lost species.

I soon tired of being blasted by the wind and took refuge in my car.

From there I kept driving on the same road until I reached an intersection. I was tempted to turn right and head up to Betancuria, but it was getting late in the day for sightseeing. Instead, I drove down through the rocky undulations to Antigua. Here and there, a property owner broke the monotony of the landscape, a planting of trees sheltering a dwelling or lining a drive. Such owners were few. For the most part, the land looked abandoned. What I did notice of interest was the way farmers banked up ridges of earth around their small fields, creating flat-bed basins to trap the water when it rained. I read somewhere that when the rain came here, it was torrential. Needs must, but what an effort.

Another ten minutes and I slowed for the approach to Tiscamanita.

As I crawled down Calle Cabrera and caught sight of all the cars parked out the front of Paco and Claire's, I wanted to do a three-point turn and head off somewhere, anywhere else, but people had seen me, and Claire was standing on the pavement looking my way. She waved, and I cringed. There was nothing I could do other than find a place to park.

The closer I got, the more interest Claire took in my presence, waving me on and pointing to where a car was pulling away from the kerb. Looked like guests were leaving. Thank goodness!

I was fortunate the parking space was almost by the side gate, which hopefully wasn't bolted on the inside. Looked like I could make an easy dash after a quick wave of acknowledgement. Before leaving the car, I fumbled my laptop into a tote bag and stuffed the Spanish scribblings into my pocket and plastered an appropriate expression of good cheer and sympathy on my face.

My plan to escape to my quarters was scuppered the moment my feet hit the pavement when Claire hurried over.

'Where did you get to?' she asked.

'I went for a drive to clear my head.'

'Anywhere special?'

'Just around.'

She didn't quiz me, for which I was grateful. But I had no choice other than to follow her to the main entrance where some of the funeral party were gathered. Suddenly, I found myself doing the rounds of introductions, Claire leading me first here, then there, on the pavement, in the front garden, through a vestibule and on to various spots around the interior patio. I adjusted the tote bag on my shoulder as I shook hands and offered sympathetic smiles to all and sundry. No one seemed keen to engage me in conversation, which came as a relief. The atmosphere was subdued, the predominant colour of apparel black, but people chatted amongst themselves and occasionally laughed. No sign of the dog.

I had no idea why Claire was bent on having me meet everyone, but eventually, she left me to it, and I found myself standing alone near the living room. I thought to disappear, a desire inflamed when I spotted Juan's uncle emerging from the kitchen with Paco beside him, but it was too late.

'Trevor,' Paco said, beckoning me over. 'Come and meet Mario.'

There was no choice. I walked towards the two men as my instincts headed off screaming in the other direction. The two men exchanged a few words as I approached. Mario was grinning.

'Mario tells me he recognises you from the gym. I had no idea you keep fit.'

'I try,' I said laughing and turning to shake Mario's outstretched hand with my own, clammy one. 'I am sorry for your loss,' I said, almost mechanically, holding Mario's gaze, hoping Paco would translate. He did.

There was a long moment of silence. I had no idea how to fill it. My expectation that Mario would throttle me or make wild, or perhaps not so wild accusations vanished in his presence. There was no sign he harboured any suspicions or animosity towards me whatsoever. My mind flitted back to that moment in the toilets when I had overheard his conversation and then the look of disgust on his face when I emerged from the cubicle. That look really was because he thought I was about to leave the men's without washing my hands. He could have had no idea I had cottoned on to a thing he had said.

He had no idea about the rucksack either, or he really would have throttled me by now. It looked as though I was in the clear. Yet I could not slow my heartrate in his presence. He was, as far as I knew, a dangerous man, a drug dealer of some kind, mafia most likely. I didn't want to be anywhere near him, but I lacked a cue to walk away.

'How's the writing?' Paco asked, which had to be the worst possible question in the worst possible moment.

'Fine,' I said, knowing I had to say more. The situation demanded it, if only because there was no other topic of conversation to be found. 'I am finding the island is filled with inspiration. Fuerteventura is very beautiful.'

'You think so? Most tourists complain it is too dry.'

Paco offered Mario a quick translation.

'Yes, dry,' I said, feeling like an automaton.

'When it rains, the land turns green.'

'Will it rain soon?' I said, relieved to be talking about the weather.

Paco laughed.

'Not until winter. Will you be here then?'

'No. I will be in England.'

We were interrupted by a sudden rise of chatter at the front door. A late arrival, it seemed, and I caught a glimpse of the behemoth's back. Fresh fear invaded my being and yet again I repressed an impulse to bolt.

'Mateo,' Mario said.

Mario had seen his friend, too. He headed for the vestibule, and I seized the chance to ease away, making it across the patio and out of their line of sight.

Once I was certain I was out of view, I darted across the living room, ignoring the couple seated on the couch, and made my way through the patio door and on to my apartment, ferreting inside my pocket for my key as Zeus cornered the side wall and bounded in my direction.

I managed to get the door open and myself inside before the mongrel reached me.

With the door safely closed and locked behind me, I exhaled. Keen to get as far from the reception as I could, I bolted upstairs.

Even up there, safely ensconced by thick stone walls, I could hear voices drifting on the wind, the odd burst of laughter. I went and stood by the window, opening it a crack. Below, Claire was chatting to a squat and swarthy looking local in dark blue pants and a white shirt who I thought I had seen at the gym. She pointed at this and that in the garden, and I thought she must be explaining the layout or future plans.

Then I overheard, 'He was staying in Tefía, but the place had a rat infestation.'

'Rats?'

'Apparently.'

'Be careful, Claire,' the man said in heavily accented Spanish. 'You don't know a thing about him.'

I held my breath, convinced she was about to tell him how we met. I pictured the scene, me frantic on the beach, approaching all and sundry, trying to offload the rucksack.

Thankfully, all she said was, 'I am sure he is harmless. He's a writer.'

It was a close shave, and the fact remained I had no idea what Claire, or Paco for that matter, had told the other guests. Worse, I could hardly ask. There was nothing for it but to trust that neither of them had mentioned the rucksack and if they had, then they had also told the interested party I had handed the whole thing over to the police.

My guts churned and my bowels clenched and I rushed to the bathroom.

I had no reason to fear Mateo other than he had followed me home from the gym. I didn't even know if he had been following me. I did know I couldn't shake the terror I felt, and it was making me bilious.

The room darkened, and the sunset filtering in through the patio window bathed the little corridor in pink. It was dinner time, but I had no appetite. I needed a distraction, something to occupy my harried mind. Hoping to find a new ghost-writing assignment, I opened my laptop and checked my emails. There were none. With much reluctance, I turned to the only project I had on my desktop, the Spanish translation.

As I typed in the next section of the tiny Spanish script, I anticipated being thrust back into the scene at the well, but instead, the story changed, and I found myself immersed in a story of a child growing up in Tenerife. Was this the same guy? Had to be. As soon as I was sure, I took the liberty of inserting the raven at the beginning. If the author was employing a motif, then it needed to appear throughout and not slip from the reader's view.

21

GROWING UP IN TENERIFE

I HAVE A SISTER, DEAR BIRD. A WOMAN WITH HAIR AS BLACK AS YOUR plumage, although I have only known her as a child and must conjure the woman she is, the woman she has become.

Maria is two years my senior, and she was a little matriarch, even at seven.

When I was a young man, women in my society were expected to blend in with the background. They were to be meek and mild, obedient to all male authority. They were to keep house and have babies and more babies and nurture them all.

My mother was the exemplar of the perfect woman, a carbon copy of the immaculate Mother herself, and in naming her firstborn "Maria", I suppose she was hoping to hand down her goodliness and obedience like a pretty pink bonnet. Alas for my mother, Maria didn't turn out like that.

JOSÉ SQUIRMED IN HIS SEAT. 'You're hurting me!'

'Sit still while I fix your hair.' Maria tapped José's head with the back of her brush, leaving behind a sharp sting to go with all the tugging and tying she'd subjected his hair to this last hour. Her own hair was pulled back, neat and tidy and parted in the middle, two long plaits that began behind her ears and ended somewhere below her shoulders in pretty white bows. She had a round, almost angelic face, the determined set to her jaw betraying the force of her inner nature.

Maria forced her brush through José's hair, matted now through some vigorous back combing. He let out a piercing scream and received a slap on his thigh for his trouble.

'Shush. Mama will hear you.'

She primped his hair some more, until it was all but standing straight up on his head. Seeing his startling visage in the mirror, he giggled, and she giggled along with him.

'That's silly,' she said, forcing him into the large blue dress their mother gave Maria for dress ups.

'I don't want to wear this dress.'

'Nonsense. You must, because you are the bride and I am going to marry you.'

'I can't be a bride. I'm a boy.'

'You have to be the bride because I don't have a sister, and Dolores is busy.'

Dolores was Maria's best friend. On Saturdays, Dolores visited, and the girls played dress ups, and José was left alone. Sometimes, Dolores couldn't visit, and Maria faced the choice of boredom or playing games with her younger brother. She had to choose José for Jesús was younger still, and only three and perfectly useless to play with.

Normally, José didn't mind his older sister's games. Sometimes, they played with her dolls in the courtyard, or he was required to sit at a small desk and receive instructions from teacher Maria. She could be nasty with her ruler, but otherwise, she was comical and made him laugh. There were times she insisted he be a baby, and she tucked him up in bed and tried to feed him sloppy food with a spoon. He was passive. He opened his mouth when instructed, happy to accept more.

One day some months before, their mother had given Maria a soft dress of the palest blue, a dress too big for them all, and Maria soon developed a fixation with imaginary weddings in which she lorded it over proceedings as the priest.

José hoped she would tire of her game and invent another one, and he no longer had to have his hair groomed and don a flouncy dress which he did not care for at all. He was a boy, after all, and boys didn't wear dresses, and even at the tender age of five, he was aware of the ridicule should another boy in his neighbourhood ever find him in a fine, blue dress.

Another change came later that year as Maria prepared for her first communion. As it dawned on her that she was to become a bride of Christ, the blue dress was deposited at the bottom of an old trunk and forgotten.

OH, raven, you who will wear the same black suit your whole life. Yet if you were to dye your feathers – let's say pink – would you change on the inside? Or would you dye your feathers pink because you have changed on the inside? Besides, I didn't choose to wear the blue dress. It was thrust over my head. But it came to symbolise all that I am.

You are you, dear raven, and I am me. We were born the way we became. The seed is destined to grow in its own unique fashion. The blue dress did not make me gay, and I did not choose to be gay. I came to know I desired men as the seed in me burst forth from my loins. And there was nothing I could do to change that. I could not dye my feathers to transform my own desires. We know, do we not, my raven friend, we know what the world cares not to know. We are who we are. Final.

The raven turns away, its interest distracted by a soft rustle behind us. My eyes are drawn to the face of the cliff rising up to either side of me, jagged columns of dark rock plummeting to the impossible deep.

22

A CONFRONTING REVELATION

José was gay and it was obvious to him as it was to me that his sexuality had nothing to do with pretty blue dresses.

The story had an historical setting. A young man suffering social rejection for being gay didn't fit in the contemporary zeitgeist, at least, not in the western world. Even in the Canary Islands, after General Franco's repression came to an end, attitudes must have shifted, modernised, and they definitely had by the millennium when presumably the author of this protagonist would have been a child. Therefore, it stood to reason that if the script was memoir, and it was set in an age more traditional than this, the 1950s, say, then the author could not be the young man washed up on the beach. Unless Juan wrote the manuscript in the style of memoir. I took a closer look at the pages, trying to ascertain the age of paper and ink, but it would need an expert, not me, to make an assessment.

The story was more than likely pretending to be memoir. A memoir of an unhappy young gay man sitting on the edge of a cliff, reflecting back on his childhood. Then there were those passages set somewhere else, where a man was forced to draw water from an old well. That must also be José. Unless the script was just a collection of disconnected ramblings. I hoped not. Although, I kept pushing away the thought that the story had something to do with the hostel. I had to, or I would have folded up that Spanish script and returned it to its hiding place, for every atom of my being wanted nothing to do with that trauma. It was too confronting. In all, I was curious to see how the story of José and the raven would end.

I closed the laptop and tried to get some sleep. Too soon, the early-morning light glinted through the shutters and the sun's radiant heat penetrated the glass and warmed me as I lay in my bed.

The area around my desk would be warmer still, but the story locked in a foreign language was compelling and after a quick shower, I made coffee, swallowed a Clen and resumed my work on the script.

I had to squint at the next words of bunched-up writing and entered what I could make out into the online translator. The foreignness of the language, the tiny cramped lettering, the too-often illegible quality of the prose took their toll, and I grew increasingly frustrated and impatient. Scanning the pages, it appeared the quality of the writing deteriorated further as the story progressed, and the only saving grace that kept me persevering were the page numbers. At least, I was guaranteed the certainty of knowing how the original was meant to flow. I had an image of myself as a monk or a scribe in a dark and damp chamber, faced with translating by candlelight some ancient scroll in Hebrew or Aramaic, a scroll all torn and foxed.

Over and again, I had to consult online dictionaries and cross-check possibilities to discover what the author had meant. I pressed on, determined to get to the end of the second page, where an indent in the text indicated a paragraph break.

I kept going, despite realising very early in the morning's labour, that the narrative had returned to that tortuous scene at the old well.

———

SO MUCH WATER! Two men trudged back across the rocky field, in each hand a full pail. About halfway to their destination, they passed another two men, each with two empty pails. The exchange of buckets went on for hours, and by the time the guard said, 'Stop,' the sun was fast on the way to its zenith.

I slogged back to the compound under the gaze of the lone girl waiting for her turn to use the well. When we had traversed fifty metres, I stole a glance back. She was tethering her camel to the beam where I had stood, a man doing a camel's work, now a camel doing a man's. I almost laughed, but my amusement soon faded.

There was grit in my boot. Pink grit, for that was the colour of the ground beneath my feet. Ground so dry my footsteps made puffs of dust. I had become familiar with the plain, the mountains, the searing heat and the infernal wind. I had become familiar with the aching fatigue in my bones. Hunger weakened me, and my vision blurred. I kept my sights on the windmill, the landmark guiding me back. The guard ambled behind. There was no need for him to stay close. There was nowhere to run even if I had the energy.

I arrived back at the compound to find the prisoners lined up in the quadrangle. As my feet hit the concrete, four men were ushered around the back. I heard the splash of water, the guards' voices filled with venom, the jeers.

For once, we were permitted to get clean. I would have rather stayed dirty, but I took my place in the queue. I was the last in line. The guard in the quadrangle watched on at some distance as one by one the men were summoned until it was only me left standing.

There was a shout, a pained cry, then laughter.

'Go,' the guard ordered.

'Dirty stinking whore!'

I could hear the insults before I turned the corner. The guards were in fine fettle; they slung-shot their abuses, battering us with their vitriol. But their fists were worse.

The water in the old trough was dirty. A thick film of soap scum floated on the surface. Under the wrath-fuelled gaze of the guards, I removed my clothing, reached for the soap and wet my body with the water in the trough. Another prisoner hurled a bucket of clean water on me. There was a soft murmur of amusement among the prisoners. A guard growled. I soaped myself all over my body as fast as I was able. Then, just as I was about to reach for the last bucket to rinse my soap-caked skin, the guard stepped forward with a kick, and I watched the bucket topple, and its contents pool and disappear into the thirsty ground.

The uproar of laughter that ensued came only from the guards.

The sun crusted the soap on my skin as I gathered my filthy clothes and skulked back to the cell – one of three, barn-like buildings lined up in a row below the compound.

––––––

I SAT BACK IN DISBELIEF. There could be no doubt this was the story of the hostel when it was used to incarcerate gay men. Had to be. The pink grit. The quadrangle. The windmill. The guards with their pointed "whore" insults. And then the cells themselves, which were described exactly as I had found them.

The story started to make more sense. This was not a memoir. It was a story recently written – I could tell that much from the fact that up until that single prisoner, Octavio Garcia, spoke out, the story of the prison was unknown and untold – but a question remained. What had Juan been doing writing all this? He might have been related to Paco and the guys at the gym but who had he been, really? A closet writer? Gay? Someone with close connections to one of the prisoners? Or did this writing come from someone else, and Juan had stolen it along with the cash. He might not even have known it was there.

It didn't seem to matter. What did matter was how to make full use of the draft.

My thoughts stopped in their tracks as my earlier misgivings rose up to hold sway. The soap scene had the makings of good prose and I had been seduced by that, enticed into relating a story I wanted nothing to do with. When I considered my circumstances, cooped up in this small if charming apartment, determined to avoid the owners of the establishment, unable to return to Tefía due to my ridiculous lie about the rats and forced to maintain another lie as to the whereabouts of the rucksack, it was little wonder I was happy to be side-tracked. I was on guard duty, locked away with little to do. But a short scene of conditions in the prison was one thing, an entire book another, and I reminded myself I would need to immerse myself fully in that prison, lock myself away in one of those cells as though I too, were gay, and to do that, I would need a lot of more than just those handwritten pages. I would need to partake in thorough background research into Franco's era and Canary Islands' culture, politics and society, all of it in a language I had little understanding of. I would, to all intents and purposes, need to *be* this protagonist, José.

There remained the possibility that sitting on my bed were the pages of a draft that could lead me to my grail, a prize-winning book that would make Sandra Flint genuflect before me, begging forgiveness.

I was on a precipice. I couldn't make up my mind whether to leap or resist. There was nothing for it. I opened Skype and called Angela. In the time it took for her to answer my call, I had my story straight.

'Hey, you,' she said.

I stared into her beaming face and grinned.

'I have some news.'

She shifted, reached behind her for something beyond my view, then ran a hand through her thick mop of hair and said, 'Must be good. Shoot.'

'I have decided to pursue the gay prison book.'

Her mouth fell open.

'Common sense at last! What made you change your mind?'

'I gave what you said a lot of thought. And I couldn't come up with a better idea so...'

By then, lying had become second nature, a reflex that stirred in me unease as my conscience grappled for justifications, and ambition sat back indifferently.

'How will you approach it?' she said, all eager-eyed.

'I have that worked out, too. I had this idea that the protagonist – let's call him José – is sitting on the edge of a cliff talking to a bird.'

'A bird?'

I clicked on the document, open at the first paragraphs.

'A raven.'

'Go on.'

'He narrates segments from his childhood, interspersed with scenes in the prison.'

'It's a start.'

'You like it?'

'Yes,' she said slowly. 'But why the raven? Why have your protagonist sitting at a cliff edge talking to a bird?'

I fumbled for an answer.

'You know how it goes. That first moment of inspiration. I had to get into the story somehow and that is what came to me.'

'Fair enough. I suppose you were visiting a cliff and suddenly it hit you. There are some terrific cliffs on the island. Further south from where you are.'

'They're magnificent,' I said, hoping she would move on.

'What are your resources?' she said. 'You can't read Spanish.'

My disingenuous self was quick off the mark with, 'I am paying a friend here to translate that novella I linked you to.'

'Good plan. I hope they aren't charging you too much, though. Another author friend who is bilingual dipped into that book and said there was a lot of religious waffle in it.'

'You showed the novella to another author!'

'Keep your hair on. She isn't interested. Says she has enough to contend with writing a pithy novel set in Dresden and Dachau.'

I groaned. 'Not another Nazi novel.'

'Afraid so. The market's appetite is insatiable.' She paused. 'Pity she isn't interested in the Spanish one, though. She would have done a good job.'

'And I won't?' I said, instantly defensive.

'I didn't say that. You didn't want to do it. You were categorical about it, if you recall.'

'Well, I have changed my mind.'

'Clearly so. And I am delighted for you, Trevor. I told you all along it was the story you needed to write. Might be the making of you. And I won't show that novella to another soul. Promise.'

'Please don't.'

'Before you go, word from one of the judges is your Sandra Flint is almost certainly set to win.'

'She is not *my* Sandra Flint.'

'You know what I mean. Don't be sour, Trevor. You are beginning to sound like my father. Must dash.'

She blew me a kiss and ended the call, leaving me to recover from her parting shot. Her father? That bombastic misogynist! The last time I had seen him was at Angela's wedding. He had sat near the band and sloshed champagne, eyeing his daughter's new wife with varying degrees of venom and contempt. I was nothing like the old trout!

I went downstairs and swallowed a Clen, remembering as the pill went down that I had taken one only hours earlier. I chased the fat burner with a glass of juice, then pressed on with the translation.

I had planned on tackling shoulder day at the gym, but I no longer felt inclined to leave the apartment until the translation was done and the whole draft safely on my laptop in English.

The fragmented narrative continued, and I found myself back in José's childhood.

23

MY SCHOOL YEARS

MY DEAR RAVEN, IT HAS NEVER BEEN EASY BEING ME. I WAS BORN AT THE wrong time, in the wrong place, into a punitive faith, ahead of my time perhaps, and there is no time for society to catch up, even if it wanted to, which it doesn't. My difficulties grew as I did, growing larger by the year. I will tell you how it was to be a cuckoo in a nest of pretty yellow birds and with the raven's view, you will know what happened to my soul.

A DECADE PASSED. Maria hadn't required her brother's involvement in her games for a long time. She was seventeen, and her mind floated, and whenever her eyes settled on José, they were filled with what could only be described as hatred.

It was the same spite that José saw in his brother, Jesús, a robust thirteen-year-old with a passion for sports and an ambition, barely formed and founded on adoration, to study law. Jesús was the apple of his father's eye. Maria seemed to please her mother despite her fiery temper. Two parents, two children. Plus one. Sitting in the dining room eating meatballs cooked in a thick, bean stew, a familiar feeling returned to fill his belly. It felt to José as though he was spare, superfluous and unnecessary, the tyre kept in the car boot. He had to fight for attention from either parent. He was squashed in the middle between his dominant siblings, where there was no room and no choice but to wither or rebel.

Isn't that simply a structural thing, the lot of the one in between? It might be a curse but it needn't be. It needn't crush the morale. The various agents playing their roles in the confines of the family structure, they have influence. They have free will. My in-between status is one thing, my family's rejection of me as a worthy member of the fold another.

You know, raven, Regina and Juan Ramos did not have to overlook me, their son, their middle child, with eyes that refused to settle for fear of what they might find. A reflection of themselves perhaps, one that turned their pious stomachs, for what I saw in their eyes and heard in their words was more than a nervous apprehension that all was not quite right with their once precious José.

'I should never have given them that blue dress to play with,' my mother was fond of saying. For Regina had seen me wearing that dress at the impressionable age of five, and she had observed at a near distance her darling boy fail to grow into a wholesome man. She did a simple maths sum and came up with a false answer. My gender preference had nothing whatsoever to do with that damn blue dress.

José isn't quite right. That would be my father.

Stop that mannerism; it doesn't suit you. Mother, again.

He's far too pretty.

Thank you, but I prefer "handsome".

His voice isn't quite the right pitch.

It is the same pitch as yours, father dear.

He doesn't walk right. I'm sure I saw him mince.

That was the school play.

Keep your hands still in your lap and stop flapping them about.

I never did that. I am sure of it.

He's a sissy.

I am a man.

Little wonder they ridicule him at school.

Children are cruel. They act out their parents' prejudices.

The way he giggles and prefers to play with the girls.

Always the scrutiny. Always the judgements. I am a man who desires other men and that's the end of it.

I laugh at the absurdity, a loud, guttural laugh, and the raven is startled and opens his wings to take flight.

Relax, bird. I am nothing to be afraid of.

There were many lovely times growing up in La Laguna. I can recall one of those, a very good time it was. My tenth birthday and my parents agreed to a party. We were allowed one friend each, and all our cousins came. They were from Santa Cruz and from La Orotava. The two sets of grandparents were there, as were my various aunts and uncles.

I invited my best friend Enrico, who lives in a house on the corner of our street, or should I say lived for I have no idea if he is still there. His father is or was a chemist, a peculiar man, widowed and dour, and we always played at my place.

It was a warm and sunny day in March of 1945. World War II was drawing to a close. Of course, I didn't know much about that. I didn't know about the horrors of that war, of the brutality and death and the concentration camps. I had no idea of human suffering, my own or anyone else's. The closest I had come to real pain was when Maria had done my hair or when I shut my thumb in a door. I didn't know about the deprivations of my people either, of how hard the peasant farmers worked to subsist, of the starvation and mass migrations to Venezuela. I was ten and I existed in blissful ignorance of real life, near and far. I could, therefore, have had no idea of the unreasonableness of all that suffering. I lived in a nice bourgeois home in La Laguna, and that is all I knew.

My parents' house, which was my house then, has an internal patio filled with plants and tall windows with Juliet balconies looking down on a cobbled street. It was paradise.

JOSÉ ALMOST COLLIDED with Jesús and, avoiding him, hit a potted plant. He had just spent the last hour running about with Enrico. He was dizzy from too much sugar and too much joy. Earlier, when he broke the piñata he insisted he have on this very special day – a piñata Maria helped his mother make – and the had patio exploded in an uproar of cheers and a cascade of sweets fell all around, his heart had been fit to burst in his chest.

The cake was still to come.

In case it was time, he ran into the dining room where his aunts and uncles and grandparents sat and stood around drinking little cups of this and that. Then his mother's elder brother, the pompous José Diaz, drew José aside and said, 'What do you want to be when you grow up, young man?' as though the question had been burning in his mind the whole time.

'He's too young to answer,' his mother said.

Yes, he was.

'Nonsense. He's reached double digits.' Uncle José was tall, plump and overbearing. Young José stood beneath him, nonplussed in his neat suit and making every effort to keep still. Enrico stood in the doorway, waiting and panting.

'He has very neat handwriting,' someone said.

'He'll never be a farmer, with those hands.'

'A farmer! Since when did anyone in our family become a farmer?'

He must be a lawyer, like you, José.

He's too shy to be a lawyer. Look at him.

They all looked.

Does the birthday boy speak?

'I'd like to be a waiter,' he said, recalling a friendly face in a café the other day.

Everyone laughed. His mother sputtered on her drink.

'He'll be a teacher or a scientist,' she said, covering her embarrassment. 'Something like that. Now tell me, Maria, how is your health?'

José snatched a sweetmeat from the table and ran off back to Enrico. Cake was coming, and it was all he could think of. We'd all have cake! When Maria came downstairs with Dolores and the rest of their cousins, they'd have cake, and he would have had the best day ever.

. . .

BACK THEN, I had no sense that I was different to any other boy. That's because I was in no way different from any other boy. My mother disliked my sensitivities, the ease with which I would cry. My father thought me too fragile for the world of men. They thought, they knew, I needed to be tougher, harder, louder, more robust. They compared me to other boys my age. To Enrico. I didn't compare well to Enrico.

I was saved from languishing at the bottom of the reject pile by Antonio, my mother's elder sister's youngest, who was scrawnier than me, wore glasses, and was prone to ailments. He would break out in bright red rashes too, which were unsightly. I always came out favourably compared to him. My parents would reassure each other that I'd turn out all right in the end. That is more or less what I understood at the time.

It is odd that I was not ignored. That I so troubled them. But they were the fussing kind of middle-class parents and aunts and uncles, and that might be because they had to fit into our lopsided society, lopsided because there were too few at the top who owned the land, and too many at the bottom who attempted to survive off it. This left an area in the middle, made up of small businesses, shopkeepers, managers, teachers, all the usual professions, people who lacked power but didn't suffer the vicissitudes of that lack. My parents understood the world was in turmoil, and no one knew what was to become of anyone. And therefore, they fretted. They fretted for they feared what would happen to me. That I would realise their suspicions and suffer the consequences. The entire situation in the Canary Islands at that time weighed heavy on their minds. That, and of course they never told me about my father's Uncle Alfredo, who never married before he died.

My family owned, and no doubt still own, one of the old houses in a terrace of similar abodes near the centre of La Laguna. While not on the scale of the grand rural and urban houses of the nobility – the landowners, including those descended from the original conquerors five hundred years before – the family house denotes moderate wealth and prestige with its two storeys and its Juliet balconies. Poorer families live in houses with only one storey, and my family has nothing to do with them, except for my father, on a professional basis and not necessarily in their favour. The even poorer, the underclass, crowd into smaller houses still, and they live much farther from the city centre and I never saw any of them close up.

I learned about these divisions of wealth and poverty later, much later. Growing up, all I knew were my own narrow cobbled street, the other narrow cobbled streets around the cathedral, and to and from my school; and I only knew what my family knew and what they wanted me to know. I only knew goodness and kindness and a narrow morality.

I was protected and pampered, and my belly was always full. I went to school without knowing my father paid for me to go there. I was innocent. I only existed in the moment. I had no cause to dwell on the past because I had no shame, despite my parents' anxieties. The future was a mystery I didn't concern myself with. I existed in the blissful present. Although glimmers of that other insidious, repressive and punitive reality broke into my halcyon existence at school.

JOSÉ WAS SITTING STRAIGHT-BACKED, his attention, full and complete, on his teacher, whose big desk brushed his own little one. He sat in the centre of the front row, on the left side of the classroom. The teacher, Doña Vasco, bedecked in black, top to toe, with her hair pulled back tightly revealing a stern, no-nonsense face, was her usual uncompromising self.

They were learning sums. They were learning subtraction, and José concentrated hard, eager not to make a single mistake, struggling not to let his pen slip, or his mind falter.

It was no use. His attention drifted to the map pinned to the wall, and he wondered what it was like in the lands far from his own.

He could understand removing five buttons from a jar of ten left five remaining because he had counted them and seen the number taken and the number of buttons left. That was easy to comprehend. What was harder was when there were no buttons and the entire operation took place in the abstract realm of the number alone. He kept asking himself, five what?

Mistakes were tolerated but idleness was not and incomprehension was too easily mistaken for idleness and the consequences stung. From five buttons to five lashes of Doña Vasco's wicked cane, and José's hand smarted for the rest of the day. Nine minus seven. It occurred to him to write down any number, but he stretched out his hands beneath his desk and bent each finger in turn, and then he wrote down two.

The sums got harder.

Soon the bottom number was larger than the top.

What did his father say to do?

He looked up, not at his teacher, for she was at the back of the class, but at the little statue of the immaculate Mary, and at the portrait of General Franco square in the centre of the wall.

It was the same portrait, wherever he went.

Not a bad-looking man with his thinning pate and martial brush moustache. His eyes followed you around the room.

José wished he could ask his friend Enrico, who had a talent for mathematics, but he sat in a different row. The boys walked home together at lunchtimes, and at recess they played in the shade, but it was now that José needed his clever friend.

Doña Vasco approached José from behind and took him by surprise as he used his fingers to answer the next sum. He felt the weight of her presence bearing down on him and anticipated another lashed palm.

His teacher had a different punishment in mind.

He could have had no idea she had been watching him for weeks. She had heard rumours. She noticed his preference for pinks and yellows when the children were painting pictures. And when the class painted pictures, he painted pretty princesses in long flowing dresses. He had no idea there was anything wrong in that.

'José Ramos, on your feet,' Doña Vasco said.

Stricken with fear, he did as he is told.

'Now, stand on your desk.'

'My desk?'

'Do not question me, boy.'

José clambered onto his desk and looked down at his classmates, their shocked faces. Somehow, the whole class was terrified. No one knew why he was being singled out, and they all thought it could be their turn next.

'Class,' the teacher boomed. 'This boy behaves like a girl. What do you think of that?' She singled out Carmen with her gaze.

'I don't know, Doña Vasco,' Carmen said timidly.

'You don't know. Well, the others know. What do we say to a boy who behaves like a girl?'

'Marica! Marica!' the other children cried as if on cue.

'Mariposa! Mariposa!'

And along came a string of insults.

Doña Vasco watched on with a sly smile on her hardened face.

José blushed crimson. He almost wet his pants.

I SWING my legs back and forth and dislodge a small rock. I lean forward and watch it bounce its way down the rock face and disappear. The sun faces me, scalding my skin with its rays. Below, the ocean beats against the rocky outcrops. I lean back, putting my hands behind me and using my arms as props. I am alone. The raven has left in favour of filling its belly. My own belly needs filling, but I have no food.

There's a farm further south, in an elevated valley. It's where I was last shooed from. If I wait until sunset and head back in the gloaming, I may steal some tomatoes. There's prickly pear in fruit growing by the roadside. And if I'm lucky, I might raid a chicken coop.

My problem is the dogs. It's always the farm dogs. Their owners let them roam at night. I have learned to fill my pockets with rocks. I hold my knife, sharpened on a stone, poised to kill if a threat turns nasty. I am a petty criminal, a thief, a vagrant, a nomad, an out and out low life. I am no one my family would want to know. Not now. No more. The day I was sentenced put paid to any hope of redemption I might have had.

24

SHOULDER DAY

I PULLED MY EYES AWAY FROM THE TRANSLATION ON MY SCREEN, marking my place on the script and closing the laptop. So much for literary gold. The writer seemed fixated on José's childhood. I felt cheated, cheated into translating all that verbiage when what I wanted was the meat of the story of the hostel. The more of that this Spanish script provided, the less I would need to research. As it stood, I faced the onerous task of doing most of the work myself.

I've never been one for backstory. Slows the pace of the narrative like a ball and chain. Readers these days want to forge ahead, gripped by events unfolding in the here and now. Although I can appreciate the building of the character. The importance of depicting the reality of being gay back then, even as a child. The stigmatisation. And there I was, toying with my own masculinity, turning myself over like a pebble in the palm of my hand.

Is a childhood really as defining of character and identity? Am I the result of the boy crafted by a careless father, a stricken mother and an overbearing aunt? Was I made by them, or am I who I always was, right from birth? I stopped short of thinking about Vince.

It was late afternoon, and I still hadn't eaten any lunch. The Clen had reduced my appetite to near zero, and I could already see the signs of a shrinking paunch. But I needed to re-fuel if only to have

671

enough energy for the gym. The script could wait. Especially since there was every chance it would offer me little other than a background tale. I was stiff and edgy after being cooped up all day. I need to get some air around my head and some heat into my muscles.

After straightening the bed, I put the script and the laptop under my smalls in the top drawer of the dresser. Then I went downstairs to the kitchen and fried up a couple of eggs and wedged them into a stale baguette. It wasn't like me to display such a disrespectful attitude to food, but my lack of appetite had rendered me indifferent. I regretted my attitude the moment I bit into the baguette and found I had to wrench the bread apart as the omelette slid out the other end.

It was late afternoon when I set off. Crossing the patio, I glanced in at the living room but, as seemed to be often the case, there was no one about. Paco and Claire appeared to prefer the other rooms in the house. As did the dog. Or they were still clearing up after the wake.

The only downside to the apartment was having to pass by those living room windows. They might have thought of that when designing the extension. Not everyone wants to feel exposed, their comings and goings there for all to see. A door facing south into the garden, with a path leading away from the house would have been ideal – something to allow privacy when coming and going. Either one of them could be watching me from an upstairs window, come to think of it. I glanced up, but my gaze met only shutters closed against the sun. Even so, I felt naked and stiff in my skin, sensations that only began to leave me once I was out on the pavement. My sense of being watched faded entirely once I was clear of the house.

I drove with a steely resolve. Shoulder day was not a favourite of mine. Was any day a favourite? They were all hard on various parts of my body. Punishing in every respect. My determination to get fit was being eclipsed by my muse now I had committed myself to writing about the gay prison, but I needed to incorporate balance in my life going forward, create good habits. I reminded myself I was a single man, and I needed to give my body a chance to transform and become attractive once more to the opposite sex. No pain, no gain. Besides, I had bought a membership, I had steroids pumping through me and I was downing a fat burner – the larger part of me would not countenance all that waste were I to go back to my old habits. And it was obvious the exercise was doing me good. I already felt toned.

My exchange with Mario had put my mind at rest as far as being the object of suspicion regarding the rucksack. However, as I parked in the street outside the gym, I still hoped to avoid Juan's uncle and his mates who seemed to have a preference for exercise earlier in the day. Although they might turn up at any time. Who could say?

I pushed open the door and inhaled the air-conditioned cool, the not-so-subtle scent of male sweat, the perfumed air the gym used to disguise it and as I inhaled, I steeled my resolve for the ardours ahead. I went and slung my gym bag on the floor, mounted the exercise bike nearest the door, and commenced my ten-kilometre pedal.

Luis appeared behind the counter and smiled at me in the mirror. He seemed genuinely pleased to see me. He came over as I was reaching my first kilometre and hovered near the handlebars. He didn't seem to want to leave me alone. I had no idea why. I pedalled and panted and pedalled and panted, not wanting to slow my pace.

'I was worried you weren't coming back,' he said.

'Why would you think that?' I said between breaths. I could feel the anger rising. This routine he had put me on was hard enough without him stealing my energy with conversation.

'I thought maybe I made your fitness plan too hard. That was what I thought when you didn't show.'

'I had a couple of rest days,' I said, cooling to him as I spoke. 'That's all.'

He still wouldn't go away, and I wouldn't stop pedalling while he watched, even though I knew I would soon be gasping for air. What was it with this guy? Did he have the hots for me, or what? It was a thought that prompted sudden disgust. Thankfully, a patron strode over to the counter, and Luis went to serve him.

I pedalled furiously and dismounted the bike on ten clicks just as puffed and just as wobbly as I had on the first day, but the time it had taken to complete the task had reduced by twenty seconds.

The weights routine was no easier than the first time around. I could not lift heavier weights on the military press, and with my shoulder still playing up, I struggled through the sets. On the final heave, I resented spending precious euros on the steroids. The military press, lateral raises, dumbbell front raises and dumbbell shoulder press might only amount to four sorts of exercise, but they targeted certain muscle groups that had no interest in participating. With each set the reps grew harder, and I struggled to meet the target. Yet whenever I felt the impulse to stop, I countered it by recalling Luis's humiliating comment about his fitness plan being too hard for me, and my strength would increase on an upsurge of anger. Too hard, indeed!

I was halfway through the last set of dumbbell front raises when a man came into the gym, a man I hadn't seen before. With his bag and his towel, he seemed like just another gym freak, but as he came closer, came into the light, I caught the curve of his calf muscles, the solid, sculpted thighs, the six-pack beneath his tight singlet, the polished skin of his arms, the biceps, the pecs, the curve of his neck, and then his face, his perfectly proportioned and astonishingly handsome face. I had to stop my jaw from falling open, my eyes from gaping wide. In a surreptitious manner, using the mirrors as my means as I raised the dumbbells to the horizontal, I began to drink him in. I drank him in like ambrosia, and as I did, I was awash with the strangest of desires, an animal lust that weakened me even as it made me want to charge at him and smother him in kisses. I could have devoured him, devoured that perfection there and then in full view of the entire gym. At least in theory. At least in my head. And in the very next moment, as I raised the dumbbells for the last time, the entrance door opened and in walked a woman, and the woman approached my Adonis, and he smiled at her, a smile that could only be a lover's smile, and I was angry, angry at him, angry at myself, and above all, I was angry at her, whoever she was, for stealing away my fantasy at a critical moment. And besides, unlike him, she was plain. She was, next to him, astonishingly, unbelievably, unjustifiably plain.

'Javier,' someone said loudly, and my Adonis looked up, and my spell was broken.

It was in that moment of disbelief that I realised my arms remained outstretched and, looking around, I felt everyone had their eye on me. Self-conscious and flustered, I quickly lowered the dumb-bells and returned them to the rack.

Then I realised I needed the same dumbbells for the shoulder press and went and retrieved them. As usual, the first set was relatively easy. The second set that much harder. When I came to the third, I had to use all my determination to continue.

I tried to focus on the reps, on the steady count to twenty, but I got to ten, and my mind fogged over, and I couldn't focus. I lifted the dumbbells, felt the agonising pain in my shoulders, but I was momentarily elsewhere, my body mechanically going through the motions. When I realised I had zoned out and had no idea the number of reps I had completed and therefore how many I needed to perform before I ended the set, I was aghast. I did what I thought might have been an extra three reps just to be sure, gritting my teeth, straining, pushing my arms up with all my might.

After a brief recovery, I headed to the bike for the cool down. As I pedalled, I wondered if zoning out had made the reps easier. Did focussing on the counting somehow make the exercise more difficult? Somewhere along the way, I had to meet my resistance, that point at which the body and mind no longer wanted to continue and screamed out to the conscious entity within who was determined to press on.

My thoughts drifted up to Tefía. Did those prisoners at the hostel who had been doomed to break rocks and then carry rocks all day long in the searing heat and wind, did they count? Did they count the rocks they were forced to carry? Did they take a daily tally, compete with themselves or each other over how many rocks they had or hadn't broken and carried? No. I could not imagine they had done that. It would have been ludicrous. They would have zoned out. They would have slipped into a sort of trance to block out the reality of their situation.

After a quick round of stretches, I carried that thought with me all the way back to Tiscamanita. It was easier to think about counting reps and rocks than it was to contemplate my startling reaction to Mr Adonis entering the gym.

Back in the apartment, I went upstairs and checked under the bed to make sure the rucksack was still in the suitcase. It was. I started to believe the heat had finally passed. If Paco and Claire had had any notion of me having kept the rucksack, they would have confronted me by now, especially when they had easy access to my apartment and could conduct a thorough search while I was out. And it seemed clear to me that Juan's uncle was no threat.

Downstairs, in the brightly lit kitchen, I recalled the macaroni cheese I had left in the fridge in Tefía. It would still be edible, and I really ought to head back there and finish it. More's the point, I really ought to head back there, full stop, and put an end to this interlude. I had rented that farmhouse for three whole months, and with no apparent threat in sight, there was no justifiable reason for my not being there; I considered the rent I had paid in advance a waste should I remain at Paco and Claire's.

Here, in Tiscamanita, I was alone and not alone. There was always the threat of Paco or Claire knocking on my door and disturbing my peace. I wanted tranquillity, not awkward dinners and crowds of visitors I was required to interact with.

I cobbled together a simple salad and munched my way through it as I continued to mull over my dilemma. I was in two minds where I wanted to be; there were benefits to both. Tefía was lonely and grim, yet the isolation suited me, and it was close to the action in my new literary work. I could press on uninterrupted. Then again, the set up at Paco and Claire's was sheltered and homely. I felt more in the centre of things. I hesitated. The atmosphere here might have been convivial if my hosts were not so dour. Claire was pleasant enough, but Paco was strange, although he had relaxed somewhat when I exchanged a few words with him during the wake. But I had the strong impression I was not that welcome here. It occurred to me if I did choose to stay here, I would need to offer them rent. I would not freeload, no matter how much Claire might protest. Which pretty much sealed it; I was not about to pay double rent. I would return to Tefía.

That left the problem of the rats. I did not want to arouse suspicion. Leaving too soon after claiming a rat infestation would do just that. I needed to allow a reasonable amount of time to pass, enough to allow for a response to my complaint and for pest control to come in and take action. Two days was not a reasonable amount of time by any measure, not even in this instant-fix, express-service world we lived in. I would imagine two weeks to be more likely, especially on this island backwater. Then again, the farmhouse was a holiday let and the owner would be concerned I would leave a negative review and act swiftly to avoid that. Surely there was an instant pest control service on the island. I did a quick search and discovered the first visit was an assessment, and then they would return to take the necessary treatment. In the case of rats, that meant blocking access and setting traps. Possibly also laying poison.

In the meantime, I could hardly pretend to take off somewhere else, since there was no choice but to park my car in the farmhouse drive, visible to all passers-by.

I cursed my own impulsive nature that day the behemoth had followed me. I should have waited. Bade my time. I should come up with a better reason for needing to leave the farmhouse straight away. Rats! Of all the lies I could have come up with! I had trapped myself in this situation, and I only had myself to blame. To make matters worse, thanks to blabbermouth me, Paco and Claire knew too much. But at least they also believed I had handed the rucksack in to the police.

Another thought occurred to me. Paco and Claire might be distant and unforthcoming, but they would protect me if it came to it. Alone, I was vulnerable. I still had the rucksack and the cash, and someone knew about Juan's phone and had rung his number. Twice. So I might not be completely out of danger.

It was all too much to consider. I slugged a cold beer and then downed most of a bottle of a local red as I whiled away the evening watching Netflix on my laptop, trying to keep my thoughts from drifting towards all the uncomfortable topics filling my brain.

THE ROOM WAS warm and stuffy. Music played softly in the background. I found I was walking. A bed appeared. It was large and circular and covered in fake astrakhan. There were people populating the room. I heard murmurs and groans, bodies in dim corners. My attention was drawn back to the bed. A man lay flat on his back with his manhood, hard and glistening, listing to one side of his abdomen. There were other bodies on the bed, limbs and butts all knotted together, moving rhythmically. I saw faces, faces filled with desire. As I stared, the heat in my own loins blazed, and I felt swollen, needy, urgent and then, after a glorious few seconds of euphoria, I was spent.

I OPENED my eyes on the thick black of the room in a state of complete confusion. Disoriented, I reached out for the bedside lamp and grabbed at nothing but air. It slowly entered my awareness that I was not in Tefia as I had thought, but in the bed of Paco and Claire's apartment, the top sheet wrapped around my thigh, soaking up the discharged juices of my manhood. A twin horror engulfed me. I had had another wet dream. A dream I dimly recalled and only in fragments. It came as a sickening realisation that there had not been a single woman on that bed or in any of the dim corners of my dream. The absence of women and my surging erotic desire could only mean one thing. My subconscious was telling me a simple message. I was gay, or at the very least bisexual. Angela had been right about me all along. I felt conspired against, as though I, the me I live with every day, had been hoodwinked by the complicity of my subconscious and a perceptive Angela into facing the reality of me, a reality I had been incapable of facing all my adult life.

For my sins, the sins of my repressed sexuality, I had soiled the sheets. But not my own sheets – oh no, nothing so simple as a walk down my own hall to my own washing machine – but the sheets of my hosts, who had their own washing machine I knew not where. And for the life of me I could not figure out how I would conjure a reason to use their washing machine on the third day of my stay and, under the watchful eye of an intensely observant Claire, somehow surreptitiously toss into the tub the cotton sheet all damp and crusty with my semen, and then whip it out again without her knowledge and dry it up here, on the patio, out of view. I had no idea how I would manage any of that, but I had to. The embarrassment otherwise would be unconscionable, and I was not about to sleep in filthy sheets.

Was I really bisexual? Or was I simply suffering from chronic sexual frustration? I jumped online and researched the topic of wet dreams in older men. One website reassured me there was no underlying medical condition associated with wet dreams. It was simply a natural response in men who reached orgasm in their sleep. Masturbate more, the websites said, and see if it made a difference.

At least, I was not abnormal.

Although, the bottom line this time was not that I had had another wet dream, but that I had orgasmed in my sleep while having an erotic interlude involving men. And straight guys did not do that. Ever. A man cannot be straight and have a gay subconscious. Face it.

I couldn't. It was all too much. Before the sun made its appearance, I packed up all my things and stuffed the sheets into a plastic bag to take with me. Then I heaved the suitcase and my bags down the stairs and, making as little noise as I could, I tiptoed across the patio, slid the bolt on the gate and loaded the car.

The dog did not make an appearance. They must keep it inside with them. Knowing Claire, the mutt probably slumbered on the end of the couple's bed. Even so, on my way back across the patio, I kept an eye out.

In the apartment, I retrieved my kitchen supplies and left a note on the bench, thanking Paco and Claire for their hospitality. Bugger the rats. I would come up with a plausible story if I needed to.

Back in the comfort and the ample space of the Tefía farmhouse, I started to relax. I put the sheets in the wash and then unpacked my things, leaving the rucksack in the suitcase, which I slid under my bed. In the bathroom, as I replaced my toothbrush and toothpaste in the ceramic cup provided, I thought perhaps the atmosphere at Tiscamanita had been having an adverse effect on my psyche. Maybe now, my inner turmoil would settle and I could pursue my new book project with vitality and poise.

After breaking my fast on toast and jam, I wasted no time translating the next passages of text. Seeing the sentences emerging in English, I was relieved to find the author at last striking at the heart of the story with scenes of his arrest and then scenes, dismal scenes set in a Tenerife prison cell. The washing machine beeped the end of its cycle, and I dashed to the laundry to deal with the sheets. After that, I didn't stop until I had another thousand words to play with. Reading them over, I knew I had reached that point where I needed to dig deeper into the real story of the prison. I couldn't rely on the hand-written manuscript alone. Besides, I wanted to know more. I felt a sense of urgency about it. I took a Clen, planning on working through the entire day without a break.

I forgot about the money in the rucksack in the wardrobe. I forgot Juan and his uncle. I was oblivious to Paco and Claire back in Tisca-manita, who had possibly already found my note and were wondering what they had done to upset me. I lost myself completely to the Spanish script. When I had translated another page, I could do no more. Instead, I began researching the Canary Islands in the period between the 1930s and the 1950s. Not only did the English version need my touch – for the original was thin on detail and heavy on reflection and far too angst-laden for my taste – but to write with any authenticity, I needed to know my subject.

The only break I took from my labours was to retrieve the sheets from the washing line and grab the occasional glass of water. I read up on what it was like to be gay in Spain under Franco. I re-visited the blog posts I had found about the prison. I took notes and started embellishing the draft.

At sunset, I was a wreck. My head ached, and I needed to unwind, but it would be a waste of an evening. Instead, I focussed on the section of writing leading up to when José found himself in the prison in Fuerteventura.

25

GUILTY AS CHARGED

He was an explosion of pain. So many thoughts and feelings vied with each other, hitting the forefront of his mind like photographic stills from a newsreel. The moment was incomprehensible. All he could do was bow his head and walk in a straight line from the café to the awaiting van. On each side of him, shoving him on, was an officer of the Guardia Civil.

His feet trod the pavement. He wasn't seeing the dark sky, the buildings, the onlookers, yet he felt others there watching the horror of the moment, his fate.

Was one of them his father? Was one of them Juan Ramos, prized lawyer, come to watch his son as he was taken away, come to spit in his face? No, his father was tucked up in bed with his wife.

He trudged on, head hanging low, eyes to the pavement. He had no clear idea what was about to happen to him. He had been singled out, that was all he knew, singled out by a thin, weasel of a boy who had taken it upon himself to identify the guilty parties.

José was shoved in the van to sit with the others. He was gripped by disbelief and choking fear. The van bounced along on the cobbled streets. It was not long and José was manhandled by the burly policemen and locked in a cell. A cell with metal bars floor to ceiling facing a corridor. A cell with a very high window. A cell of cold brick with low wooden benches. Two other young men sat on those benches. José didn't want to be near either of them.

He recognised one of the men he was forced to spend the night with. A prostitute who called himself Violeta, but whose real name was Manuel. José had never spoken to Manuel. When the young man tried to catch his eye, José looked down at his feet.

'I have done nothing. Nothing,' he said.

'You can be arrested for looking at another man for too long. Maybe you did that.'

'They have spies everywhere.'

'But it was Antonio who identified me to the police. Why would he do that?'

'To save his own skin.'

The following morning, he was told he was to be cross-examined, but the two policemen glaring at him from across the wooden table had no ears for his pleas. The sternest, meanest of the pair told him he was to be condemned to prison under the "Ley de Vagos y Maleantes" – the Vagrancy Act. That law! He knew about that law. It was created in 1933 under the Second Republic, ostensibly meant to deal with vagrants, the homeless, pimps and other low lives, anyone society deemed antisocial. Later, Franco used the law to persecute the Republicans. Then he had the idea to include homosexuals. Every gay man in Spain knew the risks. José knew the risks. It was why he would never, despite the desires filling his heart, break his virginity. He would rather condemn himself to celibacy than jail. He had fought his whole life against himself, against those longings in his heart and his loins. He existed in a state of perpetual anguish and guilt. His only sin was in choosing to socialise in the one café known to attract homosexuals. And now the law was brought down to bear on him.

José Ramos, just eighteen and due to be conscripted for his year of military service, and one of the first to be convicted.

There was no trial. Not in the sense of a fair hearing. Instead, he was assumed guilty and sentenced. The police commissioner seemed to relish in the sentencing. A triumph. There were no sympathisers in the room. His mother, his sister and brother were not there. Only his father came to watch his eldest son bring disgrace to the family name. His father, who stayed long enough to look José in the eye, scowl and leave, a public condemnation so absolute and final.

'Why, in God's name did you have to get caught?' Those were his words to José in a private moment. Words from a lawyer who defended real criminals.

'I did nothing wrong, I swear it.'

'You must have done. You were arrested. You were charged.'

'For looking someone in the eye!'

FROM BLISSFUL IGNORANCE to full awareness through one lingering gaze. What do you make of that, raven dear, you who cares to settle by my side? Could you have seen that coming? Are you sitting by me now as messenger or harbinger? Tell me which, my all-seeing friend. Perhaps neither. For I am fearless in your presence, that is all I know. With you by my side, I can face my assured future with the courage I need.

I suppose the authorities wanted to make an example of someone, get the ball rolling, put the fear of God into all the other homosexual men in Tenerife. The irony is the punishment has turned me into the very antisocial person for which the original law was created. Before my conviction, I was the most sociable young man. I wore a smile on my face, and I had a suit on my back. I mixed with the best in society, and I had a paid job. I was even prepared to endure military service despite every cell in my body wanting to bolt to Africa to avoid it.

I was a dutiful son too, and I made every effort to get along with my siblings despite their adolescent rejection of me. For I saw no good in returning hatred for hatred. Above all, I wanted to prove my worth, and I had decided I would do that through hard work and dedication.

I was a good boy. I had done no wrong. I would stare at my reflection of my flesh in the bathroom mirror and wonder at what lurked on the inside of me, the pestilence that coursed through me, filtered into every atom, taking control of my desire.

When I reached eighteen, I left school with good grades, excelling in Spanish literature and history, and secured a position in the centre of Santa Cruz as a copy boy for a local newspaper. I had high aspirations. I wanted to be a journalist or an editor. I craved a position of importance. I wanted to be significant, to contribute, to be respected, even feared.

My regular haunt before, during and after work was Café El Aguila down Calle del Castillo, a side street off Plaza del Principe in the city's cultural heart. I enjoyed that part of Santa Cruz de Tenerife, the narrow streets flanked by old buildings with their arched windows and Juliet balconies. I could walk to work from my uncle's house where I had lodgings, and I would stride along, owning the town, confident, proud, eager. I was no longer tormented by the jibes and taunts and the threat of violence from my peers at school. I was an adult stepping out into the world and making friends with my new work colleagues, and none of them eyed me with suspicion, none of them whispered names as I went by, none of them bumped into me on purpose in the corridors with the intent of knocking me flying. I wasn't judged. I was accepted, for the first time in my whole life. I worked hard and that was all that mattered to the other staff and the bosses at the newspaper.

The café was a meeting place for writers, artists, journalists and musicians. Business people and ordinary working people came too, and the place was full and vibrant day and night. Later, in the early hours when men were loose and their pockets more so, prostitutes would wander in or hover outside, but I was rarely if ever around to see them.

Anyone who was anyone went to El Aguila. I met many great artists, my raven friend, although you may not have heard of any of them, you being a Gran Canaria bird. But these were the giants of Tenerife, of the Canary Islands and therefore of Spain. Why should I not name them, since I am so proud to have been among them. Like artists Enrique Lite and García Miguel Tarquis and Antonio Vizcaya Carpenter and Pedro Gonzalez. I rubbed shoulders with Pedro García Cabrera and Emeterio Gutiŕrez Albeto, who were the avant garde poets of the "Generation of 27" and worked on the prestigious *Gaceta de Arte* magazine. I spoke to Felix Casanova de Ayala and Agustín

Millares Sall and Isaac de Vega. And Rafael Arozarena and Francisco Pimentel and Antonio Bermejo and José Antonio Padrón – those members of the Fetasiano movement who opposed post-war social realism in literature in favour of introspective, interior works, something I can only agree with as to me, the interior space is where real truth, repressed truth lives. These were great men, all of them. All the artistic giants of Tenerife and beyond came to El Aguila, or so it appeared to me. How could I not know these men, even if they did not really know me? To them, I was a boy, a pretty boy who worked for *El Día*, a cute boy with entertaining banter and big dreams. A boy who turned heads. And they didn't mind me standing at the bar, listening to their bluster.

We were socialists. I had had no idea about socialism until I started at *El Día* and mingled at Café El Aguila. I quickly learned of its importance. Of the underground struggle that went on and on in the repressive regime of Franco. Pedro Cabrera was the most outspoken. It was dangerous talk, I knew that much. These were the dissenters. They talked of the appalling conditions among the campesinos and the farm labourers. They talked of oligarchy, a word I had to look up. They talked of uprisings, strikes and other unrest back in the 1930s when I was born. Conditions were still the same in the 1950s. The business class supported Franco's coup d'etat. As did the military and the offices of the administration at all levels. Clandestine migration was rife. Those who could, went to Venezuela. 'Wine, cochineal and bananas,' Pedro was wont to say, 'The wine numbs our brains and the cochineal stains our skin while we slip and fall on our arses on banana peel.'

I loved mingling among all those important men, radical men, interesting men of conviction. I read Lorca and Ceruda. I discussed Joyce and Orwell and Hemingway. I was respected.

Frequenting El Alguila were intellectual and creative straight men and intellectual and creative gay men. There were businessmen and businessmen who were gay. There were government officials. And government officials who were gay. Consequently, there was a lot of judging and scrutinizing.

Was it the barman, the taxi driver, the cleaner, the storekeeper or the tobacconist – both in from across the street – who had called the police that night? The watchers. Everyone knew we were being watched. The young, especially, were watched.

I was at the bar with a work colleague, Mario. I sipped my coffee, sugar-laced how I liked it, and caught the eye of Alfredo, the old maricon who seemed to have homed in on me as his next adventure. A café regular, slipping from home when his wife was tucked up in bed, Alfredo was a respected and well-connected businessman who pretended to himself and the world that he was entirely heterosexual. I should have looked the other way. The man was ageing, pot-bellied and repulsive. Yet there was that alluring glint in his eye, and I was momentarily fascinated by it. Me, a virgin, taken in by the surreptitious assignations of a man my father's age. I was not a prostitute. I was not a boy for hire under any circumstances, and neither was I about to follow him to the park for a fumble in the shadows.

None of that mattered, for as I held Alfredo's gaze, he smiled at me and winked. I smiled back as I looked away. I did not return his wink. I swear I did not. Mario was right beside me, and he knew I never winked at old Alfredo. But someone must have said I did. One of those watchers informed the police that I was having relations with some unidentified maricon.

Yes, unidentified.

Convenient, for him.

Later that night, much later when the crowds had thinned and the prostitutes were mingling with the men, only then did the police raid El Aguila. I should have gone home long before then, but Mario was drunk and thirsty and I did not want to leave him alone to stagger back to his house in that state.

As the front doors flew open amid much commotion, I tried to exit through a side door, but it was blocked, blocked by Alfredo who stared at me with his leery grin before vanishing, the door closing behind him as I felt something clench my arm.

Or rather, someone. It was a hand. The hand soon became handcuffs after the wizened weasel picked me out of a small group of young men as one of the offenders.

Before the night was through the interrogations began. No one was interested in the truth or justice.

One lingering gaze at the wrong man in the wrong place on the wrong night and I lost my freedom and my life. In the days that followed, I and four others that night joined ten more and, after a spell in prison in Tenerife, we were transported by boat to Fuerteventura and then by military truck to the Tefía to be incarcerated in the Colonia Agrícola Penitenciaria.

A prison farm!

We were to labour like campesinos, only unlike poor peasant farmers, we would see none of the fruits of our labours. We would enjoy no freedom. We would never, not once, look up at the sky and smile.

At Tefía, I inherited an altogether different sort of family to the one I had enjoyed in El Aguila. None of us wanted to be in Fuerteventura, the Canary Island closest to Africa and one I knew little about before I went there, other than its shape and its location and the fact that it is bone dry. The authorities could not have come up with a more desolate location – a former military airport in the middle of nowhere.

Can you imagine that place, raven friend? You, perched here beside me at this cliff edge, pointing your beak this way and that, cocking your head at me as we sit here facing into the breeze. We are neither of us suited to a sun-drenched, wind-beaten clime.

My feet sway. I sense the void beneath them, and my mood darkens. What will become of the friends I made in prison? Of Ruben and Raphael and Jorge? And Manuel? I fear the most for Manuel. I fear the most for Manuel because I feel the most for Manuel. My Manuel. My love.

My mind wanders back and hovers above two men, two men in the thick darkness of night, two scrawny sparrows of men, huddled in a loving embrace, our stinking, sweat-coated flesh, bone pressing into bone, our kisses, tongues entwined, our longing, our eventual sex. And we came in the thick of that cold night, we came together, silently, not daring even to shudder, and I became the sinner I had been imprisoned for.

It was just the once. We took the risk in the days before my release.

Now Manuel is a lover I can never again meet.

And I ache for him, for more of him, yearn to bury my face in his. My mouth hungers for his mouth, my heart for his heart. And he loved me, too, as passionately as I him. But the day I was released, he still had a month of his sentence left and he knew he would be sent to a different island to serve his time in banishment under the ever-watchful eye of a judicial delegate. For a whole year, none of us are allowed anywhere near our own families. For another five, we must report to the authorities each month. If we do not, they will find us and imprison us once more.

My bird companion preens and ruffles his feathers, and I lift my gaze from the watery void far below to watch. The bird soon sits still, and we lock gazes.

What would you have me do, then, raven, you who stare into me, staring right into my soul? Do I get up and walk away from this precipice? Do I make my way back to the police station to report as it behoves me to do each month?

Or?

26

A CRISIS

A MARATHON RUN AT THE TRANSLATION AND WHEN THE CLEN HAD finally left my system, I fell in a heap and slept for twelve hours straight. When I woke up, the room was bright, and at first, I wondered where I was. When it came to me that I had returned to the farmhouse, I got up and went to the window and stared at the wind-mill, trying to make out the compound that was the hostel. I couldn't.

After my shower, I rubbed the scented moisturiser into my dry and flaking skin, gave the bathroom a once-over with a cloth and then went and made my bed. I collected the dirty clothes from the back of the chair and went to the laundry to do a wash. As I dropped my gym gear into the drum, I thought once it was dry I would head to the gym. Having missed the day before, my muscles were already feeling fidgety.

I swallowed a Clen with my coffee, and after the small bowl of tinned fruit I chose for breakfast, my appetite diminished to near zero. I was swallowing the last sliver of slimy sliced peach when my laptop signalled a Skype call. As anticipated, it was Angela. I hit the accept call button and gazed into her ebullient face.

'How's the literary tiger?' she said.

'Not too bad. Yourself?'

She ignored my question. 'You look different.' She peered at me. 'Have you done something to your face?'

'I have lost weight, Angela, if that's what you're referring to.'

'Well done! In just two weeks, too. That's amazing. Are you fasting?'

'Sort of,' I said evasively. I was not about to tell her about the Clen.

A serious look appeared in her face. 'What did you end up doing with the rucksack?'

'I handed it in, as you suggested.' Lying had become second nature.

She nodded and leaned in towards the webcam. 'Now tell me, is the muse being kind to you?'

Ever persistent Angela. I cobbled together a response.

'I've been deep in research as you can imagine.' Which was the truth and, 'I found some material that was a big help in developing the protagonist and his backstory.' Total lie – I had gleaned all that from the Spanish script. Then, 'I'm easing myself into the prison itself. I have to say, though, it is confronting. I'm having to meet my own resistance to engage with the conditions there.' Wait for it. 'And, of course, not being gay makes it all the more difficult regarding authenticity.' The whopper lie.

Angela rolled her eyes.

'Stop going on about not being gay.'

'I'm not, gay, I mean.'

'And I'm a monkey's uncle.'

'I concede I might be bisexual.'

'That's a start.'

'What do you mean?'

'On your path to acceptance.'

'Stop teasing.'

'Is that what I'm doing?' She gave me her mocking smile. 'Before I forget, they'll be announcing the winner of the literary prize tomorrow.'

'Tomorrow! That's come around quickly.'

'Not really. The shortlist was announced a month ago. I didn't want to tell you until you were safely tucked away in Fuerteventura.'

'Why ever not?'

'You were incredibly upset, Trevor. I was worried the news might tip you over the edge.'

What was she talking about? She made me sound suicidal. I was not suicidal. I have never been suicidal. Anything but. Back then, I was in a slump and that was hardly surprising given the situation. Jackie's lawyer had been ruthless, and I hardly saw the kids. But a month ago, I was on the up. I had bought my little retreat in Norfolk. Life had started to feel promising again.

I pretended to be distracted with something on the table out of her view and tapped the keys to reinforce the idea.

'Glad you are still on task,' Angela said and blew me a kiss. 'Gotta dash.'

Her face disappeared. I heard the washing machine on spin. I browsed the articles I had downloaded onto my desktop. There was a doctoral thesis, in Spanish, concerning Tenerife up until 1945. Various blog posts on the prison, all saying more or less the same. Some newspaper reports. A lengthy review of that novella by the professor who had interviewed Octavio García, whose testimony broke the prison story. Gleaning information from all that text was laborious, but I pressed on, taking notes as I went.

When the washing machine beeped, I went and pegged out my clothes, making sure my gym gear was in full sun. I would drive into the city after lunch. By then, my shorts and t-shirt and socks would all be dry. And I needed to do a workout. Not that I cared for chest day. I didn't much care for any of my designated workout days, but the effects were already apparent and my muscles craved the punishment. I cautioned myself against letting my new literary fixation override my need to take care of my body.

I went back inside. In the kitchen, I checked the time on my phone and noticed I had a new text message.

It was from Claire.

Where are you? Why did you leave? Worried.

I was about to hit reply when my phone sprang to life with a call. I swiped green without paying attention to who was calling. When I heard Claire's voice, I sensed that oversight was at the very least foolish. Now I would need to fudge and lie on the spot. At least texting gave me a chance to think about how to tackle the rats story. It occurred to me to hang up and text her later saying my phone had died, but who would believe that?

'Hey, Claire,' I said, casual as you please. 'How's it going?'

'We heard you leave, and then we read your note. What's happened? Didn't you like the apartment?'

'The apartment was lovely.'

'It obviously didn't suit you. Where are you now?'

'Tefía.'

'At the farmhouse? What about the rats?'

'The owner got straight onto pest control. They've dealt with the problem by blocking the access points and setting some traps.' I was relieved I had had the presence of mind to research the matter.

'Wow, that was fast!'

'I think they were worried about the review I would leave if they didn't expedite the matter.'

'True. Even so.' She paused. 'About the sheets.'

'I stripped the bed. Thought I'd wash them.'

'There really was no need. We would have done that.'

'I can't have my hosts left with all that cleaning. It was the least I could do.'

'Only, we were wondering why you left the pillow cases. Didn't you use them.'

What on earth could I say? 'An oversight. I realised when I got back here.'

'And the key. Do you have any idea where you left it?'

I cringed. I'd left it on my keyring. 'I have it,' I said.

'Would you mind...' Claire broke off. I heard voices, muffled, and then, 'We were planning to visit the garden centre. We can swing by yours on the way. Say, in about an hour.'

'An hour?'

'Were you planning on being out?'

'No, no. An hour's fine.'

I raced out the house and almost ran to the supermarket. The woman behind the counter looked up in surprise as I burst through the door. I located the household items on the hunt for traps and was relieved to sight four, displayed on their sides beside the fly spray. They seemed small, but the word "ratón" reassured me and I grabbed all four, hurried to the counter to pay the woman and left. The phrase '¿tienes ratónes?' trailed behind me.

Back at the farmhouse, I set the traps with a small crumb of cheese and placed one in the kitchen, one in the laundry, one out in the internal patio and another in a storeroom where there was a gap under the door. I stuffed the gap with scrunched up newspaper. Satisfied I had done all I could, I went and fetched the sheets and popped them into a plastic bag ready for Claire, and then I removed her apartment door key from my keyring.

They arrived in under an hour. In fifty-three minutes, to be precise, which I knew as I had been keeping an eye on the oven clock ever since I hung up. I went to the door, bag of sheets in hand and her door key in the other, thinking I would thrust them both at Claire, close the door and that would be the last I would ever see of the strange couple, but it wasn't to be. The wind caught the door and blew it wide open. Paco seized the chance to push his way inside, and I had to step aside to let him pass. Claire followed, eyeing the sheets in my hand as she went by.

I felt invaded.

I almost slammed shut the door before trailing them to the kitchen, where I proffered her key. This time she took it. 'Cheers,' she said.

'Can I get you tea or coffee?'

'Coffee would be nice,' she said and sat down on one of the stools at the bench. I filled the kettle as I noticed Paco looking around at the floor. He disappeared into the small dining room that led on to the living room at the front of the house. Next, I saw him go by on his way through to the other rooms in the house. The kettle boiled, and I scooped coffee into the plunger and added the water.

Leaving the plunger to stand, I grabbed three cups from the cupboard beside the stove and asked Claire if either of them took milk or sugar.

They didn't.

Paco came in as I was pouring the coffee.

'Increíble,' he said in Spanish. 'Who did your pest control?' He eyed me with suspicion.

'I have no idea,' I said. My eyes darted to the bin, betraying me in an instant. Paco followed my gaze, went to the bin and extracted the rat trap packaging.

'Ratónes,' he said, holding the cardboard up for Claire to inspect.

'Mice?' she said doubtfully. 'But you said you had rats, Trevor.'

'I thought I did, too. That was what I saw. The owner told me they were mice.'

'Mice.'

'And pest control came and set mouse traps?' Paco said. 'And left you with the rubbish?'

'Evidently.'

'And stuffed newspaper in the gaps under doors?'

'I saw that,' I said.

'Tell me who these people are. Did the owner give you a name?'

'Leave it, Paco.'

Paco turned to Claire. 'Go and look at those mouse traps. They are cheap rubbish. The sort of trap you buy at the local shop. Not from pest control. Whoever did this needs to be put out of business. It is unprofessional.'

'I have no idea who did it.'

Paco swung around and glared at me.

'Then, you must ask.'

The heat rose in my cheeks, and I felt a sudden urge to release my bowels. The Clen. I looked from Paco to Claire, gave her a sheepish grin and excused myself and raced to the bathroom.

Upon my return, as I neared the kitchen door, I overheard a conversation being conducted in low voices. I paused and hid out of sight to listen.

'If he's lying about the rats, what else is he lying about?' That was Claire.

'The rucksack.' They both spoke at once.

A gasp.

Then the female voice said, 'I bet he didn't hand it in.'

'Must be why he was so keen to leave the apartment.'

'No wonder he's so awkward.'

I walked in at that point as I could bear the speculation no longer and if they were going to carry on like a pair of sleuths, they could ruddy well do it elsewhere.

'Fabulous day again, don't you think?' I said loudly, striding over to my coffee cup. I slugged the tepid liquid in three large gulps and turned to face my guests, pasting a broad grin on my face to mask my irritation.

'We must be getting on,' Claire said. 'We're holding you up.' She stood and headed for the sink. I moved away to give her room. She put her cup on the draining board.

'Thanks again for letting me stay at your place,' I said, smiling at Claire and handing her the sheets, which this time she took.

It was a relief to see them go, and I hoped I would never have to see them again. As their car pulled away from the kerb and disappeared up the road, I realised I knew nothing much about either of them. Clearly, they had no children. But how had they met and who had the money? One of them had to be loaded to afford such a grand house, and neither of them had mentioned they worked. Odd.

Thinking of work brought me to the foot of the real dilemma I now faced. They suspected I had held onto the cash after all, and not gone to the police. It was only supposition on their part, but it was true. How long would it be before they came around and robbed me, attacked me, sent someone else round to do the very same? I needed to get off the island, and I needed to act fast.

I went and got the washing in. It was dry, and I could have donned my gym gear and headed into Puerto del Rosario for a workout, but I was not about to leave the rucksack unguarded. Instead, in a desperate bid to restore some equanimity, I channelled all my apprehension and indignation and humiliation into the translation, completing another two thousand words by nightfall.

I awoke early the next morning craving exercise. My muscles commandeered my reasoning. Might be the last time I used the gym before I left the island and no one, not even Paco and Claire, would turn up at dawn to raid my house. If that was the path they were going to take, they would need to create a plan and that took time. As long as I headed out the door and returned in under two hours, the rucksack would be safe.

I downed a Clen, ate an orange, and drove to the city on sunrise. The journey was made difficult with the sun at the horizontal blazing through the windscreen, but I put my foot down, squinted and peered beneath the visor. The clock was ticking.

Pushing open the entrance door, I was amazed to find the gym full. All the bikes were occupied save the one at the end near the weight machines. I adjusted the seat and the tension and mounted the bike, pedalling faster, much faster than I had previously.

When I was about halfway, Mario sat on the leg press nearby. Luis joined him. Mario seemed irritated. To my astonishment, they both spoke in English, but I soon realised why.

'You need to do something about Javier. Why do you let him in here?'

Javier? No, no, surely not...

'I have no reason to ban him.'

'Find one. Juan was in big trouble. Javier and his gang were after him when that drug deal went bad.'

'Do you think they killed him?'

'All I know is they came to my workshop looking for the cash. I told them I knew nothing about it.'

Javier? My Adonis? A gang leader?

'Do something, Luis, before someone else gets killed.'

I looked down at the monitor and found I had pedalled fifteen kilometres. I hopped off the bike onto wobbly legs, grabbed my gym bag and went over to the chest machines, keen to get the workout over and done with as fast as I could. But the bench press, table pec flies, incline dumbbell press and the decline machine press were all in use. Tunnelling my gaze, I turned around and walked out of the gym, narrowly missing colliding with the behemoth making his way inside. He seemed about to say something, and I recalled I was due for another Tren injection. A moment's hesitation, the memory of the coughing fit the last time, and I ignored the steroid-pusher and hurried to my car.

As I pulled away from the gym, I knew I would never be back. A three-month membership and an expensive injection of steroids and I hadn't even managed a fortnight, but I refused to let that part of my mind calculate the loss. I couldn't get off the island fast enough. Never mind Paco and Claire. Javier was the one after the cash. My beautiful Javier, the guy who I had momentarily lusted over. The man who triggered a wet dream and had me convinced I was gay. *A drug dealer.* If that was where my same-sex predilections were taking me, I wanted no part in it. I would rather be celibate. I'd been betrayed. Betrayed by a man fit to be a statue and by my own lust.

The moment I was back at the farmhouse, I booked a ticket on the next available flight to Stansted, departing in two days. I had no idea where I would stay in England and I was disappointed to be leaving Fuerteventura so soon, but needs must. Besides, if I kept the money I didn't need to worry about such trifles. The bigger issue all along had been what to do with all that cash. I still didn't feel entitled to it, but who was? Not Juan's family, that much was now certain, since it was evident this was the proceeds of crime, and I was not about to let Javier lay his hands on a cent of it.

I had no idea how much cash I was allowed to bring into Britain, but fifty thousand euros did seem suspicious. I could do a money transfer. It would create a paper trail, but at least I could siphon off some of the amount.

My thoughts started back at the beginning, and I wondered if I should simply hand in the rucksack and give myself peace of mind. I shook myself out of the conundrum and decided to funnel the anxiety the dilemma was causing into finishing the translation. After all, Javier knew nothing about me. He didn't even know I existed. Clearly, he was Mario's rival or enemy. If in the next two days, Paco and Claire told Mario their suspicions about the rucksack, Mario would not tell Javier. The worst that could happen was Mario turning up with his hand out. If it came to that, I would hand the rucksack over.

I went and downed another Clen with a glass of juice, took a shower and went back to work.

I worked through the rest of the day. At six in the evening, I took another Clen, planning on working all night. Around seven, I switched off my phone and shut down the internet on my laptop. No more distractions, especially from Angela. I didn't want to know about Flint and the award. That piece of news could wait until the morning.

Once I had all the words translated into English, I began working on the story. I was driven, focussed, certain that this would be my best work. The harder I strove, the more I saw my coming to Fuerteventura as fated and by sunrise, as I hit the save button, I relished the moment I would send the results to Angela.

PART II

27

THE HOSTEL

DAWN, AND THE SUMMER SUN STRUCK A GLANCING BLOW ON THE shutters of the north-eastern wall, pouring radiant orange on my face. I squinted into the blinding bands of light, ventured a raised arm to shade my eyes, then eased myself onto my side to stare into the dimness of the cell. The lacerations on my back from the flogging I received the day before – swollen and weeping, the blood dried and crusted – stung with every move I made.

A flogging for what reason? There was no reason, none that was justified. The guard had blamed me for the sun being too hot. That was not the truth but what difference would it make if it was. I was flogged because I stepped between a guard and a wizened wretch of a prisoner too weak to lift the rock he had split. Part of me wished I hadn't, but I saw frantic despair in the man's eyes.

The day was already warm. Dust-laden air drifting in from outside circulated in the space, doing nothing to lift the rank stench of unwashed clothes, filthy bodies, sweat and stale urine, our breath. I raised myself up off the mattress – so thin I could feel the wooden slats beneath – swung my legs to the floor and paused for the head spin to ease as my feet touched the floorboards.

The cot opposite creaked, and I looked over and nodded to Raphael as he caught my eye. He lay still. He was in no hurry to rise.

No one was. It was Saturday, our one day of rest. I hesitated. Why dress when I could just as well have dozed? I could give myself no answer.

My pants and shirt were hanging from a nail on the wooden beam above my cot. I stood to unhook the clothes and put them on, taking care as I eased the shirt on, tucking the thin fabric into the trousers the way I used to when I dressed each morning for work.

Brown pants and grubby white shirts were hanging everywhere from the barn ceiling, airing, crowding the already crowded space. The cell, one of three, was a small, narrow rectangle. There were twelve of us sandwiched in an area that was about the size of my parent's bedroom. Seven cots on the windowed side facing five cots squashed between two doors. Centred in the far wall at the end of the aisle was another doorway leading out to a concreted anteroom and on to the adjoining cell where another twelve men slept. Two cells for twenty-four men and all of us were gay.

The third cell, unconnected, housed another twelve prisoners. They were the non-gays, among them at present were three hardened criminals, two professional thugs, an alcoholic, three drug addicts, two political prisoners and a simple youngster with the mental age of about six. Pablo had no idea why he was here except that he knew he must have done something very bad.

I came from a family of five, and I found myself in another family of five. There were Jorge and Ruben and Rafael and, the closest to me, Manuel. We were all from Tenerife and all about the same age, brothers bound together not by our sexuality but by our various affinities and experiences. A little brotherhood of five, for all the good it would do us.

The other seven in the room were from Gran Canaria. While all of us twelve were friendly enough, the Gran Canarians tended to stick to their cultural group and we to ours. Each island was different. We spoke in different dialects and had somewhat different attitudes and traditions. There was no hostility among us, we had no energy for that, but congregating with our own kind made things easier. The other cell comprised men from La Palma, La Gomera and even tiny El Hierro, along with two men from Lanzarote. Seven islands, seven distinct cultures, and one simple binding force: our sexuality.

I had the cot on the windowed side of the room, two down from the end and below the shuttered window that looked out across the plain at the mountains. Manuel had the cot beside mine. Ruben and Raphael occupied cots on the other side of the aisle, Raphael's nearest the door. Jorge's cot was hard up against the wall on the other side of Manuel's. Manuel's was so close to mine if we wanted, we could reach out and hold hands.

We never did. Our sexuality had everything to do with why we were all here and nothing to do with the relationships we formed with each other. Yet our sexual preference hung in the air, ever present, an atmosphere, almost a smell, the smell of masculinity and forbidden desire and self-disgust and shame. We existed within this vortex of instinct and emotion as we endured the worst deprivations any of us could ever have imagined despite what had so recently taken place in Germany, in Poland.

All of us wished we were dead, that they would kill us instead of making us endure the misery.

There was a commotion outside. I stood on my cot and peered through the shutters. Two guards, who had hurried down from the military headquarters situated on the rise above the cells, appeared at the end of the cell block, running towards the chicken coop, weapons to the ready.

Brito, the prison director, emerged from inside the coop, yelling. He held out in one hand a mess of white feathers and blood and as he came closer to the cells I saw it was a chicken. A well and truly dead chicken, what was left of it. Small spats of blood stained the dirt behind him. He disappeared around the corner of the last cell, on his way up to the compound. The guards followed on behind.

The men in the cell who had been determined not to wake, began to stir. I pulled away from the window and sat down on my cot.

'What is going on?' Jorge groaned, groggy with sleep.

'There's been a massacre in the chicken coop. A dog, I expect.'

'Then we have no chickens.'

'No eggs,' Manuel murmured. He still had his eyes closed.

Jorge observed him with scorn.

'We never get eggs, darling.'

'Or chicken,' I said.

'Chicken!' Manuel's eyes sprang open. 'Oh, what I would give for a slice of breast!'

My stomach clenched in response. What I would have given for any half-decent food. For fresh bread and roasted goat meat, for grilled fish and wrinkled baby potatoes. Tomatoes!

Saliva built in my mouth. I swallowed hard.

It was best not to dwell on food. It was best to pretend that food did not exist. Otherwise, the hunger only intensified. The hunger that never went away. It would be sundown before we ate.

Raphael got up, dressed and sat at the end of Ruben's cot. Jorge joined him, the two men facing me. Behind them, Ruben was still lying huddled beneath his grey blanket.

In the cot next to mine, Manuel threw off his covers, put on his clothes and sat cross-legged on his cot. In a bizarre moment of self-preening, he began picking dirt from beneath his toenails and sniffing at the results. I half anticipated he would put the toenail cheese in his mouth. He didn't. None of us had the energy to tell him he was being revolting. No one really cared.

'Do you think there will be anything left?' Jorge said.

'Of the chickens?' I said. 'I doubt it.'

'Whose dog was it?' Manuel said without looking up.

'Does it matter, darling?' Jorge, ever the marica, couldn't help taunting the equally effeminate Manuel. We all ignored his tone.

'That farmer,' said Raphael. 'The one who waves at us sometimes when his wife isn't looking. He has a dog.'

Jorge said, 'They all have dogs.'

No one disagreed.

'Brito will be livid,' I said, reflecting on how that stark fact would affect us.

'Maybe he'll go on the rampage,' Raphael said with a snigger. It was no laughing matter, yet we couldn't help but laugh. The man, Brito, behaved like a headless chicken himself. Or maybe not. More like a rabid dog.

'Like the dog that killed the chickens,' Raphael said, reading my thoughts.

'Snarling, growling, rearing his upper lip.' Manuel bared his teeth.

'Drooling,' Jorge said, serious now, and grim.

Raphael, whose gaze hadn't left my face, said, 'He will be genuflecting and pleading with the Blessed Virgin.'

'What for?' Manuel said.

Jorge laughed. 'Who knows what for, sweetheart. Brito is deranged.'

'He will be pleading for absolution and begging for mercy.'

We all laughed this time, but none of us was certain he knew what Raphael meant. Eyes fell on him inquiringly.

'For being a maricon, of course. He probably sees the chicken massacre as his punishment for being gay.'

Jorge scoffed. 'That has to be your most absurd thought yet.'

Raphael ignored him. 'He'll never admit it. Even though this is what is sending him mad.'

'Yeah, he would blame us, not himself,' I said.

We fell into silence.

Manuel hunched over to attend to his other big toe. I could see his ribs, like rungs of a ladder through the skin of his back. My eyes drifted to the others. We were all emaciated. Raphael's bones showed through his flesh. Jorge's face was drawn, his eyes sunken. I guessed mine were the same. It was hard to know how gaunt I had become as I never cared to look at my reflection even when I could, which wasn't often.

Ruben turned over in his cot, curled in a foetal position and drew his blanket up around his shoulders. A look of concern flashed into Raphael's face. Ruben had been ill for weeks, ever since we got soaked in the rain in a sudden spring downpour while we were out breaking rocks in a nearby field. A bad cold he could not shake had now turned nasty. He was feverish. He wheezed when he breathed. The warmer weather had not helped and now it was early summer, and as the days grew hot, he wilted.

We couldn't help him. We prayed, for all the good it would do. We willed him well with what little strength we had. At night, I had to resist closing the window to protect him from the cool night air. Resist, or get arrested.

It was not worth the beating.

Ruben coughed. His cough became a hack, and his whole scrawny body shook. The day he arrived, he was a strapping young man of twenty-two. Originally a farmer's boy from Vilaflor in the dry south of Tenerife. His tenant father paid such a high tribute for his tiny scrap of land to the absentee landowner who preferred to live in the island's north, that there was little left for the family to survive on. Twelve-hour days and near starvation. Hunger drove Ruben to Santa Cruz, initially to a life of scavenging. Then he learned the ancient art and grew strong and fat on the pesetas of the old maricones, doing whatever they asked of him in the urinal or the cinema or the park. Now Ruben huddled sick in his cot, a bag of bones. I could almost hear him rattle. I feared we would lose him.

There was another commotion outside, and I went to the window and peered between the shutters.

Brito was charging towards the chicken coop, arms flailing. As he neared a bemused-looking guard, he yelled something, stopped, swung around and stormed back up to his office. The guard scanned the cells as though making up his mind which to choose. His gaze settled on ours. I withdrew from the window and sat on the end of my cot.

Moments later the door flew open. The men at the other end of the room murmured under their breath. Every man in the room avoided the gaze of the guard. Everyone except Manuel who was slow to twig. The instant their eyes met, Manuel knew his mistake.

'Come with me.' The guard looked at me. 'And you, and you and you,' he said, stabbing the air at Jorge and Raphael.

We stood slowly and pulled on our shoes, bending to tie up the laces. None of us was in a hurry.

Reluctantly, we made our way to the door beneath the uneasy gazes of the other prisoners.

The moment we were outside, the guard herded us along the narrow concrete path that fronted the cells, down the side and across the gravel to the chicken coop that had been erected beside a disused barn. There, we huddled together, bracing ourselves for what was to come. The sound of clucking that would normally have greeted the ears had been replaced with an uncomfortable silence. Another guard came barrelling down the slope and shoved buckets and a hessian sack into our hands before marching off again. We went through the rickety coop door, ducking on our way in, filing past the remaining guard who looked determined to stand where he was.

The coop was a mess of feathers and blood. The dog had savaged every bird and eaten most of its kill. All that remained of the ten birds were feet and severed heads, mangled wings and entrails.

In the nesting-box shed, we were hidden from the guard's view. I scanned around. Two other guards were making their way down the hill, but they veered to the cells on another matter. I turned and leaned my back away from our solitary sentry and whispered to Jorge to stand in the shed doorway. Realising in an instant what I meant, he obliged.

Some flies had come to join us.

I ripped feathers from some chicken skin and shoved it in my mouth, scarcely chewing the raw, blubbery, squelchy mass before swallowing it down. The entrails were easier to chew, to bite into, but the desire to do so was slim. I downed whole what I could. Raphael and Manuel, seeing me eat, did the same. Manuel blenched on a mouthful of chicken liver and whatever it was attached to. I hissed at him to swallow. When I had eaten what I thought my share, I stood at the entrance to the shed and let Jorge eat his fill. Raphael wrapped entrails in some skin and stuffed it in his pocket. I looked over in alarm. 'For Ruben,' he mouthed. Manuel found the blood-drenched sawdust easier to consume. Jorge had managed to find some flesh.

Our feast ended as fast as it began. We left the worst, the meat encrusted with chicken shit, the skin trampled into the dirt, the heads; we left enough to convince the guards we had not feasted on the dog's leftovers.

'Hurry up, whores!'

A fork or a rake would have helped. As it was, we had to gather up by hand the blood and shit encrusted feathers and bone shards off the floor of the shed and the outdoor area of the coop, and as we did, we were bent over like chickens ourselves.

'Filthy bitches, get your asses out of there.'

We were almost done. I backed out of the coop, full bucket in hand, as the guard brought his rifle down on my shoulder. I winced, the blow unexpected. Realising they would each be in for the same treatment, my friends flinched as they exited the coop.

Three heavy whacks.

With the guard growling insults behind us, we trudged up the hill and deposited the bloody garbage in the incinerator.

The sun beat down on our faces as we walked back down to the cells. The wind, as though summoned into action, roared across the plain, blowing the fine grit kicked up by our footsteps and hurling it into the faces of those who were behind. The howl, and I no longer heard the rhythmic crunch of shoes on the gravelly ground. The cells buffered the wind and as we drew closer and entered the narrow strip of shade cast by the buildings, I welcomed that brief moment of still cool air, pausing, not wanting to re-enter the cell. Not that outside was much better. The site was exposed, the hillside strewn with dried-out weeds. There was nothing in the landscape to commend it. Even the mountains with their sculpted shapes stood as reminders of the sort of place Tefía was. Nowhere I wanted to be.

The reprieve vanished. We were shoved inside by the surly guard to swelter in the gloom, to wait it out as the sun rose to its zenith. And from then, as the sun arced towards the west and baked the walls of the cells, we would sit on the floorboards and sweat. It was hard to know if a day of rest in summer amounted to any rest at all.

When it came to tolerating the heat, Raphael fared the worst. He was from the cool northwest of Tenerife, from the wine region of Icod. Powerful ancient families owned the vineyards there, some of them nobility. Raphael's family were not among them. He came from a poor working family, and when he realised he was gay, he knew he couldn't stay in Icod. He fled to Santa Cruz where he got work in a bar. He managed to keep a low profile and got through his national service without anyone detecting his sexuality. It was when he was back in Santa Cruz, working in a different bar, one frequented by some of the more prominent maricones, that the trouble started. He was twenty-two when he got caught in the act of fellatio in a cinema.

There was nothing to do but sit or lie around and talk softly. As the minutes passed, my thirst grew ever more urgent, a thirst I had been ignoring since I woke, a thirst made all the stronger by the impromptu vulture's feast, and I got up and went to the other end of the cell where a bucket of water sat on the floor. I dipped in the communal tin mug and braced myself for the salty tang. I drank fast in large gulps. No one watched. No one wanted to watch. As I walked back down the aisle to my cot, not one man looked up at me. No one wanted to be reminded of the foul brackish water that sat in that bucket, or the resultant waste that had come out of each of us that sat festering in the bucket beside it.

We heard Brito outside, berating the guards. A door creaked open to the adjoining cell. Curious, I went and peered through the keyhole.

At first, all I could see was Brito's broad back some five yards away. He had his hands on his hips and looked typically pompous in his uniform. The guards appeared, manhandling a reluctant Paulo between them. Paulo let himself go limp, and the guards were forced to drag him up to the main compound. What on earth had he done?

Paulo was from La Palma and had been at the prison among the longest. Brito, it seemed, had found a target for his wrath. I cast my mind back to the day before, to the chicken coop and Paulo working nearby in the field beyond the compound. He could have had nothing to do with the dog savaging the chickens, but in Brito's deranged mind, being close, being the last prisoner seen in the vicinity, would be enough. I thought those guards dragging Paulo away looked relieved, relieved the pressure was off them. Or maybe they were looking forward to giving their own violent natures another airing.

There was no sign of the other guards. In this slender moment of relative freedom, I caught Raphael's eye and glanced at Ruben. Raphael nodded. I then nudged Manuel, whispered to him to follow me without question across the room, and together we sat on Ruben's bed, crowding over him.

Raphael took his chance and ferreted in his pocket for the chicken scraps. I shook Ruben and when he looked up at me, I pressed my fingers to my lips. I then directed my gaze at Raphael. Ruben did the same. The moment he cottoned on to the offering in Raphael's hand, he let out a soft groan. I coughed loudly to mask it. Manuel started tapping his foot on the floorboards as though beating a rhythm. I appreciated his effort to mask the sounds coming from Ruben, but it wasn't helping. If anything, tapping would only draw the attention of the others and no one must know of our illicit feast. If they didn't rip open our guts for a share, they might tell the guards out of spite.

Ruben devoured the offering in several large chews and swallows. When he was done, I went and fetched him some water. Manuel returned to his cot and Raphael to his. I joined Manuel, who had managed to acquire a copy of Lorca's *Poem of the Deep Song* which he had inserted into the covers of his Bible, the only book Brito allowed us to have, and we read the words together as though we poured over scripture.

The men at the other end of the cell sat in small clusters, some playing games they had created out of scraps of paper and pencils, others talking quietly.

A sudden glint and I saw Jorge was checking his face for chicken blood in the small mirror he kept hidden in his mattress. My eyes darted around the room. If the guards caught him, I would not want to see his back after the beating. The sudden movement of my torso shot me a stark reminder.

Jorge was the most demonstrably gay of the five of us. He liked to put on airs. I put his at times outrageous behaviour down to his upbringing in the cosmopolitan atmosphere of Santa Cruz. His family, like mine, was not beholden to rich landowners. He was the son of a modestly wealthy export merchant trading in bananas. Back in the 1930s, his father had staunchly opposed the banana workers' strikes at Fyffes and backed the ensuing repression and the disappearances of the ringleaders. Like all the other men in the business class of Santa Cruz, his father supported the governance of the day. When the Second Republic was replaced with the fascism of Franco, Jorge says his father had not batted an eyelid. It was business as usual. At least it was until the day he realised his son was not quite right. In fact, his son was much more than not quite right in his father's eyes. Rigorous schooling, endless counselling by priests, nothing made a jot of difference. In the end, his father gave him a small allowance and told Jorge to rent a room in the centre of the city and never darken his doorstep again. Jorge's mother was distraught at the time, but there was little she could or would do. Jorge said his father's strong reaction had more to do with his own private leanings than those of his son. Alone and free, Jorge managed to get himself arrested and sent to Tefía on the eve of the day he was due to begin his national service. Raphael, in one of his more acerbic moments, told me he thought Jorge had contrived his arrest to avoid the military. And a brutal time of it he would have had.

Jorge was still staring at his reflection in the mirror.

'Put it away,' I hissed.

Just then, the door swung open. I turned to see which guard it was as Jorge inserted the mirror back into a slit in his mattress. All eyes looked nervous as Brito himself stood in the doorway and bellowed for us all to get off our filthy asses and go and line up in the quadrangle. The men were slow to move. Ruben lifted his head off his pillow and his face contorted in dismay. Brito stormed out and was replaced by a guard who reinforced Brito's command with one of his own. 'You heard. Get your sleazy asses off those beds, whores!'

It was the same guard who had ordered us to clean out the chicken coop. A short and stocky man with narrow hips and wide shoulders and a malicious curl at the corners of his lips, his face arranged in a permanent snarl.

Raphael helped Ruben to his feet and the two men headed out, Raphael making sure he was on the left of Ruben to take the blow he anticipated. The guard whacked the butt of his rifle at Raphael's shoulder as the two men went by. I filed out next and Jorge and Manuel followed. We each received a blow as we passed the guard, the rifle butt landed on our shoulders as it had before, adding to the bruise that never went away.

Prisoners of the other cells were already lined up two-deep on the quadrangle. We were about to head behind them, but Brito had other ideas and made us stand in front. Raphael and Ruben were ahead of me. Third in line, I got to stand in front of Paulo, who stared blankly from his bloodied face. Manuel came and stood beside me, then Jorge. None of us dared speak.

The sun bore down on the quadrangle, baking the concrete beneath our feet, the low buildings which fringed the quadrangle trapping the heat. The temperature was raised still further by a desert-dry wind that blew in our faces. Already, I felt the sweat build in my armpits.

The moment he had us all lined up as though to fry in the full blast of the sun, Brito began his tirade.

It was our fault, apparently, that the dog had found its way into the chicken coop and massacred those poor chickens. Our fault for being the filthy scum we were, not worthy to be called human, the scourge of the planet, filled with an evil so corrupting only the most severe rehabilitation would drive the beast from our souls.

'A pestilence lives in all you men. In you and you and you. You are diseased, do you hear me? All of you, diseased! And you must be purged. God knows it is my burden to purge you and the task is as onerous today as it was the first day I set foot in this camp. God will smite thee down, you heathen whores.' Brito signalled to a guard who walked off and disappeared down the side of the main building.

'Now you filthy bastard whores, you will sing the national anthem and show yourselves to be the proud Spaniards you are not.'

We remained silent.

'Sing!' Brito roared.

Someone at the back sang, 'Facing the sun in my new shirt,' and slowly we all joined in.

'Louder,' Brito yelled over our voices as we got to, 'If they tell you that I fell,' and we opened our chests and we sang with a heartiness none of us felt. And when we got to the end of *Cara el Sol* Brito made us start over.

When we were halfway through the second time, the guard reappeared and our gazes were drawn to the military figure who had a dog in his arms.

Brito bellowed to us to keep our eyes straight ahead and sing. The stocky guard stepped in from the wings to act as maestro of our bedraggled choir, urging us on with his glare and his arms that bounced a rhythm in the air.

The guard handed Brito the dog. An emaciated Podenco, brown and white with over-sized upright ears, a farm dog I had seen roaming the fields around the camp. It was doubtful this was the dog that had killed the chickens; its belly was hollow, not bloated or plump.

Not the guilty party, just the sacrifice, Brito the irate headmaster determined to find someone or something to blame.

We kept singing. Brito gripped the dog. I caught the dog's whimpers in the brief pauses between the verses of the song.

What happened next was not unexpected. Flashing into my mind as Brito held the dog aloft on outstretched arms was a similar image, of a goat that time. A goat Brito had savagely slaughtered after his olive grove, a grove of five hundred saplings we had laboriously planted and tended at his behest, an olive grove we had protected with scarecrows made out of newspaper, an olive grove we guarded on pain of a beating, shooing away the rabbits and birds and lizards, was finally destroyed by goats and a hail storm while we were all at church. Brito couldn't punish the hail so he punished the goat.

High in the air, the dog held its tail between its legs. It was trembling, eyes wild with fear. Brito held it there like an offering to some god and as an example to us all of the cruelty that beat in his heart. At the end of the anthem, he brought the dog down and held it to his chest as though in a cuddle. That was no cuddle. Brito was attempting to squeeze the life out of the poor canine. When he got fed up with that technique, he stretched out his arms to the horizontal and ceremoniously dropped the dog on the ground. Then he raised his foot and brought it down hard on the poor animal's rib cage.

The dog was not dead. It cowered and trembled, ears thrust back and it tried to raise its head.

I could scarcely look at what came next.

Not satisfied he had meted out enough cruelty, Brito kicked and stomped on the poor animal. He was an animal himself, arms thrashing about, his eyes wild with a sort of frenzied insanity. His mouth hung open and he let out soft grunts as his steel toe capped boots landed on the sack of bones that was the dog. And all the while we sang. We sang at the tops of our lungs, our throats dry and hoarse. And the guard waved his arms as though he were in a fancy auditorium, and the dog lay still. There was no sign of life in that battered and bleeding body. I thought of Paulo behind me. I dared not look around, but I sensed him there, sensed the pain in his own battered body.

At last Brito stopped his brutality, but our torment did not end there. Brito ordered the singing to stop. He picked up the dog and walked down the line of men, forcing us each in turn to take a long hard look at the dead creature.

'Let this be a lesson to you all. This is what will happen to criminals like you. I command this prison, let there be no mistake, and if any one of you steps out of line just remember, what happened to this dog will happen to you.'

While Brito continued on with his gruesome presentation, two guards rushed forward and built a pyre of twigs and logs and newspapers and anything else they could find that would burn. Brito joined them and ordered the pyre lit. Once the wood had caught and the fire blazed, he threw on the dog, and we all stood bearing our faces into the fiery wind, forced to inhale the wood smoke and then the stench of scorched dog fur and eventually its burning flesh.

Our ordeal was over when the fire died and all the charred remains of the dog were taken to the incinerator. Brito left the guards to take us back to our cells, while he stormed off back to his office, no doubt to gloat over a job well executed.

Once the guards had gone back up to the compound, we all sat on our cots or on the floor subdued. At first, no one spoke.

Then Antonio, one of the Gran Canaria men, said, 'That man is a monster.'

His comment sparked an outcry and soon everyone was talking at once down that end of the cell. At my end, Jorge sat on his cot hugging his knees, and Raphael was slumped on the side of Ruben's bed. His hand gripped Ruben's. Manuel, who had begun to shake from the trauma, burst into tears.

I watched his face redden, the tears making clean streaks on his cheeks. New to Tefía, Manuel was having a hard time adjusting.

He was from Santa Cruz, and had been a prostitute since he was about fifteen. He spent a year in Gran Canaria's capital, Las Palmas, where he hung out in the bars around the Santa Catalina Park. The area was near the port and it was known to be seedy. He went there for the drunken lustful orgies, for the money the foreigners who frequented the port city splashed around, foreigners hungry for pretty Canarian boys like Manuel. He told me he had existed in a perpetual state of fear combined with an insatiable desire for clandestine sex. That he was paid for his nightly trysts only added an extra layer of danger, for the parks and cinemas and urinals around the port were raided from time to time and then things turned violent.

Having narrowly avoided arrest for the umpteenth time, a friend and fellow prostitute told him to get away from Las Palmas fast. The authorities were on to him, and it was only a matter of time before he was caught. He returned to Santa Cruz and continued in his chosen line of work, partly because he genuinely enjoyed the thrills, and partly because he could do nothing else.

Watching him sob and shudder was too much to bear and, risking a beating should a guard walk in, I went and sat on his bed and put an arm around him and smoothed back his hair. Not that my efforts had any effect.

'I have to get out of this place,' he said, sounding hysterical. 'Help me escape.' He clutched my arm. 'You have to help me escape.'

'You cannot escape,' I said, my own stomach clenching at the thought. It was an odd reaction, and I realised in that instant that I desired him.

'But I must. I must.' His voice became shrill.

'Calm down,' Jorge said.

Manuel pulled his hands from his face and glared at Jorge indignantly.

'I can't do this anymore. That man Brito is insane. We'll be next. He'll start burning us on pyres before long. Burning us alive, probably.'

'Stop being melodramatic, darling.'

I shot Jorge a censorious look then turned to Manuel.

'He won't. Not even Brito will do that.'

'How do you know. He was wild up there. I thought I saw froth at the corners of his mouth.'

It was true. The guy was a complete maniac.

'Please, help me, José. Help me get out of here.'

I reached for his hand and gave it a squeeze.

'There is nowhere to go. Antonio will tell you. His friend tried, remember. Or was that before you arrived? Look, even if you manage to run off this plain, there is only one way off the island. You would need to get a boat at Puerto Cabras, and no one is going to let you do that. They have spies everywhere. This is an island that loves Franco. Don't you understand? These campesinos think he is just wonderful. Believe me.'

'Surely they do not. Not all of them.'

'And how would you know which do and which do not. And even if you could tell that, they are all Catholic, and they all hate us. You see the way they look at us. Have you ever seen any one of them wave or smile? No, you haven't. You haven't because it has never happened. Don't you see, Manuel? You would need help to get off the island, and no one is going to help you. Believe me. If you try to escape, you will be punished. After he was re-captured, Antonio's friend was taken to another prison. Antonio overheard the guards talking about it.'

All my words fell on deaf ears.

'I can't stay here. I can't do this.'

'You have to stay here, and you can do this.'

'I had to stop myself from bolting to the fire for a piece of charred dog,' Raphael said grimly, and thankfully changing the subject.

'Same,' Jorge said. 'I was salivating.'

'I can hardly believe we have been reduced to this,' I said.

'Better than goat droppings.'

'True.' It was my turn to sound grim.

'Or rancid food parcels.'

'At least you know your family cares,' Manuel said plaintively.

Manuel could have had no idea that no one had received a visit from a family member in all the time I had been incarcerated – ten months now – and no prisoner in our cell had ever received a letter from his family.

'I miss my mum so much,' he said. He looked set to burst into more tears.

I stroked his back.

'We all do.'

'We do?' Jorge said.

'Or our sisters or our brothers or our friends,' I said quickly. I didn't want to get into a conversation about Jorge's mother.

'You mustn't think like this,' I said softly. 'We are your family now. You must be strong. It can't go on forever. Three years is the maximum.'

'And Brito will hold us all for that whole time. I bet he will.'

'You don't know that.'

'He sends reports back to the authorities. He has complete control of us.'

Manuel pulled away and started pinching the skin of his arms.

'What's the matter with me?' he said with disgust. 'Why did I have to be born this way? Why can't I just be normal like everyone else.'

'Darling, shut your mouth!'

I gave Jorge a rigorous shake of my head.

'Is it my biology, like the priest says?'

'Some say we have overly pampering mothers,' Raphael said, his tone mockingly philosophical.

'My mother never pampered me.'

'Jorge, we are all sorry you had such an awful mother.' I hoped that would satisfy him.

'They think we are perverted hedonists,' Raphael said, 'relishing our carnal pleasures.'

'So what if we are?' Suddenly, Manuel was defensive, and I was pleased and relieved to hear defiance in his tone. That was the energy he needed to survive here. Nothing else would see him through.

Our conversation waned as the sun, now on its afternoon descent, started to bake the front wall of the cell, its heat radiating inside. Little escaped out the shuttered windows and there was no through breeze. The room soon became an oven, stuffy and oppressive, and as the afternoon wore on, the stench of the urine and the shit that had accumulated in the bucket by the other door grew ever stronger. Many of us lay down on our cots to ride out the worst of it half comatose, covering our noses or burying our heads in the stink of our own armpits, which was a preferable sort of stench to the one emanating from our defecations.

It was dusk before we ate. The guards threw open the door, letting in a sudden rush of hot dry air. One guard stood in the doorway as the other delivered us each a tin bowl filled with corn-meal and raw onion porridge. The prison version of gofio escaldado and delicious when traditionally cooked. Gofio escaldado was made from roasted maize flour combined with broth to form a smooth paste. Garlic, onions, salt and the all-important olive oil were added for flavour and consistency. I adored the dish the way my family prepared it, served with a spicy sauce. Here, all the vital ingredients were missing. The result was a flavourless stodge that was almost impossible to swallow. It was an insult to our culture and only marginally better than the rooted sweet potatoes and peas shot through with weevils that we were also given to eat. The only way to eat the gofio slop was to chase it with gulps of water. Knowing this, once the guards had left the cell, Antonio went around with the bucket, and we each scooped out water with our tin mugs. Meals were the only times we felt driven to slake our thirsts with the salt-tinged water from the well.

I spooned the grainy, tasteless porridge in my bowl and sipped my water with each mouthful and swallowed hard, forcing the contents of my mouth down my throat as best I could. As I did, I relived the episode in the chicken coop, tasted the raw flesh and skin and entrails. The blood. None of those flavours or textures were pleasant but they were no worse than our daily repast. I watched Manuel and Jorge and Raphael and Ruben struggle through their food, willing them to eat every scrap, not give cause for puzzlement as to why any of us was off our food. For the conclusion would be obvious, even to those dim-witted numbskulls outside, that we had feasted on the scraps left by the dog.

And then I was back to thinking about the Podenco and the awful stench of its incineration. I almost gagged.

The guards returned half an hour later to collect our bowls. Antonio was ordered to remove the stinking bucket that served as our communal toilet and empty it over the stone wall. It was the only time the bucket was emptied. We all knew the guards chose that time of day on purpose, to make us endure the stink of our own excrement for the longest possible time and make our mealtime even more unpleasant than it already was.

At sunset, came the mandatory and daily religious instruction meant to make us repent and change our carnal ways. With the guard standing at the back of the room, we were lectured by another prisoner, Miguel, who came from a religious background and had been appointed the role. It was the same every night. We had to gather round. He began by instructing us in the First Letters. Then he spoke of the story of Jesus. After that he read selected Bible passages. Then came the Rosary prayers. It was like going to Mass every single night. We all knew the stories of the faith, and we all knew the subtext embedded in the instruction. We were sinners, and we needed redemption. We had a disease for which there was no cure, we would never be saved and would be condemned to hell once we died, and all we could think of as we listened was we were already in hell, right here in this cell, and why didn't God strike us down and relieve us from this misery.

As Miguel spoke, my mind drifted. I pictured Mass at the church in La Laguna. How I confessed to the priest my homosexual desires and he told me I would struggle my whole life and never find acceptance and it was best to bury my desires and never act on them. I listened and I didn't, but my gaze betrayed me and here I was anyway, regardless.

Next, I pictured the walk we faced in the morning, the three-mile walk to the church in Casillas del Ángel and the three miles back. A pointless, fruitless walk across the dry and rocky plain to hear the priest talk his talk of sanctity and purity and Christ. And then I will confess and be lectured yet again that I had been separated from society because I was, we all were, a danger to our families, our neighbours, to all who came into contact with us. We were child molesters and prostitutes, a menace to society for which there would never be a pardon. And as we walk, there and back, the people in the houses we pass will stare and their children will point at us and say 'look at the prisoners' and their families will close the doors and windows.

And on the long walk back, we will pass the field where the olive grove stood, and I will picture the goats and the hail storm that ruined those sapling trees. And picture Brito and his rampage that culminated in the sacrificial slaughter of a goat.

Once, I told the priest our Carmelite prison director was a repressed homosexual and that he was deranged. We all tried to tell the priest, but our words fell on deaf ears.

And I blocked my mind to the days ahead. To the hours and hours we would spend in the fields breaking rocks. The hoeing and the carting of rocks and dirt. The toil out in the baking sun and the roaring wind and the relentless tirade of insults from the guards who made the smallest thing our fault. Never allowed even once to pause lest we suffer the whip, the lash, the beatings.

With the fading light, the lecture ended, and the guard left us. We talked softly, someone sang a song. Eventually, all went quiet, and I heard sobbing, the gentle sobbing not from Manuel, but from another man further down the aisle.

I closed my eyes on the horrors of the day. I closed my eyes on the demented Carmelite who had been put in charge. I closed my eyes on his henchmen guards who had not one ounce of compassion between them. I closed my eyes.

———

Raven, why do you eye me with such an inquiring look. A war was fought to put an end to the sorts of atrocities that went on at Tefía, a war fought by an alliance of the good guys, yes the good guys who were from Britain and France and Canada and the USA. And those nations, what do they do now that the war is long past? They surely have no intention of having another war to oust Franco. Not in this new era in which the enemy as they see it is not fascism but communism. Franco suits them. Franco and his hatred of communists and Republicans and gays.

As for the futility of my incarceration, futile because it turned me into the gay man that I am – oh birdy love, you with your wings and your freedom, you could never know the effect a caged life has on the soul. No one cages a raven.

How I yearned for the comfort of home in that place. How I begged and pleaded for a chance to atone. How I wept quietly at night for a loving familial embrace. I wanted to claw back time until I was but an egg and a sperm and beg God to make me heterosexual.

And no one wrote and no food parcels came and it felt as though my own flesh and blood had washed their hands of me. Maybe they had. To this day I have no idea. I cannot see them. I wrote and told them I was free, but they did not reach out to me and wish me well even then.

In Tefía, we all felt abandoned by our families. And many of us had been. But what were they to do? What could they possibly have achieved? The answer to that is simple. Nothing.

It was only when I was set free from the camp and sent to Gran Canaria that I learned of the struggles of a mother desperate to free her only son. How no one lifted a finger to help and especially not the rich gays whose aberrant needs were met by impoverished prostitutes. This mother spoke to the mayor, to police officials and business leaders, the colonial director and the comandante of the guardia civil. Doors were slammed in her face. No one did a thing. They were all indifferent to her plea. She was told her son was a maricon and was better off in prison. This woman was a housekeeper. She worked for a wealthy don. He was also a maricon.

Jorge was fond of saying we were all lucky not to have been assassinated or deported to the mainland, or kidnapped or murdered in the night – hurled off a cliff or shot – as many political dissenters had been. Jorge, who upon his release went and hurled himself off this very cliff. He had always been dramatic, and it was his final flourish, yet with his feminine ways which were ingrained into every cell of him, he had no life in this world.

Now I feel nothing. My family are estranged to me. Six years have passed since I last saw them, yet what has changed in the world to allow me to return to Santa Cruz? What can possibly change? It's 1961 and Franco has been in power for more than two decades. He will never leave. His spies keep him in power. The condemnation of my kind will go on. And on. Through the eyes of my family, I am contemptible. I am bad seed. I cannot return and ask for their forgiveness because that would be asking them to accept me for who I am. I cannot prove to them that I have changed. I have not. I am the same as I ever was. Worse.

I could pretend. It occurs to me often to pretend. I could follow in the footsteps of Ruben and find a woman and marry her and do what the rich maricones do. Ruben, who recovered from his illness and was released three months before me. He moved to Las Palmas where he met a peasant farmer's daughter and poured what charm he had on her, convincing her to marry him and dooming himself to live a lie.

Or I could find some rich old maricon like Raphael who, I heard, had prostituted himself to servitude in La Palma.

Then there was Manuel, my beloved Manuel, who was taking the biggest risk of all. He lived on the streets down by the docks of Las Palmas, giving himself to those tourists crawling by, risking further imprisonment and even his own life.

But, Raven, I cannot marry a woman or prostitute myself to an old maricon. I must be true to myself. For I have learned what it is to love another man and to lose that love. I have learned what it is like to hate your own flesh, to want to claw at your insides, rip out whatever it is inside that warps the lusts. If being gay is abnormal, then being gay is the embodiment of a kind of torture worse than Tefia.

There is only one way to end this torment, raven. When you leap off this cliff edge, you will spread your wings and soar on the thermals.

Me? I have no wings. Like Jorge, I will die.

PART III

28

A LONG WALK

I LEANED BACK IN MY SEAT, ROLLED MY SHOULDERS AND THEN stretched my arms behind my chair, feeling the release of the tension. On the laptop screen, the cursor flashed below the last sentence. There was no more to be made of the Spanish script, and nothing more to be gleaned from my frenetic research. The draft, the best I could manage, was sitting on just under twenty-thousand words, which was too short, much too short to be even a novella, but too long to be a short story. A novelette? Novelettes were just about unheard of. Who wrote a novelette? Besides, they were typically light and romantic and frivolous, not heavy and charged with significance as the draft on my laptop. I had no idea what to do with a novelette. Did novelettes win prizes? I wondered if there might be ways to expand four-fold on what I had and turn the draft into a novel. I would need to sit on it for a while, probably some months. Even then, there was every danger whatever I added would be padding. Still, I really ought to lengthen the narrative. But I did not want to embellish on the tortured introspection any more than I had previously wanted to expand on José's childhood. What interest was any of that to English-speaking readers? The original Spanish version ended abruptly with José jumping off the cliff and, abrupt as that was, I wanted to keep it that way. Looking back over what I had, I could see it was no prize winner.

The Clenbutoral had worn off and left me feeling harried yet not in the least bit tired. Before I closed my laptop, I logged onto my emails. There, as anticipated, was one from Angela. I didn't need to open it. The subject line told me all I cared to know. Sandra Flint had won the prize.

Of course, she had won the prize. My jaw set picturing her grin, the triumphant sparkle in her eyes, her, a woman short on conscience, a woman who had failed to so much as offer gratitude to her ghost throughout the entire process. She had either erased my efforts from her memory or was too scared I might pipe up and lay claim to the work in some public fashion. In denial? A coward? Which was it? Both? I was glad I didn't live in her skin.

In the kitchen, I filled the kettle and prepared myself an omelette. I hadn't eaten since sometime last evening when I shovelled a whole litre tub of strawberry yoghurt into my mouth. And I had been up all night. Whether my stomach felt like food or not, it was getting some.

An hour later, and I had cleaned the breakfast things and showered and donned fresh clothes, and I stood around not knowing what to do next. My flight wasn't until the following day, and it was too soon to pack. My mind was fuzzy from hours and hours of mental exercise, and my body had had too little sleep. I needed to get out of the farmhouse, that much was clear, and into the fresh air, and I needed to make a move before the day grew too hot. I thought of the rucksack and decided if Paco and Claire planned on stealing it or claiming it, they would have done so, and they hadn't. I guessed theft and confrontation wasn't their style. More likely they would leave well alone, especially if Mario had told them Juan had been involved in a drug deal gone wrong and that Javier had been after him.

I considered a drive. After all, I had not seen that much of the island, and I was meant to be on holiday. Morro Jable was said to be nice, and then there was the southern heel of the island beyond. Although when I studied the map, I saw I would need to drive through Tiscamanita or Puerto del Rosario to get to my chosen location, unless I went up and over the mountains of Betancuria which would take forever and require too much concentration on twisty windy roads. When I considered all the driving there and back in my current sleep-deprived state, I decided using my own feet would be less of a risk to my life. Besides, I felt a niggle, an internal itch. I had spent much of the last week deeply immersed in the story of the concentration camp, and I wanted to pay homage to those men, those gay men, all one hundred of them who had been incarcerated and suffered unspeakable deprivations.

My literary brain snatched the idea with vulpine relish. Another chapter for the novelette? Enough content to tip the scales in favour of a novella?

I snarled inwardly at myself for even having the thoughts. I was reminding myself of Flint. This was about the men, not the ruddy book.

Every week, those men tramped to the church in Casillas del Ángel, and even if I chose not to include a chapter in the novelette depicting their weekly ritual, it seemed the least I could do was follow in their footsteps and walk to the church and back. I would walk cross country just as they had and feel for myself some of their suffering. After all, I had not only translated that script, I had transformed it, given it shape, and I would continue to do so. And maybe a touch of the experiential was all I needed to further expand on the work. Through me, English speakers might read about this overlooked prison, and a piece of history would be known and acknowledged.

It didn't escape my notice that my literary self had once again taken possession of the noble act of pilgrimage, but I felt more comfortable with the way I had my rationale framed.

I studied the map. There was a dirt track I could pick up near the eco-museum. A couple of doglegs to look out for, but the track pretty much took me straight to Casillas.

Wisdom had me slathering myself in sunscreen, and I found the blue, canvas hat I had packed and had so far never worn. Then I pulled on my plimsolls, filled my water bottle and grabbed some fruit. As I closed the front door, I had to shoo away a twinge of anxiety about the rucksack. I reminded myself yet again that Adonis drug-dealer Javier didn't know me. Paco and Claire definitely knew too much, but they probably didn't know Javier, and they certainly wouldn't tell him even if they did. They were not the type to land a poor author in that kind of trouble. The most they might have done was nab the rucksack for themselves through some twisted sense of entitlement, but they were dripping in wealth – that was obvious from the house they owned – and they had that trouble-free air that comes from being wealthy. I really needed to stop worrying.

Then there was the fact – and it was unequivocal and so out of character that I went so far as to call it such – that what I was about to do was more important than the money.

A curious sensation washed through me. I did not recognise the feeling, but if I had to name it I would call it goodwill. And I surprised myself with my own resolve. I had never before acted with such an altruistic purpose.

A paltry twenty-thousand-word novelette might not cut muster in the literary world, but that draft represented something more, something personal. On the one hand, I needed to atone. I needed to atone for not wanting to rise to the challenge of writing a novel based in or on the prison. I needed to atone for my dismissive attitude which I saw now as remarkably self-centred. On the other hand, I needed to pay my respects to those men who had suffered so terribly for being gay, whereas I, Trevor Moore, had dithered and fretted and toyed with my own sexuality as though I were cat boxing in front of the telly.

What a difference in social mořés forty years could make! That, and democracy. Although values had not shifted that much in many quarters, and it was only my own – what? – vanity, or maybe self-indulgence which had provided the impetus to even consider my own sexual preference. That, together with a couple of wet dreams, my lesbian best friend and ex-wife, and Vince. For many, being gay was as big a deal now as then. Lesson learned.

The sun had already started its assault on the plain when I set off, joined by a fearful wind blowing me along from behind. I soon traversed the strip of narrow footpath and carried on along the roadside until the turnoff for the museum, ignoring the grit in my shoes. From there, the going was easy. With the exception of a handful of small farmhouses dotted here and there on the plain, there was nothing to observe other than the mean-looking mountain I was walking towards, steep-sided with a peaked cap of dark brown. To the south of the mountain, a long saddle made a gradual descent. A low hill rose up behind. Once I had navigated a couple of doglegs, all I needed to do was stick to the track. The going was easy, although I saw up ahead that the flat path across the plain would soon come to an end.

I had been walking for about twenty minutes when the track started its ascent. What had been a reasonably pleasant – for Tefía – walk, suddenly became strenuous. The mountain, with its dark cap, towered above me. Below the cap, twin gullies resembled a pair of hooded eye sockets, the ridge between them a long and fanning nose. A grim visage, like a monolithic overlord, one that suggested something menacing about the entire landscape. I started to feel I had entered a fantasy novel, and at any moment, some strange magical creature would appear.

No doubt a troll.

You could go mad out here. That thought grew prominent as I pressed on, the grit in my shoes prickling the soles of my feet.

Despite the discomfort, I kept up a decent pace but before long, I started to pant. My legs stiffened, and my calves started to burn. I knew the pain had more to do with my poorly stretched muscles than it did the actual activity, and I was annoyed with myself for not heeding Luis's advice and stretching daily.

I took a breather, emptied my plimsolls of grit, stretched my calves and took a swig from my water bottle. Common sense kicked in, overriding my eagerness to get out from under the mountain's gaze, and I continued at a slower pace. There was no need to turn the walk into some sort of marathon, and in so doing make the pilgrimage all about myself when I was meant to be tuning into what it might have been like for the prisoners. And I knew already that even, no, especially for them in their emaciated, starving and beaten state, this walk would have been arduous.

A few paces on and more grit had entered my shoes. I chose to ignore it. The further I went the steeper the path became, until I had to take care not to slip on the gravel. The last thing I wanted was a pair of grazed knees.

As the path climbed the saddle and the mountain was no longer in my line of sight, my gaze was drawn to my right, to the gentle rise and fall of the plain, the patchwork of fields, the various shades of creamy and reddish browns. The view drew me, but I had to keep a careful watch on where I was walking, as the path narrowed and the decline beside me grew higher and steeper. I stopped now and then, not to empty my shoes, but to take in the haunting desert atmosphere, the cruelty of the wind that never relented, the vicious sun from which there was no escape. Not one tree.

About halfway up the saddle, the track curved around a bulge and then went on into the vee of a gully, the flanks rising up steeply to a rounded crest at the apex. Here, the path narrowed still further, and the ground fell away sharply at the side. The prisoners would have had to walk single file. I craved a handrail or some sort of protection to prevent me from toppling over should I slip. The height wasn't dizzying, I couldn't say that much, but there was nothing to break the fall.

Taking tentative steps, I exited the gully and rounded another curve. Here, the path was even narrower, the ascent steady, the track little more than a scratch coursing the side of the saddle. I paused now and then, and leaned into the rocky scree rising up beside me and took in the view below. The further I went, the more challenging those pauses became.

Another curve and the track ascended steeply for a stretch, although it appeared in no hurry to surmount the ridge. Instead, it meandered on its way until the saddle flattened out. The land falling away beside the track had become disconcerting. At the final gully, shallow this time, the side of the saddle was especially steep and the path disappeared beneath a small rockfall. I picked my way along, testing each step, unable to imagine making this trek every week. Never mind the tremendous view, the sense of exhilaration I felt. The prisoners would have been indifferent to these surroundings. They would have lumbered on not looking around, not considering the sense of space except to despise it. And on the way back, their hearts would have sunk as they saw the plain opening up before them, and they knew where they were heading, and they would be in no hurry to get there despite the heat and the wind pushing up hard against them. As I trudged on, in my mind so did they, and we walked together as one, me, an overweight Brit with gym-sore muscles and feet pricked by grit, about to return to a comfortable single man's life in which I could choose to be gay or straight and deal with the consequences. Them with no future, no future at all unless they married some woman and held up a pretence, and what kind of life was that?

Then, at last, I reached the top of the saddle, and the land to the east opened up, and I could see the village in the near distance below. I stopped and looked around as I regained my breath. I lost all thought of the prisoners. They would not have been permitted a rest break. They would have carried on walking, heads bowed. The guards would never have let them stand as I was, king of the world, beholding a vista that was panoramic and magnificent, the various ranges in all directions rising up out of the gently undulating plain. Not a patch of green anywhere. All was russet and pinkish brown and creamy stone. I could even see the ocean, a pleasing blue to the east and the west, and I got a sense of the size of the island which was long and rather narrow. Everywhere the mountains, their long ridgelines, and while there was not much to choose between the land to the east and the west, it was plain to see that the mountains sheltered the eastern land from the wind. As those same mountains buffered the wind on the western side, so the wind funnelled and intensified as it made its journey southward. It was basic physics.

I faced into the wind again, holding onto my hat as a sudden gust the very next moment nearly blew me off my feet. Flashing into my mind were those poor parachutists forced to jump and make landfall, and the terror they would have felt being dragged along by their own parachutes. Somehow, standing up on this saddle in my gritty plimsolls, able to survey the entire scene, brought home the full force of the tragedy. What a fated location, as bleak and exposed as anywhere could be, and as I turned to continue on my way, I felt oddly privileged to have taken part – by treading this very track – in some of its history. Others, I thought with a measure of wry cynicism, walked the Camino.

The rest of the walk was downhill and with the wind behind me – a touch less powerful as I dipped below the crest of the saddle – I made good progress across the stony, arid land. The temperature felt hotter in the lee of the mountains, and hotter still when the track cut a deep path between empty fields and I was intermittently cut off from the wind. The village had disappeared from view, and it was a long time before I saw the cluster of white cuboid dwellings again. Tramping on between the empty fields with not a sign of life in sight, I imagined I had taken a wrong turn and become hopelessly lost. I could walk for days and be dead before anyone found me. Or savaged by a pack of Podencos. Were those dogs savage? I heard a bark not too far away, and alarm rang through me. I picked up a rock, just in case.

Then suddenly, there was the village right in front of me, or rather a sprawl of farmhouses on the outskirts. I guessed the village would have been much smaller in the 1950s and perhaps the church visible from where I stood. As it was I felt temporarily lost. I had no idea which streets the prisoners had been forced to tramp, but facing a warren of them, I had to rely on the maps app on my phone to find my way to the church.

On the corner of an arterial road in the village centre, I saw a bar advertising wine and tapas. The smells coming from its kitchen were welcoming and, without thinking, I ventured in, consumed by sudden hunger and an eagerness to escape the sunshine.

The café was cheap and cheerful. I sat down at one of the three empty tables and when the waitress came over, I ordered the tortilla on display and a cold beer. The waitress took my order without a smile or a care and removed herself from my presence. Alone, my mind began to acknowledge my body in sections, first my tired feet, then my stiff calves and quads. I felt a twinge in my left knee, and I realised I was developing a headache.

A few cars went by, but otherwise, the village was quiet. When my order came, I downed the beer quickly, quenching an urgent thirst, the bitter and fizzy liquid disappearing down my throat, and it wasn't until I drained the last dregs that I thought of the prisoners, their thirst, the brackish water they were given to quench it, the exhaustion they would have felt by now having trekked this far, the urge to find themselves inside the church where at least it was cool, and an equal resistance, given they would endure yet further recriminations from the priest for being gay.

It was only when I set down the empty beer bottle I had so urgently consumed that I realised I had inadvertently ruined my experiential understanding of what those men had gone through right at the very peak of their weekly ordeal. Ever the Trevor I was born to be, I thought grimly. Chastened, I hurried the tortilla into my belly, paid and left, emptying my shoes of grit on the pavement outside.

From the café, the church was easy to find. I headed down a narrow lane, and there it was, not a hundred yards thence. I rounded the side wall and noticed two men standing in the shade of a tree on the other side of the small plaza; I thought they were most likely the same men under the same tree as those I had seen the last time I visited the church. The men were chatting and didn't seem to notice me. I headed for the church entrance, and it was then that they both turned and stared. As I made to push against the church door, I noticed one of the men raising his hand. He called out to me, but I had no idea what he was saying. Seeing the door open, he let his hand fall and turned to his friend with a look of surprise.

Entering the church, I resumed my attitude of pilgrimage, albeit ever so slightly intoxicated. The air inside was cool and still and a blessed relief from the heat building in the plaza.

I made my way to the rear pew and, as I sat down, a foul smell hit me. The smell reminded me of rotting meat left unwrapped in the garbage. It was putrid and under other circumstances, I would have left the church. Instead, I remained seated in the pew and tried to ignore the olfactory assault. I was here for the prisoners. I wanted to picture them sitting here beside me and then lining up for confession. I wanted to sense their anguish and hopelessness and despair. I bowed my head and closed my eyes and imagined the suffering, the injustice, the hypocrisy. The unrelenting cruelty. Then I opened my eyes and stared at the altar; I pictured the priest all decked out in his finery, and my upper lip curled in contempt.

Christ spoke of forgiveness and goodwill and loving one's neighbour; he taught parables like the Good Samaritan, and he judged no one. All that judging came later, from the minds and mouths of the new priesthood. Setting the gospels and all the wisdom they contained aside, what remained was an edifice of condemnation and contrivances, built up over millennia, there to rule the masses and keep them in check; a church that would just as happily turn on its own flock should the occasion arise. The Inquisition was not so long ago, I thought, not so long ago at all, although long enough for humanity to forget all about it. And José and his friends suffered another inquisition tailored especially for them. And no one much cared at the time or since, because they had all been taught by the Catholic Church that being gay was a sin and those men who displayed gay tendencies were sick or diseased or corrupted somehow and needed to be banished or cured. Not so long ago. The 1950s, the 1960s, those decades were recent history. My grandparents' generation. All part of the modern era. When I considered even now there were countries and peoples who condemned others for their same-sex choices, outrage stirred, outrage on behalf of Angela, to anyone who was not heterosexual, even Jackie.

The point I had arrived at in my musings disturbed me for another reason. It had taken my literary appropriation, an act borne of opportunism, for these realisations to occur and for this empathy to stir. Could good come from an act that was fundamentally wrong? Obviously, it could. But that did not absolve the act itself, and with my new awareness, I realised I would need to live with the reality of my own shortcomings and strive to improve myself. I pulled myself up, yet again, catching myself falling into the mire of introspection. Where was the empathy when my thinking was all about me?

I sat and I stared and I thought. I conjured José and his friends in my mind as best I could. But eventually I could not pay my respects to those men. The smell was too distracting.

Hoping to escape the worst, I walked down the aisle to the altar, only to find the smell growing stronger. I anticipated finding a garbage bag left by a vagrant. Or schoolchildren who had used the church as a hangout to have a carnivore picnic and grown bored of the repast.

I looked around but there was no garbage of any kind on the floor, under the altar table, in the confessional, in fact not in any nook or cranny at that end of the nave.

The smell was strongest around the entrance to the sacristy. I knocked on the door. I was answered by a fly determined to enter with me. I knocked again. Silence. I hesitated with my hand on the doorknob, wondering if I were entitled to make such a bold move, unsure of what I would find.

I opened the door and immediately wished I hadn't. All thoughts of a pilgrimage left me the moment my eyes met a large lump of human flesh spread-eagled on the floor.

The corpse faced away from me. I glanced around the room. Cupboard doors and drawers were open. There were papers strewn about. But the worst of things were the flies. The flies, everywhere, feasting, and as my ears tuned into their incessant buzzing, the smell was so intense I blenched and covered my mouth.

Much of the body was thankfully obscured – the priest hadn't managed to take off his vestments – but when I ventured around to the other side of him, the face, the bloated face with its look-of-horror eyes imprinted itself on my mind.

I stumbled out of the room, closed the door and ran back through the nave, pausing at the front door to gather my wits before I stepped outside. I didn't want to appear stricken to whomever was out there. When the lingering stench outweighed my traumatised state, and I pulled open the door and stepped into the bright sunlight, the two old men were no longer standing chatting. The little plaza surrounding the church was empty. I was relieved.

The last thing I wanted was to end up in a police station reporting the death of a priest. But I had to report the death. Those men had seen me enter the church, and they might be the same men who saw me enter the church last week. Someone would find the priest, and gossip would whizz around; if I did not contact the police, I would end up the prime suspect. I would no doubt end up the prime suspect in any event, but reporting the body would go in my favour surely.

On unsteady legs, I went straight back to the café, and seeing I was again the only customer, I ordered a brandy from the young woman who had served me before in such an indifferent fashion. This time she looked surprised and concerned, and she asked me in Spanish if I was all right, but I pretended not to understand a word. When she broke into English, my instinct was to pretend I didn't understand that either, but common sense kicked in, and I said I was okay. She clearly didn't believe me, so I told her a dog had leaped out in front of me and given me a fright. She said, 'Oh, that animal should be locked up, I keep saying,' and she gave me a sympathetic smile. I knocked the brandy back in a single gulp and asked for another. She obliged. I drank that down as well, and she stood and watched for a few moments, poured me a third brandy and then she walked away. Taking advantage of the momentary privacy, I used my online translator and obtained the Spanish number for the police.

I dialled. As the number rang, my eyes fell on the headline of a front-page article in the newspaper folded in half on the counter beside my drink, and I hung up. I recognised the name of the church, the village – Casillas del Ángel – and a photo of whom I presumed was the priest, the same priest currently bloated and being eaten by flies. But it wasn't those two facts that had caught my attention. It was the amount written in bold. Fifty thousand euros. My stash. Everything fell into place. Juan must have stolen the cash from the priest to pay Javier back over that drug deal and then fled the scene. Maybe, like me, he thought he was being followed and went and hid the cash until he figured out a game plan.

I snatched up the newspaper and took it and my glass to the far table, opened the translator on my phone and proceeded to figure out what the article, dated ten days ago, was saying.

The priest, with the help of a huge community effort spanning all of the Canary Islands and an entire year, had managed to raise the fifty thousand euros for the Merida Orphan Dogs and Rescue Centre, a charity for needy dogs in Venezuela. Venezuela? Why there? I imagined Paco and Claire donating a tidy sum. The priest had been due the next day to fly to Caracas and then journey to the other town to deliver the funds in person.

What an idiot! Why had he not put all that cash in a bank and arranged an international transfer? The article waxed on about the money being a symbol of the goodwill of the people of the Canary Islands, who had a strong connection with Venezuela through centuries of migration. My former question answered, I began to lose interest. I kept returning to the fact that the stupid priest should have put all that cash in a bank.

Maybe he had been on his way to a bank that very day. Or maybe he didn't trust the banks in the Canary Islands or Venezuela, or they charged huge fees and he wanted the money, all of it, to go direct to the doggy carers themselves.

With that amount of cash, he should have hired bodyguards.

There was no indication in the article that the money had been stolen. As far as the newspaper was concerned the money was happily on its way to Venezuela, safely tucked away in the pockets of the priest. A money belt, one would have hoped. I returned to the article and forced my way through the last two paragraphs, typing sections of the text into the translation website. The reporter announced towards the end of the piece that the church would be closed for two weeks until the priest's return. *He never left.* I searched his name online and found no articles about him, the money or the dog charity since the day he was supposed to have departed. Whoever was involved in the delivery of the funds at this end, they must all be thinking he had made it to his destination.

Why had no one raised the alarm at the other end? Ten days! Surely someone at the dogs' home would have phoned, emailed, messaged a contact here to discover the whereabouts of the priest? I searched online again, this time targeting Venezuelan news, but I could find no mention of the priest, the money or the dogs' home. Something wasn't adding up. Then again, judging by the headlines that appeared in my searches, Venezuela was in considerable democratic chaos. Curious, I looked up on maps and found that Merida was quite a distance from Caracas. Maybe there were communication issues in Merida. Maybe Merida was the kind of small town still locked in the last century or the one before, and people expected things to happen eventually and not necessarily when they were scheduled to occur.

That might explain why no one this end was concerned. And why would they be. There was no reason to suspect there had been any foul play. No one could have smelled that odour from outside the church. The sacristy had no windows. And everyone assumed the church was locked.

I puzzled over the two men who had seen me approach the church last week. Maybe they were not religious and knew nothing about any of it. Maybe they were not the same men as those I had seen as I entered the church this time. Maybe.

I gulped down the third brandy and got up and asked the waitress for the bill, and without waiting for her response, I shoved a ten euro note at her and waited for my change with scarcely suppressed impatience and rising terror. The woman appeared nonplussed. When she handed me the change, I offered her a quick smile by way of apology and headed out the door.

It was uphill all the way to the crest of the saddle. The sun was high and bore down on my back. The wind was non-existent in the sections of track cut below the fields and the temperature notably hotter. Sweat formed little rivers coursing down the sides of my face and trickling down my spine. My plimsolls filled with grit. My penance. I refused to slow my pace. I needed to get as far away from that church as possible, and fast. As I neared the saddle, the gradient steepened considerably, and the fields gave way to barren land. Up here I felt exposed. The peaked cap mountain loomed on my right. The wind that had barely shown itself now blew in my face, cooling my skin and slowing my pace all at once. I pressed on, and by the time I neared the top, my heart was pounding, I was drenched in sweat and gasping for air. Then I crested the saddle, and the wind, which had been hiding as though lying in wait all this time, blasted me. I stopped and doubled over, putting my hands on my thighs. As I did, I imagined the prisoners groaning inwardly as they reached the same point, before shambling on, straining to hold themselves upright. Then, like me, they would have seen the track ahead, the track which took them back to Tefía, and their hearts would have sunk into their boots. Ahead, for them, awaited their stinking, crowded cells, hard labour and brutal beatings, revolting food and brackish water.

I could not share in their despair. I had a more immediate concern. The wind had taken my hat, and the sun was burning my scalp. I turned around and saw the blue canvas caught on a rock someway down the slope. My feet would not countenance trudging down to retrieve it. Instead, I forced my way along the narrow path, clinging to the face of the saddle as the wind and the sun assaulted me, and I decided Tefía had to be about the most inhospitable place on earth and I would never come back here. That much, I shared with the prisoners. Little wonder the locale was not filled with holiday lets. Only diehards came up here.

When I reached flat land, I all but ran back to the farmhouse.

29

A NIGHT IN A HOTEL

INSIDE THE KITCHEN, I DRANK ONE GLASS OF WATER AFTER ANOTHER, before ripping off my sweat-drenched clothes and taking a long cool shower. Back in the kitchen, I ripped open a can of tuna and slopped it, oil and all, onto a hunk of stale bread. A mash with a fork and I sank my teeth into the salty fishy bread and chewed rapidly. I could feel panic setting in and I knew the best thing I could do was call the police and hand in the rucksack and tell all. I would look like an idiot or an opportunist and possibly an outright liar, but at least I would have done the right thing. The money was not mine, and I would feel morally bankrupt keeping cash meant for a charity. If anything, I was the hero of the piece, for if I hadn't stumbled on that rucksack, the world would be impoverished twofold. No charity money and no gay prison story.

There was no need to mention the story. Whoever had put it there would presume their pages had been lost once the news broke. I knew with as much certainty as it was possible to have, given the evidence was circumstantial, that it was Juan who had murdered the priest, stolen the rucksack and put it in that cave to hide the cash until such a time as it was safe to retrieve it and enjoy the spoils. The story was not Juan's at all. He had inadvertently stolen it as well.

My thoughts halted at the realisation that the story had been put there for the dead priest to find, or if not the priest, then whoever was expecting the cash in Venezuela. An anonymous writer wanting to point the finger at the Catholic church, or Franco, and release the story of the prison to the world? It was rather a pathetic gesture, given the location of Merida. A publisher in London or New York would have been a better bet.

I instantly saw my surreptitious translation as a vital service to humanity, for the priest, if he had found that manuscript, may have ripped those pages into tiny pieces and burned them. Or, if he had been a good priest, he may have tried to do something with them but to what avail? Whatever the case, it was my duty to turn those words into the finest prose there ever was.

When I did call the cops, I would avoid all mention of the manuscript. I had to repeat the thought a few times to ensure I didn't make a slip. Before I made the call, I also needed to calm down. Taking some notes while the walk was still fresh in my mind, seemed a good idea. I sat down at the dining table. As I opened my laptop, Skype burst into life and my heart leaped into my throat.

It was Angela.

I must have looked surprised to see her for she squinted at me, then grinned and said, 'Am I disturbing you?'

'Not at all,' I lied.

She peered at me, her face filling the screen. 'You seem, I dunno, flustered.'

'I've been out for a walk.'

'A long one, by the look of you.'

'It was, as it happens. Did you want something?'

'I just wanted your reaction,' she said, shifting in her seat with a smirk.

'What reaction?' I said, puzzled.

'On Sandra Flint.'

'Oh, that,' I said, instantly deflated. I really didn't want to discuss Flint and her ill-gotten prize.

'But it's incredible, don't you think?'

'That she deserved to win? Hardly. I wrote it.'

Angela looked confused. 'But what do you make of her statement. I think it'll be for tax purposes to be honest, but still.'

I grew impatient. 'What are you talking about?'

Her mouth opened a fraction as the realisation I hadn't a clue what she was on about filtered into her mind. Then she said, 'Sandra Flint is donating all of her prize money to charity.'

I allowed myself a private sneer. Flint had more wealth than she knew what to do with. Angela was probably right; the donation might have had something to do with Flint's taxes, and it was also a terrific strategy to gain maximum publicity, and no doubt book sales would go through the roof.

'What charity?' I asked, not the least bit interested.

'Hang on.' She disappeared from my view for a moment. When she returned she said, 'The Merida Orphan Dogs and Rescue Centre.'

I nearly fell off my chair.

Angela misinterpreted my reaction and said, 'Yes, I thought her choice rather strange. But Juliette tells me Flint's hubby is from Venezuela.'

'Unbelievable.' It was all I could think of to say.

'I knew you'd find the news astonishing. Gotta dash.' She gave me a cheery wave. 'Enjoy yourself and may your muse inspire you.'

Astonishing? That hardly covered it. My mind was reeling with the news. Flint had gifted the Merida charity the fifty thousand the dead priest had intended to deliver. Her generous gift felt like divine intervention and recompense for my ghost-writing effort all at once. The charity would get its money, and I could hold onto my stash with a relatively clear conscience. The case, involving two deaths and the missing cash, would remain unsolved and without the crucial evidence of the rucksack, the police would have a hard job linking the dead body on the beach to the dead priest in the church, but what did I care. Let the cops do their sniffing. Maybe they would solve some other crimes in the process. By taking the cash I was doing Paco and Claire and Mario a favour, too, by helping to preserve their deceased relative's reputation. Whereas, I thought, suddenly thrilled to be exonerated from the burden of guilt, if I was to hand over the cash, Juan would be the prime suspect in the priest's murder, unable to offer his defence from the grave.

In my mind, Juan had killed the priest, taken off with the cash and the manuscript, and had gone and hidden his booty in a sea cave. On his exit from the cave, as he tried to make his way back to Puertito, he got caught in a current and swept down the coast until he drowned and was then washed up on that isolated beach. Let the likes of that author Angela mentioned – Richard Parry, if I recall correctly – let him come up with fictional alternatives to that scenario. Let him be the one to inject complexity in the form of other suspects. I did not want to consider the possibility that someone else killed the priest and Juan as well, and Fuerteventura had a murderer on the loose. Besides, if that were the case, the police would no doubt figure it out.

I started packing up my things, eager to put the farmhouse and Tefía behind me. My flight didn't leave until the following morning, but I thought I would check into a hotel in the city, see if I could get some of the cash transferred.

In the bedroom, I removed the contents of the rucksack and scattered them across the four-poster bed. The clothes and shoes and sunscreen I stuffed in a plastic bag, planning on tossing them in a garbage bin in Puerto del Rosario. The cash I packed in my suitcase. That left the phone. Curious, I switched it on. There had been two missed calls I had no intention of responding to, and one solitary message. I opened it.

Did you board your flight okay? Hope you are having good weather in Caracas.

The phone belonged to the priest? Stood to reason. It was more damning evidence that the murderer and the possessor of that rucksack were one and the same person.

I pressed the off button in case the phone sprang to life with another call. I needed to get rid of it. Not in the garbage in Puerto del Rosario. I would take it with me to the airport and dump it in a bin there, minus the SIM.

Before I left the bedroom, I took one last look out the window, at the view of the rocky plain and the windmill marking the site of the prison. Rainless clouds billowed. A car tore down the road heading south. I doubted I would ever return here, and it was with a measure of solemnity, that I turned back to the room and gathered up my suitcase and the rucksack.

I loaded the car then did a final sweep from room to room making sure I had not left anything behind. As I closed the front door and deposited the key under the doormat, I succumbed to a wave of nostalgia. The farmhouse was meant to have been my home for some months. I bid the old stone goodbye.

Inserting the ignition key aroused a fresh wave of anxiety laced with anticipation. I was about to escape with my booty; ahead of me back in England, I faced a bright new future filled with promise. In under two weeks, I had transformed myself from a depressed wretch wallowing in divorce misery and various resentments, to an optimistic man poised to commence his own literary career. A ghost no more.

The journey across the island was pleasant. The sense of leaving, the knowledge that I would not be driving in the other direction, led me to wonder what it must have felt like when those prisoners were freed. Unlike me, they did not fly off to start a brand-new life afresh. They faced a kind of purgatory without any heaven at the end of it. Unlike me, they had travelled into a future that was grim and uncertain and dangerous. A future of compromise or condemnation. Or, no future at all. Unlike me.

My first task in Puerto del Rosario was to find a wire transfer service. I called in at a bank, made my inquiry and was directed to a place in Corralejo. Surely there was somewhere in Puerto? As if I was about to drive all the way to Corralejo! The man eyed me with disdain and informed me in adequate and, dare I say it, sarcastic English, that the only place on the island where people wanted to do that sort of thing was in Corralejo. He looked behind me as though to attend to the person next in line. There was no next in line. With an inward scowl, I left the bank and scanned the pavement. The city was busy, no one was taking any notice of anyone else. There was a small waste bin in the plaza across the street. I reached into my trouser pocket and extracted the priest's phone, sidestepping over to the wall of the bank to extract the SIM. Then, with a casual gait, I wandered over to the bin and rid myself of the phone. I kept walking. I took a side street and then another. When I was sure no one was watching I dropped the SIM in the gutter. It occurred to me perhaps I should have tossed the SIM out the car window, but it was too late now. I hurried back to my car and drove off, leaving the city congestion behind and heading south, the direction of the airport.

I checked into an expensive hotel on the waterfront on the city outskirts and found myself in a spacious and modern room with a window overlooking the ocean. Stunning as it was, with little to do to occupy my time, I read over my story on my laptop, mulling over points of expansion. After all, there was no way Trevor Moore was about to settle for having written a novelette. I thought I might have José marry and repress his sexuality rather than jump off a cliff – that ending really was too melodramatic and cut off numerous possible scenes. Really, the suicide was the sole reason the work was too short.

After the prisoners had completed their sentences they were not allowed to return to their islands for up to five years. They were subjected to surveillance by judicial delegates. They had to report to the police station once a month or end up back in Tefía. It was almost impossible to find work because they had a criminal record. No one wanted to know them. They ended up working as semi-slaves or as prostitutes. Probably, a lot of the men did jump off cliffs. I could incorporate all of that and have my protagonist survive to tell the tale.

There was something about the idea of a double life that drew me. José could become a devoted husband and father of numerous children and harbour deep cravings he would be bound to repress. A tortured soul forever at odds with his own desires. A man riven, living a lie, a charade that over time would shape his psyche, warp his inner musings, fuel all manner of distortions and disturbing dreams. And he would never, not once speak of Tefía, not to his wife and certainly not to his children. Should he ever encounter another prisoner in the street, he would stare blankly with no recognition in his eyes as he walked by.

The re-write would transform the story into something both less and more disturbing; at the same time expand the work enough to warrant the novella label. I drafted out scenes, conjured characters and researched settings.

The only break I took from my writing was a dash out on the hunt for a municipal bin to dispose of the plastic bag and its incriminating contents. Not the most pleasant of drives – I ended up having to head all the way back into Puerto del Rosario – and my eyes were everywhere anticipating the police or worse, someone from the gym. After at last finding a bin down a side street, I headed back, pulling up in the car park and scurrying back into the hotel. As I went, I noted the compound-style architecture – a long, low-lying building with large arched windows out front and a flat roof – reminiscent in a curious way of the hostel in Tefía and, also like Tefía, set in the middle of nowhere, admittedly at the end of a stretch of wild-looking beach. Behind the hotel was the dual carriageway that was the island's main arterial road, a smattering of housing estates and then the mountains. It was as though the hotel had been plonked in its own ideal spot awaiting some sort of companion.

Not wanting any unnecessary eyes on my face, I went straight to my room and ordered room service. I spent the evening quaffing a delicious red and downing oysters followed by a marvellously cooked steak. Satiated, I scanned through my emails and accepted three ghost-writing gigs. A pleasant glow infused me. I even felt predisposed to write Jackie an email letting her know I would be back in London the following day. Then I sent Ian and Felicity an email each, telling them I missed them and hoped they were doing fine and keeping up with their studies and asked if they could spare a few hours of catch-up time with their old dad. I thought of the expensive gifts I could buy them with my newfound cash. Not too lavish, I wouldn't want to arouse suspicion, just enough to let them know how much I cared. I hadn't heard from either of them all trip. But I hadn't expected to. I fished out a photo of them I kept tucked in my billfold, smiled down at their cheery, innocent faces, Felicity with her wire braces straightening her teeth and Ian with a touch of acne. That was an old photo, taken in a photo booth on a day trip to Madame Tussauds. I slipped the photo back in my billfold and switched on the television.

The following morning, I repressed my anxieties enough to enjoy a sumptuous buffet breakfast – filling up on eggs, bacon, sausage, fried mushrooms, grilled tomatoes, toast, coffee, juice, a Danish pastry – and it was only when I went to fetch a second coffee that I picked up the local newspaper. I did not need an online translator to understand the headline. The priest had been found. I looked around the dining room. No one was taking any notice of me. I forced myself to drink my coffee before standing and walking casually back to my room. There was no need to panic. There was nothing to tie me to the murder. Nothing. The only evidence was the rucksack and I had that safely in my possession.

I composed myself and left the hotel, arriving at the airport two hours before my flight was due to depart. The day was warming up, and holiday-makers in dribs and drabs were making their way into the building. I parked the car, grabbed my luggage and followed the others. As I neared the doorway, I saw that inside, the entrance was guarded by two police officers. I thought perhaps that was normal or there had been a security scare. I thought that in an effort to quell the nausea rising up in my belly as my breakfast curdled. As I entered with my luggage, one of the officers stepped back to let me pass which I found a decent gesture and I relaxed.

Depositing the car keys in the box provided by the rental service seemed to draw a line under my presence on the island. I would be boarding the plane and away over the Atlantic and in my mind, I was already moving into my new home in Norfolk.

I sauntered over to the check-in desk and joined the queue, maintaining a nonchalant expression on my face and avoiding gazes. The queue shortened in fits and spurts as large family groups were followed by a few couples. As I neared the desk, I noticed two uniformed men standing behind the check-in assistant. They stared into the queue and, for a sickening moment, I felt their gazes on me. I told myself to shake off the paranoia, fast. The last thing I wanted was to arouse suspicion, not with fifty thousand euros in my suitcase. I cursed myself for not trying harder to find somewhere in Puerto del Rosario to make an international transfer. Perhaps I should have listened to that haughty teller in a bank and gone to

Corralejo, but I had not been in the mood to travel up the coast and back.

I glanced behind me and the two police officers I had passed on my way into the airport stood like statues staring down my queue. Someone ahead of or behind me was obviously in some kind of trouble.

It was only when I reached the desk that I realised the attention of all four officers was on no one else but me. Before I had a chance to place my suitcase on the scales, one of the officers said, 'Are you Trevor Moore?'

'That is correct.' I could hardly lie.

'Come with us, sir.'

My insides plummeted. I felt the eyes of every tourist in the airport piercing me like so many small daggers as the officers led me away. My mind raced. Who had informed the police? Someone at the gym? But none of them knew a thing. The old men outside the church? But how did the police make the link between the stranger they had seen and me? Same went for the waitress in the café. Or did it? And what about Paco and Claire? What if they had read the same newspaper as me and, suspecting I had held onto the cash, they had informed the cops? I sort of hoped they had. For it would at least absolve me of the crime of murder.

I was taken to a small, windowless room and told to sit down.

BOOKS AND WEBSITES CONSULTED

Richard Cleminson and Francisco Vázquez García, *'Los Invisibles': A history of male homosexuality in Spain, 1850-1940.*

Carlos David Aguiar García, *La provincia de Santa Cruz de Tenerife entre dos dictaduras (1923-1945). Hambre y orden,* University of Barcelona, 2012.

Miguel Ángel Sosa Machín, *Viaje al centro de la infamia*, self-published, 2012

Dr. Daniel Vallès Muñío, *La Privación de Libertad de Los Homosexuales en el Franquismo y su Asimilación al Alta en la Seguridad Social,* University of Barcelona, 2017.

Video - La Memoria Silenciada Tefía 1https://www.youtube.-com/watch?v=-wW-7XHuwz8\&t=571s

Video La Memoria Silenciada Tefía 2 https://www.youtube.-com/watch?time_continue=9\&v=GU20-exy8q4

Video Carcel de Tefía https://www.youtube.com/watch?v=RT19zfxIA-J8\&t=179s

Newspaper article - http://eldia.es/vivir/2005-07-31/1-centenar-gays-estuvieron-presos-Fuerteventura-franquismo.htm

Online article - http://www.nodo50.org/despage/Nuestra\%20Historia/verdad\%20historica/estrellarosa.htm

Online article - http://www.tamaimos.com/2012/06/28/memoria-historica-canaria-xii-la-colonia-agricola-penitenciararia-de-tefia/

Newspaper article - http://eldia.es/canarias/2008-05-18/6-Auschwitz-Fuerteventura.htm

Online article http://www.javilarrauri.com/represaliados/octavio_garcia.html

ACKNOWLEDGMENTS

This book could not have been written without the support and encouragement of my mother, Margaret Rodgers. I am also indebted to my old friend Domingo Diaz Barrios of Haría, Lanzarote, who told me about the prison in 1989, and Miguel Medina Rodriguez, also of Haría, who spoke to me of the prison many times and even drove past the prison on one of our visits to the island and pointed it out to me. Warm thanks to all who encouraged me to tackle this theme. A special thank you to my editor, Veronica Schwarz for her sharp eyes and diligence. And my gratitude to Miika Hannila and the team at Next Chapter for your ongoing support and belief in my writing.

ABOUT THE AUTHOR

A Londoner originally, Isobel Blackthorn has chalked up over seventy addresses to date, in various locations in England, Australia, Spain and the Canary Islands. Elements of her extraordinary life have a habit of finding their way into her fiction, providing her with a ready supply of inspiration.

Unlike her characters, Isobel now lives with her little white cat in Queensland, Australia. In her free time, she enjoys gardening, learning Spanish, visiting family and friends and travelling overseas, especially to the Canary Islands.

———

To learn more about Isobel Blackthorn and discover more Next Chapter authors, visit our website at www.nextchapter.pub.

Canary Islands Mysteries - Books 1-3
ISBN: 978-4-82417-276-1
Hardcover Edition

Published by
Next Chapter
2-5-6 SANNO
SANNO BRIDGE
143-0023 Ota-Ku, Tokyo
+818035793528

31st March 2023

Milton Keynes UK
Ingram Content Group UK Ltd.
UKHW041832280823
427655UK00003B/59